Also by Tom Arden in Victor Gollancz/Millennium

The Harlequin's Dance
FIRST BOOK OF THE OROKON

The King and Queen of Swords
SECOND BOOK OF THE OROKON

Sultan of the Moon and Stars
THIRD BOOK OF THE OROKON

Sisterhood of the Blue Storm

Fourth Book of THE OROKON

TOM ARDEN

VICTOR GOLLANCZ
LONDON

The right of Tom Arden to be identified as the author
of this work has been asserted by him in accordance with
the Copyright, Designs and Patents Act 1988.

This edition published in Great Britain in 2000 by
Victor Gollancz
An imprint of Orion Books Ltd

Orion House, 5 Upper St Martin's Lane,
London WC2H 9EA

To receive information on the Millennium list, e-mail us at:
smy@orionbooks.co.uk

A CIP catalogue record for this book
is available from the British Library

ISBN 0 575 063734

Typeset by Deltatype Limited, Birkenhead, Merseyside

Printed in Great Britain by
Clays Ltd, St Ives plc

TO
Keith Nash
1917–1991

The Sisterhood Song

They ride with lightning on a swirling sky,
The strangest strangers sweeping down from high:
What's left for us? What but to say goodbye?
  They come, they come! I see them taking form –
  The Sisterhood of the Blue Storm!

They once united in a sacred chain,
Now what unites them is a Web profane:
What do they bring? What but a spider's bane?
  They come, they come, their evil to perform –
  The Sisterhood of the Blue Storm!

When islands vanish from the oceans blue,
With sands and orchids, jungles and bamboo:
All gone, all gone? What can it be but true?
  They come, they come down like a deadly swarm –
  The Sisterhood of the Blue Storm!

In lust of power they search and search the seas,
And when they come they will not hear your pleas:
What, plead with them? What man does more than flees?
  They come, they come, and still your trail is warm –
  The Sisterhood of the Blue Storm!

But now the lightning fills the swirling sky,
Now come the Sisters sweeping down from high:
There's nothing left! My friends, goodbye, goodbye!
  They're here, they're here! Look, now they've taken form –
  The Sisterhood of the Blue Storm –
  The Sisterhood of the Blue Storm!

Players

JEM, *the hero, seeker after the Orokon*
RAJAL, *loyal friend to Jem; fellow seeker*
LITTLER, *their small companion*
CAPTAIN PORLO, *a pirate, master of the* Catayane
PATCHES, *his long-suffering cabin boy*
SELINDA, *a noble lady of the Isle of Hora*
MAIUS ENEO, *beloved of Selinda*
RA FANANA, *a nurse; slave to Selinda*
TAGAN, *a eunuch; also slave to Selinda*
LEKI, *who is nothing like Tagan*
UCHEUS, *who is nothing like Leki*
OJO, *who is nothing like Ucheus*
JODRELL, *father to Selinda; a Triarch of Hora*
FAHAN *and* AZANDER, *his fellow Triarchs*
PRINCE LEPATO, *suitor to Selinda (Innerman)*
LORD GLOND, *suitor to Selinda (Outrealmer)*
BLARD *and* MENOS, *drug-abusing sentries on Hora*
CHIEF ADEK, *of whom they go in fear*
MARGITES *of the Sea Vagas, a travelling player*
Other PLAYERS *in* The Javandiom
SAXIS, *who is either a philosopher or a sorcerer*
The SEA OUABIN, *a notorious corsair, master of the* Death Flame
SCURVY, *a crook-backed dwarf; his familiar*
VERNEY, *former trusted associate of the Sea Ouabin*
YOUNG LACANI, *an old man; slave on the* Death Flame
BONES *and* PANCHO, *also slaves on the* Death Flame
ROBANDER SELSOE, *the celebrated castaway*
WHALE, *fat first mate on the* Catayane
WALRUS, *buck-toothed boatswain on the* Catayane
PORPOISE, *slithery helmsman on the* Catayane
SEA-SNAKE, *well-endowed cook on the* Catayane
ALAM, *a survivor from the* Death Flame
MAIUS CASTOR ('CASTOR-UNCLE'), *father to Maius Eneo*
MYLA, *Rajal's missing sister; a child of great magic*
SHIA MILANDROS, *a bitchy young girl*

3

FAZY VINA, *ditto; her best friend*
FATHERS *to Shia Milandros and Fazy Vina*
KOFU, *the unman who tended Ojo*
ARD IRED, *the unman who tended Ucheus*
GOODY PALMER *and her* FIVE DAUGHTERS
The BLISHA DOLL, *much-abused doll of Selinda's late mother*
PAREUS ENEO, *Dynast of Aroc*
PRIESTS OF AROC, *their religious leaders*
The GATHERING OF THIRTY, *rulers of Hora*
KEEPERS OF THE LAW *on Hora*
The AUCTIONEER *on Shaba Lalia*
GUARDS, SLAVES, SAILORS, MERCHANTS, HARLOTS,
ISLANDERS OF NUMEROUS ISLANDS,
STREET-CHILDREN, CANNIBALS
&c.

SOME IMPORTANT PEOPLE, PRESENTLY OFF-STAGE:
CATA, *the heroine; beloved of Jem*
POLTY (POLTISS VEELDROP), *his implacable enemy*
BEAN (ARON THROSH), *accomplice of Polty, beloved of Rajal*
LADY UMBECCA VEELDROP, *evil great-aunt to Jem and Cata*
NIRRY, *her runaway servant; staunch friend to Jem and Cata*
EAY FEVAL, *friend and spiritual advisor to Umbecca*
CONSTANSIA CHAM-CHARING, *former great society hostess*
TISHY CHAM-CHARING, *her unmarriageable daughter*
SILAS WOLVERON, *father to Cata; not really dead*
BARNABAS, *a magical dwarf; certainly not dead*
LORD EMPSTER, *Jem's treacherous guardian: see also* AGONIS
TRANIMEL, *Ejland's evil First Minister: see also* TOTH-VEXRAH
EJARD BLUEJACKET, *unrightful King of Ejland*
QUEEN JELICA, *his wife, the former Miss Jelica Vance*
'BOB SCARLET', *highwayman and rebel leader*
HUL, *his deputy; once a great scholar*
BANDO, *friend to Hul; veteran rebel*
RAGGLE *and* TAGGLE, *sons to Bando*
LANDA, *a beautiful young Zenzan Priestess*
BAINES, *also known as the 'One-Eyed Beauty'*
GOODMAN OLCH ('WIGGLER'), *husband to Nirry*
MORVEN *and* CRUM
Various other OLD FRIENDS, ENEMIES
&c.

4

VARIOUS DEAD PEOPLE:
ADRI, *a scrawny and nervous youth*
NICANDER, *known as 'childlike Nicander'*
INFIN IJAS, *a dreamy youth whose eyesight was poor*
ZAP, *a bit of jester, said to be 'boneheaded'*
JUROS IKO *and* JENAS IKO, *twins and singers*
LEMYU, *a sailor in a stripy shirt*
CAPTAIN BEEZER, *formerly master of the* Catayane
SULTAN KALED, *formerly ruler of Unang Lia*
RADENINE, *son to the Dynast Pareus Eneo*
ANIANI, *a young maiden; his beloved*
BELROND, *her father*
TRIARCH SPEKO, *maternal great-father to Selinda*
WILEY WAN WO, *steward of Castle Glond*
MANI, *daughter of Wiley Wan Wo*
BLACKMOON, *sometime companion to Robander Selsoe*
SELINDA'S MOTHER, *former abuser of the Blisha doll*
SCHUVART *and* HANDYN, *the great composers*
THELL, *ancient author of* The Javandiom
VICTIMS *of the Sisterhood of the Blue Storm*
VICTIMS *of the Triurge*
&c.

ANIMALS OF VARIOUS SORTS:
RAINBOW, *a most remarkable dog*
BUBY *the monkey*
The BLUE RAVEN
KYRA, *an unfortunate heifer*
EJARD ORANGE, *a marmalade cat*
BOLLOCKS, *a marmalade cat*
PUSS, *a marmalade cat*
The OXEN OF THE MOON
The ORCHESTRA AQUATIC, *in Javander's palace*
TAXIDERMISED BIRDS *and* MOTHS UNDER GLASS
Numerous FISH, *both dead and living*
PONIES, MULES, SERPENTS,
RATS, FLIES, FLEAS, LICE
&c.

GODS AND STRANGE BEINGS:
OROK, *Ur-God, father of the gods*
KOROS, *god of darkness, worshipped by the Vagas (purple)*
VIANA, *goddess of earth, worshipped in Zenzau (green)*

THERON, *god of fire, worshipped in Unang-Lia (red)*
JAVANDER, *goddess of water, once worshipped in Wenaya (blue)*
AGONIS, *god of air, worshipped in Ejland (gold)*
TOTH-VEXRAH, *the evil anti-god*
The LADY IMAGENTA, *his mysterious daughter*
AMAS, *son to Javander, Prince of Rocks (purple)*
EON, *son to Javander, Prince of Winds (green)*
ISOL, *son to Javander, Prince of Shells (red)*
OCLAR, *son to Javander, Prince of Tides (blue)*
UVAN, *son to Javander, Prince of Sands (gold)*
The SPIDERMOTHER, *leader of the Sisterhood of the Blue Storm*
WEBSISTERS *of the Sisterhood of the Blue Storm*
The SIBYL OF XARO, *a wall full of holes*
The SIBYL OF INORCHIS, *another one just like it*
The THUNDERER AROC XARO, *a mystical volcano*
The THUNDERER AROC INORCHIS, *another one just like it*
The TRIURGE, *a terrifying metamorphic land-monster*
The MANDRU, *a terrifying metamorphic sea-monster*
KALADOR, *beguiling alter-ego of the Mandru*
The FLYING ZENZAN, *a haunted ship*
ABORTIONS *writhing on Theron's floor*
The HARLEQUIN
Other CREATURES OF EVIL
&c.

The Story So Far

It is written that the five gods once lived upon the earth, and the crystals that embodied their powers were united in a circle called THE OROKON. War divided the gods and the crystals were scattered. Now, as the world faces terrible evil, it is the task of Prince Jemany, son of the deposed King of Ejland, to reunite the crystals.

Already the anti-god, Toth-Vexrah, has burst free from the Realm of Unbeing. Projecting his powers through his Creatures of Evil, Toth is determined to avenge himself on Orok, the father-god who rejected him. If Toth grasps the crystals, he will destroy the world. Only Jem stands in his way.

An unlikely hero, Jem was born a cripple, but gained the power to walk after falling in love with the wild girl Catayane. Cata was later trained as a lady, and Jem's old enemy, Poltiss Veeldrop, sought her for his bride.

Escaping her tormentors, Cata was briefly reunited with Jem, but now they are divided again. Cata is a member of Bob Scarlet's rebel band, fighting Ejland's Bluejacket régime; meanwhile Jem must continue the quest.

Jem has found three crystals so far. His companion Rajal now bears the purple Crystal of Koros; Cata, the green Crystal of Viana; Jem, the red Crystal of Theron. But Jem's guardian, Lord Empster, will no longer help them, and Toth's powers are increasing fast.

Now, on a flying carpet from the desert realms of Unang-Lia, Jem, Rajal, their friend Littler and the magical dog Rainbow soar towards the far-off, mysterious Isles of Wenaya, desperate to find the missing blue Crystal of Javander.

Little do they know that the shady old buccaneer Captain Porlo is following them for a reason of his own.

And Toth-Vexrah is on their trail.

INORCHIS
THE FLYING ISLAND

THE TWINNED ISLES OF AROC

THE SIBYL OF INORCHIS

SAROM

BLUE STORM

JAVAN WENAOB

AMBORA ROCK

HORA

SHABALALIA

ISTHMUS of MARIC

Straits of Javander

Salt Sea of Sardoc

MAELSTROM OF THE MANDRU

EYE OF THE SEA

XARO
The Isle of the
MANHOOD TRIAL

THE SIBYL OF XARO

D·S

PART ONE

The Lost Boys

Chapter 1

A MOUNTAIN ON FIRE

Like hundreds upon hundreds of bright flowers, flung carelessly across the surface of the sea, the Isles of Wenaya stretch away from the mainland of El-Orok in a great ragged arc. Quite where the isles end is a mystery, at least to the sailors of El-Orok – Ejlanders, Zenzans and Unangs alike. Some say another continent lies beyond, of an extent even greater than their own; some say that where the isles end, the earth ends too, with the sea sizzling away into a fiery trench. There is talk of fish-people, monstrous sea-serpents, and much worse besides. Superstition, no doubt; but even on the many-sailed ships of Ejland, mightiest of the nations of El-Orok, tarry fellows are known to quail as they venture deeper and ever deeper into the watery labyrinths of Wenaya. The isles, and the seas in which they lie, are feared as places of dark magic.

So Prince Jemany had read in books of travels, long ago during languid days in Lord Empster's library. Back then in Agondon, Jem would have found it hard to imagine that he would ever come to these isles – let alone on a magic carpet.

Sighing, he stretched out on the hot fabric, shutting his eyes against the sharp morning light. Incense rose from the soft wool. How luxuriously he had passed the night, sunk in these fragrant hollows! Embraced in the genie's magic, he had felt no fear. Now, he was certain, the magic was dispersing. But might it not last just a little longer?

Warm winds rippled through his dishevelled blond hair and once again he felt himself, not quite unwillingly, drifting back into sleep. Lightly he circled Rainbow with a protective arm. The stripy dog lay panting, blinking, his head on his paws, his new silver collar flashing brightly. The collar had been a gift from Princess Bela Dona, the strange, beautiful girl Jem and his companions had befriended in Unang Lia. The Princess had assured them that the collar had magical powers. But the magic, if magic there were, had yet to manifest itself.

Dreamily Jem listened to Rajal's voice, and Littler's. They were wondering just when the carpet would land.

It was a good question.

'Can you see anything, Littler?' Rajal was saying.

Cross-legged, hunching over, Littler stared into the Orb of Seeing, his own mysterious gift from Princess Bela Dona. The young Unang boy was hardly interested at all in the real scene passing below; with his gleaming new talisman, he endeavoured instead to see their destination. Wenaya, yes – but where?

When Jafir the genie had set the carpet in motion, Jem and his companions had simply been glad to be on their way with all speed. They had given little thought to how their journey might end.

Now, they were beginning to wonder if Jafir had either.

Littler strained his eyes into the orb. Princess Bela Dona had not actually explained to him how to use it – if, that is, she had known. Was there, perhaps, some special way of looking? Blue reflections shifted in the rounded glass.

'Something,' he murmured, 'some kind of . . . blue—'

'That's the sky, you idiot!' said Rajal. 'Give me a look—'

'Hands off! The orb's mine—'

'Well, look harder.' Impatiently the Vaga-youth toyed with his own talisman, the Amulet of Tukhat that he now wore round his wrist. Could it really protect him from harm? If so, he thought ruefully, it would have quite a task, judging by his past experiences. In Unang Lia, he had come close to death – and to things, perhaps, still worse than death. He shook his dark-haired head, as if to banish painful thoughts.

He did not quite succeed.

'We must land *soon*, mustn't we?' he said impatiently.

'Yes,' said Littler. 'But where?'

Deep in the jungle, heat hovers like a mysterious menace. Moisture coils up steamily from the earth and drips back down from curling, riotous leaves, from clustering flowers and speckled, huge-capped toadstools. Sunlight, even in the brightness of morning, glimmers and fractures through the lattices of green.

There were sounds of crashing. Then came voices.

'It's our last chance.' It was a boy who spoke.

'Didn't you say we'd had that already?' said another, leading a protesting heifer.

'We're alive, aren't we? Uchy, don't be such a follyface.'

'Me, a follyface? Ojo, what about Leki?'

'He's more than a follyface, he's a madmaster.'

'That's not what I mean – I mean, what will he say when he finds out what we've done?'

There were two of them, both aged perhaps fourteen or fifteen orbits. Ojo, the one in front, was thickset, stocky; Ucheus, who tugged at the heifer's rope, was slender, almost delicate. Both boys had skin the colour of bronze and dark, unkempt hair, Ojo's a shock of ragged curls, his

12

companion's a crudely hacked mass of spikes. Downy growth furred their upper lips and their limbs were webbed with scratches. They were dirty and the tunics they wore, though once ornate, had long been reduced to rags. They struggled uphill through the enveloping jungle.

Ojo said, 'Leki should be glad that someone's taken charge.'

'Leki thinks *he's* in charge,' Ucheus said doubtfully.

'Yes, and look at the mess we're in.'

It was difficult to argue. Ucheus set his mouth and followed in silence for some moments, pausing from time to time to tug, always a little harder, at the rope around the sickly heifer's neck. How he hated to look into her big, sad eyes! He hoped he could avoid those eyes when Ojo cut her throat – at least, he hoped it would be Ojo who cut her throat. Ucheus might have spent more time on Castor-uncle's farm, but after all, it was Ojo whose father was a Priest of Aroc.

If only it were over. 'Kyra, come on!'

Ojo rolled his eyes. 'Follyface, did you *have* to give her a name?'

'I give all the animals names. Didn't you learn anything in Sacred School, Ojo? A name's a charm against evil.'

'Doesn't work then, does it?'

'Not for Kyra, I suppose.'

'Nor for us.'

'What?'

'We all had names. And we're dead.'

'Not all of us,' said Ucheus. '*We're* alive, you said so before.'

Ojo pushed between sticky vines. 'And seven of us aren't.'

'Seven? No, Ojo – six.'

'Maius Eneo? You don't still wish you'd gone with him, do you?'

Ucheus said glumly, 'Of course I do!'

His friend's reply was brutal. 'Maius Eneo's drowned, Uchy – drowned on the first day. Leki's right about that much, at least.'

'Leki? You said he was a madmaster!'

'Not about this – face it, Uchy!'

The slender youth cast down his eyes. How could Ojo speak this way? Wasn't it bad luck even to utter such doubts? In the end, if only one of them lived, it had to be Maius Eneo – dear, marvellous Maius Eneo . . . no, he could never have died at sea. Hadn't he been the best swimmer of them all – hadn't he been the best of them at *everything*? To be sure, Maius Eneo would reach the Isle of Hora, he would bring help – why, even now he might be on his way back!

Anger welled in Ucheus and he wished he had the nerve to fling himself forward, wrestling Ojo to the ground, making him take back the stupid thing he had said.

But they could hardly fight amongst themselves, could they? Not now.

13

There was an ominous rumbling beneath their feet.

'The Thunderer's angry with us,' Ucheus murmured.

Quickly, with no more words, the boys clambered through the tangled shadows, making their way towards the Plateau of Voices.

Kyra tugged at her rope.

'The Crystal of Javander?' Littler murmured.

Rajal's voice was wry. 'That's what I said. Just look for *that*, hm – save us a lot of time. Say, you don't think Jafir's spell will take us right there, do you – land us right on top of the blue crystal?'

Littler, concentrating on the orb, did not reply.

Miserably, Rajal looked around him. How tired he was of the magic carpet – tired of the billowing fabric beneath them, that was barely big enough to contain them all; tired of the wind in their faces and hair; tired of being cramped, hot, and hungry ... Very hungry, by now.

Ruefully reaching into a pocket, Rajal drew forth the bag of gold that Fish had thrust into his hand, just before their journey began. Good old Fish! Hearty meals, many of them, were easily within their reach – if only they could find a nice comfortable tavern.

Some chance.

It had been at dusk, the evening before, when they had left behind the hot desert wastes. In the night, the scene beneath had been a watery shimmer, scattered with dark humps of islands and faintly, here and there, with a flicker of fire. Now it was a brilliant shade of ultramarine, sparkling as if with scattered diamonds. For some time there had been no islands. Had they gone beyond the Waters of Wenaya? Rajal peered cautiously over the carpet's tasselled edge. In one direction there were only open seas – then he turned his head and saw clouds of smoke.

He jerked upright. 'Look!'

'Wh-what?' Jem started awake.

'Hey! Don't rock the carpet!' Littler protested, grabbing the orb before it rolled over the side.

Rajal pointed. 'That mountain – it's on fire!'

They turned their heads. A smoky trail scudded across the sky, issuing from the apex of a high, wooded island. The island was still far away, and there was no other land in sight.

Jem yawned, stretching. 'Raj, it's only a volcano.'

'A what?' said Rajal. 'Jem, when have you ever seen a mountain like that?'

'Well, in a picture,' Jem admitted. 'It smokes, that's all.'

'Like a tobarillo?' Rajal said dubiously. 'But *why*?'

'Explodes too, doesn't it?' said Littler. 'Well, sometimes – I'll look in the orb.'

'I'll throw that thing overboard in a moment,' said Rajal. 'It doesn't work, anyway.'

'Of course it *works*,' said Littler. Shifting on to his haunches, he stared into the glass again. 'It just hasn't yet.'

Rajal rolled his eyes. 'How is it,' he wondered, 'that a genie who can send us soaring across the sky, across half the world, couldn't stop one little brat – not to mention his dog – from clambering up beside us? How are we going to be able to find the Crystal of Javander, if we're worrying all the time about this pest?'

'Littler's been a good friend,' said Jem.

'He's a baby – *and* he's brought his dog with him!'

Littler's eyes flashed. In his short but turbulent life he had endured insults worse than these. He was not afraid of Rajal. 'I'm not the one who doesn't even know what a volcano is,' he sniffed. 'Jem, I helped you out in the dreaming dimension, didn't I? I'll bet I've got out of more scrapes than the pair of you put together. I've been a thief for as long as I can remember, I think fast, I'm quick on my feet – and now,' he added proudly, 'I've got a magic orb. You'll see, I'll be worth my weight in gold.'

Rajal weighed the bag of gold in his hand. 'Jem, how much do you think Littler weighs?' he said mischievously.

Jem ignored him. 'I'm sure you will, Littler. Rainbow too, hm?'

Smiling, he fluffed the dog's stripy fur. Whether Littler and his colourful friend would help or hinder them was neither here nor there. There was no turning back. The four of them were together now, and heading into danger.

Chapter 2

ULTRAMARINE

'Follyface, careful of that spear—'

'It's my eyes, I'm dazzled—'

Ojo and Ucheus were standing on the Plateau of Voices. In truth, it was not so much a plateau as the merest rocky shelf, jutting above a sea the colour of ultramarine. Ucheus set down his spear, but still held tightly to Kyra's rope. He screwed up his face and shielded his eyes. Far above, he was aware of smoke from the volcanic summit of the island, drifting slowly in the cloudless sky. Below, the sea foamed gently against the rocks.

'On a morning like this,' he murmured, 'it's hard to believe we ever had the Blue Storm.'

'Look at us now,' Ojo said bitterly. 'Doesn't that tell you the storm was real?

Ucheus supposed it did. Only a moonlife had passed since the night of the storm, but already the time before seemed sundered from them as if by an abyss of years. What terrible magic that night had wrought! He gazed over the sea, thinking again of the wild whipping winds, the flashing blue lights that had taken Inorchis, their companion island. 'Sometimes I wonder if it's still there – still there, only we can't see it.'

'What? The storm?'

'Inorchis, of course. What else?'

Ucheus sighed, then so did Ojo, saddened by even the name of their lost home. With a resigned air the stocky youth took Kyra's rope, tethering her to a rock by the sacrificial slab. 'Uchy,' he said, more kindly than before, 'why don't you get some branches for the fire? Leki could well be awake by now. If he sees that Kyra's gone, he might guess what we're doing – hm?'

They worked in silence, tearing at the dry, salty vegetation that sprouted from cracks in the rocky shelf. Beside the slab was a shallow pit, blackened with traces of innumerable fires that sun and wind had yet to blanch away. When they had filled the pit, Ojo dug the fire-lens from a pocket of his tunic. He stood splay-footed over the branches and leaves. Focusing the sun's rays, his face twisted in concentration as if it were his mind and not the brightness above that would set the pit to burn.

Kyra lowed piteously, as if she knew what the fire was for. But she was

16

too weak to resist now, wasn't she? Ucheus gulped, avoiding the sight of her face with its blinking, huge, sad eyes.

Beyond the slab, gaping impassively, were the hundred mouths of the Sibyl, or rather a hundred holes in a sheer wall of rock, the largest perhaps the size of a man's head. Not for the first time, Ucheus trembled in the presence of these holes, so dark, so ominous against the sun-drenched plateau. Some said the holes reached far beneath the sea, perhaps into the very depths of the world.

The leaves began to smoulder; Ojo slipped the fire-lens into his pocket again. The two boys exchanged glances. Ojo gulped. Could he really go through with this? Priest of Aroc his father may have been, but what did that matter? Neither boy had seen a sacrifice before, let alone officiated at one. On Inorchis, only those who had passed the Manhood Trial had been permitted even to witness such acts. But Ojo knew he must take the lead. If Ucheus placed his faith only in Maius Eneo, Ojo would show him . . . yes, he would show him!

He picked up his spear. Kyra scrambled back.

Ucheus said quickly, 'Not the spear, Ojo.'

'You're right.' Hanging from Ojo's belt was his kos-knife, the only one that remained to the three who were left. Ucheus had lost his long ago; Leki's had snapped against a sow's breastbone; whatever had killed their six companions had been careful to leave no weapons behind. Ojo gripped the flattened, cracking handle, testing the blade against his thumb.

Dull, but it would have to do.

'Hold her, Uchy.'

Through what followed, Ucheus tried to keep his eyes closed. If only he could have blocked his ears, too – and his nose! He had killed pigs and rabbits, but this was worse, much worse: this was Kyra. Flinching, he heard her desperate squeals; he felt her violent thrashings, convulsing up through his rigid arms. The stench of fear rose hotly all around him, mingling with the acrid smoke from the pit. He forced down all his weight on the rearing shoulders.

'Hurry – Ojo, hurry!'

'I'm trying—'

In a crude piece of butchery Ojo hacked bluntly, then stabbed back and forth into the sagging throat. Blood spilt across the slab, squirting first like milk from a pulled teat, then rushing in stinking, steaming gouts. Ucheus felt the hot stickiness splashing over his hands and running around his hard, bare feet. Then Kyra's bowels gave way. Ucheus gagged. Vomit filled his mouth and he would have broken free, but Ojo, with curses, commanded him to stay.

The slender boy screwed his face tighter, swallowing hard and

17

struggling not to breathe as the dying heifer first kicked, then writhed, then shuddered beneath him. At last the throbbings in the neck were still. Ucheus reeled away. Smoke blinded his eyes and he felt the battering wings of birds, swooping down desperately.

'Come back, damn you!'

'It's finished, isn't it?'

'Finished? It's only begun!'

Ojo was right. Blankly, Ucheus stumbled back. First they turned over the hot corpse, exposing the dugs that he had milked so many times. *Teat-sucker*, the others had called him, but though the slender boy had minded the name, he had not minded the task. When Kyra was sick and her milk was running dry, he had indeed sucked goadingly at the rough teats, as his cousin Maius Eneo had shown him how to do, long ago on Castor-uncle's farm. The memory had been a fond one, but all thought of his old life was terrible to Ucheus now, the merest mockery.

Ojo grabbed his spear again. 'Hold back the legs.'

Ucheus gulped in breath, as if about to dive, while his stocky friend first gouged holes with the spear, then took his kos-knife to the soft underbelly, hacking clumsily through the stinking guts. New, more terrible waves of stench assailed them. By now both boys were covered in gore. Blood dripped from their hair, from their eyelids, from their lips and fingers; their tunics were sodden. But there was no stopping: before their work was done, they were tearing with their hands, gasping at the strength it took to rend the slithering skin, to part the hot bones.

At last the entrails were steaming on the slab; the meat burning in the pit. The birds were frenzied. Ucheus was sobbing and could barely breathe. Ojo lurched upright, clutching Kyra's heart in his trembling hands. Exhausted, he staggered to the wall of a hundred holes.

He bit his lip, struggling for words. If Ojo had never witnessed such a ritual, still he had peered into the sacred texts; he had heard his father, and other Priests of Aroc, intoning the lessons in Sacred School. Whether what Ojo would say was even vaguely right he did not know, but after all, he barely cared. They had come this far; they must end it now. He flung himself forward, crashing painfully to his bare knees.

'Hundred-voiced Sibyl,' he began softly, 'all-wise one, sister of the Sibyl of Inorchis, who is daughter of the Thunderer Aroc Inorchis, who is brother of the Thunderer Aroc Xaro – before you we come with this offering of flesh . . . Hear us, Sibyl of Xaro, and tell us what we ask, for you are the last chance that remains for us now . . . Sibyl, speak to us in your hundred voices – tell us, how will we ever be restored to Inorchis? Tell us, will the Thunderer spare us? Sibyl, how will we survive this ordeal?'

18

Ojo breathed heavily, Ucheus too. The birds, as if fearful, had suddenly scattered. There was no sound but for the fire, the sizzling meat, the soft wash of waves. Lying on the reddened, slippery rock, turning away from the smoke and blood and entrails, Ucheus gazed across the empty sea. How strange it was, how impossible to think that this vista of ultramarine had once been filled with an isle like this one, identical in everything, but for the towns and farms that had flourished upon its slopes! He thought again of the storm; he thought again of the Sibyl, and wondered what she could say that might help them now.

If only they had asked about Maius Eneo!

'Uchy,' Ojo moaned at last, 'it's no use—'

'It is, it has to be!' his friend flung back.

Ucheus was right: for now, something was stirring within the rock. When the sound began, it rose slowly above the threshold of awareness. The boys might have thought it a gust of wind, playing fleetingly over the placid sea; they might have thought it one of those deep interior groanings, those mysterious stirrings of the smoking mountain. Only when the sacrifice seemed worthless, when Ojo had laid down the stiffening heart and Ucheus, after crawling to the edge of the rock, stood poised to dive into the cleansing sea, did the song of the Sibyl come drifting around them.

Terror consumed them.

Rajal murmured, 'That mountain's getting closer.'

Smoky trails scudded across the sky.

'We are, you mean.' Littler leapt up, twirling excitedly.

'What are you doing?' said Rajal.

Littler, it seemed, had forgotten his orb. 'Oh,' he cried, 'if only we could explore all these mysterious isles—'

He capered and cavorted.

'Get down, idiot!' Rajal pulled him back from the carpet's edge. 'Don't worry, before all this is over, we might just explore every single Isle of Wenaya. How many did you say there were, Jem?'

But Jem was barely listening. With foreboding he gazed into the weave of the carpet, rippling beneath them on the waves of the wind. The design was one of extraordinary intricacy. There were whorls and spirals, there were peacock eyes, there were rivers and trees and shooting stars; there were mysterious figures in robes and turbans, reaching forth hands that held dazzling jewels. He traced the rays of light, stitched in azure thread, that stabbed out brilliantly from a sea-blue stone. It was – it would have to be – the Crystal of Javander.

The foreboding in Jem's mind became sharper and he touched the stone he possessed now, the Crystal of Theron that he wore beneath his tunic. His eyes closing, he saw again the vision of Toth-Vexrah that had consumed him just before this red crystal came into his possession. If Toth's crazed words were to be believed, the powers of the anti-god had been massively increased, feeding on the spiritual energies that had burst forth, like waters from a collapsing dam, with the destruction of Unang Lia's most sacred temple. Jem breathed deeply, tightening his grip on the crystal. Only a day had passed since he had found it, yet already it felt like a part of his being, and would remain thus, he knew, until he found its blue sister.

It was then that the carpet lurched, just a little, and the Orb of Seeing rolled towards Jem. He reached for it, but just as he was about to clutch it, saving it from plummeting over the edge, he felt a sudden stabbing in his eyes. It was the face of Toth-Vexrah, leering at him from the depths of the glassy sphere . . .

'The orb!' wailed Littler.

'Forget the orb,' said Rajal. 'Look!'

They swivelled round. A flock of seabirds came plunging towards them, talons glittering, wings outstretched.

'They're coming right for us—'

'Hang on—'

They clung to the carpet. Rainbow's claws dug deeply into the weave. Like thunder, a hundred wings beat above them, shrieking filled the sky, and the carpet shuddered, beginning to spin. Jem gritted his teeth. In an instant, he was certain, he would feel beaks and claws, slashing through his tunic like razors. Instead, just as the birds were upon them, the carpet veered away, dropping like a stone through the dazzling sky – and the birds did not follow.

Rajal gasped, 'Are they going to turn back?'

'They weren't after us,' said Jem, 'they were . . . fleeing!'

'Then they've gone?' said Rajal. 'Thanks be to Koros!'

'To your amulet, you mean!' Littler returned.

Princess Bela Dona's gift to Rajal flashed brilliantly against his brown, tensing wrist. Perhaps it was really a charm against evil: for an instant, Rajal might have believed it. But only for an instant. The birds had vanished, but still the carpet went spinning dizzyingly down. A blue vortex whizzed beneath them. Rainbow barked. Rajal closed his eyes, bracing himself – but the splash never came.

The carpet spun downwards at a sharp angle. Surging into view came the wooded slopes of the island. Littler praised the amulet; Rajal blessed it, then cursed it again as the smoke from the volcano closed around them like a black, choking curtain. Sulphur filled their lungs. They swooned; they coughed; tears sprang from their eyes. From below, they heard the sinister bubbling of the caldera.

'We're sinking!' Rajal cried. 'We're sinking!'

Chapter 3

A BUZZING OF FLIES

Of the hundred voices, some were high, some low, some sweet, some strident, but all sang the same riddling song. Slowly Ojo raised his eyes to the Sibyl, pushing back his dripping, bloody curls; Ucheus did not even dare to turn back. Fearful that some vision might accompany the song, he remained gazing out at the sea and the pale, cloudless canopy of the sky. How strange it was, how deeply strange, to think that all the time they had been on Xaro, this daughter of the Thunderer had been with them, just as her sister had been on Inorchis, this unseen being who lived beneath the rocks! They had wondered at her, feared her, longed for her guidance. Never had they imagined the reality of her presence.

The song, with its own terrible thunder, boomed around them in the smoky air.

> Children who call upon my sacred fame,
> For trial of manhood to this isle you came:
> Like those before you, to spin on the gyre
> In waters of doubt and the truth of fire.
> > But just what drowns and what it is that burns
> > Are secrets hidden in the wheel that turns.

> Children who dare to play my sacred game,
> Fears lie behind you that I dread to name:
> Fears still must come to a terrible birth
> As waters claim all but one from the earth.
> > But which for the waters, which for the ground
> > Are secrets hidden till the wheel goes round.

> Children who marvel at my sacred claim,
> In one way alone may your fates be the same:
> Strike down the pilot from the bright light's glare,
> Till waters cover over the one from the air.
> > But which are the waters – which are the skies?
> > Such are the secrets in the wind that flies.

When it was over, the silence was deeper than before. The smoke was clearing. Still Ucheus stared across the sea; slowly, Ojo turned to him. The boys had known each other for as long as they could remember; they had even been best friends once, before Ucheus met his cousin Maius Eneo. Now they seemed almost shy of each other. Trembling, Ojo gripped his friend's slender arm. When he spoke at last, the stocky boy had lost all bravado, all pretence. If there was much in the Sibyl's words he did not understand, still he recognised a terrible foreboding.

'Uchy,' he whispered, 'we're going to die.'

The reply was a whisper too. 'But she's told us . . . nothing.'

'We're going to die,' Ojo said again, 'all but one of us—'

Ucheus gulped, 'No, Ojo, no – Maius Eneo, he's going to save us . . . there are things – things you don't know . . .'

Ojo's voice cracked. 'Follyface, we're going to die, I tell you!'

'Madmaster! How can you say that?' Now Ucheus was angry too. His friend's grip was tighter and he flinched as the nails dug into his flesh, but still he did not break away, still he did not turn – and so it was not until the last moment that they saw it, breaking from the smoke at the Thunderer's summit, reeling down from the sky behind them. At once, Ojo let his hand fall. He shuddered. He pointed.

'Uchy, look . . . the pilot from the air.'

'Hang on,' shouted Jem, 'just hang on—'

But in a moment, the ordeal was over. Blackened, weak and gasping, they found themselves on the other side of the smoky curtain. The carpet, spinning no more, scudded over the jungle. Cautiously, Jem and his friends relaxed their grip on the reeking fabric. They brushed their eyes. For many moments their vision was hazy and they could barely make out the scene below.

Jem breathed deeply. 'Thank the amulet,' he said, 'indeed.'

Rajal looked suspiciously at his wrist. 'If this is a talisman,' he said, 'I'd prefer one that didn't get us into trouble in the first place.'

'At least you've still got it,' said Littler. 'What about mine?'

'Now that *definitely* didn't work,' said Rajal.

Littler bristled, but restrained himself. They lapsed into silence as the carpet descended, gently now, down the wooded slopes of the island. A soft beach lay below. Few sights could be more peaceful, but Jem thought again of the vision of Toth, staring at him from the orb. Perhaps it had been an illusion, no more, but secretly he was glad that the orb was lost. With a shudder he wondered if Toth had been watching them, if he could be watching them even now.

Then it happened. The BOOM! filled the air like a clap of thunder.

'What the—'

'Dive!'

Where the burning ball came from, they had no time to see. They knew

23

only that it was headed straight for them, plunging towards the carpet like a fiery comet. Viciously the flaming thing tore through the fabric, then Jem and his friends were falling into the jungle below.

Long moments passed. Silence.

'Wh-what happened?' said Rajal.

Sourly he looked at his amulet. A thick clump of ferns had cushioned his fall, but his limbs were in a tangle and he was quite sure he was bruised all over. Clumsily he struggled to stand.

'I think we know *what* happened,' said Jem, tugging himself free from a web of vines. 'The question is *who* – and *why*.'

The jungle pressed around them, dripping, dense and green. Tickerings and strange, breathy flurryings sounded about them in the hot, moist air. Hanging from a branch was a scrap, still smouldering, of the magic carpet. Sadly Jem gazed upon the blackened fabric.

'You look as though we've lost a friend,' said Rajal.

Jem glanced round worriedly. 'Actually,' he said, 'we *have* – in fact, two. Where's Littler? Where's Rainbow?'

They called their names, but neither the expected cry, nor a bark, sounded above the hushed flurryings and tickerings. Jem reached out, parting a screen of vines. He glimpsed the beach, a distant dazzle through gaps in the foliage.

He screwed up his eyes. 'They must be close.'

They called again.

Still no reply.

'We're stranded, aren't we?' Rajal said glumly.

'Maybe – maybe not. You don't think we're *alone* on this island, do you – like Robander Selsoe?'

'Maybe – maybe not. *Rainbow!*'

'*Littler!*'

Their cries were spirited away, muffled quickly by the tropical growth. They peered through the gloom, this way and that. Branches and vines screened out the sky but offered no relief from the oppressive heat.

'Jem,' said Rajal after a moment, 'who's Robander Selsoe?'

'Really Raj, it's a famous story – a true one, too. He was a shipwrecked sailor. On an island he was, just like this – oh, for years on end. Whole cycles – all by himself, and a ship never came ... *Littler!*'

'*Rainbow!*'

'Jem,' Rajal said next, 'what if this island's like Robander Selsoe's? I mean, what if there's no one here except us – the four of us, I mean?'

'There has to be. Otherwise, where did that fireball come from?'

'I thought it sort of ... dropped from the air.'

'Balls of fire don't just drop from the air.'

'Not even round these volcano things?'

'Well, all right. But that was shot from a cannon. *Rainbow!*'

'*Littler!*' Rajal looked up dubiously through the leaves. 'What about when we were flying overhead? I didn't see any signs of life, did you?'

'Only trees, trees and trees.'

'Typical. Just when we need a nice, comfortable tavern. I've even got the gold to pay for it, you know – got the gold, and nowhere to spend it. Just typical. *Littler!*'

'*Rainbow!* This is crazy – they can't just have vanished.'

'They could have been knocked out – by the fall, I mean.'

'I hope not. Who knows what may be lurking round here?'

'Lurking?' said Rajal. 'What do you mean?'

'Snakes, poisonous spiders—'

Gulping, Rajal hoped his amulet was not really useless. He had wondered if they were searching in the most effective way, and thought that perhaps they should split up; now he thought that he would not suggest it. Acutely he became aware of the soft, strange sounds that filled the dense greenery, the bubblings, the hissings, the tock-tock rhythms of insects in bark.

So it was that Rajal, not Jem, was first to hear the peculiar, intent murmuring that sounded from beyond a screen of vines.

'Jem, what's that?'

'What's what?'

'I don't know – listen.'

But before Rajal could pull him back, Jem parted the sticky vines. At once the sound was louder, not a murmuring but the relentless buzzing of hundreds of flies. Without quite knowing why, Rajal was alarmed.

'They're busy,' he muttered.

'Yes,' said Jem. 'But with what?'

They soon knew the answer. First came the sweet overpowering rottenness, wafting towards them as they floundered forward. If the stench was enough to drive them back, their curiosity was stronger.

The object of the flies' fervour was something heavy, something pendulous, hanging from a high branch. The foliage here was especially thick, the shadows deeper, but still there was light enough to see the twisted neck, the bloated face, the blackened, hanging hands.

Rajal stumbled back. 'Jem! Come away!'

Jem only stared at the flyblown corpse. 'Raj, look at his clothes—'

'What? Jem, I don't want to look at him at all!' Rajal's hand covered his mouth and he shuddered as Jem stepped forward, pointing solemnly to the knickerbockers, the belt, the ragged remnants of a stripy shirt. On and on buzzed the flies; maggots, yellow and writhing, tunnelled through the flesh of the dead man's face. By now, even his dearest friend might not have recognised him, but one thing was clear enough.

'He's an Ejlander,' said Rajal. 'An Ejlander sailor.'

'But how did he get here? And get like this?'

'Suicide. Well, you would, wouldn't you? I mean, if you were stuck here – like Robander Selsoe.'

'Robander Selsoe didn't kill himself, Raj. Look at this man's belt. Someone's ripped away his purse – and his knife. What about his cutlass, where's that gone?'

'He lost it in the wreck – Jem, come away.'

'This man's been murdered, Raj.'

'A long time ago. Just look at him, Jem!'

'A long time? In this climate?'

There was no time to say more. Suddenly, through the trees, came a sound of barking.

'Rainbow? Raj, this way – quick!'

Vines closed on the scene of death as they sprang forward, running in the direction of the urgent sounds. A clearing lay ahead. The barking seemed to come from there, but still they could not see Rainbow's bright fur.

Then, all at once, they were swept through the air.

'A trap! We've tripped a wire!'

Chapter 4

GREEN MANSIONS

'Jem?'

'Raj?'

'Your elbow's in my eye.'

'Yours is in my ribs. Can't you shift?'

'That's what I'm asking you!'

Rajal sighed. To be swept suddenly into the air was an alarming experience; still more alarming it was to wonder what might happen next. His limbs were twisted up at angles and the mesh of the net cut painfully into his skin. His eye, the one with the elbow in it, watered profusely; the other could barely focus. All he could see were the bright rays of the sun, stabbing down through the deep green.

'What is this, anyway? An animal trap?'

Jem's voice was rueful. 'Look below, Raj.'

'I told you, your elbow's in my eye—'

'Well, just be glad it's not a spear.'

'Hm?' For a moment Rajal wondered what Jem was talking about; then, blinking, he became aware of reddish, peculiar shapes moving below. His heart lurched and he felt something prodding at his throat. He gulped and saw a slender youth standing beneath him with a long sharpened stick, upraised and threatening. A stocky fellow was covering Jem. Both were very ragged and very dirty. With matted hair and dark discolorations over their faces and limbs, they looked as if they had recently fallen into mud.

And what was that smell?

The stocky youth, who seemed the more aggressive of the two, twisted his spear at Jem's throat. 'Who are you? What are you doing here?'

Jem said, 'We could ask you the same question.'

'Don't provoke us – we *know* what you are.'

'Then you've no need to ask, have you?'

'Jem,' Rajal hissed, 'are you trying to get us killed?'

'They're just muddy boys, Raj – younger than us.'

By now, Rajal's eyes had cleared. 'I know the light's not good here, Jem, but look a bit harder.'

'You mean they're older?'

'I mean that's not *mud*—'

'Shut up!' barked the stocky youth. His eyes flickered over the two captives, sunlight playing ominously on the tip of his spear. 'Now answer this question: which of you is the *pilot from the air*?'

The leaner youth looked troubled. 'Ojo, I'm still not sure about this. What if—'

But the youth called Ojo was not listening. Threateningly, he repeated his question.

'I don't know what you mean,' declared Jem. 'We're from Ejland.' Then to Rajal, aside: 'I don't suppose you could offer that bag of gold, could you? I mean, it *might* be worth it.'

Sotto voce: 'What, waste it on them? If we had some bright beads, I might just buy the island. But the gold? There has to be a tavern somewhere, you know.'

Ojo spat, 'You were on that mat – that rug.'

'Carpet, actually,' said Rajal, 'which *you* shot down. Now why did you want to go and do that?'

'The cannon?' said Ojo. 'No, that wasn't us.'

The one called Uchy shook his head. 'Oh no! We didn't—'

'But we would have,' said Ojo.

'We would?' His friend looked at him sharply.

Jem said, 'You knew it was a cannon?'

Suddenly, the stocky youth was angry. 'I ask the questions! And I want answers!' He dragged his spear across Jem's throat. It was as well that the tip was blunt, or it would have drawn blood. 'But I think you've already answered my question. It's not just the way you talk – it's your hair.'

'Now I *really* don't know what you mean,' said Jem.

The stocky youth looked grimly at his companion. 'Just like Lemyu, eh Uchy? Sun-coloured hair, a sure sign of evil—'

'But Ojo, Lemyu wasn't evil, he was *good*—'

'He *died*, didn't he?' Jem heard desperation in Ojo's voice. It was almost as if the stocky youth were trying to convince himself of what must happen next, of what he must do – as if this were his last chance . . . 'Oh, I think we've got our pilot all right, Uchy – and the Sibyl says we have to strike him down. *To strike him down*,' he repeated slowly.

'Ojo, we can't – *you* can't.' Nervously the slender youth looked up at Jem – then blurted, as if suddenly he could not restrain himself, 'Did Maius Eneo send you? Did you come from Maius—'

'Shut up, just shut up!' Ojo whipped round, clashing his spear against his companion's. Wrong-footed, Ucheus blundered back. Ojo advanced on him, trampling down the undergrowth. The leaner youth held his spear aloft, warding off blows, but he was clumsy, and fell. An instant more and Ojo was astride him. The stocky youth had flung his spear

28

aside, but now he grabbed the kos-knife from his belt. Ucheus gasped as the bloody blade pressed against his throat.

'Ojo! What are you doing?'

Only for a moment did it seem that Ojo might really drive in the blade. His eyes narrowed with bitterness as, clumsily, reluctantly, he released his companion. 'Just shut up, Uchy – I've told you, *I'm* handling this—'

'But not well,' said Ucheus defiantly, scrambling up. He knocked the kos-knife from Ojo's grip. It fell into the undergrowth. 'You're acting like a fool, Ojo. It was the *heart*, wasn't it? Ever since you held the heart in your hands, you've been like . . . like a madmaster. Just remember, the sacrifice was your idea.'

'Sacrifice?' whispered Rajal. 'That's it, Jem – if we ever get out of this, I'm throwing this amulet into the sea.'

'You could try throwing down the bag of gold.'

'Right now? I don't think they'd notice.'

Angrily Ucheus grabbed the kos-knife, stuffing it into his own belt. It was as if he were daring Ojo to fight him again. Earnestness filled the slender youth's face as he turned back to Jem. 'Sun-haired one, tell us – do you come from Maius Eneo?'

Jem bit his lip. *Say yes. Just say yes.*

Rajal blurted, 'Maius who? Look, we don't know what you're *talking* about—'

Jem groaned; Ojo smacked Ucheus in the chest. 'Told you! Didn't I tell you?'

The two youths gazed at each other levelly. There was a silence. The heat of the day was rising, pressing insistently through the gloom of the jungle. Dapples of light sparkled on the greenery and steam, fecund and reeking, curled up from the undergrowth.

Jem cleared his throat. Later, perhaps, he would abuse Rajal, but this was not the time. 'I don't suppose you'd consider cutting us down?' he asked their captors.

'No, but we might consider killing you,' said Ojo.

He retrieved his spear, jabbing it up towards the net again.

Ucheus moved forward, placing a hand on his companion's arm. His voice, this time, was gentle. 'Ojo, don't you remember how you believed in Lemyu, how you trusted him? You agreed with Maius Eneo about him, you know you—'

The stocky youth cursed, shaking off the hand that tried to hold him back.

But now Ucheus would not let him go. 'Maius Eneo was right about Lemyu, wasn't he – right about *that*, at least? And Lemyu – he was sun-haired, wasn't he? And—'

'Raj, do you get the feeling we've met this Lemyu?' Jem muttered. He raised his voice, foolishly no doubt, since the youth called Ojo was angry enough. But Jem was angry too, and could not resist. 'This Lemyu,' he said sharply, 'I don't suppose he's a sailor-fellow hanging from a tree, with maggots in his face and flies buzzing all around—'

Rajal gasped, 'Jem, what are you—'

Shock registered in the bloodied faces. Ojo cried out, 'Now do you see, Uchy? They know too much – they know everything!' He shook away his companion's grip. He swung back his spear.

He charged forward. 'Die, pilot!'

Ucheus cried, 'Ojo, no—'

Jem braced himself. But before the spear could plunge through his flesh, there was a crash of foliage and another voice, high and fierce, rang through the clearing. A blade hacked down, dashing the spear from Ojo's hand.

In the next moment, the stocky youth was lying on his back, howling, bested by the new challenger who sat astride him, waving a rusty cutlass in the air.

Rajal said nervously, 'Who can this be?'

'Let's just hope he's on our side, Raj.'

From the net, Jem and Rajal could see no more of this new challenger than a knobbly brown backbone and a headdress which appeared to be made from feathers and leaves.

'You've been a bad boy, Zandis Ojonis,' he was saying. His voice was cracking, crazed. 'First Kyra – oh, I know about Kyra, never you mind. If I could have stopped you, I would. I'm your leader, aren't I? If there was an offering, it was mine to make – mine!' The cutlass swept down, stopping just short of Ojo's neck. 'Do you understand, Zandis Ojonis?'

From Ojo came only a humiliated moaning.

Ucheus stood by, twisting his hands. 'Leki, please—'

'Madmasters, what did you think you were playing at? Look at the pair of you, covered in blood! Ucheus, I'm surprised at you, letting him go through with it. And now this – is this the way to treat our guests?'

'Guests?' echoed Ucheus.

'Yes, follyface!' screeched the youth in the headdress. Springing up from Ojo, he turned to the captives.

Jem drew in his breath. Beneath his headdress, the newcomer's face was painted with stripes, and over his chest hung a necklace of bones. His only clothing was a loincloth – fashioned, it appeared, from the tatters of a tunic such as his companions wore.

But there was something else, too. Around his hips was a loose, broad belt, and hanging from the belt were a curving scabbard, a sailor's purse and a brace of knives. He slipped the cutlass back into the scabbard.

'Lemyu's things?' Rajal murmured.

'No doubt about it,' said Jem.

The painted youth smiled, bowing with exaggerated courtesy. If Jem found Leki alarming, he found him puzzling too. In Lord Empster's library there had been many engravings of savages. Jem had learnt that they were ignorant, brutal and warlike, and that some, perhaps all of them, dined on human flesh; he recalled the horror of Robander Selsoe when a party of cannibals landed upon his island, bent upon conducting their vile orgies. Epicycles ago, when reports of such creatures had first reached Ejland, men of learning had been thrown into a conundrum. How was it, they wondered, that human beings, created by the all-benevolent father-god, could be capable of such depravity? In time, an explanation had been found. Savages, it became clear, were not human at all, but mockeries of humanity, Rejects of Orok, who merely assumed the semblance of human form.

Whether this was true, Jem did not know, but he knew one thing: this youth who stood before them now was a most unusual savage. Perhaps, thought Jem, he was no savage at all.

'Allow me to introduce myself,' said the youth. 'I am Lekis Sanis Saxis, governor of this island.'

'What?' said Rajal. 'Governor?'

Jem dug his friend in the ribs. 'Raj, keep your big mouth shut this time, please?' He raised his voice. 'Governor ... indeed this is a privilege,' he attempted. 'My name is Jemany, and my friend is Rajal. We are poor travellers, driven by ... by poverty from our native land. Cursed by an evil enchanter, we were destined – why, to fly to the very edges of the earth, had we not the fortune to descend over your island.'

The eyes glittered in the painted face. 'Cursed by magic? Then it seems we have much in common.'

Jem's interest was aroused at once, but Leki only bowed again and gestured to his companions. 'You have met my well-intentioned, if blundering subordinates. You accept my apologies, I trust, for their somewhat ... *precipitate* actions? This Isle of Xaro, you will understand, is a place of many dangers ... but curse me for a follyface, what can I be thinking of? Ojonis, Ucheus – cut down our guests, cut them down at once!'

As it happened, it was the governor and not his subordinates who performed this duty. The youth called Ojo was only just rising, clutching his ribs, assisted by the concerned Ucheus. Leki's cutlass swished back through the air. Blunt metal hacked at rope. The net began to sway, then slowly revolved.

31

'Hang on, Raj!'

'To what, Jem?'

Their fall, fortunately, was cushioned by the undergrowth. Really, it was not so bad: with cramped legs and arms, Jem struggled against the chrysalis of twine, managing in a moment to kick himself free. Rajal had a little more trouble; he groaned elaborately. With a laugh, Jem plucked at his friend's bonds.

'Come on, Raj, on your feet!'

'Feet? Have I still got any?'

Rajal lurched and would have fallen if Jem had not grabbed him. In the next moment, they were both stumbling. The shuddering began without warning, rippling beneath the jungle floor like the stirring of a monstrous, buried beast.

Or like thunder. Thunder under the ground.

It was over in a moment. For a second time, Jem scrambled up from the sticky, steamy vegetation, brushing himself free of clinging leaves and spores. Around him, the others were rising too. Only Leki had remained standing, riding the convulsions with a splay-footed glee, waving his cutlass excitedly in the air.

Grinning, he turned to his frightened subordinates. 'You see, Zandis Ojonis?' he said in a carefree voice. 'It was all for nothing, wasn't it? Did you think your paltry sacrifice could appease the Thunderer? I told you Kyra would never be enough, and I was right, wasn't I?'

'We didn't want to appease the Thunderer,' said Ucheus. 'It was the Sibyl we went to, the Sibyl. We just wanted to find out what would *happen*, that's all—'

'*Happen*? The Sibyl?' Leki flung back his head and laughed. 'You're madmasters, the pair of you – as if the Sibyl would tell *you* anything!'

The painted youth turned back to Jem and Rajal, resuming the manner of moments before. If his words were controlled, his voice retained a crazed edge. 'Our guests are unhurt? But of course, of course – a rumble, no more. On an island like this, one must expect a little *rumble* from time to time . . . But come, we dally here to no purpose – you must be in need of rest, not to mention food.'

'Oh, please *do* mention it,' said Rajal.

Leki smiled. 'Then let us go to Sarom. Come.'

'Sarom?' said Jem.

'Indeed, where else would I take my guests? Ucheus, gather up the net, hm? We'll set it up again later.'

With that, slinging the cutlass over his shoulder, the painted youth moved off jauntily through the jungle. Turning, he beckoned Jem and Rajal to follow. Uncertainly, they exchanged glances. To be sure, they could run for it, but what would be the point? They were trapped, leagues from anywhere, on this strange island. They were also very hungry.

Better to play along, at least for now.

'Uh,' Jem attempted, as they pushed through the foliage, 'I don't suppose any of you have seen a little boy, about – oh, so high, and a dog the colour of the rainbow?'

Leki turned sharply. 'Boy? Dog? They are your friends?'

'Our very good friends, lost when we . . . landed.'

'Indeed? Ah, but there are many dangers on this Isle of Xaro.' There was a faraway note in Leki's voice. It was rather as if he had dismissed the subject, but a moment later he turned again and said sharply, 'Ojonis . . . Ucheus! No . . . Ucheus, just you. Look for the boy and the rainbow-coloured dog.'

'Me?' Fear glittered in the lean youth's eyes.

Leki smiled again at his guests. 'But come, come.'

In the jungle, words fade quickly. As soon as Leki's party had trudged away, pushing through the green mansions of leaves, no sound of their voices echoed back to the damp, fecund place where Jem and Rajal had swung in the net. There remained only silence, or rather, that peculiar jungle silence which is not silence at all but compounded of a thousand tiny cracklings, hissings, rustlings. Steam rose acridly, shimmering in the dappled light, and on a mossy, rapidly rotting log sat a large toad, swelling out its throat and blinking its bulbous eyes. Coiled languidly round a branch was a tree-snake, coloured black and gold like a tiger.

There came a sound of fluttering. It was a bird, not a seabird, but a Wenayan jungle bird, a raven coloured not black but a deep, mysterious blue. Descending, perching lightly, the raven stabbed its beak into one of the bright fruits that hung, hugely engorged, amongst the leaves. Sweet juices squirted and dripped. The serpent uncoiled, as if to pounce, but just then the toad gave a bilious croak. The raven stiffened and flitted away.

Darting here, darting there, the strangely coloured bird was nervously alert, fearful of what dangers might yet lie concealed amongst the sweltering chambers of leaves. Several times its sharp little beak snapped up juicy beetles and worms that gleamed suddenly in the sun-dappled shadows. But the raven did not linger. Always its bright eyes swivelled and flashed. Onwards, onwards it hopped and flew. Soon the treacherous snake was far behind.

Then it was forgotten. Skittering above a path of trampled ferns, the raven became aware of a sweet mysterious pungency, headier than the perfume of any fruit or flower. With it came an enticing music, the buzzing and blowing of thousands of flies. Pushing between vines, forgetful of its fears, the raven alighted on a spindly branch. Curiously it took in the source of the pungency, the heavy, hanging thing with its twisted neck, its bloated face, its blood-blackened hands. Eagerly it eyed the maggots in the flesh, plumper than any it had seen before. Greed stirred in the raven's breast and it would have swept forward, defying the flies, but something held it back. In this place of death the shadows were deep, yet still there was a fugitive shaft of light, flickering over the grinning, decomposing face as it swung slowly in a breeze, back and forth, back and forth.

But no, there was no breeze amongst this stagnant heat. The raven's feathers ruffled and its heart became rapid. On and on went the mad music of the flies, but it seemed to be changing, becoming something more. The sunshine flickered, almost like a pulse, as the first twitching came in the dead man's leg; then a hand was moving, reaching up to claw at the rope around the neck. Rotted in the heat, the rope gave way. The corpse crashed stiffly to the steaming ground.

There was a pause. The flies flurried in confusion. The blue raven watched, unblinking. Then came a stirring in the undergrowth. The corpse staggered upright and began to walk, crashing and blundering through the vines and leaves.

Chapter 5

THIS SIDE OF PARADISE

'Ra Ra, come! Ra Ra, quick!'

'My lady,' came a gasp, 'you're too fast for me!'

'But the sea – it's lovely! Oh, how can you tarry?'

The exchange took place on another island, many leagues from Xaro, where at that moment a girl in flowing robes paused on a path, looking back, laughing, as her plump nurse – burdened, so it happened, with a heavy basket – struggled towards her down a steep incline. Bright stones, dislodged by the nurse's feet, scurried before her like eager little animals, bent on plunging into the warm, glittering water.

It was an eagerness, evidently, that the nurse did not share. Breathless, she joined her young charge, setting down her basket with a loud, undignified bump.

'Silly Ra Ra,' the girl grinned, oblivious, 'how ever should you hope to catch a suitor?'

'Suitor?' What could the girl mean? Ra Ra – or rather, Ra Fanana – would be content to catch her breath. The nurse was not old – really, she was still young, or almost – but since coming into the Triarch's service she was, she had to admit, rather heavier than she used to be. Of course, her basket was heavy too – very heavy . . . 'Suitor, indeed!' she forced herself to add. 'My lady, I wonder where you get such ideas!'

'From you, Ra Ra!' The girl twirled excitedly, gesturing over the sea, bangles clattering on her slender olive wrist. 'Don't you remember that isle of yours?'

Colour played high in Ra Fanana's cheeks. Oh, but she must be careful! Had she not struggled for control? Indeed, but what of it? Discipline, discipline, always discipline – then would come a night when the sea glimmered brightly, and the perfumes of the garden stole headily on the air, and music drifted up from the palace courtyard . . . and then would come Ra Fanana's foolish stories, stealing like magic into the eager girl!

'An isle,' cried the girl now, 'where jasmine fills the air, and all the maidens are beautiful, and the young men too, and marriages are decided by a love-chase! Didn't you tell me how the nubile girls pursue the young men, and when a girl catches the one she wants, then he is hers, and they are bound in wedlock? Silly Ra Ra, you must remember!'

And the girl hugged herself, and closed her eyes, and sighed.

The nurse sighed too, for a different reason. 'It is true,' she forced herself to say, 'that there is talk of this Isle of Jasmine – ah, and indeed it may be real, not just the stuff of a nurse's tale. The world is wide, and its ways are many. But my lady,' she added, 'such are not – most *definitely* not – the ways of Hora.'

Ra Fanana's tone was solemn and she would have reached forward, taking the girl's lovely face in her hands, as was her wont when impressing (so she thought) this or that vital truth upon her young charge. But she did not have the chance. The girl giggled and darted away, skidding down the remainder of the steep, stony path.

Wearily, Ra Fanana picked up her basket again. Dear Lady Selinda! There were times, it was true, when the girl was thoughtless, times when she was perverse, times when she was no more than a silly little fool – but to think ill of her was impossible, at least for Ra Fanana. The girl was young, that was all. Try as she might to be the stern nurse, ready with reprimands and sage advice, Ra Fanana could not help but indulge her young charge. Let Lady Selinda enjoy her high spirits, at least for now – marriage would clip her wings soon enough!

'Ra Ra, come! Ra Ra, quick!'

'Why, there's jasmine enough in the air hereabouts,' mused Ra Fanana, as she unpacked her basket on the beach. 'Quite enough!'

And so there was, wafting down on a breeze from the lush royal gardens, mingling with the seaweed and the seaplants and the brackish, warm air. Did the girl know she was living in paradise? Just look at this sheltered cove with its carved, bejewelled pebbles strewn here and there, its smoothly rounded boulders, its carefully draped seaweed and aromatic plants! If only *all* seashores could be thus!

Artificial, yes – but artifice was often better than reality.

'I'm a mermaid! Ra Ra, I'm a mermaid!' Happily, her robe discarded on the sand, Selinda splashed in the soft waves.

Ra Fanana rolled out an ornate rug and set down dishes of silver and gold. All around them, concealed behind the foliage, merging into the rocks that bounded the cove, rose the high walls of the Triarch's estate, secluding them from the world. To Ra Fanana, this was a comfort, for she cherished their safety; Selinda would think of the world beyond the walls not with trepidation but with eager impatience.

'Ra Ra,' she said now, as she cast herself down on the sand, 'if I could chase *my* suitors, which should I catch?'

Ra Fanana was setting out pressed meats, arranging them neatly on the plates. She had been humming to herself, contented, preoccupied; now she looked up sharply. 'My lady, really! What can you mean?'

Droplets rolled down Selinda's slender arms and her bathing-slip clung wetly to her small, girlish breasts. Reaching for the hava-nectar, she upended the amphora into her mouth, taking a long, unladylike drink. Ra Fanana would have protested, but Selinda wiped her mouth and said, smiling, 'Lord Glond or Prince Lepato? Which one? Please tell me – *please!*'

Ra Fanana pursed her mouth. Games of pretend were all very well, but this was going just a little too far. 'The choice, my lady, is hardly *yours*, and still less should it be mine – do you forget, I am a mere slave?'

The girl pouted. 'Ra Ra, you're such a dull-wit!' And scrambling up, she seized a pebble, flinging it into the sea. 'It's not fair!' she cried. 'One of them's going to be my husband – mine – and I won't even get to *speak* to him till my wedding day!'

Ra Fanana went to her, more than a little guiltily. Now why had she told the girl about the Isle of Jasmine?

'Come, child,' she pleaded, 'is this the way for a lady to behave? Think of your poor Nurse Fanana, if you will not think of yourself! Think what a hapless task is hers, to make you fit for the life that lies before you! Should she fear she has failed? And what, I ask you, will become of her then?' She gripped the girl's wet face and pulled her round, embracing her. 'Poor lady, you are young yet, but when you are in the world, soon you will be grateful for the lot that is yours. What of it, if you cannot choose your husband? Is it not enough that he will be a great man, and you, as his consort, will be a great lady?'

She drew back, lifting up the girl's chin. Tears, as she had expected, blurred Selinda's eyes, but the girl blinked them away before they fell. 'I know, Ra Ra, I know you're right. But why can't Father just make up his mind?'

It was a question Ra Fanana had often asked herself. The two lords who sued for her young lady's hand were both fine specimens of manhood: Lord Glond, with his blue robes, his long braided hair, and the little flashing jewels embedded round his eyes; and Prince Lepato, garbed in red, with his gold-capped teeth, his hoop-like earrings and his beard plaited into a tight, pendulous cylinder. Why, either might make an admirable husband – and both were in the prime of their lives, too! No doubt about it, Lady Selinda was lucky. What did marriage mean for many a girl of her value, but the caresses of gnarled hands, the weight of a bloated belly, the lust that glittered in rheumy eyes? Could Triarch Jodrell – a man who determined, each day, the most burdensome affairs of state – be stymied by such a choice as this? Other daughters of the Hora-nobility were promised in marriage-bonds from the moment of their birth. Ra Fanana had no doubt that Triarch Jodrell loved his daughter, but it seemed he was playing a game with her destiny.

Without doubt, it was a political game – and, Ra Fanana guessed, a dangerous one.

But what good would it do to tell the girl?

'Child, would you question the Triarch's wisdom? Your father loves you. Is he to rush his decision, with your happiness at stake? Foolish girl, to be so insensible of your blessings! Now come, let's have ourselves a nice picnic, shall we? I've brought your box harp. Perhaps you'll sing to me afterwards? You know, I still haven't heard that ballad you've been learning . . .'

For a moment, Ra Fanana worried that the girl would flounce away; instead, to her relief, Selinda smiled and took her place on the rug, lighting eagerly upon the pressed meats, the dried tomatoes, the olives and the cheeses and the candied fruits that the nurse heaped generously upon her plate, accompanied with a rich, spicy dressing. Besides, the hava-nectar was relaxing the girl; Ra Fanana always added to the mixture just a drop of a certain treacle, as the royal physician had instructed her to do. (Truth to tell, the nurse quite liked the treacle herself and often dipped her finger into the sticky-sided pot at this or that odd time during the day. Foolish of her, no doubt – no wonder she was plumper, just a little plumper, than she used to be.)

'You're ready for your crumble-cake, my lady?' she urged, when Selinda's plate was clean. Ra Fanana was certainly ready for hers – best to lighten the basket, after all, for the climb back to the palace!

The nurse could have commanded any number of inferior slaves to accompany them on these picnics, bearing all burdens, waiting upon them, dressing and undressing them, flapping fans. Tagan, her lady's eunuch, was positively affronted that *he* was not invited. But it would not have been the same. For Ra Fanana, these afternoons alone with the girl – entirely alone – were the greatest of her pleasures since coming into Triarch Jodrell's service. If Lady Selinda was to be married soon, Ra Fanana would not spoil their last days together. But then, she thought, the very knowledge that these were the *last* days must cast a dark shadow over these pleasures.

And fear clutched again at the nurse's heart.

Chapter 6

FINGERS DOWN MY THROAT

Ultramarine. Verdant green.

Littler could only screw up his eyes. The sun, glittering sharply on the waves, seemed to paint more boldly the blue fields of the sea and the dappled mansions of the jungle, at once dark and dazzling. Close, too close, the verdure pressed around him in its rising, reeking richness. He shifted, wondering if the branch would hold. There was a sharp *crack!* and a bird crashed up from somewhere below, coloured a deep blue and cawing, perhaps in warning, perhaps in joy. Once, twice it whirled round Littler's head, then swooped away, arcing above the rocks then vanishing suddenly into the trees again.

Littler clung to the branch, breathing heavily. He supposed he was lucky. When the carpet tore apart, his small body had been flung far off, spinning through the air. It was a close thing. With a shudder, he looked below. Just a little further, and he would have crashed into the great wall of rock that banded this particular stretch of shore, dividing the ultramarine from the green. But his present situation was hardly enviable. He edged his way back along the branch, reaching for the spindly trunk of the tree. At this height, the trunk felt scarcely more solid than the branch. But where was the next branch down – and the next? And would they hold? So dense was the foliage, so dense and dark, that Littler could not see how to climb down . . . and his limbs were so small . . . But he had to try. He braced himself. There was a creak, then another, sharper *crack!*

Down, down Littler tumbled.

'Are we there yet?'

Rajal's tunic was sodden with sweat and his breath came in heavy gasps. He leaned against a mossy, upright slab of rock, pushing back his dripping hair. By now the sun was high overhead and the jungle had thinned. For some time they had followed a sinuous path flanked by drier, paler trees. Rajal strained his ears. Once he had thought he heard Rainbow's bark, somewhere up ahead, or perhaps behind. He could not hear him now. How high had they climbed?

Jem, further up the path, turned back. 'There's something up ahead.'

'More of those houses?'

'You're leaning against one now, Raj.'

Rajal looked behind him. It was true: the mossy slab was not rock, but the mud-brick wall of a low, crumbling dwelling. Several times as they pushed their way uphill they had glimpsed similar ruins, largely concealed beneath leaves and vines. Rajal would have liked to ask about them, but could not. Leki strode too far ahead; Ojo crashed in the rear, always concealed behind the last twist of the path.

Idly Rajal patted at a pocket. Then he gasped, 'Jem!'

Jem had already moved ahead. 'What now, Raj?'

'The bag of gold! I . . . it must have fallen out, somewhere back in the jungle.'

Jem rolled his eyes. 'What do you want to do, go back?'

'But . . . oh Jem, what are we going to do?'

'Forget the gold! Think about Littler. Think about Rainbow.'

'I am. Don't you think we'll all need a nice comfortable tavern, if we ever get off this wretched—'

Rajal said no more. Just then Ojo appeared, clutching at a stitch in his side. With peculiar intensity his eyes flickered over Jem, then Rajal, then Jem again. His lips trembled and a vein in his neck was pounding hard, rather as if he had something to say, but could not quite force out the words. Rajal's brow furrowed. He staggered towards the youth and would have shaken him, but just then Leki called back cheerfully, 'Come on, slugfeet! We're here – Sarom!'

Ojo pushed forward. Wonderingly, Rajal clambered over a last twist in the path. He screwed up his eyes. Trees and vines forced themselves from cracks in the ridge, but here there was space for the sun, too. Light poured liberally over jagged rock and splashed across a host of tumbledown dwellings. Shadows, swift and irregular, scudded across the brightness. Looking up, Rajal saw the dark smoke of the volcano, closer now, and realised that the rock beneath his feet, so solid, was trembling a little. How he wished he was in that nice, comfortable tavern!

'Come, my friends!' Leki, cutlass in hand, bade his guests a solemn welcome. 'A hard climb, but worth it, is it not, for the splendours that lie about us now? Sarom – what can this name mean but pride, bursting pride, in the breasts of all us Islanders of Aroc? Sarom – higher than all but the vents of the Thunderers, taproot of tradition, cradle of culture, hope of history, locus of law! As the Thunderers are the source of divine wisdom, so it is from Sarom that earthly wisdom flows! Sarom – seat of the Dynasts since even Brother Time was the merest infant, mewling and puking in his nurse's arms!'

For a moment Jem and Rajal stood blinking, wondering if their host had finished his effusion. They also wondered what to make of it. A ponderous joke? With Leki, one could not quite tell. This place called Sarom, if their eyes disclosed the truth, consisted of a number of shabby mud huts. Did Leki really see a mighty castle? A vast, ornate palace?

Curiously, Jem counted the huts. Nine? Ten? 'There are more of you, I suppose?'

'Not any more,' Ojo muttered.

Leki turned, silencing him savagely. 'Did I ask you to speak? You fat follyface, do you think our guests want to listen to you? Now hurry up and get the banquet ready!'

Jem's brow furrowed. Rajal bit his lip, embarrassed. From a sunken, bubbling pit in the rock there rose strands of steam. A rank smell hovered round the huts and once again there was the buzz of flies. Fresh rumblings sounded underfoot.

Leki laughed. 'Fear not, my friends. To visitors, perhaps, the Thunderer is alarming, but to us Islanders of Aroc, he is commonplace enough.'

'Aroc?' Jem had noted the word before. 'But that's not the name of this island, is it? I thought it was Xaro.'

'Indeed,' said Leki. 'But we are Islanders of Aroc, are we not?'

Jem would have asked more, but Rajal said apprehensively, 'Does it just rumble, then – the mountain, I mean?'

Leki leaned towards him, jaw uptilted. 'You want it to do more?'

Rajal was a little taken aback. 'Well, I suppose you'd hardly live on an *exploding* island,' he laughed.

'Would you take me for a follyface and a madmaster?'

Conscious of the cutlass, Rajal shook his head.

Laughing again, Leki directed his guests to a burbling spring, concealed in a grove of scrubby trees. 'You'll wish to refresh yourselves, I'm sure, before the banquet?'

In truth it was Ojo who most needed refreshing, but the blood-covered youth was already hard at work, blundering in and out of one of the huts, bringing forth pineapples and mangoes and avocado pears, breadfruit and bananas, yams and coconuts, mats made of dried leaves and armfuls of flowers. Carefully, breathlessly, he arranged them round the pit. The stocky youth was trembling with fear. Leki stood and watched.

Meanwhile, in the grove, Jem and Rajal splashed their limbs, their faces, their hair. The spring was warm, almost hot, and at first they were surprised, until they realised that the heat, like the tremblings of the rock, was the work of the Thunderer. They let the water run down freely, soaking their tunics. After some moments, Rajal even stopped moaning about the lost bag of gold.

Outside, Leki began a little capering dance, slapping his thigh with the flat of the cutlass. As he danced he sang softly, almost mournfully, in a tuneless voice:

> *Carry me to Sarom, mother,*
> *Let me make my vows –*
> *When I am a man, mother,*
> *I shall live on Sarom . . .*
>
> *I shall live on Sarom, mother,*
> *When I am a man –*
> *I must make my vows, mother,*
> *Carry me to Sarom . . .*

Rajal jerked a thumb towards their host. 'Let's hope he never auditions for the Silver Masks,' he grimaced, with a professional entertainer's fastidious disdain for the blundering efforts of an amateur. 'Harlequin and Clown would have turfed him out by now – unless, of course, he were *particularly* fetching. Which he's not.'

'What I wonder,' said Jem, 'is why the others obey him.'

Rajal smoothed his hair. 'The cutlass, for a start?'

'But there're two of them, and only one of him. No Raj, that fellow's got some sort of magic – evil magic.'

Gulping, Rajal looked out through the branches of the grove. Leki, whistling now, gazed upon his cutlass. From time to time he turned the blade, catching the brightness of the hot sun; meanwhile Ojo was probing into the pit with a stick of bamboo, fetching up strips of steaming, pale meat. Repelled, Rajal looked away.

'Jem,' he whispered, as they returned to the others, 'what about Rainbow? Once or twice as we climbed up here, I thought I heard him bark again.'

'Me too – but I couldn't tell the direction. Then I wasn't sure . . . not sure I'd heard him at all.' Jem sighed. 'On an island like this, I wouldn't be surprised if there were noises in the air – funny noises, if you know what I mean.'

Rajal nodded, and wondered if it had been magic – Leki's magic? – that had separated them from their companions. He would have said more, but the painted youth, stirred back into life, ushered them eagerly into their places. The rich aroma of meat filled the air, driving away ranker smells. Hunger at once overspread Jem's face; Rajal, more dubiously, eyed the exotic fruits. Imitating the others, he squatted on his haunches, but waved away the strip of meat that Ojo held before him, draped over the bamboo stick. In Unang Lia, where vegetable foods were in abundance, Rajal had managed to avoid the flesh of animals. He was not keen on taking it up again. But how did one eat this big, spiky thing?

Or this round, hairy thing? Cautiously he took up a squashy, reddish fruit.

'Our offerings are not to your taste?' Leki, for his part, tore eagerly at the boiled meat. Juice dripped down his skin and his bared, yellow teeth gave him an alarmingly wolfish appearance. Chewing with his mouth open, he went on, 'This cauldron of rock, bubbling miraculously, is one of the Thunderer's greatest gifts to us. Here our meat swims, safe from heat and flies, until the time comes to partake of it . . . What shall I think? That hunger does not trouble the denizens of the air? But your sun-haired friend has a stomach, I see.'

'Come, Raj, you must be starving,' Jem urged. 'It's not as if you've never had flesh before.'

Rajal muttered, 'What would Sister Myla think?'

'This Sister Myla,' said Leki, 'is a goddess of yours?'

'Oh no,' Rajal picked at the skin of his fruit, 'she's my sister.'

'There is another in your party?' The eyes flashed in the painted face. 'Besides the boy and the dog?'

Rajal wondered why the youth was so alarmed. With pretended casualness he assured Leki that no, his sister had been lost long ago; then all at once he was ashamed of his unfeeling words. He looked down. In their days in the Vaga-vans, Rajal had envied his magical little sister, resenting her powers, resenting her place in the Great Mother's heart. What a fool he had been! Since Myla had vanished, he wished devoutly that he could find her again. Perhaps, in a future he could scarcely imagine, he might embark upon a quest of his own, to discover the fate of one small girl.

Miserably he brushed away a buzzing fly. He bit into his fruit, then spluttered violently. 'Maggots!'

'Poor Raj,' Jem had to laugh. 'I think you'll have to break your Vaga-vows, old friend!'

Leki reached for a coconut, cracked it, and held it out for Rajal. 'Drink? I would offer you milk of a commoner kind, but alas, the fair lady who was to provide it is with us no more.' He glanced sourly at Ojo, then turned back to his guests. 'You see how great is the Thunderer's gift? Where flies cluster in the moment of the kill, and even the freshest fruits are quickly corrupted, this cauldron before us is a blessing indeed. Come, dark one, partake of its bounty.'

'It's remarkably good,' said Jem, chewing. 'Really, Raj.'

'Huh! And how I was looking forward to that tavern!'

With a weak grin, Rajal accepted a strip of Leki's meat, and wondered why they bothered with the fruits at all. Freshest fruits, indeed! There were nuts, too, which looked more promising – but he supposed he had already offended their host . . . The meat slid down his throat. It was extraordinarily salty, like the salt-pig on Captain Porlo's ship, but moister and very much hotter – quite without the aid of the captain's beloved mustard.

'It's pig?' said Rajal, struggling to be gracious.

'Pig?' said Leki, and smiled again. He leapt up and did another little dance, cavorting in a merry circle round the pit, first clockwise, then anti-clockwise. Accompanying the performance was a second tuneless song:

> *Pig, pig, what do I care?*
> *How can it matter to me?*
> *I couldn't care a fig for a pig,*
> *I couldn't care a fig!*

With that, the painted youth sat down suddenly, like an eager child playing musical chairs. It was as if the dance had never been.

'It's pig,' said Ojo matter-of-factly. 'We killed it yesterday – at least I did, while Uchy stood by.'

Rajal looked round. He had almost forgotten the one called Ucheus. 'Littler and Rainbow must be hard to find. Do you think your friend . . . do you think he's all right?'

'Uchy can take care of himself,' said Ojo.

Leki said archly, 'You're so sure?'

'About Uchy?' said Ojo.

'I meant about the pig.' Ignoring Ojo, Leki looked back and forth between his guests. He gestured to the mud huts. 'Ten. Hm, sun-haired one? You counted, didn't you? That's how many of us there used to be.' With the bamboo rod, he fished up more meat. Smiling, humming his pig song beneath his breath, he wafted his prize under Jem's nose, then Rajal's.

Rajal's face grew suddenly hot. Quite what Leki meant he was not sure, but a terrible suspicion flashed into his mind. He twisted away, sticking two fingers down his throat.

Jem cried out. He scrambled up, running into the trees.

Chapter 7

THE YOUNG ENCHANTED

Captain Porlo sighed.

'Now there's grub for you!' The old sea-dog leaned back, belched and wiped his sleeve across his mouth. 'Salt-pig, mustard, and hard tack for afters – nice juicy weevils and all!' He fixed his companion with a beady stare, as if challenging the boy to disagree. Sunlight shone brightly through the cabin window, glittering on the greasy pewter of cutlery, tankards, pitchers and plates. Brackish heat hovered in the air. 'Proper grub,' the captain repeated, 'not like none of your foreign muck!'

Patches faltered, 'I . . . I never eats no foreign muck, Cap'n.'

'Aye, that I'll grant you, Patches.' With drunken clumsiness the old man reached for his rum; the cabin boy winced, certain that the tankard was about to go flying. Fortunately, it did not. 'No, you be a proper Ejland lad,' the captain mused. 'How could you be anything else, answer me that, with your creamy skin and freckles and gingery hair? Aye, I could tell you was no dirty foreigner, lad, first time I clapped eyes on you!'

Patches looked suitably proud; roughly, the captain fluffed his coppery curls. 'All me cabin boys be Ejlanders, you know, here on the old *Catayane*,' he went on. 'Why, even poor Scabs – remember Scabs, lad?' Patches could hardly have forgotten his pustular predecessor – who had jumped ship, so far as he could tell, in Unang Lia. 'Aye, he was a good Ejland lad, was Scabs – though I suppose you wouldn't know *what* he was, eh, under all them red blotches and big yellow-headed swellings of pus? Used to worry he'd burst, I did, and then where'd we be? Swimming in the muck . . . Poor old Scabs!'

For a moment the sea-dog was morose – but only for a moment. He rallied, holding out his tankard for a refill; Patches happily complied. Watching them from the cabin wall – nibbling at a weevily biscuit, grinning, blinking with her big eyes – was the captain's old companion Buby the monkey, her tail coiled round the jutting horn of a rhinoceros, a little arm curved, as if affectionately, round a stuffed tiger's head. From time to time certain gaseous emissions would waft from beneath the little creature's tail; her human companions barely noticed. In the tropical heat, captain and cabin boy alike smelt rankly of sweat; their breath was foul; fumes rose, too, from the pot that was chained beneath the captain's bunk. The pot shifted with the shiftings of the tide, sometimes sloshing its contents over the deck.

'Aye, Patches, I knows all about them dirty foreigners, I do,' the old man was saying – and launched, not for the first time, into a long tale of his wanderings round the watery world which had given him the experience to speak as he did. At this point another boy might have been bored, hearing all this for perhaps the hundredth time; but Patches drifted into a pleasant haze of wonderment, thinking yet again of old Faris Porlo – but no, amazingly, of *young* Faris Porlo – and his days as Cap'n Beezer's cabin boy, and the *Catty* as she had been so many years ago.

On and on the captain would beguile the boy with his stories, and thrillingly swashbuckling they were, too – tales of barbarian raiders and sieges and bombardments, of jungles and icebergs and desert wastes – but always he would return to that tragic night in Qatani, when a lustful young lad had climbed the Caliph's wall, eager for a look at *them lovely harem ladies* – a folly he would regret for the rest of his life.

'Them cobber-as!' the captain would cry. 'Them cobber-as, them's what done me in! Now who but dirty foreigners would keep pits filled with cobber-as, answer me that, to stick their hoody heads into a poor boy's wounded leg?'

Patches could only shake his head. Who indeed?

'Aye, Patches, you can't trust them foreigners – just can't trust 'em. Look at me tars here on the *Catty*. There be a few foreigners, it's true – can't be helped, can it, when a sea-dog's far from home, roaming the wide seas, and has to take on hands? But I means me main men, Patches, I means the ones I trusts. Take me first mate – good old Whale! Take me boatswain – good old Walrus! What about me helmsman, eh – good old Porpoise? Ejlanders to a man – and me cabin boy, too!' Again the captain swigged heartily at his rum; fiery liquid ran down his chin. He looked affectionately at the freckled boy. 'Mark me words, lad, should you ever have a ship at your command – aye, and don't grin like that, for wasn't old Faris Porlo just a cabin boy once, a cabin boy like you? Indeed he were – no, lad, I tells you, it's the Ejlanders, the Ejland-fellows, not them dirty foreigners, them be the ones you can trust.'

Dubiously Patches thought of blubbery Whale, of buck-toothed Walrus, of slithery-looking Porpoise, and was not quite convinced. Would he trust even *one* of those shifty-looking fellows, whether or not they were Ejlanders? And besides, wasn't the captain forgetting something?

The boy piped up, 'Cap'n, what about that fellow called Lemyu? He were an Ejland-fellow, weren't he? The one you put ashore?'

At once, Patches wished he had not spoken.

'Lemyu?' Rum spluttered across the captain's table. '*Lemyu?* He were a dirty Zenzan if he were anything, make no mistake! Could an Ejland tar betray his old cap'n, answer me that! Stupid boy!'

With that, the captain cuffed the boy, hard, on the side of the head. It was not for the first time – and Patches, not for the first time, went sprawling to the deck. The boy lay there miserably, and wondered if he would ever really command his own ship.

Buby snickered, her yellow grin flashing.

Ra Fanana sighed.

Waves lapped gently at the artfully constructed shore and the jasmine and the seaweed and the salty plants stirred together into a balmy incense. In the cove even the tropical sun, that beat down so fiercely on the palace above, seemed milder, sweeter, pouring around them like warm, soothing cream. Like the cream on the crumble-cake, the cream – or the treacle. Ah yes, the treacle . . . Ra Fanana's eyes drifted shut and a rich, pleasant sadness filled her for places – no, for a particular place – she would never see again. What stories she could tell! Why, she had barely begun her stories . . .

'Ra Ra, you must have been pretty when you were young,' mused Selinda, when the crumble-cake was gone. The girl licked her fingers, one by one. 'Must there not have been suitors aplenty, eager to pluck so rich and plump a fruit? How is it, then, that you have no husband? Silly Ra Ra, did you never *wish* to marry?'

'Hm?' The words seemed to float towards the nurse – who had supped rather more heavily on the hava-nectar than the girl – as if from a great distance. Like the hiss of the waves, the gentle sadness washed over her again. Marry? Oh yes, there had been a time when Ra Fanana wished to marry – and then, of course, there had been her *actual* marriage . . . But these were not the stories she would tell! She would speak of her girlhood, of the days of her innocence; she would speak of those happy times on the Isle of Jasmine – for yes, it was a real place -- before the slave-ship took her away . . .

Not of suitors. Not of marriage.

She roused herself, flustered. 'My lady, your question is . . . is to no purpose. Do you forget, choice no more governs my destiny than yours – do you forget I am a slave, a mere slave?'

It would not, perhaps, have occurred to Selinda to ask if her nurse had always been a slave. When a girl grows up surrounded by the coerced and the captive, she accepts them as part of the order of things. One is a slave, as one is a woman, or a man – yet the girl, it seemed, had little idea of just what it *meant* to be a slave.

Selinda lingered over a last creamy finger. Now she became thoughtful. 'Soon I shall be married. But dear Ra Ra, what will you be then?'

'Why, I will still be a slave, will I not? And one day, perhaps, I shall care for your daughter, as I have cared for you.' And Ra Fanana smiled, and with a lazy hand waved aside an insect that hovered, with equal lethargy, over her plate.

'Perhaps,' said Selinda slowly, 'I could set you free.'

It was as well that Ra Fanana was so very drowsy. This, she began to think, was not a game she liked. Freedom? The very word caused a pang in her heart. And yet, had not the nurse seen enough of the world, enough to know that captivity here, in the Triarch's domain, was *better* than freedom in many places? Ah yes, if only it could go on! When Ra Fanana had come here, five orbits before, it had seemed to her that her young lady would always be a child. But she had grown so fast!

'My dear lady,' was all the nurse said now, 'won't you play your new song? You know how much I look forward to your songs.'

The girl, as it happened, had been working back to the question she still wanted answered. Glond or Lepato? Lepato or Glond? Might not Ra Fanana, with a little persuasion, treat her to a proper opinion of the suitors? Might she not, with just a little more, agree to carry a message – even arrange a meeting? If Selinda had lived a sheltered life, nonetheless she had a certain natural cunning; more than this, she knew her father well. That there were ways of swaying his decision, she was certain. But first she must make her own choice. Lepato or Glond? Glond or Lepato? The campaign was vital; but then, too, it was a delicate one, and Selinda knew she must bide her time – softly, softly . . .

The song, yes: then she would go to work again.

Selinda spent much time with the box harp, or the chord harp, sometimes even with the double lyre, but she was not, in truth, particularly musical. What was music but a skill she must learn, a necessary accomplishment if she were to be an ornament to her future husband's home? Reluctantly she took up her little instrument, opening the ivory-inlaid lid and turning the dial to the appropriate key. The song, a 'ballad oblique' from the days of Old Hora, was taken from the scroll-books in her father's library. This would be the first time she had sung it without the scroll . . . Let's see, could she remember the words?

Softly, softly, she picked at the strings.

> *Under the covers*
> *The girl dreams of lovers,*
> *But where, where can they be?*
> *Waiting for strangers*
> *What knows she of dangers*

48

> That dare, dare to roam free?
>> For Father has made no decision for her:
>> Fool of a man, such a fool to defer –
>> But he shan't hear the call
>> From behind the stone wall.

Selinda's voice wavered with vibrato, but was sweet and clear. Listening to the soft lilt of the melody, Ra Fanana felt her sadness ebbing away. Of course she paid no attention to the words, only to the lilt, the lilt . . . Was this a melody she had heard before? She did not think so. On the Isle of Jasmine, there had been different melodies, very different. And later, after they had taken her to Unang Lia? But she did not remember . . . no, she did not want to remember.

The nurse stretched out on the rug, luxuriating in the sun.

> Woken at midnight
> By juddering lamplight
> The girl hears of the death.
>> Questions assail her
>> But wild words soon fail her
>> And tears, tears choke her breath.
>>> Had Father still made no provision for her?
>>> Fool, what a fool, could he really prefer
>>> That his sweet child should call
>>> From behind the stone wall?

Selinda, for her part, thought only of the fingerings and the key, which she found a little too high. The melody, she knew – so calming, so sweet – was strangely at odds with the words she sang. But this was only a dim awareness. What were the words in these old songs? Nonsense, an excuse for a tune, no more . . . No, twisting the dial, modulating into the last verse – now *this* would be difficult – Selinda wondered not about the words, but why she had not chosen a simpler song.

But the words, beneath the surface, worked a curious spell.

> Into the darkness
> The girl feels the starkness
> And knows, knows this is doom.
>> Are no strong shoulders
>> To shift back the boulders
>> That close, close and entomb?
>>> If Father had but had a vision for her!
>>> Ah, it's too late when they come to inter
>>> This girl who now must call
>>> From behind the stone wall!

When she laid down the box harp, Selinda was trembling. Deeply but obscurely, the song had moved her, and again she wondered why she had chosen it. Had something more than the melody drawn her? A girl ... lovers ... a father? But what did it mean? And why was the father such a fool? What was this wall, this stone wall?

'Ra Ra—' she began.

But the nurse was sleeping.

Well, really! Selinda sprang up. Restlessly she wandered the beach. She pushed back her hair; she kicked at seaweed; she picked up a pebble then threw it down again, watching it vanish in the foam of the tide. It was then that a knowledge came seeping into her, a knowledge or a memory.

All that morning the girl had felt a certain pressing strangeness just on the threshold of her awareness, as if something unexpected might be happening, or about to happen. The song had sharpened the feeling; now she recalled a dream that had come to her during the night and knew why she had thought again, so ardently, of her marriage! On waking, she had thought the dream had vanished; she had struggled to remember it, until the rituals of the day took over. Now the dream filled her again. For a moment, she heard fantastical flutterings of wings; then the wings subsided and soft caresses ran across her skin, then soft, caressing voices filled her ears, creating strange, rhyming dialogues:

> — *My lady, let me kiss you. Hear my sighs.*
> — *So bold a lover? Let me see your face.*
> — *What care you for my outward carapace?*
> — *I care but for this trembling in my thighs!*
> — *My lady, do you shudder, quake and quail?*
>
> — *But innocence surrounds me like a veil!*
> — *A veil I rend apart! I feel the place!*
> — *But stranger, let me see you with my eyes.*
> — *My lady, see this soaring bird that flies!*
> — *So high? But ah, this bird I shall outrace!*

At the very memory, Selinda's face grew hot. Whose were the voices? Could one of them be hers? And whose was the other? Oh, but this dream was alarming, even shaming!

The girl looked around her, this way and that: at the ornate gardens that rose behind the beach; at the softly rolling waves; at the curving walls that enclosed the cove almost entirely from the harsher currents of the outward sea. Her restlessness beat inside her like – yes – like fluttering wings. If only she could fly from this place, soar up on high! The break in those rocks – a gateway, it seemed, to a forbidden vastness – had always filled her with a certain fascination, a certain excited fear.

Once – oh, moonlives ago now – she had tried to swim out that far, but Ra Fanana had seen her, and screamed and screamed.

She would not see her now.

Selinda turned, considering.

If only she had not had that crumble-cake! Could she really make it out so far? The sun was growing brighter, sparkling down directly on the blue, calm water. Shielding her eyes with her hands, the girl let her gaze travel to the end of the beach and the boulders that abutted artfully against the larger, rocky wall. Could she climb up on that wall, and walk most of the way? Worth a try, she thought. But as she moved further towards the wall, further away from her sleeping nurse, she saw that the boulders would be hard to climb. Hard? Impossible. It was the way they were shaped – the smoothness, the slope, the distance apart. Ah, but the builders of her little world – her little prison – had not left much to chance!

Selinda looked over the cove again. She sloshed out from the shore. And it was then, when the water reached her waist, just as she was about to launch herself forward, that she saw the debris, bobbing on the tide. What could it be? She touched it: a torn, unravelling shard of leaves, skins, vines. She looked towards the gap in the rocky wall. This thing, she was certain, whatever it was, had washed in from the outward sea.

At once, Selinda felt a touch of fear – then rapidly, in its place, a surge of excitement. She screwed up her eyes. Yes, there was another bobbing shard like the first, further out, knocking at the edge of the wall – then another, much larger, back near the beach, caught between the boulders she had thought she could not climb. She made for it. A boat: from the windows of the palace, Selinda had seen many boats, but none like this, so small, so primitive.

The boulders rose around her, shadowy and looming, as she turned over the wreckage: the shattered hull, the snapped mast, the ragged skins of the little sail.

Her heart hammered hugely. Her feet slipped on seaweed. A trapped fish slithered out through the vines and she gave a little gasp. The sea slurped and gurgled against the boulders and smaller rocks and shells and waving algae. Then, from somewhere in the shadows, Selinda heard the groan. Her hand covered her mouth, but she edged her way forward.

Of course, of course: as there was a boat, so there was a sailor, face down, barely breathing, clad only in rags. The girl reached for him fearfully, touching his back. The texture repelled her – scaly, like a lizard . . .

Then, her eyes adjusting to the gloom, Selinda saw that the sailor was burned by the sun, burned badly. Compassion filled her. This, she realised, was no grizzled sea-dog but a youth, a boy. Who could he be?

51

Was he going to die? She touched him again and he turned suddenly, coughing, and gazed into her eyes. In the same moment the sun shifted overhead and a shaft of light fell across his face and naked chest.

Selinda stumbled back.

'Ra Ra, come! Ra Ra, quick!'

But why had she cried out? The girl was not frightened. On the contrary: she was enchanted, and more than enchanted. For now – or so it seemed to her – there came the fluttering of wild, desperate wings; voices fill her mind, and she knew that these were the voices she had heard before, and that one of them, undoubtedly, must be her own:

> — *My stranger-youth, come tell me who you are.*
> — *My lady, let me tell you how I love.*
> — *But come you from the seas? Or skies above?*
> — *From drowning come I, come back from afar.*
> — *From drowning? Gods be thanked that you are saved!*
>
> — *But soft the sea, when deep this flesh she laved!*
> — *And soft this flesh, that trembles like a dove!*
> — *That trembles? Feel it judder hard, and jar!*
> — *Ah, what is this inside my flesh? A war?*
> — *Volcanic soon with passion will you move!*

There are things we know at once, with or without experience, reason, or motive. Selinda, in this moment, knew just such a thing. In this moment, her innocence was rent from her like a veil – and gloryingly, laughingly, she watched it flutter away. Images, awarenesses crashed inside her again that no longer shamed her, no longer alarmed her, but filled her only with a wild, desperate longing. Visions came with the voices, and she saw herself entangled in the stranger-youth's arms, saw her lips smearing hungrily over his, saw herself and the stranger rolling, tumbling together on slithery silken sheets, rising to the heights of a hot, ecstatic passion . . . Yes, he had come to her! Yes, she would have him!

This was her dream. Her dream was real.

Chapter 8

LEKI'S LIGHT

All Littler could do was screw up his eyes. Strained through the network of heavy hanging leaves, a hundred pinpricks of sunlight flared, silver and gold, against the curves of coppery ferns. With a pang, he wondered where his friends might be; shuddering, he wondered if they might be dead. But then, perhaps, so was he – dead, or about to die. After all, as the shudder passed through him he became aware of the strange, firm grip that held him; then, too, he was aware of the voice, drifting into his awareness as if from afar. *Maro . . . Maro, come . . .* Maro? What could it mean?

Littler's eyes roved round the branches and leaves. Struggle as he might to twist his neck, still he could not see, not *really* see the captor who bore him now – swiftly, slung back over a shoulder – through the enveloping jungle shadows. What had happened? *Come, Maro . . .* Down, down Littler saw himself crashing through the green mansions, then the mansions fading to black. Then the arms, the hands, plucking him from death amongst the coppery ferns. But whose arms? Whose hands? *Maro, come . . .* A large, dark figure: that was all he knew. But there was something about him – something about his . . . *skin.* Even at the beginning, Littler knew that much. *Come, Maro . . .*

Leaves and vines rasped Littler's face and he heard a dog bark, somewhere close by.

'My friends, come back!'

Leki laughed, delighted at his joke. Could they be cannibals? The very thought! Rushing into the trees, he retrieved a pile of pig-bones, flinging them about him with a merry clatter. 'It's pig, pig – doubt *me* if you will, but would Ojo lie? Ojo the Staunch, Ojo the Stolid? Good old, dull old, constant Ojo? The thought is monstrous! No, our friends have not fed this cauldron. If only they had, and we would know what had become of them – eh, Ojo?'

Only reluctantly did Jem and Rajal return to their places. The meal resumed, but now Rajal contented himself with nuts, while Jem set about inspecting a pineapple. For a time Leki kept up a steady banter, ribbing his guests about his splendid joke, about the look on Rajal's face, about the speed with which Jem had scrambled up. He embarked upon an anecdote about a tribe of flesh-eaters – barbarians, he called them – who had first killed all the inhabitants of their surrounding islands, then eaten each other in an orgy of blood-lust.

It might have been a droll story, but the way Leki told it made it difficult to follow. Jem and Rajal could only smile dutifully. They were alarmed now, and their alarm was growing.

Furtively Rajal's gaze roved about him, as if fearful of some imminent threat, some ambush. In the rocky wall behind the ridge, almost concealed behind the mud huts, he noticed the dark mouth of a cave. It made him uneasy. For a moment he glimpsed something inside the cave, something glimmering in the shadows, hunched and mysterious. He would have nudged Jem, but became aware of Leki's eyes, studying him playfully.

Rajal cleared his throat. 'What happened, then – to your friends?'

Leki only smiled.

'All dead? They're all dead?'

Leki whistled the pig song again.

'The man in the jungle . . . the sailor. How did *he* die?'

Leki stirred the cauldron, retrieving more meat.

Rajal became aware that Ojo, beside him, was sweating profusely. The sun, it was true, was *very* hot; so was the cauldron, and Ojo was plump. But the youth trembled too, almost as if he were gripped by a fever. Several times he might have been about to speak, but did not. What could it mean? With sudden intensity Rajal was aware again of the cave-mouth behind them, and the glimmering thing inside. Hunched. Mysterious.

Jem made the next attempt. 'I divine, Governor, that you and your – your *subjects* are not natives of this island. Clearly, you are creatures of a fine civilisation . . . Tell me, how is it that you find yourselves here?'

Looking up from his meat, Leki licked a slippery finger, sniffed, and wiped his chin. Politely he indicated that Jem should do the same.

Jem paused only for a moment. In an airy voice he continued, 'There was a mariner of my country called Robander Selsoe, whose fate it was to be cast upon the shores of an empty isle. Bereft of all consolation of society, this hardy mariner created a world in miniature, sufficient to sustain the wants of one man . . . Governor, you are more fortunate than my countryman, accompanied as you are by others of your race; still, I wonder if a fate not unlike Robander Selsoe's has been yours?'

So finely phrased a question deserved an answer, but Leki merely leaned back on an elbow, cracked open a coconut and, in between gulping back its juice, enquired laconically, 'But tell me, my friends, about yourselves. Your magic, I mean – how long have you had these *powers*?'

'Powers?' said Jem, puzzled. 'Governor, you misjudge us. Do you really think we have *powers*?'

'You fly through the air, do you not?'

'I told you, we were cursed by an evil enchanter. Raj, have we got *powers*?'

'I think your *friend* has powers,' said Leki.

At that moment there was a distant barking. Rajal laid a hand on Jem's arm. 'Jem, can you hear it?'

But Jem did not stir. His eyes were locked on Leki's as the painted youth said coldly, 'Yes, your *friend* – I mean the fellow with skin the colour of yours . . . hair the colour of yours . . . eyes the colour of yours. I mean a fellow who might be your brother.' Leki laughed, 'Such *powers*, but so forgetful? Did you not mention him but a moment before? I speak of a certain stripy-shirted fellow, who lodges amongst the trees. He is lonely now, with only flies for friends – *bzz*, *bzz*, how they madden him! – but has he not had *other* friends? Friends who make no *bzz*, *bzz*, yet are equally agents of corruption?' Through the steam of the cauldron, the painted face swooped forward. Jem jumped back. 'Has he not been *your* friend, too?'

'Jem, what's he talking about?' Rajal wailed. Appealingly, he looked to Ojo. The stocky youth was standing, pacing, circling the cauldron. At one moment his face was in his hands; at the next, he shook his head violently, as if trying to toss free some maddening irritant of his own, caught amongst the ragged curls of his hair.

'Lemyu,' he muttered, 'Lemyu.'

Leki looked at him sharply. 'Ojo, shut up.'

Instead, Ojo reeled round. 'Lemyu, Lemyu, Lemyu!'

Leki strode to him, struck him with the flat of the cutlass. Rajal gasped. The stocky youth crumpled. Rajal went to him, but the youth pushed him away. Ojo lay whimpering, clawing at the ground. Blood flowed from his forehead.

Rainbow, if it was Rainbow, barked again.

Rajal leapt up. 'Rainbow? Where are you, boy?'

Was he in the trees? Was he on the path? Rainbow was close now, he had to be. Confused, Rajal would have blundered in search of him, but the cutlass slashed through the air and barred his way.

Trembling, Rajal sank to his knees. He gazed round him wildly. Beyond the jagged edge of the ridge, he saw the sea, shimmering silver, shimmering gold. He saw the grove with its burbling spring; off to the side, he saw a narrow trail, leading to the pinnacle of the trembling mountain. But there was something else, too. It was the mysterious thing, the hunched thing, crouched inside the dark mouth of the cave. The thing flashed again and suddenly Rajal saw it for what it was.

The cannon. Yes, they had known there was a cannon.

Now Leki turned back to Jem. 'Lemyu,' he repeated softly. 'Lemyu, Lemyu, Lemyu . . .'

Levelly, Jem said, 'You speak of one who is dead—'

'I speak of an Ejlander—'

'An Ejlander unknown to us—'

'For shame, sun-haired one! You would disown your dear brother?'

'My *dead* brother! I mean . . . no, he's—'

'Ah! But you know him, do you not?'

Thwack! went the cutlass. As if beating time to a rhythm only he could hear, Leki advanced, hitting the flat of the blade against his palm.

Thwack! Jem scrambled back.

'Governor, this dead man was no friend of ours—'

'For shame, I say! We have given you the finest hospitality of Sarom. Now you would beguile us with your Ejlander lies?'

Thwack! Then came the dance. The song.

Jem and Rajal looked on in astonishment.

> *Tell me the measure of an Ejlander,*
> *How long is a tangle of twine?*
> *Tell me the measure of an Ejlander,*
> *How deep is a goblet of wine?*
>
> *Goblet is deep enough to drown in,*
> *Tangle will stretch to the moon –*
> *Ejland's a land that's far away,*
> *But coming closer—*
>   *Beware!*

The last word was a guttural cry. With that, Leki broke off. He darted at Jem.

'But what could we expect? Have we not taken the measure of your race? Hah, and you pretend you arrived only today! Have you not been here all this time, spying upon us, scheming, observing us from the trees, from the rocks, from the air? How many times have you circled us in secret, waiting to pounce like carrion birds? Evil ones, you have had your fill, but no more! Your reign is out, and the Thunderer shall have you!'

'What are you talking about?' Jem blurted. 'I don't understand—'

'You killed our companions—'

'No! You're mad—'

It was then that the ridge rumbled beneath them, violently, this time.

Scalding water shot up from the cauldron. Ojo screamed. Rajal ran. Jem darted for Leki, striking the cutlass from his hand.

There was a struggle. They crashed to the ground.

'I tell you, the Thunderer wants you!' cried Leki. 'Feel his impatience, throbbing through the rock—'

Jem swung back his fist.

Then came the light – light, in searing rays, bursting from Leki's eyes.

'Jem!' Rajal swivelled back, but the light struck him, too.

For an instant, the world was a flash of brilliance. Then it was dark.

Chapter 9

THE AMALI SCREEN

— But youth, you are a stranger. Tell your name.
— I tell it: now you know it: I know yours.
— But there is more I know: I know your cause.
— You know I play no merely idle game?
— I know you come to take me in your arms!

— And what is there that matters but your charms?
— Forget all else! Come take me! Passion soars!
— I feel it sear me like the brightest flame!
— My love, my love, my passion is the same!
— My love, my love, fling open all your doors!

'Ra Ra, come! Ra Ra, quick!'

With furrowing brow, Ra Fanana had been gazing over the city when she heard Selinda's call. From the girl's apartments she could look down over the agora with its milling crowds, its cloister-walk, and the high, forbidding steps of the Temple of Thirty. In the background – pierced through with gold in the early evening light – lay the docks, source of Hora's wealth, webbing the sky with masts and rigging and sails. Ra Fanana sighed. Turning back to the large, luxurious chamber, she hurried to the alcove where their *guest* lay – if guest he could be called.

So, was he stirring at last? Had his eyes flickered open? Suspiciously the nurse looked to the stranger-youth on the couch, and the girl who tenderly grasped his hand. Ra Fanana was alarmed, deeply alarmed. What thoughts had been filling her lady's mind? Why, the girl was flushed, breathless, as if in the grip of passions hardly becoming to an innocent young lady – or any *lady* at all!

'Selinda,' the youth breathed, 'dear, kind Selinda ...'

'Thanks be,' said the girl, 'I thought you were dying!'

'Thanks be,' her nurse echoed, in a different tone. 'I'll ring for Tagan now, shall I?'

It was a statement more than a question.

Selinda turned sharply, her voice almost a cry. 'Ra Ra, what can you mean? You don't think Maius Eneo's ready to leave here?'

'My lady, I don't think he should be *here* at all!'

How they had got the youth into the girl's apartments unseen, the nurse would never know. True, the beach was private enough, and the gardens mercifully empty in the afternoon heat. But the burden! Weakened, stumbling, the youth had hung upon their necks – principally, of course, upon Ra Fanana's. Really, they should have called the guards! But the girl would not hear of it. As the youth, while they laboured uphill, had gasped out his story – something about a storm, something about a boat – Ra Fanana could see that her young charge was enchanted. When the youth had swayed and collapsed – oh, *very* conveniently – on the threshold of Selinda's apartments, the nurse knew that the girl would never see reason. All afternoon she had simpered over the youth as if he were a soldier, grievously wounded. It was absurd! Not much wrong with him other than a few bruises and a touch of the sun, so far as Ra Fanana could see. And she had thought her young lady was a girl of spirit!

But then, she was a girl – a newly nubile girl . . .

Enough was enough. Ra Fanana crossed to the bell-rope.

'Ra Ra, no!' Selinda sprang up. Bright threads flashed in her robes as she darted after her nurse. She spread her arms behind her, standing before the braided, tasselled rope.

Ra Fanana shook her head sadly and glanced back at the youth – this Maius Eneo, if that were truly his name. Slowly, rubbing his eyes, he rose from the couch. What did they know of him? Might he not be the worst of rapscallions? Anxiously she thought of her lady's virtue – then of her lady's necklaces and bangles and brooches and rings, her painted ivory playing cards, her powder-urns and nut-cutters and jewelled and lacquered combs. And look at that Amali screen! It was difficult to know which was more splendid – the screen, with its inlaid patterns of herons and gulls (in sixty delicate resinwood shades) or the beaded headscarves and chains of beads, strewn so casually over the zigzagging top. Why, the rapscallion could fold that screen and walk out with it under his arm, just like that!

Ra Fanana wrung her hands, wondering if she should simply call the guards. What had the youth to do but reach out, and wealth would fill his pockets? Wasn't he looking at that earring box? That perfume cabinet? Not to mention that icon in the corner – the death-icon of the girl's mother? With the doll that sat on a shelf beside it – a battered Blisha doll, a favourite, evidently, of the departed lady – it formed a solemn shrine. Would the rapscallion think twice about desecrating that shrine? Oh, there was quite a trade in death-icons, or so Ra Fanana had heard!

She burst out, 'My lady, really! He *can't* stay here, can he?'

'But I don't trust Tagan! Where will he take him?'

'Don't trust Tagan!' Kind, loyal Tagan? The irony was hardly lost upon the nurse. 'Child, I think you forget yourself.'

Selinda looked blank. Of the many slaves who attended upon her, Ra Fanana was the only one in whom she had any faith. What were the others but resentful functionaries? Trust Tagan? Was she wholly naïve? Besides, Father said you could never trust a eunuch.

The girl said as much, and her nurse's eyes flashed. 'Indeed, my lady, you seem to forget that Tagan – like that Amali screen, the security of which means *nothing* to you at all – is a eunuch of the highest quality! Was he not of gentle birth? Had he not the highest expectations, before he was captured, enslaved and gelded? Of common eunuchs say what you will, but of Tagan I am certain – he is loyal, steadfast and true ... Besides, he knows already about our *guest*, does he not? Had Tagan been inclined to go to the guards, I imagine he has had *ample* time by now.'

Selinda looked down. It was true. The eunuch had met them in the blossom-walk, beneath the canopy of interlacing trees, as they helped Maius Eneo through the gardens. At once, Tagan's concern had been only to assist Selinda in getting the youth to her apartments in secret. He hurried them to the back stairs, then checked that the way was safe. Then, a little later, when she had dismissed him summarily, Tagan seemed distressed, as if there were so much more that he would do.

But what might that be?

'Ra Fanana, I'm frightened.' Selinda frowned uncertainly, not at her nurse, but at Maius Eneo. The youth hovered close by, eyes cast down. 'Where will Tagan take him?'

'Out of this palace, of course!'

'But he's sick! He's—'

'Child, don't be silly! Tagan will sort out something. A Triarch's daughter – his *virginal* daughter – can hardly keep a young man in her apartments, can she?'

Again the nurse motioned to the braided rope; again, Selinda barred her way. Exasperated, Ra Fanana cast up her eyes. Should she push the girl aside? The chamber, in the evening light, was a cavern of shadows and hazy gold. On the looking-glasses and the powder-urns and the unlit lamps, on the death-icon in the corner and on the battered Blisha doll, with its polished wooden face and its eyes made of shells, a thousand little fires flashed like stars. Again Ra Fanana glanced at the ragged youth. She shuddered, her fear growing.

Make no mistake, he was a powerfully built fellow.

'I'm sorry, my lady, I'm calling for Tagan.' Firmly, Ra Fanana took Selinda's arm. 'You forget, child, that I am responsible for you. What would your father say, if he knew you were *entertaining* this young man? I shudder to think!'

The youth began, 'My lady—'

Selinda burst out, 'But Ra Ra, the guards! They nearly caught us on the way up! Oh, they'll throw poor Maius Eneo into the dungeons, I know it!'

And the girl, as if to save him from this fate, flung herself across his breast. In the rags he wore, the youth's firm chest was almost wholly exposed. He winced – from the bruises, no doubt, that darkened his ribs – and might have been about to speak again, or attempt to speak, when Selinda crushed the breath from his body. Wild with grief, wild with longing, the girl heard again the rush of mighty wings, and sank once more into the ecstatic union that had filled her as her beloved had lain unstirring. In an instant, the rapture swept over her again:

— *My love, I hold you hard as hard can be!*
— *This passion knows no limit and no check!*
— *But hold me tighter! Save me from this wreck!*
— *What wreck mean you? Your boat upon the sea?*
— *But hold me tight! Come, fill me with your love!*

— *What mighty wings are these that soar above?*
— *This bird flies far! It fades into a speck!*
— *But now it swoops down mighty! Hear my plea!*
— *I hear it! Lady, give yourself to me!*
— *How sweetly fall your kisses on my neck!*

Selinda gasped sharply, several times. Then she sighed.

Ra Fanana sighed, too. 'My lady, really! Now why should the guards lock up this young fellow? It's not as if he's done anything *wrong*, has he?'

This was disingenuous, and Selinda knew it. Maius Eneo heaped wrong upon his head, wrong and more wrong, with every moment he remained in her apartments. What would excuses profit him, were Father to find out? The girl shook herself, struggling to forget her strange new pleasures, and think only of the present dilemma.

'He's ... he's intruded into the Triarch's estate!' she burst out. 'Remember what happened to those fisherboys when I was a little girl – the ones who blundered by accident into the cove?' Selinda shuddered, and tears sprang to her eyes. 'Ra Ra, you won't ring for Tagan, will you?'

Absurd girl! Ra Fanana's hand hovered over the rope.

'Tagan,' she said, 'might at least know what to *do*.'

Carefully, the youth extricated himself from Selinda's grip. 'My lady – ladies – I would go, if by staying I should cause you the least distress. Grateful as I am for your assistance, I am sensible that it must of necessity have an end – then, too, that I have a mission, one I must prosecute with the utmost urgency.'

Selinda cried, 'Speak of no mission, until you are well!'

61

'Mission? What can you mean?' said Ra Fanana.

Why, she had known this fellow was up to no good!

But now the stranger fixed her with his eyes – his very dark eyes – and it occurred to her that his voice, belying his rags, was really quite genteel. Eyeing him with what she hoped was frank suspicion, Ra Fanana betrayed, instead, frank admiration. No doubt about it, this Maius Eneo was remarkably handsome . . . But the danger, the danger!

She tightened her grip on the braided rope.

Selinda rushed to her. 'Ra Ra, no!'

But before the nurse could ring the bell, the door burst open and in stumbled Tagan of his own accord. The eunuch slammed the door behind him, leaning back upon it, breathless. He was a long, lean creature with a gamin, much-powdered face, and large dark eyes outlined in kohl. On any ordinary day, he would have looked immaculate; now he was sweaty and his toga was disordered, rucked up around his long thighs.

'Tagan,' Ra Fanana cried, 'what is it?'

'Triarch Jodrell,' he gasped, 'he's on his way here!'

Selinda and Maius Eneo exchanged bewildered glances.

'Here? Now?' wailed Ra Fanana. When did the Triarch ever visit his daughter? Once or twice a moonlife, that was the answer – and never unannounced! Did he know about the stranger? The nurse reeled round, despairing. The beautiful youth was doomed . . . they were all doomed! 'Tagan, you must take him away!'

'No time! Quick – the Amali screen!'

Grabbing Maius Eneo by the hand, Tagan ripped the youth from the girl as if he were a garment and spirited him behind the screen. Beads clattered, headscarves fluttered down, zigzag panels swayed as the eunuch emerged with an innocent smile, adjusting the disorder of his dress; then quickly he turned to the disorder of the chamber, picking up beads, plumping up cushions, pushing a footstool back against the wall.

Ra Fanana looked to the lamps. Now where were those tapers? And the incense braziers? And the shutters – she must close them! From outside the doors came the thud of many feet, then the thud of ceremonial drums.

Selinda slumped to the floor, trembling.

Swiftly, Ra Fanana pulled her up. The girl clung to her. Distantly, like an ironic counterpoint, music and laughter drifted up from below.

The doors opened, a little too soon, and a guard-senior, flanked by subordinates, announced the great man. With a high laugh, Ra Fanana flung Selinda aside, as if their embrace had been a stray diversion, no more, and bade Tagan, in a loud, affected voice, to see to the lamps, the incense braziers . . .

And what about the shutters?

'Really – eunuchs!' she laughed.

The guard-senior did not smile, but instead stepped back to reveal a shadowy figure, advancing slowly along the column of men. Just in time, a lamp flared into life. Ra Fanana abased herself; Selinda and Tagan did the same.

The guards, at a nod, turned and left.

Triarch Jodrell was a tall, heavyset man with dark eyes and a glistening curly beard. He was not old: the sum of his orbits could have been no more than thirty-five or forty, but he looked as if it were many more. It was not to be wondered at: circling his forehead, like a weight bearing him down, was a golden band inset with precious stones – a ruby, an emerald and a sapphire, each immense, and cut to identical dimensions. This was the Tricrown, emblem of his office: at the time of his coronation, as tradition prescribed, the crown had been screwed into the bone of his head, and was to be removed only when he died. Ra Fanana winced at the very thought. Really, the poor man must be in constant pain! Was such pain worth it, she had often wondered – worth it, even to enjoy such immense worldly powers?

Tonight the question had a peculiar urgency. Always the Triarch looked hollow and weary; now it seemed that the infirmity which for so long had lingered about him had suddenly, alarmingly advanced. Could it be that he was trembling? Oh indeed, he looked like an old, old man!

'Come, my darling, and sit by me.' The Triarch gestured to the nearest of the couches. In his hand he gripped a jewel-topped cane and he was dressed, despite the evening's heat, in ponderous, trailing furs. Tagan and Ra Fanana hung back, uncertainty in their eyes, as the great man laboriously positioned himself, then reached for his daughter, pulling her down beside him with a clumsy abruptness. 'Dear child, something alarms you. Can it be that I fill your heart with fear?'

'With . . . with fear, my father, only that I might fail.'

'Fail?' A smile. 'In what might you *fail*, my daughter?'

'In . . . in the duty I owe you, as my lord and master.'

It was the required response, recited as a litany. Often the father and daughter would exchange such lines, in a spirit of banter; tonight, of course, Selinda was really afraid. Her eyes darted to the Amali screen, and it seemed to her that she could hear her beloved's breathing, his heartbeat, the blood in his veins booming on the air all around her. How could her father not hear it too?

'Well spoken, my daughter,' was all he said. 'Should you show such meekness to the man you marry, indeed you will be a credit to your sex.'

That came from the litany too. Selinda smiled shyly; Ra Fanana snatched up a petit-point frame and sat, with studied deference, a little away from the father and daughter. Quickly, as if remembering herself, she dismissed the hovering Tagan with a twist of her mouth. Really, eunuchs! Could he imagine his presence was required? The Triarch, Ra Fanana knew, would request no refreshment. Only in his retiring-chambers did food – let alone drink – pass his lips, and only then when it had been tried on a trio of royal tasters.

With awkward tenderness the great man stroked his daughter's hand. But where could this be leading? Had he come here only to ask the customary questions? To Ra Fanana it seemed that there was a nervousness, an apprehension in the Triarch, too. But why?

He said, 'You carry on, my darling, in your round of innocent pleasures? But do not, I trust, neglect those studies which, should you but prosecute them with ardour, can only raise your value – great as it is already – to inestimable heights?'

If Selinda did not quite understand this question, she guessed its meaning well enough. 'Yes . . . yes, dear father. Daily, Ra Ra and I enjoy the cool waters of the cove, that leave me braced and glistening – but each day, too, never does your daughter neglect to work with her little spelling-scroll or her little ivory-brush or her little needle, such as her dear nurse plies before us now.'

And such, it so happened, as Selinda had never plied in her life. A shiver of guilt ran through the girl – still, never mind: when her husband was chosen, there would be examples enough of needlework to beguile him, should the matter concern him at all. Good old Ra Ra was seeing to that . . . But – her husband! A pang filled Selinda's heart; the nurse peered closely at her intricate work – inspiring, it would seem, the Triarch's next remark.

'My darling, but I trust you not to strain your eyes, nor risk the wrinkling of your flawless brow.' He smiled. 'Think of your husband's righteous anger, should imperfection soil so dear a purchase.'

'Indeed, my father, I . . . I think of it *constantly*.'

Had the girl ever really thought of it? Ra Fanana shuddered. Banter it might be, but she did not like it, and with a thud of dread she recalled certain incidents in her own past, before the mercy of her sale to the Triarch's household. Of righteous anger, the nurse had known enough – and wished only that her young charge might be spared such experience . . .

The Triarch said, 'And your music, my dearest girl? Remember, if it is in the *person* of his wife that a husband takes most pleasure, foremost of her other accomplishments are her playing and her singing – such, indeed, I found with that pretty child who died so soon after giving you life, whom still I honour each sunround on the day of your birth. How sweet was her voice – how inexpressibly sweet! Honour her too, my darling, honour her each day, with each melodious key you press, with each taut, vibrating string you pluck.'

And reverently the great man stared past his daughter towards the death-icon, glowing above the scented candles. It was then that Selinda saw tears in her father's eyes, and tears came into her eyes too. If it was true that the girl was afraid of her father, nonetheless she also loved him deeply, and loved him most of all when he spoke of her mother. That their marriage had been a happy one, Selinda could not doubt. How many times had she gazed upon that death-icon – a pretty child, indeed! – and seen in that sweet face an inexpressible love? Dear, dear Father! That he should hold his daughter's destiny in his hands was hardly something Selinda could question – at that moment, at least. For an instant, she even forgot the Amali screen, and was glad only that she really practised her music. 'Why, Father, is there a day on which I am not busy on the box harp – or the chord harp, or the double lyre? Just this afternoon – did I not, Ra Ra? – I played a new song from the ballad-scrolls.'

'A new song? Then you shall sing it to me, before I depart. But do you not wonder, precious child, why I should visit you at this unaccustomed time?'

Ra Fanana's fears surged anew; so did Selinda's. 'Dear Father, is it my place to wonder at your ways?'

'My darling, I see your nurse has trained you well . . . it is good, it is good.' And the Triarch gazed admiringly at Ra Fanana. 'To think, slave-woman, there were those who said a she-native of your Isle of Jasmine would never be suitable in a post such as yours. Did I not say there could be none finer than a woman accustomed first to unnatural dominance – who *then* had been brought to a proper submission? Who better to understand the ways of womankind, and the snares that might drive her from her destined path?'

This speech caused Selinda not a little wonder, or would have done, had there been time to indulge it. Ra Ra? Unnatural dominance? Modestly the nurse cast down her eyes. Busying herself with her embroidery, she seemed indeed the model of prim, obedient woman-hood, a fine example for her young charge. How could the Triarch know that inwardly she was in turmoil?

Turning back to Selinda, the Triarch gripped her hand. 'Beloved daughter, you know there is a confidence between us, such as is seldom found between a father and his girl-child. Many is the man who would send his girl to her bride-ceremony wholly unapprised of what might there await her, but such was never my way. Have I not told you of those

65

who sue for this silken hand – why, even to the extent of giving you their names?'

'Father, I . . . I am sensible of this great benison.'

'Good, good. Yet there is much, too, that I have concealed from you – concealed, and must now reveal.' The great man's voice was a dry rasp, and a vein thudded under the band of his crown. 'Ah, but my heart is sore, and requires ease!' He leaned forward, as if in illustration, a pained expression passing over his face. Still he gripped his daughter's hand and she felt the pressure tighten. She had known her father was unwell: now she knew how terribly unwell. 'Woman,' he said to Ra Fanana, 'bring me a little . . . hava-nectar.'

The nurse gave a little gasp. Had she heard correctly? But this – this was unprecedented!

'H-Hava-nectar, O Mighty One? I'll – I'll ring for Tagan.'

She jangled the bell.

Chapter 10

ZIGZAG

Zigzag. Zigzag.

So frail a barrier!

'Eunuch, more nectar. Quickly, quickly!'

'Poor Father! But what can be wrong with you?' Fearfully, all else forgotten now, Selinda gazed into the beloved eyes. Ra Fanana was worried too, but not only by the Triarch. From time to time – how could she help it? – she found herself glancing towards the Amali screen.

'Enough, O Mighty One?' Tagan, hovering by the great man, had no such concerns. The eunuch, it seemed, could barely conceal his delight. At the sound of the bell, he had appeared instantly, and on his gamin face was a triumphant smirk. Now, with every drop of hava-nectar that passed their master's lips, how eager he was to fill the goblet again! It was not to be wondered at: was he not obliged to *taste* the mixture each time? In any case, Tagan had decided that this was so, and the Triarch, intent upon his daughter, made no objection. Ra Fanana should have liked to snatch the hava-jug and set it down firmly where the eunuch could not touch it.

Just here, for example, beside her own chair.

Zigzag. Zig. Zag. The lamps shone softly on the lush fabrics, and the great man's crown, and the Amali screen. But what was the Triarch saying now?

'You ask what is wrong? My poor child, I am dying.'

Ra Fanana gasped. So did Selinda.

'Dying! Father, it cannot be!'

'My darling, yes – it is a doom I have long feared, like all men; yet, like all men, I believed the time of its coming would be far, far away. There are those who would think me in the prime of life; in truth, a malignancy gnaws at my vitals, and my prime was long ago. Now my physicians say I near my end, and all their art is powerless to save me. Thus it is that a crisis is upon me, for like a fool I have delayed in deciding your future – and would not die with it so, for then indeed it could only be terrible.'

'F-Father?' Selinda did not quite understand.

Ra Fanana suppressed a cry. She understood only too well. Suddenly she thought of the song her young charge had sung that afternoon, the song about the stone wall. Oh, how could she have been such a fool, to let the girl learn it? Why had she not ripped it from the ballad-scrolls? In her stupor of sleepy-treacle, the nurse had let the melody wash over her like a balm . . .

Pray, pray that the girl did not know what she sang!

But now the Triarch was saying, 'Yet, dear daughter, I am bound to wonder whether indeed I have been a fool. Listen, and I shall explain just why it is that I have never, though you have lived these many orbits, agreed to dispose of you to any particular man.'

Selinda's heart thudded hard.

Zigzag. Zigzag.

Burnished in the lamplight.

And a clacking, too. A breeze stirred the beads that hung across the screen and rustled at the diaphanous, trailing fabric. Tagan, retreating behind the Triarch's couch, raised an eyebrow at Ra Fanana and sipped surreptitiously from the hava-jug. Ra Fanana was alarmed. True, Tagan was her best friend amongst the slaves, but could it be that even a *quality-eunuch* was as rickety, in his way, as the zigzagging screen?

He was beginning to sway.

'I wonder, my dear Selinda,' said the Triarch, 'quite what you have divined of how this realm is governed. Politics, to be sure, is no affair of your sex, nor would I trouble your pretty head with intelligences which, alas, can only alarm you.' He sighed. 'Ah, but on this Isle of Hora there are forces at work, grave forces you would do well to understand – if, that is, you are to survive after I am gone.'

'Father, please – how can you speak so?'

'Because I must, my darling – come, wipe away those tears and listen, listen. You know, do you not, that for long epicycles it has been the pride of this realm that no tyrant has been suffered to hold sway – that its government is determined in a just and equitable fashion?'

Puzzled, the girl nodded. If her life had been sequestered, her lessons only those in the womanly arts, nonetheless she had partaken eagerly of those scraps, those morsels, that had fallen in her way from the wider world. Had she not stood in the Daughter Gallery, watching the proceedings in the Temple of Thirty? If girls were taken there only for display, nonetheless Selinda had listened, at times, to the proceedings of her island's wise governors.

'Why, Father, I know that there are barbarous lands where a single man holds sway – and when he dies, his son reigns in his stead. Long ago, this was our way too, and the people of our isle knew great suffering. In time, they rose up and overthrew their oppressor, vowing that never again should tyranny reign on Hora. Since then, we have lived under the noble system of isocracy, in which all men have power; in effect, power is decided by the process of election. Men of property choose the Gathering of Thirty, that great council in which law and policy are debated.'

Surprise flickered over the Triarch's face. Such knowledge, in one so young? Such knowledge, in a *girl*? 'Indeed, my dear child, our isocracy is a noble system, and glad am I that you understand it so well – glad, though such knowledge is hardly, as I say, the province of your sex . . . You are aware, then, that it is the duty of that Thirty to choose from their ranks those three supreme governors – those who decide the issue of the debates – of whom it has been my privilege, and my burden, to be one? – Burden, I say, for on this Isle of Hora, what is the Triarch but proxy for god? And what is any mere man, that with impunity he may assume such a mantle?'

Sadness hung heavily in the great man's eyes.

'And yet,' he added, 'there are many, too many, who would take up that mantle only too willingly, for nothing so beguiles a man as power – or rather, its promise, before this crown circles his skull, like a fetter tighter than any a prisoner wears.'

'Poor Father . . . poor, poor Father.' Selinda gripped the dry, strangely cold hand; Ra Fanana, shuddering, thought of the screws turning bloodily in the skull-flesh, then driving deep into the bone beneath. What terrible things went on in this world – things she could never even have imagined, in her innocent days on the Isle of Jasmine! Yet the Triarch, for all his sufferings, spoke of Hora as if it were a paradise, the pride of the world. He even seemed to believe in this isocracy of theirs, as if it were true that all on this isle had *equal* power – wasn't that what *isocracy* meant?

The nurse shook her head. In a previous life – so it seemed to her now – she had known something of politics, its entangling labyrinths, its intractable mysteries. Men would speak of justice, but keep slaves; of equity, while their womenfolk knew none. Yet what, thought Ra Fanana, would freedom mean to her now?

Zig. Zag. The Triarch called again for hava-nectar; this time Tagan, pirouetting away, almost fell against the Amali screen. Ra Fanana drew in her breath. The screen rocked precariously, and so did Tagan.

Really, how much hava-nectar *had* he tasted?

'Dear Selinda,' the Triarch went on abstractedly, 'you are aware that for many moonlives the Lord Glond and the Prince Lepato have sued for your hand. Each is of the Thirty, yet more than this, each has his chance of triumph in – yes – a greater election.'

His hand strayed to his temple.

'Alas, of my two fellow-kings, I had thought Triarch Fahan – so ancient is he, so frail – would be first to be replaced; then, too, Triarch Azander has never been hale, for all that his years may be barely more than mine. Fool that I am! In the thick of life, in the pride of pomp and power, what is a man but a deluded infant, if he dreams not that his doom may fall at any time? For my presumption – *all* my presumption – I am cruelly punished.'

The hand at the temple pushed painfully, just for a moment, as if the great man would sweep his crown aside.

But no. It could not be.

'My darling,' he sighed, 'let me explain the delay which, I know, has long troubled your heart. Glond or Lepato? Lepato or Glond? Both are nobles of the highest rank; both are fine in person, character and fortune. Such indeed are hardly my concerns, for if a man is to sue for a lady's hand, his bid must first be registered with the Keepers of the Law. To them he must demonstrate his worthiness to wed, and only if he does so to their satisfaction is a father obliged to consider the suit . . . No, I have deliberated over no *manly* attributes, but waited for the issue of something more vital. How often have I looked into the faces of the Thirty, wondering which way their votes will fall? How eagerly have I listened to the words of my spies, or pondered over the auguries in the stars and moon. Lepato or Glond? Glond or Lepato? Which is to be Triarch?

'Ah, my child, but your eyes glow, and I see that in your inexperience – like the unjudging world – you imagine I would marry you to the victor, only the victor. Would I shock you if I say that my thoughts have been quite opposite? Do you start, if I say that I would favour the vanquished? Yet if I must choose between these two noble suitors, I must ask which would best provide for my daughter's happiness – must I not?

'Consider this: when once a man has stood for election, he may not stand again. To the vanquished, all worldly ambition is at an end, and he must retire even from the Gathering of Thirty. A harsh fate? – better, far better, is the lot of such a man! Ah, sweet Selinda, that is doubt I see in your eyes – but there is so much you do not know, so much I have kept from you, fearful as I have been not to mar your innocence! I tell you, sorrow could only be your lot, should it be your fate to be a Triarch's wife!

'And yet, how much have you sorrowed already – as I have sorrowed – that you have never known a mother's caress? That pretty child, I said, died in giving you life, as many a member of your sex must do. Such are the dictates of fate, no more. But I lied – and not only lied, but like a villainous coward instilled in you a guilt that was never yours to feel. It was not your coming that took your mother's life – she lived, and would

70

have thrived! My daughter, the guilt belongs to your father, to your foolish father and his vaulting ambition!'

Again the Triarch's voice grew strained, but before he could call for nectar, Tagan swayed beside him. Gulping down the liquid, the great man rose to his feet – he was unsteady too, but for a different reason – and paced slowly back and forth before his daughter.

And his story unfurled.

Zigzag. Zigzag.

Inlaid herons, inlaid gulls.

'From the moment I reached the age of manhood,' said the Triarch, 'I longed only to rise to this position that now is mine. The odds were in my favour. My father had been a great man of trade. When he died the fortune I inherited was vast, and all this I dedicated to my campaign. My success was guaranteed. I was handsome; I was young; I had trained myself in all the arts of oratory, all the arts of flattery and bribery too – though then I would forbear to name them such. When I entered the Gathering of Thirty, I knew it would be but a matter of time before I rose yet higher.

'To be sure, many orbits seemed certain to pass before a member of the Triarchy was gathered into The Vast. But it seemed then that all the world was working in my favour, for soon afterwards Triarch Speko collapsed, clutching his heart, and my destiny was certain. Curse me, that I felt but a factitious sorrow for this noble lord! In truth, I could only glory in my coming fortune, when I should have been abashed, even then. Often have I wondered if a member of my faction . . . but no, there is enough to give me pain, without pursuing such entangling byways!'

Watching the great man pace back and forth, Ra Fanana was increasingly alarmed. Her embroidery, forgotten, had slipped to the floor. Oh, the Triarch was sick, sick! Once or twice it seemed he might fall. Sweat flowed from under the band of his crown and his gestures were increasingly wild. Once he blundered close – alarmingly close – to the Amali screen; twice he paused before the shuttered windows, as if he would fling the shutters aside. The light in the apartment was soft and low, but glittered intensely on the jewels in his crown.

He swigged more nectar – Tagan, by now, had fetched a second jug – and went on, 'Nor, my dear daughter, is there need to tell you of the election, for you see its issue in this band that circles my skull – this band I once desired as if it were life itself. Alas, that I had not confined my desires to that greater blessing that was vouchsafed me in the sweet child who was to be your mother! Pretty she was, and I took the pleasures she gave, but not until she was taken from me did I realise my love for her

71

... Do you know who your mother was, my Selinda? To whom she belonged? But the truth, I am afraid, can only make me seem more corrupted, more depraved!'

Stricken, the great man paused before the death-icon of his wife, and the doll that sat beside it, shell-eyes flickering in the soft flame. For a moment his hands covered his face and his shoulders shook. What to do? Tagan, as if arming himself for action, swigged liberally from the refilled jug; Ra Fanana rose to her feet; but it was Selinda who went to her father. She reached for him – was about to touch him – when he turned. 'Your mother,' he said, 'was Triarch Speko's daughter, and he gave her to me just before he died.'

Uncertainly, Selinda stepped back.

'How my faction revelled in his choice, for what could this seem but the anointing of an heir? Yet what irony, to speak of heirs! On this island of ours, what evil could be greater than a dynasty? So it is that to avert this evil, other evils must be enacted – would it were not so!'

'Father, please ... what can you mean?'

'Puzzle not, daughter of mine, for soon my meaning shall be only too clear to you – and soon, knowing what suffering I brought upon your mother, perhaps you shall shrink from me in revulsion, in fear. Yet believe me, as my green days lie far behind me now, so I have repented of them, long and hard. If guilt has not tormented every fibre of my being, what then is this distemper that gnaws inside me like rats through the hull of a foundering ship? I think of that sweet child who gave you life, and despair grips me at what I have been, at what I have done.'

'Oh Father, Father.' By now, Selinda was trembling violently, and longed only to fling herself into her father's arms – but could not. The great man looked into her face, then at the icon, then again at his daughter, and the strange thought came to her that her mother's name had been Selinda too. Why did this fill her with so sharp a pang?

Her father's voice was soft, but suffused with a bitter intensity. 'At first I thought her a badge of my prospects; then that she was an ornament to my high station. Fool, wicked fool! Could I have bound her to a Triarch's hand, had I weighed the sorrow that was sure to be her lot? – Sure, I say, for I knew well enough the rules that bind this station: indeed I did, and gloried in them. How I longed for the moment when this crown would circle my skull! In her innocence, the sweet child longed for it too. Yet in that moment, swelling within her womb, was the seed of new life. That seed' – now he clutched his daughter's hand – 'was to become this most precious of things that remains to me now – but alas, my daughter, it was also to become your *brother*, too.'

Ra Fanana, sidling towards Tagan, had wrested the hava-jug from the eunuch's grip and was sating her own thirst when she almost dropped the heavy vessel on her foot – or on Tagan's. Milky liquid spattered over the floor.

As for Selinda, she only looked bewildered.

'Yes,' her father said, 'for you should have had a brother, as I should have had a son, had it not been for my cursed ambition! What cared I, as they crowned me, for the cruel ordinance that would have my sons destroyed? My heart vaulting in ecstasy, had I not declared my vows – this amongst them, that no dynasty, no prospect of dynasty, should be suffered to spring from a Triarch's loins! What was a son against justice, peace, isocracy – isocracy, lodestar of the Horan way!

'Of my vow, your mother knew nothing. To be sure, she was present at my coronation, but my evil words were recited in High Horan, the ceremonial tongue. As a woman, she could not understand, and sometimes I wonder if I could, myself. But I understood well enough, and she did too, at the second great ceremony of my Triarchy. How the crowd applauded, how they cheered, as an infant denied even the dignity of a name was held aloft by the High Keeper, his tiny brains dashed against the Stone of Isocracy! I stood strong and stoical, the embodiment – as I had longed to be – of my people's faith and hopes. But inside I was crushed, destroyed with sorrow and shame, longing only to collapse – sobbing, moaning – as your stricken mother could not help but do.

'Daughter, it broke her.' Now the Triarch – awkwardly, almost shamefaced – took the battered doll in his arms and held it out to Selinda like an uncertain offering. She did not take it, but looked, trembling, into the painted lifeless face as her father continued, 'Do you see Blisha here, with her woollen hair and eyes of shells and this hole smashed in her forehead? It was your mother who made this hole. For three moonlives the sweet child roamed this palace, raving and crying, hugging the doll against her breast. When she broke off, it was only to beat Blisha's head against the stone flags of the floor; then she would take up the doll again, as if she had snatched it from the arms of another, stroking it, sobbing over it with renewed vigour . . . The poor child! She would not speak. She would not eat. One infant remained – but alas, dear daughter, if I had hoped she would take comfort in *you*, I was mistaken. Such was her madness, that when the slaves brought you to her, your mother thought you the spectre of your murdered twin. Her eyes grew wide with horror, and her grief more frenzied.

'Increasingly the slaves were obliged to restrain her. It seemed she might spend her life in a sickroom, a pitiful prisoner, but it was not to be. Slowly she came to seem reconciled, or at least calmer. My physicians held hopes for her recovery, and again she was permitted a measure of freedom. There were times when she forgot her game with Blisha, laying

73

the tormented doll aside. There were times when she bathed in the cove. There were even times, my poor daughter, when she sat by your basket, looking with strange wonder at your sweet, unformed face. What, I ask myself, were her thoughts at that time? I could not know. Not once, after the day of your brother's death, did your mother speak to me – no, not even to utter crazed, unmeaning words. If I approached her, she would only turn away, in confused alarm. Entreaties availed nothing; often she seemed unaware that I existed. Perhaps it would have been better had I not.'

The Triarch held Blisha high in the air. Selinda's tearful eyes travelled upwards, following the doll as her father said, 'Four moonlives after her son's death, your mother climbed on to the roof of this palace and cast herself down.'

Blisha fell to the floor with a crash. Tagan gave a little squeal; Ra Fanana let out a moan. Selinda might have scooped up the doll, but could not.

She slumped down, shaking.

'This then, my Selinda, is the terrible truth that has so shaped your destiny. How could I risk a recurrence of this tragedy? On the day of your mother's death, on the bloodied path, as I held her crushed body in my arms, I made a vow – a vow stronger, though I tremble to say it, than any I had made to the Gathering of Thirty. This it was, that you, my darling child, should never suffer as your mother suffered. Never should you be wife to a Triarch of Hora! Do you understand, then, the pain that assails my heart now? For soon I shall die, and must give you away – must, I say, for it is a choice a father must make, and to neglect it is . . . no, I shall not neglect it. But how, then, am I to make a choice? Glond or Lepato? Lepato or Glond?'

Zigzag. Zigzag.

Beaded headscarves. Beads.

Sitting beside Selinda, the Triarch gestured for nectar. Tenderly he held the goblet to his daughter's lips. 'Dear daughter, of all the isles scattered over these southern seas, none is greater than Hora. As a spider, at the centre of its web, radiates a power far beyond itself, so this small isle of ours holds dominion over a vast compass. And yet – eschewing, as we do, the ways of the tyrant – for long epicycles we of Hora have slaughtered no rivals, neither pillaged nor plundered, imprisoned none, nor fired shots in anger. Commerce, rather, is the source of our power, for as a magnet-stone compels certain metals to itself, so the great port that lies below this palace draws to us gold and silver from far across the seas. In all the history that is known to us, never has there been a realm more victorious, never a progress more triumphal. Yet now, from our very success, there comes a crisis that may tear this realm apart. Already there have been skirmishes in the streets of this city. What battles, what bloodshed may there yet be? And all because we would steer by that lodestar, isocracy!'

Ra Fanana was confused. What did this have to do with the Triarch's poor wife? Or the girl's marriage? Or anything? She wondered if she should pick up poor Blisha, who still lay on the floor where she had fallen. Instead, her hands reached for the hava-jug.

Tagan's grip was tenacious.

Selinda, meanwhile, continued to look on blank-eyed as her father went on, 'In the growth of our great trading empire, many a man of Hora has spent his life abroad, making his home beyond the seas. Thus we may wonder: what *is* a man of Hora? Many have been the marriages with women of other islands; many have been the offspring born far from these shores. When they come here, these sons from afar, they find themselves strangers in this land that yet is theirs by ancestral right. We call them *Outrealmers*, as those born to these shores are known as *Innermen*.'

Ah, but the nectar was soothing! Sinking down, Ra Fanana would even have taken up her embroidery again, but on the first stitch she pricked her finger. She cursed under her breath and cast the frame aside.

What was the Triarch talking about?

'Now it happened that until the time of Triarch Speko, your father-forefather, it was the custom that only Innermen could be elected to the Gathering of Thirty. Outrealmers, considered foreigners, were denied such a right. For a time this seemed just – no more, as it were, than the way of the world. Yet inevitably, as each election was held, resentment simmered amongst the Outrealmers. In this fulcrum of the world, not only were their ranks great in number; many, after all, were men of property, as great or greater than their Innermen counterparts. Protests grew; some feared for our polity; still worse, some feared for the disruption of our commerce. So it was, at the instigation of your father-forefather, that there came about the Act of Augmentation, extending the vote to those Outrealmers – as I say, there were many – who fulfilled our criteria of position and place. There was much celebration, and the word *isocracy* rang in the air like a clarion bell.

'Yet even then there was disquiet in some quarters. Would the Outrealmers, some asked, be content merely to vote? Would they not field their own candidates too? How long before Outrealmers filled the Gathering of Thirty – before they aspired to the Triarchy itself? There were those amongst the Innermen to whom the very prospect was an infection, a disease attacking the body politic. Others dismissed these fears, or thought them too remote to be of concern. With the Thirty, and the Triarchy too, altering only when a member died, how many orbits must elapse to bring about changes of any importance? No, said these sceptics, Hora was safe, and should have no fear . . . Yet it was soon after the death of your father-forefather, when I took his place in the Triarchy, that an Outrealmer assumed the place I vacated in the Thirty. Dear child, that Outrealmer – a robber-baron's son, that is all, from the far-off fiefdom of Ambora Rock – was Lord Glond.'

Selinda looked wonderingly into her father's face. After a lifetime, it seemed, of languishing in mystery, suddenly she had heard almost too much. What was she to make of it all? What did it all mean? Then – gazing into the dark, beloved eyes – she thought only that her father was dying, and nothing else mattered.

But it did. It had to.

'You see, then, the crisis that has come to pass. On one side the Outrealmers and their champion, Glond; on the other, the Innermen, determined that Lepato – and no alien, as they put it, no mongrel foreigner – should wear the Triarch's crown. So evenly are these factions ranged, so certain is each of victory, that the outcome of the election is impossible to foretell. Thus do I hesitate to give you away. Then, too, talk has reached me that my choice might yet serve to *sway* the election! Lepato or Glond? Glond or Lepato? What does it matter, when if I choose either, his faction will see it as a badge of favour, an anointing – as did mine when my marriage-father, your father-forefather, gave his daughter to me? My very choice could swing the election, this way or that!'

It seemed like the moment for a little more nectar. Generously Tagan sashayed forward, but caught his foot on an edge of carpet. Only Ra Fanana saved the day, pulling him back just as the nectar was about to cascade over Triarch and daughter alike. Fortunately the great ones were preoccupied, barely aware of the hovering slaves. Staggering, Tagan caught the Amali screen, gripping it for support. Just in time, Ra Fanana took the hava-jug from his hand. She smiled uncertainly. Oh, she wanted to giggle . . . no, to guzzle!

Zigzag. Zigzag. Ziggyzagzag.

The screen rocked. Tagan hung from it.

The Triarch was reaching his peroration. 'My dear girl, there is but one thing certain: whichever man wins, there will be bloodshed in the agora. Am I to die, knowing I have delivered you into the heart of this storm? It cannot be – and yet there is a way . . . Glond or Lepato? Lepato or Glond? Sweet child, you shall marry neither! The suitors, having been accepted, must be compensated, and the sums, I fear, will tax my fortune sorely. But pay them I shall. Tomorrow, before the Thirty, it is my determination to declare the existing suits null and void, and call for new ones. But this

I say: neither of the factions which divide this Isle of Hora shall claim Triarch Jodrell's daughter as their own!

'I see now I have been a fool, in this as in so much else. Never, as a fond father, could I permit you to go unwed, but what is this isle if not a place where foreigners come from far and wide? Your husband must be a man who resides far from Hora, one who shall take you away from the coming conflagration. Daughter, it is your destiny to leave this place. Oh, I fear time is short, and my death is creeping closer, ready to clutch. But let me not die, is all I ask, before I have found the man to be your new protector!'

There was a loud crash.

Selinda cried out. The Triarch turned. Astonishment overspread his face. In a heap on the floor lay the Amali screen. Beside it, hiccoughing and giggling, was the nurse; underneath it, moaning, was the eunuch; but behind it – now revealed – was a youth the Triarch had never seen before, clad in barely more than a loincloth, like a beggar.

That evening the Triarch had uttered many words. Now he was speechless, and so was his daughter. Thus it was the youth who spoke first, in a noble voice that belied the rags he wore.

'Triarch, you have found the protector you seek. I am Maius Eneo – *Prince* Maius Eneo. I am ... I am Dynast-Elect of Inorchis, and I have come for your daughter's hand!'

Chapter 11

DEAD MAN'S LOOKOUT

Swiftly, swiftly, shadows fall
From the brightest sky:
That darkness has his outriders
No one can deny!

Faster, faster, darkness comes,
Blanketing the sea:
That shadows have their avatars
All men must—

Ucheus broke off his singing and listened intently, standing like a statue in the glimmering light. What had he heard? Only the hiss of marshy steam, the drip-drip of wet leaves. Somewhere a fly buzzed; somewhere a ripe fruit tumbled down, its fall muffled by the undergrowth. The jungle, thought the slender youth, was full of phantoms. But then, there were things that were all too real – the insect, tunnelling into the back of his neck; the silent, slimy thing that passed over his feet. If he stood, statue-like, for a moment longer, would moss fur his flesh? How he longed to hack away this jungle growth! How he longed for the clean, stark whiteness of Inorchis – the stripped hillsides, the neat, logical farms!

Ucheus tightened his grip on his spear. Life was a good thing, life not death; but on Xaro, he thought suddenly, there was too much life, life out of control, diseased and rampant. But no, he did not believe that, not really – it was death that was out of control, and all this life, this seeming life, was really an emanation of death, no more. He slapped behind his ear, but the maddening insect was still there, drilling, burrowing. He scratched, drew blood, then pushed his way onwards.

He was making for the beach. For a time, it was true, he had blundered here and there, searching for the boy and the rainbow-coloured dog. By now, he barely believed they existed. But then, did Leki believe it either? Perhaps it was a trick – perhaps it was all a trick, these newcomers with their strange ways. Ucheus sighed. What a fool he had been, hoping they came from Maius Eneo! With a thud of dread, he could think only that some new, fresh evil must indeed be at work. This time, he vowed, he would not be drawn into it. He would escape, as he should have escaped with Maius Eneo.

He slithered down an overgrown trail. His arms wheeled, grabbing at vegetation, and he burst his way into the open air. From here, the path was stony and dry, winding down to a citrine, curving beach, glazed by soft surf. This was Xaro Bay, the place where they had landed – how long ago it seemed! – on the day when they had begun their Manhood Trial.

Ucheus flung himself along the strand, suddenly running. He hurled his spear skywards; arcing down, it jabbed into the surf like a leaning flagpole. He looked across the empty sea, his heart aching. 'Inorchis,' he whispered. 'Inorchis, Inorchis.' He swivelled back, hating this desolate place that was not his beloved bay, yet so mockingly like it. He thought of his father; he thought of his home. 'Inorchis,' he whispered, 'I would be a gelded slave, I would be a horse, I would be a dog, if I could walk your pale streets again . : .'

That was what Maius Eneo had said, the day before he left.

Blank, massy walls of rock divided the jungle from the citrine sands. Ucheus left his spear where it stood and advanced with deliberation towards the rocks. It was then, just as he turned his back, that a curious object came rolling up the beach, borne on the soft slitherings of the tide. It was strange, for the object looked heavy; one might have expected it to sink beneath the sea. The tide sucked out, and the object, which was spherical, flashed in the sun, rolled towards the spear, circled it, and began to spin.

Ucheus, had he looked that way, should certainly have seen this curious sight – and been startled; instead, he clambered between boulders, slipping on algae, splashing in pools. There, in a place like a cave without a roof, he came upon a coracle of skins and vines. It was almost finished – but not quite. He laughed aloud and jumped down into the coracle. If the Sibyl's prophecy had frightened him, suddenly he didn't care. So, Maius Eneo could not come back to save them. Then what could they do but go to Maius Eneo? Of course: that was what the coracle was for. 'Soon,' he said, 'soon.'

Seabirds whirled in the sky above; a darkness welled inside Ucheus and his mind drifted into reverie, borne back into the past like a boat against the current. Hugging himself, he nestled down in the coracle.

On the sands, the orb kept spinning.

The History of Ucheus

1

When Ucheus was ten orbits old, he was sent for a season to the far side of Inorchis and the house of his uncle, Maius Castor. While the boy's father was a great man in Sarom, Chief Councillor to the Dynast, Castor-uncle was – so he liked to put it – a simple farmer, remote from all thought of power, either temporal or spiritual. This, Ucheus would realise in time, was disingenuous: as a member of the Manhood Caste, as a landowner and slaveholder, Castor-uncle possessed power whether he would or no; he voted with the Elders on matters of state, and his son, should he succeed in his Manhood Trial, would be eligible – as Castor-uncle had once been eligible – to be chosen as Dynast. Yet what of it? When his uncle claimed to despise the Court, Ucheus had no doubt that he told the truth.

For the young Ucheus, life until then had been a regimented business. It was a convention in Sarom that Untried boys had little contact with their fathers and none at all with their mothers, being tended instead by unmanned slaves. Ard Ired, the unman assigned to Ucheus, was a sour, joyless creature whose solitary consolation was to punish his young charge with malicious relish for his every misdemeanour, no matter how slight; but Ucheus, fortunately, had a consolation of his own. In the afternoons after Sacred School he was permitted to play with Ojo, the son of one of the Priests of Aroc. It is desirable, after all, that boys should have friends: it breaks down shyness, builds comradeship, and fuels competition – all good preparations for the Trial that is to come. A pity, then, that Ojo was a lugubrious creature, given to dour complaints, uninventive in games, and too fat to run fast. When a bout of jubba-fever swept over Sarom, it was inevitable that the stocky boy should succumb, his life lingering in the balance – inevitable, too, that his slender friend should be sent to the safety of Castor-uncle's farm.

For Ucheus, the farm was a new world. Long after the visit was over – back in Sarom, trailing in boredom to prayers with Ard Ired, or sitting straight-backed in Sacred School – the boy would remember this different, strange place of cracking roughcast walls, of laden hedges and trees, of black volcanic soil with its buried carrots and yams. How he would long for the dog-like, hairy pigs, the saggy-throated oxen, the silky roughness of the horses' manes! In the evenings, cursed by Ard Ired for the slumpings of his shoulders or the leftovers in his bowl or the flecks of mud on his crisply laundered tunics, Ucheus would close his eyes and see a long rugged table with splintery benches where all the family of Castor-uncle, his wives, his daughters, even his slaves – but he did not call them slaves – ate together without restriction, winking at each other, smiling and joking. Ucheus loved them all; most of all he loved his cousin, Maius Eneo.

2

How to describe the splendours of his cousin? How to describe the glories of their days? With Maius Eneo, Ucheus explored the thousand delights of Castor-uncle's domain, from the sun-warmed musky barn to the encrusted mossy troughs, from the cobwebbed storeroom with its cool urns and barrels to the prickly hedges and the stonecropped fields. With the alacrity of a prisoner set suddenly free, he burrowed into hayricks, sending rats scurrying; he prodded at serpents under curing-sheds; he squeezed the creamy hotness of milk from a teat. Then there was the red, dark hotness of blood, flowing over the blade of a knife, or bursting from the breast of a plummeting bird. Ucheus whittled arrows; he strung bows. Soon he shot with unerring ease, expertly screwing up his eye to aim. If he did not much like killing – in truth, it repelled him – still it seemed he could do anything if only Maius Eneo were beside him. The two boys ran, they leapt, they laughed; naked, they swam in a glittering stream. One afternoon, whooping joyously, they swung across the length of a tangled orchard, never once touching the ground.

They should have been brothers, Castor-uncle would say – Twinned brothers, like the two Thunderers of Aroc. But Ucheus never wanted his cousin for a brother – let alone a twin. If Maius Eneo was the same age as Ucheus, to Ucheus he seemed older – much older. Then, as now, he was at least a full head taller than most boys his age, and possessed already the lineaments of a man. He was lithe, taut-muscled, and extraordinarily handsome.

In many of us, in our early lives, there is a longing for a mentor, a guide, to lift us – gently, understandingly – from the prison of our inadequacies; in Maius Eneo, Ucheus found his guide.

To be sure, Maius Eneo was not so gentle. He was a boisterous boy; he pinched, punched and pummelled; his voice could be a coarse, bantering cry. It sounded like a laughing bird – but how Ucheus longed for that laughing bird! *Nearsider, you fool*, it cawed, or *Nearsider, come on*, or *Nearsider, that's not the way*. Soon it seemed to Ucheus that his name indeed was Nearsider – and yet he knew this was not a name at all, only the term, in these parts, for those who came from the other side of the island. It carried with it a certain contempt: where Ucheus came from, Farsiders were pitied as ignorant, rustic; but Farsiders, for their part, pitied Nearsiders. Who would wish, said Castor-uncle one night, to spend his life staring over the Bay of Aroc to Xaro? He looked at Ucheus, as if daring him to differ; then Maius Eneo laughed, like a laughing bird, and Ucheus laughed too. Who would wish? Oh, who would wish . . .

Sometimes, in the cluttered attic they shared, Ucheus would lie awake in the quietness of the night, staring with a delicious, sad happiness at the sleeping Maius Eneo. How peacefully his cousin's breath rose and fell, rose and fell beneath the thin covers! How taut, but how loose, were his cousin's limbs! He thought of his cousin's limpid eyes, his full lips, his lean, angular face, and felt consumed by an aching, shuddering longing – a longing he could barely understand. From time to time a breeze made the open shutters creak; nightjars called distantly; heat, and the perfumes of fruit and flowers, hovered on the air. Oh, thought Ucheus, but they *should* have been brothers ... Then the sad happiness would become simply sadness, and he would wish that somehow, in some way, their bond could be stronger. Time was passing: before long, Ucheus knew, he must leave, returning to Sarom, to his father, to Ard Ired. Many times, with sudden bitterness, he wished the jubba-fever would take them all. Then shame would consume him at a thought so unworthy.

Two moonlives had passed, perhaps three, when the message came to summon Ucheus home. The danger had passed: all would be as it had been before. But how could it? When Castor-uncle, smiling broadly, told Ucheus that his friend Ojo had lived, the slender boy barely registered a smile. It was not that he had no regard for his stocky friend – far from it; only that his friend seemed to belong to another world, a world Ucheus had long left behind. How he ached to stay with Maius Eneo! How he longed for that stronger, deeper bond!

3

It was on the night before he was to leave when the incident occurred that was to mark Ucheus's life for ever afterwards. Some days earlier, the boys had gone climbing, not in the trees or on the crumbling walls, but amongst the rocks that rose behind the farm, jutting up towards the cone of the Thunderer. Their destination was a certain high outcrop that Maius Eneo called Dead Man's Lookout. Many times he had promised they would go there, but always, before now, the mission had been postponed. There was too much to do about the farm; Castor-uncle would be angry; besides, Maius Eneo would grin, the view to the horizon was so clear, the sea so wide and empty, that it would turn a Nearsider's wits ... Ucheus denied it vehemently, but Maius Eneo was unmoved. Now, when they knew Ucheus would be leaving soon, Maius Eneo declared suddenly that they would make the climb. Ucheus's heart beat hard with excitement. Obscurely he was aware that this was a test, a test he must not fail.

In the afternoons, when the heat was at its height, no one worked on Castor-uncle's farm. Castor-uncle reclined on the verandah, rocking back and forth in a big curving chair; the family retired to their rooms; the slaves, who were not slaves, dozed in the shadows of the sheds, broad hats covering their faces. This was the time when Maius Eneo, creeping and whispering, led Ucheus out towards the rocks. Looking up, a hand shielding his eyes, Ucheus could barely make out Dead Man's Lookout.

No matter: he knew that it was high above, too high, and he knew that the rocks were steep, too steep. Sweat ran down the back of his neck.

The climb began slowly; it soon became slower. Hand after hand, foot after foot, Ucheus imitated his cousin's holds. In moments, his tunic was sodden and his legs and arms ached; moments later, he began to be frightened. To look up was dangerous – to look down was worse. The searing sun beat at his neck like a hammer against an anvil. His breath came in gasps. Then the rocks were steeper, sheerer, sharper. Time, called the laughing bird, to prove what a Nearsider can *really* do.

The climb was just beginning; Ucheus gritted his teeth. Particles danced before his eyes, pitching and tossing in the dazzling air. He was a puppet – his master was above. This way: that way: hands: feet. But the confident easy swing of his cousin's limbs was something Ucheus could never imitate. Soon Maius Eneo was far above. The slender boy flattened himself against the cliff-face.

How much higher? He turned his head.

The sea was wide and empty.

Ucheus screamed.

How had he got to the ground again? How could he say? All he could remember was the laughing bird, taunting him at the foot of the cliff. So, the Nearsider had proved himself at last – proved himself a coward! Oh, but the game had been brief – really, it had lasted no time at all . . .

Grinning, Maius Eneo scrambled up. Where should they go now? What should they do? Soon they would swing in the cool of the orchard; soon they would bathe in the cool of the stream. But Ucheus's shame burned inside him, burned and beat in him like the hammer of the sun. Every day, it was true, the laughing bird had taunted him, but this was different – now, when he must go away, Ucheus knew just how different. If only he had been a hero, not a coward! To stand beside his cousin on Dead Man's Lookout: what could this be but the bond he had wanted? Now, he would be gone and his cousin would remember him only as a weakling.

4

Ucheus felt the desperation rising inside him. On his last night, he lay awake later than ever before. Gently, on and on, Maius Eneo's breath rose and fell; moonlight spilled goldenly over the rough floor. Like a thief, Ucheus crept down through the house. Later, he would pretend he had been sleepwalking – but then, perhaps he had. Why else would he would make the climb again, alone and in the dark?

The moon, a different hammer, bore down on him coldly. He must not turn – he must not look. He thought of his cousin, of the handholds, of the footholds, of the swing of his limbs. Perhaps that was why, when terror gripped him again, Ucheus would have cried out his cousin's name. But no: the cry froze in his throat. His fingers clawed at rock. Must not look – must not turn. He clung precariously to a narrow ledge. But then, impossibly, the hand was there, reaching for him – reaching *from above*.

He gripped it, hard. His cousin hauled him up to the ledge.

'Do you know why they call it Dead Man's Lookout?' said Maius Eneo. His handsome face glimmered in the moonlight, giving him a strangely unearthly look. 'They say the dead want to come back to life, so they stand here and wait, watch and wait for climbers.'

'Do they push them down?'

'No, they help them. Funny story, isn't it? They say if you grip a dead man's hand, you'll change places with him – then you'll be dead, and he'll be alive.'

Ucheus, in sudden terror, gazed at his cousin.

Maius Eneo laughed. 'Of course, it's only a story – just a silly story . . .'

The sea, wide and empty, glimmered under the moon as Ucheus murmured at last, 'Maius-cousin, how did you know I'd be here?'

'Why, Nearsider, didn't I hear you call?'

'You *heard* me?'

'It's not far—'

'But . . . I didn't call.'

'Nearsider, are you so sure?'

They said no more, but it did not matter. Next day, trundling back in the wagon to Sarom, Ucheus felt a calm deep within his being. What had he to fear? The moment of transfiguration had come; it had passed; nothing would ever be the same again.

5

Later – once alone, several times with Ojo – Ucheus would return to Castor-uncle's farm. Each time Maius Eneo was bigger, stronger, more boisterous than before; soon, alarmingly soon, there were tales that he had acquired something of a reputation amongst the fair sex. More than one slave-girl from the farm, it appeared, had had to be sold, or exchanged for male-slaves from neighbouring estates, owing to the depredations of Maius Eneo.

When Ucheus asked his cousin about these tales, Maius Eneo would only flash his bright smile, taunting him goodnaturedly in the voice that had already deepened from a bird-caw into a smooth, rumbling bass. But of course the tales were true, and secretly they delighted Ucheus. If girls, whatever their place in the world, would swoon at the mere mention of his cousin's name, was this to be wondered at? Everyone must love

Maius Eneo, whatever he did. Didn't they say he would be Dynast-Elect, as soon as he passed his Manhood Trial?

Only Ojo seemed doubtful about Maius Eneo. Quite what his friend saw in this rowdy, vain cousin the stocky, lugubrious Ojo could never quite understand. In truth, he envied Maius Eneo; often he hated him; his cheeks burnt hotly when the bigger boy tormented him. Ucheus saw all this; he was even sorry for Ojo, but how could he explain? What was he to say if Ojo could not see the deeper, truer Maius Eneo that ran like a buried stream beneath his cousin's outward character? One day, Ucheus was sure of it, the buried stream would break through again, sweeping them all to their destiny.

Never again did they climb Dead Man's Lookout. But an image haunted Ucheus. He saw himself with his cousin again on that precarious ledge, this time not in darkness, but in daylight.

Chapter 12

DEEP PURPLE

Swiftly, swiftly, shadows fall
From the brightest sky:
That darkness has his outriders
No one can—

What is that song?

Jem stirs. With cramped limbs he lies on rock, his knees drawn to his chest, his back curved like a question mark. Pouring around him is a golden light, that may or may not be the light of the sun; from somewhere he hears a sound of barking. Rainbow? There is a rasp in Jem's throat. He would call out, but cannot even whisper, so parched are his lips and tongue. He rubs his eyes and the scene before him judders into focus. A slab. Bones, bleached. Blood, blackened.

He rises to his feet. Why is he alone? Bringing a hand to his temples he sways, just a little, like a branch in a breeze. But no breeze stirs the languor of the sweltering air. Only a buzzing, a subdued unrelenting drone of flies, blowing and blundering just beyond the field of his vision. Then the barking again. Jem turns. He looks across the sea that is deep and wide and empty, vanishing into the haze of the horizon. Smoke from the Thunderer scuds across the brightness.

Jem turns back, and it is then that he sees the most important thing: the wall of a hundred holes. How did he get here? No matter: moving forward, he knows at once that a presence looms in the dark holes. What it might be he cannot be certain, but he glimpses, or thinks he does, the fugitive blinking of a glaucous eye. He breathes deeply. As if he has partaken of a drug, Jem feels his mind beginning to spin; then he is aware of the crystal at his chest, burning scarlet through the fabric of his tunic. But something else is burning, too. Flames, glassy and shimmering, leap around his feet. Then Jem knows he is dreaming; he must be, for he feels no pain. He stares and stares into the wall of holes. The eye blinks again and there is a glimpse of green; the green, perhaps, of slimy scales.

Jem swallows hard. The flames are glassy, shimmering; smoke clouds his eyes, but still the only heat he feels is the crystal's, searing like a brand at the flesh above his heart. From the holes comes a low but fearsome sound, a long, shuddering exhalation of breath. Somewhere the flies still blunder and buzz; then, in the hundred voices, some hissing, some shrieking, some drawling languidly, come the words, the song, and Jem knows that this is not just a dream: this is prophecy. The Sibyl sings as if Jem had questioned her, yet Jem knows he has not spoken at all.

> *Key to the Orokon, seeker of the stone,*
> *What shall your hands hold if you seek alone?*
> *Should you fail to heed these words from me,*
> *Empty, empty those hands shall ever be:*
> > *Key, you may come at the prize you would take*
> > *Only if you follow in magic's wake!*

> *Voices, too many, whisper in your ears,*
> *Choices, too many, only rouse your fears:*
> *Key, there is somewhere an island in the clouds,*
> *Somewhere a citadel the sea's depth shrouds,*
> > *Somewhere a magic you cannot understand,*
> > *Magic you must follow to a magic land!*

> *Seeker of the Orokon, key to the stone,*
> *Where lies the clue to your quest, to your throne?*
> *Scattered over islands by the winds that fly,*
> *Whipping in a wild storm, blue in the sky:*
> > *Key, but in truth, there is one key alone –*
> > *Follow the magic to the magic stone!*

By the time the song is over, Jem has sunk into the fire, prostrated by the force of the hundred voices. His chest burns; tears stain his face. Fragments of the last lines echo in his mind. *Storm ... Blue ... Stone ...* And there is laughter too, trembling like the tremblings of the glaucous eye. Then the laughter fades and there are only the flies, buzzing louder now than before ...

Jem looks down. But what can have happened? Has time run in reverse? Where the bleached bones were, and the blackened blood, the blood instead is rich, and running from huge, stinking chunks of meat. Round and round swirl the madding flies. Sickened, Jem lurches back, just in the moment when a hand grips his shoulder.

Jem woke with a start. 'Raj! Where are we?'

Rajal grimaced. 'Take a look around you.'

At first Jem was aware only of a reddish brightness. He screwed up his eyes and saw that it was the sun, sinking now, spiking its rays through a jagged arc of rock. They were in the cave at Sarom, just the two of them – Jem, Rajal. Where were the others? Jem scrambled forward. The cave was stifling and his limbs were cramped. But when he tried to climb out into the evening air, he hit his head against an invisible wall. With an oath, he lurched back.

'I was going to mention that,' said Rajal.

'Glad you were so prompt,' said Jem, rubbing his forehead. Cautiously this time, he reached out a hand. The barrier tingled against his fingers. He traced it from top to bottom, from side to side. 'Adamantine is the word I'd use.'

'Adam what?'

'Just say I'm going to have a bump on the head.'

'Me, too. But Jem, that's not the most amazing thing.' Holding up a crudely fashioned bowl, Rajal sipped from it, then passed it to his friend. 'See this? This wasn't here when they first dragged us in – nor this.' He lifted a palm-leaf. A chunk of boiled meat, some suspicious-looking fruits and a pile of nuts lay, like an offering, on a platter of bark. 'It was a while ago now. I still couldn't move my limbs then, but my eyelids flickered – that was when I saw him, you see.'

'Him?'

'The fat one. Scurrying in, then out.'

'So Ojo's brought us some provisions. And?'

'That's just it. There was no barrier – not for him.'

Thoughtfully, Jem peered through the invisible wall. In the waning light, the rocky ridge lay deserted. Steam curled languidly from the cauldron in the centre; the silence was thick, but to Jem it was a silence of anticipation, as if the world were holding its breath. He gazed across the sea and his dream came back to him. Never, in all the time of his quest, had Jem felt so strongly that here was a sign, a clue he must follow. *Follow the magic.* But what did it mean?

Barking, brief and distant, drifted over the air.

'That barking's so strange,' said Jem. 'Where *is* Rainbow?'

'What about Littler? It's almost dark. I'm worried, Jem – really worried, now.'

'Me too.'

They looked down morosely and, as if to underscore their fears, the floor of the cave began to shudder. Skittering down from the roof came sharp little shards of rock. They cuffed them away, as if they were flies. Jem reared up and would have paced back and forth, but the cave was too low. He slumped down again, wiping his forehead. The heat was unbearable, the stench worse. Did the barrier shut out even the air?

He burst out, 'I don't get it! Leki said the Thunderer wants us. Why stick us in here – why not just take us up the mountain and throw us in?'

Rajal laughed. 'Easy – they're waiting for the right time.'

'You seem remarkably certain,' Jem said.

'You forget, I've been sacrificed before. Well, sort of.'

'Yes, but *that* was in a civilised country.'

'Are you there? Are you still there?'

The only reply was the rustling of dark, sinister leaves. It was not the first time Littler had called out. Perhaps the stranger had gone away. But Littler, lashed to the trunk of a tree, suspected that his captor was still there, lurking silently behind him in the foliage. Shuddering, he recalled the shadowy presence that had bound him tightly with these thick vines; then the hand, a little later, that had reached around the trunk, holding fruit to his parched mouth. Littler thought of the texture of that hand. Terror consumed him at its alien strangeness.

The hand was blue. Blue, with scales.

Nearsider, come – Nearsider, quick.

Ucheus rose gently back to consciousness. Filling his mind was an awareness of a voice, a calling voice; it was an awareness that had come to him before. He gazed up solemnly. Darkness was falling; evening, mottled in vermilion and mauve, poured and pulsed over the rocks with their reeking algae and clinging, nacreous shells. The slender youth shifted, not without awkwardness. It was damp in the coracle and his limbs were cramped; he was hungry – but somehow, just now, he did not care. Curiously he touched the sides of the primitive little boat – skins, mud, vines, bark. But thicker than before – tighter, firmer. Could it be true? It had to be!

Nearsider, come – Nearsider, quick.

The first time, he had not believed it; the second, he had not been sure. But he knew it now. Slowly, as the voice echoed in his mind, more of the coracle had formed itself around him, as if directed by occult powers. Oh, in the beginning the coracle – this particular coracle – had been his own handiwork, his and no other's. And how inept he had been! True, he had watched the building of that certain *other* coracle, but he had watched it idly, understanding little. Besides, how much time could he spare for the work on this one? Bent on secrecy, he had not even told Ojo what he was about. The coracle was a dream. But yes, that was it: the coracle was a dream, or came in dreams. The voice. The vision. It was all true!

Nearsider, come – Nearsider, quick.

The voice, until now, had sounded only in the slender boy's mind. How could it now echo on the air? It bounced from the rocks, it boomed from the trees, it tolled inside the coracle, as if the coracle were an inverted bell. Ucheus sprang up. Doubt had assailed him too many times.

89

No more. Had the Sibyl strengthened him? All he knew was that destiny was upon him. Could Maius Eneo be lying dead, food for fishes at the bottom of the sea? No, he was calling him! Soon the coracle must be completed ... Soon, soon, the journey must begin!

Ucheus stumbled out from the rocks.

Skin: he needed skin.

Gripping the kos-knife he had taken from Ojo, he plunged towards the darkening jungle. What would he do, there in the gloom? Seize the huge, hot body of a pig, wrestling it, squealing, into the undergrowth? Absurd: but then he thought of Kyra's hide – yes, that was *just* what he needed for the coracle ... He darted back along the beach. In the purple evening, he could barely make out the stony path, leading back to the thickly wooded heights.

Ah, but the figure stood out clearly enough. The dark outline, ragged and lumbering.

His voice trembled. 'Lemyu? *Lemyu?'*

'Perhaps we could blast our way out,' said Rajal, not quite unseriously. He gestured behind him and Jem saw that his friend leaned against the hunched, rusted cannon.

Jem moved behind the gun-carriage. Looking along the line of sight, he lit an imaginary touchpaper and put it to the vent, then leapt back, as if from the recoil, a spitty explosion bursting from his lips.

'Watch it!' Rajal protested.

'Good shot, eh?' said Jem.

'Hah! At this range I could spit in your eye too.'

'I meant,' said Jem, 'the one that shot us down. What do you think would be the odds against that?'

'Bull's eye on a large, brightly coloured object? Odds *against*? Quite high, actually – since I don't see any powder hereabouts ... or tindersticks ... or cannon balls. Besides, this old thing's rusted solid ... Jem, do you get the feeling that life's stacked against us?'

'I get the feeling that Leki's more powerful than we feared. Curse it to Toth!' And Jem picked up a small stone, flinging it at the invisible wall. Rajal ducked to avoid it as it bounced back, but it only struck the cannon's muzzle, letting out a dull clang. 'Raj, there must be a way out of this!'

A voice came. 'Ejlanders, I'm sorry, but there's no way.'

Jem swivelled round. Squatting outside the cave-mouth was Ojo. The stocky youth had brought a fresh bowl of water and with a diffident smile he extended it to the prisoners. Jem watched, intrigued, as the dark forearm, with a fizzing of sparks, penetrated the barrier.

He seized the arm suddenly.

Water scattered. Jem twisted.

'Let me go, let me go!' Ojo cried.

The stocky youth struggled, but not hard enough. In a moment, he was through the barrier. Jem sat astride him, pinning him down.

'Jem,' sighed Rajal, 'what good will this do?'

'None, no doubt,' said Jem, 'but there are a few questions I want answered.'

'Such as?' said Rajal.

Ojo flashed Rajal an uncertain smile; Jem, looking intently at his plump victim, said rapidly, 'Such as what is this place, who are you, who's your friend with the bright eyes, and what does he want with us – hm?'

'I thought we'd worked *that* one out already,' said Rajal. 'How about making him get us out of here?'

'Now there's an idea,' said Jem, and bounced menacingly, several times, on the cushiony belly. 'You're the gaoler, you've got the key – haven't you?'

Ojo turned green. 'Sun-haired one,' he spluttered, 'I . . . this is none of my doing. Oh, I thought you were evil before, I know – I was confused, and . . . but then Leki came, and . . . and I wanted to tell you before, and I was *trying* to, but Leki . . . oh, don't you see, I know I'm wrong *now*? I'm wrong, Uchy's right – I'm on your side, I swear it . . .'

Jem bounced. 'Oh? Then how about letting us go?'

'I would – but only Leki . . . only Leki has the power.'

With another bounce, Jem considered this remark. 'You just came through that barrier, didn't you?'

'Yes, I can enter . . . but only for an instant. But you've kept me too long . . . now – now I'll be trapped in here, too.'

'What?' Jem groaned.

'Typical,' said Rajal. He considered aiming another stone at the barrier, but decided it would only rebound and hit him. 'Let him up, Jem. I think he *is* on our side – well, sort of.'

With ill grace Jem released his prisoner. 'All right,' he scowled, 'he can prove it by answering a few questions. Such as what's been going on? Such as why is he here – him and his friends? Is he marooned, or what? Just what's been happening?'

'Yes, tell,' said Rajal. 'Tell all.'

There was a pause. The three of them sat cross-legged in the cave. By now, evening was drawing in apace, and the air around them had darkened to a deep, purple glimmering as Ojo looked up solemnly and said, 'My friends, your questions are brief, but my answers must be long if you are to know *all* that has come to pass – if you are to understand,

91

truly understand, the tragedy that has befallen our Twinned Isles of Aroc.'

Jem was confused. 'Twinned Isles? But there's only one.'

'Indeed,' said Ojo, 'for its companion, its twin, has vanished like – like a phantom. Like a vision. Like a dream.'

'Vanished?' Rajal echoed.

'Dream?' echoed Jem.

The word tolled in his brain like a bell, and he thought again of his own mysterious dream. Slowly its meaning was becoming clear to him. *Follow the magic.* What was this magic, what could it be, but the carpet, but Leki, but this vanishing island? But follow – how? Jem would have urged Ojo to go on, but it was Rajal who spoke next, bursting out in exasperated jest, 'What, has the sea swallowed this other island? Or a mighty whale? How can it be that an *island* vanishes?'

'You doubt me?' said Ojo. 'My friend, three moonlives, no more than three, have passed since the days when Inorchis stood proudly on the other side of the bay, for all the world like a reflection in a looking-glass – a looking-glass I say, for not only in magnitude but in every dimension, in every zigzag of ragged rock, in every curve of sandy coast, these Twinned Isles of Aroc were exactly the same.'

'Exactly?' said Rajal. 'But that's impossible—'

'Raj, shh!' said Jem. 'What have you learnt from all our adventures, if you say that anything's impossible? But Ojo, did your peoples on the other island live in the manner that you live here? Your leader fooled me at first, but I cannot believe you are savages.'

Ojo's look was solemn. 'Then you see, sun-haired one, that your friend is right, for beyond the reckonings of height and breadth and width, beyond the mountains and the contours of the coast, indeed there was a difference between these Twinned Isles of Aroc. This it was – that while Xaro, as you have seen, is a place wild and unkempt, Inorchis was the locus of our civilisation, its slopes smoothed into roads and farms, its ridges built high with fine dwellings, its peoples bedecked in jewels and gold and brightly dyed garments of the finest cambric and kersey.'

'A strange civilisation,' Jem reflected, 'that would cluster on one isle, with another so close. My own race, I dare say, would long ago have spread to the empty one too.'

'Only if it were empty?' Rajal said archly.

Ojo did not appear to follow these remarks. Jem wondered why. Could it be that these Islanders of Aroc were a docile people, unversed in that lust of conquest which coursed so fiercely through the blood of his own countrymen? He thought of Leki, and it seemed unlikely; but maybe Leki was an aberration.

In a faraway voice, Ojo explained that his peoples had lived peacefully on Inorchis for epicycles, united in worship of Aroc Inorchis, guided by the Sibyl Inorchis Ija, and the benevolence that flowed, like sweet honey, from Sarom ... The youth was evidently repeating, in mechanical fashion, some scrap of a lesson learnt long ago.

Jem said, 'So Sarom was on the other Isle – the *real* Sarom, I mean?'

'Yet this is a Sarom of sorts. Must not this Isle have a Sarom, when it has the Thunderer Aroc Xaro and the Sibyl Xaro Ija?'

Rajal was about to ask what this Sibyl was when Jem leapt in, 'This Thunderer ... these Thunderers – these are your gods? But I thought Javander was the deity of Wenaya? Javander, goddess of water – no?'

Ojo looked puzzled. 'There are many gods, as there are many tribes and races. On the Isles of Aroc it is the Thunderers who grant life or death. Is it not natural that we should turn to them in worship? But alas, I fear Leki's worship is not mine.'

'I'm glad to hear it,' said Jem. 'But come, friend, on with your story. What catastrophe overcame Inorchis? Were you and your companions the only survivors?'

Ojo took a deep breath.

Ucheus exhaled slowly. 'Lemyu, you're ... *alive*?'

But of course he knew the answer already. Where could it be but in the angle of the neck, in the sharp, foul stench, in the crazed, relentless whirring of the flies? Terror, or madness, gave him sudden strength. He lunged forward, screaming, stabbing, and the kos-knife stuck into the corpse's face. Blood, pus, sickening corruption burst out in a viscous leap.

No good, no good ... Lemyu – but it was not Lemyu – only lashed out and continued to trudge heavily, impassively, towards the sea.

Ucheus's head reeled. Vomit coiled from his lips. He staggered up, floundering, in the suck of the shallows. Desperately his eyes darted here, there. He saw his spear, still where it had fallen, spiking up from the sands. The tide swilled round it, glimmering in moonlight.

He made for it. Seaweed tangled round his ankles and he fell again, crying, coughing as the corpse slammed towards him. He screamed – but all the corpse did was to crash past him, as if obeying some terrible summons ...

The Thunderer shook. The spear juddered.

Then Ucheus saw it. He had thought it was moonlight, shining in the water – but no, it was a glassy sphere, an orb, gleaming and golden, bobbing in the shallows, knocking and knocking at the vibrating spear.

Stiffly, slowly, the corpse reached down. The Thunderer shook again and Ucheus felt his heart shaking too, almost bursting as the corpse turned, holding aloft the orb in its rotting hands.

93

What happened next was the most terrible thing of all. With a wild cry, the corpse smashed the orb into the black, dripping place where its face had been.

For a moment the brightness guttered, like a lamp on the point of extinction. Then the corpse pulled its hands from its face and stood, unmoving, in the gathering darkness – and then, as if from a single, immense eye, light streamed from the rotted visage and the corpse began to blunder back to shore.

Ucheus scrambled to his feet again at last. He ran, sobbing and shuddering, to the stony uphill path.

Chapter 13

THE MANHOOD TRIAL

Pieces of eight! Pieces of eight!
Gold and diamonds, rubies and silver plate!
Are they lying in a wreck at the bottom of the sea?
Where, tell me where can me treasure be?
Yo-ho-hee! A sea-dog's life for me!
But where, tell me where can me treasure be?

The squeezebox groaned like a wheezing old man and Captain Porlo –
who *was* a wheezing old man – desisted for a moment from his raucous
shanty, looked about him in the lamplight and called lustily for rum,
more rum. At once the trusty Patches was on hand, sloshing fiery liquid
into the captain's greasy tankard. The old sea-dog grinned, grabbed the
boy by the arm and commanded him – not for the first time – to sit with
him for a while.

Another boy might have sighed or grumbled inwardly. Patches, after
all, had spent much of that afternoon in the captain's cabin, with the old
man alternately fluffing his curls affectionately or boxing his ears in
sudden anger. It was all a bit much – and besides, the cabin boy was
neglecting his duties. The first mate – the fat fellow called Whale – was
suspicious of him, calling him a *shirker*; Walrus, the boatswain, had called
him an *arse-licker*, while the helmsman, Porpoise, had not only called
Patches something still more obscene but had taken to tripping the boy
up, pinching him and punching him at every opportunity, then daring
him – just daring him – to go crying to the captain.

Was it all worth it? To Patches, there could only be one answer. As he
took his place again at the captain's lonely table, a desperate tenderness
filled the boy and he felt the beginnings of tears in his eyes. It was almost
as if the captain were his father – a father he loved, and would love, in
spite of everything.

Quickly he blinked away his tears and gazed about him at the tiger's
head and the rhinoceros horn, at the Rivan pennant and the Torga-shield,
at the brass musketoon and the rusty scimitar that hung precariously
from the cabin walls, flickering and shimmering like promises of magic.
With marvelling gratitude the boy took in, once again, the yellowed
maps and charts, the musty, leather-bound volumes of the ship's log and

the captain's hunched, copper-banded sea-chest. Patches sighed. The heat might have been stifling, the stench foul, but what did it matter when he was in the captain's cabin? He was happy, and his happiness could only grow as the captain sloshed him out a measure of rum and Buby the monkey – who had perched, parrot-like, on the captain's shoulder – now leapt across to the cabin boy and curled up in his arms.

The captain's eyes twinkled. 'I think that little miss has taken a liking to you, Patches. Funny, she never seemed to get on so well with Scabs – but then, I suppose it was them big yellow blobby things all over his face. Afraid they might pop all over her, she was, and get her nice fur all stuck up with pus – that's my guess. Bloody big, them pustules, when you're as little as Buby, eh girl?' Buby snickered, released a gaseous emission and scratched at her mange. 'Aye, she's a good little girl, is Buby – the one member of her particular sex who be welcome here on the *Catty*.'

The one member? Patches considered this.

He ventured, 'But what about Miss Cata?'

'What about her, boy?' The captain's brows knitted and Patches thought it best to be careful, just in case he should enrage the old man again. Strange, how for long moments the captain would be kindly, drunkenly rambling on with his old stories – then be moved, suddenly and without warning, to violent anger. It was all part of being a father, Patches supposed; it was how fathers behaved. But hadn't the captain been sorry to leave behind Miss Cata – and Master Jem, and Master Rajal, too – when they made their sudden departure from the Lands of Unang? That Lord Empster had been a shifty character, that much was certain – but Miss Cata had been a good sort, hadn't she?

And after all, she had the same name as the ship.

What happened next left Patches not a little perturbed. The captain leaned forward – squeezebox protesting as it squashed against his belly – and gripped the boy's hand. The grip was hard, so hard as to hurt, but what startled Patches was the sudden intensity in the captain's eyes – an intensity almost fearful. 'Listen to me, lad, and listen good. Ladies is *bad luck*, you hear? Does we want no ladies on the *Catty*? No, we *don't* want no ladies on the *Catty*! And don't you go saying no different, lad, or I swear I'll knock them wretched brains of yours clear out of your earholes! Does you understand me, lad?'

Patches could only gulp and nod; he knew enough, on this occasion at least, not to risk a blow by asking the captain to explain himself. Relief flooded him as the old man leaned back, squashed at his squeezebox and bellowed out another raucous verse of his shanty:

> *Bullion bars – stamped with a crest!*
> *Ah, how they'll flash when I opens that chest!*

96

Is it buried in the sand 'neath a far-off desert sky?
Where, tell me where can me treasure lie?
Yo-ho-hee! A sea-dog's life for me!
But where, tell me where can me treasure be?

When the captain paused again to swig from his tankard, Patches sought the opportunity to address a new subject – as if, perhaps, he would obliterate the strangeness of moments before. The shanty, after all, was about a treasure hunt, and what was the voyage before them now? Eyes kindling – and no, not for the first time – Patches asked the old man to tell him about the challenges, the excitements and the dangers ahead. Longingly, as if it were happening already, he imagined the captain's liver-spotted hands reaching for a certain yellowed chart, and the stiff, pudgy fingers with their blackened nails tracing over a confusing criss-cross of lines, almost like a web, to the place at the very edge of the map – at the edge, it seemed to Patches, of the world itself – that was marked, ominously and thrillingly, with the **X**. Becoming excited, the captain would tell how he had acquired this map from a certain very special acquaintance, long ago, and planned this voyage ever since, intending it as the climax to his long and illustrious buccaneering career. What splendours awaited them, the old man would claim, when they sailed through the perils of the Straits of Javander into the unknown seas beyond! That was when their voyage – their *real* voyage – would begin! And Patches, listening wide-eyed, would find himself growing almost feverish with anticipation.

All this happened as the boy had hoped. Oh, how he loved the old man!

'But Cap'n,' he cried, 'when does it begin? When does we go through them Straits of Javander?'

'When, lad?' Only now did the captain grow vague. 'Well, there was that Lord Empster—'

'But we's finished with him now, ain't we, Cap'n?'

'Aye lad, we be having no more truck with that shifty character – no Ejlander he was, if you ask me. Now there be just one more thing in our way—'

Patches was bewildered. 'But Cap'n, what can that be?'

'Why, lad, it be a place called the Isle of Hora. There be a little business I've been meaning to look up there, and I don't be thinking we can set off for them Straits of Javander until we's seen a certain fellow I knows on Hora—'

'But Cap'n,' cried the impatient Patches, 'how can we be a-stopping anywhere, when we be on a treasure hunt?'

The captain bristled. 'What, lad, you be questioning my command? This is not mutiny, is it?'

Patches gulped, 'Cap'n . . . Cap'n, no!'

And again he was grateful as the Captain seized his squeezebox, roaring out the last verse of the strange, familiar shanty:

> *Crystal of blue – lost long ago!*
> *Powers, they be such only gods can know!*
> *Is it true the glowing crystal holds the secret of the sea?*
> *Where? Don't I know where me treasure can be?*
> *Yo-ho-hee! A sea-dog's life for me!*
> *Where? Yes, I know where me treasure can be!*

The moon rose rapidly, goldenly, over the ridge. Again there was a trembling in the rock, more dangerously this time; geysers spurted from the pit outside and spattered, fizzing, against the barrier. Jem's heart was filled with foreboding. He looked out across the ridge and wondered if the fate that had overtaken Inorchis – some terrible destruction, he supposed – was about to be visited upon this island too. For all the stifling heat inside the cave, he found himself shivering. He crossed his arms around his knees, telling himself to listen, just listen to the tale Ojo had to tell.

The tale began like this.

'Visitors from Ejland, you wonder why our peoples clustered on one of our Twinned Isles, when the other ran wild. But you misunderstand the way we lived. For long sunrounds Inorchis was our home, but there had been a time when Inorchis was the wilderness, and we lived instead on Xaro – then, too, a time before that when our home was Inorchis, not Xaro, and before that a time of Xaro, not Inorchis . . . Inorchis, Xaro . . . Xaro, Inorchis: so it had been throughout our history. For a time, perhaps for epicycles, we would live on one isle, rising to proud heights of worldly riches; then at last, as we knew he would, the Thunderer would decree that hubris had overtaken us, and destroy our fine dwellings and cultivated slopes. Time and again our civilisation perished, swept away in the fury of molten fire . . . but always there were those of us who crossed the bay, there to begin, on our companion isle, a new chapter in the history of our race.

'My friends, you look bemused; your countrymen, no doubt, would long ago have ventured to other lands, leaving behind this ever-imminent doom. I tell you simply that this was our way, sanctioned by long generations of our forefathers. Our wish was only to serve the

Twinned Thunderers, living in submission to their mighty will. So, at least, said the Priests of Aroc who mediated between us and our mighty gods: in truth, things were not so clear.

'It happened that, by the time of my birth, three epicycles had passed since the last eruption of Aroc Xaro had forced our peoples across the bay to Inorchis. Never, according to the Tablets of Sarom, had we sojourned so long on a single isle. Never had so many generations passed, while the Thunderer had yet to punish us. Our civilisation had grown to new heights; so, alas, had our pride. By now, there were those who ventured beyond the Twinned Isles, returning from across the seas with the bright fruits of trade – and sometimes, too, the brighter fruits of plunder. Our long isolation was coming to an end, and eagerly, the Dynast Maius Ejanus urged these developments, insisting that we had entered a new phase in our history.

'But all was not well. For the first time, the Priests of Aroc clashed with the Dynast. Certain that hubris would always meet its nemesis, they warned that a delayed punishment must be all the greater. Many a time they repaired to the hundred-voiced Sibyl, eager to confirm the destiny before us, but her prophecies were oblique, her intimations of doom never sufficient to sway our worldly ruler. How could they? Was it not clear that the present generation had been especially favoured? If only it had been so, for then we might have been spared the blue doom which was to sweep upon us from the storm-tossed ocean!'

Jem looked thoughtful at the mention of the Sibyl. Had he not heard her hundred voices, echoing in his dream? He knew how oblique her words could be – but knew, too, how vital it appeared to be to obey them.

Ojo shifted his stocky limbs. 'But I run ahead of myself. Ejlanders, you see that we have survived a catastrophe, but we are not survivors in the way that you might think. You imagine us, perhaps, clinging to driftwood, swept upon these shores with waterlogged lungs? No, we came here in no desperate struggle, no wild escape – not chaotically, but organised, as our fathers accompanied us across the bay, in a stately procession of plumed boats. Elaborate ceremonies with incense and orations, benedictions and prayers had marked our departure from the docks of Inorchis; on the sands of Xaro, the old ones embraced us, circling our necks with wreaths of hibiscus, pungent and tightly twined. Tears blurred our eyes, but we held them back, and as the plumed boats returned across the bay, abandoning us here, we stood looking seawards in a stiff, unblinking line. Such were the protocols of the Manhood Trial.'

'Manhood Trial?' said Rajal, alarmed.

Ojo's look was grave as he carried on his tale.

'There were ten of us that day, ten who had reached the age when boyhood must end. Since then, so little time has elapsed, yet when I look back it is as if I am looking already, as into a magic glass, at a scene from a past I can barely imagine. I see myself glance furtively between Ucheus, playmate of my tender years, and Maius Eneo, the courageous, resourceful cousin he worshipped. How I remember Uchy's clenching fists, and the apple in his throat bobbing up and down! How I remember Maius Eneo, firm and unflinching – the oldest of all of us, or so it seemed, though like us all he had passed but fifteen orbits! Often I had envied him – resented, too, his place in Uchy's heart. But this was not the time. If only one of us were to survive our trial, I was sure it would be Maius Eneo. Already some were saying he was certain to be made Dynast-Elect, for all that his father had turned his back on the Court: I believed it.

'Of my own fate I felt less certain, and still less certain was I when I thought of the others. Of scrawny, nervous Adri . . . of childlike Nicander . . . of Infin Ijas, with his head in the clouds and his weak, straining eyes. There was boneheaded Zap, our boisterous jester. There were the twins Juros Iko and Jenas Iko, identical, like the Thunderers, and cursed, said some, because the Thunderers would envy them and drive them apart. Then there was Leki, the strange one, the loner that no one really knew.'

Ojo paused. His eyes were impassive and his voice was level. 'Together, that day, we began an adventure that for some – so we thought – would end in death, for some in disgrace, but for some in the privileges and pleasures of manhood. For five moonlives, it would be our destiny not only to eke out a living from the wilds, but to preserve, as best we could, the values of our civilisation. Only if we passed this test could we join the Manhood Caste, with its benisons of marriage and the siring of sons. Of the failures, those who died would be luckiest; those whom our fathers found starved or crazed, or living like ungodly savages, would be consigned to the ranks of the unmen, or gelded slaves.'

'Gelded?' gulped Rajal, who could not forget how nearly he had met just such a fate in the course of his own recent adventures. There were times since then when he had woken in terror, thinking himself back in the Palace of Perfumed Stairs. He looked sharply at the stocky youth. 'What manner of race,' he burst out, 'would enslave its own people? What fathers would preside over the gelding of their sons? You speak of all this, yet speak of civilisation? Why, this is barbarism!'

'Such has always been our way,' was all Ojo said. 'If, since time immemorial, our race has lived in expectation of flight, so those who would call themselves men must prove they could survive such a catastrophe.'

Spluttering, Rajal would have attempted further protest; Jem hushed him, intent on the tale. But Jem, too, felt alarmed at Ojo's manner. The stocky youth, for all his earlier, clumsy violence, seemed in truth a good and gentle fellow. How could he speak with such equanimity of these vile, depraved customs? But then, thought Jem, to live within a society is to ignore much: tradition excuses all manner of crimes. Sadly he thought of the terrible deeds that were enacted daily in his own empire. What challenges faced him if he ever became its ruler!

Earnestly he urged Ojo to go on.

'How my heart hammered, how my face flushed,' continued Ojo, 'as I waited to turn from the retreating boats – yet though a thousand fears clustered round me, like excitable serpents ready to spring, I reckoned without that insensibility that steals over us mercifully, after a time, when dangers have yet to come to pass. I deluded myself well. I thought of old Kofu, the unman who had tended me, and Ard Ired, who had tended Uchy, wondering how it was that they had failed this Trial. Could it really be so hard? Five moonlives lay before us, it was true, but this Isle of Xaro was a place of abundance. There were pigs and cats and monkeys; fish filled the waters; boughs hung heavy with fruit. What was there to concern us? It was the calm season and the air was warm. We had our kos-knives, an axe, a fire-glass. Our rescue was certain; our homes, and our fathers, lay just across the bay.

'Then there was Maius Eneo. If I was able to be so sanguine, it was all owing to him. What shame I felt for the envy he had once inspired in me! From our first day on Xaro, it was Uchy's intrepid cousin who assumed command. Declaring that we must keep together, he permitted no resentments, no rivalries, no factions; above all, he said, we must remember that we were Islanders of Aroc, bound by the conventions and codes of our race. I knew he was right. Had it not been for Maius Eneo, I am certain, our little party would soon have degenerated. Who else could have united us? Could dreamy Infin Ijas? Could snuffling, shy Nicander? Could Adri, with his cast-down eyes and bitten nails? Could Uchy? Could I?

'As for Leki, he barely spoke to us. He was a philosopher's son, but his father, once eminent in the Court of the Dynasts, had long since vanished from public life. Until now, the rest of us had barely seen Leki: if we thought of him at all, we thought of him as an outsider, never as one who might lead us. No, it was Maius Eneo who organised the gangs for hunting and fishing, Maius Eneo who taught us to whittle spears, to weave nets, to lay traps for wild pigs. With Maius Eneo, we made a coracle of bark and vines, enabling us to fish in deeper waters and skirt with ease round the rocky coast. He presided over our prayers to the Thunderer, ensuring that we kept to our sacred devotions; he said that our camp should be made here, amongst these ruins of an ancient Sarom. Where better, when from here we could gaze across to Inorchis, remembering where we came from, and to where we must return? Besides, there was the cauldron: what meals we had, what banquets, when Maius Eneo was here!

'You see, it was not so solemn. Those early days had their dilemmas, but often our faces were creased in smiles. How we cavorted, how we laughed, when the joker Zap suspended a banana and two plump pears from a cord about his hips! Round and round the cauldron we pursued him, wielding our kos-knives, determined to deprive him of those monstrous parts.

'This became our favourite game, but there were many others, too. We boxed; we wrestled; we duelled with spears; we crashed interminably in and out of the jungle, playing at chase or hide-and-go-seek. We raced along the sands, we swam in the sea – Adri proved himself a reckless diver, wheeling from the rocks like a plummeting bird; Infin Ijas became a strong swimmer; Nicander led us on many a merry caper, shinning up coconut trees like a monkey. In the midst of our Manhood Trial, perhaps, we were more truly boys than ever before – but our games, we knew, were readying us to be men. Our little civilisation thrived, and so did we. All this was down to Maius Eneo – but our idyll was not to last.'

There was an ominous sizzling from the pit outside.

'Who are you? What do you want?'

Again Littler squirmed in his bonds. It was useless. The vines were too tight and his strength was gone. He might have sobbed, but he would not be so weak. He was brave, wasn't he? As brave as Jem? Braver than Rajal, he thought defiantly; then Littler gulped hard, wondering what had become of his friends. Again he called to his mysterious captor, 'You're near, aren't you? I can feel you near!'

Or could he? Perhaps all Littler could feel was the fearsome, pressing intensity of the jungle night. Sinister hissings, tickerings and writhings sounded from the dark branches and leaves.

Then came the barking.

'Rainbow ... Rainbow, is that you?'

But soon enough, the barking was gone again.

Chapter 14

LEGEND OF THE TRIURGE

> — *My love, I run my tongue across your skin!*
> — *Such ecstasy! But tell me, where are you?*
> — *What matters it? But one thing must we do!*
> — *My head is swirling! Down and down I spin!*
> — *I feel my manly firmness swell and rise!*
>
> — *How moistly run the juices from my thighs!*
> — *In passion hot we roll in clouds of blue!*
> — *How can such sweet sensations be a sin?*
> — *Your thighs are open, deep I slide within!*
> — *My love! My love! Ah, can this bliss be true?*

But of course, it was not.

Selinda moaned, turning on her couch. She kicked away the covers. She plucked at her nightdress that clung stickily to her breasts, to her belly, to the unaccustomed, shocking moistness of her thighs. How she longed to rend the frail garment, to cast it from her, to fling it contemptuously across the floor! Oh, but if only she could sleep, sleep! Yet how could she sleep when she felt herself possessed by Maius Eneo, dear Maius Eneo?

A candle flickered beside her couch; a moth fluttered around the flame. Selinda watched it, envying its swooping, soaring flight. And if she could fly? Ah, then she would be a stranger to herself! And did she not long to be a stranger to herself? But what was she now, what had she become, in the space of only a day? In a day, the girl had run the gamut of emotion. All these torments she had never known before, and now it seemed they were just beginning!

She thought of her father, of the terrible tale he had told. She thought of her mother, then of the brother she had never known. What was all this, if not torment enough? But then came her beloved Maius Eneo, thudding inside her like her own heartbeat. She thought of the crashing of the Amali screen, and Father sweeping suddenly, imperiously from her apartments, demanding that the guards bring the stranger-youth. But where, where had her lover been taken? Had they flung him into the dungeons? Would she ever see him again? Would she never, in truth, know his sweet, imagined touch? Oh, she could not bear it! She thought

103

of her lover condemned to die; then she thought of herself condemned too, and knew that if Maius Eneo died, then so would she.

The girl moaned again; as if at her summons, the blundering moth swooped a little too low, searing away its wings in the flame.

Selinda flung herself from the couch. She paced the floor. The splendours of her apartments blurred before her eyes. What did it mean to her, all this luxury, if she were not to know a lover's caress? She ripped at her nightdress. Long ago, with angry cries, she had dismissed Ra Fanana, screaming that the nurse was useless, useless, that she hated the sight of her. Poor Ra Ra! But Selinda could not bear to ring for her now.

She seized a scroll from beside her couch, the scroll from which her nurse would often read aloud. What was this but the girl's old favourite, the one she used to call the Monster Scroll? With sweaty fingers she unrolled the parchment. Inscribed here were tales of fantastic things and creatures, all the many horrors of Wenayan legend. What delicious, innocent shudders Selinda had enjoyed as she listened to these old, foolish legends! There was the Legend of the Flying Zenzan, the accursed ghost-ship that plied the skies, riding the night on the howling storm. There was the Legend of the Mandru, greatest of sea-monsters, whose mighty coils lay deep beneath the waves, at the bottom of a strange and swirling maelstrom; ah, but what terror would erupt when the Mandru burst to the surface! Then, worst of all, most delicious of all, was the Legend of the Triurge.

The Legend of the Triurge! How many times had she made poor Ra Ra read it? Again and again; and all the nurse's protests that the girl would have nightmares had been as nothing against her insistence. How thrilling the tale! Of all the monsters of Wenaya, could any be more terrifying than a Triurge? Such creatures formed when a spore of evil animated a rotting corpse. Returned to a terrible semblance of life, the corpse would swallow into itself first one living man, then another, becoming the sum of all three men.

What mayhem, what murder swiftly followed! Selinda thought of the Great Triurge of Torga, that had rolled into its rotting, monstrous immensity the bodies not just of three men but of four, then five; then, growing unstable, as a Triurge must when it engorges more than three men, the creature had sought out a virtuous maiden, to gather her into the Swallowing Marriage that alone could save it from certain destruction. How Selinda had squealed with delighted terror, imagining a Triurge upon her trail, desperate to grasp her in the Swallowing Marriage!

Would a Triurge, she wondered, want her now? Was she, in truth, still a pure maiden? And would she, if a Triurge took her, be returned in time to her own natural form?

For yes, it was possible to escape from a Triurge, even after one had been swallowed. Only with great destruction could the creature be killed; but of those who had been gathered into its fearsome mass, the one who was purest of heart could survive, to be specially sanctified for ever afterwards.

Ah, the Triurge! Selinda gazed over the lurid engravings that once had so diverted her. What were they now, what were these tales, but weary, flat, stale and unprofitable? What were such fears, such fantasies, against the real fears that filled her now?

She flung the scroll away. She pinched out the candle and lay, burning, in the hot darkness. Sobs came to her throat. Tears filled her eyes. She tossed. She turned. Then came the voices, the visions, teasing her, taunting her. If only Maius Eneo were with her now! If he were here, what sufferings would mean anything?

Not thoughts of her mother. Not thoughts of her brother. Not even thoughts of her father's death.

Swiftly, swiftly, shadows fall
From the brightest sky:
That darkness has his outriders
No one can . . .

The stocky youth had fallen silent for some moments when, quite suddenly, he broke into song. His voice was softer, more tuneful than Leki's, but in a strange way more troubling; the melody coiled smokily through the moonlit cave, and Jem and Rajal wondered what it could portend. Jem toyed uncertainly with the crystal under his tunic; Rajal shuddered.

Ojo broke off, and carried on his tale.

'In the evenings,' he said, 'when we were exhausted, Juros Iko and Jenas Iko would sing the songs of our homeland, their high young voices twining together in a purity that brought tears to our eyes. Of the songs, our favourite was "The Shadow Song", with its slow, mournful refrain that we had never quite understood, for all that it made us deliciously sad.' Briefly he hummed the melody again. 'We had been here for almost a moonphase when the first shadow fell over us. This, indeed, was an outrider of the dark.

'It began like this: one afternoon, during a long game of hide-and-go-seek, Infin Ijas found himself lost somewhere on the far side of the isle. His limbs were firmer than they had been before, but still his eyes were weak. When he found his way back to us, he could say only that he had been somewhere we had never explored. He remembered a leafy glade, but not how to find it; he mentioned, as an aside, the lowing of an ox – or a cow, perhaps. Never mind: Maius Eneo was excited. Pigs he had expected, but never had he thought that cattle might survive on this isle. How extraordinary that we had never seen them before! At once, he determined that we must trap them. What visions of glory filled his mind – milk . . . beef-steaks . . . tanned hides! What praise would flow from the lips of our fathers, when they saw what we had done! What blessings would the Thunderer rain down upon us, when we sacrificed at his steaming summit not swine, but a monstrous black ox!

'The next day we set out early, all ten of us, a little army laden with kos-knives, nets and spears, with ropes fashioned from plaited vines and shields made from bark, glued in strips with rubber sap and daubed brightly with ochre. Merrily we crashed through the jungle, the treetops ringing as Juros Iko and Jenas Iko led us in songs more raucous than the songs they sang at night.

'As we left the familiar ways we became more subdued. The jungle grew thicker; there were no beaten paths. Maius Eneo hacked at foliage with the axe. Perhaps my memory tricks me, but I think that it was then that a strange foreboding began to steal over me. When, from time to time, we glimpsed the sea, there was no longer the comforting sight of Inorchis, only endless fields of ultramarine, shimmering in the sun.

'At what point we separated, I cannot remember. If there were oxen on the isle, Maius Eneo was sure we could find them. Could huge, unwieldy beasts move through the jungle, yet make no sound? But then, he went on, there might be but a few of them, mere remnants of a larger herd . . . We must break into smaller groups, fanning out; whoever saw something was to whistle three times at a certain pitch – Maius Eneo showed us how. That would be the signal to bring us back together.

'In the event, what brought us running was a sudden, desperate cry. It was Leki's, and not the last he was to utter that day. What happened must have been the work of an instant. There was Leki, padding cautiously between dank ferns, parting a curtain of vines, when all at once an immense black ox came rearing down on him, smashing through the foliage. Screaming, Leki thrust his spear into the creature's flank. When we found him, he was collapsed over the carcass, sobbing; blood flowed all around him, and his spear had snapped. He must have stabbed and stabbed until the monster was dead.

'Maius Eneo was furious. Grabbing Leki, he pulled him up roughly, shaking him, slapping him. "Fool! Don't you know what you've done? Don't you know this ox could be the *only one*? Fool, stupid fool!"

'The attack astonished me. Later, Uchy insisted that his cousin was in the right, but still I wondered whether Maius Eneo had expected Leki to let himself be killed. I was sorry for Leki, but did not dare say so. In the days that followed, Maius Eneo made us search for the herd again, then again and again until the quest that had begun so merrily left us all sick and disgusted. Pushing our way through the jungle, I was terrified that at any moment another monstrous ox would come – this time, for *me*. In the event, all we found was a placid heifer and her sickly calf. The calf soon died, but we brought the heifer here. She gave us milk until . . . but I run ahead of myself.'

Ojo paused, rubbing at an eye.

'It's easy, looking back, to say that everything changed after the business with the ox. I'm not sure it did. Soon enough, after all, we were back to our hide-and-go-seek, our races, our duels, our mock-geldings of the joker Zap. Nicander shinned up coconut trees; Infin Ijas swam and swam – but something was wrong with Leki. It was on a hunting trip that I first noticed the change in him. There were two hunting parties, five of us in each: Maius Eneo led one – Uchy, reluctantly, the other. I was in Uchy's with Adri, Zap, and Leki. Deep in the jungle, after killing a wild boar, we were resting one day on a rotted tree-trunk, cracking open coconuts, when Leki leaned close to me and whispered in my ear, as if it were the lightest, most carefree of remarks: "He doesn't want us to be *men*, you know. He wants us to be *slaves* – unmanned slaves."

'If I was alarmed by this confidence, it was more by its unexpectedness than by the actual words. Moments passed before I realised what Leki meant. "He's tyrannical," he went on, in the same careless whisper, "don't you see? He pretends to be saving us, *all* of us – really, he only wants to save himself. What will our fathers say, when they see him ruling us?" I turned, pushing Leki away. For a moment, perhaps, I was tempted by his view; perhaps, too, he knew that I was, sensing the envy I had tried hard to bury. But now I longed to bury the doubts he would stir. He only laughed and I saw, for the first time, a strange glow in his eyes.

'This was just the beginning. Soon Leki was whispering in the same way to Adri, to Zap, even to Uchy; I know he got to Nicander – to Infin Ijas, too. Every chance he could, Leki spoke to us of Maius Eneo. "Don't you realise what he's made us?" he'd say. "His slaves, his willing slaves! He'll be the man, just him, and we'll be the unmen, all of us – it's a trick, don't you see?" Perhaps Zap was fool enough to believe him, I can't be certain. I only know that most of us thought Leki was crazy, and one of us – I think it must have been Infin Ijas – told Maius Eneo what Leki had said. There was a terrible scene. Maius Eneo beat Leki savagely, and Leki blundered off into the jungle. He did not come back to the camp that night. That was the night before the Blue Storm.'

'*Blue* . . . Storm?' said Rajal.

'*Blue* . . . *Storm*?' said Jem. Memory stirred in his mind and he thought again of his mysterious dream. Could this be the magic he was meant to follow? At once he knew there could be nothing more important than to hear the story of this Blue Storm.

Ucheus drew in his breath. Wistfully he began to speak of Infin Ijas; each morning, he said, their weak-eyed friend used to rise earlier than the rest of them.

'The glare of the sun hurt his eyes; he liked to swim before it grew too bright. Often, stirring from sleep, I would hear him make his way down the jungle path, blundering a little in the half-darkness; later, I would hear him coming back. On the morning before the storm, he did not come back. We thought he was still swimming, and Maius Eneo was angry, because he wanted to hunt before it grew too hot. His mood alarmed me: the fury of the night before had not abated. I said I would run down and fetch Infin Ijas. How often, since then, I have wished I had not!

'I found him on the sands – sprawled on his back, face to the sun. The posture surprised me; how could he stand not to cover his eyes? Then my surprise turned to fear as I called to him: "Infin Ijas!" – then called to him again, louder than before: "Infin Ijas . . . Infin Ijas!" I flailed forward. At once I knew he was dead, but at first, in my confusion, I thought he had been drowned, and washed ashore.

'Then I saw the blue, twisted bruises that ringed his neck. I collapsed beside him, shuddering. The sand was scuffed in all directions, as if Infin Ijas had struggled against his assailant, desperately but hopelessly. Only later did I realise that there were no footprints leading away from the scene . . . There was no time to think of that now. Shock gripped me, as if the murderer's hands circled my neck too. I had known that Leki was mad: I had never imagined he could be a killer.

'I blundered back to the others. When Nicander learnt what had happened he screamed, rolling on the ground. Adri collapsed. Juros Iko and Jenas Iko broke down in tears. Uchy only stared and stared. But it was Maius Eneo who terrified me; he screamed too, but his scream was like a battle cry: "I'll kill him! I'll kill him!"

'We divided into our hunting parties – but that day's hunt was a hunt for Leki. What would happen if we found him, I did not want to imagine; I only hoped it would be Maius Eneo's party, not ours, that saw him first. But as I crashed through the jungle, spear at the ready, crazily it seemed to me that I could hear Leki's voice, a sinister whisper, hissing and sniping from the trees and ferns: "Ojo," he would say, "you're a fool, a fool! Do you think he cares about Infin Ijas? Fool, I say! He's fretting, that's all, fretting that his kingdom is collapsing around him! What will happen then? Will they make him an unman, just like the rest of us? Oh yes, yes – that's if they find us! But perhaps they never will! Think of it, Ojo – perhaps they never will!"

'I shut my ears against the mad words, desperate not to admit even to myself how much I resented, even hated Maius Eneo. Wildly I imagined Leki here, Leki there, laughing, grinning; again and again I raised my spear, ready to hurl it through the green gloom. If I hoped that we would find him, and find him soon, it was only so that the whisperings would stop.

'We never found him, not that day. The storm came first.'

Ojo paused, breathing deeply.

'Go on, Ojo,' Jem urged.

But just then there was a guttural cry. Jem reeled; Rajal leapt up, striking his head on the roof of the cave. Ojo, his story forgotten, slammed his fist against the fizzing barrier, desperate only to escape his confinement.

He knew that voice. He knew that cry.

Jem, and a moaning Rajal, clustered behind him.

Their eyes widened. Staggering across the moonlit ridge was Ucheus, dishevelled and bloodied. Ojo called to him and the slender youth turned deliriously, turned this way and that like a hunted animal, exhausted by the chase.

'Uchy – what is it? Uchy – what's wrong?'

Ucheus collapsed by the mouth of the cave.

Chapter 15

ORPHANS OF THE STORM

Mighty one, master, measure of all things—

In the heat and the clouds and the rising steam, Leki sits cross-legged, staring down. Darkness surrounds him, but here, there, through the tatters of the clouds, comes a shard of moonlight, flashing on the lake that lies below, viscous and festering, hissing, bubbling. Sulphur fills his nostrils but he seems not to mind, nor does he see – his eyes, though open, stare only on blankness. Entranced, he is enclosed within the cavern of his skull and even his chant – rather, his mantra – is only an echo tolling bell-like, bounding and rebounding in that closed, interior space. Round and round he revolves in the air, circling slowly with the tattered clouds – cross-legged not on the shore of this lake, not on the precipitous rim, but above it. Like a tethered balloon he hangs over the caldera, held aloft as if by the force of his mantra.

Mighty one, master, measure of all things—

What does he know? Perhaps there is nothing but this bounding and rebounding; perhaps there is only this turning like a wheel. But then, perhaps, there are visions that twine round the mantra, like smoke or like harsh, unexpected flowers. Visions, or memories – say, of a boy gazing at an endless sea, as if it were an emblem of his loneliness; of a boy in a boat, crossing a bay, struggling to hold back the fear that overcomes him. Thinking of the trial that lies ahead, does he promise himself he will not be weak? Until now, Lekis Sanis Saxis has been anything but weak. But then, perhaps, the boy he has been and the thing he is now are too far apart to be thought of as the same.

Mighty one, master, measure of all things—

Lost to the old life, Leki turns and turns; but if indeed the memories come twining, maybe they take him back to a day when he crashed through the jungle, deep in the green dilapidations of light. Pushing through tangled, unfamiliar ways, first he looks here, then he looks there; then – but it is inevitable – he finds himself alone. And that is when the terrible, black malevolence comes smashing through the foliage, rearing down on him; that is when the scream rends the air, and the spear thrusts and thrusts into the creature's flank, thrusts until it snaps and all the green world is vermilion and flowing and the voice fills his mind, as if from nowhere—

110

Child, are you dreaming – do you dream on still?
Blood-soaked, can you feel the power of my will?
Now comes destiny, twining like a trail
Of smoke from my caldera, setting sail!
Weak have you been? Weak shall you be no more,
Now you have bathed in this dead creature's gore!

Child, once child of my thundering brother,
Now you become the child of another!
Why? But you must know it was destined soon—
Child, have you not killed the Ox of the Moon?
You are the child, as I knew you would be:
I am the Thunderer – child, come to me![1]

– and Leki, collapsed over the carcass, feeling the power coursing through him, knows – in sudden despair, in sudden ecstasy – that the blood that covers him might be his own, for in killing the creature he has killed himself, too. But why it might be that he was chosen for this act – if indeed he *was* chosen – he does not understand; there is only the power, the coursing power ... And now the power shall grow. When dawn comes, the Fjlander called Jem must die, and the one called Rajal must die, too. The Thunderer has demanded it: his glory demands it. And flooding Leki's mind is a great joy, for when the prisoners are dead, his power shall be greater. The Thunderer has promised – greater and greater ...

Mighty one, master, measure of all things—

Out on the ridge the cauldron hissed like a serpent slithering menacingly closer; the moon throbbed in the sky and Ucheus, from time to time, whimpered or moaned. Despairingly Ojo gazed out at his friend, but how could he help him? The invisible barrier refused to yield. All he could do was turn back to his companions in the cave and ask if he should continue his tale. Jem nodded; Ojo shuddered, wiped his forehead and resumed, pausing from time to time to glance anxiously whenever the stricken Ucheus stirred.

The Blue Storm, said the stocky youth, had struck suddenly. Where it came from, he did not know; when it began, he could not say. Sometimes, he said, it seemed to him that the storm was like the ox that

[1] Cf. Professor Mercol's invaluable unpublished MS, *Legends of the Primitive Tribes of Wenaya* (this may be consulted in the Royal Ejard Library, University of Agondon) for the definitive account of the legend of the Oxen of the Moon. This particular ox may be assumed to be a survivor of that great herd, said to be controlled by the Thunderers of Aroc, which would possess the Essences of any who dared to kill them.

Leki killed, hidden and secret until the moment of its attack. But no, that was not quite true – it was only that they did not see it, at first, for what it was . . .

'It was late afternoon, almost evening, when Zap gave us the first warning. All day, like mad things, we had blundered uselessly through the tangled gloom. We were tired, we were hungry, but still Uchy drove us on, as if sparks of his cousin's fury had set him ablaze too. It was strange: later, after Maius Eneo was gone, Uchy would never have that force in him again. He might have been a puppet whose strings had been cut – but that, I say, was later. For now, there was only the search for Leki – and the search was going badly. We had lost touch with Maius Eneo's party; for all we knew, Leki might be dead already, skewered like a pig on the end of a spear. I wanted to go back to Sarom, but Uchy would not hear of it. "We've got to go on! Think of Infin Ijas!" he cried, almost crazily, and I had no reply; all I wanted to do was rest.

'Then, hacking through a wall of leaves, we found ourselves on an unfamiliar ridge, looking out over the sea. I suppose we must have been on the far side of the island, for Inorchis was nowhere in sight. I blinked, screwing up my eyes. Then Zap cried out, pointing to the horizon: "Look!"

'For a moment I thought this was one of his jokes, and I was afraid, for Uchy might be angry. But there was something – something *there* . . . It was small, it was blue, a sort of column – a pillar, shimmering . . . No – moving, moving closer, and at a frightening speed . . .

'I clutched Uchy's arm. "What – what *is* it?"

'He only shook my hand away, muttering, "Nothing. A trick of the light. Now forget it!"

'But I could not, and nor could Zap.

'"It's coming this way," Zap insisted. "Uchy, it's a storm – Uchy, it could be dangerous!"

'Uchy struck him on the side of the mouth. The action shocked me – it was so unlike Uchy. "Leki's what's dangerous!" he cried. "Think of Leki, and think of Infin Ijas!"

'I wished Uchy had not said those words, for now it seemed to me that I could hear Leki's voice again, that terrible taunting whisper in my brain, and the words it said were, "*Forget Ucheus – forget Ucheus, and Maius Eneo, too. You know they are false, and I am true. I am your leader now, and you are mine.*"

'I cried out, as if the voice had been real. I looked wildly at my companions; they looked back at me, blank-eyed. Could none of them hear it, this terrible voice?

'Uchy only demanded that we go on, go on.

'"But Uchy," cried Adri, "we'll be caught in the storm!"

112

'Uchy didn't care. He plunged back into the jungle.

'We followed reluctantly. We had not gone much further when we felt the first of the tremblings in the air. By now, I was sure that something terrible was happening, more terrible by far than what had happened already. When the light through the trees began to flicker strangely, and dank droplets shuddered at us from the leaves, our fears broke out again, clamorously this time. Adri began to wail; Zap would go no further; he cried out that we must get back to Sarom, to the cave. Uchy would have struggled with him, but I grabbed his arm.

'"Uchy, Zap's right! A storm's coming, and we must find cover!"

'He shrugged me off, and might have struck me too; instead, he only shouted, "Sarom! Sarom!"

'There was no time. With sudden, shocking rapidity, the storm was upon us. First the dense foliage creaked back and forth, and through the parting trees we glimpsed the sky churning and scurrying as if it would flee. A dull roar filled the air, growing rapidly louder, a gathering low drone accompanied by a dissonant, high-pitched whine . . .

'We floundered back to the ridge. Only then did we understand just what it was that was bearing down. Terror gripped us. Moments before, there had been only a blue pillar, far-off and shimmering; now the storm was tearing towards us, consuming the horizon, churning the sea into a furious, foaming maelstrom. Below us, breakers crashed against the rocks, flinging up vast explosions of spume; all around us the wind rose, hurling us back, wrenching leaves from the trees; palm fronds scurried through the air like ungainly, doomed birds. Soon, too soon, the sun was blotted out; there was only the weird illumination of the storm, its spinning column bluer than the sea and surrounded by brighter, dazzling bolts of blue, cracking and fizzing round the screaming clouds . . .

'No, there was no time to get back to Sarom. When the storm hit, all we could do was cling for our lives to the rocks and trunks of trees, or huddle in the undergrowth. How long the battering lasted, it is impossible to say. The rain came first, slamming against us with explosive force; at once we were overwhelmed by the drenching, relentless cold, the screeching in the air, the *whip-whipping* of the leaves and straining branches. Pebbles, rocks, coconuts cannoned through the air; vines lashed my back; somewhere in the chaos, most terrifyingly of all, I was aware of the blue lightning – cracking, searing . . . What had become of my companions, I had no time to think, but suddenly I saw Adri, close by, clinging to the trunk of a sturdy palm. I shouted to him – "Adri, get down, *get down*—" – but the winds ripped my words away . . . and then the mighty trunk was ripped away too, and Adri was in the air, billowing, limbs flailing . . .

'I screamed; from his open mouth I knew that Adri screamed too, but our voices were like silence against the wildness of the storm . . . Then came the lightning. Adri was still in the air when the blue bolt struck him. His limbs spasmed, his neck jerked back – like a mad puppet he danced in the sky, caught in the searing, blue aurora; then all at once the winds bore him away, and that was the last I saw of Adri . . . Desperately I flattened myself into the ground, clutching my arms around my head.

'By the time it was over, it seemed to me that I had lived through an eternity of torment. I was battered, I was bruised – worse still, I had imagined again and again the agonised form of Adri, dancing in the blue light; then, too, I had heard the whisper, audible over the storm because it was inside my head: "It's all over, Ojo – it's over, don't you know? Didn't I say I was your leader now?" How I struggled to shut out the voice . . . But when it stopped I heard instead a cacophony of voices, teasing me, taunting me, shrieking, hooting, dinning into my brain above the violence of the storm. In a crazed vision, it seemed to me that I flew off with Adri, riding the wild winds on his jerking corpse, whirling round and round in the vortex of blue – and all the time there were the voices, the mad cries, the laughter . . .

'The silence came suddenly – I say silence, but it was a silence filled with the creakings and groanings of tormented vegetation, with the rapid drippings and runnings of water, with the whimpering, here, of a crippled monkey, the sobbing, there, of a broken-winged bird . . .

'I stumbled to my feet – wondering, for desolate moments, if I might be the only survivor of our party. But no . . . I saw Zap first, shambling towards me in the blue, mysterious pallor that was the only light. His face was bloody; one of his arms hung limp, but he could walk. For long moments we clung together, sodden and shivering. "It's over," I said uncertainly, then shuddered convulsively, for these were the words that Leki had used.

'Carefully, Zap cradled his damaged arm. "Over? Look at this blue light. It's not over, Ojo – this is only the eye of the storm."

'I nodded bleakly.

'"Quick," said Zap. "Sarom – the cave."

'As we pushed our way through the dark ruins of the jungle, I asked him if he knew what had happened to Adri. This time it was Zap who nodded bleakly. It was as if all the life had gone out of him, leeched out of him with the blood from his arm . . . We found Uchy a little later, shaken but unharmed.

'It was morning before we made it back to Sarom. We sheltered in a hole in the ground, the three of us, while the storm's wild force battered the island again. Huddled with my companions, I struggled to shut out the terrible voices that I knew were all around me, whirling in the air

114

with the wind and rain. Could Uchy hear them? Could Zap? Over the violence of the storm, we could not speak. I plunged into fresh, hideous torments ... and the next thing I knew, Uchy was slapping my face, tugging at me, pulling me from the muddy, dangerous hole. I suppose I must have lapsed into a merciful unconsciousness. I blinked: I shielded my eyes. It was morning; the storm was over, and a sharp shaft of sunlight stabbed down through the trees.

'"Ojo, come on! Let's see if the others are alive!"

'How hard my heart thudded as we trudged back to Sarom, our path choked by mud, leaves, branches, vines! When we began I was shivering; by the time I laboured over the brow of the hill, I was panting like a dog and my hair was sodden with sweat. A thousand questions filled my mind – then they vanished, blown away like chaff, as a ragged, muddy figure came floundering down towards us. Nicander!

'"We thought you were dead!" he wailed, collapsing into Uchy's arms. Moments passed before Nicander would learn that Adri, whom he had loved, was indeed dead; for now, he could only embrace us joyously, calling back behind him, "Everyone – it's Uchy ... Zap ... Ojo!"

'The next thing I knew, we were back on the familiar ridge of Sarom, bathed in the sunlight of a clear, still day. Uchy cried excitedly as his cousin stepped forward. They hugged each other, hard, but when I saw Maius Eneo's face hanging, mask-like, over Uchy's shoulder, I knew at once that something was wrong. A soft refrain drifted on the air. It was a song we knew, only too well:

> Swiftly, swiftly, shadows fall
> From the brightest sky:
> That darkness has his outriders
> No one can ...

'I turned to the singers, but no joy filled the faces of Juros Iko and Jenas Iko. They stood close together by the mouth of the cave; then they drew apart. I gasped. Standing behind them was Leki, almost naked, his face painted like a savage's and his eyes glowing like fire. He moved forward, weaving around us, slowly circling the bubbling cauldron. The rest of us all were paralysed. Shadows of the Thunderer's smoke passed across the ridge.

'"It's *over*," Leki said softly. "It's all over now."

'I said hoarsely, "Leki, what's over?"

'In reply, Leki only smiled, and pointed out to sea. I turned. That was when I saw the empty ocean, the empty ocean where Inorchis had been.'

Jem looked down, troubled. Ojo had paused. Out on the ridge the cauldron still hissed, the moon still throbbed, and Ucheus moaned again.

But there was something else.

115

'Jem!' said Rajal. He raised a pointing finger.

It was Ojo who turned first. Beyond the cauldron, through the shimmering curtain of steam, stood the watcher. How long had he been there, silent and impassive?

Littler languished in a purple haze. Not quite awake, not quite asleep, he had sunk into a swirl of strange visions. How many times had he seen his lost orb, hanging like the moon in the velvet darkness? The orb was thrumming, pulsing with light, and deep within the light he saw a blurred, shadowy face. Whose face? Once he thought he made it out, but the face became a bird, then a dog, then a bird and a dog, mingled grotesquely into one – Rainbow, sprouting wings from his back, barking as he blundered through the dark leafy mansions, high above the level of the undergrowth. More than once, Littler mouthed the dog's name; sometimes he cried it aloud.

But could he really hear the sound of barking?

Chapter 16

THE MYSTERIOUS STRANGER

Uneasy lies the head that wears the crown: especially so, should that crown be screwed into the skull.

In the depths of the night, it may have been that Triarch Jodrell slept at last. But how could he sleep, for all the soft caresses of luxurious sheets, for all the perfumes that drifted upon the air, for all the sweet potions his slaves had prepared? Round and round inside his head went thoughts of all that had passed, and even his fears of death were as nothing to the fears he held now for his daughter's fate. Fool of a man, such a fool to defer! His death, though soon, might be many moonlives away, but his daughter's fate would be decided upon the morrow. He thought upon the arrangements he had hastily made, and prayed that nothing would go awry.

But did he really pray? Or did he attend, rather, to the voice, then to the visions, that crept so mysteriously, so insistently out of the darkness?

> — *I think, my lord, you know why I have come?*
> — *How strangely streams this knowledge through my brain!*
> — *Have not you reached the climax of your reign?*
> — *The climax, yes: my fears beat like a drum.*
> — *What need of fear? Your daughter's love is mine!*

> — *I see it in your eyes! I see it shine!*
> — *Such love shall never come her way again.*
> — *Such love indeed! Its splendour leaves me dumb.*
> — *And Father, yet what depths I still must plumb!*
> — *As deep as deepest seas, I see it plain.*

It was Leki.

Ojo reared up, clawing at the barrier.

'Leki, I'm trapped – Leki, let me out!'

No reply. Sparks fizzed.

'Leki, it's Uchy – there's something . . . *wrong* with him!'

No reply; Leki turned away.

'*Uchy*, Leki – Leki, help him!'

Beside the cave-mouth, Ucheus moaned again, but Leki only squatted by the steaming cauldron. Hunched, his knees huddled to his chest, he turned his back both to the stricken youth and to the captives in the cave. Thus he would remain until morning. If he slept they could not tell, but his head did not slump; he seemed only to be staring across the sea, into the moonlit emptiness of the night. Beside him, the steam from the cauldron might have been a ghost perpetually fluttering, struggling to rise ... Intently, Jem studied the painted youth. What were his secrets? What were his powers? To understand *him* would be to understand much ... Through clenched teeth, Jem vowed he would do just that – if Leki, of course, did not sacrifice them first.

Was there no way out of this cave?

The night wore on – and Ojo, inevitably, resumed his story. He spoke in a low, bitter voice, glancing from time to time towards Leki's impassive, averted figure.

'After the storm, there could be no question that Leki was our leader. Before, I had wondered if the others could hear the voices; now I was sure they could. Often, in the urgency of my despair, I tried to talk to Uchy, to Maius Eneo too; but we were wary, as if Leki would root out and punish any disloyalty. It seemed he could see us, hear us, even when we were far from him ... That first day, I saw burns on Maius Eneo's chest and thought he had been struck by lightning during the storm. Then I learnt the truth. It was Leki – Leki's eyes.

'Leki demanded a banquet to celebrate our freedom. "Freedom?" I laughed, but Leki looked at me murderously. I don't think he cared that the storm had taken our homeland; I don't think he even wondered *how* it had happened. He certainly didn't care about our fathers. We had our own island, was all he said – we were men now, on our *own* terms. But how could I believe that? None of us could. We were eight boys, that was all, eight boys in a desperate situation. And Leki was making it so much worse.

'Only childlike Nicander dared defy him. "We must go to the Sibyl," he said piously. "The Sibyl will tell us what to do."

'Leki became enraged at the thought. "Shut up," he spat, but when Nicander began to snivel and cry, a searing ray burst from Leki's eyes. Nicander leapt back, yelping like a dog, and the stench of burned flesh hovered in the air. Uchy looked at Maius Eneo: Maius Eneo looked at Uchy. I looked at them both. What could we do but follow Leki's orders, searching through the jungle for undamaged fruits, clearing the cluttered paths, rooting out the surviving pigs?

'The banquet that day was a splendid affair – or at least it was for Leki. Fondly he spoke of the future before us, for all the world as if a glorious kingdom had come into our possession – or rather, into *his*. Then he led us in a stomping dance ... Later, as we sat drowsily round the cauldron,

118

Leki made Juros Iko and Jenas Iko sing. Twining and twisting on the still, empty air, their voices seemed to have in them a quality of mystery we had never heard before. On and on came the songs of our homeland. Tears pricked our eyes – but we were careful not to let them fall . . .

'Days passed, and in the heat the island rapidly recovered itself. Battered foliage sprang back to life and the verdure seemed richer, wilder than before. It was hard to believe there had ever been the storm; hard to believe, sometimes, there had been an Inorchis – but only sometimes. Each day our hunting parties set out; we sharpened spears, wove nets, threw chunks of meat into the simmering cauldron. We danced, we sang – but always we were certain this could not last. Terrible things were still to come. We knew this, knew this as surely as we knew that our hearts were beating.

'Only Leki seemed oblivious. Though he looked like the wildest hunter of us all, seldom would he come with us when we set out to hunt. Much of his time he spent on the summit, communing with the Thunderer; of what passed there, he would not speak, but our destiny, he would say, was assured – assured, whatever happened . . . What could he mean? When he spoke like this, I shuddered in fear – and not only when he spoke like this. Sometimes at night I heard him pacing round the camp, like an animal caged behind invisible bars. Often I saw him hunched, huddled, arms around his legs, staring up at the moon . . .'

'Like now?' said Rajal, gesturing out to the ridge.

'Just like now. At such times, his eyes would be blank, unseeing discs, and I would wonder – hope, even – that something inside him had snapped at last, that he would never come round from this mysterious trance. Then in the morning, he would be as before. Had the storm made him this way? But then, I would think, it was *before* the storm that I had first heard Leki's voice inside my head! I would try to remember what I had known of him in the days before the beginning of our Manhood Trial. I could only think he had been a philosopher's son, and I wondered what philosophies his father might have taught him. Had I not known that his father had gone away, many orbits earlier, leaving his son in the care of slaves?

'It was, I suppose, almost a moonphase after the storm when the rumblings began. Of course the island, from time to time, had always trembled a little, and we had thought nothing of it; the same happened on Inorchis. Now the earth shuddered frequently and loudly – rocks rolled downhill, fruit shook from the trees, monkeys screamed and scurried about the branches. Never in our lives had we known an eruption, but now we wondered if one was about to come. Adri said no; had not the Thunderers always taken turns to vent their wrath? If Aroc Inorchis had not erupted, how could Aroc Xaro? It was the inhabited island, always the inhabited island . . . but then, said Maius Eneo, it was Xaro that was the inhabited island now.

'It was soon afterwards that Nicander went missing. He had been gathering fruit in the cool of the morning; when, by late afternoon, he had not returned, all of us were worried. That day, the Thunderer had shaken us more violently than before. Could something have happened to Nicander? Maius Eneo insisted that we search for him. Leki's eyes flashed, just a little, but he agreed.

'We were right to be worried. We found Nicander on a steep path that wound beneath one of the island's many jutting, rocky ledges. The corpse sprawled at an odd angle, the flies already buzzing thickly around. Blood splattered the dusty path. The Thunderer, it seemed, had shaken down a rocky fragment, cracking open Nicander's head . . . Shocked, tearful, we clustered round our dead friend. Only Leki seemed unmoved. He looked down at the corpse and laughed.

'That was when Maius Eneo confronted him at last. He sprang up, shouting, "The Thunderer's appeased! Is that what you think, that the Thunderer's appeased?" He pushed Leki in the chest and Leki stumbled back. I was terrified. Fire flashed in Leki's eyes and for a moment I thought he would sear Maius Eneo into powdery ash. Why he didn't, I don't know – turning curtly, all he did was command us to get rid of the corpse, and get rid of it quickly. We heard him laughing again as he pushed his way back along the tangled path.

'Maius Eneo stood trembling with rage. Uchy went to him. Carefully, experimentally, he touched his cousin's arm.

'"His power's weakening," muttered Maius Eneo. "Why didn't he kill me? I don't know what magic has him in its grip, but I tell you it's weakening."

'"Can we be sure?" said Uchy. "He's playing some sort of game, we know that much – I wonder if he's just biding his time."

'"I don't care what he's doing, I'll defy him, I swear it."

'"Come, Maius Eneo – Nicander, poor Nicander, is our concern now."

'Maius Eneo nodded slowly. "The coracle," he said.

'"Coracle?" echoed Uchy.

'"Indeed," said Maius Eneo. "Would you have this cursed ground close over Nicander? Already the flies have supped from his brain; let not their maggots slither between his bones as he lies beneath this vile, shuddering earth. Let us take him to the coracle, and set him upon the waters."

'Though Uchy looked doubtful, Adri nodded. So it was that Juros Iko and Jenas Iko picked up the corpse by the legs and arms. As they bore him down to the beach, the saddest of their songs became his funeral dirge:

120

Swiftly, swiftly, shadows fall
From the brightest sky:
That darkness has his outriders
No one can deny . . .

'By the time we got to the beach, the song had twined itself so firmly round my skull that I was unsure if the brothers still sang or whether I heard only their mournful echo, resonating in my brain. I was in the rear and all the way down the path my footsteps followed a bloody trail; the dripping of the blood, or so it seemed, came in time to the rhythm of the song. How much longer could the song go on? How much blood could flow from Nicander? But as it had flowed on to the rocky path, so the blood would flow into the powdery sand.

'The coracle was behind a screen of rock. Earlier, Maius Eneo had been amazed that this little vessel had survived the storm; but then, he had said, it would be needed for something. Strange, the prophecy in the idlest words – but the coracle, as it happened, would never go to sea with Nicander's corpse . . .

'I was looking down, scuffing blood into the sand, when Maius Eneo cried out. It was then that I knew that Juros Iko and Jenas Iko had indeed still been singing, for their song stopped suddenly, and I looked up, startled – and there on the beach, washed ashore, barely free from the lapping waters . . . was a *boat*.

'It was a rowing-boat, we knew that much, but a boat of quite foreign design and shape. Maius Eneo approached it carefully. Then he cried out again, for lying in the bottom of the boat . . . was a *man*.

'We gathered round, astonished. We had heard that there were men in the northern lands with hair of such fairness – like yours, sun-haired one – but never, at that time, had we seen such a man.

'"Is he dead?" goggled Adri.

'"He's breathing," said Maius Eneo, prodding the recumbent form. Suddenly poor Nicander was forgotten. (We would dispose of him later, in a hastily dug grave at the edge of the jungle.) For now, there was only the sun-haired man who reared up, blinking, and asked us in a parched croak who we were. Maius Eneo said, "I think it's for us to ask the questions." The man grinned faintly, and said that perhaps it was.

'From the moment that I saw this mysterious stranger, I felt that our destiny had shifted. Who he was, how he came to be here I did not yet know, but his presence filled me with a strange excitement. Perhaps it was because we had thought ourselves alone, and now we were not. Perhaps it was because we had hoped to be men, and now one who was truly a *man* had come amongst us. Perhaps I thought Leki's reign would now be over . . . And yet the stranger seemed devoid of power; on the

121

contrary, he was weak, almost starved, and burned badly by the sun. He pointed to his parched lips and Adri ran into the trees, returning with the halves of a cracked coconut; questions burned in our minds as the stranger's hands, shaking violently, held the brimming shells of milk to his lips. Afterwards, with much slipping and stumbling, we helped him up the hill to Sarom.'

'That was . . . kind of you,' Jem said, in a voice heavy with implication – ah, but what need was there for *implication*? 'You say he was sun-haired?'

'Perhaps,' said Rajal, 'he wore a shirt with stripes?'

'A purse,' said Jem, 'and a cutlass . . . a knife?'

'Perhaps,' said Rajal, 'the flies buzzed around him? But no, I suppose that was not until *later*.'

Outside the cave, Ucheus stirred suddenly, his fingers fizzing against the barrier – then he was still again. Awkwardly, Ojo murmured that his friends were getting ahead of him . . . just a *little* ahead.

Lemyu, he said, was an Ejlander, but one who had long been absent from his homeland. In the days after his arrival, as they nursed him back to health, the boys learnt the history of his wanderings. What had prompted his exile, said Ojo, they had never quite divined, but Lemyu claimed that as a boy he had yearned for adventure. His wish, it seemed, had been granted in abundance. When he spoke of his visits to exotic lands, the boys were enraptured; when he spoke of the peoples he had met, they were intrigued – except, that is, for Leki.

'It was Maius Eneo who would urge Lemyu on,' said Ojo, 'when the rest of us were shy, or overawed. Often as we clustered round the Ejlander I found my gaze shifting from the rugged, bearded face to Maius Eneo's shining eyes. It appeared to me then that time had turned back, and the able, excitable Maius Eneo was again our leader. Delusion, of course – but through all this, Leki kept strangely in the background. That he would take part in Lemyu's care was hardly to be expected; what surprised me was that he seemed barely *interested* in the sailor at all. Later, of course, I realised that Leki was only biding his time.

'The events which had brought Lemyu amongst us were swiftly told. After the failure of a certain smuggling venture, our new friend had been cooling his heels in Kjeda, one of the southerly outposts of Unang Lia, when he heard that an elderly sea captain, an Ejlander like himself, was taking on hands. Lemyu put himself forward at once. Where this captain might be going he did not care – only that he should soon be gone. This, said Lemyu, was a rashness he would later regret. Only when he was at sea did he realise that this captain was no mere trader, or buccaneer masquerading as such; this captain – there could be no doubt of it – was crazed. To sail south was one thing; to sail beyond the Straits of Javander, as this captain proposed, was suicide. Didn't every tar know that? If the others were fools, Lemyu was not. He remonstrated fearlessly and the captain raged at him, calling him a villain.

'It had almost been Lemyu's fate to walk the plank; only on the intervention of the first mate was he consigned, instead, to the destiny that brought him to us ... In the little boat, Lemyu told us, he had thought that his death had merely been postponed. What other fate could await a lone sailor, adrift on the open sea with no food, no fresh water, and the sun beating down? There was no telling, he would say, how lucky a tar could be ... Ah, but what irony we would soon find in these words!'

Ucheus paused. Rajal would have urged him to go on at once, but a suspicion – a fancy – had stirred in Jem's mind and he leapt in, 'This sea captain – Ojo, you don't know his name?'

The stocky youth shook his head. 'Your Ejlander names are strange to me. Perhaps Uchy might remember – if, that is, he remembers anything,' he added miserably.

Jem urged, 'Porlo? It wasn't ... Captain Porlo?'

Rajal turned to him. 'Jem, really! There must be hundreds of sea captains floating around these waters – Ejlander captains, too. Well, quite a few of them – traders, mercenaries, buccaneers and whatnot. Besides, Porlo wasn't *crazed*, was he? Just a drunken old coward. If you ask me, all he wanted was to escape Lord Empster and scurry off home, quick smart. I can't see "old Faris Porlo" sailing for these Straits of Javander, can you – if they're really so dangerous?'

Jem looked thoughtful. 'Hm, I suppose you're right – yes, you'd have to be right. A drunken old coward, that's about the measure of Captain Porlo.'

Impatiently, Rajal turned back to Ojo.

'But Lemyu,' he said, 'what about Lemyu?'

Chapter 17

ON THE BEACH

The night had been a long one, but was almost over. Soon the first shards of dawn would come, purple and gold, prising at the edges of the dark horizon. Jem felt a tiredness hammering behind his eyes, but matching it, resisting it, was the foreboding that prickled his skin, that crawled through his veins, that tightened his chest. What would happen when morning came?

Of the five who were there on the ridge that night, only Ucheus appeared to have slept – though perhaps, in truth, the slender boy was unconscious. By the cauldron, Leki had begun to hum, softly at first, and only slowly, but after a time, the humming grew louder – faster, too. In the cave, Ojo bit his lip and carried on with his tale. After a time, he had to raise his voice a little.

Lemyu, he said, had been a hardy man, surprisingly so after all he had endured. Within days of coming amongst them, the sailor's strength had returned. If he had begun by telling tales of his colourful past, soon his attention shifted to the future. By now, the Thunderer was shaking the island five, perhaps six times daily; the smoke from the summit was thicker, darker. Gazing across the sea to where Inorchis had been, Lemyu came to a desperate resolve.

'I's seen these 'canoes before,' he said. 'Believe me, lads, this one's going to blow. There's one thing for it, only one thing.'

Excitedly, Maius Eneo asked what this could be.

Lemyu looked at him, surprised at the question. 'We got boats, ain't we – two of 'em, to be precise? Now what's the good of a boat if it ain't on the sea?' He licked a finger and stuck it in the air. 'Feel them winds? I knows the charts for these waters pretty well. If I's not mistaken, we be fair on the trade route for Hora.'

Maius Eneo gasped, 'But that's leagues away! With a sloop, yes, but a rowboat . . . a coracle . . .'

'You'd rather be roasted alive?' said Lemyu. 'Come, young fellow, I don't knows about no Blue Storms, but right now the sun's out, the trades be blowing – and anyway, we can't stay here.' He looked squarely at his young companions, eyes squinting earnestly. 'Listen, lads, this here tar owes you a lot. He could take off himself, he could, all on his lonesome – but does he want to see you all roasted? Look, we could do it in a few days – the crossing, I mean. Besides, there's many a ship bound where we'll be going – chances are, we'll be picked up soon enough. But say, ain't none of you lads ever been to Hora? Island-dwellers be always out on the seas, ain't they?'

'Not, I suppose, if they're Islanders of Aroc,' said Jem.

'Indeed,' Ojo sighed. 'Easy to reach Hora might be, but to us, it might as well have been a world away. History told of wars long ago, when the natives of Hora had sought to conquer us. Since then, we had never been reconciled to these old, bitter enemies. On Inorchis, we would hear of Hora only in tones of execration. While for long epicycles we had kept to ourselves, shuttling back and forth between our Twinned Isles of Aroc, the Horans had built a great trading empire. In Sacred School we learnt of the decadence of their wealth, the corruption of their politics, the pollution of their race by the blood of outsiders. The Horans, we were told, were a terrible warning, and soon would bring doom upon themselves.

'Instead, they thrived, and secretly, I knew, many of us envied our wealthy neighbours. Once, I recall, Uchy asked Maius Eneo why it might be that the Horans did not try to conquer us again – this time, after all, they would surely succeed. To me it was a mystery, but Maius Eneo – repeating, I suppose, the wisdom of his father – said that really there was no mystery at all. In the time of the wars, the Horans had been just beginning their expansion; since then, they had learnt that their power would lie not in conquest, but rather, in commerce. In these southerly seas, the Horans were the greatest of trading peoples. What need had they of our volatile islands when a hundred others were in their debt?

'Reflecting on this, I saw that what Maius Eneo said must be right. But how galling, how infuriating, to think we were not even worthy of conquest! Often, far away on the horizon, we had seen ships plying the route to Hora, and our hearts had been filled with longing. Of course, we kept these longings secret.

'Not any more, though.

'"Lemyu's right – we can't stay here," said Maius Eneo. He looked at us intently, then added, suddenly, surprisingly, "Yet what of it? Our old lives are over, but the world is wide." And gesturing to the sea where Inorchis had been, he grew expansive. "Forget Inorchis – forget our fathers! If they came back now, we'd *all* be unmanned. Hora-port is massive, and open to the world. Once we get there, we can go where we please – just think what adventures lie before us!"

'There was madness in these words. Perhaps we knew it; perhaps Maius Eneo knew it even as he spoke; later, I would hear him sobbing for Inorchis, hoping only that somehow, in a future we could barely imagine, our lost homeland might yet be restored to us. But for now, such thoughts were banished from our minds. In our eagerness, we would have set forth at once, had Lemyu not told us we must *prepare* for the journey. Impatiently, over the next days, we laid up provisions, salting meat, smoking fish, drying mushrooms and apricots in the sun. We plaited new ropes; we wove new nets; Lemyu worked on the rowing boat, improvising a mast and sail, while Maius Eneo, assisted by Uchy, strengthened the coracle with fresh bark and vines. The plan was to tow it behind the larger boat. It was all so easy; it was all so exciting. In the evenings, Juros Iko and Jenas Iko now sang only happy songs.

'But the shadows still loomed in wait, ready to fall.

'Only Leki dared question our enthusiasm. "*Two little boats,*" he whispered to me one day, "just *two little boats*. Do you really think there's room enough for us all?"

'I barely registered what he meant. He leaned closer to me, and all I could think of was the way this voice had echoed in my mind, back at the time of the Blue Storm. '"*Two little boats,*" he said again, and this time I pushed him roughly away.

'He sprawled on his back.

'"Shut up," I said, "just shut up, or we'll leave you behind!"

'Madness, madness indeed! Had Leki been minded to destroy me at that moment, he might have unleashed all the fearsome powers of his eyes . . . Instead there came a crashing in the undergrowth and Jenas Iko burst upon us, his arms scratched and bloodied and his face stained with tears.

'What shocked me was not only his appearance, but the fact that he was alone. He babbled hysterically.

'I grabbed him, slapped him. "Jenas! Where's Juros?"

'Helplessly, Jenas Iko pointed into the jungle. He clawed at me – demanding, without words, that I come, come.

'"*Two little boats!*" shrieked Leki. "*Two little boats!*"

'He lay where he had fallen, lolling in the undergrowth, his laughter ringing behind us as we blundered away. But there was no time to think of Leki now. Only one thing hammered in my mind, hammered so hard it might break through my skull. *Dead. Juros Iko was dead.* But the sight that awaited me was worse than I could have imagined.

'Jenas Iko collapsed, sobbing. I turned away and retched.

'The brothers had been gathering vines to plait into ropes. They had lost sight of each other only for a moment, the merest moment, amongst the enveloping green – but that moment had been enough. Juros Iko had not had time even to cry out – and after that he could not cry out, for the vines had been plaited tight around his neck . . .

'When Maius Eneo learnt what had happened, he called a council of war. There could be no more delays, he said; this island was cursed and we must leave at once.

'"Now?" we gasped.

'It was hardly the time to set to sea. The coracle was not ready; we needed more food; night was falling and the sky was blood-red. But then the Thunderer rumbled, violently shaking the ground beneath our feet, and suddenly we knew only that we must escape, escape.

'Juros Iko was barely in his grave before we began loading Lemyu's boat. By the time we were ready it was dark and the moon shone, huge and sinister, over the vast blackness of the waters. Our nerves jangled like maddening bells as the terrible rumbling came again.

'It was time. We were leaving.

'Someone cried, "Leki – where's Leki?"

'Maius Eneo spat, "Forget that madmaster!"

'But it was then, as if to confirm these very words, that a wild screech came ringing out of the darkness – "*Two little boats! Two little boats!*"

'I reeled round. Fire burnt in Leki's eyes, this time more terribly than ever before, and his whole frame was surrounded by an evil incandescence. He advanced slowly, pointing at Lemyu with a trembling, accusing finger.

'But the words he spoke were for the rest of us.

'"You never realised, did you? Fools, did you really think it was the *Thunderer* that killed Adri ... and Infin Ijas ... and Nicander ... and Juros Iko? It was Lemyu, can't you see?"

'Maius Eneo cried, "Leki, what are you talking about? Lemyu wasn't even *here* when Adri died – or Infin Ijas, or ..."

'"Fools, I say! Don't you know he's been here all this time, hiding in the jungle? Sailor, indeed – he's a Creature of Evil, and a wily one ... But no more of his tricks! The Thunderer's told me everything, and the Thunderer wants him to die! *Die*, Creature of Evil!"

'As Leki approached, Lemyu had staggered back against the boat, terrified, his manly strength gone. Now the fire shot from Leki's eyes. In an instant, the boat was ablaze. Screaming, Lemyu darted away, but Leki turned to him – and then came the most terrifying thing of all, for suddenly it seemed that the radiance around Leki was rushing towards the rest of us, capturing us all in its evil glow. Now all volition was taken from us. *Die, Creature of Evil!* rang the words again, but this time I heard them inside my own skull.

'What happened next is almost too horrible to tell. Let me say only that Leki stood by laughing, watching the burning boat, as we raced after the hapless Lemyu, intent upon destroying him ...

'You know the rest.

'Afterwards, Leki told us that everything would be all right now. The evil was gone, the Thunderer appeased ... But as the glow of Leki's magic subsided, we all knew in our hearts that he had to be wrong.

'Soon we would find out just how wrong. A day passed: and the Thunderer rumbled again. Another day: and again. Another: and Zap was dead, mutilated hideously. He must have bled to death. What had happened to him I shudder to reveal; suffice to say that it was rather as if he had played again, but this time not with bananas and pears, a certain game that had once so diverted us.

'Yet still Leki's power held us firmly in its grip; he was our leader; our doom was certain. Only Maius Eneo dared think of resistance, and one day, while Leki was communing with the Thunderer, Uchy's brave cousin called us to him. Knowing he would speak against Leki, we were terrified, for it seemed to us that Leki would know what we were saying, what we were thinking, and punish us terribly.

'"The coracle," said Maius Eneo. "He didn't burn the coracle. It was nearly ready, I can make it ready – it's our last chance, don't you see?"

'"Madness!" I cried. "You don't think we could make it to Hora, do you? In that thing – alone?"

'"There are ships," said Maius Eneo. "A ship might pick us up, didn't Lemyu say so?"

'"It's madness – we'd sink in the first day!"

'"What, you'd rather die *here*, like the others?"

'Jenas Iko's lips trembled. "Leki says there'll be no more killings. He says the Thunderer ... the Thunderer's appeased now."

'"That's what he said before Zap died, too. That's what he'll always say, over and over, until we're all dead but him. Forget the Thunderer! Don't you see it's *Leki* who's been killing us? Leki ... and he won't stop till he's killed us all!"

'"But why?" I burst out. "It doesn't make *sense*—"

'"I don't know why!" cried Maius Eneo. "Evil magic ... something to do with the storm ... oh, what does it matter? We've just got to get off this island, that's all!"

'"What about Leki?" said Jenas Iko. "He'd send his fire after us, I know he would!"

'"Jenas Iko's right," said Uchy. "Leki – why, he'd never let us go!"

'Maius Eneo sprang up angrily. "You mean you won't come with me? None of you?"

'"We may be murdered here," I had to say, "but I'd rather chance that than commit *suicide*."

'"We can't ... we can't leave Leki," said Jenas Iko, his brow furrowing strangely.

'"No, cousin, it would never work," said Uchy.

'Later, Uchy would be astonished to think that he had ever uttered these words. Cursing himself as a coward and a fool, he would wonder what had come over him, so devoted was he to his extraordinary cousin. But I think we both knew: I think we had both heard the whisperings in our brains. No matter: Maius Eneo had given us our chance, and it was a chance we had failed to take.

'Next morning, the coracle was gone – and so was Maius Eneo. Whether he drowned, I don't know. I can hardly imagine he reached Hora.

'That was almost a moonphase ago. Since then, there's been another death. Poor Jenas Iko – one of us should always have stayed with him. He was never the same after his brother's death – never sang again, either . . .' Ojo gulped, brushing his eyes. 'I wonder if I'll ever again hear such pure voices. The sound was like . . . like liquid gold. How bitter, then, that one was strangled, and the other's throat cut from ear to ear!'

There was little more to say. Ojo might have added that sometimes he dreamed of Maius Eneo – as Uchy, he was certain, did as well. In the dreams, their old leader was not dead, nor had he abandoned them. He had gone to get help, that was all, and one day he would be back, bold as life, to save them . . . But no, this was too forlorn a hope – Uchy might believe it, but how could Ojo?

All through the last part of the story, the three in the cave had been aware of Leki's humming, like the tuneless blundering of a persistent insect. Now the humming suddenly stopped. The Thunderer rumbled and the captives, turning, saw Leki, wraith-like through the cauldron's steam, standing against the reddening morning sky. But redder than the sky were his glowing eyes as he stretched out his hand towards the mouth of the cave. There were cracklings, sparks – then the captives were free.

But only for a moment . . .

'Jem,' hissed Rajal, as they stumbled on to the ridge, 'what can he do to us – really, what *can* he do?'

'With those eyes? Quite a lot, I should think.'

'But Jem, there's only one of him. We could make a break for it, couldn't we? Ojo's on our side, Uchy's out cold—'

'I wouldn't be so sure,' Jem muttered.

'What do you mean?'

But no words were needed to answer *this* question. Slowly Rajal let his gaze follow Jem's and he watched, startled, as the stunned Ucheus rose to his feet, bathed in the aurora from his evil leader's eyes. The slender youth's own eyes showed only blankness, the blankness of a creature devoid of will.

'Uchy . . . Uchy?' Rajal breathed, horrified.

He turned to Jem, then both turned to Ojo, as if their new friend could say something, do something – but now it seemed that Ojo too could only gaze back unfeelingly, bound together with Ucheus in Leki's evil spell.

'Raj! Run for it!' cried Jem.

Impossible. The Thunderer shook the ridge again, with a violence even greater than before. For a moment it seemed that the rock would buckle, bending and breaking, cracking like a crust of stale bread.

Triumphantly, Leki rode with the thunder.

Jem lurched. Rajal sprawled.

'Seize them!' came the cry.

Chapter 18

CLOUDBURSTING

Light glimmers through the overburdening leaves; soon it will be morning. Littler struggles against the vines again, his mind clearing after the night's visionary haze. How cramped are his arms! How cramped are his legs! There is a fluttering in the branches – the blue bird, vanishing with a harsh, almost mocking beating of wings. But there is something else, too. Littler becomes aware that the earth is trembling, shuddering. Heat prickles the air; there is a sulphurous smell, and the thought comes to him that he is high on the island, closer to the Thunderer than to the watery shore.

But now fear beats up in Littler like the bird through the branches as he sees his captor, moving out of the shadows into a shaft of light. This time, Littler sees him directly, even the face. But Littler is no coward, and does not scream.

'Wh-what,' he falters, 'do you want with me?'

There is no answer, not really. The strange hand – but the hand, compared with the face, is barely strange at all – rips away the vines. Now, perhaps, Littler might cry out; but the action is neither clumsy nor violent, and the voice is not unkind.

'Come Maro . . . Maro, you must come.'

Littler says, 'Maro . . . Maro?'

Again, he is gathered into the stranger's arms.

'See that rock? It's wobbling.' Rajal glanced ruefully at a large boulder. 'Jem, do you think this place is going to blow?'

'Learn fast, don't you, Raj? Just think, a day ago you'd never even *seen* a smoking mountain – now it seems you know all about them.'

'I just said, is it going to blow?'

'Right now, I couldn't care less.'

'You never know – a distraction, in the nick of time. Just what we need, maybe.'

'Actually Raj, that would be *more* than a distraction – that would be a disaster.'

'So what's this?'

There was no escape. As the bloodied dawn spilled across the island,

131

the captives found themselves hustled, staggering, up the narrow track to the Thunderer's summit. Ucheus and Ojo – their strength, it was certain, much augmented by magic – held them fast and their wrists, in any case, were bound behind them with sticky vines. By now the violence of the volcano had relented, but ominous shivers still passed underfoot. Like fleeing rats, little stones scurried downhill as Leki strode briskly, brashly ahead. From time to time he would turn back, urging his henchmen to hurry, hurry . . . He was almost insouciant; he even smiled. For now, the fire was gone from his eyes and, but for the paint that daubed his skin, he might have been any ordinary boy intent upon some exciting game. He whistled; he skipped; he swept his cutlass at the scrubby vegetation.

'Some heroes we are,' Rajal muttered angrily.

'It's hardly been a fair fight,' said Jem.

'I suppose not . . . Jem?'

'Raj, if you're going to say it's been nice knowing me, stop right now. I don't want to hear it – really, I don't.'

They were climbing higher. By now, the bright morning air had given way to a blanket of sulphurous, reeking mist; by now, the vegetation was sparse, scrubby; the rocks beneath their feet were sharper, hotter. They stumbled. They gasped. They rounded a last twist of path. All at once they had reached their destination. The clouds overhead rolled thick and dark. They were standing upon a hot, crumbling edge. Sickened, Jem and Rajal gazed down into the bubbling core of the volcano. The heat was overwhelming. Steam and smoke swirled around them, intoxicating, choking; but for the gripping hands of Ucheus and Ojo they would certainly have lurched and fallen.

'Raj?' gasped Jem. 'You were going to say?'

'I *was* going to say it's been nice knowing you, Jem.'

'You too, Raj . . . But Raj? Shut up – please.'

The caldera was narrow – no wider than the length of four men laid head to foot – but this only made it all the more fearsome, so great was the constriction of the liquid, glowing rock that pitched and heaved in the searing bowl, that growled and belched and shot up in spurting, spasmodic leaps. Leki skipped playfully, fearlessly along the rim. Stretching out his arms, he breathed deeply. 'Mm, smell this bracing air! Come, Zandis Ojonis – Ucheus, come . . . Hold your charges a little closer, *hm* – closer, that is, to the *crumbling* edge?'

Jem twisted, struggling to no avail.

Rajal cried out, 'Jem, I'm slipping . . . Jem, I'm going to die!'

But not yet – and Leki, with a laugh, said as much. 'But soon, my friend, soon. Ojo, make sure you grip him tight. His wrists are still secured? Good . . . let him hang just a little further over these bubbling depths, *hm*, since he seems to enjoy it so much. But careful, careful – in common politeness we must greet the Thunderer, must we not, before we present him with our fine offerings?'

Jem's head reeled and he coughed, choking on the acrid air. He blurted, 'Leki, this is madness – you know it's madness . . . Leki, fight against this evil inside you!'

'Evil?' Leki twisted suddenly. For a moment it looked like he would slip into the caldera, but effortlessly he regained his footing – borne up, perhaps, by his mysterious powers. To Jem's blurring eyes, it seemed indeed as if the painted youth were no longer balancing on the edge, but hovering above it, just a little . . . And now the voice became a crazed screech: 'You speak of evil, sun-haired one? *You*, a vicious murderer – *you*, the brutal killer of my companions?'

'Leki,' Jem cried, 'you know that's not true! How could we have killed anyone? Didn't you shoot us down only yesterday? We weren't here before, you *know* we weren't here—'

'Ejlander tricks, Ejlander magic—'

'No, no . . . Leki, I don't know what evil has you in its grip, but I'll be bound it's the same evil that killed Infin Ijas and Adri and Nicander and Juros Iko and—'

Leki spun round. Jem gasped, for all at once the crazed youth was directly before him, prodding with his cutlass, thrusting forward his wild-eyed face.

But how could that be? In the grip of the mesmerised Ucheus, Jem hung precariously above the caldera.

His eyes darted down. It was true.

Leki stood only on air, on steam.

'Sun-haired one,' the hiss came now, and it might have been the hiss of the Thunderer's heat, 'how can you even *dare* to defy me? Do you not know this is my kingdom, my realm, my absolute monarchy?' His voice rose and he lashed out, striking Jem's face with the flat of his cutlass. 'Mine! *My* kingdom, do you hear – mine, damn you!'

Jem gasped and his head lolled back, cracking against the shoulder of the blank-eyed Ucheus. Leki twisted and cavorted in the air. All through this exchange, the angry caldera had shuddered and pulsed; now came a new, violent convulsion and a red, heaving wave reared up from below, splattering its glowing spume against the rocky sides of the bowl. Delighted, Leki leapt up and down on a billowing cloud, shrieking again of his kingdom, his reign.

Jem raised his head, breathless in the heat and fumes. Tears ran from his eyes and his throat was parched, but he forced himself to fling out the words, 'Leki – Leki, listen to yourself! Can't you see it's a kingdom of *one*?' He jerked back, gesturing with his jaw, to Ucheus, to Ojo. 'Are these your loyal subjects? They obey you only because of your magic – and

133

even if they didn't, what of it? Two subjects . . . two boys . . . and the rest all *dead*? What kind of kingdom is that, Leki? You can kill Raj and me, but you'll *all* be dead soon. This place is going to blow, Leki – sky high . . . Let us . . . let us help you, Leki! There's a world beyond this! We can try and make it to – to Hora, we can . . . Leki . . .'

Jem would have struggled on, but he knew it was useless. The crazed youth leapt back and forth across the caldera, danced around the rim, burst in and out of cloud after cloud, eyes glowing red, cutlass slicing through the smoke and steam. As he cavorted, he seemed to be chanting, uttering incantations, but Jem could not make out the words. Gritting his teeth, he writhed again in his captor's powerful, magical grip. There was one chance – one last chance . . .

'Uchy,' he flung behind him, 'this isn't you. You don't want to do this. Uchy, think of Maius Eneo – Maius Eneo, Uchy, coming back to save you!' Jem raised his hoarse voice, shouting as best he could, 'Uchy – Ojo, you too – fight against Leki, fight against him now!'

For a time Rajal appeared to have passed out, but at Jem's words he rallied, urging Ojo, too, to defy his evil master. He cried out the names of the lost boys. 'Infin Ijas . . . Zap . . . Adri . . . Nicander . . . Juros Iko . . . Jenas Iko – Ojo, Uchy, it was Leki who killed them, Leki, it must have been! Leki, Uchy . . . Leki, Ojo!'

'Maius Eneo!' shrieked Jem. 'Ojo, Uchy . . . Maius Eneo!'

'Infin Ijas . . . Zap . . . Adri . . . Nicander . . . Juros Iko . . . Jenas Iko!'

'Maius Eneo . . . Maius Eneo!'

There is a magic in names; some say all magic is a matter of names. In the clouded air Leki reeled and reeled, eyes blazing, as the names rained around him, echoing at the sides of the trembling caldera. Below, something was happening. There was the shifting of a footstep, the loosening of a grip. Then the cry broke from Ojo's lips; then Ojo – Ucheus, too – was stumbling back, slithering on the crumbling edge, and Rajal, then Jem too, was falling. Lava surged towards them. Heat flayed their flesh.

Then Leki was laughing. The fire burst from his eyes, sweeping over the falling figures, gathering them, spinning them upwards through the air. Suspended, billowing, they hung amongst the clouds as Leki joyously soared around them, twirling his cutlass, diving and plunging through the steam and smoke. Far below they saw Ucheus and Ojo, dazed, scrambling, flailing.

And now the voice came in Jem's ear, 'An instant, just an instant, and the Thunderer will claim you – but not yet, not yet!'

Leki bounded round the rim of the caldera. Already he had performed the first incantations; now came the last, ecstatic summoning. It was a song without rhythm and without melody, or rather, with a rhythm and a melody so strange that neither Jem nor Rajal could follow them. Round and round on the air it boomed, as the names of the lost boys had boomed before, but it seemed that no line of this mad song died away, only reverberated beneath this new line and that, and that and that and that . . .

In the chaos, it was impossible to make out the words, but to Jem, as to Rajal, it seemed that Leki's caterwaulings from the day before had returned, transfigured – *Tell me the measure of an Ejlander* and *Carry me to Sarom* and *Pig, pig, what do I care?* churning together with a hundred demands, entreaties, supplications to the shuddering god, if god it were, that went by the name of Aroc Xaro . . .

'The noise,' shouted Rajal, 'I can't bear it—'

Jem struggled with the vines around his wrists. 'Raj, do you think we could *swim* through these clouds? Sort of waft ourselves away – while Leki's not looking?

'What? Swim . . . waft? We're going to *die*, Jem!'

'We thought that a moment ago, didn't we? Come on, Raj, you don't think this is the end, do you? It can't be!' Jem ripped his bonds and the vines dropped below, sizzling into nothingness before they hit the lava. He reached out, gripping his friend's arm. 'Quick, out of those vines. If we can just get clear of this soupbowl . . . Raj, quick!'

'They're . . . they're cutting my wrists—'

'Raj,' Jem laughed, 'if *that* were your only problem—'

'It might be! At this rate, I'll bleed to death before the Thunderer has a go at me . . . Urgh! That's torn it!'

'Torn the vines? Good, now quick—'

'Not just the vines—'

'What—?' Jem's gaze darted below and he saw something hard, something rounded spiralling down, flaring in the volcanic glow. 'The amulet? Well, you said you wanted to throw it away! Now – swim, Raj, swim!'

It was hopeless, of course. They flailed against the choking smoke, but hardly moved. Below, Leki's mad song was reaching a climax. Surging out of the cacophony came *Mother, mother* and *Beware, beware!* and *How long?* and *How deep?* and *I couldn't care a fig for a pig*, mingling with the Thunderer's sacred name, then the thunder of the god himself, shaking the island again and again . . .

Yes, it was hopeless, for just as Rajal thought he had pushed himself forward, the world and the caldera and the air and the clouds seemed to lurch precariously, pushing him back.

'Jem,' he gasped, 'it's no good—'

'Don't give up now, Raj—'

But Rajal was right. They billowed and tumbled in the violent air.

'It's over, Jem! I've even lost my talisman now ... I *do* want it, you know. Now I haven't got it, I *do* want it—'

'At least I've got mine.' Jem dug into the pocket of his breeches, holding up an ornate golden coin. It flashed in the lava-light as they turned, turned. For a strange moment they were suspended in time; the booming, wild music was far away, and their voices came dreamily, as if in truth they were not about to die, or in any danger at all.

'Nice,' murmured Rajal, eyeing the coin. 'Well, at least ... at least it's practical – or would be, if there were a tavern round here.'

'Droll, droll. It's Cata's coin – the harlequin gave it to her when she was a child.'

'Hm. And tell me, what does it *do*?'

'It's a symbol of our love.'

'Oh ... well, I see.'

'Do you, Raj?'

Rajal said no more. Turning in the air, he found himself thinking of a certain lanky fellow and wondered if ... if *it* could have amounted to anything. Aron Throsh ... Bean ... Polty's friend – Polty's accomplice, who had run back to Polty, who had vanished, in the end, when Polty had vanished, in the Sanctum of the Flame in Unang Lia. Oh, it was mad ... Rajal turned, turned ... And Jem, he knew, was thinking of Cata ... But what was Cata now but another dream, just as much a dream as Aron and Rajal, Rajal and Aron? Jem held the coin between his fingers, gazing upon it as if in a trance.

It was a trance that could not last.

For nor could Leki's song. Rapidly – too rapidly – the echoes died and there remained only the surging, rising thunder; then with a scream, perhaps of pain, perhaps of joy, Leki was soaring like a rocket through the clouds, surging between the billowing captives. Jem careened back, feeling the coin slip from his fingers. He cried out; his treasure was lost – but then the very *thought* of his treasure was lost as a new horror was upon them, rearing up from the caldera's bubbling depths.

It was a surging, searing column of fire.

It was a monstrous, glowing fist.

It was a hideous face.

No, it was more – more, and worse. It was a molten giant, rising, swelling, gathering the substance of the lava into itself.

Jaws opened immensely.

Claws reached up.

Chapter 19

THE PRINCE OF TIDES

'This can't be the end! It can't, it can't—'

Wildly Jem clutched the crystal at his chest. He rolled through the air, crashing against Rajal. Below, on the caldera's edge, Ojo and Ucheus scrambled back; all around them Leki's laughter rang like a high, hysterical jangle over the grinding, the groaning, the bursting and booming of the terrible thing rising from the lake of lava.

Then Rajal cried, 'Jem! Look—'

His hand flung out, pointing. Was there something else? Some new horror? They flailed together, spinning, clutching each other, just out of reach of a sizzling claw. One moment more and the claw would rise higher, high enough to grasp them. Jem struggled to focus his clouded eyes; it was then that he was aware of the crystal at his chest, glowing red through his clutching hand, then Rajal's crystal too, glowing purple. The rays locked together in dazzling shards. What was happening? Could they be in the presence, already, of the blue crystal?

But there was something else, Jem knew, that could make the crystals glow.

He saw it.

'No! It can't be—'

Smoke shrouded the astonishing new creature that had now appeared on the caldera's rim. The body was darkened, like a black shadow, but nothing could obscure the golden, glowing orb that shone from the face like a single, huge eye. It was Lemyu's corpse, monstrously animated, but as the golden eye swept evilly over him, Jem knew he was looking not at the dead sailor but at Toth-Vexrah, projecting his being through the orb.

He cried his defiance of the anti-god just as the orb began to flicker and pulse, sending out beams of mysterious power. Floundering, Jem and Rajal were drawn down helplessly, towards the source of the golden light . . .

Above, Leki whirled round and round like a monstrous insect, suddenly enraged; below, the caldera sizzled and swelled. Huge bubbles burst, lava leapt into the air and all at once the molten giant had achieved its full height, head flung back, jaw swooping, claws tearing the clouds – and tearing at Jem and Rajal too.

Swipe! Swipe!

But no – just in time they were out of range and the monster's claws connected instead with the insect-thing that whizzed round and round its dripping, burning head – swatted once, twice, then plucked the hapless victim from the air . . .

'Thunderer . . . *Thunderer, no!*'

Leki's screams echoed like his song; then, like his song, they were gone.

Jem's head jerked back, eyes wide with horror. But there was no time to think of Leki, no time for Leki or the Thunderer either, for now the lava-monster too was gone, beaten down by new and more powerful energies pulsing from the thing that had once been Lemyu.

'Raj, fight against it . . . Raj, it's Toth, he—'

'Jem, I can't . . . Jem, it's too strong—'

'The crystals . . . Raj, we can defy this—'

'Jem, look – *Ojo! What's he doing?*'

Jem would have cried out, shrieked at Ojo not to be a fool, but there was no time, no time. On the edge of the caldera, rising up beside the rotting corpse, Ojo lunged, as if to bring it down; the Lemyu-thing staggered, fixing the stocky youth in the full force of its beam.

Ojo stumbled back, blinded, slipping . . .

Jem plummeted – Rajal, too . . .

Down, down they spun towards the lava-pit, only to be wrenched up again at the last moment as this new beam from the golden eye scooped them violently back through the air.

Already, below, Ojo was rallying, blundering towards the Lemyu-thing with fists flailing.

Ucheus leapt at him. 'Ojo, no! Ojo—'

But he never reached his friend. The corpse's arm struck out, knocking Ojo flying. Ucheus lurched back; then Jem, then Rajal, were slipping closer, precipitously closer to Lemyu's corpse, cowering as the rotted hands reached through the air, ready to pluck the crystals from their chests. Faster, faster flickered the golden light. Nauseated, Jem saw, smelled, almost touched the vile corrupted flesh with its ragged wounds, its suppurating pus, its tunnelling, waving maggots. Still the flies buzzed and blundered, ecstatic at the stench and decay.

They must not yield. *Must not. Must not.*

Jem struggled. Reaching for Rajal, he would have beat his way back through the air, back into the steam, back into the clouds, as if he could fly of his own volition – but Toth's grasp was too strong . . . Dazzled, Jem looked into the light of the orb, and within the light he saw the face of the anti-god, leering as it had leered beneath the Great Temple of Agonis when the evil thing had smashed its way through the magic glass, bursting its way back from the Realm of Unbeing ... And as if it were real, as if it had *happened*, Jem saw the corpse ripping away his crystal, Rajal's too, then flinging their bodies like discarded husks into the annihilating fury of the caldera.

Must not. Must not. Hands reached out. Jem clutched his chest. Hands grasped at his hands, pulling and tearing; the air was a chaos of smoke and light.

Then Ucheus leapt up, screaming, pointing.

Jem gasped, 'Raj, look! Who—'

'Jem! What the—'

From somewhere there shone a beam of blue, clearing a path through the obscuring clouds. For an instant the Toth-monster's grip slackened and Jem and Rajal caught dazzled glimpses of a mysterious new figure, rising on the opposite rim of the caldera. Outlined in auroras of fluorescent blue, the figure appeared as a silhouette, no more, but a silhouette of formidable size and strength, standing statue-like, arms upraised.

And there was something in the arms. A burden. A body – a tiny, human body. Then the arms flung the body forward; swooping, soaring it plummeted through the haze towards Jem, towards Rajal, towards the Toth-monster as it grabbed again for the crystals, raging now in a blind fury ...

Jem cried, 'Littler! But how—?'

'He's alive! Jem, what's he doing—?'

Littler's limbs flailed. Screaming, he careened into the frenzied corpse. The corpse reared back, raising an arm to beat him away.

It was too late. Littler was fearless, feeding on the energy of the pulsing blue. He plunged his hands into the rotting face, clutching at the radiant, pulsing orb; with a wild, wrenching action, he ripped it free.

Back, back he tumbled through the fractured light. A scream filled the air; then the corpse was tottering, collapsing into the lava; then the orb slipped from Littler's hands and Littler and Jem and Rajal too were falling, down, down after the spinning, guttering orb, and all at once the figure in silhouette took flight, swooping forward in a blur of blue, sweeping them up in its auroral force.

'It's over,' gasped Ucheus. 'Ojo, it's over.'

Ojo mumbled incoherently; Littler looked dazed; Rajal, blinking, wondered what had happened, while Jem, astonished, gazed up at the figure that stood above them, statuesque in the strange blue light.

The figure presented an extraordinary spectacle. If indeed he was tall – half as tall again as an ordinary man – so too his skin was alarmingly odd, blue in colour, scaly, slimy, and with curious finny excrescences about the face and neck. Formidably muscular, he wore a greenish, brownish toga, belted at the middle, which might have been fashioned from seaweed. But only in appearance was the stranger fearsome. He carried no weapons, or none that Jem could see, and there was a benevolence, almost a warmth, in the yellow, fish-like eyes.

When he spoke, his voice was soft.

'I am Oclar,' he said, 'Prince of Tides. Seldom – very seldom – in the epicycles of my reign have I manifested myself to those of humankind, but no longer can concealment be my way. What choice have I, when destiny is at hand, and upon the merest moment this world's fate may turn?' He turned to Littler. 'But your small friend will forgive me, I trust, for holding him captive. Had I not readied him to play his part, he would not have been able to save you – then you, Prince Jemany, and all your companions would have been doomed.'

The aurora had faded; the clouds were clearing, too. The mountainside had ceased its violent tremblings and stillness crept over the caldera below. But now Jem's mind was in turmoil instead, racing with a hundred questions.

Oclar smiled – smiled, perhaps, as if he already knew not only the answers, but the questions, too. 'For the length of many orbits I have roamed these Waters of Wenaya,' he said, 'seeking, seeking ... but no, there are some things that need not trouble you. Let me say only that I have long awaited the evil which, I knew, would be enacted this day – long awaited it, and long vowed that it must *not* be permitted to triumph.'

'You ... knew?' said Jem.

But the Prince of Tides did not answer *this* question. Instead, his scaly hand fluffed Littler's hair and he said reflectively, 'Great as my powers are, they are much diminished, and can only diminish further in this present, ruinous condition of the world. To confront directly the powers of evil is not within my scope, nor shall it be until ... but that, I hope, you shall see in time. Suffice to say now that I took this child, who alone could pluck out Toth's golden eye. Treasure him, my friends, for he is a hero, and before this drama is over he shall, I am certain, play a greater role.' And Oclar leaned down, staring into Littler's wide-eyed face. 'But can you forgive me, Maro? It was never my wish to imprison you ... Maro?'

Was Littler still in the power of enchantment? In any case, the little boy only nodded dumbly, and it was left to Rajal, in a puzzled voice, to echo 'Maro?' – and Jem to ask the Prince of Tides whether he were a god, and what clues he might provide to the quest that lay before them.

But just then, Ucheus cried out.

'Ojo! Ojo, no—'

For some moments the slender youth had been struggling with his friend – struggling, that is, to help him stand. Several times Ojo had swayed dangerously; now he collapsed, his eyelids flickering, his breathing stertorous, his limbs jerking as if in the grip of a fever. At once Ucheus knelt beside him, grave with concern, there on the caldera's precipitous rim. Uselessly his hands slid over the convulsing legs and arms, as if he could calm them through force of will.

The others gathered round, all else forgotten.

'What's wrong with him?' cried Rajal. 'It's as if he's—'

'Possessed!' said Jem. 'But what the—'

'It's destroying him, consuming him—'

Jem cursed, gazing into the pit below. How could this be happening, how could it happen *now*, when the evil that had threatened them had sizzled to nothingness?

But the Thunderer's lava still bubbled and plopped; steam still rose with a sinister hiss.

'Lemyu!' Jem burst out. 'Ojo took the full force—'

'Blue man – do something!' Littler wailed.

Oclar's look was grave. 'I told you,' he said, 'my powers are much diminished. If Toth's evil consumes him, there is no chance, no chance—'

'His eyes!' moaned Ucheus. 'Look at his eyes!'

Ojo's eyes had flickered open, but their colour was occluded by a thick, milky film. Sweat poured from the stocky youth's forehead; his teeth chattered; when he tried to speak, it was in a strangled gasp. Choking back tears, Ucheus cradled his stricken friend's head, bending close to catch the words.

'Uchy ... Uchy, it's all going dark ...'

'Ojo, no ... the clouds are clearing ...'

'For you, Uchy ... for you, not me ...'

'No, Ojo ... you'll be all right, you'll see ...'

Fresh convulsions racked Ojo's frame. For a long moment he could not speak, and it seemed as if he were slipping out of consciousness. Desperately Ucheus gazed up at Oclar, at Jem, at Rajal, at Littler.

Littler turned, clawing at Oclar's toga. 'Blue man, if there's nothing you can do, can't I? Can't I? I saved Jem ... I saved Rajal, you said I did ...'

But Oclar could only sweep Littler up into his arms. Tenderly he stroked the little boy's hair, sadness filling his yellow eyes. 'Child Maro, if only ... But you and I, we have woven already the spell we had to weave. If what we see is the rage of Toth-Vexrah, burning on in all its terrible force – alas, against Toth we can do no more. Not here. Not now.'

The sun brightened through dispersing clouds, its radiance spilling

141

over the rocky mountainside. To Jem, it looked as if the Thunderer's shudderings had been resumed inside the body of Ojo. Only slowly did the spasms die again; only slowly did Ojo, milky eyes staring up blindly, force further words from his trembling lips.

He reached for his friend's hand.

'Uchy ... Uchy, are you there?'

'I'm here, Ojo ... I'm here.'

'Uchy ... it's not true that he's dead, I'm sure of it ... I've heard him in my dreams, Uchy ... I can hear him now.'

'Ojo, you mean ... Maius Eneo?'

'He's still with us, Uchy ...'

'I know ... I know ...'

'Oh, I envied him so much, but I was wrong ... wrong about him being dead ... Inorchis will return ... and he'll come home too ... he'll be Dynast, Uchy, he'll be a great man ... no, it's not over ... nothing's over ...'

'Of course ... of course ...'

'A great man, Uchy ... a great man, with all that means ... but remember ... just remember, I'm ...'

'Ojo ... Ojo?'

Ojo's words were lost in a long, rattling breath. For a moment it seemed that he had slipped away and Ucheus gripped his friend's hand tighter, as if he could will him not to go. Blank-faced, the tears spilling obliviously from under his eyelids, he whispered, 'It's not over ... Ojo, it can't be ...'

Now the hand returned his grip – tightly, so tightly.

'Remember,' the voice resumed, 'I was ... your friend.'

Then the hand went limp, and it was over.

With a low, terrible moan, Ucheus fell over the body of his friend. There was a silence. The sun etched the scene with a harsh, unshadowed clarity; Jem bowed his head, touching a hand to the crystal at his chest; Rajal, in awkward reverence, sank to his knees.

Oclar looked away. In his arms he still held Littler, but slowly he let the boy slip to the ground.

'Blue man,' Littler murmured, 'blue man, why?'

But just then there came a sharp barking and a bright, stripy form bounded amongst them.

Jem turned first. 'Rainbow?'

'Rainbow!' Littler cried.

And the little boy, rushing to embrace the beloved dog, was torn between the sorrow that still consumed him and a sudden, guilty joy.

Chapter 20

LEMONSILK TRAIN

'Cap'n? Cap'n?'

Patches was relieved when there was no reply – none, that is, but a snorting snore. The captain's head had sunk to the table; his mouth hung open, drivelling, revealing his few remaining, stumpy teeth. The lamp had gone out and morning light pressed at the casement, glittering and dancing. Stiffly, blank with tiredness, Patches juddered back his chair. Buby was still in his arms and slept soundly too, looking like a remarkably desiccated infant. Carefully the boy laid her on the captain's bunk. What a long evening it had been! The captain had been in fine form, too fine a form, and Patches had paid the price. Never had he endured so many pettings – so many pummellings, either. But did he mind? In the doorway, the boy looked back fondly on the drunken old sea-dog, still clutching his tankard loosely in curling, black-nailed fingers.

Making his way to the upper decks, Patches screwed up his eyes against the early morning sun. He breathed deeply, luxuriating in the freshness of the air. A breeze rippled through the sails; it was almost cool, for now at least. This would be the best time of the day, before the tropical heat rose to its usual fiery strength. He yawned, heading for the prow. On the decks around him there were few stirrings. A turbaned Qatani swabbed the decks – the boy winked at him; a Sosenican, dressed in a loincloth, plaited rope – Patches called to him merrily. Dirty foreigners these common tars might be – oh, he knew that well enough – but would they not smile at his many-patched costume, joke with him and laugh, and sometimes let him puff on their tobarilloes or Jarvel-pipes? No, Patches didn't much mind the common tars; it was the first mate Whale, the boatswain Walrus and the helmsman Porpoise that he didn't like. Not that he could tell the captain.

He sighed and hung over the prow, looking down at the chipped wooden lady who was the ship's figurehead – the lady called Catayane. Patches liked to come and look at her; sometimes he would even talk to her too, and pretend she talked back. She was kind, sweet. Good old Catty! Dear old Catty! But now Patches was troubled, thinking of the captain's outburst against ladies. If the cabin boy didn't know much about ladies, he knew that Miss Catty – the real one, that is – had been a fine lady indeed. How could she have been *bad luck*? And where did that leave this wooden lady, who looked so much like her? Indeed, Patches was troubled, but what really troubled him was the captain himself. Could there be something wrong with him? And what was all this talk about going to Hora – Hora, some boring old trading port, when they were supposed to be on their treasure hunt? Several times during the long night, growing incautious, Patches had asked why they couldn't just set out on their treasure hunt now, without delay; each time, inevitably, the captain had called him a fool and clouted him to the deck. Poor Patches! His head was aching!

The boy reached for a nice, comfortable coil of rope – comfortable, that is, for him – and was about to curl up in the ship's beak, the pointy part above the figurehead, when all at once came a tar's rough cry: *Land! Land ho!*

Patches scrambled up.

Hora? This might not be the place where they would find their treasure, but if they had to come here first, then didn't that mean their treasure was closer?

Perhaps, in a way, their adventure had begun.

Patches rushed below. 'Cap'n! Cap'n!'

'My lady, keep still—'

'Ra Ra, I'm sick of this—'

'Sick? Well, I like that! You'll have a lot more to be sick about soon if you don't look your best!'

Fuss fuss, fumble fumble went the nurse's fingers, pinning up the girl's train. Selinda's heart gave a painful thud. 'Do you think it matters?'

'A lady's appearance always matters. Always.'

'Even when she's going to be condemned to death?'

'Especially then,' Ra Fanana said automatically, then broke off, flustered. 'Oh, now look what you've gone and made me do – you and your silly talk!'

The pins down one side were all askew.

There was a testy silence. Nurse and young charge stood before the looking-glass in the slanting morning light. From the agora below came the sounds of the crowd and the sharp high tootings of thirty horns, proclaiming that the Gathering would soon be in session.

There was not much time. Ra Fanana removed the offending pins, sticking them in a row between her pursed lips. For a full shadowphase she had arranged the girl's finery, the carefully draped folds of the gown, the jewels, the bangles, the beads, not to mention the heaping-up of the

144

hair and the dreadful business of paint – oh, paint! Eyes, lips, cheeks – it was unending, and Ra Fanana was still not sure she had got it right.

She sighed and carefully adjusted the train. In the glass, the lemon-yellow fabric glowed, catching the sun in a soft dazzle.

Now, again: *pin, pin, pin.*

If Ra Fanana was irritable, it was hardly to be wondered at: this was a eunuch's work, not a nurse's. The nurse should have been merely an onlooker, prodding idly at her petit-point, sipping from time to time at a goblet of hava-nectar as Tagan's slender hands fluttered here and there and palace gossip burbled from his lips. Many a pleasant morning they had spent in such a way, when the girl had nowhere particular to go – now she faced a terrible ordeal, and where could Tagan be?

Pin, pin . . . Pin, pin?

Oh, *that* wasn't right!

If Ra Fanana had not been so annoyed, she might have been worried, very worried indeed. The last she had seen of the eunuch, he had been making a reluctant exit – he had glanced back, grimacing – behind the Triarch and the boy. What the Triarch wanted with the boy – this Maius Eneo, or whatever he called himself – was hard enough to fathom, though throwing him in the dungeons seemed a likely prospect. But Tagan? Seeing her friend disappear into the night, flanked by guards, had given Ra Fanana quite a turn.

Since then, nothing. Only the girl's tears, and her hysteria in the night – then a guard at dawn, bringing the message that the Thirty would be in session, and the girl must be in the gallery for all to see.

But what could it mean?

Pin, pin. Pin? Oh, curse this train!

Restless again in a different way, Selinda began to hum, though at first she had forgotten what it was she hummed. The melody, so it seemed, had stolen on her unawares; then, unbidden, the words came back.

> *. . . But he shan't hear the call*
> *From behind the stone wall—*

She turned. 'Ra Ra, what does it mean?'

'My lady, keep still—'

'This song – what does it *mean*, about the stone wall?'

Pin, pin – prick!

With a little cry, Ra Fanana snatched back her hand, fearful that blood might fall upon the train. Such exquisite lemonsilk! Why, it was of a quality so fine that the smallest stain would run and run through the delicate fibres, never to be expunged!

'Ra Ra? Ra Ra, what's wrong?'

'Nothing . . . nothing.' Sorrowing, the nurse sucked at her finger. Of course she should have scolded the child, but somehow she could not bring herself . . . It was all too much . . . The *stone wall*, indeed! As if they didn't have enough to worry them now! And only a day ago, hadn't they been living such a pleasant life?

Now, slowly: *pin, pin* . . .

What did it mean? Well, thought Selinda, no use asking Ra Ra. She gazed into the looking-glass. She looked ridiculous, but did she care? Her mind lurched and the sensation came to her that she was looking at a stranger. The paint, perhaps – Selinda had never liked paint, but Tagan applied it with a grace, a delicacy her nurse could not emulate . . . Still, Ra Ra said it must be plastered thick. What was to be done when a girl's cheeks were blotchy and there were dark rings under her eyes?

Pin. Nearly there. *Pin* . . .

The guard's summons, like a knell of doom, filled Selinda's mind. Was she to be denounced in front of the Thirty and all the assembled watchers? Was Maius Eneo to be condemned too? She could not believe it. But why, if he were not angry, had Father left so suddenly, so abruptly, after the fall of the Amali screen? And where had he taken poor Maius Eneo?

Selinda felt the tears filling her eyes again and blinked them back quickly. Ra Ra would be so angry if she made the paint run – again! But then, what was Ra Ra's anger against the thought of Father's?

Pin, pin. Pluck, pluck.

Still not right?

Selinda closed her eyes, steeling herself. Well, that was the intention: instead, she found herself thinking again of her strange and terrible interview with her father. Of the Amali screen, crashing down. Of Maius Eneo, his lips, his hands, his hair, his eyes . . .

> — *But oh, my love, can you be lost to me?*
> — *No, never lost, though far from you I go.*
> — *But hasten back! This absence is a blow.*
> — *I fear I must fly far across the sea.*
> — *What trial is this, when from the sea you came?*

What could this mean? But then there was only the thought of those hands, running over the slickness of her skin. Ecstasy burst again in Selinda's mind, like the Flying Zenzan over stormy seas; like the Mandru rising from its terrible maelstrom. Down, down she plummeted, as if into the all-enveloping darkness of the Triurge. How often had this passion possessed her in the night! How often had her fingers pushed beneath her nightdress, gouging between her tormented thighs!

> — *What trial divides us, till you share my name?*

146

— No words, no words, just give me love's bright glow!
— Ah, yes, I feel this hardness like a tree!
— Possess me with your love and set me free!
— Yes, deep within I shoot my loving flow!

Ra Fanana pursed her lips. *Pluck?* Just one more?

Oh, but the girl was shuddering, moaning!

'Leave it, leave it!' Selinda swished away and the silken train first billowed out behind her, then caught between the zigzags of the Amali screen – and ripped free.

Ra Fanana wailed. 'All my good work, spoilt – ruined!'

Selinda turned contemptuously. 'What do I care! What does it matter?'

Ra Fanana only wailed louder. No, Selinda didn't care, she really didn't! Like a moth beating at gauze she flung herself against the window-mesh, gazing despairingly at the scene below. How colourful was the crowd! The robes, the cowls, the mantillas, the plumes, the capes, the kerchiefs, the turbans, the togas. Already the sun had risen up, up, and flowed laving, lemon-yellow, over Outrealmers and Innermen and Neithers too, glistening on the hilts of cutlasses and swords. Flashing on the horns of the thirty clarion-callers, ranged in rows up the high steps of the Temple.

Beyond them, the great portals were opening, the crowds filing in.

Thud, thud!

Ra Fanana gasped.

The guards had come for them.

Chapter 21

CEREMONY OF THE SWORD

'My lady, keep still—'

'Ra Ra, I'm sick of this—'

'Shh! Remember, all eyes are upon you!'

'Don't be silly! They're watching the tier-stage.'

'Yes, but they're glancing up at you – whenever they can. Oh, if only you hadn't torn that beautiful lemonsilk!'

The whispers – there were many more – hissed back and forth in the Daughter Gallery, widest and most prestigious of the great galleries that curved through the upper reaches of the Temple of Thirty. With restless eyes, Selinda gazed down at the robes, the cowls, the mantillas and all the rest, packed together tightly now beneath the high, transparent dome. Crystalline shades of light streamed down, many-coloured, through stained-glass spirals; a treacly heat was rising in return.

Selinda plucked at her hot gown. Back and forth, back and forth, elaborate punkahs flapped to no avail. Guards swayed, swords held aloft, while on the tier-stage an old man droned on, his wizened head nodding as he spoke. Dressed in robes of heavy purple, he was the Law Speaker, chief Keeper of the Law, and it was his duty to recite all the laws that had been broken, and by whom, since the last Gathering. Whether detailing murders or tax-evasions, thefts in the agora or ransom-demands, his tone never changed, his posture never shifted, and his head kept nodding in the same clockwork way. This was how the Gatherings always began, and of course no one really listened, unless the crimes, or the punishments they had merited, were particularly spectacular. Today they were not. At least, not yet.

'Ra Ra, I can't stand it—'

'Wait, my lady, just wait—'

'To be condemned? Condemned, or—'

'Shh, I say! Shh!'

Selinda sighed; the old man droned. Behind him, ranged on the lowest tier, were his fellow Keepers; above, in rows of nine each, robed successively in green, red and blue, were the Underlords of the Thirty, surmounted on the fifth tier by their leaders, the Triarchs, in their golden robes and bejewelled, irremovable crowns.

Fahan. Azander. Jodrell.

148

A majestic staircase swept up towards them, cutting through the ranks of the lesser Lords. By this staircase – so steep, so high – petitioners of various sorts might approach their rulers. But how could they dare? Gazing upon her father now, Selinda could barely believe that the stern, forbidding Triarch was the same man who had come to her last night – the same dying man . . . From time to time, across the gulf that divided them, she would try to catch his eye. It was impossible – his face was like a mask. But Lord Glond, robed in blue, glanced at her sharply. And Prince Lepato, in red, flashed a golden smile.

Selinda turned away, confused, troubled.

'They say she still can't decide *which is which*,' came a voice from somewhere on the gallery. It was a girlish hiss, a whisper, insinuating itself between the throng of noble daughters, attendant mothers, nurses, eunuchs, guards.

'What do you mean,' came another, *'which is which?'*

'Which is her husband, silly!'

'Well, neither is – silly!'

'I mean *will* be.'

Selinda stiffened. Cautiously she peered around her, gazing over the ornately dressed girls.

She knew those voices, didn't she?

A giggle. 'They say she's driven her father mad – all her fussing, all her fretting. Still, what do you expect? She always was a stuck-up little horror. That's what comes of being too liberal, Mother says – spoilt her, he has. Letting her choose? Whoever heard the like? Besides, she's nowhere *near* as pretty as everyone says – let's face it, *no* man would want her if she weren't a Triarch's daughter!'

'Hm – I don't believe it.'

'Don't believe it? Look at that gown!'

'No, I mean *letting her choose* – he can't be, can he? No father would allow that – least of all a Triarch.'

'Hah! They say he's gone funny.'

'Funny?' A new giggle.

'Not ha-ha. Something to do with his wife.'

'The dead one – I mean, the *mad* one?'

'The fruitcake – that's right.'

Fruitcake! Beneath her paint, Selinda's face was burning. The source of the whispers was clear enough – Shia Milandros and Fazy Vina, huddled together, sniggering over their heartless bitcheries. Typical! Had they forgotten how well voices carried, up here in the gallery? Or perhaps they didn't care – but then, why should Selinda? What was a Milandros or a Vina to her? Her father *was* a Triarch, wasn't he – and theirs only

Underlords, and Green ones, too? For a moment – it was an old feeling – the girl felt a rush of superiority.

Then she thought of a Triarch's trials and was rather less sure. Her anger ebbed away and despair filled her instead.

'My lady! Eyes to the front!' said Ra Fanana.

The next phase of the Gathering had begun. First a Green Lord – today it was Fazy Vina's father, and a fat, ugly fellow he was too – would speak of some new law, some new measure, some *something* it was necessary to enact, or enforce, or do, or not do, and the Lords, in their wisdom, would debate the matter; the onlookers, though of course allowed no say – were not the Thirty their representatives? – might nonetheless sway things a little with their cheering or baying or stamping or hooting, or occasionally their fighting amongst themselves.

Thus things would proceed with a Red Lord, then a Blue one, introducing issues of ascending seriousness, before the Triarchs at last would enter the fray, then weigh and consider, weigh and consider, before pronouncing what was to be done. Bursts of music – trumpets, drums, chord harps – punctuated each phase of the proceedings.

'The commerce of the seas is the lifeblood of this island,' Fazy Vina's father was saying, his finger wagging importantly in the air, 'yet still the widening of the harbour is delayed! Is this not an outrage? Is this not a calumny? Let me present certain statistics . . .'

'Hang your statistics! What will this scheme cost? And who is to pay for it? Answer me that, now!' cried an old Blue Lord, springing to his feet.

'Our harbour,' burst out a Red one, 'is the widest in Wenaya!'

'Widest in the world!' shrilled a Green one, as if no more needed to be said.

If only . . .

Selinda slumped over the balcony, or did until Ra Fanana dug her in the ribs. How long would this last? It was Special Injunctions that the girl waited for now, heart thudding in trepidation. Even on an ordinary day, these were by far the best parts of the Gatherings. Each Triarch, his deliberations done, was permitted a command of his own that – so long as it fell within certain bounds – would be lawful *without debate*. Such a man, Triarch Fahan might say, was to be ennobled; such a man, Triarch Azander might say, was to be pardoned of his manifold, but not particularly serious, crimes.

And Triarch Jodrell? What might Triarch Jodrell say – today?

Selinda trembled. Oh, when would it be time?

'She's not her best today,' hissed Shia Milandros.

'Not her best? She looks a fright! Did you see her *paint*?'

'Her *pancake*, you mean! And where's her train?'

'Pity her husband, if she doesn't buck up her ideas!'

'I'd pity him anyway.' Fazy Vina smacked her lips.

Selinda twisted hers. Down below, Fazy Vina's fat, ugly father – he had had his way with the statistics – droned on and on. And on. And on ... The men, it seemed, found it fascinating; Selinda, for her part, began to think how much Fazy Vina's father resembled Fazy Vina – or the other way round. She really must tell Fazy. Yes, she *must*.

She would have contrived to edge her way along the gallery, just a little, so as to deliver this intelligence – but could not quite manage it. First Ra Fanana's hand restrained her, then came a jostling from the other side. Someone – politely, no doubt, but firmly – was pushing through the crowd.

At once Selinda forgot about Fazy Vina. 'Tagan!'

Smiling, the eunuch took his place beside her.

'And what,' urged Ra Fanana, 'happened to *you*?'

'Where,' burst out Selinda, 'is Maius Eneo?'

'My lady, shh!' – Ra Fanana and Tagan, together.

Then Tagan: 'I always come, don't I, Fa Fa? Just a little *late* today, that's all.'

The eunuch wore a clean toga, his face was freshly painted and his eyes outlined anew in darkest kohl. But Ra Fanana saw that he was tired, desperately tired.

'You've been up all night, haven't you?'

'Well, yes. Things ... things to get ready.'

Selinda gripped his arm. 'Tagan, please.'

'Let's just say my skills were needed – as I see they were *elsewhere*,' he added, glancing, appalled, at the girl's paint. 'Really, Fa Fa, I don't know what you thought you were doing,' he hissed. 'Getting an *old slapper* ready for a sailor's tavern, perhaps?'

'That's your job, not mine—'

'Taverns, Fa Fa? *Me?*'

'Paint, Tagan!'

'So I see.'

Selinda urged, 'But Tagan—'

'Shh!' There were shushings all round. A Red Lord had stood, and much excitement filled the Daughter Gallery. This was not occasioned by anything this particular Underlord might say – it was, in fact, to be a disquisition on the export trade – but rather by his considerable charms. Was there ever a man so fine? There was a certain amount of swooning, much fluttering of fans, and envious eyes flashed at Selinda, which was ironic – Selinda, for her part, being the only girl who displayed no interest at all in the dashing Prince Lepato ... For what was Prince Lepato after the charms of Maius Eneo?

'She's hard, she is,' whispered Shia Milandros.

'Doesn't deserve him,' hissed Fazy Vina.

'Hasn't *got* him yet, of course.'

'Hope she never – *then* she'll be sorry.'

A snort. 'She'll just have the other one, then.'

'The Outrealmer?' A snort again. 'A mere robber-baron's son, from the far-off fiefdom of Ambora Rock? My dear, I hardly think *he's* a catch!'

'What do you mean? He may come from Ambora Rock, but look at him now! Besides, my sister thinks he's the biggest dish – and do you know ... so do I?'

'Fazy, he's an Outrealmer – trouble!'

'Oh, I've never believed that ...'

'No? Well, watch and see.'

For, as it happened, the red-garbed Lepato had now been replaced by the blue-garbed Glond. Suddenly the temperature in the hot temple was higher, as Glond launched into a savage denunciation of Horan policy towards Outrealmers. In the last moonlife, he claimed, Outrealmers had been savagely attacked, a warehouse had been burned and a cargo ship capsized as it approached the docks. And *what*, he demanded, had the Keepers of the Law done to prevent these outrages?

Selinda rolled her eyes. As if anyone cared! 'Tagan—'

'Patience, dearie. Just a little patience. There's a big surprise on its way for you, and *not* what you think!'

'Surprise? Tagan, what—'

'Shh!' – from all around.

But angry voices were stirring below; Glond's soared above them like a clarion-horn. There was only one way, he declared, to ensure justice. The Horan guard – Innermen to a man – must at once begin recruiting Outrealmers to their ranks.

'Hear, hear!' cried a Blue Lord.

'Preposterous!' cried a Red.

But there was more than this. The Gathering must resolve that Outrealmers, Outrealmers alone should be eligible for election, until the time came that their representation was proportionate to their numbers on the island.

A Green Lord sprang up. 'Traitor!'

'Dearie me,' said Tagan, 'that's torn it!'

It had. By now the hall was in an uproar, with skirmishes breaking out amongst the men below. Fists flew, swords clashed, while Shia Milandros squealed with delight, and Fazy Vina just squealed piercingly.

Shaken, Selinda huddled close to Ra Fanana. For some moments the great chamber was in chaos, before the guards descended, imposing a sullen silence.

There was a pause. Punkahs flapped.

'But he *is* dishy, isn't he?' whispered Shia Milandros.

Fazy Vina nodded fulsomely.

It was time for the weighing, time for the considering. Looming down from the highest tier, first it was Triarch Fahan who came forward, glinting with gold and jewels, to deliver his judgement on the matter of the harbour. As it happened, he was all for it – the widening. The Triarchs nodded sagely behind him. And his Special Dispensation? Further noble titles for Fazy Vina's father, what else?

'An afternoon in a steambath might be more use,' muttered Tagan. 'Or rather, a whole moonlife.'

Selinda flashed him a grateful look.

'But Tagan,' she urged, 'tell me what you know!'

The kohl-eyes glittered. 'Patience, it seems, is not one of our virtues! Worry not, dearie. I said a marvellous surprise was on its way, didn't I? Any moment now.' He smirked. 'And *I* did the costume, all last night – the paint, too.'

'Tagan? What are you talking about?'

Triarch Azander had risen now, and was deliberating at length on the matter concerning the export trade. What it all meant, what it was about, Selinda neither knew nor cared. All she could think of was Father. How could he sit there so calmly? The girl's gaze roved wildly over the packed hall below, where everything – robes, cowls, mantillas, all the rest – looked damp and limp and dead. Sweat beaded her brow; her paint, she was certain, was beginning to run – *had* run . . .

Oh shut up, Azander, shut up, shut up!

'Tagan?' Selinda gripped the eunuch's arm. Yes, she decided, she was prepared to dig. With her nails. And deep. She pressed threateningly into the hollow of his elbow. 'Sweet Tagan – Tagey-wagey – *won't* you tell me what you know?'

Selinda dug; the eunuch shook her free and rolled his eyes. 'Dearie, I've had worse done to me. And upped me no end, you know – my *value*, I mean. Tripled? Quadrupled – which all goes to show that less is more . . . *As* I was saying,' he added, with a gesture at the girl's paint.

'Ta-*gan!*' Selinda grabbed his arm again.

Tagan slapped her hand away. 'Pert little minx, hm?'

The girl pouted. 'Oh, Tagey-wagey, tell me – *please* tell me what you know!'

There were black looks, shushings.

Sighing, the eunuch leaned close to her ear.

'Tagan, don't forget *me!*' Ra Fanana huddled in too.

'Let's just say,' Tagan whispered, 'that quite a lot has come clear. The mighty one wanted to be sure, of course – had a few questions to ask – but really, I think he made up his mind at once – at *once*, I ask you, after all this time!'

'Tagan,' said Ra Fanana, 'you don't mean—?'

'Indeedy-deed! Oh, I've heard all about our little friend, Fa Fa. Would you believe, he's an Islander of Aroc?'

'From Aroc? But Tagan,' said the nurse, 'so are you!'

The eunuch nodded. 'Truth to tell, I thought there was something *familiar* about the fellow. Of course, my dear old father always lived a secluded life, but I'd heard about Castor Eneo and his marvellous son . . . Anyway, it turns out old Castor-sugar's *well* known to Triarch Jodrell, would you believe? One of the few Arocans to venture beyond their shaky little isles, as it happens – in his younger days. Quite the explorer, old Castor-sugar was – and *like father, like son*, it would seem . . .'

'Castor-sugar? Shaky?' said Selinda, bewildered. 'Tagan, what *are* you talking about?'

'I warn you, dearie, expect convulsions – in more ways than one . . . *Well*' – the eunuch smacked his lips – 'what I'm saying is, it seems little Maius – or big Maius, as I may *authoritatively* say, after my duties in the dressing-chamber – has not only been anointed by the Dynast as Dynast-Elect, having passed his Manhood Trial with flying colours – they're *big* on manhood on the Twinned Isles, make no mistake, my dears – but, as a badge of his new status, they've sent him here on a *trade mission*. Opening up to the world, they are – the Islanders of Aroc, I mean. Well, hardly before time . . . Anyway, it *seems* our little friend's ship was attacked on the way over – someone thought he was an Outrealmer, I suppose – and he was left to drown . . . Lucky to make it here alive, he was . . . Lucky, in fact, it wasn't *slavers* that got him, if you ask me—'

'Poor, dear Maius Eneo!' sighed Selinda. 'But Tagan—'

'Tagan,' said Ra Fanana, '*exactly* what are you—'

By now, her nails were poised to dig too.

Tagan burbled on; on and on, tormentingly, heat poured down through the stained-glass dome – and on and on, too, went Triarch Azander. Now the great man was making his Special Dispensation, something about tax – rope-tax or lanyard-tax or hawser-tax or something . . . Something *that dull*.

There was scattered applause.

'But quality,' Tagan was saying, 'definitely quality. As well as *width*.' Grinning, he nudged his young mistress in the ribs. 'Now there's a combination and a half for you, you lucky little minx—'

Selinda was trembling. Could Tagan mean, could he really be saying what she thought he was saying? Her fingers dropped from his arm and her furrowed face was pleading, desperate. Kohl-eyes crinkled. The eunuch had to smile. The girl was impossible, wasn't she? But it was impossible, too, to be angry with her – for him, at least.

He said simply, 'Dearie, you'll marry your Maius Eneo. Right now, down in the harbour, they're fitting out a ship to take you back to the Twinned Isles, and the luxurious Palace of the Dynasts—'

'I don't believe it! Oh, Tagan! Oh—'

'Believe it, dearie! It's *true*—'

Selinda squealed. She clapped her hands. She jumped up and down. 'Tagan, what about *us*?' said Ra Fanana.

'That's the best bit, Fa Fa – we're going too!'

And the nurse and the eunuch squealed in turn.

'*Shh!*' Angry shushings came from all around. '*Shh!*'

Triarch Azander had trailed off at last and now, in the place of judgement, stood Triarch Jodrell. From on high, godly in gold, the great man appeared still more impassive, still more formidable, but now Selinda's fear had gone. Her eyes misted and all she could feel was a desperate love. To think she had questioned a father's judgement! To think she had doubted a father's love!

His crown shimmered in the many-coloured heat. Oh, but was he trembling? Was he swaying? Selinda's tears flowed and she gripped Ra Fanana's hand, Tagan's too. Poor Father! At once, in the wildness of her heart, Selinda resolved that he must come with her, come with all of them, when they set sail for their new home. Free at last from the burdens of state, far from the scenes of old tragedy, might not his terrible sickness abate? How lovingly she would nurse him! How tenderly she would hold the nectar to his lips . . .

Excited, Selinda would have blurted out her plan, but alarm filled the faces of her companions. She looked below. There was jostling, shouts. Once again, violence was looming and only the guards, swords at the ready, restrained the tumultuous feelings of the crowd.

Father raised his hands and silence fell.

A strained, resentful silence.

'The issue of Innermen versus Outrealmers,' he said, his voice flapping wearily like the punkahs in the heat, 'is the gravest one that faces this Isle of Hora, and one that much troubles my Brother-Kings and me. Lord Glond's case – the case for the Outrealmers – is one that he states with formidable and admirable eloquence. Yet the noble Lord, I am afraid, is more than a little mischievous, for this, as he knows, is not a matter that can be determined at a stroke. He speaks of fairness. He speaks of equality. But if, in pursuit of these aims, we throw aside our very constitution, what have we achieved? Already we have made it permissible for Outrealmers to be elected officers of state, as Lord Glond's presence on this tier-stage shows. It is well known to us, too, that the noble Lord now aspires to an office yet higher.'

Glond shifted awkwardly.

'Yet would he have that office without a fair and free election? Are we to betray the wisdom of our forefathers and risk again the tyranny they fought so hard to banish? Ours is a system of isocracy, and must be seen to be such. If Outrealmers command the support they claim, their power will display a natural increase with each new election. And if this increase is a dilatory one, is not that a just and fitting thing, giving us time to adapt and grow?'

If there were some – on the tier-stage, and in the great chamber too – who might have agreed, there were many, it was clear, who thought differently. As the Triarch spoke, murmurings had broken out below and guards moved decisively to avert a skirmish.

Glond looked murderous; Lepato looked wry.

Punkahs flapped, flapped; the Triarch, raising his hands again, staggered a little. Selinda gasped, but there was nothing to fear. Swiftly but reverently, a slave ascended the stairs, bearing a golden goblet. On the tier beneath the Triarch, he turned, tasted from the goblet, wiped its rim with a silken cloth and held it aloft for his master.

The Triarch drank liberally.

'Oh, very stylish,' Tagan said enviously, eyeing the retreating slave. 'Now why couldn't I do that?'

'After last night? You'd probably trip over,' said Ra Fanana.

'Well, really!'

'*Shh!*' – from Selinda, this time.

'No,' the Triarch was saying, 'there is to be no sudden decision on matters of state so momentous, so grave. And yet, if I may turn to my Special Dispensation' – Selinda's heart lurched – 'there is a matter on which I may pronounce, a matter not unconnected with these. For long moonlives, speculation has been rife about my daughter's wedding. How, some ask, could a fond father leave a girl-child so dangerously unbetrothed?'

Murmurs again, noddings.

'And yet, may I not ask in return, are not the dangers of betrothal equally great? What am I to do, if in selecting her suitor I should be seen to favour one or other of the factions that divide this isle? How could this not be folly in a Triarch, when we see today, even in this great and historic chamber, even in this cradle of Hora's isocracy, how strong the passions run?'

The Triarch signalled for nectar; the slave appeared again.

Glond looked murderous; so did Lepato.

'My Dispensation,' said the Triarch, 'is this: that neither Lord Glond nor Prince Lepato, fine and noble though each may be, shall be the man to whom I give my daughter. Each shall be compensated, as the law decrees, for the failure of his suit. But there is another who shall take Selinda's hand, and in taking her, shall take her from this isle!'

The crowd could be restrained no longer.

'Shame!'

'Robbery!'

'This cannot be!'

'Who is this stranger?'

'Foul, foul! There has been no *suit*!'

'The Keepers of the Law – have they seen this man?'

Glond was on his feet, Lepato too. 'Compensation?' cried one. 'Failure?' cried the other.

Then, together: 'The girl is mine!'

'Guards!' – the Law Speaker.

Guards again; again Selinda's father raised his hands, waited, and punkahs flapped, flapped.

Again, the nectar: and the Triarch's voice trembled.

'Who, you say – how? My people, the man who would have my daughter waits at this moment beneath this stage. Would you question the legitimacy of his suit? Already, in this night that has passed, I have called to me the Keepers of the Law, and all has been done as protocol would have it. There is no doubt that he may marry my daughter.'

'None indeed,' Tagan said archly. 'I was there.'

'*Shh!*' – Selinda.

'Now,' declared the Triarch, 'as custom dictates, my daughter's new suitor shall come before us, bearing with him the Sceptre of Entreaty. In law, he makes a request, no more, that his suit may be ratified before this Gathering. But let me declare, to end all doubt, that my mind, so long divided, is at last made up – my daughter's marriage shall take place forthwith.'

Lepato shuddered, shook with rage. Glond glowered; but guards were at the ready.

'Oh, Tagan! Ra Ra!' – hugs, tears.

Spite: 'That little bitch!' – Shia Milandros.

'She was always a show-off,' spat Fazy Vina.

'Still, we haven't seen the suitor yet! Let's hope—?'

Some hope. With a last flourish, Triarch Jodrell announced Maius

157

Eneo, Dynast-Elect of the Isles of Aroc. There were trumpets, harps, drums. A trapdoor opened and rising, turning, showing himself to the crowd, was a magnificent youth in a silvery loincloth, his hair striped in a rainbow pattern, his chest draped in jewels, his flesh elaborately painted in bright coils and curlicues. Held before him, jutting up at – oh, forty-five degrees or so from the level of the loincloth, was the massive, weighty ceremonial sword.

Selinda swooned; so did Ra Fanana.

So did Shia Milandros and Fazy Vina.

'My masterpiece!' said Tagan proudly. 'See the angle of the sword? That was mine – my suggestion, I mean. Didn't do *that* for Glond and Lepato now, did I? Well, Lepato in particular – lucky escape there, dearie, take it from an old hand . . .'

But the women were not listening.

Awe-struck, the crowd lapsed into silence as the youth slowly ascended the stairs. Soft drums thudded, soft strings plucked, and Selinda's father held out his arms. Up, up went Maius Eneo; up, up, soared Selinda's spirits like joyous fireworks exploding in her mind. Love enfolded her like an element of its own and she forgot the tragedies that had been, the tragedies that might come, and the bitter hatreds and rivalries that seethed all around her in this great, broiling chamber.

There was only Maius Eneo, sweet Maius Eneo.

    — *Now, let me, with my tongue, explore this fold.*
    — *Ah yes, I feel you slithering inside!*
    — *Already do you feel the mounting tide?*
    — *I do! Can bliss yet more this garden hold?*
    — *A woman's secrets fill my heart with awe!*

    — *Ah, let me writhe and cry out! More, yes, more!*
    — *Yes, more and more! For such is woman's pride!*
    — *Such treasures! More than silver, more than gold!*
    — *Such beauty! Yes! Such vision you behold!*
    — *Yet, spent, I almost feel that I have died.*

Selinda doubled over, moaning.

Then it happened.

One step, just one step more, and Maius Eneo, in time-honoured fashion, would have held the sword to Selinda's father's breast; Selinda's father would have touched the blade to his fingers, bringing the tip to his mouth to kiss. Such, on Hora, is the challenge of a girl's suitor to her father. What can it be, symbolically, but the ceremonial slaying of the old by the young, remnant of a barbarism darker even than the tyrannies the islanders remember with dread?

Countless times this ceremony had been enacted, and all had gone as it should. So what happened this time? Whether it was that Maius Eneo tripped, just a little, on that stair before the last stair, and the Triarch, lurching forward, sought to save him; whether it was that the Triarch, befuddled with hava-nectar and swaying in the heat, lost his footing as he leaned down to the sword; whether it was a matter to be ascribed to malevolence – that someone distracted one, or both, who could say?

In any case, the result was the same: in the moment when he would have touched the sword, Triarch Jodrell fell forward, impaling himself on the glittering blade!

'Father! No!' Selinda screamed.

Maius Eneo staggered back, astonished.

Bloodily, the body thumped down the stairs.

Later, some would speak of a sudden collapse. Some would speak of suicide. Some would speak of poison on the tip of the sword. Some would swear they had seen the young stranger viciously lunge, thrust.

But in any case, again, the result was the same:

'Treachery!' cried Glond.

'Murder!' cried Lepato.

'Guards!' cried the Law Speaker. 'Seize the boy!'

Chapter 22

THE BURIAL OF THE DEAD

'Dormant? I don't think so.'

'Damped down a bit, that's all?'

'Not dormant – that much is certain.'

Black against the bright day, the cloud curled away towards the horizon.

'Still, what does it matter?'

'Hm? What's that, Raj?'

'We've got the sea.'

It was irony, of course. Dubiously Rajal looked across the bay. The calm, he was certain, was deceptive. Or rather, calm or not, it hardly mattered. Who would cross that watery expanse in nothing but a flimsy coracle? It was madness; from the moment Ucheus had told them of the coracle, Rajal had been convinced of that much. But what else were they to do? Again he felt the trembling beneath his feet and glimpsed the dark scudding of another cloud, twisting forth from the Thunderer's summit.

'What a choice! Water or fire!'

'Hardly,' said Jem. 'Water or nothing.'

'*Now* I appreciate the carpet – I preferred air!'

Jem did too. But he gestured to Oclar. In the shallows of the bay, their mysterious new friend loomed above the coracle. From his hands, passing back and forth over the little vessel, came flashes of blue; soft chanting wafted from his lips and slowly the coracle began to spin. 'At least there'll be some magic to help us on our way.'

'You think so? I'll bet he's just showing off.'

'Oh, Raj!'

They sat on the sands, Jem cross-legged with his back hunched, Rajal aslant, leaning on a splayed hand. Further down the beach Littler played with Rainbow, tossing a stick and clapping and laughing each time the brightly coloured dog retrieved it.

Such high spirits, thought Jem, were hardly fitting when Ojo had been buried but a short time before. Should he tell Littler to be quiet? But no, the little boy meant no harm. Besides, if he did not indulge this joy, he might give way to sorrow.

Curiously, Rajal eyed the frisking Rainbow. He thought of the barking they had heard in the cave, indeed all through their strange captivity.

160

Where had Rainbow been? Had the barking been real? To Rajal it had been a ghostly sound, echoing not on the air but in the senses. His brow furrowed and he looked at the collar round Rainbow's neck. Already their adventure in Unang Lia seemed far off, but Rajal recalled vividly the day when he had first seen this mysterious band. It had been at Princess Bela Dona's Ritual of Rebonding. What had been the words of the silver suitor, as he came forth with his gift? *Princess, I offer you the last of the Lichano bands, retrieved from the furthest reaches of Amalia. For epicycles, tomb-robbers have sought these mystic arcs, that once graced the foreheads of the Lichano priestesses, massively increasing the powers of their minds . . .* And what had the Princess said, much later, when she gave the gift to Rainbow? *Already it has given voice to a girl who was dumb; what powers it will grant Rainbow I do not know, but soon enough, I dare say, you shall see . . .* The power to bark in people's minds hardly seemed like much, Rajal thought. Still, the Lichano band, useless though it might be, was the last of Princess Bela Dona's gifts they still possessed.

'Ojo!' The cry came suddenly. 'Ojo, come back!'

Rajal swivelled round. Behind them, his back turned to them, Ucheus gazed up to the Thunderer's clouded peak. It was rather as if he thought his friend might still be there, living, lingering, instead of lying under the rich volcanic earth. When they had buried Ojo, Ucheus had kept his eyes hard; now it seemed that the emotion banked inside him must burst forth, just as they were ready to leave this Isle of Xaro. A second cry escaped him and he slumped down in the sand; his shoulders shook and his hands covered his face.

'Uchy?' It was Rajal who went to him. Tentatively he touched the slender youth's arm. Did he expect a sudden, repelling shock? 'Uchy, it's all right,' he added, though what was all right he could not begin to imagine. If Ucheus had pushed him contemptuously away, Rajal could hardly have been surprised. Helplessly, shaking his head, he turned back to his companions.

Jem looked alarmed. Rainbow cocked his head. In the shallows, the blue light still shone from Oclar's hands and the coracle spun faster.

'Uchy?' Rajal said again.

'Sorry . . . I'm sorry,' Ucheus sniffed, wiping his wrist across his nose and eyes. 'I can't believe it, that's all . . . can't believe he's gone. All of us here . . . now only me. I thought at least there'd be . . . at least me and Ojo . . .'

'Isn't there Maius Eneo too?' said Rajal.

At once, he wondered if he should have been silent.

Ucheus gulped. How could he speak of what he really felt? How could he speak of the guilt that gnawed inside him? He had not really cared about Ojo, not since he had met Maius Eneo – and now it appeared he

161

had been punished for his neglect. Yet even now, thought Ucheus with a pang, should his marvellous cousin appear on this beach, he would run to him joyously, with no thought for stocky old, stolid old Ojo. There could be no doubt about it. But what was it Ojo had said at the end?

Remember . . . remember, I was your friend . . .

Fresh sobs burst from the slender youth's eyes.

Rajal stole an arm round the shaking shoulders. With a surge of sorrow he thought of his own losses, of Myla, of the Great Mother . . . then of Aron, a different kind of loss. He breathed deeply, aware with sudden alarm of his own pressing tears. He gulped, 'Just remember, he said it's not over . . . nothing's over yet, Uchy.'

'Nothing?' The reply was sharp. 'I threw dirt on his cold face, didn't I?'

And shrugging Rajal away, Ucheus scrambled up. Perhaps he would have run off along the beach, but all he did was stumble and fall back down. Out in the shallows, there was a flash of blue light, brighter than before, and Oclar turned back to his young friends, beckoning them forward.

'It's time. Come on, Uchy.' And Rajal, with a strained smile, extended his hand.

Back at the caldera, an observer might have wondered whether that morning's scene had ever happened. Had the Thunderer been appeased? It seemed not. Again violent tremblings shook the rocky earth; again, beneath the dark, billowing smoke, the lava-lake was alive with sinister bubblings, ripplings. Excitably – or so one might have fancied – shards of rock cracked and rained down, like little anticipatory sallies of doom; hissings and gurglings and subterranean rumblings threatened at any moment to gather themselves into a sudden, irresistible momentum. Yes, to an observer, had one been there, the events of that morning might never have happened, never happened at all. But then, just what would the observer have seen? Tearful, almost blinded, could anyone have guessed that something more than smoke, more than lava, more than the violence of the earth was stirring here?

The burial of the dead does not always last for long.

'You're sure it's safe, Oclar?'

The blue man only smiled.

Diffidently, Jem clambered into the coracle. How small it was, how flimsy! With the provisions they had piled into the bottom – apples, mangoes, coconuts, salt-fish and salt-pig, precious spring-water in a stoppered amphora – the sides of the vessel dipped low in the water; but then, thought Jem, without this ballast the little boat might have blown away ... Awkwardly he hunched up his knees, searching for a comfortable way to sit. His knuckles brushed the rough, moist interior of the hull and doubt overspread his face.

Skins? Vines? Bark?

'Say, where *is* Hora, anyway?' said Rajal.

The coracle bobbed as he clambered aboard.

Ucheus, sloshing in the shallows, waved vaguely, sadly towards the horizon. 'That way, I think. On Inorchis, we weren't supposed to know.'

'I hope Maius Eneo had a reasonable idea,' said Rajal. 'But how *far* is it?'

Jem said, 'Three days, according to Oclar.'

Rajal groaned. 'Three days, in this little thing? If we're not on the bottom of the sea by then, we'll be stark, staring—'

Rainbow shook out his wet fur, spraying Rajal copiously.

'Hey!' Rajal protested, and Jem had to laugh.

He stopped himself abruptly as Ucheus climbed aboard. By now, the vessel had sunk still lower in the water and Jem's doubts grew.

Vines? Bark? Skins?

They could only hope that Oclar knew what he was doing. But perhaps he did, for when the blue man appeared in the coracle too – and it was, indeed, as if he had just appeared, standing massively in the centre of their little, cramped party – they no longer seemed to sink and the blue glow flickered again about the mast and the bows. 'Worry not, my young friends – or at least, not yet. The future stretches before you. Do you not remember the words of the dead boy? It is not over – not yet over.'

Worriedly, Rajal looked away from Ucheus.

Oclar's gills dilated; slippery lids dipped over the yellow eyes. The words he said now would long resonate in Jem's mind – in all their minds – even if, at first, they could not quite believe them. 'Did I not say we had reached the time of destiny? But that is not a time when things come to pass which simply were ordained, and must always have been so; rather, it is a time when the future hangs in the balance and must be decided this way or that.'

The blue man spread his arms wide, and slowly, then faster, the coracle began to move. Soon, whether through magic or sudden fortune, the sail ballooned with wind and they were on their way.

Bark? Skins? Vines?

'Goodbye, Xaro,' Ucheus murmured. 'Goodbye, Ojo . . .'

Jem looked troubled; Rainbow barked; Littler whooped, bouncing up and down until Rajal admonished him. Then they were all were silent, solemn too, gazing first back at the mysterious island, then ahead, across the vast sunny fields of ultramarine. Only Ucheus kept turning back, letting his eyes linger on the place they were leaving. Again he thought of the rich volcanic dirt, falling from his fingers on to Ojo's face.

Littler fluffed Rainbow's fur. More than once since their reunion he had leaned close to the strange dog, whispering his questions, *Rainbow, where were you? Rainbow, what happened?* Silly, perhaps; but slowly, visions formed in Littler's mind – a pit; a tunnel; honeycombs in the ground. Had Rainbow been trapped, struggling to escape? But how had his barking sounded around the island?

The dog's silver collar flashed brightly in the light.

Rajal shifted uncertainly. On impulse, he looked down at the amulet on his wrist – but no, only at the place where the amulet had been. Not for the first time, he felt a bereavement, and wished he could have his talisman back. Hah! But he was a fool, wasn't he? What luck had it brought him?

Like Rajal, Jem thought of the talisman he had lost. How could he do without the harlequin's coin? The loss was dire, for now it felt to Jem that he was severed from Cata, and the love that linked them through all that fate could bring. Softly, almost furtively, he reached for the crystal under his tunic – at least he still had *that*. Oclar was right. Destiny: he must think of destiny. But then Jem saw again the corpse's fingers – Toth's fingers – reaching for the crystal, and despair flooded in. They had defeated Toth, hadn't they? But barely: only just. Without doubt the anti-god would appear again soon in a new, more terrible manifestation. Jem gripped the crystal hard. It dug into his hand, which began to hurt. In a moment the flesh would break, bringing forth blood.

But it was then, with a start, that Jem became aware that Oclar was singing softly, beneath the swell of the wind and tide. Jem strained to hear, then was astonished, for the song was the one he had heard in a dream. His hand fell from the crystal and for a moment he could do no more than listen, trembling and wondering:

> . . . *Seeker of the Orokon, key to the stone,*
> *Where lies the key to your quest, to your throne?*
> *Scattered over islands by the winds that fly,*
> *Whipping in a blue storm, wild in the sky.*
> > *Key, but in truth, there is one key alone:*
> > *Follow the magic to the magic stone!*

Did the others hear it? Jem reached up, touching Oclar's arm, and whispered hoarsely as the blue man turned, 'You never really said who you are—'

'Did I not say I was Prince of Tides?'

'But . . . are you a god?'

It was a question the blue man did not stay to answer. All at once he laughed, twirled, then leapt from the coracle with a mighty splash, vanishing in an instant beneath the waves. Littler wailed, anguished; the others cried out and Rainbow barked as water cascaded over them. For a moment the coracle listed and they thought they would capsize; then the blue light flashed round the mast again, like a candle that had guttered then resumed its burning. Already Xaro was far away, and the waves had grown higher; the sound of the wind was louder in their ears.

'I don't understand,' sniffed Littler. 'I thought he was coming with us.'

Jem gripped the tiller. 'We're on our own now, Littler.'

'Hm.' Rajal looked down.

No, the burial of the dead does not always last for long.

Back to the caldera, one last time. Look into the pit, look down deep – deeper, deeper through the curtaining fumes. Oh, of course our vision is obscured – the heat is overwhelming, the smoke, too. But wait: can you see something flashing in the depths – something silver, something gold? Or, just perhaps, something made of glass?

Look again – down through the reeking darkness. Can it be true? Can something be stirring?

Rising from the bubbling lava comes a fist.

Then there is a face, with a single, glowing eye.

END OF PART ONE

PART TWO

Terror of the Triurge

Chapter 23

A GAME OF CHESS

To call it a tavern would not be quite right – indeed, not at all, especially since amongst this evening's patrons are nautical gentlemen of the type known variously as corsairs, buccaneers, privateers or pirates. 'Tavern' – so crude an appellation – suggests, in conjunction with such fellows, an establishment louche and rowdy, hard by the salty, suppurating docks, where the sawdust floor is sticky with ale, where the darkness is foul as the blackened mouths, and wenches plastered thick with paint ply their poxy trade.

This place – you may find it, though it is somewhat concealed, on the Isle of Hora – is different. Here no raucous squeezebox splits the air; there is no lusty bellowing; no stripy-shirted tars, tankards in hand, threaten at any moment to burst into violence, with oaths and lunges and flying fists. Here, the patrons dress beyond extravagance in robes and togas of the finest fabrics; the air is perfumed with sandalwood and civet; the music is a dulcet tinkling, a cool glissando, issuing not from drunken patrons but from a trio of immaculate young men on a dais, plucking and pressing at instruments an Ejlander might think of – but they are not quite the same – as a harp, a gittern, and a clavichord. (Why, is that not a trio by Schuvart, or the early Handyn, transcribed for these unaccustomed players? Such elegance, so far from an Agondon drawing room!)

As for the women, they are discreet hostesses; wraith-like, demure, they weave their way beneath the muted lights, bearing no coarse benisons of ale – let alone rum – but the richest wines, cocktails and liqueurs. How lightly flutter the veils across their faces! How softly glitter the jewels in their hair! Ah, and how gently the laughter ripples round the tables ... Merriment, it seems, can only be urbane in such an establishment, a gentlemen's club so exclusive that only the most *exclusive* gentlemen know that it exists.

See, here they are, the great and the powerful: are those not two members of the Thirty, reclining languidly against the plush upholstery, studying the chessboard on the table between them? Is that not Hora's richest trader, twirling that tumbler in his plump hand? That old gentleman, grey-bearded, inspecting certain etchings – could he be the Chief Keeper of the Law? It seems likely ... But wait. Were we not promised a privateer, a pirate? A buccaneer, a corsair? What, are these wicked fellows here in disguise, ready at any moment to burst forth, cutlasses flashing?

Not this time. Come, look more carefully through the velvety light. See those curtains, lavishly ornate, draped all round the walls? Behind them – see, one is pulled back just a little – are booths, plushly padded, where gentlemen seeking a *particular* privacy might withdraw from observing eyes. What might we see, could we look behind these curtains? A hostess, perhaps, her posture less demure? A pillar of society, his demeanour less urbane? Even a Triarch in his telltale crown, indulging in vices shocking in one who stands, on this isle, in place of the gods?

All this and more. But let us consider two particular booths: one to the left of the little orchestra; the other, to the right.

LEFT

Not through the club, but through a plush-lined door in the back of the booth, come CAPTAIN PORLO, *the monkey* BUBY, *and the cabin boy* PATCHES, *shown to their places by a veiled hostess.* PORLO *is awkward as he lays down his crutch, adjusting his wooden leg beneath the table; suspiciously* BUBY *sniffs the perfumed air;* PATCHES *looks round wide-eyed, his gaze lingering on the girl as, with swift, smooth motions, she sets down wine in ornate beakers, one for* PORLO, *one for* PATCHES, *one – no, not for* BUBY, *but (evidently) for a third party, yet to appear.*

Hovering, the girl would appear to be waiting for a gratuity; PATCHES, *misunderstanding, ogles her instead.* PORLO *cuffs the boy's head; the girl, casting up her eyes, swishes out through the curtain into the club.*

PATCHES (*rubbing his head*): Eh, what's that for, Cap'n?

PORLO: Didn't I tell you about them cobber-as, boy?

PATCHES: I knows all about them cobber-as, I does. What's that got to do with clipping a poor boy round the earhole, I asks you?

PORLO (*bristling*): Lust, boy! Don't you remember why I falls in that there cobber-a pit? Looking at the lassies when I shouldn't, that's why! So let that be a lesson to you – better a few less brains in your head than to be without a *leg*, eh? (*The captain quaffs, then spits out the wine.*) Bah! Foreign muck! Haven't they got any good *rum* in this place? – Girl ... girl! Now where's that lassie gone?

170

BUBY, *leaping on to the tabletop, laps eagerly at the spat-out wine;*
PATCHES *peers curiously through the curtains.*

PATCHES: It's all right, Cap'n, I sees her ... Girl! Hey, girly!
(*Turning back:*) Coo, this be a swish sort of place, eh? And
we was broke, you said! Don't tell me, someone's died and
left you a fortune? What, and you didn't even tell me?
PORLO (*impatient*): What in Toth's name you be talking about,
boy?

A hand – but not the girl's – pushes back through the curtains, and
PATCHES, *albeit accidentally, is cuffed round the ear a second time.
Resentfully, then with astonishment, the boy looks on –* BUBY *hisses,
muzzle red with wine – as a blue-garbed figure with long braided hair
exclaims, then holds out his arms to the captain.* PORLO *struggles to
stand again; the two men embrace.*

PORLO: Me little Glondy! Can it be me little Glondy?
GLOND: Oh, Captain ... my Captain!

RIGHT

*The booth is one of particular luxury, fit for a Triarch, perhaps, or a
foreign ruler of equal (or greater) stature: lusher fabrics, plumper
cushions, and the table, a low slab in the Unang style, is furnished
already, not with beakers of brimming wine but with a hookah, hava-
nectar, and plate after plate of glittering sweetmeats.*

*With the incense that curls from ornate braziers, with the soft glow
of the lamps, with the strangely transcribed Schuvart – or is it, could
it be, early Handyn? – creeping though the curtains, how could
happiness not reside in such a scene? But all is not well. Awkwardly,
two figures occupy the booth; but a third, it is clear, is expected, and
has yet to arrive.*

*Sighing heavily, muttering sometimes, the first of the figures paces
before the drawn curtains, then round the table, then back and forth
by the plush-lined door. It is a fellow we have seen before: red-robed,
with long curly hair, teeth capped in gold, hoop-like earrings, and a
beard plaited into a tight, pendulous cylinder, it is, of course,* PRINCE
LEPATO.

*But who is this with him, skulking by the door, snivelling a little,
wringing his hands? Dressed in the raiment of a common servant or
slave, the unfamiliar figure – one of surpassing ugliness – is a dwarf,*

171

crook-backed, with a nut-brown wrinkled face and blackened stumps of teeth that he exposes, a little too often, in an unctuous grin.

His name? His role? Ah, but that should be clear to us soon enough.

LEPATO: Come, Scurvy, is this not intolerable? Can you not *see* that this is intolerable? Has your master no thought for my status?

SCURVY (*his voice a feline hiss*): Noble Prince, that is why he sent me. Already I have delivered his apologies, have I not?

LEPATO: Apologies I can scarcely credit. Can it be that so ruthless a corsair, like a timid novice in a house of contemplation, keeps to such rigorous times of prayer?

SCURVY: It is true, it is true! Would my master's career be so illustrious, did he not give thanks to his god? Five times a day, let the day bring what it may, always he will bow his obeisance at Catacombs, Green, Dust, and Wave. And this one: Stars. (See, I know them well, these times!)

LEPATO (*bridling*): Scurvy, do you think me wholly ignorant? Is not your master of the Tribes of Ouabin?

SCURVY: Indeed, noble Prince.

LEPATO: Yet those are the prayer-times of the Unangs![1] If your master is a Ouabin (though a strange one, to be sure, to roam not the desert sands but the seas), must hatred not consume him at the mere thought of the Unang-kind, of all their works and ways?

SCURVY: Noble Prince, I know nothing of Unangs – or indeed of the Ouabin, other than my master. I say only that he is a man of faith – you do not imagine he would lie to you?

LEPATO (*archly*): Dear Scurvy! You know my respect for your master is unbounded! – But hold, he comes!

SCURVY, *with a little yelp, scurries back from the plush door; it opens; there is a murmur, as of a lord dismissing slaves, or perhaps, instructing his guards to wait. With a flourish of black robes – a disguise, evidently – the dwarf's master enters. So tall a figure! So imposing!*

LEPATO *bows deeply, but not, perhaps, deeply enough: haughty eyes flashing beneath a dark cowl, the Ouabin – if Ouabin he be – takes a sharp stride forward and strikes him, hard, across the face.*

---

[1] Cf. *Sultan of the Moon and Stars*, Ch. 7, for more on the religious customs of Unang Lia.

PORLO: I declares, Glondy, I can hardly believe it! Who'd have thought me little scamp from Ambora Rock could grow into such a great man? See, Patches, there's hope for you yet ... But Glondy, can it be true what they says, that soon you'll be in charge of this whole island?

GLOND *laughs*: Not quite *in charge*, old friend! (But your wine, drink your wine!) Let's just say that, come the election, I'm in with a chance.

PORLO (*who does not drink his wine*): In with a chance! Aye, I likes that! As if me little Glondy wouldn't get anything once he'd set his mind to it! Such a scamp he was, Patches, back on the *Catty*, after we saved him from that raider fellow—

PATCHES *is silent; slumping glumly, the cabin boy tries to prevent the agitated* BUBY *from leaping out through the curtain into the club. Ingeniously, he has wrapped her tail round his wrist;* BUBY *stares at him with slitted eyes.*

PORLO (*rushing on*): Why, Glondy, remember the time I locked up all me hard tack, so you wouldn't get your piggy little snout in 'em? Eating us out of house and home he was, Patches, and then what does he do? Picks me lock, that's what, and before I knows it he's up in the crows' nest, having himself a fine old beanfeast!

PORLO *and* GLOND *collapse in laughter.*

PATCHES (*aside, to* BUBY): I guess you had to be there.

PORLO: But what's with this hole-in-corner meeting, eh Glondy? Don't you remember, dry land always sets me stump an-aching? Why, aches something shocking, it does! Come, wouldn't you'd like to dine with me on the *Catty* instead? Salt-pig and mustard, just like the old days? Hard tack too, of course, all you can stuff down your piggy snout?

GLOND: Old friend, what more could I want?

PATCHES (*aside, to* BUBY): To be one of them Tri-Kings, for a start!

GLOND: Alas, but for my need of circumspection—

PORLO: Eh? Well, I don't knows about your foreign customs, but it warms me old heart to see you again, Glondy, it does! – He'd have made a fine cabin boy, eh Patches, if I'd never took him back to Ambora Rock. – Didn't want to go, did you, Glondy? Ah, but where would you be by now?

PATCHES (*to* BUBY): Keel-hauled, I hope.

GLOND's *eyes twinkle*: Captain of my own ship? Admiral of my own fleet? Think, old friend, of the veritable navy that might by now have been ours to command, had you but allowed me to stay by your side! Think how we might have circumnavigated—

PORLO: What's that, Glondy?

GLOND: I mean, old friend, we might have sailed the five seas, a brotherhood of buccaneers at our command such as the world has never seen! Should we not have been invincible? (But drink, drink your wine!) Why, I think a certain corsair would have scuttled his own wicked galleys, before my dear Porlo ever had need to engage him again! Such a fleet—

PORLO (*laughing*): Come, Glondy, you was no rapscallion like young Patches here – foreigner you may be, but a quality-lad you was, with a heritage and a home—

GLOND (*slyly*): Indeed, old friend, your thoughts were all for my father, hm, and the reward he'd offered you to take me back?

PORLO: Reward? Glondy, you know I thought only of your own good—

GLOND: Of course you did, old friend, of course you did! – Your wine, your wine. (*To* PATCHES:) Told you all about it, has he, boy? Why, how could he not? Now there was an adventure for a young fellow, eh? Captured from our castle on Ambora Rock I was—

PORLO: Kidnapped, you was—

GLOND: Ransomed, I was—

PORLO: Snatched in broad daylight—

GLOND: Manhandled—

PORLO: Manacled—

GLOND: By the Sea Ouabin!

A pause is necessary, it would seem, upon the utterance of this infamous name. PORLO *and* GLOND *appear suitably awed;* BUBY *endeavours to beat her tail, which is difficult, as* PATCHES *still has it looped around his wrist. The monkey decides she will bite his hand instead, but getting her little jaws in place is not going to be easy ...*

PATCHES (*eventually*): Sea what?

PORLO (*impatient*): What, boy, were you dozing off when I told you about the Sea Ouabin? Catching forty winks? Or perhaps you were paying court to *Goody Palmer and her five daughters*, all furtive-like, under me table? Don't you remember the most notorious corsair in these here tropic waters? Now there's a scurvy fellow and make no mistake. You'd better listen to your Cap'n, lad, and listen hard, or you'll go to the bad like that there Sea Ouabin too!

PATCHES *cleans out an ear with a finger, a little ostentatiously*: Oh aye, the Sea Ouabin! Oh aye, Cap'n ... Eh! Buby, stop that!

GLOND: D'you know, boy, your captain's the only fellow ever to have vanquished that wicked chap? Pitched battle it was, and I the prize ... why, they say that to this day, every time the Sea Ouabin bows to his heathen gods, he tells them to curse the name of Porlo ... But old friend, really! You haven't touched your wine!

PATCHES: He spat some out.

GLOND: Hm? Ah, what a fool I am! It's fiery rum an old tar wants, eh, old friend? (*And pushing back the curtain, he signals discreetly to a hostess.*)

PATCHES (*aside, to* PORLO): Cap'n, I don't like it.

PORLO (*aside, to* PATCHES): What, boy? Don't like what?

PATCHES (*aside*): Him. He's a shifty character, mark my words!

PORLO (*aside*): Fool of a boy, what you be talking about? Don't you know it's Glondy here who's saved the *Catty*?

GLOND (*turning back*): An unorthodox order, but one our lovely hostess can fulfil, I'm sure ... What's that, old friend, did I hear you murmur again the name of *Catayane*? The great lady is, I trust, somewhat recovered from her recent debilities?

PORLO: Recovered? Never been better! Why, Glondy, them fellows you sent, old Faris Porlo's never seen the like! Banging away all last night they were—

PATCHES (*with a yawn*): I'll say—

PORLO: Caulking they were, every crack in me timbers, a-hammering and a-heaving, a-patching and a-painting, till me dear old girl's right fit for a Queen! And here's me thinking foreigners were all shiftless idle beggars – present company excepted, of course, me lovely. And did I see them barrels, barrel after barrel they was, a-rolling down to the hold? Did I ever! – Glondy, Glondy, how can I thank you?

GLOND: Old friend! What is all this but my way of thanking *you*? Have I not longed for this chance, all these orbits since my days in your charge? To think, if it hadn't been for you ... but here's the rum. A toast, eh boy, a toast to your captain?

175

PATCHES (*aside*): Smarmy foreigner!

BUBY *tries again to bite the boy's hand.*

PORLO (*gulping rum*): Ah, and that new bedding! No fleas in
that lot, eh, Patches? Not yet, anyways ... I declares, I
never seen the like! Them curtains ... them plates ... them
chamber-pots – why, they wouldn't shame even a fine
lady's arsehole ... But come, Glondy, you must dine on the
Catty, at the very least! Let your old friend do something to
thank *you*, eh?

GLOND: Alas, I am circumscribed—

PORLO: Aye, so you said. Bloody heathens ... but Glondy, it's
your stomach I'm talking about. Just a little dinner, hm?
Salt-pig and mustard? Hard tack? Rum? In me cabin? Like
the old days?

GLOND *looks down, smiling, shaking his head*: Alas, impossible—

PORLO: But Glondy, after all you've done ... isn't there *one* little
thing old Faris Porlo could do for you?

PATCHES (*to* BUBY): Oh no!

GLOND (*looking up*): Well, old friend, there might be *one* thing.

PORLO (*innocently*): And what might that be, me lovely?

RIGHT

SEA OUABIN: So, Red Prince, this establishment is yours?

LEPATO (*swallowing*): Its ownership, Sea Ouabin, is not
commonly known, but ... yes, it is mine. A fine
establishment, is it not?

SEA OUABIN (*indifferent, it seems, to the lavishly laid table, he peers
through the curtains*): This squalid little bordello? Do not seek
to impress me, Red Prince: I ask only, is this house *secure*?

LEPATO: But of course: what prying eyes attend us here, in this
illicit and secret sanctum?

SEA OUABIN: Red Prince, I have no need to doubt you?

LEPATO: Never, I swear! Sea Ouabin, think of me what you will,
but believe me, all is in place ... and shall be as we
planned.

SEA OUABIN (*sharply*): All, Red Prince? So, your bribes have
been successful?

LEPATO (*gaining confidence*): Bribes? – Let us say that I am sure
of one thing: that Lord Glond will never raise the votes he

needs. What is this election but the merest formality? I tell you, Sea Ouabin, the Triarchy is mine!

SEA OUABIN: Ah, Red Prince, what I should give, to see them screw that crown through your head!

LEPATO: But Sea Ouabin, you may! Did I not say this noble house is mine? Know then that within the pitching roof is a viewing platform, cunningly contrived, where you may observe what passes in the agora, certain that none may observe you in their turn. Will you not watch my triumph from there? You and your good Scurvy too?

SEA OUABIN (*aside*): See, Scurvy, how he ingratiates himself? See the splendours that attend upon power – the power of a corsair who has *never been defeated*?

LEPATO (*oblivious*): Ah my friends, what glory lies before us—

SEA OUABIN (*flaring out*): Hold, Red Prince! You have mortgaged your destiny to me, yet would call me friend? Am I not rather your lord and master?

LEPATO *quails*: Indeed, Sea Ouabin, oh indeed! (*Then, wheedling:*) But you know my debts shall soon enough be paid. Might we not consider our relations – in the longer term, of course, in the longer term – rather those of . . . *partners*?

SEA OUABIN: So the Prince grows bold! And what can it be that turns his head? The thought that soon he shall wear the Triarch's crown?

LEPATO: Not bold, Sea Ouabin. Shall we say – cautious?

SEA OUABIN: Red Prince, you are cryptic. Would you not say he was *cryptic*, Scurvy?

LEPATO: Cryptic, if I refer to certain – disappearances?

SEA OUABIN (*bridling*): What mean you, my *mortgagor*?

LEPATO: Only, Sea Ouabin, that these disappearances have . . . have raised much talk amongst the common people.

SEA OUABIN: And what care I for the common people? Indeed, Red Prince, what care *you*?

LEPATO (*quickly*): Nothing, Sea Ouabin! But care I, must I not, for the security of . . . *our* kingdom? After all, talk spreads, hm? Should connections be made . . . should suspicion fall . . . Sea Ouabin, I am not Triarch yet.

SEA OUABIN: What, dissembler? Did not you say your victory was certain?

LEPATO: Of course! But these disappearances – these kidnappings . . .

SEA OUABIN: Kidnappings? Fool, do you know what it takes to

177

keep a fleet like mine afloat? Do you know the rate at
which my slaves die? Must I not keep my galleys stocked?

LEPATO: Of course, of course! But Sea Ouabin, think of the
slaves – the hundreds, the thousands – who shall fall to
your lot when my Triarchy begins!

SEA OUABIN: You mean, when you pay your ... *mortgage*?

LEPATO: That's it, exactly! Sea Ouabin, can your men not
restrain their ardour, just a little ... just a *little* longer?

SEA OUABIN (*flatly*): Do you question me, Red Prince?

LEPATO (*frightened*): S-Sea Ouabin?

LEFT

PORLO (*intent*): What's that, Glondy? A precious cargo?

GLOND: To me, old friend, more precious than all the treasures
of the world.

PATCHES: Then isn't it *one* of them – of the world's treasures?

GLOND: The new lad is sharp. But let us not bother with the
nature of this cargo. Old friend, of you I ask no more than
this: but bear this treasure to Ambora Rock, to that castle
that once was my father's, and now is the base of my
Outrealm power ... The task is not too hard, hm? (*He
smiles.*) After all, you know the way.

PATCHES (*aside, to* PORLO): Cap'n, I don't trust him.

PORLO, *however, glugs back his rum, burps, wipes his mouth and
grins*: Dear Glondy, after all you've done ... how can an
old sea-dog say no?

PATCHES (*bursting out*): But Cap'n, our quest! You said we had
to sail for the Straits of Javander, before the season got any
more—

PORLO: Hush, boy, what you be speaking of? Stupid lad!

He cuffs the boy's head, hard this time – but misses, striking BUBY
instead. With a shriek, the monkey breaks free from PATCHES, *leaps
up to the curtains, then swings backwards, making the curtains billow.*

When they billow back, BUBY *is gone and* PATCHES *is off after the
monkey.*

But what's this? PORLO, *glugging at his rum again, has eyes only
for* GLOND; *and* GLOND *is quite uninterested in a mangy monkey.*

GLOND (*slyly*): Old friend, so you plan a long voyage? No, look
not alarmed: do I enquire after the plans of a buccaneer?

178

Let me say but one thing: Javander's straits are far from here, and the seas strange and perilous. For such a voyage, a captain needs a sound ship, but does he not also need *gold* to pay his crew and procure his many supplies? Treasure we need, if we are to *find* treasure, hm?

PORLO *shifts uncomfortably*: Treasure? No, it's you be talking about treasure, Glondy!

GLOND *grins*: Of course, old friend, of course. But listen: already I have provided the sound ship. Accomplish but this task I set (so simple a task, is it not?), and when my galleon reaches Ambora Rock (be assured, I follow as soon as I can, once I have discharged my political cares), then, old friend, when we meet again, into your hands I shall place a purse of – (*he pauses, considering*) – shall we say, twenty thousand Hora-ducats?

PORLO's *eyes widen. This is a fortune!* Twenty thousand? Oh Glondy, Glondy, what a friend you be!

Centre

Almost at the end now? So it would seem: if the players betray no eagerness, no vulgar hastening to the final chord, still it seems certain that this little trio of – the middle Handyn's, is it not? But no, Schuvart's – will soon be over. And then? Some other, similar divertimento, *then another, then another, for the night has barely begun ... But as if this were an image of eternity, all in this urbane place is as it was before. A hand hovers above the chessboard, considering the next move in the game. Laughter – but softly – ripples round a table. An old, bearded gentleman puts aside an etching (*erotica *they call it, not pornography) and takes up another.*

But wait. The old gentleman's brow is furrowed; all at once, the furrows grow deeper. What's this? What can it be? So far, he is the only one to register the disturbance: but in so exclusive an establishment as this, if one patron is perturbed, is that not enough to constitute an alarm?

A ragged urchin – his garb, it would appear, made entirely of patches – skulks between tables, keeping low, peering alternately between the legs of the patrons, then up towards the heights of the lush curtains. And what is this he is whispering? The words – but the old gentleman may not hear correctly – would appear to be 'Psst! Buby!'

SEA OUABIN: But come, Red Prince, be not perturbed by my menacing ways. You know but fragments of my long history, but if you knew all, you would know that betrayal – bitter, painful betrayal – has shaped the course of my life. Am I to be betrayed again? Am I to be defeated? Never! So you see, Red Prince, I must be sure of your loyalty, must I not? – Must I not, Scurvy?

SCURVY: Yes indeed, Master – indeed, indeed!

SEA OUABIN: But Red Prince, this I know: should you be true, your reward shall know no bounds! What is the Triarchy, but the first step in our plan? With my backing, shall you not rid yourself of your fellow Triarchs? Shall you not be *absolute ruler*?

LEPATO: Sea Ouabin, Sea Ouabin, but say it shall be so!

Gibbering with emotion, the treacherous LEPATO *sinks to the floor, clutching, tugging at his companion's dark robes. But what's this? That sound . . . could it be another gibbering, close by?*

In an instant, all this happens: turning sharply, the SEA OUABIN *sees* BUBY *hanging from the curtain; he reaches into his robes, whipping forth a dagger; his robes, torn at by the traitor, pull away, revealing the desert garb beneath. How suddenly, how whitely it flares in the lamplight!*

A commotion of the curtain. SCURVY *scuttles excitedly. There is a gasp, and a stranger, a boy dressed in motley – can it be motley? – bursts in: 'Buby, there you are! Buby, you naughty girl!'*

The dwarf grabs for the boy; the boy grabs for the monkey, then staggers back, gulps. His eyes goggle at the sight of the SEA OUABIN.

SCURVY *seizes the boy. The dagger glitters.*

Out in the club, the trio ends. Handyn, late Handyn – it has to be.

Chapter 24

DAZED AND CONFUSED

'The sea.'

Pause. 'The sea, the sea.'

Pause again. 'The sea, the sea, the sea.'

Again. 'The sea, the sea, the sea, the—'

'Oh, shut up!'

Pause. 'Well, sorry.'

Grunt. 'You get on my goat, you do.'

Pause. 'What goat?'

Grunt again. 'You're on it.'

The next pause lasted longer. Gulls, here and there, wheeled lazily through the rising morning light and waves crashed monotonously on the rocks below. Scrawny Sentry Menos screwed up his eyes, looking out glumly from the shadowy hollow where he stood side by side with his grunting companion; the companion, big-bellied Sentry Blard, scratched himself, spat, then took off his heavy helmet and unbuckled his sword.

'Should you do that?' said Menos.

'Do what?' said Blard.

'Make yourself comfortable.'

'How long are we *here* for, Menos?'

It was a fair point. This cavern in the cliff-face, at the end of one of the rocky arcs that enfolded a certain cove, was the furthest of many sentry-posts surrounding the Triarch's estate. It was also the dullest. If only it had looked *into* the secret cove, instead of away from it . . . Well, Menos supposed, it hardly could, the cove being secret: but he would have liked that, wouldn't he? Blard, too: Blard, especially. Sand. Bejewelled pebbles. A girl, bathing – hm, yes . . . This way there was nothing – unless you counted the occasional slave-galley, far out to sea, plying the Unang-Wenaya route.

'Still,' Menos sighed, 'at least we're safe. No Outrealmers, no Innermen – no bloody frays.'

'Bloody what?'

'Frays – like, fights.'

'Hm . . . no.' Blard, being – unlike Menos – a big bruiser of a fellow, might not have minded *that*. But at least, he admitted, there was no Chief

181

Adek to bother them here. If there was one fellow in this world Blard hated, it was Chief Adek.

Menos was just frightened of him. 'You're *sure* he never comes this way?'

Blard gestured behind them. The corridor, stretching back through rock, was narrow, smelly and dank – dark, too, but for the pools of light that spilt at long intervals through tiny vents bored into the low ceiling.

The fat sentry grimaced. 'Did he *ever* come down there?'

Few did. In truth – sentry-funding being what it was – this particular station often went unguarded. What of it? The sea was deep; the coast was all just cliffs and rocks, rocks and cliffs, for league upon league. No ship – no swimmer, probably – could penetrate the gap between open sea and cove. Of course not: but the guard had been doubled since Triarch Jodrell's murder and no station, not the least, was to be neglected. All the sentries were on double shifts, and cursing the vicious murderer at every chance they got.

When they weren't cursing Chief Adek, that is.

'He's getting worse, they say,' Menos ventured.

'Let him,' scoffed Blard, 'he won't come here.'

And the fat sentry, as if to show his confidence, grinned and produced from beneath his breastplate a short-stemmed clay pipe and a small, flattish pouch.

'Blard!' Menos was shocked. 'Not on duty!'

'From the Jarvel Coast – the finest,' Blard grinned again, opening the pouch to reveal a weedy substance – green, pungent, and festooned with spores that would crackle deliciously when the substance burnt. Indeed it was the finest – a pleasure indeed for fellows used to hard, impacted grass-clippings. Some might wonder how a sentry's pay could stretch to such delights – but after all there are innumerable ways in which an enterprising fellow might increase his earnings. And what was Blard, if not an enterprising fellow?

Fat fingers stuffed the pipe.

'Blard, please—'

'Come, Menos,' said Blard, misunderstanding, 'what do you think I am? You'll have *your* hit, don't worry.' A grin again. 'Even though you get on my goat.'

'Hm? Rainbow?'

Flap-flap, flap-flap.

The nose was hot, its nuzzlings weak.

Rajal flopped out a languid hand, patting the dry, brittle fur. A rough tongue licked at his fingers, or tried to lick. Poor Rainbow! Rajal smiled

182

weakly, struggling to open his eyes. It should have been easy. From the reddish churnings that played at his awareness he knew the sun had risen at last. Another day ... But how many more? His eyelids were gummy; he would have moistened a finger and rubbed, but didn't even have enough spit in his mouth.

Flap-flap, flap-flap.

Now where was that amphora?

Rajal pulled his eyelids apart and for a moment – it was all he could do – lay gazing up the sky, a cerulean pallor beyond the flapping sail. There were birds, wheeling high ... a few clouds, just a few – white wisps ... But then, the last thing they wanted was a *storm* ... Gentle rain, that would be nice – wisps, just wisps ... *Huh*. Rajal felt the familiar, heaving ache in his stomach, churning in time to the rhythm of the sea. Vagas, they called his people – vagabonds. *Huh*. So, they were supposed to be good at travel? *Huh*. Land travel, yes, now that was different – a nice trundling van ... But when did you ever hear of a Sea Vaga? Rajal groaned. The magic carpet had been bad enough. This coracle was a thousand times worse.

He rolled his head, ready to retch.

But where *was* the amphora?

The others were sleeping. Beside him, pressed against his thigh, Rajal felt the huddled, hot form of Littler; Ucheus, who should have been keeping watch, drowsed over the bows; Jem lolled back, his tunic open and the Crystal of Theron hanging heavily from his burned, reddened neck. Poor Jem! Pale skin was not always an advantage. All the same, with his haystack hair bleached almost white, Rajal's friend looked just a little like a fallen god – a shabby one, at any rate ... With a pang, Rajal recalled the days when he had loved Jem, or thought he did. Well, he still did now, but in a different way – Jem, and Cata too. If only they could find each other again! Was that asking much?

Right now, it seemed so. Much too much.

Meanwhile, Ucheus was deep in a dream.

UCHEUS'S DREAM

But is this really a dream, or a vision? Again and again since his beloved cousin left, the slender youth has fallen into these trance-like states, when it seems that Maius Eneo is calling him, calling him, reaching invisible hands to him from far across the sea. Is he not leading them towards him now? What strange powers must Maius Eneo possess? Did he always possess them, or has he acquired them somehow, in the course of his voyage? Ah, but has not Ucheus always known that his cousin is magical?

Marvelling, he will think of that night on Dead Man's Lookout, long ago on Inorchis, when he had left his cousin sleeping and climbed in secret, yet found Maius Eneo already there before him, waiting for him, reaching down for him from that precarious ledge. Now the memory makes Ucheus shudder, for he imagines Maius Eneo in the glimmering moonlight and it is as if he is seeing his cousin in death, as if Maius Eneo has died somewhere on these heaving, implacable seas. More than once when they were still on Xaro, did not Ucheus set out for Dead Man's Lookout – the Dead Man's Lookout that must, he assumed, exist on Xaro too? With what wild hope, with what wild fear, had he thought he might find Maius Eneo there, waiting for him as he had waited before? But the thought was foolish; besides, the Dead Man's Lookout on Xaro was obscured by deep jungle growth. No, Maius Eneo is alive: of this Ucheus is certain.

And now, again, from a haze of swirling blue, he sees the figure forming. Deliciously he anticipates it becoming clear: the handsome, high-cheekboned face, the dark eyes, the dazzling smile, the long-fingered, reaching hands. Then shall come the splendid voice, rumbling in his brain with its eager, urgent command of Nearsider, come! Nearsider, quick! *Oh, how he longs to obey that command! Oh, how he longs for the moment of reunion!*

But wait! What's this? Can it be that the dream has changed? Who is this new figure, forming in the place of his beloved cousin? Can it be . . . a girl? Can it be a girl with long, dark hair, dressed in a flowing lemonsilk train? Ucheus sees at once that she presents a regal figure. But more than this, more: is she not as beautiful as Maius Eneo is handsome? And can it be that in her softer, caressing voice, she utters his cousin's familiar words? Nearsider, come! Nearsider, quick! *Ah yes, all this can be. But who, Ucheus wonders, can this strange girl be?*

His heart hammers hard and he wakes, astonished.

'Uchy?' croaked Rajal. 'Uchy, are you all right?'

There was no reply. Ucheus lay across the bows, spent and moaning. Rajal looked at him wonderingly. He would have reached out, shaking their new friend's shoulder, but he could hardly summon the strength. He knew only that he must find that amphora. Poor Rainbow looked as if he could use a drink too.

It was then that Rajal felt a dampness near his feet and wondered if the amphora had cracked. Now *that* was all they needed . . . But no, this was worse – a leak in the hull, just a trickle, but insisting its way steadily through the skins and vines, leaves and sap. All they needed, indeed. Patching time again!

But first, the amphora. There it was.

Rajal was filling Rainbow's bowl, a little too generously, when the bright dog began to bark, frisking up against the ragged bows.

In an instant, Littler was awake. 'Land!' he cried.

Jem, startled: 'Land? Call that land?'

Ucheus, blurting: 'Cliffs, I call it!'

Rajal: 'Rocks! And we're heading straight for them!'

'The sky.'

Giggle. 'The sky, the sky.'

Giggle again. 'The sky, the sky, the sky.'

Again. 'The sky, the sky, the sky, the—'

'Oh, shut up!'

The sky was swirling. Still giggling, Menos struggled upright, leaning against the rocky cavern mouth. Then his giggles subsided and he only breathed deeply, not without difficulty. Was he feeling sick? He wasn't sure. No doubt about it, this stuff – the real stuff, from the Jarvel Coast – did funny things to a fellow. It was almost too much for him. Blankly, dazzled, he stared again at the sky and the clouds, churning unreally, somewhere far away from him.

And the gulls . . . And the rocks . . . And the waves, crashing . . . And the sunlight that spilled across the cavern floor as he lay back again carefully, carefully. Blard had taken off his breastplate now and his fellow-sentry found himself staring, fascinated, at the rise and fall of the belly beneath the tunic.

'Lard?' said Menos. 'I mean . . . Blard?'

Blard gave a grunt, but a gentle grunt. 'Hm?'

'Adek . . . Adek better not come this way *now*. Hm?'

'Adek?' grinned Blard. 'Who's Adek?'

'You'll remember . . . if he comes.'

And Blard only grinned again, waving the pipe in his companion's direction; Menos was about to wave it away, then took it after all. How the spores crackled! The smell alone was splendid! Menos expelled the smoke slowly, watching wistfully as the sea breeze snatched it, dispersing it on the air. Fondly thinking he might follow the ghostly smoke, looping and curling away with it through the sky, Menos almost started forward. He could fly, he could fly!

'Menos, hey!' Blard laughed, snatching back his fellow-sentry from the brink.

Or perhaps he was just snatching the Jarvel-pipe.

Menos grinned, 'Lard . . . Blard? You know this Jarvel?'

'Finest,' slurred Blard, 'from the Jarvel Coast—'

'I know . . . but where's it *from*?'

Pause. 'Jarvel Coast. Didn't I tell you?'

'Hm. But where . . . where did *you* get it, Blard?'

Grunt. 'Docks, of course.'

'I know. But Lard ... how did you *pay* for it?' A shudder passed through Menos. 'You didn't ... you didn't get anything from that dishcloth-headed fellow?'

The scrawny sentry was referring to a certain foreign corsair – ah, but we have met him – who had taken some of the sentries into his employ, paying for information about this and that, that and this, that might be going on in Hora. Menos was more than a little dubious about the arrangement, and by no means keen to get mixed up with so dangerous a fellow. What risks they ran! It would be the dungeons for them, or worse, if Adek found out!

He said as much, his voice cracking.

'Calm down, Menos! No, I think old dishcloth-head might be useful later – we'll keep him stringing along, never you mind – but I'm afraid he's yet to come up trumps. No, this is something else.' Blard was squatting on his haunches now, knocking the burned weed from the pipe. Looking up, he grinned again, his belly rolling, lava-like, over the belt of his toga. 'Remember that girl? That girl I took you to see?'

Menos flushed. 'Girl? Not the one you—'

'No, Menos, no – the one ... *on the beach.*'

Had Menos not been befuddled with Jarvel, he still would have taken some moments to realise what Blard meant. As it was, Blard had to curve his hand lasciviously in the air, then gesture in the direction of the hidden cove, before Menos had an inkling.

He drew in his breath.

'Blard! Not Triarch Jodrell's daughter?'

'Nice girl, that – or *was*,' Blard grinned, then began humming to himself, as if there were no more to be said.

Menos found his mind suddenly focused. If the Jarvel was strong, so was his urge to unravel this little mystery.

It had been a moonlife ago or more, last time they were on duty here, that Blard had led him back down the tunnel to a certain low door, cut in the rock. Blard explained that the door was an emergency defence-route, in the event that an invader were to make his way to the beach. With a finger to his lips, he led Menos into glaring daylight and onto the bright sands of the beach. There, from behind the artfully placed rocks, the sentries had watched in lustful wonderment as Triarch Jodrell's daughter, clad only in filmy silk, bathed in the placid waters ... Afterwards, Menos had wondered fearfully what would have happened if Adek had come.

But now he wondered about something else.

He struggled against the Jarvel. 'The ... pebbles?'

Blard grinned. 'Got it, friend.'

Menos was staggered. How could Blard run such risks? As they spied on the bathing girl, he had noticed – idly, at the time – that Blard's attention drifted to the bejewelled pebbles decorating the beach. When they were leaving, Blard had made Menos go first, saying he would check, just check, that they had left behind no tell-tale signs . . .

Menos wailed, 'You filled your pockets, didn't you? Oh Lard, what if they find out?'

'What's to find out? Those pebbles are *long* gone.'

'On a ship, are they? What about customs inspectors? Lard, if they trace this back to us . . .' Menos moaned. 'You think it was worth it, for a bit of silly green *weed*?'

'Worth it? Don't you?' Defiantly, Blard rose to his feet. 'So worth it, in fact, I'm going to get more – pebbles, I mean. Come on, let's go back to our secret door.'

Menos gripped Blard's arm. 'Lard . . . Blard, you can't!'

'Menos, come off it – Adek's not coming, no one can see us. And I don't think that *girl*'s on the beach today, hm?'

'How do you know? *Why* isn't she?'

Blard rolled his eyes. 'Dead, that's why.'

'Dead . . . what? She can't be!'

'Well, she will be soon! Don't you know anything about what's been going on, you dozy fool? At any rate, the girl's not there – take my word for it. Come on, I'm filling my pockets again – and you'll fill yours, if you've got any sense.'

With that, Blard lurched off down the tunnel.

Menos followed, dazed and confused.

Boulders, stage left.

Boulders, stage right.

Downstage, steps from the palace gardens.

And upstage is Tagan, hunched in the sand. His sharp elbow jabs into his kneecap and his cheek rests in his willowy, curled fingers. Tears, more than once, have welled this morning in the eunuch's eyes; each time he brushes them away, a little more irritably. Blinking, he looks out over the calm of the cove. The soft hiss of waves . . . the sparkling sun . . . how they belie the turmoil in his heart!

In the sand, abandoned on the day that Maius Eneo came, is the picnic basket; there are plates and a blanket, a robe of Selinda's, and her little polished box harp too. Tagan sighs. He has come, at last, to clear away these things, but has not even begun. Disconsolately he inspects the flies and ants that crawl over the remnants of cold meats and crumble-cake and round the sticky lip of a hava-pitcher.

187

Empty – a pity.

He bundles the plates and blanket into the basket, then reaches for the box harp. Its nights outdoors have done it little good. Already the delicate veneers are peeling; have the tiny pegs inside fared any better? Hm ... but under the lid, the strings are still taut. Tagan plucks experimentally. Filling the stillness with a gentle discord, he thinks of the times he has heard his lady play.

Poor Lady Selinda! What will become of her?

For now, the girl is imprisoned in her apartments, under heavy guard. But this – if Ra Fanana is right – is just the prelude to a fate far worse. Can it be otherwise? The girl is not married, and her father is dead. That he *decided* her destiny, just before his death, matters not a jot. Can a girl marry her father's murderer? That the youth *is* a murderer, the Thirty all agree. Only the motive remains in doubt. Some say he is an Islander of Aroc, and is that not enough? Have not the Arocans always hated the Horans? Must not the youth have bewitched Triarch Jodrell, that the great man would even consider marrying his daughter to an inhabitant of those benighted isles? No doubt; but others have more specific explanations. To Prince Lepato, the youth is an Outrealmer agent; to Lord Glond, an Innermen plant, sent to discredit the Outrealmer cause.

In the Thirty, and all over Hora, passions run high in support of both men – and both men have seized upon the murder to whip those passions higher. Tomorrow, secluded from the eyes of their people, the Thirty shall elect a new Triarch. Glond or Lepato, Lepato or Glond? One thing is certain: whichever one it is, blood will stain the agora.

But that is not the worst of it. Only after a successor has been chosen can the crown be removed from Triarch Jodrell's head. Then comes the burial – and the burial of the Triarch is the burial, too, of his unmarried daughter ...

Tagan cradles the box harp in his hands; plucking the strings again, he sings murmurously:

> *...What matters her father's decision for her?*
> *What shall they care when they come to inter*
> *The girl who soon shall call*
> *From behind the stone wall?*

And call she might, but who will hear?

Tears well again in Tagan's eyes. This time, will he let them fall? Will he collapse in heaving, helpless sobs? But what good will that do? Roughly, angrily, he brushes at the tears again – and it is then, as he stares blurrily, blankly out into the cove, that he sees something strange. He blinks; he stares again. The gap between the cliffs. Can the waves against the rocks be suddenly wilder? Yet the rest of the day is calm, calm.

Tagan stares and stares.

Flap-flap, flap-flap!

The coracle lurched, spun.

What could be happening? When Oclar had set them on their way, their course, it appeared, had been magically assured. So much for magic! Hora, they had been told, was a bustling port, centre of an empire that rivalled even Ejland's – a port set in a wide, magnificent harbour. What, then, was this place?

Cliffs. Cliffs and rocks.

'Some watchman you are, Uchy!' Littler burst out.

'Dreaming about your *friend* again, were you?' said Rajal.

Ucheus blundered, 'As a matter of fact I – I . . .'

'And I suppose this is Hora?'

'Who cares?' cried Jem. 'Uchy – hand on that tiller, hey? Come on Raj, let's turn this sail!'

But turning the sail was not so easy. All at once the wind was stronger, and so was the current beneath the coracle, bearing them swiftly, inexorably forward.

The cliffs loomed, sheer and massive.

'Raj, *strip* the sail! Just tear it, quick—'

'I'm trying! Uchy, can't you turn that tiller?'

Impossible. They were out of control. By now the leak in the hull was worse. Littler was bailing, but to no avail. Rainbow leapt and howled. In moments, the world was a blur of flying spray, of shadows and sunlight, of swooping seabirds, of great arcs of rock – two great arcs, stretching out into the sea like mighty repelling arms . . .

But there was space between them . . .

'Hang on!' cried Jem. 'We're going through—'

'But the rocks . . . they'll rip us to shreds—'

'Hang on, just *hang on*—'

Now the rocks and the wind and the waves were immense, tearing away first their sail, then their mast, then chunk after chunk of the frail bows.

'Hang on, *hang on*—'

But to what? Suddenly the coracle was ripped in two. Rajal felt himself spiralling, spiralling. Through dazzled eyes he glimpsed sunlight, darkness, rock, foam; he breathed in water, air and water; he heard Littler shriek, and Rainbow bark . . .

He saw Ucheus, borne away into the outer sea.

189

Rajal waved, gasped, 'Uchy! Uchy, no—'

'Raj!' It was Jem. 'Raj, where are you?'

Rajal struggled to the surface. He sank.

Weak, so weak . . . Arms encircled him . . .

But where was Littler . . . Uchy . . . Rainbow? For now, there was only Jem and Rajal, Rajal and Jem, sweeping forward into the placid waters.

Silence. Sunlight. And a beach ahead.

They struck out towards it with the last of their strength.

Chapter 25

ROCKS AND SAND

Sunlight. Silence.

Well, almost.

There was the gentle wash of waves, lapping at their heels, and the suck and hiss, suck and hiss of water running in and out of little pools and hollows. From somewhere far above they heard seabirds caw; there was a warm, aromatic skittering of wind; loudest in their ears was their own laboured breath.

'Raj ... Raj, are you all right?'

Rajal rolled over, coughing. 'Nothing,' he gasped, 'that a moonlife in a ... nice comfortable tavern wouldn't fix. Say, I'm bleeding. And I didn't even know—'

It was a jagged gash, cutting open his calf.

'Those rocks ... Damn!'

'Rocks?' Jem repeated. Grimacing, dripping, he forced himself up. He looked around them, this way, that way. 'Raj ... Raj, are we alone?'

Rajal nodded glumly. 'I saw Uchy, swept out ... Littler too, I suppose ...'

Jem cursed. 'But this can't be ... happening again, it can't!' He gulped in breath. 'Raj, we've ... got to find them – Littler!' he called hoarsely. 'Littler ... Littler!'

'Rainbow, too,' Rajal muttered. 'Those rocks ... Damn, damn!'

'No ...' Shielding his eyes, Jem gazed out despairingly to the rocky walls and the gap between them. The outer sea had subsided; the violence of their arrival might never have been.

He cast aside his tunic. He sloshed back into the water.

'Jem, no ... they didn't stand a chance!'

'We did, didn't we? Raj, I've got to try!'

Rajal struggled to stand, but whether to restrain his friend or follow him, he barely knew. He did neither. Pain shot through his calf and his leg buckled. He covered his face. Oh, Jem was a fool, a fool ... But Rajal knew there was nothing he could do. After a moment he drew his hands from his eyes and scanned the water for Jem's haystack hair, bobbing between the silvery, sharp flashes of sunlight.

'Oh Jem,' he moaned, 'come back, come back ...'

'Don't worry,' came a voice, 'I think he will.'

191

Rajal turned, astonished. 'Who's there?'

✷ ✷

Rocks – rocks . . .

Waves, surging . . .

Then the waves, dying away . . .

Now Ucheus was aware only of his fingers, clawing painfully into hardness and slime, and the powerful, relentless strainings of his heart. Bursting, it filled his ears like thunder – but the thunder was subsiding . . . Then there was just the billowing of wind and the softer lappings of foam below – and the sun came back, steaming against his clinging, sodden tunic . . .

What had happened? Just moments before, he had been sleeping, dreaming – that strange dream of the girl . . . To Ucheus, it was certain that the sudden storm could only have been magic. But to what end? The surge of the waves filled his mind again and he saw his companions borne under, borne away . . . Heavily, he raised his head, screwing up his eyes against the brightness above.

The cliff, at least, was on a slope. But could he climb?

Too high, it had to be . . .

But wasn't there something dark up there, too? A cavern? A cave? Ucheus struggled to shift his limbs. He thought of handholds, footholds. He thought of Dead Man's Lookout, and wondered if he would ever climb up *there* again. A great weariness filled him and he would have liked to sleep again, here on the cliff.

Then he heard the barking. Then the cry.

The paddling, just below. 'Littler . . . Rainbow!'

✷ ✷

'Who's there?'

Silence. Sunlight. Rajal screwed up his eyes. Only then did he take in the scene that surrounded him, in all its curious artifice. Downstage, the colourful, carefully arranged seaweed. Stage left, stage right, the smooth, sculpted boulders. The steps in the hillside, leading up to what looked like elaborate formal gardens. A pebble shone in the sand and he picked it up, startled to find it inset, as if by design, with a jewel.

There was another pebble, just like the first.

Then another.

'I'm over here.' A strange, high chord hovered on the air.

Rajal turned again, slowly this time, and, torn between fear and wonderment, saw a willowy, oddly beautiful creature, standing before him in the lemony light. Was it a woman? Was it a man? The stranger wore only a simple white garb and carried, crooked beneath an arm, a

192

curious, ornate box. Long fingers plucked inside the box; the chord sounded again.

'He'll be back – I'm sure of it, dearie.'

'Who . . . who are you? What is this place?'

'Why, this is Hora. Where did you think you were?'

'Not Hora. We . . . we'd heard it was a great port.'

The stranger rolled his eyes. 'Well so it *is*, dearie, round the other side – finest in the world, they say. They built up the cliffs round all the rest. Something to do with smuggling – well, stopping it, I suppose . . . trade, taxes, I don't know.' He set down the musical box, then came and sat lightly, gracefully beside Rajal. 'I'll admit I hid when I saw you coming. But somehow I think you're friend, not foe.' He inclined his head. 'Tagan's my name. What's yours? Rajal? Hm, nice. Don't know about you, but I'm from the Isles of Aroc – originally, I mean.'

'Aroc? But that's where we've come from!'

'I hear they've changed – Inorchis, in particular.'

Rajal wrinkled his brow. 'You mean . . . you know what's happened there?'

'Oh, there's a lot I know, Master Rajal. But then, there's a lot I don't, too. One hears things. But not everything. My, your friend's a strong swimmer, isn't he?'

'Jem's good at most things – well, *now* he is. Used to be a cripple when he was young, would you believe?'

'And I used to be a boy like you. What's wrong? Haven't met my type before?'

'Actually . . . I almost *was* one.'

'Well, I like that – I *do* wish people would make up their minds.'

'Menos . . . Blard!'

Chief Adek, of the Royal Horan Watch, Palace Division, was annoyed – very annoyed. Here they were with a crisis on their hands, a city on the brink of civil war, and all his men were useless – useless! It was as well he had decided on a surprise inspection. First he had gone up to the west battlements. And what had he found there? Two men, with the agora below them, drowsing in the sun like dogs, that's what! As for the east battlements, if that wasn't ferment he'd smelled on those men, he didn't know what it was – ferment, or worse . . . And the agora steps? Adek could hardly bear to think of it. Just as he arrived, his men had been caught in a skirmish. Outrealmer brats, taunting the sentries – should have found themselves clapped in irons . . . coshed, at the least. And instead? Skittering away through the crowd they went, while one sentry clutched his head and another doubled over – reeling, the pair of them, from a rain of stones! Why, Adek himself had caught one, just under his eye. The skin was broken and it throbbed painfully.

'Blard . . . Menos!'

The sharp voice echoed down the long, dingy tunnel. Had the wretched men not cleaned the wax from their ears? Adek's anger welled higher. How many turns had he taken so far? By now he could hear the surge of the waves. Just a few more bends, if he remembered rightly, and he should see the cave-mouth – and the sea, and the sunshine, and Blard and Menos. Curse the fools! A link, they said, was only as strong as its weakest chain – or was it the other way round? In any case, were there *any* strong chains in Adek's links? Or links in his chains? Oh, bother it . . . Adek knew one thing, at least: if those men weren't rigid to attention, guarding that post with their wretched lives, there'd be trouble!

'Menos . . . Blard!'

Tagan mimed the action of a knife, slicing.

'Tripled my value, don't you know? Well – quadrupled, actually,' the eunuch said proudly, then laughed at the alarm that crossed Rajal's face. 'No, dearie, you're safe with me – I'm just a slave, not a slave-master, aren't I? Still, you'll be in trouble if you're found out . . .' He scanned the water. 'Where's your friend gone? Really, one would think he'd turn back now.'

'He's determined. Trouble?' Rajal pursued.

'Coming the way you did? By the back entrance?' Tagan arched an eyebrow which, Rajal observed, was immaculately plucked. 'There's some who say it's not an entrance *at all*, if you know what I mean.'

'We were wrecked,' said Rajal.

'So said the last one.' Tagan sighed, then laughed again at Rajal's expression – puzzlement, this time. Then, alarmed: 'Ooh, but your leg!'

Rajal had been clutching a hand to his calf. Now he shifted, just a little, and through his fingers came a spurt of red. At once Tagan was all concern. Leaping up, he ripped away a strip of his costume. Dextrously, the eunuch began to bind the wound. 'This really is nasty. Just think if you got gangrene! Then where would you be? Saw an old sea-dog down the harbour I did, just the other day, stomping round on a wooden leg. Ever so uncomfortable . . .' He looked up from his work. 'Ah, there's your friend! Up on those rocks, see? Is he looking back? Wave, wave!'

Rajal waved. Jem's distant figure, standing where the coracle had foundered, brought their loss home to him. Poor Littler . . . Uchy . . . Rainbow!

Tagan knotted the bandage. 'Red, isn't he?'

'Hm?' Rajal winced.

194

'Your friend. Red. Blotchy.'

'He's burned. By the sun.'

'And fair-hairs *are* prized in these parts, too! Not permanent, I hope, these blotches?'

What was Rajal to make of this strange new friend? He said blankly, almost cruelly, '*Scabs*, we called him in the coracle. In fact—'

'Shh!' Tagan gripped Rajal's arm. 'Listen!'

❉ ❉

Sunlight. Shadow.

And a sharp dividing line.

The rocks were hard, hot and glaring.

'You didn't see . . . Rajal?' breathed Littler, after a moment. 'Or Jem?'

'No more than you,' said Ucheus. 'Just the waves . . . rocks. Rainbow tried to reach them, didn't you, boy?' He reached out, fluffing the dog's wet fur. 'We just have to hope they're alive, that's all.'

Littler felt his heart sink. The climb had been a hard one, but somehow they had made it. They rested on the ledge at the mouth of the cave, half in sunlight, half in shadow. Seabirds, close by, swooped and cawed.

'What now?' said Ucheus. 'Where to from here?'

Rainbow had already bounded ahead, barking.

'Look!' Scrambling up, Littler pointed behind them, into the darkness. 'A tunnel!'

❉ ❉

Silence. Sunlight.

Then a grunt. A giggle.

Behind the boulders, stage left.

'Blard and Menos!' Tagan whispered. 'What are they doing here? Quick, lean on me.'

And Rajal let himself be led off, hobbling, stage right. With a grimace he slumped behind the boulders. There, amongst the looming shadows and seaweed, he saw the remnants of a hull, a sail. So, someone's coracle had got a little further . . .

'Tagan,' he whispered, 'you said we weren't the first. The *last one*, you said – who did you mean?'

Tagan gave no answer. Earnestly he peered out from behind the boulders.

Voices, loud and slurred:

'Jarvel? It's just the beginning!'

'Ladies? Women? What else, Lard?'

'Travel, of course! We could go anywhere—'

Pause. 'You mean it, Lard? Like, no more Adek?'

'No more Adek! Why, we could be fine gentlemen—'
'In a far-off land? But Lard, how could we ever—'
'Fill your pockets, Menos, just fill your pockets!'
Pause. 'Lard, I don't like it! I mean, if Adek—'
'Bother Adek! Fill your pockets, quick!'
Grunting. Giggling. Stumbling.

The musical box still lay in the sand. Someone kicked it; there was a jarring chord, underscoring Rajal's unease as he asked Tagan who these fellows might be. Again Tagan did not reply. But Rajal could see that his new friend was trembling.

Fear? No, it was anger.

Tagan strode out. 'Menos . . . Blard!'

'Blard . . . Menos!'

It was as he rounded the last bend that Chief Adek saw something strange. Light, spilling across the tunnel – light, brighter by far than the sallow illuminations from the holes in the ceiling. But not the light from the cave-mouth – this light came from a doorway, yawning open in the side of the tunnel . . . At once, the Chief's fury knew no bounds. Had those men *dared* to intrude upon the cove? Roaring, he lunged forward, as if to fling himself through the doorway.

But something intervened.

A voice cried, 'Rainbow, no—'

Adek reeled. A collar flashed. Jaws ripped. He lashed out, punching—

Bright fur: green, red, impossible colours . . .

Trying to kick the thing away, Adek kicked the door instead. It slammed and he juddered back against it, slithering down.

'Come on!' A voice again, a boy's.

'Which way? This way?'

'Rainbow, quick—'

Adek heard footfalls and the skittering of claws, trailing away round the turns of the tunnel. Fools! Would they get far? But where were his men? He groaned deeply. Who would be Chief of the Royal Horan Watch, Palace Division? A murdered Triarch . . . Blood in the streets . . . And now this!

'Menos . . . Blard!'

'Blard . . . Menos!'

Rajal, still concealed, looked on anxiously.

'Lard!' Menos jumped. Pebbles showered from his hands.

Lurching, Blard only stuffed another fistful into his pocket. 'Menos, relax. He's just a gelding . . . What is it, arse-greaser? Want your share?' And stumbling a little, the sentry scooped up another bejewelled pebble, holding it up between pudgy fingers. It flashed. 'Fight me for it, will you?' he taunted.

Tagan's voice was level. 'This is my lady's beach—'

'*Your* lady, gelding? Now there's a joke—'

'My lady's beach, and you're a—'

'Look, Menos, his toga's all ripped. Turn round, gelding, let's look up your sloppy arse. Dripping, I'll bet—'

Menos hissed, 'Lard, in the water—'

It was Jem, coming closer.

Blard did not listen.

'And I'll bet, too,' Tagan said savagely, 'on what Chief Adek will say when—'

Menos wailed, 'Lard, I told you—'

Blard pushed him. Menos staggered; Blard, grinning at Tagan, stepped closer, holding out the pebble like an offering – jigging it, a little obscenely, in the air. 'Come on, gelding, I was only joking. We're friends, aren't we? Come *on*—'

Tagan struck the pebble away. 'Dirty thief—'

Blard burst out, 'Dirty? Well, I like that! You think I'll take that from an arse-greasing—'

Menos cried, 'Blard, no—'

Blard swung back his fist. 'Dirty, dirty gelding—'

Things happened quickly. First came Rajal, floundering forward, blood reddening the bandage round his calf. 'Leave him alone, you fat bully—'

Then Menos, desperate: 'Blard, in the water—'

It was Jem, springing up from the foaming shallows – pale-haired, red-skinned, like a strange, avenging god.

His fist struck out. Menos fell.

'Who? What the—' Blard reeled round.

It was Rajal's chance. Grabbing the musical box, he swept it back through the air and brought it down, with all his strength, on the fat sentry's head. A discord rang out, and Blard crumpled. Pebbles burst from his pockets, glittering all around him.

A pause. Tagan looked wonderingly at his new friends; gratefully, at the unconscious sentries; then regretfully, at the shattered box harp.

Jem breathed heavily, slumping down. 'Raj, who the—'

There was no time for explanations. From behind the boulders, stage left, came a new voice, angry, urgent:

'Menos! Blard! . . . Blard! Menos!'

Tagan's hand covered his mouth.

'Tagan, what is it?' said Rajal. 'Who—'

'Chief Adek, coming this way! Quick – up to the gardens! I've got to hide you!'

Chapter 26

VOICE FROM THE VORTEX

'Buby? Buby-girl?'

Patches turned, puzzled. Just one moment earlier the little monkey had been sitting on his shoulder, munching contentedly at a weevily biscuit. Now there were just crumbs on his shoulder and Buby had vanished. Patches cursed. He knew he should have held her by the tail! He looked round the agora, this way and that.

Crowds clustered thickly in the bright morning. They were not the usual crowds. If some thought merely of haggling and hawking, pushing round the cloister-walk with its laden stalls, today there were many others – squatting austerely on ledges or steps, or setting themselves up in the middle of the great square with cushions, blankets and picnic baskets – determined already to claim their places for the great ceremony of the morrow, when the old Triarch would be entombed and the new Triarch crowned, beginning a new era in Hora's history. Many carried banners and pennants, indicating their support for Lepato or Glond. There was tension in the air, a lurking violence, fluttering like the bright cloth of red or blue. Sentries stood by, ominous in armour.

'Buby-girl? Buby?'

Patches took in the façade of the Temple of Thirty with its high stone steps and fluted columns. How it dominated the agora, this great forbidding seat of Horan isocracy! Yet it was the smaller, flanking edifices that were important now: to one side, the tall-chimneyed Decision Chamber, from which the smoke would rise tomorrow, red or blue, indicating the triumph of Glond or Lepato; to the other, the Tomb of the Triarchs with its lowering pediment and vast doors of stone. Patches hoped Buby had not gone skittering up there – or towards the Decision Chamber! These sentries looked as though they wouldn't think twice about skewering a little monkey on the end of a spear.

'Buby? Buby-girl?'

It was then, screwing up his eyes against the sun, that Patches saw the suspicious curl of tail – could it be a tail? – hanging from the high plinth of a tall, bronze statue that stood in the centre of the agora. Flashing like a beacon in the bright light, the statue depicted a group of three – the first three Triarchs of Hora, Patches gathered, under whose benevolent reign the isle had first enjoyed the benefits of isocratic government.

Hard by the high plinth was a brightly coloured, rather dishevelled van, which had been pulled across the agora – effortfully, no doubt – by two shabby-looking old ponies. Now, watched by curious children, a group of fellows from the van – swarthy fellows with big hoopy earrings and spotted headscarves – were setting up a makeshift platform. Patches moved towards them, his steps a little on the hobbling side. No doubt about it, his left leg was bruised badly after last night, when a steward had unceremoniously ejected him – and Buby too – from a certain establishment just around the corner. He supposed he should have been grateful – if the steward had not intervened, that ugly dwarf and his master had looked capable of killing them.

But Patches wasn't grateful for much at the moment. Right now he should have been on the *Catayane*, attending to his duties. What of it? He'd risk the captain's wrath. Hadn't he endured enough of it last night, after disappearing from the club? Patches hadn't even told the captain what had happened, just endured the curses and blows. Truth to tell, the boy was sulking. He was angry with the old man, ashamed for him, too. How could an old sea-dog like Faris Porlo – the great Faris Porlo – get mixed up with that Glond fellow? If ever there were a foreigner you couldn't trust, didn't it have to be 'good old Glondy', with his jewel-embedded eyes and his braided hair? Oh, the captain was a fool, a fool!

Patches pushed his way through the children, who pawed and patted admiringly at his strange, colourful costume. He grinned at them, relenting a little in his sulky mood, and pointed up to the top of the plinth. Could they see a monkey's tail? Yes, that was definitely a tail, wasn't it? Patches cupped his hands round his mouth, calling Buby's name. Ah, but he was right! Buby looked down, snickering – then, just as Patches was about to brave the plinth, cursing the throbbing bruises on his leg, the little monkey leapt through the air, slithered and scrambled over the top of the van and vanished through a vent in the roof.

The children squealed, delighted; Patches groaned.

The hoopy-earringed fellows, busy with barrels, planks and ropes, had paid no attention to the monkey. Dubiously Patches glanced at them and edged his way towards the back of the van. There, shooing away the children, he peered in through a set of ragged curtains, into a shadowy interior stuffed full with cushions, rugs and curtains of beads. Nestling against a rumpled heap of fabric, Buby had found a banana and was peeling it eagerly with her strangely human hands.

'Buby-girl, come here!' Patches hissed.

'Let my little visitor eat her banana, at least.'

A face looked up; Patches started. The heap of fabric, he realised, was in fact an old man, dressed in elaborate robes. In the dim illumination of the ceiling vent, the old man's face looked kindly and wise. He smiled, reached for another banana, and offered it to Patches. Gratefully, realising that he was very hungry, the boy scrambled up into the van. Careful of his sore leg, he struggled a little to get himself into the proper cross-legged posture.

The old man's eyes twinkled. 'So, young fellow, this creature is yours? I think you ought to take better care of him – hm?'

'*Her*, actually,' said Patches, his mouth full of banana. 'I – I meant to hold her tail, but—'

'You forgot – hm? Ah, that is how we lose everything that is important to us, is it not? We forget – just for one moment, we forget something we ought *never* to have forgotten, and it is on such a moment that destiny turns.' The old man sighed. 'Why, I recall a little girl who travelled with us once, not so long ago – the most splendid little girl, the most talented of our troupe. What high hopes I had for that child! Ah, but when passing through the slave-ports, I ought always to have hugged her close to me – and one day, on an isle far from here, I turned from her but for a moment, and she was gone.'

'That's . . . that's terrible,' Patches breathed.

The old man sighed again, and wiped away a tear. 'The stuff of tragedy, is it not? But we have tragedies enough for our venerable troupe.' He turned, indicating a bank of yellowing scrolls that lay in an open chest beside him. 'Come, my young friend, if you are to earn your banana – perhaps even another – you must help me rehearse. Let my companions set up the stage – I am an old man, I am weak, and besides, my memory is hardly what it was. To think I once carried a hundred parts in my head – not just parts, but entire plays!' He drew forth a particular scroll. 'I'm rather rusty on this one now, and – alas – I have quite an important part. I'm the Attendant Spirit. But let's see, I think I have another copy . . . Will you read the fire-god, and the goddess of water?'

The boy looked blank. Deeper furrows appeared in the old man's face. 'What, boy, don't you understand? You realise, don't you, that we're Sea Vagas? Players? That we go from isle to isle, performing our little pieces? Tomorrow, I'm sure, the sentries will move us on, but this afternoon and this evening we should get in – oh, at least three or four performances of *The Javandiom*. It's a favourite, you know, at times like these – oh, but you *are* looking blank, aren't you? Never mind, just help me run through the first act, will you?' He proffered a copy of the scroll. 'As I say, I'm the Attendant Spirit – you can do Theron and Javander.'

Patches flushed, shamefaced. 'Sir, I – I can't read.'

The old man looked surprised. 'Well, really! And aren't you an Fjland-fellow? You're certainly not from these parts, that much is certain.' The old man took the script back, proffering another banana instead. 'But you have ears, haven't you? You can listen?' He unrolled his own scroll. 'It's a very old play – traditional. You might not understand all of it, but it's quite exciting if you can manage to follow it.'

He cleared his throat, then paused, noticing a group of dirty, envious little faces peering through the curtains. Whether they were looking at the cushions or at the bananas he could not tell; in any case he relented, letting the children scramble up into the van. Generously he distributed the last of his bananas, and with Buby on his lap and a party of cross-legged young persons sitting around him, the old man set the scene.

'Now,' he said, 'imagine a swirling vortex, coloured purple, green, red, blue and gold. Can you see it – hm? What's that, little boy? What's a vortex? Well, just think of lots of pretty colours, going round and round. Sort of like a cloud – or lots of clouds. Turn your head, they would, if you looked at them for too long . . . So: swirl, swirl goes the vortex, and then, when everyone is suitably amazed, it resolves itself – I mean, it turns into . . .' – the player spread wide his arms – '. . . the mighty vistas of The Vast! The Vast – the cloud-capped towers, the gorgeous palaces, it's all there . . . Hm? What's that, little girl? What's The Vast? Well, just think of it as a very special place – mentioned quite often in the old legends, it was – a place where not just ordinary people live, not just people like us, but *gods* . . . So, you've got it, then? Vortex, cloud-capped towers, dwelling-place of the gods – of course, we shan't be *showing* any of this, I mean it's not as if we're the Silver Masks now, are we? – but I'm just trying to get you all in the mood . . .'

Benevolently, the old man looked around him; the children, he became aware, were stirring impatiently. He rustled his scroll and hurried on, 'Anyway, imagine all this . . . then, down a great flight of celestial steps, the Attendant Spirit descends – that's me, and I speak first.' He cleared his throat again. 'We're all ready?'

The children nodded.

'So: *The Javandiom: A Masque.*'

The player began by reading from the scroll; after a time he let it fall aside and intoned the dialogue from a memory which was still, it seemed, prodigious after all; still more impressively, his voice changed, and changed entirely, with each of the characters who spoke. To Patches, it was a voice filled with magic. Marvelling, he thought of the mysterious vortex of purple, green, red, blue and gold.

ATTENDANT SPIRIT:

People of Hora, lucky have you been,
Enjoying as you do the fruits of just

And righteous government. Forgathered here
In this historic agora, we long
To learn the fate of those who seek to hold
The noblest of our offices of state.
Let us reflect on what they wish to be.

    God-like are the ones who reign as Triarch;
Nay, gods in human form they must become
Upon assumption of their sacred crowns.
What better gods for Hora? Answer not
If vain allegiances still claim your heart,
Faiths that, if once true, are true no longer.
Must it not be wisdom to discard them?

    My friends, the burden of our play is this:
To show the folly of the gods of old
And how our independence came to pass,
That, thus instructed, we might all the more
Cherish our lot. – Begin then, aeons past
When still this wat'ry realm and other isles
Gave fealty to the goddess of the seas.
Our scene, at least at first, is in The Vast,
Where remonstrations three *Javander* makes
To mighty *Theron*, red of hair and eye.

JAVANDER:

Brother-husband, fiery *Theron*, hearken!
Ere now, many earnest supplications
From all the noblest in your retinue
Have you received with stony unconcern.
Do not, likewise, turn away a sister,
As all the while you gaze upon your glass!

    Your sad preoccupation is the talk
Of all The Vast. Some wonder what it is
That so engrosses all your waking care.
Not I: for in your glass I see her plain,
The lady whose visage you look upon.
What is she, but the phantom that enslaved
Our brother *Agonis* before the wars
That proved so ruinous to us and all
The mortal ones who live upon the earth?

    The *Lady Imagenta* is her name,
A dream created by a wicked god,

203

Or rather demon. Vengeance was his goal.
With *Agonis*, success was in his grasp:
But fiery brother, can it be that you
Are subject, like the milksop, to his snares?
  Look around, your lust is all-consuming!
See, what vileness even now surrounds you
As spawn that springs unbidden from your loins
Is forming into monsters on the floor,
Loathsome, oozing, slithering abortions
Like unto the evil things our father
Would destroy? – Ugh, but I must beat them back!
My brother-husband, please, deny me not:
Put down that glass! – Ah, if even *Theron*
Whom all the world once looked upon with awe
Is now but an enchanter's fool, no more,
Then we are lost.

THERON:

                    Javander, think you not
That I can see behind these canting words?
Goddess you may be, but you are woman
Foremost. When you see me gaze upon a face
That far surpasses yours, what must you feel
But envy? – Envy, gnawing at your heart!
Woman, no more, if you would not endure
A retribution savage and condign.
Javander, go!

ATTENDANT SPIRIT:

                    Javander goes. This first
Remonstrance over, useless must it seem:
How could she come again? But aeons pass:
When still the fire-god gazes on the glass,
So comes it that his stricken sister-wife
Must remonstrate again.

JAVANDER:

                                    Of hair and eye
So red, my brother, yet so black inside?
If leathern are your wings, what of your heart?
Yet heart? – I fear that such a part you own
No longer, when shuddering I look on
Where you dwell: this Palace of Abortions!
Can this be your home? – Ah, brother, brother!
Though once the newness of your loss excused
Your meditations on this phantom girl,
I fear by now that nothing can forgive
Such rank indulgence. – Pray, do you forget
Our father's stern commands? Did not he say
It was our task to look upon the earth
And all those there who bow to us in prayer,
Until the time their lot may be redeemed?
Yet you forget your fiery desert realms!
Do not you know that prophecy foretells
The rising of the anti-god again
To captivate your peoples in the thrall
Of false religion? – Unang Lia's doom
Shall certain be, unless its god should turn
And take its destiny in hand.

THERON:

                                    Javander,
Must I tell you once again? Go from me,
Your words beguile me not. What care need I
For Unang Lia? Does not all the world,
Or much of it (the rest, I can be sure
Shall follow in good time), bow down towards
Kal-Theron, and accept my Sultan's yoke?
Think you not of *Agonis*? If traitor
To our father you would find, the milksop
Fits the bill far more than I. How much time
Has passed, yet still he wanders far away,
Neglecting to come back here to The Vast?
By your lights, his lands should be in ruins.
Yet are not the Agonists of Ejland
The only rivals to my Sultan's might?

Why, look you on your own lands, sister-wife!
Think you that your paltry, savage islands
Do you any credit? – Go! Go!

JAVANDER:

                        I go,
But utter first a different plea. – Brother!
More than brother! If not for your own sake,
Nor even for your peoples you will act,
Will not you think of me, your sister-wife,
Whose wat'ry cool once quenched your fiery cares?
How can you live surrounded by these vile
Aborted creatures, spawn of useless lust?
Might not your seed find welcome in my womb,
And there bring forth a fair and godly child?
Divine I am like you, your sister too,
And yet you treat me like the humblest slave.
For aeons have I suffered your neglect:
No more can I endure.

ATTENDANT SPIRIT:

                    He merely laughs
And turns back to his glass. The aeons pass;
But when at last the goddess comes again,
As come she must, things shall not be the same.
Now her heart has hardened. Should her brother
Spurn her one more time, she vows, then never
Will she come again. But first, just once more
Must she remonstrate. Her voice is desperate,
For desperate, thanks to *Theron*'s long neglect
Is now the pass to which affairs have come.
Fire-god, will you listen?

JAVANDER:

                    Husband! Brother!
Ugh! – Barely can I gaze upon your form,
So thick are the abortions all around,

Suppurating, bloody and repulsive
As all the vileness evil ever brings.
But listen! – Please, I beg you, one last time.
   Brother, no more plead I as a sister,
Much as yet I might: for since in sorrow
On the stern commandment of a father
We gods, departing earth, resumed The Vast,
How bitter have the aeons been to me!
Denied the sweetness of a lover's touch,
What is eternal life to me but dust?
   Yet bitter has life been for mortals, too,
And worse it can but be in times to come
Should you not act. – Come, look upon your lands!
Come, see my prophecy, the destiny
That even now is edging forward. – See:
Betrayed by you, the Unangs bow in prayer
Not to *Theron* but to an impostor.
You must know who it is! When long ago
Our father cast the evil one away,
Toth-Vexrah vowed revenge. Was it not he
Who made this glass you look upon today?
What are these abortions but his evil,
Hideously channelled through your being?
Indeed, I see his vengeance has been sweet!
While here you sit, a languid, love-struck fool,
Toth-Vexrah shall usurp not but your lands:
Your name, too, he shall take, and the praise
That once was yours. The Sanctum of the Flame
Shall fuel his resurrection. Yet your strength
Is greater far than his. But say you would
Be god, true god of your own rightful realms,
And *Toth* is gone!

THERON:

               Javander, you are weak
In mind yet more than body. What, is *Toth*
To be despised? Our brother is he not,
Quite as much as *Agonis* and *Koros*?
More, is not he father of the greatest
Beauty ever seen? And if freed he were
From the dread clasp of Unbeing, certain

It must be that this girl shall live again.
Until then, she is lost. – An image, yes:
But sister, if an image in a glass
Be fairer far than all else in the world,
By what right can you call the one a fool
Who looks not on the world but on the glass?
Let *Toth* return: he cannot come too soon!

JAVANDER:

Then things are worse than ever I have dreamed!
I see now all is over: for too long
Have I loved where I am hated, hoping
Always that your heart might change. In one thing,
Brother-husband, are you right: call me fool
Once more, and I shall not demur. – But now
I must away: and if, to go, I break
The bonds that bind me to our father's words   .
Then so be it. No more can I endure
Your detestation: as to what your realms
Must suffer now, I will not intervene.
But where to go? – My heart shall guide my way:
Through all this time of exile have I longed
For earth, where once again I might disport
Beneath those ocean depths that are my true
And natural element. So fare thee well,
My faithless love! – This place we call The Vast,
Though higher far than earth, to me now seems
A dark and dusty tomb.

ATTENDANT SPIRIT:

                              And with these words
Javander plummets from those airy heights
Where gods in secret dwell. The skies above
Her tropic realms are velvet with the dark.
Comet-like she sears them; ocean depths
Receive her; twisting, turning joyously
The goddess sinks upon her sandy bed.
At last! At last! – Ecstasy consumes her;
Exploding from her hands and eyes come rays

208

Like lightning bolts of energy divine.
And when they fade there rises from the sands
And oozy rocks that lie beneath the waves
An edifice of such magnificence
That mortal eyes, on seeing it, should think
Themselves grown mad. – Was ever in the world
Such wild profusion? So many turrets,
Domes, castellations, minarets and spires?
Such mighty, regal halls! Such sweeping stairs!
So many courtyards paved with precious stones!
And all of it aglow with light unearthly
That shimmers strangely through the cloudy depths
While through and round there flicker, swish and flash
The many-coloured creatures of the sea.
   Ah, but all the splendours that bedizen
The mightiest of palaces on land
Seem as nothing set against this sanctum,
This strangest place that ever yet must be,
Javander's city underneath the sea!

The old man bowed his head and was silent. Patches exhaled deeply. All around him, the little children were sleeping and so was Buby, curled up happily on the soft cushions; only Patches had remained intent upon the play. What it all meant, and whether the story were true, the cabin boy had no idea; he just knew he was curious to know what happened next.

'Sir?' He leaned forward, prodding the old man. 'Sir, it can't be finished, can it? Oh, say it's not finished!'

The old man looked up. 'Why, my young friend, you are a fool – that was only the first act, wasn't it? There are three more, or three that we have; some say there may be a fifth, but it is lost. In any case, it gets better as it goes along, or so I've always thought. This really is *by far* the dullest bit ... But I think I've got it now – hm, yes, I've got it.'

'You mean you're not doing any more?' said Patches.

The player rolled his eyes. 'Silly boy, of course I am! Our little troupe shall be doing it *all* – very soon, on that stage out there. Though – hm – I hope our audiences are composed rather more of fellows like you than *this* lot here,' he added, looking ruefully at the sleeping children. 'Ignorant you may be, but at least you're interested. Now this lot – why, they just don't *know* about their traditions, these young people of today!'

'They're only little,' said Patches. 'I think they're tired.'

A faraway look came into the old man's eyes. 'Ah, but that little girl who used to travel with us, she was a different matter – very different indeed . . . Now there was a child who was educated beyond her years – one really would have thought she was *much* older . . . Oh, but if only I hadn't lost her to those slavers . . .' Tears filled the old man's eyes and once more his wrinkled head bowed into his robes.

Patches looked on helplessly. Reluctant to leave the pleasant van – pleasant, at least, to Patches – he had been about to urge the old man to tell him, at least just *tell* him what happened in the rest of the play when a brown face came poking though the curtains, glowering at the sight of the sleeping children. A sharp voice, like a bark, scattered them in a moment.

'Margites – Margites, what are you doing? Out of it, you lot . . . hop it, I say, the lot of you! Come on, Margites, we're all set up! What have you been doing, you senile old fool?'

Chapter 27

THE GODDESS IN THE GARDEN SHED

Jem sighed, 'How long?'

Not for the first time.

'A long time,' sighed Rajal.

Again, not for the first time.

This time he added, 'And I'm so hungry!'

'Not,' Jem said, 'how long already.' The answer, by now, must be most of a day. 'I mean, how much longer?'

'There's hardly a choice,' said Rajal. 'Is there?'

'I don't know.' Jem looked up.

Rajal looked down. 'I'm not climbing up *there*,' he muttered. 'Anyway, for what?'

'There's a garden out there, isn't there? A big garden.'

'Yes, filled with conifers. Did you see any fruit?'

Jem shrugged. 'Must be some.'

Rajal brightened. But only for a moment. 'Sentries too, no doubt. Just like Blard and Menos, but cold sober.'

'You'd rather be stuck in this place?'

'We're not stuck here. We're waiting.'

Jem sighed again. 'For how long?'

'A long time.'

The scene was a gloomy, circular chamber, draped thickly with cobwebs and moss. Disorderly ladders, buckets and brooms, rakes and shovels and terracotta pots clustered against the dingy walls. Jem, his jaw heavy on a bunched-up hand, sat on a set of low, cool steps. Rajal, a leg swinging back and forth, perched on the sill of a boarded window. Higher windows – grilled, narrow, running round the rim of the ceiling – let in the green-grey light from the garden.

'What is this place, do you think?' said Rajal, bored.

'I think we can reasonably say it's a garden shed.'

'These carvings on the walls?' Rajal raised an eyebrow. 'And behind you, up those steps? That statue? I think this might be a temple, Jem.'

Jem looked round, and something occurred to him. The statue – it was, in fact, only the most prominent part of a bas-relief that covered all the walls – was barely visible, but appeared to depict a figure – a woman, yes

211

– with something on her head, something in her hand. A crown? A trident?

'Now this *is* odd,' he said. 'After all, we're in Wenaya.'

'Hm?' said Rajal. 'I'm not sure what you mean.'

'Raj, think. We're after the blue crystal, aren't we – the Crystal of Javander? Well, who's this?'

'You mean, why is the goddess in the garden shed?'

'I mean, why has this garden *temple* been abandoned? Remember back on Xaro – Uchy and his friends knew nothing about Javander, did they? Yet she's their goddess – goddess of *all* these isles. Well, she's supposed to be.' Jem screwed up his forehead. 'I think we need a lot of answers, Raj.'

'Hm. Tagan, where are you?'

'You think we can trust him?'

Rajal considered this. Earlier, as he led them through the shadowy gardens, Tagan had whispered, almost to himself, about his lady, and a murder, and Maius Eneo. It was all in fragments, no time for details – but the eunuch knew, or said he knew, that Jem and Rajal were not mere strangers, shipwrecked at random. Once he had used the word *magic*, though what magic he meant, or whose it might be, neither Jem nor Rajal could be sure. Still, Tagan was on their side. He'd proven that – hadn't he?

Rajal said as much.

'Proven, Raj? He's locked us in here.'

'To keep us safe, he said.'

'To starve, if nothing else.'

'Don't remind me!' Rajal clutched his belly.

'You're the one who keeps reminding us, Raj,' Jem said, not quite fairly. He shifted his jaw from one hand to the other. 'What did he mean about Maius Eneo, do you think? Sounds as if he's in trouble.'

'I was confused. But he thinks ... I think he thinks we *know* Maius Eneo.'

'Well, Uchy does – or did.'

'Poor Uchy!' Rajal sighed. The light from the garden was growing dimmer. Once again he felt the emptiness rumbling inside him. He picked at his bandage, as if to distract himself. 'Something must be keeping Tagan,' he said, hopefully.

'So you *do* trust him, Raj?'

'He bound up my leg. This is his toga – well, part of it.'

Jem looked dubiously at the bloodied wrappings. 'They had fellows like that in Unang Lia,' he murmured, after a moment. 'Didn't they?'

'Fellows?' A strain entered Rajal's voice.

212

'There's something about them,' said Jem. 'Oh, I'm sure we shouldn't trust him, Raj!'

Rajal said quietly, 'I was nearly one of those fellows.'

'Hm?' Jem had not heard. Not quite.

'It's not his fault – what he is, I mean,' said Rajal. 'Quadrupled his value, getting his bits chopped – he's *proud* of that, would you believe?'

'Raj, what are you talking about?'

'He's a slave. Eunuchs are big business – for their owners, I mean. Didn't you know?'

Jem shook his head, appalled; Rajal felt his face grow hot. As soon as he spoke his next words, he knew he regretted them. 'Things happened, Jem. When we were apart – in Unang, I mean. I . . . oh, it doesn't matter.'

Didn't it? Jem was not so sure. Intently, through the gloom, he searched out Rajal's eyes. He would have urged his friend to go on, but just then they heard the sound of a bolt drawing back in the curving doors. Jem sprang up, suddenly tense. Had the eunuch betrayed them? They were about to find out.

'Master Rajal? Master Jemany?' Tagan slipped inside.

Rajal began, 'Tagan! You didn't bring any food, did—'

He broke off. Tagan pushed back the door behind him, but in the briefly brighter light, Rajal saw that the eunuch was hunched, limping – saw, too, that on one side the dark-hued face was darker, the make-up smudged.

'Tagan, what happened?'

Tagan leaned back against the door, breathing deeply. 'Adek held me . . . Adek and his men. Said I knew where you were . . . said I must be hiding you. Thought they might have searched . . . might have found you. Thanks be they didn't! Adek . . . so angry . . . Something about boys, and an animal . . . a stripy animal.'

'What?' Jem and Rajal exchanged glances.

'I didn't understand,' said Tagan. 'Said there was no one on the beach, no one . . . said Blard and Menos made it all up. Seems I convinced them . . . in the end.'

'Stripy animal? Boys?' said Jem. 'Does that mean—'

'But Tagan,' urged Rajal, 'what did they do to you?'

'Doesn't matter . . . doesn't matter.' The eunuch was dismissive, almost angry. 'Adek believed me, that's all. Blard and Menos . . . Jarvel-weed . . . he knows what they're like.' Turning, he peered through the crack between the doors. 'But I've had to be careful,' he muttered. 'Getting away was hard . . . and getting you out of here . . . *that* might be harder. But I've got a plan . . .'

'Tagan, what is it?' Jem's voice was gentle now, trusting. If he had doubted the eunuch before, his doubts were gone now.

In truth, he was a little ashamed.

❊ ❊

Tagan's plan was simple. It was also dangerous.

The garden slaves, he explained, were quartered in the city, and each day at dusk would leave through a particular gate – he pointed in the direction, just down the path from where they were now. The slaves, he said, generally worked in pairs – and left in pairs too, as they slowly made their way from their various parts of the gardens. On their wrists they wore bronze bands, each one stamped with a number, and when they passed through the gates would hold out their arms to the sentries, who transferred corresponding numbered tokens from the 'in' box to the 'out' box.

Jem began, 'I don't quite see . . .'

'Right now, there are two boys on duty in this quarter. Before they leave, they'll come here to leave behind their hoes, shovels, shears, whatever. That's when you jump them and take their wristbands – their robes, too, of course. There are cowls, and you can draw them around you – but don't worry, the sentries won't look at your faces.'

'They'll look at our wrists,' said Rajal. He grabbed Jem's; it flashed whitely. 'That's no Wenayan!'

Tagan brushed the objection aside. 'Master Rajal, this is Hora, crossing-point of the southern seas – why, slaves here are of *all* hues. Is your friend the first fair-hair to stray into our waters? No, I see no difficulty in getting him past the gate . . .'

'What then?' said Jem. 'I mean, when we're past it?'

The eunuch spoke quickly. 'You'll find yourself in an alley. Follow it and you emerge in the agora. Cross it to the opposite corner – just look for the Temple of Thirty: Decision Chamber side, not Tomb of the Triarchs side – and there, in the second side street, west-south, five doors down, you will find the house of my father.'

Rajal said, surprised, 'Your *father* lives here?'

Jem was intent on the directions. 'Temple of Thirty? West-south? Five down?'

There was no time to say more. 'They'll be here soon. Don't forget the wristbands – then down the path to the Oclar gate.'

A pointing finger, a smile, and Tagan was gone again.

Jem looked at Rajal. 'Did he say *Oclar*?'

Rajal looked at Jem. 'Did he say *father*?'

'I think he did – yes, his father's house. But what did he mean about that stripy animal, that's what I want to know? Oh, there are mysteries here, Raj, mysteries heaped on mysteries!' Jem was inspecting the garden

214

equipment. After all, they might need a weapon. Or weapons. 'Now, let's just hope these gardeners really *are* boys.'

'Instead of eunuchs? Or do you mean girls?'

'I mean, Raj, instead of big, hefty men.'

'Let's hope so. But Jem? What sort of father would ... I mean, why is his *father* ...'

They heard voices. 'Shh!'

Jem, grabbing a terracotta pot, took up his place just inside the doors. 'Raj,' he whispered, 'I'll do it. But take this shovel. Just in case ... But Raj?'

'Jem?'

'Whatever you do, don't hit *me* – hm?'

Rajal nodded, and his leg began to throb.

Chapter 28

IN THE CLOSET

'Littler? Littler, where are you?'

Ucheus spoke only in the faintest whisper. Much time had passed; the labyrinth, by now, appeared endless. But what was happening? Only moments earlier, with Littler and Rainbow, he had crouched back amongst the columns of brickwork that lined a particular stretch of the passage. Behind one column was Ucheus; behind another, Littler and Rainbow; approaching, with a steady thud, were the footsteps of sentries. Barely daring to breathe, Ucheus had pressed himself hard against the wall. Then, with a soft click, it gave way behind him.

'Littler, are you there? Littler? Rainbow?'

Was there a door? Was there a handle? Was there no way back? Ucheus felt only a smooth wooden wall. He turned slowly. In the labyrinth, pools of light had trickled through the ceiling; here the darkness was entire and there was something else, something stranger. Replacing the stale, sour smell of the labyrinth was a lush, intoxicating scent – a feminine scent ... Cautiously Ucheus took a step forward. Something brushed his arm and there was a susurrus, like a sigh. Trembling, he reached before him. With one hand he felt a slither of silk; with the other, a rasp of velvet.

'Littler?' he whispered again. 'Littler ... Rainbow?'

Should he call their names aloud? Should he beat the wall behind him? But that might only bring on new and greater dangers. He clenched his fists. Curse it, curse it! The labyrinth had been bad enough, but at least he had known that Littler was safe, Rainbow too – not like poor Jem and Rajal!

But what was he to do? Was this place really Hora? Would he find Maius Eneo? All he knew was that he had to try. He stepped forward again, pushing his hands through rustling fabric, parting it like thickness after thickness of curtains. Then, at waist height, came a circle of light – a keyhole ... Crouching carefully, Ucheus looked out.

The first thing he saw was the sparkle of jewels: a long necklace, hanging over a screen. He made out a pattern of resinwood, gleaming in the afternoon sun. His gaze flickered to an incense brazier – a perfume cabinet – a lamp ...

Then he heard the voices.

'So many! How can there be so many?'

'My lady, there will be many more. Now we see only those who would stake an early claim, careless alike of their comforts and their duties. On the morrow, you may be sure, the crowd will be swollen to twice its present size.'

Through the thin veneers of wood that separated him from the apartment, Ucheus made out all the words clearly. Then he saw the girl and her older, plumper companion, shadowy against the brightness of an open window.

'Twice?' came the girl again. 'Could the agora contain such a number?'

'Why, more – indeed, more. There was a time, so I have heard, when it held *thrice* as many – four times, perhaps.' The companion, Ucheus surmised, had attempted a forced cheerfulness; now, a little abruptly, she turned from the window, as if perhaps she had said too much. 'That was before I came to this isle,' she added, beginning halfheartedly to tidy away a set of bangles, a scattered deck of cards.

'But Ra Ra, when was this?'

The nurse shuffled the cards, as if considering. 'Why, child,' she said airily, 'they say it was the day of your father's election – yes, it must have been.'

'Ah.' The girl remained by the window; to Ucheus, she was still a shadow against the light. But there was something about her, something that made him long for her to turn, revealing herself to his secret gaze.

When she spoke again, her voice was strained. 'Yes, I imagine it – can you, Ra Ra? How they must have cheered, as they shall cheer tomorrow, when the smoke rises from the Decision Chamber! And then? Why, the coronation! Only when the line is secured can the crown be removed from the old Triarch's head – that is how it works, does it not? Yes, how they must have cheered, as the screws were driven into poor Father's skull! But Ra Ra, did they cheer what came then, when old Triarch Azander, the last offices over, was spirited away into the darkness of his tomb?'

Now the girl turned and Ucheus saw a vision that almost made him gasp. The girl from his dream! In sudden rapture, he gazed upon her beauty. It was no ordinary beauty. The girl's hair was dishevelled, her face drawn; for all the luxury of her surroundings she wore only a shapeless white shift. In her arms, cradled like an infant, was a shabby doll. Ucheus felt himself trembling violently, but whether with love or worship, he did not know. For a moment he thought he had given himself away, that the lovely eyes could see him crouched there in the darkness.

But the girl's gaze was fixed on her nurse; her voice, for a moment, became almost harsh. 'To be sure, they must have cheered; tradition had been fulfilled. But Ra Ra, what of tomorrow? Shall they cheer then?'

It was as if they were playing a game; but the nurse, it was clear, was a reluctant player. Still she held the cards; slowly she placed them on a little low table, as if fearful that they would spill from her hands. 'I'm sure,' she quavered, 'that *all* shall—'

There was a sound of jangling; there were raised voices. Ra Fanana swung round, grateful rather than alarmed. There was the click of a door and Ucheus saw a willowy, strangely feminine young man skittering into the apartment as if he had been pushed; it seemed he had. His hands fluttered like harried birds and his black-outlined eyes flashed in rage. His painted face was smudged, almost as if it were bruised.

'Well, I never! If manners maketh the man, I'm more a man than some, that's all I can say!' the new arrival called back over his shoulder. 'Begging your pardon, my lady. Really, Fa Fa, those *guardsmen* just have no respect any more. Do you know what one of them said? Said he knew where I'd be, this time tomorrow, and he'd be coming for me! Well, I never!'

'Tagan, shh!' Ra Fanana, alarmed after all, glanced at her young charge, then hissed anxiously, 'Tagan, just look at you! You haven't been down at those docks again, have you? At this time of day?' She cast up her eyes. 'Oh eunuchs, eunuchs! And where's the box harp? Remember, I said we'd mislaid the—'

The girl asked, 'And where, Tagan, *will* you be tomorrow?'

Tagan grimaced. He could hardly tell the girl that he feared he might meet the fate of many a *used eunuch*, finding himself consigned to the stews – after all, if that happened, it would happen because his mistress was dead ... But that wouldn't happen. Hadn't he told his father everything? Hadn't he pleaded, hadn't he cried? And hadn't the old man come up with a plan? No, Lady Selinda would not die – and nor would Maius Eneo.

The eunuch smiled brightly. 'Where, dearie? Tomorrow? Why, where but here – making you up for the grand occasion? I've planned something *very* special, is all I can say – and I warn you, we'll be starting early!'

Selinda glared. 'Smooth-tongued, aren't you? Both of you!'

Exchanging glances, the slaves sank back; to Ucheus, they slipped from view, disappearing on either side of the keyhole. From his perfumed prison he saw only the girl, and again it seemed to him that she saw him, staring intently from behind the thin veneers. For a wild moment he could have moaned aloud, giving himself away there and then.

'So I don't even have my box harp,' she was saying. 'Did you hear that,

Blisha?' She stroked the head of her battered doll. 'Tomorrow, then, must we sing without it? Very well, we shall sing without it.' And the girl, twirling slowly, rocking the doll like an infant in her arms, began softly to intone, at once enchantingly, eerily:

> Where is my lover?
> I long to discover
> Just where, where he can be!
> Lost and forsaken,
> Yet I'm not mistaken,
> I know, know he loves me!
> Had Father not made his decision for me?
> What price his life, if he could but foresee
> His child condemned to call
> From behind the stone wall?

The girl might have been making up the words as she went along, but it was the melody more than the words that moved Ucheus strangely. He ached with tenderness. Images from his dream welled confusingly in his mind and he could have burst from his confinement there and then, sweeping the girl into his arms. Instead, he found himself straining to hear the slaves, whispering worriedly through the veneers.

'Couldn't you at least have found the—'
'It's smashed. But Fa Fa, you'll never guess—'
'Smashed! Tagan, you clumsy—'
'I didn't *lose* it, did I? Now listen—'
'What good's listening? Look at her—'
'But there's a way! I told you, my father—'
'Enough! What good's your senile old—'
'And Fa Fa, something's happened! Strangers—'
'Enough, I say! Oh my poor, poor lady—'

> *. . . Had Father not still had a vision for me?*
> *Is it too late, though they come to decree*
> *That now this girl must call*
> *From behind the stone—*

'My lady!' It was Ra Fanana who blundered forward, reaching out her arms. The girl pirouetted away, angry, blazing-eyed.

'Don't touch me! Did you think I didn't know? Did you think I couldn't guess? Cruel Ra Ra, you have treated me like a child, but I am a woman now!' Fiercely the girl clutched the Blisha doll to her breasts. 'Protect me, would you – save me, until you can save me no more? What, would you have me face the morrow, ignorant of the fate that is to be mine? I *know*, Ra Ra – of course I know!'

The nurse wailed, 'Child, there is hope—'

'More than hope!' Tagan burst out. 'My father—'

Ra Fanana might have hushed him violently, but her eyes were all for the girl. Selinda flung up her arms; the doll fell to the floor. 'Don't lie to me!' she screamed. 'Don't lie to me any more – don't you think I know I'm going to die? And that Maius Eneo will die, too?'

'No!' The crash came suddenly, sharply as a shot.

Tagan leapt; Ra Fanana reeled; Selinda only gasped as the closet door burst open and Ucheus – draped, half-concealed, in a slithery silken garment – sprawled to the floor at her feet.

❈　❈

Ra Fanana rallied first. 'Guards! Guards!'

'Fa Fa, no! It's a friend, I'm sure of it!'

'Friend? Tagan, what are you talking about?'

There was no time to answer. The doors opened; Tagan tugged the nurse towards him. Standing together, they shielded the silken heap.

'There was a cry.' Uncertainly, the guard looked at Selinda, then at Ra Fanana; but it was Tagan, muttering that the lady had dropped her doll, who flicked the guard contemptuously away. Later the action might cost the eunuch dearly, but the guard, at least for now, remained respectful of the Triarch's daughter.

Superstition, perhaps. He bowed, withdrew.

Selinda swivelled round. 'Stranger, who *are* you?'

Ucheus gazed up at the astonished girl. 'My lady,' he gasped, struggling to disentangle himself from the gown, 'in my real life I have never seen you before, but in my mind you have shone bright as a goddess. I come to you with only honour in my heart, and offer myself as your—'

'*Lover?*' Ra Fanana burst out. 'Well, there's cheek!'

'Fa Fa, shh! Can't you see he likes to dress in women's clothing?' said Tagan, snatching back his lady's gown. 'I hardly think . . . But boy, you had companions? A fair-haired fellow? And a dark one?'

But the youth, for now, had eyes only for Selinda. 'I am Ucheus, son of Zada, High Councillor to the Dynast of Aroc. Last of the last of the Tested of Xaro, I come at the call of Maius Eneo, my beloved – and yours, my lady, yours. I swear, if I can save him, and save you too, then this I shall do; and should my life be the forfeit, I should pay it gladly. Call me Maius Eneo's cousin, call me his companion, call me his friend. Most of all, call me his servant – and yours, my lady, yours.' With that, the youth's forehead scraped the floor.

'Well, I never,' said Tagan, once again.

Selinda kneeled; she clasped the boy's hands, then raised him up.

'Good Ucheus,' she whispered, in a lover's voice, 'I am to die; there is no hope now – and alas, my beloved must die too. Only one night lies before us, one night before death divides us, one night when I may yet pretend I am with—'

Ra Fanana's eyes widened. 'My lady, really—'

'Wait!' said Tagan. 'Boy, how did you *get* in here?'

Selinda ignored them both. 'Good Ucheus, before I die, this service, this one service I beg of you. Speak of him, speak of your cousin, your friend, your master, speak of my beloved till your throat is hoarse, till your lips crack, till—'

'Really, we'll give him *some* water!' Tagan flung back. 'Hava-nectar, even.'

He plunged into the closet.

Ra Fanana reeled. 'Tagan, what are you doing?'

'Oh,' Selinda wailed, 'but what sufferings must befall my sweet beloved? Maius Eneo, my Maius Eneo!' And breaking from Ucheus, almost pushing him away, the girl flung herself down on a couch. A hand trailed the floor, searching for the battered Blisha doll; Ucheus, kneeling beside her, held it out to her. She snatched it, clutched it to her breast. 'Maius Eneo,' she sobbed, moaned, 'Maius Eneo, what have they done to you?'

'My lady,' said Ucheus, 'I can be certain only that he loves you, loves you more than—'

'Life itself,' snapped Tagan, reappearing. 'Boy, I asked you: *how* did you get in?'

Ucheus, as if the matter were of no moment, told him.

Ra Fanana wailed, 'A secret door! In my lady's apartment?'

'What, it surprises you?' Tagan disappeared again. 'But if this boy can get *in*—'

What new foolishness was this? Resignedly, Ra Fanana shook her head, gathering up the gown that their strange visitor had shed like a skin. Already she had chosen her lady's garments for the morrow; the thought came to her that this one would never be worn again. Tears blurred her eyes. Ah, but until they took her to the dungeons, or sold her again – the tears began to flow – Ra Fanana would care for this gown, and care for everything of her dear, dear lady's!

Tagan was thumping at the back wall of the closet. Then came a thumping at the doors again.

With a start, Ra Fanana flung the gown back over Ucheus.

'Lord Glond to see the Lady Selinda.' The guard's eyes flickered suspiciously round the apartment.

Ra Fanana gasped, 'But my lady . . . a moment, a moment!'

She turned desperately as the man withdrew.

Tagan's head popped out of the closet. 'Rock solid! I don't understand it—'

'Never mind that!' wailed Ra Fanana. 'Lord Glond is here – waiting outside!'

Tagan clapped a hand over his mouth. 'Quickly, Fa Fa, get the girl into that gown – or something.' He grabbed Ucheus. 'Come on, missy, it's back into the closet for you. Just keep your hands off those gowns this time, all right? *Control* yourself . . . and if you find the way out, let us know.'

'What, by thumping?' flung Ra Fanana, hauling the confused Selinda to her feet.

'No thumping, hm?' Tagan turned the key in the lock. 'And nothing else either, while you're in there. I've met your type before, never you mind.'

He swivelled back to his distraught lady.

'Glond?' Selinda was sniffing, wiping her eyes, staggering as the nurse pushed and pulled at her, forcing her into the gown, manipulating her weakened limbs like a puppet's. 'But what can Glond want? Has he come to . . . to gloat?'

'Oh my lady, my lady!' Anguished, Ra Fanana smoothed the gown. The silk was of the finest, embroidered with intricate designs. Sudden bravery filled the nurse's heart and she clutched the girl tightly, as if to transfer the strength between them. 'Remember you are the Triarch's daughter. On the morrow, Glond may take your father's place, but for now, your rank remains higher than his. Face him as the fine lady you are – pretend your father is looking down upon you!'

The words had a visible effect on Selinda. When the doors opened again, her eyes were hard and proud.

Chapter 29

A MOTHER'S LOINS

There is magic in a company of players, no matter how shabby that company might be. Margites and his band of Sea Vagas were very shabby indeed, but nonetheless an eager audience had gathered round their makeshift stage. From the steps of the temple and from the shadowy cloister-walk sentries watched the players suspiciously, but would not move them on, not yet. After all, they were a distraction for the crowd during the long wait for the ceremonies of the morrow; their performance, too, was devoid of inflammatory intent.

Margites and his band were no fools. In their long ramblings round these Isles of Wenaya, loading and unloading their rickety van and their two elderly ponies from one merchant-sloop or merchant-galley after another, one brig or barque or barquentine, they had learnt more than just what would play with this audience or that. They had learnt, often by painful experience, what would best preserve their own safety. There were times when gravity would be most unwise; times when nothing was so apposite, say, as the bawdy *Comedy of Capers* or the burlesque *Tragedy of the Triurge* or the biting satire *Triarch True-Wit's Glorious Reign*, with its hilarious attack on Horan isocracy, or 'whore's hypocrisy' – a great hit, that one, on the many isles of the Outrealmers, as well as in the coarser taverns by the Horan docks.

The Javandiom, by contrast, or some version of it, was always a safe bet on solemn state occasions, wherever they might be. Fourth of the Theatricals of Thell, that hoary cycle about the lives of the old gods, what was the play, after all, but a legend that no one believed any more? How long since Javander had been worshipped in Wenaya? Why, epicycles ago! That was what was good about the ancient plays: they created a certain mood of earnest respect, while meaning nothing and disturbing no one.

By now the performance was well advanced. It was hardly impressive, consisting of little more than a line of robed, masked figures, bedraggled in the hot sun, stepping forward in turn on a creaky wooden platform to declaim this or that ornately formal speech.

To be sure, they performed their parts well, in all the high solemnity of the classical style; after each act, the most junior of the players, weaving his way amongst the crowd, would collect a healthy purse. Yet how often, I wonder, even as the noble lines left their lips, did Margites and his friends find their thoughts straying to a certain lost child, a certain little Vaga-girl who had travelled with them for a time, until the slavers had snatched her away? Had that child been here, soaring melodies would have surged from her throat, in rich counterpoint to the verse the players spoke; fantastical images would have risen like magic into the minds of those in the audience, holding them spellbound.

But did we not say there is a magic in a company of players, no matter how shabby those players might be? If the magic was not all it might have been, for some, nonetheless, it might have been enough. Perhaps there were some such – even one such – here today, among the many jostling, craning figures who clustered round the stage, watching the second act of *The Javandiom*.

ATTENDANT SPIRIT:

So it is that time resumes its cycles
Immemorial. So it is that secret
Beneath the rolling waves, betwixt the isles
Where those who worship at her shrines abide,
Javander holds dominion. Here she brings
The spirits of the faithful: when their lives
Upon the lands that lie above are done,
Wenayans rise not to The Vast but sink
Beneath the waves. – How great then is their joy!
How great the many marvels! Born again
Cerulean in new aquatic forms,
With seaweed hair, with fishy scales, with fins
And bubbling gills, their privilege it is
To serve their rightful goddess as her slaves.
   But there is more. Are there not the *Daughters*
Of Javander, for such she calls that caste
Of woman priests which, on each of her isles,
Directs the prayers of those who worship her?
Indeed, united with her in a Web
Of psychic power, in which the goddess sits
In central place, these *Daughters* rule her realms
And all her human charges in but name,
As those who tend the province of the gods
(And not the merely temporal) must rule
In lands where ancient faiths are strong. – Indeed:
For such in these days is *Javander*'s lot

When throughout these Waters of Wenaya
Her *Daughters* do her bidding in the world;
Indeed (though later she shall rue her trust)
These *Daughters* seem the offspring of her loins.
But only seem: and how can they do more?
   For yet within her heart *Javander* aches
With loneliness. Ah, how she longs to look
Again on *Theron*'s face, yet knows (alas!)
That he is lost to her. – Come, let us hear
Her solitary musings.

JAVANDER:

          Fiery one,
In all its turnings time cannot erase
The love for you that still I must avow.
But of my passion no more shall I speak,
For there is pride in me as well as love.
Spurn me, would you? – Very well, I spurn you
In my stead. If severance eternal
Be my destiny, I flinch not from it.
But O, my heart, my heart! How shall I pass
The aeons? Humans, in whatever form
Are hardly fit companions – transfigured,
Untransfigured, they still can be but slaves.
My *Daughters* are no daughters, I can see:
Nobler recompense my solitude
Requires. Must not there be a way? – Think. Think!
   But hold! If rays sprung from my hands and eyes
Might make this citadel, what might my loins
Not fashion in their stead? What matters it
That arid is my womb of milky seed?
Divine am I: already have I left
My father's realms and nothing ill has come,
No retribution. Would I not do more?
Indeed, *Javander* shall enchantress turn,
In her magic wilfully usurping
Her mighty father's generative powers.
Might not I bring real daughters into life?
But yet – if daughters, might I not have sons?
Yes, sons – the noblest boon a mother knows!
Sons would I have, to love me all my days!

Godly fire that burns in me I charge you,
Make good the empty aching of my womb:
Ignite the spark that brings forth progeny!
Immaculate in me would I conceive
Such sons as never earth (nor yet The Vast)
Before has seen, possessed alike of strength
And nobility surpassing, and fair
To me beyond all gods and men. – Yes, yes!
Already stir the seedlings! Children, come!
Upon you would I lave the love that else
Shall fester like a wound. – But one son? Two?
No niggard mother, fecund would I be.
What, three? Four, perhaps? Nay, more! – Already
Works the magic, and I am great with child.

But ah, the pain! Will not this swelling cease?
I feel my belly fit to burst, and still
It grows and grows. – No more! Enough! My hands
Cannot forbear from rending at my flesh!
I rip! I tear! As if I were at once
Both hapless prey and monster of the deep
That hunts it down, in agony I gouge
My womb apart! – But ah! My sons, my sons!
Miraculous, you spring to sudden life,
Five mighty beings so various of hue,
Possessed at once of manly height and strength
And beauty such as breaks a mother's heart.
Why, but look upon your coloration!
To mark you each from each is finny flesh
And hair of purple, green, red, blue and gold –
The pattern sacred of The Orokon,
Translated here to this aquatic sphere!

But can it be that all is not quite well?
Close indeed your mother's act has rivalled
Her father's when he gave life to the gods:
Yet, alas, she knows her strength is weaker,
For can presumption come without a price?
Diminished is *Javander*! Grievous sore
Your birth has left her: never shall she be
Quite as before: she fears perhaps her powers
Have been divided: damaged in its fabric
Is her being. – Yet what of it? Need she care
When you are with her now, and is the price
Not one she gladly pays? But speak, my sons,

226

And tell me who you are. What are your names?
For sure, names must you have: as I was born
Already woman, not but bodily
But in identity, so you, my sons,
Are men. But which shall be the first to speak?
Flame-fleshed One, of all my sons your beauty
Is most dazzling. Come, speak.

FLAME-FLESHED ONE:

                              Mother, goddess
Of every wat'ry place, of burbling springs
And sinuous rills and rivers tumbling free
Down mountain and o'er plain: of willow-draped
Unstirring hidden ponds, and lakes immense
That glow beneath the sun and moon alike
As if they were unearthly fields of fire:
Goddess, most of all, of this pervasive
And elemental source of life and death
Surrounding all, this place of bounties great
And terrors too, this firmament revers'd,
This empire of the seas: we five have come
Your consuls here to be, and each from each
In provinces these realms we would divide.
   But to our names. My darkest brother first:
Come, to our mother bow, and kiss her hand.
Is not he handsome? Mother, cherish him:
Purple like the weedy growths that cluster
On many rocky shores that lie above
Is he: his name is *Amas of the Rocks*,
For rocks that might bring death to mariners
Shall be the ocean province he shall rule.
   Green comes next, green like the ocean's surface
When scooped in arcing caverns perilous:
This being's name is *Eon of the Winds*,
And tempests of the sea his hands shall guide.
Yes, kiss him, mother, love him. – Now for blue:
Shall not you love him more? Like yours his flesh
Is coloured, and like yours his nature bold
Is of the very essence of the seas:
Who can he be but *Oclar of the Tides*,
Whose heart beats with the beating of the surf

227

Upon the shores? – And see his brother here,
His almost-twin, this being of dazzling gold,
Gold such as is strewn with rash abandon
Upon the coasts of all the isles above
Our tropic waters? – *Uvan of the Sands*
This golden son is called, of all of us
The gentlest and most sweet. With such a son
Might any mother rest content. – But ah,
I see you look to me, this *Flame-Fleshed One*
Who speaks: intent are you upon a form
So like the one that spurned you in The Vast.
   Mother, hold! Think not that I am *Theron*
Incarnated new: flaming may I be
But not with fire, unless it be the spark
That kindles being. Is blood not coloured thus,
The fluid that means death, but also life?
My province is the living things that thrive
Beneath the waves: the minnows and the whales,
The sharks and tender rays, the coral reefs
Sublime; the little rearing seahorses,
Cephalopods with tentacles a-waving,
Seals, swordfish, starfish, cuttlefish and crabs,
Eels and oysters, lobsters, clams: the bright things
That flicker through the shallows in the sun,
And dark misshapen monsters of the deep.
My name is *Isol*: *Isol of the Shells*,
For in the meanest shells that strew the sands
My province lies as much as in the great
LEVIATHAN, for life in every guise
It dons in these dominions is my charge.
   But mother, let me kiss you.

JAVANDER:

                O my sons!
Need I care if weak I am, diminished
Sorely by my harsh travails, when consuls
Of such splendour have I now? But consuls?
Shall I not call you Princes – the Princes
Amas, Eon, Oclar, Uvun, Isol!
   (*Isol!* Impartial must a mother be
Between the various issue of her loins,

Yet am I to deny my greater love
For one who is to me the fairest far?
Perforce I must: yet I cannot! My lips
Would linger on his kiss, my fingers would
Caress him lovingly and long: my flesh
Would sear beneath his hands! – My burning boy,
Already you divine my love, I know:
How I but pray you love me in your turn!
Oh *Isol*, dearest *Isol* . . . but enough!)
    Come, my sons, and celebrate our fortune
In thus uniting in these bonds sublime:
Filial, fraternal and maternal
Is our love, and greater thus than passions
Of a merely carnal stamp. See, the lights
That play about my mighty palace swirl,
And all is made yet stranger than before:
Domes, castellations, minarets and spires
And all my ramparts pulse with joyous life.
    See you not this ORCHESTRA AQUATIC,
Of dolphins, lobsters, manta-rays and eels?
See you, too, their fellows all about us
With joyous tentacles and fins and claws
Entwining in a mazy dance? – And look!
Now come the finest dishes of the deep
That human slaves in finny form can bring:
A banquet of the gods indeed is ours,
To mark this day our happiness begins.
    My sons, my sons, I love you all: again
A mother's kiss would not you feel? – Come, yes,
Kiss me, *Amas* . . . *Eon* . . . *Oclar* . . . *Uvan* . . .
Isol . . . *Isol* . . . *Isol* . . . *Isol* . . . *Isol!*

This scene with the sons was not, alas, the most compelling part of the performance. Since there were not enough players to be all five sons, a certain amount of doubling was necessary, with two fellows switching from a green mask to a gold, or a purple to a blue.

If these mechanics occasioned a certain mirth amongst the watchers, the player who took the part of Javander – the only woman in the little company – was, at least, moved by her own performance. If behind her mask she was just a blowzy old Vaga-woman, hardly possessed of the glories of a goddess, nonetheless she had the feelings of a mother. And yet it was not by the issue of her own loins that her strongest passions

229

were stirred. Sorrowing, she thought of the Vaga-child they had lost. If only that child had been her daughter! To be sure, this Javander – this pretended Javander – might have been guilty of certain base motives. With that child and her mysterious magic, this shabby little band might have soon been something more – might, perhaps, have become a great company, leaving behind taverns and public squares for the glories of courtly patronage.

But it was not for these lost chances of glory that the players, any of them, missed the little girl; they missed her because they had loved her, and would never see her again.

The second act was over; it was time to collect the purse.

Chapter 30

AN OFFER FOR SELINDA

'My lady.' Glond bowed deeply.

The nobleman still wore the blue robes of his station, but his long braids were gone and his hair had been shaven close against his skull. With a start, Selinda realised that this was in preparation for the donning of the crown – her father's crown. Was the election over already? No – the arrogant man merely thought he knew its outcome, and would imagine no other. When he looked up he was smiling, and his eyes in their beds of little jewels glowed softly, as if with love.

Selinda shuddered.

Tagan had gone to procure hava-nectar and would hover, decanter in hand, through much of what followed. Briefly Ra Fanana resumed her tidying, but the nobleman, with impatient fingers, flicked her away. So it was that she sat dutifully with her petit-point, needle raised, eyes downcast, but was not to attempt a single stitch. From Selinda's first words, the nurse was trembling violently.

'My lord,' said the girl, 'do you come to mock me? Why else should you intrude upon me at this solemn time?'

'Mock you, my lady? What man would mock such beauty?' Glond stepped closer. 'What man would mock the woman he had chosen for his bride?'

'I was unaware, my lord, that the *choice* was yours.'

'It was my choice, was it not, to make my suit?'

'And my father's to grant it – need I remind you that he accepted another? Were there any justice on this island, that suit would now be honoured.'

'No justice?' The man's voice was soft; reaching out, he would have grasped the girl's hand, but she turned away. His next words were harsher. 'Forgive me, my beauty, but the facts are simple. You remain unmarried, and your father is dead. Think of our isocracy, and how your father prized it. Is it not justice to follow our customs, showing no favour even to the highest? And certainly it is justice to punish a *murderer*.'

'You envy Maius Eneo – envy him and hate him.'

Glond's eyes flashed – or perhaps it was just the jewels. He gestured to the window. 'My beauty, on the morrow your young Islander of Aroc meets his death before the mob. A fine testimony to our isocracy, is it not,

231

that even one of gentle birth should be treated thus? My own fate, if I may say, shall be *somewhat* different – yet you say I am envious?'

'I say you are a monster!' Selinda slumped to a sofa, rubbing her forehead. Ra Fanana's heart thudded painfully; Tagan was on hand with the hava-nectar, but the girl brushed him aside. Glond clicked his fingers, commanding the eunuch to serve him instead; impatiently the nobleman quaffed the soothing liquid. He breathed deeply; he drummed his fingers against the Amali screen.

'My beauty, you are unkind. True, I have no love for your Arocan – indeed I am shocked that any feeling other than horror should stir in *your* heart for your father's murderer ... Yet what am I saying? You are the merest girl, and weak-minded as girls must be; the distresses of these last days have disordered your wits. What testimony to a loving nature that a father's passing should move you so strongly! Indeed, I see I was wise to choose you!'

Selinda rolled her eyes – to think this man had almost been her husband! Handsome he might be, but there was a cruelty in his nature, a cold selfishness that nothing could disguise. He moved forward, taking his place on the sofa beside her. Again he attempted to clasp her hand; again she moved away.

The man's voice was caressing. 'No, you cannot love the Arocan; you, as much as your father, are his victim. Has not his inferior race long resented our dominance in these seas? What we have seen is a bid for vengeance – but such a foolish one! The Arocan shall die, and his race shall be subdued. Shall foreigners overturn all we hold sacred?'

Selinda swallowed hard, gesturing for the hava-nectar after all. She would not shed tears before this man, she would not! She said coldly, 'My lord, *you* are a foreigner, are you not?'

'An Outrealmer of Hora; a foreigner, no – yet think you that I would see any man die – any woman, either? But what is to be done, when the woman is ownerless, and the man the one who has made her so?'

Selinda burst out, 'You know that's not true!'

She darted up from the sofa, pacing angrily.

The man paced beside her. 'My beauty, I was there. And so were you.'

'Yes, that's why I know the truth. Did Maius Eneo drive in the sword? Father fell. He was sick – dying. Ask the royal physicians, you fool!'

'Too late, my beauty!' Was that laughter in his voice? 'Are the entertainments of the morrow to be cancelled now?'

'Tormentor, indeed you mock me! Just remember, the crown you covet has yet to circle your unworthy skull. You have no claim on my duty – go from me, just go.'

'My beauty, hear me!' The man clutched at her; Selinda slapped his face. He caught her wrists. 'Hear me, I say! If but for protocol, my beauty, hear me!'

'What care I for protocol, when on the morrow I die?'

Ra Fanana forgot herself. 'Cruel man, leave her!'

Tagan gasped, 'Fa Fa, shh!'

But Glond barely heard. Holding the struggling Selinda in his arms, he spat out his words through clenched teeth. 'Foolish girl, do you think I would let my own beloved die? Listen to me, and listen well. When I am elected, as is certain to happen, I must uphold the traditions of my office, never deviating from the sacred laws. Your sentence of death I cannot avert – but what if you were to vanish *before* the morrow?'

'Vanish? Wh-what are you talking about?'

'I *am* an Outrealmer, am I not? Vast estates across the seas are mine. When I am Triarch, my Domain of Rest shall be an isle of my own, many leagues from here; there, no jurisdiction shall there be but mine – and there you shall live. My beauty, don't you see? On Hora, all shall believe you have vanished. Spirited away by a jealous god – abducted, perhaps, by enemies of our realm! In truth, you shall be my *secret wife*—'

'Oh, monstrous!' Ra Fanana burst out.

'You're mad!' Selinda cried. 'Let me go—'

'My beauty, hear me out! Don't you see what this means? It means that I love you, as no other man has loved you! Lepato wanted you only for political ends. Why should he marry the Triarch's daughter, but to ensure his own election? As for the Arocan, he has beguiled you with lies, when in truth you are nothing to him but an instrument of revenge—'

Tagan struggled to silence Ra Fanana; Selinda, kicking and clawing, shrieked that the cruel man knew nothing, nothing.

'I know that I love you! My beauty, soon these present sorrows shall fade from your memory like a bad dream!' With one hand, Glond kept a tight hold on Selinda; with the other, he gestured sweepingly. 'On Ambora Rock – I speak, beloved, of my private isle – a palace shall be yours, compared to which these present environs shall seem the merest hovel! Why, there you shall reign as unchallenged Queen, no want unsatisfied, no luxury denied! Already that palace is being prepared for you; already, I have made arrangements to transport you there – tonight!'

Ra Fanana punched Tagan.

Tagan jabbed Ra Fanana in the ribs.

Selinda, for her part, stopped struggling.

Astonished, she looked into Glond's glittering eyes. 'I don't believe it. You're lying.'

'My beauty,' the man laughed, 'it could not be simpler. The guards shall be dealt with; you shall be smuggled out in a chest. And your slaves?' He smiled, winningly, at the eunuch and the nurse. 'Why, they shall go with you. Is not your happiness my *paramount* concern? Do I not love you more than life itself? Ah, but I see you have come to your senses ... Come, embrace me, kiss me, give me but one foretaste of the pleasures that shall soon be mine – that shall soon be ... *ours.*'

He held out his arms. Selinda smiled.

She kicked him, hard, in the groin.

❋ ❋

Glond doubled over.

Ra Fanana shrieked.

'In the jewels! Not the jewels!' Tagan, all solicitude, darted at once to the groaning nobleman. 'My lord, she ... she didn't mean it – what can a pure, innocent young maiden, surrounded all her life by eunuchs and she-slaves, know of what makes a man a man? She merely meant to be playful, I'm sure ... the girl's over-excited, of course she is – the thought of that private isle ... that palace ... *us* for her slaves ... why, knowing her as we do – she's like a daughter to us, really she is, except of course that *we* are the merest, abject slaves, and *she* a lady of the finest quality – we'd say *that* bit particularly excites her, hm, Fa Fa? So you see it's all a bit much, but just *give her time ...* '

'Tagan!' Selinda burst out, disgusted.

There was a thudding at the door. Ra Fanana rushed towards it, opening it just a crack.

'Prince Lepato,' said the sentry, 'to see the Lady Selinda.'

Glond, appalled: 'Lepato? He ... he mustn't see me!'

Selinda, confused: 'Lepato? I ... I won't see him!'

No one heard her. The lady required a moment, just a moment, smiled Ra Fanana and turned back, flustered, gazing at Glond. What all this meant, the nurse could barely imagine; she knew only that this nobleman had offered to save her lady's life, and that nothing, nothing at all, must endanger his plan.

Not her lady. And not Prince Lepato.

She gasped, 'The closet, quick—'

There was a flurry; Tagan screeched, 'Wait – not in there! The ... the Amali screen! Quick, my lord, quick – lean on me ... just try not to *moan* again, hm? Ooh, I know it's dreadful for a gentleman of fine endowments – and yours, I can tell just by looking at you, are *very* fine indeed – when someone gets him in the jewels ... well I don't, not really, that's one of the advantages of ...' Rapidly, Tagan adjusted the zigzagging screen, hissing as he did so, 'But might I just mention, I always thought you by *far* the finest of the suitors? And ... and I don't suppose I could be Head Slave, could I? On Ambora Rock?'

234

Clumsily, almost brutally, Ra Fanana adjusted her lady's gown; impatiently, Prince Lepato burst through the door.

Chapter 31

ANOTHER OFFER FOR SELINDA

'Darling girl!'

Now Selinda's second suitor came sweeping forward, arms out-stretched, red robes billowing. His curly hair had been shaven; perfumed unguents oiled his skull; heavy rings, gold like his teeth, hung from the distended lobes of his ears and circled the tightly plaited cylinder of his beard.

'Prince Lepato, please!' Selinda turned from his clumsy embrace. How she cursed her weakness! Why had she not been more decisive – shouted, screamed that she would not see him? 'Prince, am I to assume that you forget yourself?'

'How can I not, when I think only of you?'

'Beguile me no beguilements! You think of me, yet forget that I am in mourning – that tomorrow, too, is the day of my *own* death?'

'And also, darling girl, the day of my election.' The man, crossing to the bright window, gestured expansively to the crowds below.

Selinda only stared at him, disbelieving. Scion, was he, of one of Hora's oldest families? Once, fool that she had been, she had imagined that a man of such noble bearing would possess nobility of heart as a matter of course. Instead, Prince Lepato seemed wholly without feeling. Just like Lord Glond.

She said coldly, 'There is another, is there not, who might claim your glory?'

The man paced past the Amali screen. 'You refer, darling girl, to a certain treacherous Outrealmer? To a lying, avaricious foreign opportun-ist whose very election to the Thirty is a monument to our corruption? Whose campaign for the Triarchy is the climax of our folly, which should, if any sanity prevailed, have been disallowed by law? Who shall, in the first act of my Triarchy, be first denounced, then banished – better yet, publicly executed? Why, were the Triarch's crown to circle the head of such a monster, the very fabric of Horan life would be ripped into tatters!'

Tagan glanced anxiously at the screen. To an acute ear, and the eunuch's was *very* acute, in the last moments there had been at least one scuffling from behind; one, perhaps two, sharp intakes of breath; possibly

236

also a gnashing of teeth. Fortunately the new visitor was intent upon his rantings; still, this pacing up and down was alarming.

Selinda said, 'But Lord Glond *might* win, might he not?'

Tagan quailed, but Lepato surprised him. Relaxing, the Prince merely snapped his fingers for hava-nectar and strolled, goblet in hand, towards the confused Selinda. 'Darling girl, you are delightfully feminine – the sweetest of the sweet! And here I am, troubling your little head with *matters political*.' The golden smile flashed, dazzling in the sunlight; the unguents glittered on the oily skull. 'Know only this: that as my victory is certain, so is your salvation.'

'You mean,' Selinda said bitterly, 'when I am dead?'

The smile became a laugh; goblet cast aside, Lepato was upon her, imprisoning the girl's hands before she could escape. Repelled, she was aware of the pendulous cylinder of his beard, pressing hard between her small, girlish breasts. 'Foolish child, don't you understand I am to set you free? Don't I know how greatly, how grievously you have been abused? You have been a tool of policy, no more – Glond's, then this so-called Dynast-Elect of Aroc's. These impostors have pretended to fine feelings, but I, Lepato, am the man who *really* loves you!'

'Liar!' Selinda burst out.

It was just as well, since a curse, at the same moment, sounded from behind the screen. Tagan coughed theatrically; fortunately, Lepato was preoccupied.

'Darling girl, shall I not *prove* my love?' The man was excited now, and in a manner quite different from before. Pacing again, holding tight to Selinda's wrist, he almost dragged the girl after him across the floor, back and forth, back and forth, as he cried out that Glond's defeat on the morrow must spell the end of Outrealmer power. 'What have the late reforms in our laws been but a catastrophe for this isle and its peoples? To think, that mere Outrealmers should vote in our elections, should serve upon the Thirty, should contest the crowns of the Triarchy itself! If such is allowed, are not all our laws the merest mockery? Glond and his ilk have corrupted us, but tomorrow a new era dawns in Hora's history, and all the errors of the past shall be expunged. To begin it – and no man, I am certain, shall dare defy me – what shall I do but *annul* your cruel, unjust punishment, declaring that no such fate must befall a Triarch's daughter?'

'Bless you, bless you!' Joy overspread Ra Fanana's face; forgetting herself, the nurse blundered forward, attempting to kiss the hem of the Prince's billowing cape. Tagan, with a squeal, stilled the sudden rocking of the Amali screen.

Only Selinda remained unmoved. 'And Maius Eneo?' she burst out. 'What of *his* cruel and unjust punishment?'

Lepato ignored the girl. By the windows, he gestured in the direction of the crowd. 'Think how they will cheer, how they will weep, when they hear of the reprieve of their beloved Lady Selinda! Ah, and how they will weep, how they will cheer, when, before them, we plight our nuptial vows! Darling girl, shall they not love you more, far more, than if you had *never* been threatened with death? Why, your position will be inviolable!'

'And yours, Prince? Indeed, I see I am a tool of policy!'

'My lady,' Ra Fanana wailed despairingly, 'embrace and kiss your blessed deliverer!'

'Fa Fa, shh!' Tagan struggled to drag the nurse away.

Selinda writhed in the Prince's grip. The pendulous beard swayed, its golden hoops flashing. 'Indeed, darling girl, embrace me, kiss me – for tomorrow, tomorrow, you shall be mine for ever!'

She broke away. 'Vile man, you are wrong! Would I plight my troth to a monster, on the very day when an injustice crueller than my own death is to befall the man I *really* love? Would I *ever* marry you? I am Maius Eneo's, and Maius Eneo is mine! If he is to die, I die too – and gladly!'

'No, my lady, no!' wailed Ra Fanana.

But Lepato only laughed, delighted at the girl's innocent folly. Lurching forward, he would have clutched her again, but she darted from him. She made for the Amali screen, as if to bring it down.

Tagan grabbed her. 'Prince, excuse the poor child—'

'She's overwrought, that's all,' gasped Ra Fanana. 'The blessing you bring her is too much to take in all at once. Just *give her time*—'

'Prince, you fool! Why, at this moment, Glond—'

Tagan slapped a hand over the girl's mouth.

The scene, it seemed, could end only in a new and more terrible confrontation. Instead, still laughing, Lepato crossed back to the door. 'Darling girl,' came the mocking words, 'Take heed of your slaves, for theirs is wise advice, and when I am your master, they shall prosper greatly. Call me *fool* if it gives your heart ease, but shall I let you be taken to the place of execution – do you think, do you really imagine, that when the time comes to seal your father's tomb, you will be standing *behind the stone wall*? I must away – arrangements must be made . . . But darling girl, think of the morrow, when at last I take lawful possession of your heart!'

With that, the man's lips pursed in an airy kiss, he laughed again, and with a flourish of his cape he was gone.

Selinda bit Tagan's hand. 'Ooh, minx! Dearie, that hurt!'

'Tagan, what were you doing? Ra Ra, how could you?'

The nurse wrung her hands. 'My lady, he's – he's going to save your life!'

'And not Maius Eneo's! Ra Ra, don't you—'

The screen descended with a mighty crash. They jumped.

Glond's bejewelled eyes blazed with fury. With what effort, what superlative denial, he had restrained himself as his rival held the stage! Now the torrent of words burst forth. Ra Fanana and Tagan staggered back, alarmed.

'Foolish nurse, would you listen to the Innerman's lies? Wicked eunuch, would you be his accomplice? Do you not see the corruption, foul and rotting like flyblown meat, that festers in one who would be Triarch, with all its pomp and privilege, yet fling away, like chaff in the wind, the very laws of this isle? The man is a fool, and crazed – were he elected, anarchy would be the only outcome. But he shall *not* be elected – he stands no chance!'

The man stepped forward; Selinda stepped back. All at once, his anger gave way to a tone of tenderness. 'My beauty, hear me, and hear me well. In your girlish folly, knowing nothing of the superior sex, you imagine yourself enamoured of your young Arocan. He has duped you, as only the innocent may be duped – but is it not for your innocence that I love you?'

Selinda sighed. 'What are you saying?'

'I may not yet be Triarch, but already many great privileges are mine.' Glond's hand plunged into a pocket of his costume, bringing forth a set of gleaming, jingling keys. 'From tomorrow, I must uphold the honour of my new office, never deviating. But tonight, my beauty – just say you will be mine – I shall *release* your Maius Eneo. He shall be taken to the harbour, supplied with a ship, and left to make his escape.'

Tagan jumped; Ra Fanana almost slumped to the floor.

Selinda cried, 'This is a trick, it must be! How can I believe you?'

'Remember, my beauty, should you resist my desires, I shall have you kidnapped in any case. Here are the choices I put before you.' His arm stole, snake-like, around the girl's shoulder. 'Number one, you may come to Ambora Rock as my prisoner, denied all comforts, enduring all hardships. Now I hardly think you will be so stubborn as to take *this* course, will you? Especially since you shall be without your eunuch and your nurse' – he glanced at them, smiling – 'who will, no doubt, be swiftly executed when it is discovered that they have lost their mistress. Public beheadings, I dare say ... So I think that leaves only the *second* choice, does it not? My beauty, simply say, without demur, that you will be mine, and your Maius Eneo goes free ... Why, my poor child, you are shaking. But may I take your silence as consent? May I not, eunuch? May I not, nurse?'

'I – how *can* I believe you?' Selinda said again.

Glond looked wounded. 'What, would I deceive the woman I love? By all canons of justice, Maius Eneo must die. But if his freedom is the price of your heart, is that not a price I am willing to pay? There is no deceit here, my beauty.' And with seeming tenderness, Glond stroked Selinda's hair; for the moment, the girl could not resist. 'Fear not,' said the beguiling man, 'I shall have the Prince brought before you, that you may bid him a fond – if chaste – farewell before you embark for Ambora Rock ... What, is that surprise I see in your face? Jealous of you I may be, for my ardour is fierce, but must not a girl, in the time before her marriage, indulge certain frivolous infatuations? I have wisdom enough to see that this is so; am I not a man of the world? – Then, too, I am a man of honour, unlike a certain red-garbed villain who would fling aside the very laws which underpin the great office of state he foolishly, he *absurdly* imagines he soon shall hold. My beauty, forget Lepato – forget Maius Eneo. Glond, and only Glond, shall possess your hand!'

By now, Selinda was struggling again, but the man merely affected a delighted laugh. 'What a pity we must postpone this kittenish play! Never mind, my beauty, soon there will be time enough for all your girlish tricks – yes, and what *womanly* pleasures I shall teach you, too! For now, one kiss – just one kiss – and I take my leave.'

In the doorway, he turned back triumphantly. 'Tonight, my pretended kidnappers come for you, to take you away to our secret retreat. But fear not, I say – for soon, when the formalities of the election are over, I shall join you to consummate our union. Ah, what eternities of bliss lies before us!'

Chapter 32

BETWEEN THE ACTS

'What am I to do? Tagan, Ra Ra, what am I to do?'

Selinda slumped down, her face in her hands. Moments earlier she had been angry with the slaves, thinking they had betrayed her; now she saw only the dilemma before her. It all seemed hopeless.

Gingerly, Ra Fanana sat beside her. The sun burned at the window, a hazy gold in the afternoon heat. Below, the sounds of the crowd were louder, obscuring the soft, irregular scratchings that came from inside the closet.

'My lady,' said the nurse, 'I think the way is clear.'

Selinda drew her hands from her face. 'You do?'

Ra Fanana chose her words carefully, at least at first. 'Lord Glond is a fine figure of a man, is he not? But he is, let us say, not entirely to be *relied* upon. Oh, he presents a mask of confidence, but his election is hardly so certain as he maintains. Were the contest an open one, perhaps it might be; but remember, only the Thirty can vote for the Triarch. Would they not favour an Innerman, from an old Horan family? No, Prince Lepato is a better bet, you mark my words – besides, his offer is *much* to be preferred. Would you rather be a Triarch's wife here on Hora, boldly and openly, celebrated by all? Or spirited away, still under the cloud of a death sentence, to some nasty little isle we've never seen? Ambora Rock, indeed! Glond might promise all the luxuries of the world, but you would still be kept there as a prisoner, in fact if not in name. No, my lady, Lepato is the one, it's clear. Quite clear.'

As the words flowed forth, seemingly so reasonable, seemingly so right, Selinda found her face setting hard. To be sure, she had no wish to be hidden away on Ambora Rock. But was this not a fate she would choose a thousand times, if in so choosing she were to save her lover's life? She turned on her nurse suddenly, angrily.

'Cruel Ra Ra, I thought you loved me! How little, in truth, you even know me! Can't you see that life is nothing to me without my beloved? What would I care if I ruled the universe, if Maius Eneo were not by my side? If I follow your way, he will be executed!'

Tagan, in the course of this exchange, had busied himself with the hava-nectar; the scratching, meanwhile, was now a regular tapping. The nurse did not heed it; Tagan felt for the key in his pocket.

But first, just a little more hava-nectar.

'My lady,' Ra Fanana wailed, 'I swear I want only what is best for you! Yes, you are young, your passions are strong, but there is much in this world that must be denied us, for all the longing that burns in our hearts. Oh, I know you love the young Islander of Aroc, but you met him only a short time ago – in fact, you met him only *yesterday*.'

Selinda cried, 'What is time, measured against love?'

'Quite, quite' – Ra Fanana barely paused – 'but really, my lady, you hardly *know* the fellow! And time is more than you think, I'm telling you! Look at it this way: if you *just* agree to marry another – a personable man, a powerful man, a wealthy man – then the life before you is long, the good you may do immeasurable, the happiness you may yet know certain to be great. Yes, it's true, the young Islander of Aroc must – *die . . .*'

Selinda looked as if she might be about to scream, even attack her nurse; Tagan downed the last of the hava-nectar and turned swiftly, smiling. 'But he *won't*. Really, my dears, that's what I was *trying* to tell you.'

The tapping had become an insistent rattling.

'Tagan, what are you talking about?' said Ra Fanana.

'Didn't I mention my *father* had a plan?'

'Did you?' said the nurse.

Ra Fanana had been only too grateful for the interruption; now her gratitude faded as quickly as it had appeared. Didn't she know all about Tagan's father? Skipping forward, the eunuch was about to launch into his story. Instead, the nurse burst out, 'None of your nonsense now, you silly capon! You know your father's just a senile old fool.'

Tagan flushed. 'That's not fair, Fa Fa. He *is*, as it happens, a powerful enchanter.'

'An enchanter who can't save his own son from slavery? Not to mention worse things.' The rattling became a relentless banging, accompanied by kicks and cries. 'And open that closet, why don't you?'

'Fa Fa, I tell you he has a *plan*!'

'And I'm saying I'm not listening to your wretched father! Enchanter, my foot!'

Reluctantly Tagan repaired to the closet; Ra Fanana turned back to Selinda. She grabbed the girl's hands. 'My lady, listen. You're right, Prince Eneo can't be allowed to die.'

'What, so now I should have *Glond* after all?'

'It would buy time,' said Ucheus, stumbling forth from his confinement.

'Time?' Tagan rolled his eyes. 'What good is time if you're stuck at the ends of the earth? Ambora Rock, indeed! As if there could be any decent society in such a place . . . and do they have kohl? Silly boy, she can't go with Glond! Now my—'

'She might *have* to go with him, mightn't she?' Irritably pushing the eunuch aside, Ucheus looked intently at Ra Fanana. 'So how are you going to hide her when the kidnappers come?'

Ra Fanana had forgotten Glond's kidnappers. Her hand went to her mouth. 'Oh, my lady!'

'We'll barricade the doors,' said Tagan. 'Including the secret one. But I'm telling you—'

'They'll batter down the doors,' Ucheus returned. 'Or bribe the guards. Or something. No, Glond's more or less got her already.'

'Ooh, hark at Miss Misery!' Tagan snapped. 'I've a good mind to shove you back in that closet. Now, who wants to hear about my father's plan?'

Selinda, alas, was not listening. She scooped up the battered Blisha doll. One of the doll's seams had split and sawdust, or perhaps it was sand, ran steadily from inside. Tears sprang to the girl's eyes and she hugged the doll tightly. Hopeless. It was hopeless. Poor Maius Eneo!

'Wait!' said Ra Fanana. 'The boy's right – about buying time. Why, it could be – oh, many phases before Glond actually *goes* to Ambora Rock. So what if he didn't get our lady at all? I mean, Glond's men – what if they didn't *really* capture her? What if they just *thought* they'd got the right girl, and . . .'

Selinda's brow furrowed. Carefully she lowered the Blisha doll.

Tagan's patience was entirely gone. 'Fa Fa, you're talking nonsense! As usual. Now my father—'

'It's not nonsense,' snapped Ucheus. 'Don't you see? Glond captures the Lady Selinda – or thinks he has. He puts it about that she's been kidnapped – therefore she can't be executed. But really, she's still here on Hora. In disguise. And *we* do all we can to save Maius Eneo.'

Tagan began, 'As I was saying, my *father*—'

Selinda clapped her hands. 'Ucheus, it's brilliant!'

'Just one thing,' said Ra Fanana. 'If they don't kidnap our lady, then who *do* they capture?'

At once Tagan seemed to forget his ill-temper. He sighed. Ra Fanana was right: his father *was* senile. Marvellous new prospects filled the eunuch's mind. Darting to the closet, he returned with an elaborate gown, various sashes, kerchiefs and veils. In dumb show, he looked sadly at his companions. Fa Fa? Too fat. Himself? Too tall. But Ucheus?

He smiled broadly at the slender boy. 'Well, you *do* seem to like women's clothing.'

'Buby, no! Just keep still!'

Patches tightened his grip on the little monkey's tail. Why he hadn't left her back on the *Catayane*, the cabin boy didn't know; but she had scurried after him, looking up at him with such pathetic eyes, that Patches could not resist. He only hoped the silly thing was not going to get into trouble this time.

He wound his way back through the crowded agora, limping a little on his bruised leg. For a time, guilty at his absence, the boy had returned to the ship, where preparations were well in train for their departure for Ambora Rock. At once Patches felt so despondent that he determined to come back to the agora and try to see more of the Vaga-play. He knew he would be in trouble if the captain called for him, but the boy was still in a defiant mood. He would go back to the *Catty* when he was good and ready. For now, he was intent on only one thing. He craned his neck to see the brightly robed players.

This was the third act of *The Javandiom*.

ATTENDANT SPIRIT:

> So it is that time resumes its twistings
> Labyrinthine, such that all the twinings
> Of a thousand lengths of string, when followed
> With all vigil, nonetheless might never
> Lead to freedom's door. – Beneath the turnings
> Of the tides, beneath the tempests' tossings
> And the tropic rays of heat, *Javander*
> Still holds sway, presiding like a spider
> In its web: at once secure and central
> Yet divided, as in a dimension
> Of its own, the creature lodges distant
> From its anchoring extremes, yet senses
> With awareness keen each tremor of intent
> Upon the tensile cords that hold it fast.
> Thus from the Briny Citadel there flows
> To far dominions all *Javander*'s might:
> Held tight as she may be in webs self-spun,
> To worshippers upon her many isles
> It seems the goddess hangs in phantom form
> Immense above their sands. And so it must,
> As on the isles her *Daughters* still hold sway,
> And worship back along the silky cords
> Comes thrumming. – So it seems eternally
> *Javander*'s reign must last: but forces work

Towards her ruin. Soon the bonds shall break.
Already has she not reduced her power,
Her strength divided, profligate in birth?
Does not she languish now in foolish love,
Enraptured by the redness of an eye,
A cheek, a hand, while *Isol* all the time
Returns her kiss not with a lover's warmth,
But ardour suited only to a son?
Meanwhile far from home range *Isol*'s brothers,
Sore-grieving at their mother's partial love.
   Ah, *Javander*! Fool you are, so swiftly
To sweep like cobwebs through those family ties
That might alone have held your empire firm!
For there is more that threatens. – From The Vast
A spying form now peers down through the waves
And gazes on your Briny Citadel.
The eyes are red, and from them anger shoots
In flames. – Is Theron, then, oblivious
No longer? Has he set his glass aside?
Within him envy churns, and from his lips
Fall harsh, avenging vows.

THERON:

               So, sister mine,
Not only would you flee your brother's side,
But leave The Vast? How grave is your offence!
Did not the father-god who gave you life
Command that you must be my complement,
Both wife and sister, passive in each part,
With neither will nor judgement of your own?
Then would you turn against the stern decree
That we must leave the earth and not return?
Yet more, you build this Briny Citadel:
Guilt set forth defiantly in turrets,
Domes, castellations, minarets and spires!
   What, you would establish a dominion
Of your own, divided from your father's
And from mine? – But greatest of transgressions,
Worst by far (why, hubris gorged to madness),
You take it on yourself to forge new gods!
This usurpation of our father's power

245

Deserves the strictest punishment, and death
Could be but certain, goddess though you are,
If still your great creator did not lie
Unmoving, dark, inside the Rock of Being
And Unbeing. – Yet shall you not be punished
All the same? – Alas, I fear I cannot
Take your life: not all my fiery power
Is great enough to kill another god,
Or one, at least, who shares with me the same
Degree of being. – Yet what need of death?
No: you shall suffer in another way,
Not just for a moment but for ever.
Defy me, sister, would you? – Very well:
You shall pay the price!

ATTENDANT SPIRIT:

                Thus Theron muses,
Writhing with the rage that burns inside him.
What vent, then, is his jealousy to find?
He gazes round his chamber at the vile
Aborted creatures that ooze and slither,
Reeking, on the floor. On one, a hideous
Maggot-serpent, glittering, pulsating,
Bloody like the entrails that a butcher
Flings away, he looks with sudden ardour.

THERON:

Misshapen monster! Loathsome thing! Of base
And self-polluting lusts the spawn you are,
Deserving only swift and brutal death.
Yet cannot your . . . *father* show compassion?
Indeed, for he would fashion you anew,
In form more fair, and charge you with a grave
And vital task.

ATTENDANT SPIRIT:

                  Thus it is. – Flashing fire
From eyes and hands, the jealous god creates
A creature to beguile and to betray
Such as *Toth*, and barely *Toth*, could equal:
The simulacrum of a being divine!
The vision forms amidst the clearing smoke:
Yes, after aeons in the ooze of vile
Abortion all around, this changeling spawn
Becomes, it seems, his father's noble son,
Alike to him in every way. – The name
By which he shall be known is *Kalador*,
A nobler name than he has used before
(But let us not reveal that evil name).
   Now the task: the fire-god, with endearments
Falling smoothly from his lips, with caresses
From his hands, and lavish with his promises
Of future recompense, says *Kalador*
Ambassador must be, and set out on
A mission to the Briny Citadel.

THERON:

There you shall beguile. There you shall betray.
Then shall my foolish sister rue the day
She turned from me! – But come, my son, draw close.
I whisper my instructions in your ear:
Do but as I ask and I shall love you
Ever more. Now go! – What's that? Your brothers?
Of course, shall I not make them handsome too,
When you have proved yourself? – Their destiny
Is in your hands. Now go!

ATTENDANT SPIRIT:

                    The so-called son
Obeys. With what alacrity he shoots
Towards the briny depths, a meteor
More glowing than *Javander* e'er had been.
   At first the fire-god smiles, but then disgust

247

Consumes him, for the creatures that remain
About him, oozing on the floor, cluster
Closer, eagerly, their loathsome faces
Studies both in love and expectation.

THERON:

What, what? Oh no, no!

ATTENDANT SPIRIT:

                Flames burst from his eyes.
The air is filled with frenzied cries, shrieks, wails.
Smoke. – Then the stench of burning, rancid flesh.
He laughs; then looks again upon his glass.

THERON:

Ah, *Imagenta*!

ATTENDANT SPIRIT:

    Certain of revenge
Upon his hated sister, *Theron* thinks
Once more but of his own obsessive lust.
Before long, fresh abortions must be killed.
But next, we must to *Kalador* and see
What doom he brings *Javander's* citadel.
One thing is sure: it shall be ill, not well!

Patches felt his heart pounding hard.

Watching the unfolding drama, the boy found his response strangely divided. On the one hand he was eager to know what happened next; Patches, after all, was an ignorant boy, and the hoary Theatricals of Thell struck him with all the freshness of tales new-coined. Then, too, the boy found himself thinking more and more of Margites and their meeting that morning; each time the old man stepped forward, in his guise of

248

Attendant Spirit, Patches would think again of that comfortable, cushioned van, and the old man's kindness. So it was that when the third act ended, Patches – retreating shamefacedly from the fellow with the coin-purse – worked his way back to the colourful van.

A wild hope was stirring in him. If he had no coins to give the company, did he not have something more? Margites was an important man, and an artist, too: surely he needed a servant to look out for him, to fetch and carry, to smooth his way? Of what value might Patches be to the old man, and to the company? Why, perhaps in time Margites might teach him to read – then Patches could learn the scrolls and become a player too! Oh, he knew he was not of the Vaga-stock, but did it matter, when the players were masked? And what a life a player's must be, what a noble life – to have at one's command such gestures, such words, such enthralling stories!

Poor Patches! In his fondness for Margites, he had not considered that the old man's gestures had become more florid as the afternoon wore on, nor that his words had become more slurred. To the boy, this was all part of the performance; part of that surging theatrical emotion of which Margites, he imagined, was a revered master – for of course he thought the old man a player of genius, rather than just a shoddy old ham. Imagine, then, the boy's disquiet to find a dishevelled, unmasked Margites in the hot, smelly van, swigging heartily from a chipped urn and pawing at the Javander-lady, who no longer looked majestic but like a raddled old harlot.

Patches gulped, gripping Buby's tail with particular tightness.

'Please sir,' he faltered, 'I – I wanted to ask you—'

'What is it now, boy?' Margites snapped. 'Can't a man take a rest between the acts and enjoy a little pleasure?' He rolled his eyes contemptuously, turning back to the Javander-lady. 'Oh, if only we still had that girl! Would we still be living in this squalor, I ask you?'

'Margites, you're drunk! Don't talk about Myla that way!'

'Drunk? I'm the finest player in this company, and don't you forget it, you ugly old bitch!'

Patches flushed. He turned and fled.

Chapter 33

THE OCLAR STATUE

'The tree, the tree . . .'

It rustled in the breeze, just a little.

'The tree, the tree . . .'

Needles fluttered to the path below. Dusk glowered through the tall branches and a pendulous cone seemed to hover in the air.

'The tree, the—'

Blard turned stiffly to his grinning companion. 'You're going to stop this, aren't you, Menos?' he said through clenched teeth. 'Because I'm telling you, you're getting on my goat again, and some. And if you dare ask what goat,' he added, 'I'm going to take that spear of yours and ram it right up your scrawny little arse. Now stand up straight! You don't seem to care what a fix we're in, do you?'

There was a pause. They stood in the mouth of the long sentryway that tunnelled back through the thickness of the walls. Soon it would be time to light the tapers. The passage behind them was a velvety darkness, illuminated only dimly from the ceiling-vents.

'The tree, the—'

'Oh, shut up!'

Menos giggled, not quite voluntarily, and struggled to drag his eyes away from the tall, aromatic conifer, last of an avenue that curved round the gardens to the Oclar Gate. Earlier he had gazed with equal intensity at the mossy statue of Oclar, whoever Oclar might be, that stood on the opposite side of the path, just across from the sentryway. Menos shook himself. Really, why wasn't Blard so woozy? He supposed his fat friend was used to the stronger stuff. Menos certainly wasn't: measure after measure of the day slid by, and still he couldn't seem to shake it off.

But Menos wasn't sure he *wanted* to shake it off.

'Lard – I mean, Blard? You don't have any more of that . . . *stuff*?' he ventured. 'No? What about the dishcloth-headed fellow? You don't suppose he'd give us any, do you, if we went and asked nicely?'

'Menos, pull yourself together!' Blard's patience was almost gone. 'And forget the Sea Ouabin! What have we had from him so far? Gold? Jarvel-weed? Nothing, that's what! Just think about Adek, eh? This is our last chance, didn't he say so?'

'So? He's come by already, hasn't he?' Menos sounded vague; but yes,

Adek had been to inspect them, at the beginning of their shift. The Chief's face had been grim and this time he had not been alone but flanked by a personal guard – two of the best, called back from other duties. Adek was taking no risks – not any more. Somehow Menos had stared ahead glassily, holding down the laughter that bubbled inside him.

'He'll be back,' Blard said, 'you mark my words.'

Menos tried to do so, but now the pine-needles on the path started to form themselves into strange patterns, zooming and swirling. He staggered a little, not for the first time, conscious of the weight of his helmet, his breastplate, his spear. Disgusted, Blard thumped him in the chest; the breastplate rang like a gong.

'Buck up, Menos!'

'Rainbow, are you all right? Don't be frightened, boy. We'll find our way out, I know we will.'

Littler squatted down, nuzzling against the dog's warm flank. All around them the darkness pressed tightly, leavened only by ceiling-vents that now glowed purple instead of gold. For an eternity, or so it seemed, they had wandered through these passages. They were tired, they were hungry, and Littler thought Rainbow was frightened – very frightened. It was true there were exits – an archway, a staircase, a sliding screen. But each time they were about to emerge, Littler had drawn back, aware of the presence of men in armour, or other strangely garbed denizens of the palace. Often it was Rainbow, with swishings and pawings, who signalled the danger. More than once they had cowered in the darkness, pressing themselves into alcoves in the wall as the men passed by, armour jangling, spears rasping at the stones of the ceiling.

'Poor Rainbow! You're worried about Uchy, aren't you?'

It was long ago now that they had lost their friend, back near the beginning of these twisting, turning passages, after the first man in armour tried to attack them. Many times since then, Littler had thought Rainbow might be about to whimper and howl, giving way to his distress. It was not to be wondered at: to lose Jem and Rajal had been bad enough, but at least they had thought Uchy was alive. And safe. And *with them*.

Tenderly Littler's fingers stroked Rainbow's fur, showing in the dim light only as purple-grey. For how long had they had gone round in circles, desperate to find their lost friend? By now, Littler wanted only a safe passage out of this maze – even an unsafe one! He reached for the silver band that circled Rainbow's neck, but drew his hand away fearfully. Something strange had happened, hadn't it, with the first man in armour? Littler sighed, hugged the dog tightly, and they shambled along again. *Click-clack, click-clack,* went Rainbow's claws. How large was this palace? Did it cover all the island?

'Come on, boy, there has to be a way out. Say, what's that smell?'

Drifting towards them came the fragrance of conifers.

'We really should light those tapers,' said Blard.

'I wish it were something else,' giggled Menos.

'You'd pass out,' said Blard. 'But yes, I wish it were too. Damn, if only we'd got those pebbles ... You know, if I see those intruders again, there's no telling *what* I'll do.'

'So ... what'll you do, Lard?' Menos said, grinning.

Blard sighed, gazing along the curving path. His efforts to play the upstanding, responsible sentry were admirable; still, there were limits ... and they'd *hear* Adek coming, wouldn't they? The fat fellow hitched up his toga, scratched irritably at a certain part of his person, and slumped back against the mossy stones. How many of these wretched slaves had still to leave? They would glimpse them through the trees and hear their jingling wristbands, before they came before the sentry post – cowed, wretched fellows, holding out their wrists as if to be slapped ... weren't such creatures beneath the dignity of the Royal Horan Watch, Palace Division? It was an outrage! Would the Sea Ouabin treat such fine sentries so?

'Garden duty, I ask you!' Blard burst out.

'It could be worse, Lard.'

'Oh, and *how*?'

Even in his present state, Menos could think of many ways. Adek could have had them on a charge, for a start. Besides, what was wrong with garden duty? It was easy and pleasant; conifers scented the air, cicadas shrilled and the stone Oclar, from his mossy plinth, looked down on them like a tutelary deity – well, Menos surmised, he *was* a tutelary deity. And did Blard really want to be on the battlements – let alone on the Sea Ouabin's ship, pitching and tossing on the ocean waves? Of course not: it was just that, fancying himself a tough fellow, he had to pretend to be humiliated by this demotion ... Anyway, wasn't it all his own fault?

If Menos thought it best not to voice these thoughts, Blard sensed them nonetheless – well, some of them. 'You didn't help matters, you scrawny runt – saying they *surprised* us, indeed! We're not supposed to be *surprised*, are we – by anything?' He shifted himself back into his upright position, clamping his hand tightly round his spear. Once again he would be Blard the upright, Blard the responsible; Blard, the wholly uncharacteristic.

Did the tutelary deity look a little wry?

'They surprised Adek too,' Menos attempted. 'The other ones, I mean.'

'A rainbow-coloured beast?' Blard's poise slipped at once. 'Come on, Menos, you can't believe a word of that! If you ask me, Adek was in a blue funk – just for a few fluff-faced boys! And why? Because he's a coward, that's why! And then he has to take it out on us – I always knew he had it in for . . . Why, I've got a good mind to seek out that Sea Ouabin now, this very instant, and tell him everything that Adek's . . . Wait!' Blard stiffened. 'Menos, did you hear something?' His head swivelling, the fat fellow gazed behind him into the sentryway. 'You didn't hear . . . a footfall?'

Menos shook his head. What could Blard be thinking? Adek and his men would make *much* more noise.

Blard breathed out slowly. So who was in a blue funk?

Upright. Responsible. But he muttered under his breath, 'Damn Adek, damn him! Menos, I'd go over to that Sea Ouabin's side like a shot, if only he'd give us just one bag of gold. How can any dishcloth-headed foreigner be worse than Adek? Answer me that, now, answer me that!'

'He . . . Adek *could* have had us on a charge,' Menos said aloud. But his voice was distant. Behind them in the sentryway, or so he imagined, the purplish illumination was churning slowly, turning round and round like the needles on the path. What had Adek said about a rainbow-coloured beast? Now it seemed to Menos that just such a beast was hovering in the gloom . . . He turned uncertainly. Oh, that Jarvel-weed!

'And what about the arse-greaser?' Blard was saying. 'He knew those intruders were there, didn't he? Probably just opening up his hole for them, he was, when we distracted them – dirty little gelding! Why, if I get my hands on him, I'll show him a thing or two . . .'

'Adek couldn't punish Tagan,' Menos said, still studying the rainbow beast. Or rather, the illusion. 'Tagan's . . . off limits.'

'You wait. With that little bitch Selinda gone, it'll be a different story. Off limits? Off to the stews with the sloppy-arsed capon, you mark my words! I wouldn't mind having a crack at him myself, just to teach him a lesson. Once I can get him for a few dirty coins – why, the arse-greaser won't walk upright ever again!'

But Menos, by now, was hardly listening. He turned away from the darkening passage, where the rainbow beast – or the Jarvel-illusion – seemed larger, and coming closer.

'Say,' said Blard, peering through the twilight, 'what's happened to *them*?'

Menos heard the clink of wristbands. Snapping his eyes from the sentryway, he followed his companion's pointing finger. Round the curve of the conifers came the latest pair of slaves, one limping, one rubbing his head; their cowls pushed back, the slaves spoke together in agitated whispers, evidently unaware that the sentries could see them.

Blard let out a long, low whistle and hit his companion suddenly, hard, in the breastplate.

It rang out like a gong.

'Menos, straighten up! I may be wrong, but I think we've just found a way to get ourselves out of Adek's bad books.'

'Lard ... Blard, what are you talking about?'

'Look, Menos, look!'

'Jem ... Jem!'

It was Rajal who stopped suddenly.

Alarmed, Jem turned back. He had pushed forward, just a little, in his eagerness to reach the gate. Had Rajal's leg given way? The altercation in the garden temple had not been easy. Jem had taken a blow to the head and Rajal had managed to get kicked, hard, in his injured calf. Already fresh blood had flowed through the bandage; Jem was worried that the wound would worsen.

And what was that clang, like a mournful gong?

As if in answer, Rajal pointed ahead. 'Jem, it's Oclar!'

Jem started. 'Oclar! Raj, what can this mean?'

The statue by the gate was streaked and mossy, mottled by the sunset with purple, red and gold. But the figure was unmistakable.

And so were Blard and Menos.

'Get them!' Blard lurched forward.

Jem gasped, 'Tagan's betrayed us!'

'No – Jem, it can't be!'

Spears prodded; fists swung back; then, blasting from the sentryway, came a sound like a roar. Menos reeled, and so did Blard, for suddenly something massive and rainbow-coloured burst from the dark passage, rearing down upon them.

'The beast!' cried Menos.

'Menos – run!' cried Blard.

Quite what was happening, neither Jem nor Rajal knew. All they saw were the sentries, shrieking, blundering apart in terror, then turning back, colliding and collapsing with a clang of helmets, a clattering of spears.

'What's happened to them?' said Rajal.

'Never mind them!' said Jem. 'Raj, it's Rainbow – and Littler!' Suddenly the dog was frisking about them, his collar gleaming strangely, while their little companion stood, dazed, in the sentryway. 'Littler, what—'

'Blueman!' Littler breathed, staring up, pointing.

'It's just a statue . . . Littler, what happened to you? And Uchy, is he—'

'Blard . . . Menos!' came an angry cry.

Littler leapt. The cry came from behind him.

'Run!' said Jem. He grabbed Littler's hand. 'Raj, run!'

For Rajal, this was a tall order. Jem and Littler took off down the alley, sprinting in the direction of the agora; Rajal would have followed, but his leg buckled. He gasped. And where was Rainbow? Littler called to him; Jem turned back; he would have run to Rajal, but all at once there was Chief Adek and his personal guard, crashing from the sentryway, almost tripping over Blard and Menos.

'The fools, the fools!' The chief took in the scene at once. He grabbed Rajal. 'I'll take care of this one! You men, after the others – quickly now, quick!'

They rushed into the alley, spears at the ready.

'Littler – run, run!' Jem and Littler raced for the agora.

'Let me go!' Sudden new energy surged through Rajal. He pummelled at Adek. They floundered back against the stone Oclar; Rajal winced, pain stabbing his leg; then there was a roar again, and all at once something was there, something immense, something rainbow-coloured, and Adek collapsed, shrieking, over Blard and Menos.

Again came the mournful clang, like a gong.

Chapter 34

WHAT MAKES A MAN A MAN

'Isn't this enough? Won't this *do*?' wailed Ucheus.

'*Do*? You want to be seen through at once?'

'Through all this paint? And these layers?'

'Detail, dearie – that's how you make a lady.' Tagan smacked his lips. 'And let me tell you, there's many a lady who'd *kill* for the expert attention I'm lavishing on you now. Fazy Vina? Why, I've as much chance of growing back my jewels as that little tart has of a decent marriage. Shia Milandros? How any self-respecting eunuch could send out his lady looking like such a raddled old trollop is beyond me. But what do you expect, if you buy the cheapest eunuch in the slave market? Would you believe, I've heard he's not even *clean*? Just the jewels ... Now that would hardly have upped his value three times, would it? Let alone four. Barely doubled, if you ask me ... Now hold still, those eyebrows still aren't right.'

Ucheus sighed. Did a lady really go through this every day? The endless dressing had been bad enough; the painting was unbearable. How he longed to scratch his face! He frowned up at the hovering brush. 'What's the point? It'll all just *run*, won't it?'

'Stop frowning! Dearie, what do you take me for? This is the permanent stuff.'

'Permanent!' Ucheus did more than frown. He broke away. 'You've made me look like this, and it's *permanent*?'

Tagan grinned. 'Yes, and now look what you've done to your eyebrow. Quick, before it sets.' He skittered forward, dabbing with a little sponge. 'Permanent, you understand, is just a figure of speech. Let's just say long-lasting – an old Horan art. Of course, some ladies have their faces tattooed. Eyes, lips – cheeks even, with big red circles. Now *that* sort of thing really is common – all it says is, you can't afford decent slaves. And where are you when the fashions change? Marooned, that's where, like a castaway on an island!'

Selinda, on the window-ledge, paid little attention to Tagan's ministrations. Sadly, fearfully, she gazed out into the evening. Ra Fanana sat beside her, prodding nervously at her petit-point. By now, the scene below was clamorous. There was laughter, there were jostlings, merchants cried their wares, entertainers sang or danced or declaimed or juggled fire-sticks dangerously amongst the crowd. Tapers burned before the Temple of Thirty. The sky was purple, speared through with rays of red and gold.

The girl rested her head on her arms. 'What's your petit-point, Ra Ra?'

The nurse showed her. 'Javander – with her five sons, do you see?'

'The old goddess? Father used to say she didn't exist.'

'Now that I wouldn't know – nice design though, isn't it?'

'She looks powerful. If only she could help us now!'

Ra Fanana gripped the girl's hand. 'Worry not, my lady. I've a feeling all will be well.'

'But Maius Eneo? Will Glond really set him free?'

'We can't trust him. But even if he betrays us, there's still hope – there's always hope.'

'Not long ago you thought there was none.'

'My lady, please!' Tears glistened in the nurse's eyes. 'I'm just a foolish woman, I don't pretend otherwise. But whatever I say, don't you know I'm only thinking of you? Only wanting your happiness? You have no mother, and I no ... no child. But are you not the child of my heart?'

They fell together, embracing.

'There!' Tagan, meanwhile, stepped back from his handiwork. 'Come to the looking-glass. Or rather, don't – how could an ignorant boy like you possibly judge?'

But Ucheus took the first advice. He groaned deeply.

Tagan rolled his eyes. 'There's gratitude for you! You want those *rough sailors* to treat you with respect, don't you, as you ply the seas towards Ambora Rock? Why, a finer flower of Horan womanhood was never seen before. Except for my lady, of course,' the eunuch added quickly.

Selinda looked on, bemused at this creation which seemed at once so like, yet unlike herself. Dubiously she eyed the complex arrangements of jewels and silken sashes. 'Ra Ra,' she whispered, 'you don't think Tagan's *gone a bit far*? He had rather a lot of hava-nectar this afternoon, didn't he?'

'Come, my lady, Tagan's an artist. And the boy is ... well, a boy. Is it not wise, all things considered, to err on the side of the emphatically feminine? Let's face it, the merest hint of the *tomboy* could be disastrous ...'

Selinda supposed it could.

Tagan took the boy by the shoulder, spinning him away from the glass. 'Now, let's practise the walk again, shall we? Follow me. Like this.' The eunuch minced ahead with little tight-bottomed steps. 'And remember, don't talk.'

'Never?'

'Well, you can talk to Maius Eneo – if they let you see him. But

257

whisper, hm? Dearie me, what a pity your voice has changed already. You sound too manly by *far*, I'm afraid.'

'Oh? Perhaps *you* should have done this,' Ucheus muttered bitterly.

'Well, there would have been those sailors to look forward to ... I mean, no – I told you, I'm too tall. But yes, I do have the voice, don't I?' The eunuch preened before the looking-glass. '*And* the walk. *And* the figure. Not to mention the beauty – none of which *you* possess, dearie.' If the boy possessed other attributes which some might value more, Tagan did not wish to consider the matter. 'And that is why we have art,' he added, 'to repair the defects of nature. Well, patch them over, at any rate. I say, you don't *shave* yet, do you? But come on, walk – *walk*.'

The eunuch swished absurdly across the chamber, Ucheus following in grotesque imitation. Selinda had to laugh, but her merriment was brief. On the bench beside her lay the Blisha doll. The sawdust had emptied long ago, but the doll was full again, plumper indeed than she had been before. As Tagan worked, Selinda had been busy too, stuffing the doll with strings of jewels, brooches and rings. 'Ra Ra,' she said now, 'may I borrow your needle?'

'My lady, what are you doing?'

'I often carry her, don't I? Might I not be carrying her when I'm kidnapped? Let's just hope she doesn't rattle too much.' When Selinda finished sewing up the seam, she hugged and kissed the doll and proffered her shyly to Ucheus. 'You'll take care of her, won't you? Well, I know you will. After all, somehow you're going to have to escape from that ship. Or that island. What's inside Blisha might just be a help.'

'Oh, my lady!' Ucheus would have bowed in reverence, but Selinda caught him in her arms instead.

'You're a hero, Ucheus,' she said tearfully. 'If Maius Eneo and I are ever married ... if he is ever Dynast of Aroc ... then you shall be the finest, the noblest man of our Court.'

'Man?' Ucheus said wryly.

'But what is it,' said Selinda, 'that makes a man a man?'

Tagan *hem-hemmed* impatiently. 'I could answer that, but I think I shall restrain myself. This is all very touching, my dears, but time rushes on.' He turned a critical eye on Selinda. 'Fa Fa, didn't I tell you to get her into the boy's clothes? Oh, and we'll have to do something about her hair ...

'You're not cutting her lovely hair!' said the nurse.

'Well, put it up then – *help* her, Fa Fa. If we're going to smuggle her out of here, she's got to look like a common slave.'

'A slave, yes. But a boy?'

'Just get her out of that gown.' Tagan made Ucheus turn his head. 'I know all about boys whose voices have changed, never you mind,' he added saucily. 'And I thought he *liked* women's clothing, too . . . Boys! I think they should all be made clean like me, don't you, Fa Fa?'

'Well, I wouldn't go *that* far. Arms up, my lady.'

'Oh yes, just a few reserved for breeding,' Tagan expatiated, 'and similar pursuits. They could be kept in dungeons. Wouldn't the world be a better place? So much more *elegant*.' He fixed an eye on Ucheus. 'And if you dare ask what's elegant about a greasy arse,' he muttered, 'I'll tweak you somewhere painful, gown or no gown.'

It had not occurred to Ucheus to ask any such thing.

The eunuch clapped his hands. 'Now let's go through the drill again, shall we?'

This was the drill: presuming that Glond had bribed the guards, Tagan expected the kidnappers to burst through the doors, possibly quite shortly, possibly without warning, and possibly with a large chest in which they would bundle the struggling victim. 'Some struggling is essential,' he explained, 'but careful of the costume, hm, boy? One rip in the wrong place and we're in trouble. Now, do you remember what to say to Maius Eneo?'

'To go to your father's house. And how to get there.'

'And that I love him,' Selinda flung out.

'If the boy *sees* him,' said Ra Fanana. 'I just don't trust that Glond.'

Selinda said, 'You trusted Lepato, not so long ago.'

'Well, he is from an *old* Horan family . . . There, my lady, the breeches almost fit, too! But what about your hair?'

'A cap,' said Tagan. 'Don't worry, soon we'll all be lying low in my father's house. Then we can make *proper* plans.'

'Except me,' murmured Ucheus, clutching the Blisha doll to his padded chest. He looked thoughtfully at the eunuch. 'Say, how do you know *you* won't be kidnapped, too? You, and Ra Fanana? Didn't both suitors promise to take you?'

'A likely story,' said Tagan, 'in both cases. But as soon as we hear any noises in the hall, we hide in the closet, hm, Fa Fa?'

'What about me?' said Selinda.

'The Amali screen . . . No, the closet with us – safer.'

'It's going to be crowded in there,' said Ra Fanana.

Ucheus sighed. 'If only we could find the secret door again. That way, perhaps we could *all* escape.'

'Well, let's make a bit of room in there, shall we?' said Tagan. Opening the veneered door, he bundled out many beautiful, brightly coloured gowns, wraps and scarves. Ra Fanana took them, laying them sadly upon her lady's bed. How they would miss her many fine things!

'Let me have just *one* last look for that secret door,' said Ucheus, stepping back into the wardrobe.

It was a fateful action. He cried out.

Tagan spun round. 'Glond's men? Are they here?'

'The closet,' gasped Selinda, 'the closet!'

'My lady, come away!' Terrified, Ra Fanana shielded the girl; Ucheus staggered back, struggling to shut the doors. No chance. A sword slashed through the thin veneers and suddenly, bursting forward, came a fierce, red-garbed form.

'Lepato!' cried Tagan. 'Lepato – *not Glond*?'

Viciously, the Prince grabbed Ucheus by the arm. 'Foolish girl, could I risk the caprices of your heart? Did I not say you should never be taken to the place of execution? Excuse my violence, but what can I do? Tonight I make you my prisoner – tomorrow, I make you my lawful bride!'

The sword flashed in the air; Lepato swivelled round, dragging away the disguised, struggling Ucheus.

Hollowly, the secret door thudded back into place.

'That's torn it,' said Ra Fanana.

'What are we going to *do*?' said Tagan.

Selinda sobbed, 'Ucheus . . . poor, poor Ucheus!'

The Blisha doll was left behind, face down on the floor. Shuddering with emotion, Selinda scooped it up; Ra Fanana reeled, moaning. Tagan slumped to his knees, beating at the floor.

The eunuch's despair was justified. In the next moment, there was a commotion in the hallway, the locks burst from the doors and three burly thugs in the garb of sailors erupted into the apartment, cutlasses flashing.

'Give us the Lady Selinda, in the name of Lord Glond!'

'Wh-what happened?'

Rajal looked down at the inert figures of Blard, Menos and Adek, then up at the other inert, mossy figure that presided over the scene.

'Oclar?' he whispered. 'Oclar, are you there?'

No answer; after all, it was just a statue.

But then there was Rainbow. Barking, frisking, the dog appeared from behind the mossy plinth, his silver collar glowing against the evening's deepening purple. Faltering – but his leg, all of a sudden, felt much better – Rajal followed Rainbow out into the alley.

Two ways. Now which way?

Swiftly they moved off in the direction of the docks. With Rainbow beside him, Rajal felt strong, almost invulnerable. That he would soon be reunited with his friends, he had no doubt. Ah, but how swiftly his hubris would be punished!

It happened in the docks, as Rajal turned, alarmed, realising he must have come the wrong way. First he heard a scuffling. Then he heard a laugh. Then two dark figures leapt at him from an alleyway.

But Rainbow would save him! Wouldn't he?

There was no time. The oblivion-cloth covered Rajal's face. Then a door slammed behind him and he was gone, vanished as if he had never been – and Rainbow was left, alone and whimpering, in the dank, gathering gloom.

Rigging patterned the sky like a spider's web.

Chapter 35

A PLAYER'S STAGE

'Jem? Jem!'

'Littler? Littler!'

Jem swivelled round. Littler struggled, caught between a merchant's wickerwork baskets and the curtain-like skirts of a fat old woman. The crowd closed like a dividing sea.

'Didn't I tell you to keep hold of my hand?' Jem shouldered his way back, wrenching Littler after him.

'There was barking – I thought it was Rainbow!'

'If only! I think we've lost *him* again – and Raj, this time.'

'Then don't you want to find them?' Outraged, Littler tried to break away.

Jem knelt down. He gripped Littler's shoulders. 'Of course I want to find them. But Littler, look around you – what good will it do if *you* get lost, too? Right now, the one we've got to find is Tagan's father. He's our best hope, if we can get across this agora. Now stay by my side, hm? And don't be conspicuous – and don't look at the guards.'

Littler nodded glumly, letting himself be tugged along. If the crush was unbearable, so was the clamour. In places there were chants; in places songs; here and there supporters of Glond bickered, even fought, with supporters of Lepato. Waftings of incense and Jarvel and hava-nectar mingled with innumerable fouler smells.

Then came the cry of a pancake-seller.

Littler's stomach rumbled. 'Jem? Jem, I'm starving!'

'No good, Littler – Raj was the one with the bag of gold, remember? And *he* lost it. Still, I'm sure Tagan's father will feed us.'

'If we find him! Are you sure you know the way?'

'Second side street – west-south, five down . . . Decision Chamber side, not Tomb of the Triarchs side . . . That was what Tagan said, wasn't it?'

'I wasn't there,' said Littler. 'But . . . we've been this way already, Jem.'

'What? How can you tell?'

'See that pool of sick? You trod in it last time, too.'

Jem glowered, scraping his shoe on the paving stones. 'If a certain person hadn't run off, I'd have kept on course – no trouble. Now where's this Temple of Thirty?'

'If *you* can't see it, do you think *I* can?'

'You might from my shoulders.'

'I thought we shouldn't be conspicuous.'

'It's just for a moment – up you go.'

Littler squealed as he swung through the air. 'Didn't I tell you I'm afraid of heights?'

'You weren't afraid of the flying carpet, were you? Now what can you see?'

What *did* he see? At first there was only a blur, a twilight glimmer of purple, red and gold. Littler screwed up his eyes. Tapers flared. Flags fluttered. Smoke rose, steam too. There were jugglers, clowns, men on stilts. Masks. Make-up. It might have been a carnival, but a sinister, strange one. Ominously, guards in plumed helmets pushed their way through the milling commoners. Littler looked away. Everywhere there was a sense of foreboding. More guards, many more, formed a phalanx on the temple steps. Awed, the little boy gazed upon the soaring columns and the great boxy edifices on either side. Decision Chamber ... Tomb of the Triarchs ... But which was which? Littler was about to ask if Jem knew when he heard the barking, the same barking he had heard before, cutting through the music and voices. He swung round sharply.

'Hey!' Jem protested.

'Jem, it's Rainbow!'

It was not. Amongst the crowd, however, there were many dogs; there were cats too; there were serpents, mice, rats, moths, spiders, beetles, ants, fleas and lice, not to mention fish, lobsters, turtles, eels and the like – in various stages of sentience.

Then there was the monkey. Raised high on another set of shoulders, separated from Littler by the mounds of many heads, the creature turned big eyes towards the little boy, and its long tail curled like a question mark.

The creature shrieked. Then it leapt.

Littler cried out; Jem staggered; then Littler, Jem and the monkey crashed to the ground. All around them there were angry cries. Jem felt a foot in his side; a fist grabbed his collar. Then a boy, a boy he had seen before, came diving through the forest of legs, scrambling after the monkey. The boy was copper-haired, pale-skinned and freckled, and his ragged breeches and tunic were a mosaic of patches.

He cried out, 'Buby, Buby ... Master Jem!'

Jem gasped, 'Patches? Buby? What are you—?'

But Littler tugged his hand. 'Jem – quick!'

Pushing through the crowd came a party of guards. Suddenly Patches was swept aside, Buby too, borne away as if by a dividing sea, and Jem, wrenching free from an angry merchant, went skittering away, following Littler's nimble weavings.

Cries pursued them, then faded.

Jem clutched at a stitch in his side, leaning against the plinth of a tall statue. He swept back his hair. Blurring in his eyes were a juggler's burning torches. A stench assailed his nostrils. To one side of him, a swarthy Wenayan relieved himself against the plinth; to the other, two burly fellows smoked something foul and, pinching and punching each other all the while, debated the merits of Glond and Lepato.

'Don't be conspicuous, you said! That was your fault, Jem.'

Jem craned his head over the crowd. A raised platform was close by, where a party of masked figures had assembled as if for the enactment of some ritual. 'All right, Littler, it was *my* fault. But we're somewhere in the middle. How are we going to get to the other side?'

'Who was that boy? The one you called Patches?'

'Didn't I tell you about Captain Porlo?'

'Of course you did – you mean he's here?'

'That boy's a member of his crew. So, unless Porlo's given Buby away – but no, the drunken old coward loves his monkey, if nothing else . . .' Excitement flared in Jem's eyes. 'Why, Littler, the *Cata* must be in the docks! Perhaps we should just forget Tagan's father . . .'

'But Porlo betrayed us. You said so.'

'Well, he betrayed Empster – and Empster betrayed us . . . So where does that leave Porlo?'

'You're asking me?'

'Just wondering – and why's Porlo *here*?'

They would have said more, but the ritual on the stage was about to begin. At once the crowd pressed tighter, murmuring and intent, and Jem and Littler had no choice but to watch as the robed and masked players, declaiming in florid voices, swaying and gesturing broadly, embarked upon the fourth act of a certain drama. Their masks flashed grotesquely in the light of the tapers; their costumes shimmered as if they were burning or as if, perhaps, they were under the sea.

If the performance, from one point of view, was little more than a ludicrous shambles, Jem soon found himself eager to follow its strange, mythic action. He lifted Littler to his shoulders again, this time at the little boy's insistence.

This is what they saw.

Marvelling I contemplate these turrets,
Domes, castellations, minarets and spires,
These many mansions raised beneath the sea.
Such profusion wild! Such light unearthly!
To be sure, its author is a mistress
Of her art, from the fibres of her being
To spin such glory! – Then, what glory waits
The one who brings destruction to her realm?
Indeed, my father's vengeance shall be sweet
And so shall mine! – But hold, hold. Cautiously
I penetrate this briny, wondrous place.
– What, human slaves? To bar my way? Avast,
And back with you! – But see, they melt away,
For in me they must see the spark divine
And know me for a god. (For am I not
A god in truth, now *Theron* calls me son?)
   But ah, I see the object of my quest!
Fantastical in garments green and blue,
With trident in her hand and gleaming crown,
Majestic on a mighty coral throne
Javander lolls. Around her garlands wreathe
And writhe of wild aquatic flowers, and there
Beside her, kneeling like a postulant,
I see one shaped like me, if not so fair.
– And look! The godly one would draw him close
Inviting him to nestle at her breast,
To play an infant's part, and yet to share
Embraces carnal, too! – Oh, loathsome vice!
I see the son's reluctance: yet I see
He shall not long resist, for he has not
Resisted many times before. (Fear not,
My cousin, soon you shall endure all this
No longer: for no longer shall you live!)
   But ah, she sees me! – Hail, O Mighty One!
Your beauty far exceeds all I had heard:
Indeed no mere report could justice do
To charms of such superlative degree.
Blessed then be my mission, that I should come
To you! – Yet need I state why I am here?
No, for already in your eyes I see
Recognition shining like a beacon.

265

Javander, it is true! Your brother's son
Am I: yet better far, from him I come
In spirit meek, and seek but to atone
For all the error that has passed before.
Your brother's bond must keep him in The Vast:
But as an offering he sends me forth,
And begs that you shall take me. – And you must!
Could you still prefer that mewling *Isol*,
Whose stony heart rejects a mother's love?
Forget your slavish passion! Turn from him!
What would you have with self-created toys,
When now before you *Kalador* appears?
Goddess, take your brother's son!

JAVANDER:

Kalador?
Was ever name so splendid? Like a bell
It tolls inside my being: *Kalador*!
Already love is stirring in my heart,
And like a fire it burns me: *Kalador*?
Nay, but like a flood you overwhelm me,
And all my strength is useless: *Kalador*!
So like unto my brother are you formed,
That all my care must be at once for you:
Kalador! – What matters now my kingdom
Or my sons, or all this wild creation
I have made? *Kalador*, this destiny
Is all. – Come, let me take you in my arms.
Come, and be my lover!

ISOL:

Lover? – Mother,
No! Not merely lust this is, but madness!
You know how grievous was your falling-out:
Can you believe your brother really seeks
To reconcile? This creature's words are lies!
An instrument he is of *Theron*'s hate!
Why, look: deception cloaks his very form!
If fair to outward show, what matters it,

When all beneath is rotting, rank and vile?
I see his true corruption: can you not?
Beguilement, Mother, that is all this is
And nothing more. I tell you, should you take
This creature to your bosom, it is sure
That you shall be betrayed. – This *Kalador*
Is evil! Mother, see the truth!

JAVANDER:

                                    What truth?
Think you I shall listen to a faithless,
Thankless child, a child so vile as even
To spurn his mother's love? My trials of birth
Were grievous, yet you care not for my pain!
Son of mine? – Why, had I not seen you burst
Exultant from the tatters of my womb,
No son of mine could I imagine you:
In the state of grief in which I made you,
I only can suppose I made you ill.
    And how you prove my handiwork was flawed!
Not satisfied with all the meanness past,
Now envy stirs you to this feigned concern:
Yes, *Isol*, I can see through you as well!
This *Kalador* is fairer far than you,
And how you hate to see yourself surpassed,
Though you would hug your beauty to yourself.
    Go, I am done with you. – Come, *Kalador*:
My arms, my lips are longing for your love!

ISOL:

Hold, vilest of the vile, and keep away!
Mother, it is not I who is faithless:
Have not I always loved you as a son,
Resenting only freedoms you would take
Unfitting both to your role and to mine?
And yes, I know how great has been your grief,
Your pain: why, I and your remaining sons
(Whom you ignore so cruelly) long only
To assuage it. There is much we might do:

267

Happy we might yet be even now. But
Mother, I am not your brother *Theron*,
And nor is this ambassador he sends!
But enough. – What, creature, still you linger?
Go, *Kalador*, if such might be your name:
Mother wants you not.

JAVANDER:

On the contrary,
Son of mine, she wants no other! – What, whelp?
Draw upon my new beloved, would you?
To arms, in base defiance of my wish?
Indeed I know you have no love for me,
And that your punishment must be severe.
  How boldly clash their swords! – *Zing!* Fish start back
Affrighted, and tremors shake the currents
Round my throne. – *Zing, zing!* Can it be? My son,
Perhaps, is less the weakling that I thought,
And beats back his opponent with a strength
I had not guessed. – *Zing, zing, zing!* No, please, no!
Is *Isol* to destroy my brother's son?
I shall not let it happen! It must not!
– *Zing, zing, zing, zing! Kalador* advances
With a fury such that only *Theron*
Could instil. – *Zing, zing, zing, zing, zing!* Yes, yes!
The fire-god's son is victor! – But no: wait!
My hated son may yet break from this hold!
  Isol, traitor, hear a mother's curses
Echo in your being as you die: die,
I say! – What, think you that the stuff of gods
Shall save you? Think you, fool, to find a shield
In fabric torn from deep within my womb?
I laugh in scorn! – Alas, my *Kalador*
Has being on a plane like to your own,
And though he may defeat, he cannot kill
His traitor cousin: but your mother can!
Yes, my son: for as she made, your mother
Can unmake you, taking back the life
You have degraded and defiled. – See, fool?
The rays burst from my hands and from my eyes.
Die, *Isol*, die! – Ah yes, he sinks away,

Collapsing, screaming, in a bloodied mass.
   But now, what bliss awaits me! *Kalador*,
Sweet *Kalador*, see how I prove my love!
Where you have vanquished, I in turn have slain
My fairest son. – My son? But what was he?
A scrap of swollen flesh from my entrails,
No more. – But come, my sweet, and kiss my lips.
Eternities of splendour lie ahead,
Yet no more, no more would I linger. – What?
My love, where is that smile that so bewitched
My dazzled eyes? – Come, shall you not resume
That countenance in which you came to me?
Spread wide are my arms: will not you fill them?
   But what is this, a game? (No more, no more!)
My love, your face! – Your form! – It cannot be!
What is this monstrous serpent now before me,
Dripping bile of evil from its fangs? – No!
Isol, help! – Come back to life and save me!
Monster, keep away! – Monster, keep away!
Help, help! – *Amoc, Eon, Oclar, Uvan*!
I need you!

ATTENDANT SPIRIT:

             But in vain the goddess cried:
Imprisoned was she in the monster's grip,
For monster now indeed the creature was,
Grown greater, viler far beneath the seas
Than ever it had been on *Theron*'s floor,
This being that was called not *Kalador*
But rather as the *Mandru* would be known,
Most hideous of serpents of the deep.
Such, then, was *Javander*'s tragic fate,
And freedom, so it seemed, was lost to her.
   Oh, in time the sons that still were living
Took pity on their foolish mother's plight,
But all their plans to save her came to naught.
What could they do? – The *Mandru* was supreme,
And could be neither vanquished nor destroyed.
Worse, they found that though they could not kill it,
The loathsome thing could kill them after all,
By drawing on its father's fiery strength:

First one son, then another, met his end
In mighty coils or salivating fangs.
　Thus began the bondage of *Javander*:
Since then, long and strange have been the ages,
And many say the goddess must be dead.
But there are those who say she lives on still,
For after all, how could a GODDESS die?
Does *Javander*, then, for ever languish,
Enfolded by the thing she once desired
Before she saw its true and monstrous form?
　What matters it? Her empire all was lost.
From the fateful moment when the *Mandru*
Transfixed her in the guise of *Kalador*,
The bonds that bound *Javander* to the isles
Above (where once the faith was sure), these bonds
Snapped. – So in time the faith would fade and die.
No worship would sustain her. Cults and sects
Of many different sorts possessed the isles:
The *Daughters of Javander*, once so great,
No more commanded all, no more were seen,
And all Wenaya's unity was lost!
　Ah, shall we dream that yet the day may come
When once again these isles shall be as one?
Shall we dream of crystalline adventures,
Of quests that take place deep beneath the waves?
But there are secrets we must keep. – A song!
Our play is done, its moral made. – A song!
Come, can you hear? I hear celestial bands.
– A song! And then the tribute of your hands.

Jem's heart pounded.

The song was some nonsense, some fal-de-lal with the five players stomping round in a circle, linking arms; there was little evidence of celestial bands. It did not matter: Jem could think only of the tale he had heard, and what this tale might portend. At once he determined that he must speak to these players, especially to this last one who seemed to be their leader. He lifted Littler down from his shoulders and gripped his hand tightly.

But now the song was over; applause filled the air and there were renewed jostlings from the crowd, surgings, heavings. Somewhere above the clamour came the sound of a bell, tolling slowly. Jem found himself wedged again; then, turning again, he could no longer see the stage, nor was he even sure in which direction it lay. There were guards, pennants, smoke, flames, and bodies, crushing bodies.

Littler cried, 'Jem, can't we just get out of here?'

'If only we could! Just stay with me, Littler—'

Now the tolling of the bell grew louder; now, but for the tolling, the air around them was strangely quiet. What could be happening? All through the performance Jem had sensed the imminence of magic, but what sort of magic he could not be sure; now the crowd parted and an old man stood before them. He was tall, dressed in dark robes, and his beard was long and flowing. To Jem, something about him was familiar. Could this be the player who had told the story, in between the speeches of the gods and strange beings – the player, without his mask?

But this was someone else.

'Come,' muttered the stranger. 'I have assumed the guise of a holy man, and the crowd will part for me. Follow – my house is not far. Forget this foolish performance; these players speak mere words, and know not of their meaning. Forget them – I am the one who must guide you now.'

'But . . . who are you?' said Jem.

The old man looked surprised. 'Why, Prince Jemany, did you not expect to meet me tonight? My name is Saxis, and I am Tagan's father.'

Chapter 36

THE BIRDS

'Master Saxis, what sort of holy man are you?' said Jem as they pushed their way slowly to the edge of the agora. 'I mean, what are you pretending to be?'

Still the old man's bell kept tolling. 'Prince, I see you know little of Wenayan ways. I am garbed as a Predicant of the Five Sentinels.'

This meant nothing to Jem. 'And I thought Javander was the deity of these isles!'

'You have seen, have you not, how her power was lost? Now, as the player told you, there is many a different sect. On the isles of my birth – isles, Prince, that are already known to you – it is mighty volcanoes that serve as gods. On other isles there are cults of the caves, of the sea, of the sun, of the vegetable world. Far south from here, or so it is said, there are those who bow to great totems, erected on the cliffs by their ancestors. As for this Isle of Hora, that is another matter. Here it is the Triarchy that is the focus of ardour. Why else should such crowds be gathered, anticipating a mere election?' The old man let his bell fall silent. Suddenly the crowds were gone. 'But here we are. Second side street – west-south.'

In the mean alley, tight between the houses that overlooked the agora, darkness was relieved only by the thinnest seepings of moonlight. Saxis stood before a peeling doorway, fumbling for a key. But if Jem and Littler expected a squalid lodging-house, they were surprised. The door opened into a clean, well-lighted place, empty save for a staircase, solid if plain. With unexpected agility, the old man began to climb, beckoning his two companions after him.

When they reached the first of several landings, Jem attempted to resume his questions. 'Master Saxis, you say the Triarchs are gods of this isle, yet you – though you wear the garb of a rival faith – went unmolested through the thickest of crowds.'

'Prince, there is nothing on which these Men of Hora pride themselves so much as their method of government – what they call their *isocracy*. I say the Triarchs are a focus of ardour: I do not call them gods. They are proxies, at most. To the ruling orders, all that matters is the system of election: the mob may choose what gods it likes, so long as its real masters go unchallenged. Thus it is that old faiths retain much allegiance;

besides, is not freedom in such matters vital to the principles of isocracy? It means the same as *equality*, you know.'

Jem did not know, but detected the irony in the old man's tone. Twice in their progress up the stairs – the back stairs, it was clear, of a grand house – they had passed fellows dressed in the garb of slaves, hurrying, eyes downcast, as if in answer to this or that summons. Jem said, 'There are rather a *lot* of slaves on this island, aren't there?'

Turning, looking at him intently, the old man might have been puzzled, perhaps merely irritated. The irony of a moment before was gone. 'Slaves?' he said. 'And how else would a great civilisation function, were it not for slaves?'

Jem thought it best not to reply. They had reached the top of the stairs. A long, dim corridor stretched before them. Softly, through the thick walls, came echoes from the agora.

'Ask him about the blue crystal,' Littler hissed.

But Jem was off on another trail. 'Pray, Master Saxis, and who are these gods *you* worship? I mean, if your costume is to be believed.'

'Prince, were you not attending to the play? Who are the Sentinels but the sons of Javander, created to care for the realms of her domain? Not gods but Undergods, of the shores, of the deeps, of the winds and storms, of the tides, of the living things of the sea. Of course, they're all dead now – if they ever existed. Amas, that was one. Eon. Isol. Uvan. And one other. Now what was he called?'

'Oclar?' piped up Littler. 'Oclar, Prince of Tides?'

Jem still gripped the little boy's hand; he felt it go clammy. But Saxis was no longer listening. He pushed open a door and the confusion of his companions could only grow as he led them into an apartment at once cavernous but strangely crowded. Mysterious shapes loomed from the shadows; a slave moved in the background, slowly lighting many candles. Jem gasped as the shapes became clear to him.

Eagles. Hawks. Doves. Ravens. The apartment was filled with motionless, staring birds.

Littler whispered, 'Jem, I don't like it – Jem, it's sorcery!'

'And I *am* a sorcerer, am I not?' Saxis smiled. 'But alas, little boy, this is no doing of mine. Have you not heard of the art of taxidermy? You see here the collection of a rich citizen: I am its caretaker, that is all.'

Jem sensed that this was a lie – but why should Saxis lie? The old man motioned them forward. A large table, heavy and rectangular, filled the centre of the apartment. Set at an awkward angle to the walls, it might have been deposited there for temporary storage, then never shifted to a more appropriate place. Jem's gaze flickered back and forth. All round the walls, glinting behind the birds, were specimen cases filled with innumerable smaller creatures – butterflies, moths, insects, beetles. In some of the cases, the glass was cracked; shards glittered like moist, expectant fangs.

'To be sure,' said Saxis, 'my position is a lowly one, when once I was a great and powerful courtier. Still, there are compensations. Has not my son – my castrated son – told you my story? Has he not embarked upon my *Philosopher's Tale*? Hm, I dare say he – *it* – has been remiss.' There was contempt in the old man's voice. 'But come, sit by me – you shall hear of my life, and a fine repast awaits us. Come, sit.'

They complied awkwardly. Pulling out a chair, Jem noted first the elaborate carvings on the back, then the slashes in the upholstery. The table, too, was heavily scored and stained, though it appeared to be of the finest quality – perhaps, indeed, a valuable antique. Uneasily Jem looked at the birds – their beaks, their claws.

He attempted conversation. 'Hot, isn't it?'

The heat, as it happened, was stifling. Shutters lined one wall, but the slave made no effort to open them; instead he knelt at the fireplace, bellows at the ready.

Jem's brow furrowed; Saxis smiled. 'Many and varied are the protocols of magic. But there are those that possess *particular* power.' And the old man held his hand above a candle, splaying his fingers through the bright flame. Jem gulped; the smile did not slip from the withered face. 'Think of metal, molten in a forge. Think of a scroll, crisping on a hearth – blackening, crumbling. Or a house as it burns to the ground. What is heat, but an agent of change?'

Littler's voice was shrill. 'Your hand hasn't changed.'

'What's that, little boy? Well, indeed it has not.'

The old man snapped his hand away; the slave's fire, in the same moment, burst into life. With a muttered oath, the fellow leapt up. Only then did the guests see him properly. He was tall, and when he turned, they saw that his face was concealed by a mask – a disc of white porcelain, like a plate with eyeholes. For a moment Jem was aware of the eyes behind the holes, flicking over him – over Littler, too.

But wait – did Jem not *know* those eyes?

The slave bent to his master's ear, whispering earnestly.

'What's that?' said the old man. '*Two*, you said!'

The whispering resumed, then ceased abruptly as Saxis lashed out, slapping the slave about the head. The plate slipped dangerously. '*Wrong one*? What is this, another of your fool tricks? Away with you, and bring us our repast!'

The old man turned back to his guests, remarking, as if nothing untoward had happened, that he was sure they must both be hungry.

This was true enough.

Almost at once the slave returned, bearing a pitcher and a battered set of goblets. To Jem's disappointment the pitcher contained only water, and somewhat brackish water at that. Chunks of bread followed – hard, mouldy bread – and bowls of a brownish, tepid ragoût. Jem pursed his lips, eyeing the greyish meat, the limp scraps of turnip, the globules of grease; Littler could not help wrinkling his nose. There are things that even hunger finds it hard to conquer.

Jem had suppressed a resolve that was growing within him; now he took strength and pushed back his chair. 'Master Saxis, grateful as we are for your hospitality, I'm afraid we must leave. There are companions of ours who are missing, and it is imperative that we find them.'

Littler brightened. 'Yes, imperative!'

Saxis laughed. 'What, you imagine you shall find your friends tonight? Mayhap, when the events of the morrow have passed – then indeed you may do as you will. But you would save Maius Eneo, would you not?'

Jem slumped into his chair again, bewildered. 'Maius Eneo? Save him?'

'But that is why you are here!' The old man's eyes grew earnest. 'Ah, but I see that we have reached an intersection of plots. What would it mean to you, should I explain that a certain Lady Selinda has escaped her doom? Already, I trust, she has departed these shores. But what of the youth who has become her lover, the youth who is destined to be Dynast of Aroc? Unless my magic can set him free, Maius Eneo shall die before the mob. But I am old – weak . . .'

Saxis gestured to the burning candles. 'Be not diverted by common-place tricks, such as the merest stripling learns in his first term at Elio College. To save Maius Eneo my powers must be channelled, as through a prism, by a greater magic.' The old man leaned forward, gripping Jem's hand. 'Prince Jemany, *you* are that magic – you, and this little companion of yours. You have been touched by the powers of the gods – and on the morrow, I shall *focus* those powers.'

By now the heat was almost too much; Jem clawed at the neck of his tunic. Could he believe this story? Could he trust Saxis? Memories welled in him of his days in Unang Lia, of the enchanter Almoran and his servant, the girlish youth. Almoran's palace had been called the House of Truth, when really it was only a house of lies. Jem might have asked Saxis how he would proceed with this channelling of his, but at that moment the slave – a girlish youth indeed – set down the last of the evening's offerings. It was a tray burdened with little silver pots, streaky-sided bottles and flat dishes of powdery, coloured substances.

The old man clapped his hands, as if to banish grave thoughts. 'Friends, I trust you pardon the crude fare that is all a poor exile can provide? But all is not lost.' He held up a brown, stoppered bottle. 'May I recommend the Elio sauce? Were I to forget all else I learnt at Elio

College, still I should hope this most precious of receipts might never be expunged from my mind.'

Removing the stopper, Saxis sprinkled just a little of the liquid over his bowl. Uncertainly, Jem and Littler did the same.

'It looks funny,' said Jem.

'It smells funny,' said Littler.

Of course, Saxis knew what would happen next. If his guests wondered whether they should taste the sauce, their doubts did not last long. Moments later, they could think only of the food. Smiles overspread their faces. Gravy ran down their chins. Musically their spoons clicked against their bowls and when they were finished, there was no need to ask if they would like second servings.

Littler grinned, 'So long as there's more Elio sauce!'

While they waited for the slave to reappear, Saxis demonstrated other powders and potions. Mouldy bread became springy with freshness; crumbs swelled into biscuits and cakes; brackish water became sweet wine. Say what he would, Jem thought, their host was a sorcerer of prodigious powers.

And again Jem was uneasy, conscious of the birds, with their glimmering beaks and eyes, and the papery, immobile butterflies and moths. From a specimen case came a sound of clinking. Cracking.

Cracked glass, falling from its precarious place.

Saxis, for his part, seemed not to hear it. The sorcerer had other concerns, muttering irritably at the slowness of his slave. With a blackened pot in hand, the fellow moved awkwardly behind their chairs, filling their bowls with more ragoût. He was hovering behind Saxis when his ladle slipped, splattering brown muck on the old man's sleeve.

The sleeve flew back through the air. 'Stupid eunuch!' There was a clattering, then a crash. The pot, then the ladle, had fallen to the floor.

So had the slave's mask. And so had the slave.

There was an awkward silence. Saxis sighed; Littler gulped; Jem could only look on, dazed, as Tagan – for of course, it was Tagan – hauled himself to his feet again, gripping the back of an empty chair. He juddered out the chair from the table and flopped into it, resigned. Jem looked pityingly into his face, appalled at the savage bruises, the cuts, the smearing blood. If Tagan had been beaten before, it was clear that he had now been beaten again, still more brutally.

Jem gulped, wondering what more this night would bring.

Chapter 37

THE RAVEN

At the sight of his son sitting at the table, Saxis could barely conceal his outrage. 'What are you doing, sterile creature?' he cried.

'Father, I'm tired of this game – in fact, just tired.'

'Tired, when my destiny is at hand? Castrated thing, am I to look upon your unmanly, beardless face? Put back your mask! Put it back at once, I say!' Revolted, the old man turned towards Jem, as if certain of sympathy. 'How I hate to look upon his face – I always thought he was no son of mine, and now indeed he is no *son* at all! Indeed I wish he had died when they emasculated him – sliced it all away, they did, sliced it clean! Ugh, what man would not kill himself rather than live thus?'

Jem faltered, wondering how to reply, and could only be glad when Tagan said tartly, 'But then, I'm hardly a *man* either, am I, Father? Besides, don't I come to you, day after day, whenever I can spare a moment from my duties in the palace? Who would look after you if I were dead? I don't think my *brother's* going to be much use to you.'

This roused the old man to fury. 'Capon, put back your mask!'

'Father, you've broken it,' Tagan said lightly. 'See? Down there? On the floor?'

'Then get another plate! You can bore out the eye-holes while we're eating – while I tell our guests my *Philosopher's Tale*.'

'I'll bet they can't wait.'

'What, neuter? What was that?'

Tagan turned to Jem. 'Father,' he explained, 'likes to feel he has some status – so I'm afraid he can be a *little* imperious. After all, he once had a retinue of a hundred. Or was it fifty? Or ten? Or one? In any case, he was an important man, back home on Inorchis. Once.' The eunuch's expression changed. 'But Master Jem, what's happened to Master Rajal?'

'I wish I could tell you,' said Jem. 'I said we had to find our companions, didn't I? But Tagan, what's happened to *you*?'

'Besides Father, you mean? Oh, *he's* too weak to do all this, never you mind. Let's just say more rough trade, dearie – twice in one day, would you believe?' The eunuch attempted a wry look, but Jem did not smile; Tagan looked down, sorrowing, instead. 'Or – if you prefer – say that Glond's thugs were a *little* enthusiastic.'

Saxis impatiently cleared his throat. 'Time,' he announced, 'for my *Philosopher's Tale.*'

'But at least they left me here,' Tagan went on in a low, flat voice. 'My lady and Fa Fa weren't so lucky.'

'So this lady's gone?' said Jem. 'But where?'

'I *said*,' Saxis resumed, 'it's time for my tale.' He looked almost sternly at his young guests; he cleared his throat importantly.

'You have wondered,' he said, as if daring his guests to deny it, 'how a man of my station should find himself quartered thus, sequestered here so strangely, in a place far from home – how one such as I, destined for greatness on the Twinned Isles of Aroc, should find himself eking out the years of his decline on this Isle of Hora, tended only – if at all – by the unmanned thing that used to be his son, with no home but this ugly room, where the role he plays is that of mere curator to these dead, brittle-winged butterflies and birds.'

There was a pause – and another.

'I'm not quite sure I follow,' Jem said to Tagan.

'Tagan,' piped up Littler, 'but who's Fa Fa?'

'Ra Fanana. My lady's nurse. Well you see, Fa Fa—'

'Both gone?' said Jem. 'Kidnapped? But how—'

Saxis burst out, 'You *have* wondered, have you not?'

'Father, such rudeness! Have you no patience?'

'Enough, steer! You would bore our guests?'

'I'm sure *you* would,' was the bitter reply.

Jem looked uneasily between father and son. But if fresh violence seemed to fester in the air, soon it was gone. For a moment Tagan's eyes blazed defiance, then faded. His shoulders sagged; his head hung; then slowly his hands rose to cover his face as Saxis continued, oblivious, 'You *are* aware, Prince Jemany, that I am from Inorchis? It is on that lost isle that my tale must begin.'

'Lost isle? Then you know about . . .'

Jem said no more. For some moments he had felt a growing heaviness in his limbs; now the heaviness became acute. Before him, tepid and glutinous, was his replenished bowl. Saxis pushed across the Elio sauce, but now Jem felt no further hunger. Littler, already, had slumped across the table.

The tale that followed would unfold in Jem's mind like an unnerving dream.

1

What is meant by a sorcerer and what by a philosopher is a vexed question; in different lands, the same words may mean different things, or different words the same things. Suffice to say that long ago on Inorchis, it was the pride of this old man before you to style himself Philosopher Royal. And yet, this old man began life with few advantages.

Of my father I can speak but little; he died before I was born, and my mother, his one living wife, would say nothing of him. I knew only that he had left her in poverty. To my distress, his very name filled her with bitterness. I hoped that I would not disappoint her so much, yet feared my hope was vain. I was a sickly child, and when the time came for my Manhood Trial I knew that even my mother was certain I should fail, to be condemned not only to the ignominious lot of a gelded slave, but to the sure prospect of early death.

Destiny was to order matters differently. Amongst those sharing my time of trial was Pareus Eneo, who all were certain would soon be anointed Dynast-Elect, as soon as the Manhood Trial was over. A plucky, combative fellow, Pareus Eneo had marked himself at once as our natural leader. Glorying in the energies of youth, nothing delighted him more than to demonstrate his strength. But he also had in him a streak of folly and one day, when the surf was high and tempestuous, he swam too far from the shore. Soon he was in trouble, desperate trouble. His friends watched in horror, for it seemed that none could save him. Then, just as death was certain to claim him, I felt within myself a surge of power. A beam of light erupted from my hands, arcing over the water. In an instant the Dynast-to-be was lifted from the waves, spirited upwards on the searing light, and deposited on the sands before us, gasping but unharmed.

I was a hero. How had I performed this feat? No answer could I give, but none was needed. To certain rare youths, my mother had once remarked, the onset of manhood brought strange and prodigious powers. In the event, she would not be surprised that her son was such a youth. She appeared desolate, as if I were lost to her. This angered me, for to me it seemed that I was saved. There could be no doubt that I was the luckiest of fellows. Shamed before his companions, the Dynast-to-be might have resented me, but his temper was of the sweetest. Admiringly, he determined to take me into his service; I should be his Philosopher Royal. So it was that I was sent to the Isle of Elio and there, at the famous college, my powers were trained.

My training, it must be said, was a little late. All through childhood I had sensed intimations of something otherworldly stirring inside me. Had my gifts been cultivated from the first, manhood might have brought me far greater powers. Never, now, would I be a philosopher of the highest calibre, and I confess that I resented my mother, for I came to see that she had kept my destiny from me, hoping that my magic would remain dormant. Still, she had failed; at least on Inorchis, where I had no rival, my powers would be formidable.

Orbits passed; the Dynast-to-be assumed his place as Dynast and I my place as Philosopher Royal. It was the pinnacle of my life. If once, as a green boy, I had rescued my monarch, now I was to rescue him again and again, in one way or another. When his courtiers were wily, I took their measure. When his peoples were unruly, I rendered them calm. Many times I repelled the depredations of invaders. Constantly, that I might be apprised of any threat, I would repair from the Palace of the Dynasts at Sarom to the mysterious hundred-voiced Sibyl of Inorchis, whose cryptic words I comprehended as readily as a child does the scrolls of the old tales. From the hundred-voiced one I learnt of floods, of storms, of tremblings of the Thunderer; of evil schemes afoot across the seas; of enemy ships sailing near. Always, when I left her, I felt a sense of power.

But one day there was a prophecy that left me shaken. The hundred-voiced one spoke of a blue raven that would fly skywards from my monarch's palace; standing out in silhouette against the moon, the bird would presage a certain and terrible calamity. I begged to know more, but the hundred-voiced one was silent; after that day, she would speak to me no more. I was distraught, for what had I done to be treated this way? Desperately I wrestled with an inexplicable guilt.

2

It was shortly after this that I found myself summoned unexpectedly to my monarch. I thought I knew why. It happened that some time ago a certain Lord Belrond, Ambassador of Hora, had arrived unexpectedly on our Isle of Inorchis. Belrond's mission was to propose trade links between our two realms. The incentives he offered were generous, but the plan filled my monarch with secret rage. Had we Islanders of Aroc not repelled the Horans, long ago? Were we now to welcome them as traders, bowing to their commercial power, allowing ourselves to become enmeshed – slowly but inexorably – in what was an empire in all but name?

Yet much as he longed simply to reject the proposals, my monarch feared the reprisals this might bring. Telling the Horan he must deliberate upon the matter, in truth he merely delayed and delayed. More than once already he had consulted with me, seeking the aid of my magic arts; more than once, were I not mistaken, he had hinted that Belrond should meet a dark fate. My code of honour rebelled at the idea. Belrond was a legitimate ambassador, no invader. What had my monarch to fear, should he only stand firm? Thus I had told him before; thus I expected to tell him again, when this new summons came. But neither my own intimations, nor those of the hundred-voiced one, had prepared me for the direction that events were now to take.

'Saxis,' my monarch began, 'since the days of our youth you have been my loyal subject. What am I to think now? Have you turned against me? Have you become a traitor?'

The words astonished me, but my astonishment grew apace as I learnt what lay behind the terrible questions. By this time my monarch had many sons, the eldest being a youth named Radenine. Recently successful in his Manhood Trial, Radenine was possessed of striking charms. Of all the subjects that engaged the Court, few could be more fervent than the question of his first marriage. Where would his choice fall? Which lady would be so blessed? The finest virgins of Inorchis vied eagerly for the role; many, in the rashness of their ardour, vowed they would die virgins, even take their lives, should it be their fate to be rejected.

All this I knew: but now my monarch told me of a startling new development.

'You are aware, are you not, that the Horan travels with a considerable retinue? Cursed be that he does, for I see it now as part of his cunning design. Among that retinue is his daughter, one Lady Aniani. Her father has called her a great beauty. To me, this means nothing. It is a Horan's beauty, and thus a whore's – must not races other than our own be repellent to all true Islanders of Aroc? Yet now, in the worst calamity of my reign, I hear my son is in love with her – with a Horan whore!'

'My monarch, this must be false, some rumour—'

'Fool, I have heard it from my son himself! Did he not stand before me like one bewitched, here in this very chamber, declaring that he will take the harlot for his bride – Aniani, and no other? What can this be but some scheme of Belrond's, to bring these Twinned Isles into the Horan thrall? Now do you see why I know you are a traitor? You see the future, do you not? You advise me, do you not? Can you not have known where your advice would lead? Why, perhaps it is you who has bewitched my son!'

I sank down, horrorstruck. 'My monarch, believe not this of me! Vision have I, but much is obscure to me; a dark destiny, I know not what, has hidden this terrible knowledge from my sight! Punish me not, for never once has my loyalty wavered, in all the long orbits since our Manhood Trial!'

'You deny my charge? Saxis, I know not whether to believe you. Yet still, perhaps, you may redeem yourself.'

'My monarch, tell me how – anything, anything!'

But even as I made this rash promise I knew that doom hovered over me, ready to descend as if on dark wings. I dare say no surprise even flickered over my face as my monarch laid his condition upon me. It was simple. To avoid the Horan's wrath, my monarch would pretend to agree to the wedding. The announcement would be made, the guests would assemble; then, in the moment before she was to plight her troth, the Lady Aniani would collapse and die! It was to be the operation of the subtlest magic. No suspicion must fall upon my monarch; if needs be, I might contrive a plague that would kill thousands, to render more credible this one sudden death.

3

With what a heavy heart did I set about my task! Yet even as I contrived my evil spell, I knew I could never see it through. Some orbits ago I had married and fathered a son; the loyalty that had once been all my monarch's had now become divided. For the first time I saw my monarch clearly, and what I saw was a vain fool. Why, if I were to kill this innocent lady, would I not curse for all eternity the Dynasts of Aroc, and my own progeny too? It was this murder, not this marriage, that would bring doom upon Hora!

So at least I thought. Thus it was that, violating my vows of loyalty to my monarch, I warned the young Radenine and his lady of their danger, counselling them to flee while they had the chance. Indeed, I went further: I arranged a ship; I bribed the guards. Conscious of my own danger, I too would have fled the Isles of Aroc, but for the thought of my wife, who once again was great with child.

Radenine laid but one condition upon me.

'Good Master Saxis, this service you render shall bring you much credit in the life beyond this; in this life, too, I shall reward you well, if ever it falls within my power to do so. Promise me but one thing, should this plan fail.'

'Fail! It cannot!'

'But if – if.'

'Son of my monarch, anything, anything.'

'Then this. In the days of my innocence I would see you conjuring, converting crumbling dirt into grain, rank weeds into ears of corn, dull lead into gleaming gold. Once, with an incantation, you turned a slave-boy into a bird; to the applause of the courtiers, he fluttered from the window. You explained that if this bird encountered greater magic, a magic force still greater than your own, then he would again assume human form; otherwise, he would live as a bird. Do you remember, Saxis? Oh, but you must!'

Radenine sighed. 'How I have envied that blessed slave-boy, who left this hated palace for the infinite skies! Now, should it happen that my father captures us, his rage shall know no bounds. Yet I would die rather than lose Aniani. Saxis, say that, should the need come to pass, you shall liberate my beloved and me, as once you liberated that hapless slave-boy. Speak not to me of the dangers: I know we might never encounter greater magic, should we search for it all our lives. What of it? Would we not rather live as birds, swooping and soaring in the azure air, than eke out human lives in a bondage of misery? Promise me, but promise me you will do what I ask.'

I promised, but my heart hammered with dread. The incantation to which the youth referred had been a foolish one, dangerous too. Determined to amuse my monarch, I had succeeded only in rousing his ire at the loss of an expensive slave, while leaving myself weakened, hovering close to death. Remember that my powers were less, much less, than they should have been. To effect not one metamorphosis, but two, would be certain to destroy me. With a shudder I recalled the words of the hundred-voiced one, and the particular bird the slave had become. I had turned him into a raven – a blue raven.

4

Swiftly the time for the escape drew near. It was midnight; clouds obscured the moon. How many times had I told myself that the plan could not fail? In truth, it had been hopeless from the start. Thinking I had avoided suspicion, I had reckoned without my monarch's many informants. So it was that Radenine and his betrothed were stealing from the palace when suddenly out of the darkness burst the enraged Dynast, sword in hand.

'Traitor!' he cried, and lunged at me; but Radenine, in the hot folly of youth, darted forward as if to protect me. He fell, run through by his father's sword.

Tapers flared. Guards swarmed around us. Aniani flung herself across her lover's body, clutching him even as they would tear her free.

Life ebbed rapidly from the stricken youth. 'Saxis,' he moaned, 'the incantation!'

Terror consumed me. Knowing I must honour my promise, I forced the mystic words from my lips. There was a bolt of lightning. I collapsed to my knees. In the next moment, the blue raven that had once been Aniani fluttered skywards, sharp against the suddenly unclouded moon.

And on the ground, in a pool of blood, lay the youth whose one desire it was to have been her husband. For him, the incantation had come too late.

So it was that doom descended over Sarom. My monarch's contrition knew no bounds. From the days of our youth I had seen the goodness in him; now he embraced me, begging my forgiveness for his errors, as I begged him to forgive mine. Soon, I sensed, he would order the construction of a mighty temple, surrounding his son's tomb. There, for all the life that remained to him, my monarch would sit thinking upon the days that had gone; there, too, would perch the blue raven that had once been Aniani, that never would return to human shape. When she died, the tomb would be opened and the girl would lie in raven-form upon her lover's breast.

5

But this was to come. Meanwhile, stricken at his daughter's loss, Ambassador Belrond fled back to Hora, telling his masters that our Twinned Isles were cursed. For my part, my courtly days were over; my monarch would call upon my magic no more. With the pension he provided me, I left Sarom behind me, purchasing a small farm on the far side of Inorchis. There, remote from all society but that of my wife, our son, and the new child that would soon be ours, I resolved to live in humble simplicity, forgetting the magic that had brought me such sorrow.

Alas, my sorrow was but beginning, for shortly after our removal from the city, my wife died in giving birth. For any man, such a blow might be heavy, if he had but one wife and loved her dearly; for me it was especially so, for all my arts, depleted as they were by my late incantation, could do nothing to save her. Then it was that I cursed my fate, wishing only that the magic was strong in me, that I might defy the dictates of time.

I fear I became a bitter, twisted man. Mourning the loss of my beloved, so too did I mourn the power I once had wielded. Yes, it was a shadow of the power I might have had; yet what glories might have been mine, had I but used my gifts to the full! I saw now what a fool I had been; yet as my sons grew older, I knew that power might still be in my grasp. It had to be: for if my magic was leaving me, theirs was but beginning. If only I could harness their gathering powers! Closely I monitored the stirrings within them, anxious that their training should not be left too late. Ah, but what fools we human creatures be! Could I forget the raven, dark against the moon?

Tagan was the elder of my sons, and when he had reached the age of ten orbits, I arranged that he should depart for Elio College. That way, by the time of his Manhood Trial, the boy could exercise his powers to the full, and I could assist him. But Prince Jemany, can you guess the rest? Of course you can. Crossing the seas to the Isle of Elio, his ship was waylaid by a Xishan galley.

At first, this was all I knew. Despairing at the news, I could think only that I must recover my lost son, cost what it might. Rumour had it that the Xishans had been bound for the notorious slave port of Shaba Lalia, west-south of the Outrealms of Hora. Leaving my younger son in the care of a slave, I vowed that within an orbit I would return. Vain delusion! That was ten orbits ago; since then, this old man you see before you has pursued a trail through these Waters of Wenaya, failing again and again to find his son, until he came at last to this Isle of Hora.

Many an adventure might he relate. More than once he languished in foreign dungeons; once he was tempted by the love of woman, forgetting in his madness the one beloved wife to whom he would be loyal even after death; once, he too was captured as a slave, and might have died in fetters, had a kindly master not set him free. But all this is too much to tell. Suffice to say that the old man used up all his substance, of strength as of fortune. Hora was his last chance. From here, he could neither make his way home nor purchase back his son, even should he find him.

By now, he was sure he would *never* find him – ah, and how he wishes that he had not! After all, the old man often would have abandoned his quest, returning to the other son that still was his; yet, in his greed, he would think of the powers his firstborn must possess, the powers that must now be strong within him, swollen to fecundity with his burgeoning manhood. Come, laugh at this foolish old man – would you not laugh? He had thought he need only purchase a slave in order to gain back all he had lost; imagine the horror that consumed him when he learnt that long ago, before he had even embarked upon his quest, all prospect of power had been rent from his son, as he suffered a loss that can never be restored! What magic can flow from a pitiful eunuch?

So it is, Prince, that you see me here, an old man and a broken one, a servant in a great man's house. What dreams of glory once were mine! What ignominy is my present lot! Yet on the morrow, shall not my ignominy end? Think of the gratitude of Maius Eneo, when he is liberated from the Horan's thrall! What future then can there be for Master Saxis but restoration to his old and treasured role? Again he shall be the glory of Inorchis! Again he shall be Philosopher Royal!

The dream is over. Or has it just begun?

Saxis leaned back, smiling evilly. On and on raged the fire in the grate. By now, Jem was barely conscious, but struggled boldly to focus, to think. The *Philosopher's Tale* seemed to press against him like a tangible thing, hovering on the heat. Oh, but Jem's limbs were heavy! Sweat soaked his clothes and ran from his hair, dripping into pools on the table before him.

'Saxis . . . it doesn't add up.' His words were slurred. 'This tale of yours . . . it doesn't make sense.'

'No, Prince?' The philosopher was wry.

Jem felt a prickling, a prodding at his skin. What could it be? Littler lay sprawled, his breathing stertorous. Tagan was sobbing. Jem struggled to force out his words. 'Tagan . . . was never trained. So how could he have had such great powers, even if . . . even if the slavers had never taken him? And your powers . . . they're gone. You said so, Saxis. So how can you be Philosopher Royal? You're too old – and your Isle of Inorchis . . . it's gone too, vanished entirely. You're *mad*, Saxis.'

The old man, it seemed, did not hear these last words. 'Gone?' he mused. 'Vanished? But not entirely. Gone, but shall return.'

Jem thought Saxis was speaking of his isle. But perhaps he meant his powers; perhaps he meant both. The old man leaned forward, his eyes glittering like the fixed eyes of the birds. 'Prince, you *feel* my powers, do you not? Now, at this moment, do you not *feel* my powers?'

The prickling again. Maddening. Oh, but what was it? Littler, it was clear, was wholly unconscious. 'You're channelling through us, aren't you? Even now, you're just channelling . . . channelling. You'll never be Philosopher Royal, Saxis. Never again . . . never.'

'Really, Prince! Not even with my two fine *captives*?' How composed was Saxis! How calm! Still his son whimpered; still the father ignored him.

The prickling, Jem realised, was along his arm. But which one? His head had slumped to the table and he could see only Saxis, looming over him like an evil god. 'We've met madmen like you before, Saxis. And . . . and we've escaped before, and . . . we'll escape now.'

'Now?' The voice was mocking. 'That, I think, is *most* unlikely. But do you take me for a cruel man?'

'Yes.' The bearded face blurred in Jem's eyes.

'Oh, come! You're not really my *captives*, are you?'

'But you just said . . . of course we are!'

'Prince, you shall help for me a time, that's all. *Friends* help each other, do they not?'

'You're not . . . our *friend*.'

'Am I not friend to Maius Eneo?'

'I . . . what do you mean?'

'I mean what I say – I say what I mean.' The philosopher had pushed back his chair from the table and moved slowly about the crowded apartment. Distractedly, as if they were alive, he petted the dead birds –

cupped a head, ruffled a wing, stroked a glittering beak, then a claw. Jem could barely keep his eyes open, but always he seemed to see the crazed old man, pushing his way through the shimmering haze.

'Dear Prince,' Saxis mused, 'what shall become of you? Perhaps – it is, after all, a vice of royalty – you rate your own importance just a *little* too highly. Perhaps this old man now has secrets to which you – a callow boy – cannot be privy. Perhaps, in this very act of channelling, he might . . . why, might he not even *restore* his powers? Has that occurred to you? And might not Inorchis, too, be restored? Hm? Prince?'

'I . . . I don't . . .' The prickling. His arm.

'Did I not say I had *another* son?'

'Yes. But how . . .' But how did this follow?

Then Jem saw it. The butterfly on his arm. Or perhaps it was a moth. In any case, the patterns on its wings looked like eyes and Jem fancied they were staring up at him.

He forced his gaze away. 'Another . . . son?'

'Prince, for shame! You heard my story, did you not?'

How dull Jem's brain had grown! Only now did the realisation come to him. A laugh welled, unbidden, to his lips. It was the horror – the horror of it.

'It's Leki, isn't it? He's your other son . . . Leki!'

'That's right. My lost son . . . the lost one *now*. But might he not come back to me?'

'He's dead,' Jem said brutally.

'Prince, can you be so sure?'

'I can, Saxis – I *saw* him die.'

'But Prince, what is death?'

'I . . . I don't understand.' Jem's awareness was fading fast, but in the moment before he lost the struggle, joining Littler in the blackness of oblivion, he saw the butterfly – or perhaps it was a moth – twitching its powdery, papery wings. Beside his arm, a candle flickered, dripped. Then suddenly the creature flew into the flame, flaring like a beacon as its wings caught fire.

There was a laugh, then a slap. 'On your feet, eunuch! Tie these boys up. And stop snivelling, hm?'

Chapter 38

LOOK THROUGH MY WINDOW

Jem surfaced slowly, rising like a diver. Images surrounded him in a cloudy swirl. There were conifers, trembling in a midnight garden; bodies dead of plague lay about in heaps. Butterflies clustered over a massive, stony tomb, blood oozing over their papery wings; darkly the raven flew against the moon . . . Jem moaned. Far away, softly, there was a sound of breaking glass.

He blinked. Shadows. Heat. He would have rubbed his eyes but his hands were bound, crushed painfully behind his back. He was gagged, and ropes ran round his chest and feet. Slick with sweat, he struggled to shift but could move only his head, starting as the tip of a bird's wing scraped his cheek. He shuddered, thinking again of the glassy, inhuman eyes, gleaming from hundreds of hunched, feathery heads. But those were behind him: lashed into an armchair of exotic design, Jem faced the shuttered windows. Beside him in a matching chair was Littler. Similarly bound and gagged, the dishevelled little boy was still sleeping, or drugged. Bright light pushed through the cracks in the shutters; the morning, evidently, was far advanced.

Floorboards creaked. Jem heard voices:

'So then, all is ready? The strangers are in place?'

'My lord, could you doubt me for a moment?'

'Doubt every man – it is the first rule of politics.'

'Oh? Glad am I that I am no politician.'

'You call yourself *philosopher* – I call you traitor.'

'My lord! When your triumph is all my care?'

'Have you not betrayed the isles of your birth, and the Line of Dynasts whom once you served? But what care I for your history, when soon your powers shall bring me all I desire? – Well, almost all.'

'What greed is this? You would have *more*?'

'Traitor, say you haven't forgotten the girl! Ah, if I could but embrace that lovely creature in the same moment as I savour my triumph! But even now, I dare say, she is far across the seas. Could you not magic her before me this instant, that my ecstasies might be delayed no longer?'

'Indeed, my young fool – if you would squander the energies that ensure Lepato's doom!'

'Bah, your old man's heart is withered! Why, and the fug in here is suffocating! Traitor, can this heat be needful? Or these creatures you have killed?'

'You would have your magic, would you not?'

'You would serve me, would you not, when I am Triarch?'

'Of what else might I dream?'

'Unctuousness does not become you, traitor. But soon the smoke rises from the Decision Chamber; I must away.' Footsteps sounded again. 'Make sure the election is mine, that is all I ask. Remember, oceans of wealth are yours, should you but bring this to pass!'

'Lord Glond, I am certain of your goodness!'

There was the squeal of a door. A clunk.

'Certain of your treachery, more like, once your vaulting ambition is fulfilled,' the old man muttered. 'Call me traitor – traitor indeed!'

'Lord Glond, I am certain of your goodness!'

Contemptuously, Glond mimicked the philosopher's words. What goodness would Saxis receive, once his task was done? Only what might be vouchsafed him by his god, after he entered the realms of the dead! How Glond despised the enchanter! But from the moment his spies had told him of this old man, living in obscurity here on Hora, the Outrealmer had determined to harness his powers.

A little bribery had been all that was necessary. What did a foreigner care for the noble traditions of Hora's isocracy, that he would not pervert them – gladly, gleefully – for personal gain? What wild thoughts of wealth, what fantasies of luxury must even now be filling the old man's senile mind?

The blue-garbed nobleman laughed softly, the jewels glittering around his eyes. Standing by a window in the corridor, he gazed down on the agora through the open shutters. What crowds! What clamour! And all there to witness his impending triumph!

If only he could have the girl, too – now, with no delay! How splendidly she would soothe his pain after they had driven the screws into his skull! Might she not rub his head with sweet oils? Might she not lie beside him in his darkened, perfumed chamber? If only – but no, it was better, far better, to have sent her at once to Ambora Rock. He thought of the girl on the swelling ocean and felt himself overwhelmed by lust. But could he trust Porlo? Curse the old fool, curse him, if he did not protect that girl with his life! But then, what was the old sea-dog but a base and venal coward, concerned only for the reward he would receive?

Or imagined he would receive.

Glond's gaze rose above the agora to the rigging and sails that webbed the skies behind – the docks, from which the *Catayane* had sailed the night before. Anger suffusing him, the nobleman recalled those boyhood days when he had contrived – yes, contrived – to have himself kidnapped from Ambora Rock. His kidnapper had been a certain notorious brigand who went by the name of the Sea Ouabin. How the young Glond had longed to join the fellow in his wicked life of piracy! But his plans had come to nothing – all thanks to Captain Faris Porlo! For the sake of a reward put up by Glond's father, the Ejlander had pursued the Sea Ouabin far across the Waters of Wenaya, managing at last – somehow, inexplicably – to defeat him in battle, snatch Glond back and return the boy to his father.

How Glond had hated Porlo ever since! Of course, he had pretended to be the Ejlander's friend. But the old fool would find out soon enough just how much of a friend Glond considered him to be – once, of course, he had served his purpose . . .

Glond shuddered, thinking of the agonies, then the ecstasies before him. Did he feel the merest tinge of regret, that he had given up his buccaneering ambitions? But no, what had the Sea Ouabin been but a shabby criminal, hunted from one end of the ocean to the other? Glond had felt nothing but loathing for the fellow after he had been defeated by the likes of Porlo. Where was the Sea Ouabin now? Dead, almost certainly – eaten up by fishes on the ocean floor! No, the glories of Glond would be greater, far greater, than any a common buccaneer could know! The Triarchy was just the beginning. Soon, Glond was certain, he would be emperor, sole ruler, not just of Hora but of all Wenaya!

And now his shudders became convulsions. Gazing again on the agora – on the Decision Chamber! on the Temple of Thirty! on the Tomb of the Triarchs! – he moaned, almost swooned. He closed the shutters, raking his fingers against the vertical slats, rocking and gasping, racked by spasms in the thin lines of light. Oh, his triumph, his triumph would be sweet!

But the ceremony. It was nearly time.

Quickly Glond turned and went on his way.

Who was it who'd said that you couldn't trust a eunuch?

Straining to hear what the philosopher said to Glond, Jem had closed his eyes. When he opened them he saw Tagan – the treacherous Tagan – looming above him in the shadowy light. Long hands loosened Jem's gag. Rage swelled within him. He would have burst out, but his mouth was parched.

'Hava-nectar. Don't worry, Father didn't make it.'

Smiling, Tagan proffered a goblet; Jem gulped gratefully at the milky liquid, then spat it out, as if realising what it might contain. 'Another of your drugs? Tagan, why?'

'How could we trust you? Oh, I'll admit I've had my doubts about what Father's been doing. But don't you see, there's nothing we can leave to chance?' Tagan held up the goblet again. 'Come on, more. Swallow this time – just a little.'

Jem shook his head. 'You're on his side too? So much for Maius Eneo! So much for your lady!'

'Master Jem, don't be silly. I'm telling you, I don't like it any more than you do – and do you think I'd have truck with a fellow like Lord Glond? It's playing with fire. But don't you see it's the only way, if we're going to save my lady – *and* her beloved? Oh, but I wish I could tell you everything!' Shaking his head, waving a hand, Tagan seemed to intimate there was too much to explain. And not enough time. 'Master Jem, just tell *me* one thing – where's Master Rajal?'

'What, you want to capture him, too?' Jem jerked his head towards Littler. 'That *is* him. He shrank.'

'Capon,' called Saxis, 'leave those prisoners alone!'

Instead, Tagan pulled away Littler's gag. 'Father, it's hotter than a furnace in here. Do you want them dead before you cast your spell?'

Jem murmured, 'You think your *drugs* have done us good?'

Littler shuddered, moaning in delirium.

Saxis said, 'Neuter, come here! Help me into my robes!'

'Father, one moment!' Liquid ran down Littler's chin.

'It's true what that nobleman said, isn't it?' Jem pursued, his voice louder now. 'This has nothing to do with Maius Eneo. Or your lady. You're traitors, you and your father both!'

'Shh!' hissed Tagan. 'Don't get him started!'

Too late. Sweeping forward, the old man thrust his face into Jem's. 'Traitor, you say? Did I not save my monarch? In like manner, shall I not save his great-son? Prince you may be, but you are a fool if you believe my promises to the corrupt and vicious Glond. You see now why I must keep you captive.'

The angry face relaxed into a smile. 'Still, you shall serve your purpose well enough. And should you die, you and your little friend . . . is it not to the *greater good*?'

'Die?' Jem shuddered. 'You're going to kill us?'

Tagan hissed, 'Father, you can't! Jem's a good man . . . you'll let him go, won't you, when this is over? Father, please, say you'll let him go!'

'Silence! What care I for the whinings of a powerless, pathetic eunuch? Has the hole between your thighs not healed? Must you continue to squeal, squeal, even after all the orbits that have passed? Unmanned thing, if this boy's destiny is to die, then die he shall. What is his life, against the life of your brother? Think, but think, of when he has returned to us, radiant in the glory of his manly potency!'

'Yes, Father,' Tagan said glumly.

Jem said, 'You're mad, Saxis – Leki's dead!'

But the old man only turned away. 'Come, steer, gag them again and help me dress. The ceremonies of the day are about to begin.'

'Father, you won't forget Maius Eneo?'

'Castrated fool! Is he not necessary to my destiny?'

'But how will you free him? Shall he rise up suddenly with god-like power, striking down those who would take his life?'

'Vile, mutilated thing, is it not enough that I must look upon your face? Must I endure your fool questions too? Oh, how I wish you had bled to death on the day they threw your manhood to the dogs of the street! Know only this: that your brother – your manly brother – will return, and again I shall be Philosopher Royal. All this shall come to pass with the spells of this day! Spineless sterile thing, have not my motives become clear to you yet? Now gag these boys again – and help me with my robes!'

'Yes, Father – at once, Father.'

A rapping came at the door.

Tagan started. 'Father, who can it be?'

'I told you there was *another*, did I not?'

Tagan was bewildered. 'Another what?'

'Oh, never mind! The gags, capon! Tightly, tightly.'

Jem felt the ball of cloth, pushing at his lips. He rolled his head away. 'Tagan, how can you go along with that monster? Have you no courage? Have you no will?'

'I am a eunuch. I am a slave. What would I not do to save Maius Eneo? What would I not do for my lady's happiness?' The long hands were surprisingly strong.

Helpless, Jem heard the following exchange:

'Your Royal Highness ... but time rushes forward!'

'You would have me assume my place in the agora? Madman, but assure me that my victory is certain.'

'All is as prophesied. Even now, has not the Lady Selinda been made ready for marriage? Is not the young Islander of Aroc ready for death? But one element more, and your destiny is fulfilled. See, I have the strangers, bound and ready for channelling!'

'Let me look upon them! Ho, but would I venture further into this chamber, when the heat is so intolerable? And these dead things! These birds, these insects! Crazed old man, did you not say you were once a fine courtier?'

'And shall be so again, shall I not?'

'Indeed. Yet you surround yourself with such vileness?'

'You would question my magic? Fool, vain fool!'

'Ho, a feisty spirit! You shall liven up my household, I see! But again, you are certain? There can be no doubt?'

'Who is to be Triarch, but Prince Lepato?'

'And the girl – mine, too?'

'Already she is yours. It is written in the stars. But go, go! The time is upon us, and I must begin!'

'Madman, fail me not, and wealth – wealth beyond your dreams – shall flow upon you like rain!'

'Your Royal Highness, I am sensible of your bounty!'

The door banged shut and Lepato was gone.

'Sensible you would have me murdered, more like, once I have raised you to the throne,' Saxis muttered. 'Madman – madman indeed!'

Tagan began, 'Father, I don't understand! How can you –'

'Stop your squealing, castrato, and dress me in my robes! And the shutters, open the shutters! Quickly now, quick!'

'Who is to be Triarch, but Prince Lepato?'

There was a shuttered window in the corridor. Heavily, Lepato leaned against the frame, staring unseeingly through the slats. Like an incantation, he repeated the philosopher's words. Yes, no question now – he would triumph.

Lines of light slanted over his face, glittering on his earrings and his newly shaven skull. Marvelling, he reached up, tracing the circle, at once rough and tender, where soon the crown's rim would bite into his flesh. His destiny, or so he fancied, hovered above him like an imperial eagle, ready to descend. How he longed, how he ached for the tightening metal, for the turning screws! Such pain – ah, but the pleasures that were soon to come!

To think, even to think, that a man could know such glories in a single day – first the Triarchy, then his new bride! All last night Lepato had burned with lust, longing alternately for his crown and the girl. If the girl, it was true, was already in his grasp, still he had restrained himself from going to her, possessing her there and then. Must not all be done in the immemorial ways, with all the dignity of his new office?

When a man finds himself on the crest of a pinnacle, it may happen that, looking down, he feels a sudden vertigo. Lepato's vision juddered into focus and he saw the crowded agora, glaring up at him through the window-slats. He flung wide the shutters and staggered back, stunned by a shock of realisation.

It had worked. It had all worked. Prince he might be – oh, the appellation was real enough – but in the isocratic society of Hora, such titles had long ago become almost meaningless. What did they confer but a shabby glamour? Lepato's family, or rather his branch of it – cousins, mere cousins, of the old King – had been particularly shabby. As a boy, had not Lepato run barefoot with dusty urchins, stealing from handcarts, heckling traders, skittering down alleys, leaping and yelping over dirty canals? What had he been at heart but a little criminal? Yet from the first he had vowed to gain back the place his family had lost – that place, and more.

Lepato's had been no idealist's career, begun in a haze of high expectations, only to slither inexorably, inevitably, into the politician's accustomed sty. No: from the time he adopted gentlemanly garb, procuring a post as copyist to the Keepers of the Law, his progress had been built on corruption. Bribes. Incentives. Favours. Threats. What a gamble it had all been – and it had worked, it had all worked!

But this was just the beginning. Was he to share his power with those fools Fahan and Azander? Was he to heed the advice of the Thirty? Never: soon enough, with the Sea Ouabin to aid him, and the philosopher's magic too, Lepato would sweep away the system of isocracy, with all its prating of equality. There was no equality in this world. Had not his own career proved that well enough? Most were inferior. Some were superior. And soon Lepato would reign supreme!

But the ceremony. It was nearly time.

The Prince's red robes billowed behind him as he swept imperiously down the corridor. And yet, at the head of the stairs, he paused. Composure slipping, he fixed his eyes upon a certain narrow door, barely noticeable in the ornate panelling. Tentatively, he opened it. There was one last call he should pay before returning, via the tunnels under the agora, to the rampart-like steps of the Decision Chamber.

A well of light, falling from above, illuminated another set of stairs, a narrower set, leading up to the roof. Yes, he should venture up, lips brimming with unctuous pieties: *Sea Ouabin, are you comfortable? Sea Ouabin, are you happy? Sea Ouabin, do you want for nothing?* Yes, he should assure his fine guest, one last time, of all he had promised – so rashly, so wantonly – to deliver when this day was over. Lepato shuddered. How to rid himself of the corsair, once the fellow had served his turn, was a problem he had barely considered.

Echoing down the stairs came an evil laugh.

Lepato turned and hurried on his way.

Chapter 39

RED SMOKE OR BLUE?

Up. Up.

Escaped from a window, a butterfly – or perhaps it is a moth – winnows at the air with papery wings. Up, swirled by breezes, oblivious of agora, docks and bay. Up, skittering across terracotta tiles that tumble in an orange arrested slide, the creature comes to rest in a sliver of shadow under a gable's edge. Around the agora, other roofs are crammed, packed. Not here: this, pitching and plunging, is a roof to repel invaders. Empty: but not quite. Here, where the tiny wings are twitching, the little feelers quivering, what is this but a cunning screen, a grille, a mesh? A place of concealment, where only Master Butterfly – or Master Moth – furtive in diagonals of dark wood, can spy upon what is passing inside.

'How much longer? Scurvy, how much longer?'

Listless, lolling in a throne-like chair, the corsair before whom all the world has trembled does not, for now at least, present his customary fearsome façade. Sweat collects in the band around his skull. Irritably, he plucks at his desert headdress; glugs at hava-nectar; says again, 'How much longer?'

Scurvy, squatting beside the throne, avails himself of a chamber pot. Nervously, he peers at a programme-scroll; above them a punkah flaps back and forth, worked by the little hunchback's hairy foot. So much to do, and all at once! 'Soon, master, soon,' he says. 'The event shall begin – why, any moment now.'

His master's brow furrows. Idly he holds a far-glass in his hand, raising it from time to time to his eye. 'What care I for this ceremony? The merest formality, is it not? Or do you refer to the opening of your bowels? (Foolish Scurvy, to partake so liberally of our host's sickly offerings!) I mean, how much longer shall we be holed up on this isle, concealing our galleys in a secret cove, hiding our very faces from the light? Scurvy, don't you long for the bracing brine, pungently filling your deformed and slitted nostrils? Do you not ache for the sea breeze, for the heft of the waves, for the salt spray swirling round your twisted limbs, falling upon your monstrous hump like – why, like restoring balm?'

Scurvy, straining on the pot, says he does. But is the Ouabin convinced? Uneasily, the dwarf shifts. A little before he is ready, he edges himself off the pot, clasping at his breeches. Should he scuttle into the corner, avoiding the blow that soon might come? But no, can he leave the flap-flapping punkah? His foot falters; then quickly he picks up the rhythm again. He ventures, 'Such a balm, master, has yet to restore *me*.'

His master laughs. 'Ah, crook-backed friend, but I forget! You are a dry-land creature, are you not? Did I hear you say you confined your early scuttlings to – where was it, some drab northern peninsula?'

The punkah goes flap, flap; with relief, Scurvy plants himself once again upon the chamber pot. 'Tiralos, master,' he chirps. 'A watery enough place being an island – more watery, may I say, than the sandy lands of the Ouabin?'

'Is it paradox you attempt, my little familiar? Shall we put it into verse, like Imral, that wisest of Unang versifiers? Let's see: *My roamings, once, were over seas of sand—*'

The punkah goes flap, flap. '*And still are now, but sea conceals the land?*'

'Good, little familiar!' Scurvy beams; in the same moment, he achieves a second success. The Ouabin laughs again; but his mirth, if mirth it is, is short-lived. Back he looks through the screen – so cunning a screen; from this side, almost invisible – and sighs, 'Ah, that I never had made this pact!'

The dwarf busies himself with the programme-scroll. 'With the Red Prince? Master, it shall soon enough bear fruit – why, soon enough.'

'You trust him, Scurvy?'

'Master, is it for me to trust?'

'Scurvy, I see your eyes a-glitter—'

What, in the flush of his recent success? But Scurvy says, 'Master, it is *your* eyes that glitter, like chips of blue fire in your much-tanned visage – your remarkably handsome visage, if I may say.' And reaching forth a hand – still he squats on the chamber pot – through the white robes the dwarf strokes his master's shin. The great man leans back; flap goes the punkah; but punkah or no punkah, a foulness rises from the pot and on a table behind them the delicacies – their host's sickly offerings – wilt in the heat, pickle and stew. Can this be privilege? Can this be power? What is this view-box but a hot prison?

Outside, guards protect them: or keep them in their place.

And the butterfly – who might, perhaps, be a moth – perches, barely moving, in the diagonals of the screen. Is there something wrong with you, little creature? Poor thing, I think there's something sticky, just a drop, oozing from this screen. And your wings, I fear, are no longer wings to fly.

The Ouabin shifts his leg. 'Come, little familiar, think not to flatter me. You are alarmed, I can tell: I saw your eyes.'

'Master, no! We shall destroy the Red Prince, shall we not, should the cur even think to betray us?' The dwarf gazes at the hava-beaker that hangs, tilting, in his master's hand. His strong, brown hand.

He goes on resignedly, 'And yet, master, one's thoughts might turn to our vessels and men. Or rather, to their sad state. Much damage we sustained, did we not, on our late sojourn in the seas of Amalia? Many and many a slave was lost, and how much booty had we for our pains? Master, to the great world the face you show is a brave one: with me, may you not own the truth?'

A flash of eyes. 'Little familiar, how bold you grow!'

Scurvy shifts off the pot again, though he feels a fresh stirring in his bowels. Quickly, as if it would banish the stirring, he ties the knot of his breeches and stammers, 'Pray, master, chastise me not!'

'What, *chastise*, when you are so acute? Scurvy, come back. Flap the punkah, and empty that pot.'

The dwarf comes back. Is the hand about to strike?

The Ouabin says, 'No, the hand shall not strike.' He leans forward; the hand, instead, smoothes damp, dog-like hair. In the grille, the butterfly – the moth – is deathly still: and soon, very soon, shall be really dead. But Scurvy has yet to see our little friend. For now, he forgets the punkah, forgets the pot and has no eyes for the grille. He moans with pleasure; but his pleasure is tempered at his master's next words.

The words come in a whisper, hot and secret:

'Crook-backed friend, all you say is true. Then, as you are my familiar, you divine that we have financed this Prince beyond our means. In truth, could we visit our vengeance upon him, should the need arise, as well it may? These late disasters leave us in a parlous state. Ah, Scurvy, Scurvy!'

The butterfly – or moth – twitches; the dwarf's eyes are misty. 'Master, you speak as if all were over! But look, look through this invisible screen. What, after all, has yet begun? And what is this Prince but a paltry Horan? Master, remember: you are a Ouabin, bold and true.'

'Seek not to beguile me, all-licensed fool. Is this Prince, in truth, the weakling he appears? Does not rumour have it – and rumour seldom lies – that by the time this Lepato took his seat in the Thirty he was already steeped in corruption so massive, so manifold, that by all canons of justice he deserved only to die? So great is his ambition, they say, that there is no betrayal at which he would demur. And if he would betray his own countrymen, am I to believe he would not betray *me*? Scurvy, if I have learned one thing in this world, it is that treachery is a constant amongst the tribes of men. After a first act of betrayal, what then? Why another, then another. But Scurvy, look below.' The Sea Ouabin raises his far-glass. 'See, little familiar – the ceremony begins!'

But just then a thudding comes from behind.

Scurvy leaps up, fearful. 'Master, who can it be?'

'Those fool guards, of course! Would an assassin knock? What, have they some new offering from our host, to twist your bowels into yet tighter knots? I swear, the reprobate is determined to kill you, whatever else he may or may not plan. Show some restraint, Scurvy: send them away.'

Expectantly, the Ouabin gazes through the far-glass, focusing on the chimney where the smoke will rise. Suddenly he is excited by the impending drama – excited, though its outcome is in no doubt. Red. The smoke will be red. And then the Sea Ouabin will call in his debts.

He smiles. The chamber pot is stinking, close by his chair. Still the butterfly is secret, unseen. Remember the butterfly? Remember the moth? Its little wings, once wings to fly, are now but fans to beat the air.

Scurvy scuttles back. 'Master, it's those new spies we recruited – Blard and Menos. They would speak with you.'

'Now? Tell them it is my prayer-time. Tell them it is Dust.'

'They know it isn't.'

'Those peasants? How do they know?'

'I told them – I mean, they asked if you were praying. Master, it's urgent.'

'What's urgent? They want their pay? So soon?'

'Master, they say they've found something out. Something important.'

'Urgent, in fact? Very well, Scurvy, let them in. But first – empty that pot, will you?'

So it is that the dwarf, forgetting the screen – it is almost invisible, after all – flicks the contents of the pot in its direction; so it is that the butterfly – it *is* a butterfly – finds itself doused in the stinking lava.

Tagan pulled back the shutters. Jem was dazzled with light. Adjusting to the glare, he found himself looking down into the agora. Had he been able to gasp, he would have done so. Last night there had been so many people he could hardly have imagined there could be more; today the numbers were doubled, even tripled. Clustering on window-ledges, on cornices, on roofs, the crowd seemed to flow up walls, to slither down drains, to ooze like – like *lava* into every available space.

But if no surface was free of the human swarm, the clamour of the night before was gone. All was stillness, silence. All heads turned to the Decision Chamber, where soon the great chimney would cast up its long-awaited plume of smoke.

Blue for Glond – for Lepato, red.

Behind him, Jem heard Saxis cursing as Tagan helped him into his ceremonial robes. Then, with barely a pause, the old man embarked upon some mystic incantation, a strange series of mumblings and mutterings; there were no words Jem could understand. He writhed, prickly-skinned, stewed in sweat. Littler, barely conscious, could not even struggle. Jem gritted his teeth. If only he could be free! Without mercy, he would strike Saxis down.

There was a sound of breaking glass. Then another. And another. The eunuch giggled nervously. His father, a madman indeed, was making his way around the walls, smashing the glass in the specimen cases.

'Father, your hand – Father, the blood!'

The old man only kept up his mutterings.

Then the silence outside was broken too. As if in time with the crashings and clinkings there was a thud of timpani, a flourish of horns. A door slid back in the Decision Chamber; a line of guards parted and filing out on to the high steps came a succession of figures, robed heavily and ornately in purple.

'The Keepers of the Law!' It was Tagan who spoke, his voice fearful. Jem started, aware of the eunuch's hand upon his arm. 'You know what this means? The decision is made – already, within that great chamber, slaves are building a fire, heaping it with dye-reeds, blue or red. In moments, smoke will come pulsing up the spire-chimney. In moments, we shall all know Hora's destiny!'

Behind them, the crashings of the glass had stopped. Now Saxis merely crooned eerily, while below, the timpani came thundering again. Assembling on successively higher steps, following the ponderous figures in purple, came figures yet more noble, yet more magnificent, robed in green, red, blue. Intrigued, Jem strained to see when suddenly a moth – this one was a moth – blundered in front of his eyes.

Thud! Thud!

Tagan was intent on the scene below. 'It's the Thirty! See? The Underlords. Nine in green, verdant as the leaves. But the red? Count them. Only eight. The blue? Count them. Only eight. No Lepato. No Glond.' The eunuch's fingers dug deep in Jem's arm. 'But look! The Triarchs!' At the top of the steps, framed by the great door, Hora's two surviving rulers now appeared, dazzling in their golden garb and bejewelled, irremovable crowns. 'That one's Fahan. That's Azander. But oh, my poor, poor lady's father!'

Thud! Thud!

On a litter borne by slaves, the dead Triarch descended through the parting figures of Fahan, Azander and the lesser Lords, coming to rest in the foreground of the great and dazzling tableau. Flowers in the five colours of the Orokon cushioned the bier on which he lay; a gleaming sceptre rested in his hands; his robes, replacing the golden ones he had worn in life, were black. It was time for the great man to be shut into his tomb. But not quite – not yet.

Thud! Thud!

'See the walkway, leading above the agora, crossing the façade of the Temple of Thirty?' On and on the philosopher crooned; on and on came the high voice of the eunuch, buzzing like an insect in Jem's ear. 'See that stone portal? Behind that portal is the Tomb of the Triarchs. Oh, with what ceremony shall they lay him to his rest! What aeons shall pass as he lies in darkness! To think that my poor lady might have joined him there, dying slowly behind that wall! Oh, but he's not quite ready, is he? Not yet. See, his crown still glitters on his head!'

Fanfares blasted out. From one side of the steps emerged Glond; from the other, Lepato. The contenders took their places not with the Blue and Red Lords but with the dead Triarch, one on each side. Both men seemed calm, poised. Each, perhaps, had the air of a man sure of victory; each seemed oblivious to the clamour of the crowd, the cheerings, the booings, the stampings of feet, the desperate, ardent cries of *Glond!* or *Lepato!* To Jem, to Tagan too, it seemed that both men were glaring across the agora, towards the window of the philosopher's apartment.

Tagan turned. Now his father's uneasy croonings had fallen into a rising, insistent rhythm; the floorboards squeaked as he revolved in a circle, his arms flung high like flightless wings, the loose sleeves of his robes rumpled back. But there was something else, too. The eunuch gulped. Could it be that there were butterflies and moths circling excitedly round his father's head? Fearfully he snapped his eyes back to the agora.

Oh, but it was time, it was time!

In unison, the purple-robed Keepers of the Law commanded silence, and silence fell. To Jem's astonishment, everyone in the agora, from Triarchs Fahan and Azander to the lowliest beggars, turned to gaze up at the great spire-chimney that towered above them, cutting across them with its knife-like shadow. Spiking so far into the cloudless sky, as if to pierce the intensity of the sun, in that moment the great chimney was the embodiment of all their hopes, perhaps of all human hopes.

There was a sound like thunder. Again came the timpani, rolling and rumbling, marking out the moments until Hora's destiny would be known at last.

Red or blue? Lepato or Glond? The moments seemed interminable. Tagan sank to his knees, gnawing at a knuckle. Littler, too, seemed aware of what was happening. His neck was straining and his eyes were huge.

Blue or red? Glond or Lepato? Even Jem found himself holding his breath, as if the fate in the balance were his own.

That was when he became aware of the insects, crawling over his sweaty limbs, and the moths and butterflies, butterflies and moths, plunging and plummeting in the sunlight over his head. Jem shuddered with fear.

The timpani rumbled on. The crowd stared. Like a malicious sprite the sun danced on the spire-chimney, flickering in the myriad jewels and golden carvings, flashing on the rim where the smoke would come. But the smoke, it seemed, whether red or blue, could only vanish, spirited away into the dazzle of the sky, as if the sun, jealous of its supremacy, would permit no challenge to its all-enveloping gold.

The rumblings ceased.

Red smoke or blue?

Chapter 40

THE CHANNELLING

'Urgent? What can be urgent at a time like this?'

His lethargy banished, the Sea Ouabin was himself again, or rather the self that the world knew and feared. Savagely he turned from the tensed silence below and glowered like an angry deity upon the unctuous and sweaty Blard and the cowering Menos. Scurvy blinked, grinning evilly.

Blard stammered, 'S-Sea Ouabin—'

Menos choked, 'We b-bring the news—'

'The news you s-seek—'

'Such n-news, S-Sea—'

A roar, like a lion's, split the air. 'Fools! Do you forget you must kneel in my presence? To your knees – grovel!'

Blard and Menos grovelled; the Sea Ouabin circled them with ominous tread. 'Fools, twice you have come to me, bursting with expectation of reward. And what have you brought me? A eunuch cavorting with boys on a beach. An animal coloured, you say, like a rainbow. Prince Lepato, struggling down a tunnel with a girl. What care I for a *girl*? Look at you, with your breastplates covered in scratches and grease, with the straps of your helmets flapping free, with your leggings all rumpled and your scabbards askew! I see what manner of men you are! I see the Jarvel-haze in your eyes! Can it be more than a matter of time before you are executed as incompetents, if not as traitors? Fools, my eyes are many: why, already your superior, Chief Adek—'

Menos stammered, 'Ch-Chief Adek—'

Blard choked, 'He's in your pay?'

'Never mind how I learn what I learn! Know only that, like an all-seeing god, I have looked into your hearts and know that they are corrupt!' The great man ceased his pacing. Standing squarely before his hapless spies, his manner softened, and slowly he raised them to their feet again. Sunlight played on the greasy breastplates. The Ouabin's voice dropped. 'You would come with me, would you not?'

'S-Sea Ouabin?'

'You can't stay here, can you? With Adek on your trail? But friends, soon I shall leave this blighted isle: and when I leave, would you not come with me? A life of adventure, on the rolling waves? Such adventure, as few have ever known?'

302

Menos quavered, 'Ooh, I get terribly s-seasick—'

Blard kicked him. 'Yes! S-Sea Ouabin, yes, yes—'

Amusement played in the Ouabin's blue eyes. With his left hand he caressed the pudgy arm of Blard; with his right, he toyed with the bony arm of Menos. He ran his hands up their necks: then, with a sharp flipping motion, sent their helmets clanging to the floor. He cupped their skulls like coconuts.

The Ouabin's voice was dark with menace. 'Justify the faith I have placed in you and the fairest prospects shall open before you. Fail me, and as you have dashed my hopes, so – here, now – I dash out your useless brains. Now tell me your news.'

Blard grimaced. Menos gulped. From the agora below came a deathly silence, as the moment before the smoke rose was protracted interminably.

Blard stammered, 'S-Sea Ouabin, it's—'

Menos choked, 'It's Lord G-Glond, he—'

'What? You speak of Glond? I knew him when he was a green boy; even then he was a contemptible fool. Has he not just lost this election, and all chance of—'

'But Sea Ouabin, the g-girl—'

'You see, Lepato's got it wrong—'

'Lepato, he thinks—'

The blue eyes were murderous. 'Girl? You speak of a girl? Have I not heard this tale before?'

Blard and Menos felt the strong fingers tighten. That the Sea Ouabin could crack their skulls, there and then, neither sentry doubted.

'Sea Ouabin, no! It's Glond, he took her—'

'L-Lepato only th-*thinks* it's her! I mean, the one he's got, it's—'

'It's Glond! He's got her! Sent her away in a foreign ship—'

'F-Foreign, that's right! To Ambora Rock—'

Suddenly the tightening fingers were still. The blue eyes were cold as ice. 'What are you saying?' the Sea Ouabin whispered. Then he shouted: '*Fools, what are you saying?*'

But all at once Scurvy was leaping and scurrying, beating at the mesh of the view-box like an ape. 'Below! Master – look below!'

Below, the scene was electric with ecstasy and despair. Whether it was Lepato or Glond who cried out first, none could say. The cries came together, ripping across the agora like a slashing blade.

Then Glond was sinking down, despairing, cursing, while Lepato punched the air in triumph.

Red! The smoke was red!

303

Chaos filled the agora.

But the chaos, for now, was brief. There were screams, then shovings, surgings, as Glond's supporters erupted in rage. Objects flew through the air. On the steps, Glond rushed at Lepato. He never reached him. Guards flung him back. He sprawled across the steps. Then guards forced their way through the crowd too. Swords flashed. There were screams of a different kind, jets of blood – then order returned, as suddenly as it had vanished. But this would be a precarious order. Next time, the shiftings of the crowd seemed to say, nothing could cow them back into submission. For now, only astonishment held Glond's supporters in check.

Glond heaved himself back to his feet. He shook his fist across the agora, then with an angry flourish of his robes, blundered back through the ranks behind him, pushing his fellow Lords brutally aside.

Meanwhile Saxis moaned on, howling like a beast. Had he dropped to his knees? Had he flung back his head? Tagan dared not look. By now the insects were a steady, choking swarm, desperately seeking the freedom of the windows. Few found it. Some crumbled to dust as they fluttered their wings, spraying the air with powdery, pungent fragments; others collided and fell down, dead again, as they had been but moments before. Jem could have shrieked as the little, scratchy corpses stuck to the sweat of his arms, his face, his hair.

Then, at once, the milling creatures were gone. The sun pressed painfully, glaringly through the window. Firelight flickered luridly over the walls.

Tagan cried, 'Father, are you ready? Are you ready now?'

There was no reply, only more chantings, and the thump of something falling heavily to the floor. A stuffed bird.

Below, the Keepers of the Law raised their hands again. Lepato stepped forward; trembling, Tagan pressed his lips close against Jem's ear. 'There's no going back. He is Triarch Elect. See the slaves round my poor lady's father? They are setting him in place. See the implement in the Chief Keeper's hand? How it gleams, how it glitters! First, it must release the screws from the dead Triarch's skull. Then it must fix the crown into Lepato's head!'

There was a new sound from behind. A cawing, a rustling? Jem felt a tightness in his chest. Could it be his crystal, stirring, pulsing as if with life?

The whispered words became hoarser, more urgent. 'Foolish Lepato! What agony he must feel for his people's sake, as he binds himself to them with this sacrifice of blood! Can he know what pain it will entail? When, moments from now, he is paraded, insensate, back and forth across the steps, what then? What grandeur shall he know, what glory? –

But wait! Why does the red-garbed one not kneel? He holds up his hands, as if to push the slaves away ... but yes, yes! See, he would speak!'

Saxis moaned on. In his excitement, Tagan barely registered the birds that fluttered about the apartment, floundered through the window, then dropped, senseless, towards the crowd. The eunuch could only rock back and forth, long hands clutching his smudged face.

Jem glanced at Littler. Unconscious no more, the little boy was intent on the scene below, his eyes wide with wonder and fear. What agonies might soon rack his frame? If Jem could have resisted the channelling, he would. But his bonds held him tight; the philosopher's power held him tighter still.

From the apartment, Lepato's words were inaudible, but their meaning was clear enough. Before the crown was fixed to his skull, the Triarch Elect would name his bride, snatching her from the death that otherwise would claim her. First, he summoned two burly guards, who dragged between them a bruised, beaten form.

Maius Eneo!

Tagan moaned, shocked at the youth's condition. Then, flanked by a retinue of eunuchs, came a startling vision of feminine beauty. The crowd let out a collective gasp. Tagan shuddered, almost sobbed, though the vision, he knew, was his own handiwork. How like the lady the impostor looked!

As if in dumb show, Lepato produced a large and menacing dagger, holding it out to the supposed Selinda. Bangles flashed. A hand gripped.

So: it was the lady who must kill her father's killer.

'Father!' shrieked Tagan. 'Do something! Hurry!'

Saxis lowed piteously, as if in pain. Jem felt first a stab of terror, then pain of his own, suddenly urgent, lapping at his limbs, then searing out from the crystal at his chest. There was a scream, but not his own. Flutterings. Scurryings. Then the air was alive with bird after dead bird, taking flight, crashing into the walls and ceiling, cawing, crumbling in feathery cascades. Madly the shutters banged back and forth. In the hearth, the fire churned into a vortex, swirling wild shadows over the birds, over the prisoners, over the crazed enchanter and his castrated son.

Saxis howled. He dropped to his knees.

Spasms, like convulsions, shook Littler's limbs.

Gasping beneath his gag, Jem strained at his bonds. He twisted. He tugged. He juddered. He jerked. The ropes, at any moment, would rip through his skin, tear bones from sockets. He did not care. The heat from his crystal was a relentless, spreading agony, stabbing though the muscles of his legs and arms, bubbling like acid through his bursting veins.

Then it happened. The crystal blazed out through his tunic like a fire from his heart. Jem ripped away his bonds, staggering upright, tearing the suffocating gag from his mouth.

'No ... no!' Tagan flurried round him; Jem pushed him and the eunuch sprawled back, crashing into the oncoming birds. He shrieked for his father; dusty feathers, beaks, claws, broken-off wings rained down from the air.

Jem slumped against the window. Still the shutters banged, almost striking his face; then banged too hard, ripping from their hinges and falling away.

Littler. Save Littler.

But Jem's vision was reeling, spiralling upwards into the blazing sky, then down, sickeningly down towards the crowd, and the steps where Selinda – but it was not Selinda – had taken up the gleaming dagger, stepping towards the stricken Maius Eneo.

Jem felt vomit rising to his throat. How eagerly, how exultantly Lepato looked on! Uncertainly, the dagger rose through the air. Lepato reached out, complacently smiling, as if to guide the weak, feminine wrist ...

Now. Now.

Then suddenly the wrist was weak no more and the beauteous figure twisted, plunging the dagger into Lepato's throat!

The crowd broke into chaos again.

Chapter 41

TRIARCH AND TRIURGE

'This cannot happen! I am ruined – ruined!'

In his anger, the Sea Ouabin was a terrifying sight. Like stormswept sails his robes scythed behind him as he flung himself back and forth, cursing, keening at Lepato's death. As if it were all he could do, he gripped the heads of the sentries, bashing them sharply together. Blard and Menos slithered to the floor, where Scurvy kicked them viciously several times before splintering through the view-box grille with his fist and bursting out on the pitching roof with its scalding, precarious tiles. The dwarf cavorted there like a mad thing.

'Wait!' His master swivelled round. 'It's Glond now – Glond and the girl! We must ransom the girl ... set sail ... find them ... no time to lose!' He swooped down, grabbing at a senseless Menos. 'This girl – this bride? His castle, you say? Ambora Rock?'

Menos moaned, vomiting blood.

The Ouabin flung him down again and grabbed at Blard. 'This foreign ship – what ship? Whose? When did it sail?'

Blard spat teeth. The Ouabin slapped his face and the sentry spat more. 'Think, fool, think!'

Blard gurgled, 'Northern lands ... Ejland, Zenzau—'

'An Ejlander ship? Ejland, did you say?' The Ouabin gripped Blard by the shoulders, propping him up. 'Fool, think!'

Gurgle. Bubble. 'Ejlander. Called the *C-Catty*-something—'

'The *Catty-yane*,' spewed Menos, 'the *Catty-yane*—'

'*What?*' the Ouabin bellowed again, and let go of Blard.

The fat sentry fell heavily, right on top of Menos.

'No ... no!'

Scratched, bloodied, a horrified Tagan collapsed beside Jem. Birds screeched above their heads, blundering out into the brightness of the sky.

Down below, sentries sprang forth. But the mob was everywhere. The human swarm rushed, flowed up the steps. This time, nothing could hold them back. In an instant Jem could make out neither Lepato, nor Ucheus, nor Maius Eneo; but just before they vanished from his sight, he thought he saw a sword slashing down, and Ucheus collapsing over a red-garbed corpse.

Jem reeled back, just as the philosopher, in the centre of the apartment, burst into a spinning column of light. Jem thought he had broken the channelling. But Saxis had magic enough. Just enough.

The birds whirled, caught in the column of light.

Then the column was gone. Saxis fell and so did the birds, thumping to the floor, bursting open. Feathers, sawdust exploded through the air.

Tagan gripped Jem's arm. Gasped. Pointed. In the agora, a blue bird soared above the steps, vanishing into the brightness of the sky.

Tears burst from the eunuch's eyes. 'It's Maius Eneo . . . he's escaped! Oh Father . . . Father!'

And caring nothing for the riot below, or of the dead things he must crunch underfoot, Tagan started towards the prostrate old man.

'Littler . . . Littler, are you all right?'

Jem released Littler's bonds. The little boy was dazed, feverish. Jem slapped the hot face. The eyes snapped open. There was a gurgle of protest. In a rush of joy, Jem pulled the gag from Littler's mouth.

Tagan crooned over his spent, stricken father, fondling him, embracing him. Sawdust and feathers still floated on the air and the fire in the grate that had raged so unnaturally had collapsed into a smoking, ashy heap.

From below came shouts, screams. Swords clashed.

'Jem,' Littler croaked, 'remember Captain Porlo? I think . . . I think we should have looked for him . . . instead.'

Jem had to laugh. 'Littler, can you walk?'

'To the docks? I'll say! Let's get out of here while we've got the chance—'

'Some chance! There's a battle down there—'

'You'd rather stay here?'

There was a thumping at the door.

Tagan froze. 'Father, who can it be?'

It was Jem who answered. 'Remember . . . *Glond*?'

The thumping came again, louder this time.

With a cry, Saxis struggled to his knees. Angrily he pushed his son away. 'My magic . . . I knew it would work, I knew it!'

'Father, it *has* worked! We saw Maius Eneo . . .'

'Maius Eneo? Who's Maius Eneo?'

Thump! Thump! Leaden. Immense.

Littler cried, 'There's no way out!'

Jem said, 'The window—'

Thump! Thump! Could Glond thump so loud?

Tagan was babbling, 'Father, tell him it was Lepato's fault. He . . . why, perhaps Glond doesn't *know* Lepato's dead! Yes, that's it! Tell him your magic's killed Lepato!'

Thump! Thump! Louder. Louder.

The eunuch was clutching at his father again, but the old man shrieked at him, 'Don't touch me! How dare you touch me – mutilated thing!' Tagan went sprawling. 'Can you imagine that I would use my precious magic to aid a eunuch and his foolish friends? What was this but the merest pretext? What have I done but summon my son, my *only* son?'

Something smashed through the timber. A fist.

Jem was in the window, gesturing upwards. 'Littler, quick!'

'All this, and now we break our necks?'

'There's a roof, isn't there? And a ledge? Come on, I'll give you a leg up!'

But Littler could only reel round, shrieking, as the rest of the door smashed to splinters, revealing not the angry Glond but a loathsome corpse, trailing filth, reeking like the foulest grave. Flies swarmed thickly round the rancid, mud-like flesh.

Littler gasped, 'Lemyu . . . *Leki!*'

Saxis stumbled forward. 'Come to me, my magic child! Come to me, my only son!'

Gold glowed from behind the dead eyes.

'Father, no!' Tagan struggled to stand, struggled to snatch back his father from the monster.

His father struck him. He sprawled again.

Jem cried, 'Littler, come on!'

Littler: 'But Tagan . . . we can't leave him!'

'My son, what glories shall now be ours!' Drivelling, Saxis stumbled into Leki's arms.

Then the old man cried out in agony. The corpse's arms were rippling, buckling, as the Leki-thing turned into something yet viler, an immense, all-absorbing mass of corruption. Its eyes, its nose, its mouth ripped away, and pushing through the tatters of flesh came the golden orb that had blazed from the forehead of the monster on the volcano.

'My son . . . no, no!'

Old man, you have served your purpose!

Saxis screamed again, then screamed no more as his body was absorbed into the monster's sickening mass.

'Father . . . *Father!*' Tagan convulsed, clawing at the dead things that were strewn about the floor. Piss spurted from the hole between his thighs.

Jem was beside him. 'Tagan ... quick, quick!'

Tagan only looked past him, trembling. 'Father?'

Jem turned. The monster was gone again and the philosopher stood in his place, arms outstretched, as if at the beginning of an incantation.

Again came the golden glow behind the eyes.

'Father ... Father?' Wrenching the shuddering eunuch up from the floor, Jem tried to drag him to the window. But Tagan could think only of the corpse.

'Tagan, it's a trick – Tagan, he's dead!'

There was a commotion in the corridor and in burst Glond, sword in hand. He lunged at Saxis. 'Traitor, you have betrayed me!'

The sword stabbed through the corpse's midriff. Tagan screamed, but the corpse did not fall. Then it was Glond who screamed, as his arm was sucked into the ravening body.

His arm. His head. His torso.

The monster turned, slavering, bigger, viler, the sword still stuck grotesquely through its middle. Wildly buzzed the flies round the suppurating form, and the daylight seemed to darken. The sounds of the riot were far away. There were only the flies, the relentless flies ...

The golden gaze swept across Jem, Littler, Tagan.

Then back to Jem.

Littler whispered, 'No. Jem, no.'

The monster was holding something in its hand. Something bright – something shining ... Jem gasped. Could he hear strange music playing on the air? He felt the crystal, burning at his chest.

'Cata,' he whispered. 'Cata, your coin.'

'Jem, no!' Littler rushed forward.

Jem breathed, 'The harlequin's coin – *Cata's coin*.'

Littler, louder: 'Jem, no – Jem, it's Toth!'

Key to the Orokon, I hold the key to you. *Child, did you think you could ever escape me? Come, come to me and take your treasure.*

The dead hand reached out. Jem shuffled forward.

Littler darted. He struck the hand and the coin arced, spinning, through the air. He grabbed it, flung it into the golden orb.

There was a clash. A burst of flame.

The monster roared, its spell broken.

'Quick!' cried Littler, 'Jem ... Tagan! The window!'

They rushed for it. But as they were scrambling up to the gutter, a tentacle of dead, slimy matter snaked out from the spinning monster. Shooting through the window, it grabbed Littler's ankle.

The little boy screamed. Slipped.

Tagan gaped. Jem gasped.

They looked down, vertiginous, aware again of the stabbing sun, of the pallor of the sky, of the knife-like shadow of the spire-chimney, cutting sharply over the mêlée below. Their feet scrambled against the window-frame. Their hands gripped hot, dry tiles.

Upside down, terrified, Littler hung above the agora, supported only by the oozing tentacle.

Jem shifted carefully. 'Littler . . . my hand. Can you grab my hand?'

The tentacle swung. Littler swung.

'Littler . . . Littler, I'm not going to leave you. Tagan, hold me – I've got to reach him.'

Tagan shifted. Jem shifted.

A tile slipped, just missing Littler's head. The tentacle shuddered, rasping over the window-ledge.

Tagan whispered, 'It's drawing him in.'

Littler whispered, 'Jem, it's got me.'

Jem shouted, 'No! Littler, quick – my hand!'

But the tentacle was quicker. With a spasm, it whipped Littler back across the ledge, and Jem, holding fast to Tagan, could only look on, numb with horror, as the little boy vanished, screaming, into the stinking, misshapen mound of vileness that once had been Lemyu, Leki, Saxis and Glond.

And now was Littler too.

The orb blazed, bright as the sun. Jem cried out. In that moment, he might have fallen to the agora; Toth might have triumphed. But no; there are sounds from the corridor; the orb's light dies, and Glond – or it looks like Glond – turns to face the breathless old man who has sought him out.

It is a Keeper of the Law. The Chief Keeper.

Tagan pulls Jem, sobbing, to safety.

'Oh Master Jem, I'm sorry – so sorry! But quick now – over the rooftops! Quickly, quickly!'

He drags Jem behind him. 'Tagan – but look!'

At what? The pitching tiles? The chimney? The smashed grille?

Or at the crook-backed dwarf, descending upon them?

'Master – slaves! I've found new slaves!'

311

In the ruined apartment, the Chief Keeper gasps, 'My Lord, you know what this day's events mean? You know what role must await you now?'

'Events, my good Keeper? Role – what role?'

'I mean, my Lord, that ... Prince Lepato is dead.' Still the man's breathing comes in gasps. He slumps to his knees. In moments, he will be dead; for now, with awkward reverence, he fumbles inside his robes, producing the prize – meaningless now – that Glond and Lepato had coveted so ardently. 'The mob,' mutters the old man, 'they tore him to pieces ... oh, it was horrible – horrible ... but this – this most sacred thing I managed to save ...'

How brightly it gleams in the withered hands! But scraps of flesh, slivers of bone, dried blood cling brackishly to the nail-holes round the rim. And the new Triarch – or rather, the *Triurge* – flings back his head and laughs.

END OF PART TWO

PART THREE

The Old Man of the Island

Chapter 42

DEAD MAN OVER ALL

In the eye of a gull, from cloudy heights, the galley might look at first like a gash, a scarlet wound in the sea – as if the rippling waters were a skin, savaged by a predator's claws.

Closer, with its fin-like, triangular sails, with its oars like innumerable churning legs, its bows fashioned like a ravening maw, it is the vessel that looks like the predator. What can this be but a monster like the Mandru, risen glitteringly from the ocean depths – unless it is some terrible being of the air, certain at any moment to spread its wings?

And here, no doubt, any sane gull would veer sharply away, its plumage racked by shivers and its tiny heart hammering. But if it ventures closer still, what then?

For a moment let us share the gull's bulbous eyes as it swerves across the lurching upper deck, over brown-backed fellows in loincloths and turbans, earrings flashing as they skitter up the rigging and haul at the sails that are patterned in the shapes of searing flames. Heavy cannons swivel in their moorings; ropes slither like snakes across the deck; spume crashes round the dragon-like bow and ripples and foams in the galley's long wake.

It is the *Death Flame*, pride of the Sea Ouabin's fleet.

Look, there he is: in a battlemented edifice high in the bows, richly decorated with gold and scarlet stones, the great corsair stands steely-eyed, unswaying, white robes and the long flaps of his headdress fluttering like the thunderous pennants and sails. Oblivious to all but the exhilarating speed, what can he feel but a sense of glory?

But look beneath this fearful glory, through the pylons under the upper deck. In the terrible colonnades that lie below, powering the ship's formidable speed, serried ranks of boys and men strain at oars that are thick as tree-trunks. How many rows? Thirty or more: five to a bench, port and starboard. Hot beyond endurance, foetid and loathsome, this could be a vision of the Realm of Unbeing. Face after face is a rictus of pain; sweat runs relentlessly over tormented flesh; terrible groans, sobbings and gruntings hover on the air like the anguish of the damned.

Stroke! Stroke! comes the slavemaster's cry, ringing repeatedly over the agonies; with every cry, his whip cracks. Meanwhile, the Sea Ouabin's

315

guards patrol up and down, lashing out with less regular cries of *Faster, you dog!* or *Cur, put your back into it!*

But keenest of all, readiest with his whip, is a hideous hunchbacked dwarf – Scurvy. Like a mad thing he capers between the benches; he clambers up and over them, cursing this or that slave beyond reason, lashing wildly here and there. Sea-spray bursts through the colonnades; the crazed dwarf only whoops and cavorts, eyes goggling, mouth foaming with excitement. This is the life on the high seas! This is the life of a corsair's man!

Scurvy turns, brow furrowing, then lunges forward, furious, as a slave lolls suddenly over his oar. Insensate, the big bearded fellow is borne back and forth, stroke after stroke, not even stirring for all that Scurvy switches his back, reducing it in instants to bloody meat.

The fellow's benchmates, helpless in their chains, can only grit their teeth, heaving at the oar that is unbearably heavier now that their companion has relinquished his burden. How they struggle, how they strain – this fat, red-faced fellow; this savage with bones through his nose and lips; this grizzled old man in an unravelling turban, with a scraggy beard and wizened arms.

And this young man, this fair fellow with haystack hair.

He can't go on. But Jem goes on.

Again, Scurvy lashes the big man. 'Row, damn you!'

'He's dead, you fool! Would you flay a corpse?' A guard pushes forward, cuffing the hunchback out of the way.

Scurvy crashes to the deck. 'Hit me? Hit *me*?' He scrambles up, ready for attack.

'Kick you too, if you don't shut up!' And the guard calls to one of his fellows, *'Dead man over all!'* – the cry, when a galley-slave dies on the seas.

'I'll tell the master what you did!' Scurvy turns, indignant, to a second guard, who lurches forward, answering the *dead man* call. 'Did you see what he did? Did you see what he did?'

But the guards only ignore him as they push between the benches, unlocking the manacles from the dead man's wrists. Awkwardly they haul up the heavy corpse. The dead man wears only a loincloth, and as the guards move him it tears away, discharging a copious, runny burden down the necks of the slaves who are still chained in place.

At this, Scurvy is gleeful again and claps his hands as a guard, slipping on the sodden loincloth, lets the corpse crash head-first into a pylon, sickeningly breaking its neck. The bearded head skews back impossibly, blood gurgling from the hanging jaw, as if it is about to split from the body.

Cursing, the guards bundle the corpse over the side, between the strokes of two mighty oars. The splash cascades back, drenching them. Scurvy laughs again, then reels viciously, raining down lashes on the dead man's companions, just in case they should think of dying too.

Under the water, oars batter and slice into the corpse. For moments, the galley leaves a scarlet wake.

❊   ❊   ❊

'A lady on a ship – a lady . . . *on a ship.*'

'I thought there be *two*, Cap'n.'

'Two? One? A lady's a lady, lad.'

The boy splashed more rum into the captain's goblet. 'You means they be the same, like? I don't think they be quite the same, Cap'n. If you knows what I mean.'

Candlelight gleamed in the captain's eyes. 'Been looking at them ladies, have you, lad?'

'Cap'n, no! I mean – well, I *looked* at 'em, ain't I?'

The pitcher, heavy and tarnished, trembled in the boy's freckled hand. The captain caught his wrist. A leap of rum splattered the table. 'Lad, have you ever heard of . . . *Goody Palmer and her five daughters?*'

Patches was frightened, though he could not have said why. 'Wh-what, Cap'n?'

'Because I been looking into your face, Patches, and I think I can tell when a lad's been skulking off to Goody Palmer and her five daughters. Oh, she be a fine woman, that Goody Palmer, but I'm warning you, lad, make sure she's the only one you sets your sights on. There be no other lady for the likes of you, not on this ship at any rate. Understand?'

Patches did not. What was the old man talking about?

The captain thumped with his wooden leg. 'Don't you remember how I lost poor Lefty here? Just remember, lad, a lady be a curse on a ship, a curse and make no mistake.'

Patches might have pointed out that it had been the captain, no other, who had agreed to take the ladies to Ambora Rock. Wouldn't Patches have been only too glad to sail off without them, forgetting the shady Glond and his dubious offers? But the boy thought better of voicing his thoughts.

The captain shifted in his wormy chair, emitting a healthy blast of wind. 'But come, lad, sit beside me. Here, take Buby, she's getting heavy.'

Patches brightened. 'Shall I get your squeezebox, Cap'n?'

'Aye, lad, we might have me squeezebox.'

'Can I have a bit of rotgut, Cap'n? The leavings, like?'

'Aye, lad, you can have a bit of rotgut.'

Patches was happy. For a moment he petted Buby, then looked about him in the candlelight.

317

For all the recent refurbishments of the *Catayane*, little had changed in the captain's cabin. True, Glond's men had offered to replace the rickety table, the threadbare carpet and the flea-ridden bedding; one bold fellow had even wanted to strip out the *clutter* – as he called the tiger's head, Rivan pennant, brass musketoon and others of the captain's most treasured possessions. Hands fluttering, the fellow spoke of 'doing' the walls in eggshell blue, the ceiling in fuchsia, and draping the bunk and casement with matching hangings – *aubergine*, he thought, with silver-threaded *bias binding*.

The first campaign had been met by the captain with oaths and execrations; the second would have roused him to violence, had Patches not intervened just in time.

The old ship groaned on the tide.

'Shall we have a spot of squeezebox, Cap'n?'

The captain, it seemed, was deep in thought. His squeezebox fell to the floor, wheezing limply.

'Careful, Cap'n! Here, let me get it for you.'

The captain's voice was distant. 'It's the end, Patches . . . The beginning of the end. That's what old Beezer said about . . . the first time, the first time we had a lady on board.'

Patches said wonderingly, 'You means that girl – that girl Catty-yane? But Beezer didn't say nothing about her, Cap'n. Beezer, he's been dead for – oh, since you was a lad.'

To Patches, this seemed a lifetime ago. And it was.

Again the captain thumped with his wooden leg, this time like a drumbeat of doom.

'That be the beginning – then this must be the end.'

Stop that thumping. Please stop that thumping. 'End of what? Cap'n, what do you mean? Why, it's just the beginning!'

The boy looked round him. He grabbed the squeezebox. A discord split the air, and Buby leapt madly about the walls. 'Now how does it go?

> *Bullion bars, stamped with a crest,*
> *Ah, how they'll flash when I finish me quest—*

The treasure, Cap'n! Think of the treasure!'

The captain blinked. 'The treasure . . . yes, the treasure.'

Patches would have continued, but the captain cuffed him and grabbed the squeezebox. 'Give it here, boy! What use are you with a fine musical instrument, answer me that, when you've addled your brains with Goody Palmer and her five daughters?'

Chapter 43

THE TERRIBLE COLONNADES

Darkness comes rapidly in the deep tropics, falling like a veil over misty mountains, over seething jungles, over clamorous ports and desert atolls, over frigates and barques and cutters and ketches and flame-sailed dragon-mawed pirate galleys, too. The blue Wenayan waters turn silver, then grey, and the horizon glimmers intensely.

On the *Death Flame*, the sunset imparted new horror to the terrible colonnades. Stabbing hotly through the heaving columns, the glare painted the torments of the slaves in lurid colours.

Agonised, Jem screwed up his eyes. His wrists bled in his manacles, the palms of his hands were blistered and what was left of his tunic stuck to the blood on his back, pulling his weals painfully open, again and again with each stroke of the oar. When would they ring the Submission bell? Soon, Jem was certain, the muscles of his shoulders would tear away, leaving his arms hanging useless.

The bell tolled at last, sounding over the surging decks. Stars! Gods be praised, it was the Submission of Stars! At once the slavemaster stilled his cries. The whips cracked no more; even Scurvy ceased his caperings, scurrying up the ladder to the upper deck. The galley listed. Jem gasped as the great oar thumped into his chest, then juddered to a halt. Breathless, he sprawled against the galley's side, gazing blankly into the foaming depths.

How long had passed since his capture, Jem could not say. Days, to be certain, perhaps even a moonphase: but time, in the terrible colonnades, had passed into an eternity of pain, punctuated only by these brief respites. He thought of his first taste of the lash; of the manacles clanking shut; of a guard's brutal hands searching him for valuables, ripping the Crystal of Theron from his neck and tossing it, almost contemptuously, into a clinking bag of plunder. Of all he had endured, this one thing was the worst. Fear thudded in Jem's heart. What was he to do if he could not retrieve the crystal?

The *Death Flame* sloshed on the tide. Often Jem had wondered why the great galley should cease its furious progress five times a day. In his adventure in Unang Lia he had learned of the Unang prayer times: Catacombs, Green, Dust, Wave and Stars. But why should a Ouabin stop to pray? The Ouabin were not of the Unang faith, but its bitterest enemies. Besides, such piety, if piety it were, seemed bizarre in so fearsome a corsair, especially one intent on some perilous mission.

Jem rolled back his head and shoulders, trying to ease his nagging pain. Beside him was the dead man's seat, where only a set of manacles, a pannikin on a chain and a twisted, stinking loincloth testified to the fact that he had lived. The fellow's name had been Verney, and once Verney, with grim knowledge, had said that this voyage was *make or break* for the Ouabin. Jem urged him to explain, but the burly fellow could speak only with difficulty, as if his brain no longer worked well. But wistfully, during the times of Submissions, he would mutter only that *this wasn't always the way*, that *things had not always been like this*.

Quite how long Verney had served in the galleys Jem had never discovered, but there had been a time, the fellow said, when slaves were not manacled permanently to the oars but sent down into the hold for rest; when they were fed more than a pannikin of mush, once a day; when they relieved themselves by squatting over holes in the stern, instead of soiling themselves where they sat. At this, Jem would see their benchmates nodding sagely, as if recalling a lost paradise.

For now, two things were clear. The Ouabin had a desperate shortage of men – and a mission equally desperate. Nothing mattered but speed, and more speed, and if all his slaves died to provide it, the Ouabin did not care. Grotesquely, Jem's fellow slaves seemed to accept their lot, as if this were simply the way of the world.

But Verney could not have believed that, could he, even as his last agonies claimed him? Poor Verney! Jem tried to feel for the dead man, but there was nothing, only the aches in his own back and arms and the terrible numbness in his legs that made him think he was a cripple again. In the thrall of this terrible captivity he had barely given a thought to Littler, Raj, Uchy, Rainbow, let alone to Tagan. What had happened to the eunuch Jem was not sure; they had been separated early on, but he believed they had sold Tagan to a slave-dealer.

Eunuchs, after all, fetched high prices.

'Patches?'

'Cap'n?'

'It's them ladies. I'm worried about 'em, lad.'

'Aye, Cap'n. A curse on a ship, you said.' Patches looked down reflectively. 'Perhaps we could ... perhaps we could put them overboard. Make them walk the plank, like.'

'What, lad? Are you mad?'

In truth, Patches rather liked the ladies. That Fa Ra one was a bit of a dragon, but the pretty one, Miss Selinda, seemed a good sort – or would do, if only she'd give over moping.

But keeping the captain happy, that was the main thing.

The captain, however, was not happy. 'And what's Glondy going to say, answer me that, if he finds out we've gone and drowned his bride? Stupid boy!'

Patches was glum. 'But Cap'n, I thought—'

'It's not your job to think, Patches – that's my job. Don't you think old Faris Porlo knows what to do with ladies?'

Patches grinned uncertainly; the captain scowled.

'No, don't go getting ideas like that, Patches.'

'Like what, Cap'n?'

'Hah! Don't you think I knows what feverish thoughts come to a lad when he's off in the company of Goody Palmer and her five daughters?' The captain thumped his wooden leg. 'Punishment of lust, lad! Let old Lefty be a warning to you, eh? No, I'm telling you this: them ladies be unhappy. And why, Patches? Answer me that.'

'It's Miss Selinda. Don't want to marry that Glondy, does she?'

The captain's brows knitted. 'Of course she does! What lass wouldn't want to marry Glondy?'

'Well,' said Patches, 'if I was a lass—'

'What, you think Goody Palmer and her five daughters have taught you all there is to know about the fair sex? No Patches, if you knew just one thing about ladies, you'd know they'd be miserable, stuck here on these high seas with only a lot of coarse tarry fellows for company, and the cry of the seabirds, and the salt spray, and the very floor a-shifting under their feet! Dry land, that's a lady's element – dry land, with all her little feminine fripperies and fineries about her.'

Patches might have pointed out that quite a few such fripperies and fineries had been provided for the ladies' cabin.

'Them ladies be pining for land, Patches,' the captain continued. 'That's why Miss Selinda's moping like she is. That's why she's off her feed.'

'I'll say – she's *really* off it, Cap'n.'

The boy had to grin again. Every time he took a tray to Miss Selinda, it came back barely touched – and since Glondy had provided a special cook for the ladies, Patches had been eating well of late. Very well indeed.

Not that he hadn't tried to share his good fortune. Hadn't he given the captain first crack at the leavings? The other day Patches had heaped a plate high with seaweed semolina, fruitbat stew and cephalopod in brine, candied cat's tail and custard eel, but incredibly, the captain had rejected it – flinging the plate from the casement with a cry of *foreign muck!*

The captain, with the air of a man of the world, was expatiating knowledgeably on the Lady Selinda. 'Dry land, Patches, that's the key! That's why she goes on about being a prisoner – a prisoner, when soon she'll be in Glondy's arms!'

'Cap'n, that's what she's worried about!'

The captain was not listening. 'Ah, but a lady never had patience. It's their brains, Patches, tiny flibbertigibbet brains like birds! But never mind, the lass is unhappy – and if she's unhappy, won't poor Glondy be unhappy, too?'

Patches didn't care about Glond's happiness.

The captain bristled. 'And where'd we be without Glondy?'

'Off on our treasure hunt, that's where!'

'In a leaking hulk with no cash, no crew and not a side of salt-pig to speed us on our way? Why, lad, without Glondy the poor old *Catty* would have been fit only to be scuttled! Glondy's our saviour, lad, and don't you forget it.'

'But the *Catty*'s fixed now. Couldn't we just get rid of these ladies and be on our way? Or . . . or take them with us?'

The captain aimed a fist at the coppery curls. 'Why, Patches, I'd chop off your hands if it didn't mean you couldn't wait at table! Have ever Goody Palmer and her five daughters addled a lad's brains more than yours?'

Patches rubbed his head. 'Well, I suppose I *was* forgetting the twenty thousand Hora-ducats.'

'Never you mind about Hora-ducats. Now listen to me, and listen good. Them ladies are used to refined ways, aren't they? A bit of gallantry, that's what ladies need. A bit of sophistication. Patches, we're going to have ourselves a little *soirée*. A banquet, that's what – a banquet for the ladies! We'll call it . . . the Barnacled Banquet! Now, who says old Faris Porlo can't *hold his own* with the fair sex?'

※　　※　　※

A silence had descended over the *Death Flame*, a silence broken only by the clink of chains, by mutterings and sighs. Stray billowings stirred the sails and the sea lapped ominously against the galley's sleek hull. Then came a lantern's creaking sway; then the stirrings of pathetic, animal eagerness, the clutchings and cryings as the Ouabin's guards, with cauldrons and ladles, worked their way contemptuously down the aisle, slopping mush into dirty pannikins.

Jem's stomach churned. For days he had barely eaten at all. How could he eat anything, let alone the mush, here in these sewer-like colonnades? Uneasily he reached for his pannikin, imagining the mush slithering down his throat like someone else's phlegm. He squinted along the bench. The guards were coming nearer. His companions held their pannikins aloft in pleading, claw-like hands. Jem raised his, too. Suddenly he was ravenous. *Phlegm? Who cares?* Let them hawk it up in front of him, he would eat it!

But he was not fast enough. In an instant, the slopping ladle had passed and Jem's pannikin was empty.

He moaned, letting the pannikin fall. He doubled over, covering his face. Had he come to this? In the stinking darkness, surrounded by slurpings, Jem knew despair. Down, down he spiralled through the depths of horror, wanting nothing but to die, and die now.

He thought of Cata. What would she think if she could see him here? Chafings and rashes crawled over his skin; his hair was matted; his breeches squelched with shit. He sobbed dryly. It was all over. The crystal was lost; the quest was hopeless. But then, hadn't it been hopeless from the start? Cata's father . . . the harlequin . . . Empster . . . hadn't they just been playing with him, taunting him? He probably wasn't even a Prince at all! He might as well have stayed in Irion, eking out the life of a pathetic cripple!

Just then a chain clanked beside him and Jem brushed his eyes to see the turbaned old man, now his closest benchmate, struggling to reach across Verney's empty place. In his withered, yellow arms, the fellow extended his pannikin to Jem.

Jem gazed, marvelling, into the rheumy eyes.

'Bend your neck a little, matey, hm? Bit of a wrench, but I think you can. Come on, let's see that tongue – slurp it, that's the way. I always try and hold my breath and pretend it's chicken broth. Come on, a bit more . . . Lick the bowl clean, that's right . . .'

Dribbles ran from Jem's mouth as he croaked out his gratitude. Such kindness, in the midst of all this!

The old man smiled. 'If we don't take care of each other, who will? You know, I never caught your name? Well, never got a proper look at you, did I? Poor Verney was a bit big, after all.' A tear came to a rheumy eye. 'I'm Lacani – Young Lacani they call me, since I've got an older brother.'

He turned his head along the bench. By now the darkness was almost entire, but in the last glimmers of twilight Jem could make out the much-pierced savage and the fat, red-faced fellow, peering at him with curious eyes.

Young Lacani indicated the savage. 'Bones, we call that one. Doesn't have much to say for himself – well, he can't, since they cut out his tongue. Or someone did.' Bones flashed a smile. But a sad smile. 'And that's Pancho. Fat fellow, isn't he? Used to be a lot fatter, let me tell you.' Young Lacani leaned forward. 'Just remember, matey, we're all in this together. Did you say your name?'

323

But just then the gong rang, the slavemaster cracked his whip, and the *Death Flame* was on the move again.

'Stroke, you dogs! Stroke, stroke!'

Chapter 44

THE BEAUTIFUL AND DAMNED

'My lady, please! Please?'

No reply.

'Please, my lady, please!'

No reply.

Selinda shifted languidly. With her legs drawn up beneath her, with the Blisha doll clutched tightly in her arms, she sat curled in the casement-seat, gazing blankly on the shifting, glittering sea. The beauty of the afternoon meant nothing to the girl. Her hair was lank, her skin pasty and she had yet to change the ill-fitting male garb she had donned in the moments before Glond's men had come.

Days had passed since then, and Selinda had barely spoken.

Desperate, Ra Fanana knelt beside her. She sought the girl's hand. 'Come, my lady, you *must* eat. Why, you'll fade to nothing!'

Poor Ra Fanana! What was she to do? Twice the boy Patches had come to their cabin, enquiring shyly if the *ladies* were ready for what he called the Barnacled Banquet; twice, blocking the doorway, the nurse had informed the boy that the *lady*, singular, was not quite ready, not quite decked in her full finery – then glared at him until he turned away, marvelling at the unfathomable ways of the sex.

Ra Fanana sighed. Forlornly she gestured to the magnificent gown that she had laid out on the girl's bunk. 'Very well, my lady, don't let me dress you, don't let me wash you, don't let me set your lovely hair. Forget about perfume, powder, and paint. You're tired – weak. But come to the Barnacled Banquet – just come, please?'

Selinda only tightened her grip on the doll.

The nurse assumed a wheedling manner. 'Didn't I say there'll be almond anemones? Why, there'll be lung-and-seaweed pie! There'll be rack of weasel – the rarest of delicacies! There'll be curried iguana – with quince chutney, too! Not to mention a *very* special crumble-cake.'

'And barnacles?'

'Of course – freshly scraped and fricasseed in octopus ink! I even heard there were chocolate tri-crowns – tri-crowns, I ask you, here at sea!'

Selinda looked witheringly at her nurse.

'Don't think it's just salt-pig and hard tack, that's all I'm saying. Captain Porlo's got all your favourites, my lady – in abundance, too.'

'Favourites? What does he know about my *favourites*?'

The nurse attempted a smile. 'I don't think it's *Captain Porlo* who knows, my lady.' She gestured again. The luxurious cabin might almost have been the girl's apartment in miniature, replete with all the delicate veneers, the silk and jewels, the silver and gold that could fit into so small a space. Painted ivory playing cards and a delicate fan lay on a little inlaid table, slipping and slithering with the swelling waves. 'Might we not suspect a certain someone has had, shall we say, a *hand* in things? I speak, of course, of your husband-to-be.'

Selinda burst out, '*Husband-to-be?*'

Ra Fanana quailed. 'Now come, don't excite yourself—'

'I'm not excited, I'm angry! You wicked woman, you're on his side, aren't you? What, have you been on his side all along?' The girl flounced up, pacing the carpet. 'But . . . you're mad, you've got to be! Just a few days ago you said I should marry Lepato!'

The nurse wrung her hands. Oh, how could she explain? 'Please, my lady, it's not about *sides*! Don't you see, we've got no choice? I want you to be happy! I want what's best for you!'

'For *me*? To be a prisoner, on some remote island?'

'Not a prisoner, but a great lady – a Triarch's wife!'

'Glond's wife – *and* a prisoner, for the rest of my days!'

The sun flashed painfully about the rich cabin, catching on jewels and mirrored glass and flashing in the eyes of the Blisha doll that now lay unregarded in the casement-seat. Ra Fanana breathed deeply. If only Miss Selinda would see reason!

She sought the girl's hands. 'My lady, listen. Day after day the winds and waves carry us closer to Ambora Rock; day after day our new life comes closer, ever closer. Rail against Lord Glond all you will, what will it bring us but an increase in suffering? Hold him in hatred, and—'

'*We? Us?* Ra Ra, it's me that's got to marry him!'

'And me that's got to tend you, every day of your life! And where would I rather see you – in a fine boudoir, or in a filthy dungeon? In a castle, or on the streets? My lady, think! Lord Glond is a personable man, is he not? A powerful man? Why, many a woman would sell her very Essence to be his bride!'

'What care I for other women? Ra Ra, you're asking me to be a whore!'

The nurse was outraged. 'A whore? My lady, never!'

'Are you blind, Ra Ra? It's just a question of the price!' Proudly, the girl flung back her head. 'I tell you, Glond may offer what he will, torment me as he will, fling me in his dungeons, beat me, torture me – but never, never shall I be his bride!'

Ra Fanana cried, 'Then you are a fool! A silly, stubborn little fool!'

There was a silence.

As soon as the words had left her lips, the nurse could not believe she had uttered them. She staggered and sank into the casement-seat, a hand clapped fast across her mouth. Selinda glared at her and poor Ra Fanana could not bear the hatred in her lady's face. The tears that she had been holding back pressed more insistently behind her eyes.

'A fool, am I?' The girl's voice was level. 'Very well, so I'm a fool. A *fool*, not to marry an evil Outrealmer, a traitor to my country and to my father's memory, a man who holds my person and position in such contempt that he would kidnap me, a Triarch's daughter, in order to have me in his possession. A *fool*, not to marry a man who promised he would free my beloved Maius Eneo – and did not, when the act was in his power. A *fool*, not to marry a man who is as good as a murderer – a *murderer*, Ra Ra. A heartless, pitiless murderer.'

Ra Fanana was shaking. To her, just then, it seemed that it was Selinda who was heartless, pitiless. She gathered the Blisha doll into her arms. It gave her no comfort – but then, it was filled with coins and jewels. Absently she fingered the hard lumps, murmuring, 'He – he was going to have Maius Eneo brought up from the dungeons . . . before we sailed, wasn't he? He – he promised . . . promised. Why, there must have been some . . . misunderstanding—'

Selinda gasped, flinging up her hands. 'The man I love is dead – *dead*, Ra Ra! You stupid woman, can't you see that I care about nothing else? Can't you see that I want nothing else? What does it matter what happens to me now? What is there left for me but a lifetime's grieving? What does it matter if I languish in a dungeon, when life with Glond must be a life in fetters?'

The girl flung herself across her bunk. 'Oh, you're just a slave! What can you understand about nobility, about suffering? What . . . what can you understand about *love*?'

This was too much. Tears burst helplessly from Ra Fanana's eyes. She covered her face in her hands. She rocked from side to side. The Blisha doll fell, jangling, to the floor.

❋   ❋   ❋

'Ra Ra?' Shocked, Selinda rushed to the nurse's side. 'Ra Ra, I'm sorry! Oh, I know you love *me*, I know you want what's best, but—'

'Do . . . do you think I've never had a life of my own?' moaned the slave-woman. 'Or wanted one? Do you think I've never been anything but what I am now, this abused, degraded thing? Ah, my lady, indeed I love you, and now – now, and for all the days that remain to me – I would serve you, and serve you well. But what can you know of all that *once* was mine, of all that *once* I loved – and have lost?'

'Ra Ra, I'm sorry – Ra Ra, forgive me, please!'

In her confusion, Selinda barely wondered at her nurse's strange words; to the girl, it was unimaginable that Ra Fanana had ever had any other life. Selinda did not want to think of it; she would only quell this distress, and have things as they had always been.

But nothing could be as it had always been; the words that were spilling from Ra Fanana's lips, flowing forth like her coursing tears, could not be checked now. In the nurse's tone was no rancour, only a desperate sadness.

'My lady, I know suffering only too well – and dare I say my acquaintance with it has been deeper than yours? Oh, so you have loved a man, and that man has been taken from you! Oh, so you must marry another, not of your choosing, and leave behind the scenes of your girlhood! You speak of prison, but had you seen more of the world, would you dismiss so lightly a prison of gold and silver, of jewels and silk and satin? When you have lived as long as I, you will see that prison – of one sort or another – is a woman's lot, and that the wise woman takes care to be locked in only the finest. My lady, grieve for your beloved, sob for him in secret, but when there lies before you the promise of wealth and finery, speak not of languishing in a dungeon! Foolish child, you know not what you say!'

Selinda's mind reeled. Nothing could allay her hatred of Glond. Nothing could reconcile her to this coming marriage. But what was she to do? For now she could only hug her stricken nurse, longing only to comfort and be comforted. They mingled their tears.

In their distress, the two women were oblivious to a knocking at the door. The door opened and Patches gazed upon them, astonished.

Indeed, the ways of the fair sex were strange!

'P-Please, ladies . . . C-Cap'n Porlo would . . .'

Abruptly, Ra Fanana brushed her eyes. 'You'll come to the Barnacled Banquet, my lady? *Please?*'

Selinda sniffed. She nodded.

As they left the cabin she grabbed the Blisha doll, hugging it tight against her breast again.

Chapter 45

THE BARNACLED BANQUET

'But the *Catayane*?'

'Hm?'

'The *Catayane*?'

'*Why*, me lady?'

'That's right. Why?'

Captain Porlo paused, toying with the tail of the monkey that sat, blinking, on his shoulder. Leaning forward – the nurse leaned forward too – he said somewhat unnecessarily, 'Now, me lady, wouldn't you like to know?'

Ra Fanana glanced demurely at her plate, for the moment ignoring its contents which were, when all was said and done, somewhat regrettable. The bright light of late afternoon slanted sharply through the captain's casement, gleaming on the heavy new knives and forks, the delicate china plates, the goblets, the decanters and dome-like covered dishes that seemed so incongruous on the wormy table.

The banquet, for all the elaborate preparations, had not been a success. The almond anemones had been watery; the pastry had been soggy on the lung-and-seaweed pie; the weasels and iguanas supplied by Glond's men had already, unmistakably, been a little on the turn. And where were the barnacles?

It was enough to drive a man to distraction, yet had not Captain Porlo shown admirable restraint? If inadvertently, from time to time, he would let slip the words *filth* and *foreign muck*; if he had given up on the delicate, spicy wines, demanding instead his accustomed rum, at least he had refrained from flinging his prettily patterned plate through the casement and bellowing angrily for salt-pig and mustard.

In these last days – privately, she would to admit it to herself – Ra Fanana had developed a certain fondness for the captain. His manner, yes, was a little coarse, but undoubtedly he was a good man – even a noble one.

Not like some. Not like many.

The nurse assumed a winsome expression. 'This *Catayane*, perhaps, was a sweetheart of yours? Captain, do tell!'

Selinda rolled her eyes.

Patches leered.

If the captain was nervous at finding himself in the company of the fair sex, nonetheless he was determined to conduct himself with gallantry. He swigged his rum. His eyes twinkled. With the air of one moved at last to revelation, he sighed, 'Who might she be, this *Catayane*, but the *speciallest* of girls in all the world?'

'I knew it!' Ra Fanana clapped her hands.

Patches piped up, 'Gave her a bit of the old what-for, eh Cap'n?'

The captain aimed a cuff at the coppery head. 'I'll give you a bit of the *old what-for*!'

The boy ducked; his master struck him a glancing blow, but was content, nonetheless, with the violence he had administered.

'There be a few more brains gone, Patches, and a good thing too – brains like yours only leads a lad into trouble, not least of all when they thinks of nothing but Goody Palmer and her five daughters. (Oh, I knows what you been up to, Patches, never you mind.) And don't talk with your mouth full! Don't you know there be *ladies* present?'

'Only one *lady*,' smiled Ra Fanana, though if truth were told it was the nurse, immaculate in Wenaya-wimple and blue beaded gown, who looked rather more the part than her bedraggled charge. With her boy's attire and her hair in a semiturban, piled in a slovenly heap, Selinda might have stood in, as it were, that relation to Ra Fanana in which Patches stood to Captain Porlo.

But Patches would never have been so sullen.

The girl toyed with the Blisha doll, twining the coils of its hair around her fingers.

Ra Fanana girded herself for a second sally. 'The *speciallest*, Captain? The *speciallest* girl?'

The captain coloured. 'Of course, me ladies, it be a manner of speaking – I means, I don't means ... *present company*.'

'Oh, Captain!' said Ra Fanana.

Patches snickered; he was risking his brain again, but his master, all at once, grew wistful, even distant. 'I speaks, indeed, of no company of mine.'

'Captain?' said Ra Fanana.

'Cap'n?' said Patches.

The *Catayane* creaked expectantly on the tide. Captain Porlo poured himself more rum; Buby looked questioningly into her master's eyes.

'It were Cap'n Beezer named me fair vessel – I means, back in the days when she were Cap'n Beezer's. I recalls when he was on his deathbed, old Beezer, after the Battle of Badger's Island, when he took all that shrapnel in his guts and groin. (Begging your pardon, me ladies, begging your pardon.) There he was, old Beezer, a-groaning and a-rattling – that was his chest – just before he breathes his last.'

A tear splashed down the sea-dog's cheek.

'"You been like a son to me, Faris," says old Beezer. "The *Catty*, she be yours, laddie – you be her master now. Just one thing, laddie, one thing." – "Anything, Cap'n Beezer," says I. – "It's this, Faris," says Beezer. "Don't you go changing her name, now, not me *Catty* – never minds what derring-do you might get up to, Faris, never minds what flags you fly, don't be like some of these buccaneering fellows, one day a-sailing on the *Saucy Sal*, next day the *Love o' Lord Agonis*, and it be the same wicked old barnacled hulk all the while. No, Faris, this be the *Catty* – always the *Catty*." – "Always, Cap'n Beezer," says I – ah, and you'd best believe the tears be pissing down me cheeks, me lovelies, fair pissing down by now. (Begging your pardon, ladies, begging your pardon.)'

Ra Fanana inclined her head, indicating that pardon was given. 'Captain, so *you* never knew this girl?'

Patches screwed up his forehead. 'But Cap'n, what about that lass we picked up off Qatani – the one old Master Jem was keen on? Catty, that were her name, too.'

The captain's eyes twinkled. 'Indeed it were, lad.'

'*Funny lass?*' said Ra Fanana. '*Picked up?*'

The nurse was confused now, even troubled.

'Aye,' says the captain, 'and you know what Beezer says, just before his groaning and a-rattling goes quiet for good? (I means he's slipping – ah, he be slipping fast.) What should he say in them last moments but, "She's a special girl, Faris. Speciallest girl in all the world, she be." (Here's me thinking he still means the ship.) "Aye," says Beezer, "and when this girl comes aboard, remember this, Faris – remember, when you meets her . . . it be the *beginning of the end*, Faris, the *beginning of the end*." And that's when the rattling and the groaning stops – I means he dies, me lovelies, I means he dies.'

There was a puzzled silence. Tenderly, the captain stroked Buby's furry head.

'Cap'n,' said Patches, 'I don't understand!'

'Captain,' said Ra Fanana, 'did you say this girl has *been* aboard – already?'

Selinda's eyes flashed. She let her doll lie down in her lap. 'So, Captain, the *end* is upon us?'

The captain only let out a bellowing laugh. 'It's just some nonsense – Beezer's nonsense! Come on, me lovelies, eat up, eat up!'

This was hardly a compelling invitation.

❈　　❈　　❈

'So . . . you be a ship's boy . . . matey? Cabin boy . . . like?'

'Cabin boy, that's right . . . cabin boy.'

331

'Pressed you, did they? The Ouabin's . . . thugs?'

'Pressed? Oh yes . . . kidnapped.'

'Oblivion-cloth? Or got you . . . drunk?'

'Drunk? Oh yes . . . very drunk!'

'I know it . . . I know the way!'

Moonlight, like a mockery, shimmered across the terrible colonnades. *Stroke. Stroke.* On and on came the slavemaster's cries. On and on ploughed the galley through the night. Never had Jem's agonies been so great. Only now, with poor Verney gone, did he realise how much the big fellow had borne the weight of the oar.

Had he still been at his lowest ebb, Jem would have given up the struggle. Others had done it, many others. Even since last Submission, the cry of *Dead man over all!* had rung across the decks some three, perhaps four times. This voyage was mad. Wholly mad. But if Young Lacani, a weak old man, refused to give up hope, Jem knew that all was not lost. Breathless, he struggled to answer the old man's questions.

'Know any . . . others, matey?'

'Others? Other . . . slaves?'

'Lots of new blood here . . . from Hora.'

'Oh, I had . . . friends. But they're . . . lost.'

'We've all lost . . . friends, matey. But don't you see we're . . . all friends here . . . all of us . . . in these manacles? Heard of the Slave's Revolt of Sosenica, have you? Now there's . . . there's a story for you. Just starting it, that's the trouble . . . getting started. Know that hunchback? Got a knife, he has . . . seen it glinting, I have . . . in his breeches . . . now if I could . . . one day . . . when he whips my back . . .'

They rowed on. And rowed on.

But keep talking. 'Young Lacani, were you . . . pressed, too?'

'Matey, we're all pressed . . . here. Not . . . not sold, good and proper, as slaves should be.'

'You think a slave . . . a man . . . should ever be sold?'

Young Lacani did not quite answer this question. 'They'd never have got me, you know that . . . never, if it hadn't been . . .' He doubled over, wheezing. Jem was alarmed. How much longer could the old man hold out? He looked towards the Ouabin's guards, hoping that the fellows would come no nearer.

'Put your backs into it, filthy dogs!'

The guards came nearer, cursing, lashing. Jem pulled harder, pulling for Young Lacani, too.

Stroke. Stroke.

The old man rallied just in time, his withered arms tugging valiantly at the oar. 'Never,' he spluttered, 'if it hadn't been . . . if it hadn't been for the Zenzan!'

'Zenzan? Young Lacani, what . . . Zenzan?'

But then came the light of a lantern, swaying luridly along the aisle. The guards ceased their random violence, turning abruptly to the source of the light. *Oh no.* It was Scurvy, grinning insanely, scurrying before the white-garbed form of his master.

From time to time, never with any warning, the Ouabin would visit this noxious nether world that provided the power for his desperate quest. Unswaying on the heaving deck, impassive amongst the stench, the corsair would let his gaze flick cruelly from side to side, stare accusingly at his guards, and bark out orders for speed, more speed.

Stroke! Stroke!

Young Lacani jerked his head towards the Ouabin. 'They say he was a . . . great man, back in Unang.'

'A Ouabin?' said Jem. 'But aren't they just . . . nomads?'

'The desert ones . . . yes. But a Sea Ouabin . . . well, that'd be . . . different, wouldn't it?'

Jem supposed so. 'But who is he . . . really?'

'Verney knew, I think poor . . . Verney knew. In league with him, he was, till the Ouabin . . . double-crossed him. Put him down here, he did . . . to die, he did.'

'What? Verney was his . . . accomplice?'

'One of . . . many. Betrayed them . . . all, he has. But his reign . . . won't last, will it? Can't . . . can it?' Young Lacani's voice rose defiantly. 'Oh, he won't get me, matey, he won't . . . get me!'

'Young Lacani, keep . . . rowing!'

The old man missed his stroke. He didn't seem to care. 'Don't you know he was . . . defeated, once before? Defeated before, and he'll be . . . defeated again!'

'Yes, but . . . keep rowing, Young Lacani!'

'Ejland fellow, it was . . . nearly sank him he did . . . ever hear of him, matey? Fellow called . . . Porlo?'

'*What?*' Now it was Jem who missed his stroke. They were all flagging, but this was one flagging too many. There was a sound of clashing, oar against oar. Young Lacani gasped; Bones grunted; Pancho doubled over as the oar struck his paunch.

In an instant Scurvy had leapt up on their bench, dancing in Verney's empty place. In one hand, the evil dwarf held aloft the lantern, swinging it in a wild arc. With the other, he flung back his whip, striking the four benchmates relentlessly on their backs, their necks, their heads. Young Lacani sank down in his place, manacles dragging cruelly at his wrists.

'Leave him alone, you monster!' Jem lurched to one side, bashing into the dwarf. Shrieking, Scurvy fell into the gap between the benches. The lantern smashed; flames billowed up; Young Lacani slumped down, inert.

Scurvy leapt up, flames spiralling from the seat of his pants. 'I'm on fire! I'm on fire, you fools!' Shrieking, the dwarf ran up and down the aisle, until the guards grabbed him and rolled him on the deck. But this only increased the creature's rage. Cursing the guards, he called for them to kill the man who had flung him to the floor, to kill him at once.

The Ouabin turned sharply. 'Kill my slaves?' he roared. 'Fool, do you think Lepato is in power, providing us with slave upon slave upon slave? Have you forgotten that Lepato is dead? Crook-backed creature, out of my sight! Guards! Flay these men till their backs are raw meat, but just keep them rowing – speed, more speed!'

Chapter 46

PLAYING FOR TIME

'Why, Glondy, what a lad he was – a lad and a half! What about the time he gets his snout in me best hard tack, eh? Remember, Patches? What about the time he cuts the rigging on me mizzenmast, just when we's coming into a following wind – with that wretched Sea Ouabin a-pulling up me rear, too! And when he flings poor Buby out that there casement? Fair went and drowned, she did – well, nearly! (Eh, steady on, Buby-girl . . .) Good old Glondy!'

The captain paused, rubbing a tear from his eye. Candles fluttered on the hot night air and glistened on the clutter of greasy plates. If the banquet was over – or at least abandoned – the captain's carousings seemed barely to have begun.

Furtively Ra Fanana helped herself to another splash of ferment.

Selinda despaired.

'Done me a lot of good turns, has old Glondy,' said the captain. 'Did me a big one when he runs away with that Sea Ouabin, he did, trying to escape Ambora Rock.'

'Even *he* wanted to get away?' Selinda said sourly.

'Done me a bigger one now, though – that I have to say.'

'Captain,' said Selinda, 'what I don't understand is how Lord Glond has been anything to you but a trial and tribulation. From your own account, I fail to see that he has ever done you any *good turn*.'

Patches piped up, 'Twenty thousand Hora-ducats, ain't it, Cap'n?'

The captain glowered. But then his glower became a smile, exposing the brown remnants of his teeth. 'When Glondy said we had a precious cargo, I didn't realise *how* precious! It's true, I liked Glondy best before he had them jewels round his eyes and them big coloured dresses like ladies wear and his hair all done up like a tart on the tiles – begging your pardon, Miss Selinda, I knows it's such fripperies that sets your little feminine heart a-pit-a-pattering – but what better turn could one man do another than to put him into the company of two such *lovely ladies*?'

'Just one *lady*, remember,' said Ra Fanana.

'Hora-ducats? What Hora-ducats?' said Selinda, fuming.

The captain made no reply. Thoughtfully he stroked the monkey that had slipped down from his shoulder, filling his arms. 'Good old Glondy!' he muttered again. 'He *were* a lad and a half, weren't he, Patches?'

Patches began, 'I never met him—'

A gaseous emission erupted from beneath Buby's tail; the lung and seaweed pie had been a bit much for her. The captain waved away the fumes. 'Never met him? What you be talking about, stupid boy?'

'Never,' said Patches, 'when he was a *lad*.' The boy smiled surreptitiously at Selinda; he rolled his eyes; he waggled his head.

The girl looked confused. Did she think he was mad? Or merely wonder what these actions might mean?

The captain had no doubts. His fist swung.

'Yeow! Cap'n, what were that for?'

'What do you think? Hands on the table, you dirty little beggar! We'll have none of your Goody Palmer and her five daughters here – in front of poor Miss Selinda, too!'

Selinda looked a little bewildered; Ra Fanana looked *very* bewildered. The sea-dog took another fortifying swig. 'You see I teaches the lad to respect *the sex*. As I always say, what's a sea-going vessel – I means a ship, me lovelies, I means a ship – without a lady on board, answer me that? That's why us sea-dogs have our wooden ladies in the bows, to bring us good luck when we goes on our travels. But how much better off shall *we* be, eh, with a real live lady? Or two,' he could not forbear from adding.

'*One*, Captain. Only one,' simpered Ra Fanana, then thought that perhaps, from this point on, she would no longer insist upon this nicety.

No. Decidedly, she would not.

'But Cap'n,' said Patches, 'you said a lady was a curse on a ship, a curse and make no mistake!'

'*Curse?*' The captain spluttered rum across the table. 'Stupid boy! Blessing, I said! Don't you know a blessing from a curse?'

His fist swung again. Patches crashed to the floor.

'Pardon the lad, me ladies, pardon him. Means well, but it's his age, you know – every spare moment with Goody Palmer and her five daughters, till his silly little brain is addled.'

Patches, snivelling, clambered into his chair again; the captain – rather too late, one might have surmised – gave the boy a look of stern warning. 'No more talking back to your elders, eh? And no more sniffing round Miss Selinda. I means it, Patches. If I sees you poking your snout up her skirts, there'll be trouble, I'm telling you.'

'S-Sniffing, Cap'n? P-Poking?'

Selinda, to begin with, was not wearing skirts. But the captain did not deign to expatiate. His gallantry scaling new heights, he reached through the clutter of the table, grabbing her hand. His next words were suffused with fatherly concern. 'Just let me know, lovey, if this here lad comes sniffing round your rear – let me know if his dirty snout comes snuffling up your petticoats, and I'll give him more than a good clip round the earhole, never you mind.'

Selinda looked dazed; their host, for one thing, was crushing her hand. The captain felt a warm glow of righteousness. Who more than old Faris Porlo respected the tender sensibilities of the sex?

'No,' he said, 'you can tell when a lad's been skulking off to Goody Palmer and her five daughters. See that furtive, shifty look on his face? That blush across his cheeks? Those circles under his eyes?'

'But where,' began Ra Fanana, 'is this Goodwife—'

The lady, if lady she were, was not permitted to complete her question. Winking, Captain Porlo gestured to Selinda. 'Just like we can tell when a young lady's . . .'

The sea-dog paused for a swig of rum.

Coldly, Selinda recovered her hand. 'Tell *what*, Captain?'

'Captain,' quavered Ra Fanana, 'what can you mean?'

The captain grinned. In his cups he might be, but had he forgotten the demands of gallantry? 'Just like you can tell when a young lady – begging your pardon, miss – is in, shall we say, a *delicate condition*?'

Selinda blanched.

Ra Fanana burst out, 'Captain, I assure you—'

The cabin was filled with the captain's laughter. 'No, no, there be no denying it! There's none would call old Faris Porlo a lady's man, but can't he tell what it means when a certain young lady's been neglecting herself, a-moping and a-crying and a-going off her feed? What can it mean but—'

'Captain,' said Ra Fanana, 'you can't imagine—'

'What can it mean' – the conclusion came triumphantly – 'but that this certain young lady must be . . . *in love*?'

'In love?' Ra Fanana laughed, relieved. 'Of course she's in love! Isn't she on her way to be married?' The lady blushed and giggled, for all the world as if she were the *ingénue*. 'Ah Captain' – she wagged a finger – 'I can see that indeed your heart is no stranger to the ways of—'

'What are you talking about?' Selinda burst out. 'What are you talking about, both of you? Ra Ra, have you forgotten the duty you owe to me? How can you fawn so sickeningly over this pirate, this *depraved buccaneer*, when all the time he keeps us in a prison, and bears us to a worse one?'

Depraved buccaneer? The captain had never thought of himself quite in such terms. He brushed back his whiskers with a preening hand.

Ra Fanana was aghast. 'Child, what can you mean? Captain Porlo is a good man – a fine man—'

'He's a whoremonger – Glond's lackey! Twenty thousand Hora ducats, is that what I'm worth? Ra Ra, I told you I was a whore, and here's the proof!'

The girl swished to the door.

'My lady, please!'

'Lass, lass—' Captain Porlo struggled up. He would have grabbed the girl's arm, but his wooden leg caught as he pushed back his chair. He stumbled; his hand, flailing at the ceiling, cuffed inadvertently at Buby.

Buby shrieked, leaping on to Selinda's back.

The girl cried, 'Ugh! Get it off me, get it off me!'

The captain cried, 'Patches, help the lass!'

But Selinda needed no help. The little monkey spiralled through the air.

There was a splash.

'Buby! Buby, me girl!' The captain was horrified.

But Buby was agile and the sea was calm. Moments later, a dripping monkey came clambering back through the casement, while Ra Fanana joined the captain in exclamations of delight.

'Rum!' he bellowed. 'Patches, more rum!'

But Patches had gone. And so had Selinda.

'Miss Selinda? Miss Selinda, wait!'

The girl pushed through the narrow corridor, making for her cabin. Patches pushed too, blocking her way. She reeled angrily, running up a ladder to the deck. Patches followed; for a wild moment he thought the girl might fling herself over the side.

But not Miss Selinda.

He found her on the poopdeck, gazing haughtily into the ship's rippling wake. The rigging creaked.

'Miss Selinda?'

She turned, ghostly in the gleaming moonlight. 'I'm not Miss Selinda, I'm *Lady* Selinda.'

Clutched in her arms was the Blisha doll; she held it tight, like a talisman, at her breasts.

'Well, boy? What do you want?'

'Lady Selinda, you mustn't—'

'Mustn't? What *mustn't* I do now?'

Patches barely knew what to say. 'Cap'n Porlo, miss, you mustn't . . . *blame* him, I mean he – oh, he don't know what he does, Miss Selinda, he don't—'

'I'd have thought he *knew* only too well! Twenty thousand Hora-ducats – is that my price?'

Gulping, the boy gazed into the defiant face. Even in her present shabby state, the girl's beauty blazed out. Oh, she was a grand girl, was Miss Selinda!

'Miss Selinda . . . I mean Lady Selinda . . . you're worth a hundred Hora ducats, I mean a thousand, I mean a million – I mean, you're beyond price! But the Cap'n – you see, he's really on a treasure hunt, I mean a quest, and . . . well, that's what this voyage is for, there's a map, and – oh, I think he thinks it's his last voyage, and – he's *afraid*, Miss Selinda!'

'Afraid? That vulgar, violent old sot?'

How could Patches explain? 'He's a good man, Miss Selinda—'

'A good man, who beats you round the head? What, boy, are you as stupid as you look?'

'But he means well, Miss Selinda! Cap'n Porlo and me, we're like – like father and son, we are, and . . . why, miss, didn't you ever have a *father*?'

Selinda's look was incredulous.

'Oh . . . of course.' The boy looked down, flushing violently. He mumbled, 'Well then, you knows what it means, don't you? It means I knows him well – knows him like he really was me old dad, I does, and loves him like it too, and I'm telling you . . .' He gathered strength. 'I'm telling you he's *stalling*, Miss Selinda, I'm sure of it – playing for time, he is! The treasure hunt, it's like his final . . . *test*, his last – oh, I don't know, but don't you see, once he has those Hora-ducats he'll . . .'

'Wait!' Selinda's eyes flashed. 'Captain Porlo needs twenty thousand Hora-ducats, if he's going to pursue this . . . treasure hunt? That's why he's working for Glond?'

Patches nodded.

The girl gripped his arm. 'And if he had forty? If he had fifty?'

'What?' To Patches, her hand on his arm seemed to burn like fire.

'W—well then,' he stammered, 'he'd have no excuses, would he?'

Selinda smiled. She held up the Blisha doll. 'Very well. Let's see just how keen your captain is on this *treasure hunt*.'

And she pushed past the cabin boy, rapidly making her way back below.

'Miss Selinda? Miss Selinda, wait!'

They are gone.

For a moment, the poopdeck is empty. Or is it? What is this sound, this soft sound that comes between the sloshing of the waves, the sighing of the winds, the creaking and groaning of the timbers and ropes? Could it be a click-click of claws – and not just the tiny claws of a rat? Yes, for a certain stripy creature has been watching this latest dialogue, concealed behind a stack of barrels.

Now Rainbow emerges. In the darkness his fur is five shades of grey, but his silver collar glimmers eerily in the moonlight. With furtive eyes he looks around him. Then slowly he makes his way back to the longboat where for some days he has been hiding, beneath the folds of an old tarpaulin.

He is playing for time. But soon, his time will come.

Chapter 47

THE FLYING ZENZAN

'Young Lacani? Young Lacani, are you all right?'

It was a foolish question, of course. But Jem just wanted to be sure his benchmate was no worse. He leaned as far as his chains would let him, prodding at the skin of a withered arm. So cold! But the old man rallied, just a little. 'That ... Zenzan,' he muttered. 'If it hadn't been for that Zenzan ... oh, they'd never have got me then ... they'd have never got Young Lacani!'

Jem whispered, 'No ... no, they'd never.'

The night was far advanced: in Ejland time, beyond the passing of the First Fifteenth. Once again the *Death Flame* had halted; or rather, only the wind in the sails propelled it now. If there were no Submissions in the middle of the night, nonetheless the slaves must have some rest. The minimum, at least.

Along the benches, they sprawled at all angles, slumped into exhausted sleep. Fellows behind Jem snored loudly; fat Pancho mumbled; Bones, perhaps, was deep in meditation.

There would be no rest for Young Lacani. His back was a bloodied mess, his every nerve exposed. To Jem's horror, the blows of the guards had fallen most viciously on the weak old man. Perhaps they thought it was Young Lacani, not Jem, who had attacked Scurvy. Perhaps they just wanted to beat him, as if outraged at his very age and weakness.

Jem pressed the old man's hand. He must keep him talking. Yes, it would help if he kept him talking. 'Young Lacani?'

'Hm? What's ... that, matey?'

Jem struggled. 'You know how they'd never get you? If ... if it hadn't been for the Zenzan?'

'Ah, matey ... if it hadn't been ...'

'This Zenzan ... who was he?'

At this, there was life in the old man's eyes. The old spirit. The old fire. 'What, you've never heard of the Flying Zenzan?'

Eerily the sea sloshed against the hull, like a whisper continually urging *no, no*. Many a time Young Lacani slipped away. But slowly, as the great galley drifted with the winds, as the moonlight gleamed, sinister and silver, through the terrible colonnades, Jem pieced together a bizarre tale.

It was a tale, said Young Lacani, that had its beginnings long ago, when the five seas were terrorised by creatures far more fearsome than this paltry Ouabin, who thought himself the emperor of the world, but really was no more than the weakest pawn of fate. In those days, the cut-throat to rival all others was a fellow known as the Flying Zenzan, for such were his powers that it was said his ship could rise up from the waters, bearing down on his enemies like a monstrous bird.

'Why,' said Jem, 'such a man must have been . . . invincible!'

'Not . . . quite,' wheezed Young Lacani. 'When this tale begins, he had fared badly in his late campaigns and was holed up on the barren Isle of Aranthas, his crewmen and his riches much . . . oh, much depleted. The Zenzan was growing old and feared his days of glory would soon be at an end.' Young Lacani sighed and seemed about to slip into a reverie – one concerned more with himself perhaps, than with the subject of his tale.

'But his glory . . . it was only beginning?' urged Jem.

'Not . . . quite, matey, not quite. But for a while, it might have looked that way. You see, this was the time when the creature called Kalador, who was really the Mandru, had entwined the goddess Javander in his dark coils. Some say he is a myth, of course, and the goddess too . . . but they're fools. You know . . . Kalador, matey? Kalador, and the Mandru?'

Jem said that he did; Young Lacani nodded.

'You know, then, how the wicked thing would destroy Javander's sons? Already he had contrived it that the goddess herself should take the life of the son she most loved, red-hued Isol of the Shells. Then Kalador had hunted down first purple-hued Amas of the Rocks, then green-hued Eon of the Winds. Now . . . now only two remained.'

'Oclar of the Tides,' said Jem. 'The blue one. And . . . Uvan, I think? The golden one?'

'Uvan of the Sands.' Again the old man nodded, and explained how the wily Oclar had proved impossible to seek out and destroy; Uvan, meanwhile, was Oclar's boon companion, to be found perpetually at his brother's side. Together the blue and the gold sons of Javander held out long after their brothers had fallen, hiding in all manner of strange places, through all the vast expanses of the watery world.

But what, Jem wondered, had this to do with the Zenzan?

The answer was long in coming. For some time Young Lacani drifted away, with flickering eyelids and stertorous breath, before he felt able to carry on the story. How relieved Jem was when the old man's words resumed!

Kalador, he said, came before the Zenzan, addressing the cut-throat in terms such as these: 'Zenzan, you are the most fearsome of the buccaneers who terrorise these waters. I look upon your powers and sense that you, like me, might be a creature more than merely mortal. And yet, what has your evil made you but a spurned and hated outcast, lost to your kinsmen and your country too, hunted across the seas by those who would avenge the thousand wrongs you have done them? Would you not rather be a mighty potentate, a great ruler, revered and unassailable in the sway he holds not over some shabby ship but over a plenteous, populous isle, nay, a chain of isles – nay, a continent of his own?'

'What mockery is this?' the Zenzan demanded. 'Evil one, you stir me not to fear, for I fear no thing that lives. Think you that I am some callow boy, to be beguiled by the promise of a prize? But state what you would have, or you shall feel the force of my powers.'

At this, Kalador smiled with satisfaction. 'Ah, but indeed you are a fiery one! Was I not right to select you as my admiral? – Zenzan, look not startled, for to your side I would summon the greatest and most magical of companies ever assembled, a company – nay, a crew – gifted with a thousand evil powers, and all of them under your sovereign command. With such a crew, might not the Flying Zenzan be invincible in truth, not merely by repute? And Zenzan, this shall be but the beginning of your glory! Look you eager? I see you do. – This, then, is the task: to seek out and destroy Oclar and Uvan, who hide like cowards somewhere in these seas. Bring me back their corpses and a continent is yours.'

Jem felt his heart pound hard. Suddenly, for reasons greater than before, he found himself anxious to hear this tale to its end. It was like another piece of a child's wooden puzzle, slipping into place at last.

Gently, he pressed Young Lacani to go on.

For now, the old man needed no encouragement. Was the Zenzan filled with doubt, he wondered, even for a moment? Did the sense come to him even then that this mission would lead to no worldly greatness, but rather be the last he was to undertake? Perhaps the villain's brow might have furrowed, just a little. What of it? He took up the commission soon enough.

Young Lacani's eyes shone. Of the creatures that set out on that terrible quest, he said, by all accounts the Zenzan – an ugly, dark-browed mountain of a man – was the fairest. What a crew he led! There were many-tentacled monsters; there were noxious masses of squashy, formless jelly; there were clickety-clackety spiky things clad in shells like armour; there were vast malformed bird-men with beaks and wings and claws; there were men with heads like sharks and sharks with heads like men; there were hideous things in woman's shape, sirens with fish-scale skin and seaweed hair. Every abortion and deformity of the seas was there, all the most repellent Creatures of Evil that Kalador could summon from the mysterious caves and grottoes, the treacherous rocks and reefs,

343

the sucking swamps and fathomless ocean trenches where they would hide. What chance had Oclar and Uvan with such forces ranged against them?

'They were gods,' said Jem, 'or almost – sons of a goddess. Didn't they have to have *some* chance?'

Young Lacani drew a deep breath. 'Ah, matey, to tell of the long pursuits, the many campaigns from one side to the other of these watery realms would be the task of an age, and I must hasten to my conclusion. This it is: that after long travails in the icebound Seas of Soren, in the seaweed Seas of Sosenica, in the Wilds of Wendac, with its fogs that sap the will of all but the strongest men; in the Vision Gulf, and on the Coast of the Abyss; after orbit upon orbit of misery and terror, when the peace of half the world had been shattered by the Zenzan – after all this, I say, the end came at last one stormy night on the barren Isle of Aranthas, where, so long ago . . .'

'Where the quest had begun?'

'That's it! That's it exactly!'

So animated was Young Lacani now that Jem could not believe he was the same sick old man of moments before. Could he be dying? Jem could not believe it. In the moonlight, it seemed to him that the old man's eyes were filled with a strange, bright light of their own.

'But on Aranthas . . . Young Lacani, what happened?'

Withered lids fluttered over the bright eyes and the old man's manner darkened again. On Aranthas, he explained, the Prince of Sands had become ensnared in the deceptions of the sirens. Severed from his brother's side, drugged by sinister potions, so it was that Uvan was at last destroyed, his noble spirit rent from his golden form and spirited away to the Realm of Unbeing.

'The Zenzan was exultant,' sighed Young Lacani. 'Round and round the stormswept isle, like the very spirit of death itself, the evil creature whirled in his flying ship. His last and greatest victory was in sight, his imperial destiny almost upon him. Only Oclar was living now, and through the streaks of lightning and the swirlings of the storm, the Zenzan saw the Prince of Tides slumped, sobbing, over his brother's insensible form. "He is ours, we have him!" the Zenzan cried, and with all his evil crew poised, powers at the ready, he swerved the great ship around in the air, ready for the kill. "Die, Prince of Tides! Die, die!"

'But it was then that the Zenzan's real destiny was revealed to him. Lightning split the night apart and suddenly Oclar was standing, hands upraised like vengeance incarnate, as all the vast powers of the storm came channelling into his being. With blazing eyes he flung back the Zenzan's taunts. "Die? It is you who die, Zenzan!" he cried, as the lightning shot back, bolt after bolt, towards the flying ship. "Die, but in your death live on, a howling ghost that ever haunts these seas!"

'And the curse came to pass. So it is that, to this day, the Flying Zenzan, howling on the storm, is the vision most feared by all who sail these waters.'

※　※　※

Young Lacani fell silent.

The old man was shivering, as if the tale had been too much for him. Jem leaned forward, wishing he could place an arm round the quaking shoulders. He could not reach; besides, the shoulders were raw. But he reached out just enough to prod a withered arm.

'Young Lacani . . . Young Lacani?'

'They'd never have got me, matey . . . they'd never.'

'No . . . of course not.' *Keep him talking. Just keep him talking.* 'The Zenzan . . . does he curse all who see him?'

Young Lacani breathed slowly. Yes, now he was really slipping away. 'He doesn't curse. Or only those who . . . why, matey, there's some say he . . . blesses.'

Is this rambling? Just rambling? 'Young Lacani, I . . . don't understand.'

'But it was Oclar, wasn't it . . . didn't I say? Wasn't it Oclar who . . . made him that way? Don't you see? He doesn't curse, he . . . changes you . . . changes your fortune. You see, don't you?'

Jem was not sure he did. But he saw something.

'Young Lacani?' *Try, Young Lacani. Try, just for me.* 'You said you saw the Zenzan. So . . . what were you? I mean . . . before you got caught? Before you were a slave?'

'What was I, matey? Why, didn't I say?' For the last time, the old man laughed, and the laugh was almost hearty. 'I was a slaver, matey. Yes, I was . . . a slave-trader.'

Jem's heart chilled.

Chapter 48

AMBORA ROCK

'Young Lacani . . . Young Lacani, are you all right?'

Jem knew the question was pointless now. The long and strange drifting could not have lasted: neither the galley's, nor the old man's. All at once the gong had rung again; harsh orders had echoed down the decks, then heavy rapid footsteps, then whips, then cries of pain.

Stroke! Stroke! High above, the sails creaked and billowed. Below, dark waters churned to boiling foam. Again the galley sped through the night as if possessed by a demon; beside Jem, gripped by a different demon, Young Lacani only lolled and slumped. Sometimes he moaned; sometimes he coughed, blood flowing from his drivelling mouth.

There was nothing to be done. Desperately Jem, and Bones and Pancho too, struggled to make up for their companion's missing strength. They were losing the fight. Along the aisle, closer, getting nearer, came the crazed dwarf. Swing of a lantern. Swing of a whip.

'You man, there! Old man, there!'

How many times did the whip descend? What new frenzy, for a back already flayed? But still there was only the lolling, the slumping – then the guards bursting forward, pushing Scurvy brutally out of the way.

Then the familiar cry of '*Dead man over all!*'

These things, it seemed, would go on and on, a nightmare repeating endlessly until all the slaves were dead. But Young Lacani may not have been dead, not entirely, in the moment when they threw him over the side. His head was heavy and his limbs were still, but just before they lifted him out of his manacles, as a guard fumbled and cursed with his keys, Jem felt something sharp, something cold prodding his ribs.

Then came the last whisper, rasping in his ear: 'They've got me, matey . . . don't let them get you . . . not you . . . not you.'

Astonishment, like nausea, rushed over Jem and he could only cry out, clawing and clutching at the old man even as the guards lashed him away. The whip cut his hands; he crumpled back, agonised, and in the confusion, in the darkness, with the *Stroke! Stroke!* of the galley continuing all around, neither Jem nor the guards saw the thing that fell, spinning, from Young Lacani's hand, clattering to the deck between Jem's feet.

Brutal arms lifted and the corpse that was not a corpse swung up into the air. Jem sobbed, 'No ... he's not dead! No ... leave him!' Then, absurdly: 'Young Lacani ... come back!'

The splash seemed immense, though it could not have been. But it was then, as foam spattered the deck, that Jem saw, in a sliver of moonlight, the thing that had prodded against his side, then fallen from Young Lacani's hand. His chains allowed him just enough movement. Quickly he reached down, hiding the prize in the tatters of his tunic. The old man must have grabbed it when the dwarf attacked him. It was his gift. His last gift. All through that night Jem would feel it pressed against him, warming slowly against his flat, starved belly.

Stroke! Stroke! The galley ploughed on. But by Jem's bench, the guards were talking.

'It's pitiful, I tell you! These three? Plug this gap.'

'Plug it? From where? Who else can there be?'

'I don't know, one of the new ones.'

'What new ones? We've been at sea four, five days.'

'Just go down the back, eh? There's a few full benches left, ain't there? What about that Menos? What about that Blard?'

'Menos has had it. Blard's on his last legs.'

'There's a few more, ain't there? Just get me one that's half alive and plug this gap.'

'Waste of time. They're all going to die.'

'Just do it and stop moaning!'

The guards lurched off. By now Jem's mind was swirling beyond the scene, as if these horrors had severed some connection that tied him to the world. He might have been in a fever. On and on his arms worked, back and forth at the oar, but Jem was far away. When the guards came back, thrusting a ragged, shambling figure into Young Lacani's place, Jem could not even glance at his new benchmate. The hunched, dark form might barely have existed.

Instead, between the flickerings of his eyelids, Jem saw the scurrying, mad figure of Scurvy, Scurvy where Scurvy could not possibly have been, dancing on the bows, swinging on the pylons, leaping up, cat-like, to the silver disc of the moon. Then, like some horrific incubus, the Scurvy-thing came leaping down again, fixing itself to Jem's back, wrapping its claw-like hands round his throat. Jem struggled, but his wrists were chained to the oar: how could he throw off the vile abomination? He jerked. He writhed. Somehow, searing in the pain of it, he bashed and bashed the incubus against the side of the galley. *Crunch*, went the bones, *crunch* and *crunch* again.

For long through the night it went on, this unending, agonising

347

crunching of bones, until at last, in one of those strange transitions of dreams, Jem found himself alone: Scurvy gone, guards gone, all the benches round him empty, silent but for the waves and wind. He looked down at his wrists and his chains were gone too. He would have stood, would have blundered up to the prow, but that was when he saw that he was not alone at all: ahead, glimmering in the moonlight, was the Ouabin. Jem gulped: the white-garbed figure pointed, then Jem felt a sudden hotness in his chest, a burst of flame from the red crystal. Terror filled him and he sank back in his place, grabbing for the hard, sharp thing that had fallen, like a mercy, from Young Lacani's hand.

Jem hunched down, as if he could make himself invisible to the Ouabin. That was when he saw Scurvy's hideous face, grinning up at him from beneath the bench. The blackened teeth. The evil, glittering eyes. He stabbed. Vile jelly spurted from an eye, but Jem only drove the blade in harder, twisting it round in the blinded socket. Screaming, clawing, Scurvy scratched and bit at his attacker's hand. But Jem would not relent. Deeper, deeper, he drove in the blade until there came a cracking, then a bursting of timbers, and waters came flooding through the hull.

Stroke. Stroke. Jem swam. To describe the aquatic odyssey that followed, the kaleidoscope of visions that came to him under the sea, would be the task for an age. Whether they were good, these visions, whether they were evil, Jem could not tell. He only knew they were beautiful. There were cascades of dappled light; there were the strangest plants and fish, there were gorgeous, treasure-laden wrecks and reefs, garlanded with flowers that looked like jewels and jewels that looked like flowers. On and on came the tide of vision; on and on Jem swam, and as he swam he knew the crystal glowed at his chest, illuminating the hazy depths with its bright, unearthly light. But later, he would remember just one thing: the figure of a woman, imperious on a vast throne, hair flowing behind her in the undersea currents. Jem swam towards her, but never got any closer. In the dream, it did not matter: all he wanted was for the dream to go on.

Of course, it could not. At last, dawn came spilling over the decks. The gong sounded: Catacombs. Jem woke slowly, slumping over the oar. After the strange magic of the night, to be back in this noxious place was too much. He groaned, despairing. He shivered. But that was when he felt Young Lacani's legacy, felt it in the jab of the knife against his ribs. Then slowly he turned to the new presence beside him, filling the place where his lost companion had been. Jem drew in his breath. The face was gaunt, filthy and sleek with sweat. But suddenly the face was smiling.

Then Jem was smiling too. 'I don't believe it . . . Raj!'

'Cap'n, it's dark!'

'Dark? What you be talking about, lad?'

The sun shone brightly. The morning air was fresh. Captain and cabin boy stood in the forecastle, gazing towards Ambora Rock. Patches had taken the captain's far-glass and held it earnestly against his eye.

'Cold, too. Brr, it's freezing!'

'Stupid boy, give me that glass! Dark? Cold? Goody Palmer and her five daughters have done your brain in, lad, fair done it in!' The captain gestured expansively – or would have done, had the ship not lurched. His crutch skewed and he grabbed for a rail. 'Don't you know,' he gasped, 'that's Glondy's family seat?'

Patches knew this only too well. Like a strange and fearsome creature of the deep, the great crag rose immensely from the sea, thrusting blackly into the brilliant sky. How incongruous it appeared in the Waters of Wenaya! The Rock seemed to belong in chill northern reaches, where it might have been the domain of some barbarian raider, clad in a hornèd helmet and flea-infested furs.

'But Cap'n, where's the castle? Don't he have a castle?'

'Of course he does, and a castle and a half it be, you mark my words. Just wait till we rounds that headland, lad – soon enough, you'll be seeing something you won't forget in a hurry.'

The captain twirled the far-glass in his hand. Below, the quarterdeck seethed with life. To bellowing choruses of *Yo-ho-hee*, tars with flashing earrings and bright bandannas scrubbed down the timbers and polished the cannons, heaved at the halyards and hauled in the sails, ready for their arrival at Ambora Rock.

The captain said, 'Didn't I tell you old Faris Porlo spent some of his happiest days in Castle Glond? If I'm sure of one thing, lad, it's this: when you be a grizzled old sea-dog too, looking back on a long life like mine – most of it squandered, I'll be bound – one day you'll be saying the very same thing! Why, when I thinks of that banqueting hall, rafters rising high as the sky, and all them long tables groaning with—'

Patches was incredulous. '*Foreign muck?*'

'Eh? And them slaves got up in jewels and glittery capes—'

'*Tarts on the tiles?* Oh Cap'n, you can't—'

'And them sofas and curtains and carpets and—'

'*Feminine fripperies?* Oh Cap'n, Cap'n!'

But the captain was not listening. Buby clambered through the rigging over their heads, screeching and pointing at the fearsome Rock. The captain reached up, cuffing her with the far-glass. The monkey, like a swatted fly, dropped to the deck.

Patches gasped. Buby lay curled in a ball, whimpering; the captain merely ignored the little creature, bellowing to the tars to hurry round the headland. Could an eager old sea-dog, and a young one too, wait even a moment more to see Castle Glond?

Patches said miserably, 'But Glond won't be there.'

The ship listed to starboard. 'Eh? What, lad?'

'Glondy. He's still in Hora, ain't he?'

'Aye, and what does that mean but a longer stay for us?' Captain Porlo held tightly to the rail. 'Let Glondy take what time he will – I tells you, lad, by the time he gets here you'll be wishing it were longer! Why, before the sun's over that there yard-arm you'll be sticking your arse up in the air, bowing low to Wiley Wan Wo – that's Glondy's steward, here on the Rock. Good old Wiley! Fatten you up like a pig he will—'

'What, for the slaughter?'

'Aye, like a pig, or a big floppy seal! Wait till you tastes his octopus in bee sauce, Patches! Wait till you tastes his dolphin pie, served on a bed of slithery oysters—'

'But Cap'n, I only wants salt-pig and mustard! And weevily biscuits, and rotgut, and—'

'What, boy? Have you no spirit of adventure?'

Buby was struggling back to her feet. She sank down. Was she hurt? Patches almost burst into tears.

The captain continued, 'And wait till you see them serving-wenches! Don't worry, lad, you can sniff all you like up a slave-girl's rear, without so much as a by-your-leave! Too shy? Never mind, old Wiley'll fix you up! I tell you, lad, you'll soon forget about Goody Palmer and her . . . What's wrong with you, lad?'

Patches sniffed. 'But Cap'n, you hates dry land! Remember how you hated Qatani? You said—'

'Don't remind me of them cobber-as, boy. But this ain't rotten old Qatani, this is—'

The ship lurched; the captain tottered, and Patches, grabbing him, burst out desperately, 'Cap'n, you *could* take Miss Selinda's doll!'

'What, boy?' Angrily the captain swivelled away, stumping on Buby's tail. With a shriek the monkey leapt on to his shoulders. He tottered again and the far-glass rolled across the deck.

He clutched the rail, scowling at the clawing Buby.

A voice came, 'That's right. You *could* take the doll.'

It was Selinda, her face high-coloured in the whipping wind. Clutched in her arms again was the Blisha doll; the girl held it forward like an offering, like a sacrifice.

'Forty thousand Hora-ducats, Captain. Fifty.'

The captain glowered, launching at once into a fulsome description of the splendours, the wonders, the manifold feminine fripperies and fineries that awaited the ladies on Ambora Rock.

Selinda had heard it all before. She burst out, 'You're afraid, aren't you – afraid of your treasure hunt? Come, Captain, I tell you – the doll is yours!'

'My lady, please!' Struggling up behind the girl came Ra Fanana, puffing and protesting. Hearing the girl's words, she was at once alarmed.

Then she saw Ambora Rock. She staggered back, moaning, as the captain cried, 'Wait, just wait, till you see Castle Glond – finest castle this side of Ejland! Why, there couldn't be a lady in the world who wouldn't want to be mistress of such an establishment!'

The nurse lurched forward, clutching the captain by the arm. 'Faris,' she breathed, 'about this treasure hunt. Perhaps – perhaps the girl's right. After all, we – we could be together . . .'

Astonished, the captain turned to her.

Patches pleaded, 'Cap'n, you know it's what you want! Forget Wiley-whatsisname, forget Glondy—'

'And what about the girl, answer me that? What about Glondy's lady-love, that he's trusted old Faris Porlo to—'

'She's not his lady-love – she hates him, you know she does! And Glondy's a villain! A slimy, dirty foreigner, Cap'n, like you always say! Don't you see, Miss Selinda could come with us, and—'

'Stupid boy! What's a lady, but a curse on a—'

Ra Fanana said, 'Faris, you can't mean that! You don't!'

Buby shrieked on the captain's shoulder. The sea-dog whirled, as if to shake her free. Patches plunged to save her; the captain, it seemed, thought the boy was attacking him.

'Don't you dare!' Swinging back with his crutch, the captain would have struck Patches to the deck, but Selinda burst out, 'Leave him alone, you drunken coward!'

Patches reeled, shocked.

Captain Porlo crashed to the deck.

Ra Fanana cried, 'My lady, what have you done? Faris, dear Faris, are you—'

Patches cried, 'Cap'n, are you all right?'

Selinda cried, 'Look!'

They had rounded the headland. Aghast, the girl pointed at Ambora Rock.

Castle Glond was a blackened, smoking ruin.

Chapter 49

THE VORTEX

'Cap'n, it's dark!'

'Aye, Patches, and cold too.'

A chill wind circled Ambora Rock, for all the brightness of the surrounding day. Captain Porlo drew his long shabby coat tighter around him and, following his cabin boy, stumped across the desolate landing-stage. Striding ahead fearlessly was Lady Selinda, astonished and fascinated by the ruinous castle; behind them came Ra Fanana, nursing Buby like an infant at her breast. Worriedly, from time to time, the nurse would look back to the *Catayane*, bobbing impassively out in the bay.

When the ladies had insisted on coming ashore, Captain Porlo had scowled and muttered oaths; but when it was time to lower the longboat, the subdued old sea-dog had not demurred. Something had happened to Castle Glond. But something had happened to the captain, too.

He shook his head, then shook it again. The great doors of the castle hung blackened and crumbling. The windows, high above, were like blinded eyes. Still the stench of burning lingered, for all the swiftness of the strangely cold wind. 'I . . . I can't believe it. It can't have been long ago, it can't have been. Oh, if only we'd got here sooner!'

Protectively, Ra Fanana drew beside him. 'Faris, don't torment yourself. What could you have done? Come away – come back to the *Catayane*.'

The captain seemed barely to hear her words. 'Castle Glond! It used to be so warm, so happy. Where better for a poor sea-dog to take a nice long rest from his cares, and fatten himself up for the perils ahead, and study his maps and charts, and write up his log, and . . . and fall in love with a certain young lady?'

'Young lady?' Sadly, Ra Fanana stroked Buby's fur.

But the captain's reverie, for the moment, had ended.

Patches called, 'Hel-*lo*! Hel-*lo*!'

Selinda stood peering through the hanging doors.

'My lady, be careful!' called Ra Fanana.

The girl called back, 'There's debris – a lot of smoke. But I think we can go further, just a bit. Come on, Patches.'

Ra Fanana gasped, wishing she could restrain them. It was to no avail.

As if through a malevolent, swallowing maw, the young people vanished through the dark doors. Rapidly, painfully, the captain stumped behind them – with a determination, the nurse noted worriedly, that could hardly accord with the number of his legs. With an automatic gesture, almost an absurd one, the sea-dog drew his cutlass from its scabbard.

Ra Fanana had no choice but to follow. Her heart was in turmoil. For many a day she had convinced herself that nothing could be better for her lady, or for herself, than the future Lord Glond had promised them. True, her lady would bridle against it; true, the girl would feel constricted, constrained; but after all, she would be honourably married, and Ra Fanana would still be with her, tending the wife as she had tended the child. Their trials would be over, the course of their lives laid out before them as if on a map.

A map, indeed! Ruefully Ra Fanana thought of the fantasies that had consumed her from the moment when the girl, eyes blazing defiance, had flung down the Blisha doll on the captain's table. Fantasies, of course, are indulged in the more for all their apparent impossibility. Now it seemed those fantasies were about to come true. Now a different map would direct their lives, and where it might lead them, the nurse could not say.

But how much better this new life would be!

Buby stirred, whimpering, in Ra Fanana's arms. Hushing the little monkey, hastening after Faris, dear Faris, the nurse did not look back towards the *Catayane* again, nor towards the landing stage and the knocking, sloshing longboat that was tethered there.

So it was that none of the five explorers saw a certain brightly coloured canine form emerging from beneath the tarpaulin in the bottom of the longboat, scrambling up on to the slimy jetty and following furtively behind them.

Inside the great portal, Castle Glond presented a desolate scene. The hall that opened before them might have been the depths of a smoking pit, cut through by harsh sunlight, beaming through gaps in the ruined roof. Coughing, Ra Fanana caught up with the captain. He turned to her. His cutlass trailed in the ashy floor and tears sparkled in his old eyes.

'This smoke,' he said, 'this smoke—'

'Faris,' said Ra Fanana, 'I'm not really a one for dry land. Don't you know I've been on ships before? The slavers took me away when I was just a little girl – why, I've been all over these Waters of Wenaya!'

The captain looked thoughtful. 'I could tell you'd got your sea-legs, me lady—'

'Ra Fanana. Call me Ra Fa—'

'And the girl's got pluck. Oh, that much I could tell. Like I could tell about another girl, once—'

'Another?' Ra Fanana held her breath.

There was a faraway tone in the captain's voice. 'Old Wiley Wan Wo's daughter, she were. Mani, her name was – a great beauty, everyone said so, though she were just a commoner. How that lass used to love me tales of life on the ocean wave, and all me adventures and derring-do! Used to joke that I'd take her with me, I did, if her dear old papa would only let her go – oh, her eyes used to light up like lanterns, they did! Well, I thought, I thought . . . well, I was a younger man then, of course, not like now . . . But a lovely girl like that, she'd hardly want a fellow with only one leg, now, would she? Them cobber-as—'

'Oh, Faris! What became of her?'

'Died of the jubba-fever, I heard later, some time after I'd sailed away. Yes, that's right – the jubba-fever, it were.' There was no bitterness in the captain's voice. 'So I never saw that lass again, never really knew why . . . Still, there were something she gives me, I means before I go.'

Ra Fanana gulped. 'Faris?'

'Aye, the lass gives me something to remember her by. Makes me think – makes me think she might have . . . it were a map, me lady.'

'A map? *The* map?'

The young people had gone on ahead, their calls echoing back through the swirling gloom.

'Hel-*lo*! Hel-*lo*!'

Ra Fanana shifted the burden of Buby. She laid a hand on the captain's arm. 'Faris, it's no good. There can't be anyone alive left here. Come with me – come back to the *Catayane*, hm?'

'But what happened here?' said the captain. 'How—'

Ra Fanana shuddered. 'I should think that's clear—'

'There might be someone. Old Wiley—'

There was a scream.

Then another: Ra Fanana's. 'My lady!'

First Buby, as if suddenly restored, leapt from the nurse's arms. Then Ra Fanana rushed ahead. Horror overcame her. From a blackened rafter, with a hot chain drawn taut about his neck, hung the half-burned, smouldering form of a man. The man wore the remnants of bright embroidered robes and a long, dark, rope-like pigtail flopped forward over his coppery, ancient face.

Slithering, almost collapsing, the captain floundered after Ra Fanana. 'Wiley!' he gasped. 'Old Wiley – burned!'

Selinda shuddered. 'Not just burned – murdered!'

Patches staggered back through a doorway, retching.

Selinda swivelled round. 'Patches, what is it?'

The boy only pointed. Selinda surged ahead.

'No, miss, no! It's them serving wenches! They—'

Captain Porlo slumped down heavily. 'Old Wiley – poor Wiley! I . . . I can't believe it!

'Oh Faris, Faris!' Awkwardly, Ra Fanana moved to embrace him.

'Very touching, I'm sure,' came a voice.

They turned, startled. For a moment the figure before them was obscured, the merest shadow in a sharp shaft of light. Then it moved forward.

The captain breathed, '*Glondy!*'

Jewels flashed around the bright eyes. Glond's voice was urbane, amused. 'I'm pleased to see you remember me, old friend. After all, it's been – what? A moonlife, or more? So perhaps you remember your duty to me, too? A matter of – hm – twenty thousand Hora-ducats, if I recall.'

The captain blurted, 'I've brought the girl, Glondy!' He reached for Selinda. He would have grabbed her arm, but the girl drew back, affronted.

'Faris!' cried Ra Fanana. 'You can't mean—'

Patches breathed, 'This doesn't make sense. How can *he* be here, all sudden-like? Where's his ship? How did he—'

Glond said, 'Indeed, Porlo, you have brought the girl. The Hora-ducats we shall arrange in due course. First, perhaps—'

'But Glondy, what's happened here?' the captain cried. 'Your castle, your servants—'

'They were in the way. They *annoyed* me—'

'Glondy, what are you talking about? Old Wiley—'

'Slaves, mere slaves! What, I ask you, can one such as I gain from mere slaves?' The tall, blue-garbed figure waved a hand in the air, as if to brush aside the very thought. His costume, his demeanour, suggested he was still in an elegant royal court, not this desolate, smoking ruin.

He moved towards Selinda. 'Darling girl, I see you tremble. Ah, but should not a fair innocent tremble when the moment of her womanly destiny is nigh? Embrace me, my darling – embrace me, kiss me! Don't you know the time of our wedding has come?'

'A respectable girl,' began Ra Fanana, 'would hardly—'

The girl stepped back. 'Don't touch me! I said I'll never be your bride, and I—'

'*Won't?*' The nobleman had to smile. 'Such delusions – hm, Nurse Fanana? But the girl is young yet, far too young! Touching, isn't it? And pathetic too – *still* she has not gathered that she has no choice. After all, what energies, what powerful surging forces, might one such as I draw

355

from a Triarch's daughter? Yes, and what *stability* might she not confer upon me?'

Selinda gasped. Her hand went to her mouth.

'Energies?' said Ra Fanana. 'Forces? What do you—'

Since Glond appeared, Buby had hissed at him suspiciously, her teeth bared and her back arched; now the monkey leapt upon him, scratching and biting. He cuffed her away, but in the moment that he struck, Glond's face changed. It was as if he were wearing a mask and the mask had slipped, revealing, just for an instant, a quite different visage.

It was the wizened face of an old, bearded man.

Selinda breathed, 'Who are you? *What* are you?'

But then he was Glond again. 'Who, my darling, but the one who loves you?'

'No!' Boldly, Ra Fanana stepped forward. 'You're evil—'

Glond, if Glond he were, shouldered her out of the way. She sprawled to the floor. 'Away with you, Nurse Fanana – your ministrations are at an end! The girl is mine now, mine!'

'Glondy, don't touch her!' The captain brandished his cutlass. 'I may be an old man, but you got me roused! I always knew you was an evil little tyke, and why I listened to you for one moment, I'll never—'

'Evil? That's rich, – coming from a man who's spent his life, from his boyhood to his dotage, in an unrelenting course of pillage and plunder. I may be evil in your eyes, Porlo – never more so, no doubt, than when I plucked the virtue of a certain young kitchenmaid. Now what was her name? *Mani*, I believe, that was it—'

The captain's eyes blazed. 'Why, you—'

'I told her it was only a little curtain of flesh, that and no more. Of what consequence could our diversion be? Still, it seems she was prey to superstition, and decided that she must refuse your offer of marriage.' Glond looked down, studying his fingernails, quite unalarmed by the captain's cutlass. 'The little fool killed herself after you left, Porlo. We don't get much jubba-fever out in these parts, you know – not much at all.'

The captain said again, 'Why, you . . . why—'

'Oh shut up, you senile old fool.' In a casual gesture Glond raised his arm, as if to knock the cutlass from the captain's trembling grip.

It was then that his face flickered once more – first came the visage of the old man again, then another, the face of a painted savage.

The captain breathed, 'You're not . . . you're not . . .'

'Oh, but I *am* Glond – Glond, and much more! In my life as Glond, what had I wanted but to assume the mantle of Triarch? How blind I was, to be slave to an ambition so petty! Now, have I not achieved so much more? I would have been a Triarch – instead, I am a *Triurge!*'

356

Selinda gasped, 'I knew it! But I never believed—'

The captain cried, 'I don't know what you are, Glondy, but I knows you be a monster!'

'Out of my way, old man!'

With a brutal blow, the Triurge would have cuffed the captain aside, but now the sea-dog swung forward, lunging savagely with his rusty cutlass.

The blow connected.

The Triurge roared. Its faces flickered again, and not just its faces: in an instant the entire form of the creature had changed many times. First there was the old man, in the flowing robes of an enchanter; then a little boy in Unang garb; a savage in a loincloth; then Glond again, then a stripy-shirted sailor. Then, as if the force inside these five separate forms were whirled together and blended, the creature suddenly turned into a hideous, slimy, shambling monster, faceless but for the golden orb embedded in its head.

Captain Porlo's cutlass stuck into the monster like a thorn in its side. Reeking flesh swelled and the cutlass, sticky with slime, fell clattering to the floor. Searing orb-light cut through the gloom, sweeping across faces transfixed in terror.

The light lingered, blindingly, on Selinda.

The creature extended a rotting hand.

The girl staggered forward.

Patches was the first to break the spell. He rushed at her, pushed her from the creature's path. 'Run, Miss Selinda – run, run!'

'Faris!' Ra Fanana screamed. 'What about Faris—'

Desperate, the cabin boy seized the captain's cutlass.

The creature turned again, filling the air, filling all the world with its stench, its vileness.

A hand swept down. Patches hacked at it.

'Miss Fanana . . . help the Cap'n back—'

'Faris, can you manage? Quick, Faris, quick—'

The creature lunged again. The boy hacked again.

Selinda cried, 'Patches, come away! Patches, you can't—'

A new and terrible tumult came, a sound beyond screaming, beyond roaring, and the orb-light was suddenly, impossibly brighter. The Triurge was growing, rearing to a greater and ever greater height.

The ruined chamber trembled. Dust rained down.

Patches cried out. The cutlass burned his hand. It fell.

The creature was upon him, ready to destroy him.

Then it happened. As if from nowhere, a rainbow-coloured animal bounded forward, swooping into the air, surrounding the Triurge in swirling beams of light. Patches scrambled back. The others could only

357

look up, astonished, as Rainbow with his mysterious glowing collar turned and tumbled with the monster in the air. Rafters crashed down. The hall was a chaos of smoke and dust and sound, of dazzling orb-light and churning rainbow patterns.

'Now that's what I call a *dog*!' cried Patches.

Selinda cried, 'But where's he from? I—'

'Never mind that! Let's get out of here!'

They stumbled back to the doors. On and on the battle raged, with the dog howling, with the Triurge shrieking. Then as quickly as it had swollen, the Triurge withered. Faces, figures flashed again in the crackling, sparkling space where the monster had been.

And one in particular. From a churning vortex, Littler reached out, crying Rainbow's name. The dog barked and leapt, but to no avail. Then the vortex whizzed faster and faster, and the Triurge fizzled into nothingness.

'Wh-what happened?' gasped Ra Fanana. 'Why—'

'Never mind!' Patches cried. 'Let's just get out of here – while we've got the chance!' He whistled to Rainbow. 'Here, boy! I don't know where you came from, but you're one of us now.'

Rainbow frisked and panted. But the dog lingered before loping back to the longboat, looking forlornly at the place where Littler, just for a moment, had seemed to live again.

Chapter 50

ALL THE CONSPIRATORS

The *Catayane* creaks on the darkness of the sea. Below decks, it is quiet. Tonight there are no carousings from the tars, no bellowed shanties, no fierce disputations over cards and coins; the ship might be under a vow of silence.

Life, it seems, resides only in four shabby figures, clustered on the quarterdeck. One is the helmsman at the great spoked wheel – the greasy-looking, slippery fellow whom the tars call 'Porpoise'. One is the boatswain, whose buck teeth and whiskers long ago earned him the nickname 'Walrus'. There is the first mate, whose corpulence makes it inevitable that he should be known as 'Whale'. Then there is the ship's cook, a recent arrival on the *Catayane*, where food has in the past been the province of the cabin boy, or sundry common tars. A Horan, engaged by Lord Glond, and architect of the many forms of *foreign muck* that have passed of late across the captain's table, this fellow has nonetheless been accepted readily enough by the tars – especially when he has been liberal with the contents of what he affects to call, or thinks are called, 'the cellars'. His name is something silly and foreign, but his longish, alarmingly bulbous snout – or some similar nether part, if sightings are to be believed – have led him to acquire the name of 'Sea-Snake'.

Shall we listen to what they have to say?

WALRUS: But I don't understand. I thought that was all just
    nonsense, about a treasure hunt. That stuff about the Straits
    of Javander, too – that's why he threw off old Lemyu,
    wasn't it, for going on about that stuff? So what's the old
    fool on about now?
WHALE (*with a sigh*): I think we know what he's *on* about,
    Walrus.
WALRUS: What he's *on*, you mean! I tell you, mates, it don't
    make sense. Oh, I knows he was going all sea-lion, like—
SEA-SNAKE: Sea-lion? What is this, this sea-lion?
PORPOISE (*at the helm, ignoring this*): Senile? Cap'n Porlo? You'd
    better watch what you say, Walrus, or you'll be ending up
    like Lemyu, too.
WALRUS: But I tell you, I don't understand! First we're on our

way to this there Rock—

PORPOISE: You buck-toothed fool, you saw the Rock! We could
hardly stay there, could we? Or leave a lass?

SEA-SNAKE (*gesticulating*): Alas? Ah, alas, what splendid kitchens
His Lordship Glond had promised me! Oh, I shall never
recover from this loss! And the sea's harvest in those deep,
rich waters – why, I should cook him dishes fit for a King!

PORPOISE: So you bloody well should, since he *is* a King – ain't
he? Or one of them Tri-Kings? Anyway, with what you've
got in your britches, I don't see why you should complain.

SEA-SNAKE: Eh? What?

WALRUS (*impatient*): But this treasure hunt, I tells you, mates, I
don't—

PORPOISE: Cut it out, you buck-toothed fool! Didn't I tell you to
cut it out?

WHALE: There's none to hear – I can't see that little bum-boy in
the patchy pants, can you? Can you see him anywhere? I
tells you, mates, I don't like it either.

SEA-SNAKE (*carrying on*): What of me? What, am I to live
without my kitchen? What, am I to find a kitchen fit for a
King, as we wind our way through these Straits of
Javander?

WHALE: No, but you might find an early death.

WALRUS: And a quick one, too! Ain't you heard about them
savages, with blow-pipes—

PORPOISE: Walrus, I told you to shut your trap!

SEA-SNAKE: Eh? Savages? Why, the buck-toothed fellow is right.
He don't like it? *I* don't like it!

WHALE: Me neither! You don't, do you, Porpy? Not really?

PORPOISE (*considering*): Well . . . no, I don't like it.

WHALE: That's it then. You know, I'm starting to think poor old
Lemyu wasn't so cracked after all. So what we going to do,
mates – what we going to do?

✳   ✳   ✳

For long into the night the girl shifts restlessly. Sometimes she paces her
narrow, perfumed cabin, then flings herself down on her bunk again. The
casement discloses a sinister pallor, the glimmer of moonbeams on the
slapping water.

Again and again, in her clammy wakefulness, the girl imagines that
she sees the Triurge and hears the terrible echo of its roar. She thinks of
the old tales. The Triurge, she knows, has ingurgitated too much, and
now seeks desperately to stabilise itself. As Glond sought her for his

360

unwilling bride, so the Triurge seeks her for the Swallowing Marriage that alone can prevent that dissolution. Suddenly the girl is no longer keen to die. But again she imagines the orb-light sweeping across her; again she feels the desire that consumed her, like a fever, when it had seemed that the Triurge would triumph. How she had longed to be wholly consumed! Selinda shudders. Of one thing she is certain: they have not seen the last of the hideous creature.

Gratefully she runs a hand over Rainbow's furry head. Like a sentinel the mysterious dog sits, unsleeping, in the casement-seat. Selinda knows that he will try and protect her. But can he save her when the Triurge comes again?

On the other side of the cabin, Ra Fanana is wakeful too. Anxiously she peers towards Selinda, but somehow she cannot bring herself to speak. Sighing, the nurse thinks of dear Faris, after their return from Castle Glond. Standing up in the forecastle, the wind whip-whipping round his white whiskers, the captain had addressed his assembled tars. How like a hero he had looked – looked, and sounded, too. Stentorian, his voice surged above the decks, but he said nothing of Ambora Rock or the Triurge. Instead, it was all about the voyage ahead.

At last, said the captain, the time had come for the treasure hunt he had delayed all his life. He waved the crumpled map. He pointed to the **X**. Stretching forth his arms, he spoke of strange places, of the Isthmus of Maric, of the Straits of Javander, of the Salt Seas of Sardoc. Exulting, he invoked the Maelstrom of the Mandru, and a place even stranger, called the Eye of the Sea. This map, he said, was graven on his heart, like the memory of the lass who had given it to him – and every man who joined with him, following him to the treasure, was guaranteed his share.

Every man, and every woman too.

How the tars cheered! How they stamped!

And yet, how strangely hollow it had seemed . . .

Ra Fanana shifts on her pillow. If only she could sleep!

But no, she would like to be with the captain at this very moment.

Captain Porlo scratches his fleas. Gingerly, he fingers a scab on his belly – left, no doubt, by his last bout of itching. (Why, there are scabs all over him these days – getting as bad as that poor lad he is, that cabin boy, the one before Patches!) The worst of it is down below – where his stump meets his wooden leg. What must it be like down there? Raw, like raw meat? Smells a bit, too. Oh, he'd like a good scratch there right now, he would. But the captain can't reach that far any more – not, at least, when he's lying in his bunk.

The weapons round the walls clink-clink like coins. The urge to piss comes over him again. Blearily, flopping down a hand, he fumbles for the pot. What, has it slipped across the floor again? Used to be on a chain, it did, but the chain broke – oh, days ago, and no one's fixed it. Hah! Sometimes it stinks in here like the squirtings of old Bollocks, the *Catty*'s trusty puss-cat. Dear old Bollocks! How long had it been since the first mate found him under the bowsprit, stiff and cold? (Tossed him overboard, the bugger did, before the captain could so much as say goodbye!) Back in old Beezer's time, that were ... Marmalade-coloured he was, was Bollocks – one eye, one ear, but two enormous orbs, like a tart's tits, swelling under his sticky-up tail. What a rat-catcher he used to be!

Still, it was as well old Bollocks was gone. Bollocks and Buby, they'd never have got on now, would they? And Buby was a good sort, when she weren't being too contrary. Sometimes the little monkey would nestle against him – times like now, in his bunk at night. Scratch him, too – the captain liked that. But Buby weren't here now. No. Been acting funny, ever since that business with Glondy. Very funny.

The captain has given up on the pot. Doesn't matter, does it? The urge has passed, as these days it often does, leaving only a slow, spreading ache, all in the guts like. No rest till morning now ... Oh, bother it, bother it! The captain raises his head. On the ledge above his bunk, beside mouldering volumes of the ship's log, is the trusty tankard he always sets there before he puts himself down for the night. In the moonlight it gives off a friendly glint.

He reaches for it. The fire fills his throat.

Oh, he's not much of a man now, is he? Old Faris Porlo, he's coming to his end ...

The beginning of the end.

But it must be long past the beginning now.

When the captain sleeps at last, he dreams of Glondy, or the terrible thing that Glondy has become; he dreams of poor Mani and Wiley Wan Wo; most of all he dreams of the cobber-as, the evil hissing cobber-as that put paid to Lefty, so long ago. But no, not the cobber-as, the whole seething pit of them, but one, just one, rearing up and swelling to monstrous size. Why, a cobber-a that size could poison the world! The captain feels its rank breath. Venom drips from its jaws.

He wakes suddenly. Again, he reaches for his trusty tankard.

Now Selinda dreams too. But the dream is not the nightmare she has feared, all the time she has lain awake. Instead, she sees herself on the prow of the ship, not in darkness, but in bright day. Does she feel a trepidation, wondering if the Triurge might rise from the water? The breeze that stirs around her is a sweet wafting incense. Mysterious music begins to play. Then the bird – but it is not just a bird – lands as if from nowhere on her hand, and the girl, intently, with a knowledge beyond knowledge, gazes into the blue raven's eyes ... No, this dream is no nightmare. But when she wakes, Selinda shall find her pillow wet with tears.

So shall Ra Fanana. The nurse dreams of the Triurge, but her dream, too, is not the expected nightmare. Rather, it is of the Triurge withering into the merest husk, and the five figures who have formed the fearsome creature stepping forth from the husk unharmed. Look! Here comes the stripy-shirted sailor, grinning broadly. Here's the painted savage, leaping, punching the air; the enchanter, Tagan's father, shuffles forward in his long robes, raising his hands as if in blessing. Here's Lord Glond, handsome, eyes twinkling. Ah, but he is an admirable suitor after all!

And then there is the little boy.

The child comes running into Ra Fanana's arms.

❊　　❊　　❊

WHALE (*after a pause*): So what are we going to do? I think I know.

WALRUS: Oh, and what would that be, lard-lump?

WHALE: Who you calling lard-lump?

WALRUS: You, you big lump of lard!

SEA-SNAKE (*bridling*): What is this lard? Where is it? He has taken it from my kitchen, no?

WHALE: I'm warning you, Walrus! Boatswain or no boatswain, you can still be in line for a good—

WALRUS: Yes, and first mate or no first mate—

PORPOISE (*rolling his eyes*): Mates, mates! Now listen now, and listen good. So what are we saying here, eh? What are we thinking? We aren't thinking ... *mutiny*, are we?

Pause.

WHALE: I don't much fancy them Straits of Javander, do you?

WALRUS: I don't much fancy them Salt Seas of whatsitsname.

SEA-SNAKE: Ah, and this terrible Maelstrom of the Mandru!

PORPOISE: Look, mates, I don't like it either, not these maelstroms, these eyes in the sea. Not natural, is it? But aren't you all forgetting something – something *very* important?

WALRUS: What, the treasure? You don't believe the old fool, do you?

PORPOISE: What's believing? I've knocked round these parts

many a long year, long before I came aboard the *Catty*.
There are things a man hears—

WHALE (*scoffing*): Myths? Legends?

PORPOISE: What do you know about legends, lard-lump?

WHALE: What, *you're* calling me lard-lump, too, are you?

PORPOISE (*ignoring him*): Look, I say the old bastard's on to
something, mates. I say we goes with him – just a bit
further. After all, if he leads us to treasure . . . *greatest
treasure of the seas*, didn't he say?

WALRUS: A likely story! I tell you, he's gone sea-lion—

WHALE: Well, he *did* promise us a share – *all* of us.

PORPOISE (*considering*): I think I'd prefer a share for *some* – eh,
mates?

WALRUS: What are you saying, Porpoise?

PORPOISE (*suddenly*): What's that noise?

WHALE: Eh, steady on! It's just the monkey – capering up in the
rigging, like.

SEA-SNAKE: Ugh! Filthy thing! Fling it in the sea!

WALRUS: Eh, don't let the Cap'n hear you say that!

As it happens, it is not just the monkey. Above, PATCHES *is
sequestered in the crows' nest. The boy is awake, and alarmed – but
not only by the conspirators. He looks out into the darkness. All at
once, he feels that something is happening, and wonders that the men
below appear not to feel it. Ah, but they shall feel it soon enough!*

   What is this mysterious churning in the sky?

Chapter 51

STROKE! STROKE!

Stroke! Stroke!

'Jem, you can't be . . . serious.'

'Raj, how could I be more . . . serious? Look at us. We're going to die. If this goes on, we're going to . . . die.'

'Yes, but . . . two of us, against these . . . guards? Jem—'

'Not just two! Raj, don't you . . . see? Young Lacani said—'

'Young . . . Lacani?' Rajal shuddered. 'In Qatani, in the dungeons, there was a . . . madman, yelling and screaming. They called him . . . *Old* Lacani. Some . . . family, eh?'

'Young Lacani, he was no . . . madman.'

'No? But he thought that one . . . *one* knife—'

'I'll show you, Raj! Just wait, I'll . . . show you—'

From along the decks: *Dead man over all!*

The splash. Then the whips. Pain clawed at Jem's heart. For a moment he thought only of death, and all the horror that pressed around him, like a blanket filled with plague, smothering him in the tropical night.

'It can't last,' he muttered, 'this just can't . . . *last*—'

'They say we're gaining. We . . . have to be. My arms are just about . . . falling off.'

'What, Raj? Gaining on . . . what?'

'You mean you don't know? Back there, the guards . . . I heard them talking. It's Porlo . . . he's got this girl—'

'Porlo?' That name again! Sometimes it seemed to Jem that everything he had known was turning slowly in a vast circle, certain to come round another time. There was a pattern in things, he was sure of it. He felt the weight of the knife against his ribs, shifting with every stroke of the oar. 'Young Lacani said Porlo was . . . the one man who'd ever . . . defeated the Ouabin—'

'You think he'd . . . defeat him now?'

'Not while . . . we're on board, I hope! But Raj, this girl—'

'Glond's bride—'

'Tagan's mistress? She was . . . kidnapped—'

'Yes,' said Rajal, 'by Glond. But Porlo, he's in on it . . . he's taking her somewhere . . . but the Ouabin wants her, too—'

'For love?'

365

'Money . . . ransom.'

'That's it!' said Jem. 'Make or break.'

'What's that?'

'This voyage is make or break . . . for the Ouabin, they say. But Raj, it'll be break. We'll . . . break him, we will, if Porlo can't.'

With these words, Jem felt a strange exultation. Squalor and degradation fell away and he thought only of the victory to come. Young Lacani's legacy: think of the legacy.

Then the cry: *Dead man over all!*

Again? So soon?

Rajal's face was grim in the moonlight. 'Jem? It's not just the crystals we've . . . lost. Remember our friends? They're . . . dead, aren't they? All of them? Even our enemies . . . they're dead, too. That Blard . . . that Menos . . . they were on the benches back there . . . I saw them die. Everyone's dying, Jem . . . and soon . . . we'll be dead, too . . . won't we?'

Despair flooded back, filling Jem's heart. But no. He had to fight it. Never had the quest been so bleak, so terrible. But all was not lost. Somewhere on this galley, in a bag of plunder stripped from the slaves, lay two hard, dark gemstones that the guards could not possibly have seen for what they were. One was the Crystal of Theron. One was the Crystal of Koros. Somehow, in all this, Jem and Rajal must seize back the crystals. That was their challenge. If they could meet it, the quest could go on. Nothing else was important now.

'Keep rowing, Raj . . . just keep rowing.'

The waves were rising higher. A high wind whipped the air.

✳   ✳   ✳

Stroke! Stroke!

'It's almost . . . time, Raj. First Submission . . . soon.'

'Jem, I can't . . . I can't believe this will work.'

'Raj, not again! What would you . . . rather do? Sit here—'

'I'm hardly just . . . *sitting* here—'

'You know what I mean! Would you rather . . . die? Here in this . . . filth? It's our only chance, Raj. And . . . Raj?' Some rows in front, Scurvy was beating a man repeatedly about the head. 'When I'm King . . . if I'm ever King . . . men won't be treated like this . . . not ever. I'll stop it, I swear—'

'You'll only be King of . . . Ejland, Jem. We're not in . . . Ejland *now*, are we?'

'I'll stop it, I tell you!'

Jem was vicious. But he had to be. All night his resolve had hardened within him, steeling him for the conflict ahead. All night, as the galley churned on through tides that heaved more heavily, through waves that

366

were rougher and rising higher, murmurings that had begun with Jem had travelled between the chained men, catching like an igniting spark. They all knew, didn't they, that there was no other way? Each cruel curse could only tell them so, each pannikin of mush, each lash across their backs, each brutal cry of *Dead man over all!*

And after the spark, the kindling: the little ivory-handled knife that, with just a nick of its sharp blade, released the locks of a man's manacles. All night the knife had travelled in the wake of the murmurings, again and again performing its secret task. The men would leave the manacles in place, not revealing yet that they were free. But they were. Already.

And after the kindling, the fire: soon, soon. Glimmers of daylight slanted through the colonnades, orange, red and purple. When the gong rang for Catacombs, the men would rise up suddenly, and chaos would break loose. It was a desperate plan. Could these ragged slaves – exhausted, starved and without weapons – really overpower the Ouabin's guards? And the Ouabin? Perhaps Raj was right. Perhaps it was hopeless. But Jem could not allow himself to think that way.

'Roll on, Catacombs . . . it must be soon, it must!'

Down the aisle cavorted Scurvy, whip flicking restlessly. Had the creature noticed the loss of his knife? More than once he skidded, landing with a thump on the sleek deck. If Jem wanted one thing in the conflict to come, it was to fling the little incubus into the sea. The thing capered on, unaware of its doom, and Jem could not help himself. He had to laugh. Soon his torments would be over; again the wheel of destiny would turn. Jem had been a creature worse than the lowest beast: now, already, he was a man again. Bones and Pancho turned towards him, grinning. How alive they were, as if at last awoken from a long, living death! On the bench behind, on the bench ahead, Jem was aware of a fever of expectation.

Only Rajal was dolorous. Jem might have damned him: but then, it was only the day before that Rajal had discovered that Littler, Uchy and Rainbow were lost.

'Jem?' His strokes were faltering. 'How are we going to . . . find the crystals again?'

'I've told you, Raj, they're with . . . the plunder. Don't you remember that bag the guards . . . had?'

'Huh! I just woke up and . . . found myself here.'

'Well, there's a . . . bag. Rings, coins, gold-capped teeth . . . anything they could take from these . . . wretches—'

'*Us* . . . wretches?'

'Well . . . yes—'

'So where's this . . . bag?'

'I'll bet the Sea Ouabin . . . keeps it, wouldn't you? We just need to . . . Raj, keep rowing!'

Rajal was breathless. But when he spoke again he said, 'Jem . . . Jem? Do you think you can have a slave revolt in . . . in a storm?'

'In a . . . what?'

Alarmed, Jem saw that the sky was darkening again, as if the morning had approached, then turned and fled. Ominous clouds lurched across the horizon, and the galley rolled on mounting waves. For a moment the sea was black as midnight, then lightning, then thunder split apart the darkness. Jets of water splashed across the decks and Scurvy slithered down the aisle, shrieking, as the galley rose up, then crashed back down. Guards staggered. Above, the gong crashed, then crashed meaninglessly again and again. At once, the decks were a surge of men rising up, flinging down their chains. But some were swept at once into the hungry sea.

'This is mad!' Jem burst out. 'This can't happen so fast!'

'In these waters?' cried a man behind. 'Anything can happen here!'

Sheets of rain came pelting in from the sides. Waves washed the decks. Relentlessly the storm pounded and pounded, striking the galley like the fist of a god, sweeping down imperiously from the sky.

Guards blundered past. 'The lifeboats, the lifeboats!'

Jem's fist struck. He struggled. 'Lifeboats? Not for you, beasts! Raj, get the other one!'

But a surging wave bore the guards away.

Stroke! Stroke!

Now he was swimming. Now he was running. Now he was clutching and clambering madly. Darkness, then light, slammed across his vision. There were cries. Cuts. Blows. How he fought his way up from the lower deck, Jem would never know. Tightly he clung to Rajal's hand, as if he would never release his grip. Desperately they slammed against guards and slaves alike, struggling to escape the waves that threatened to drag them into the sea. Somehow they must find the crystals. But how, in this storm? It was hopeless, it had to be!

Then suddenly Rajal's hand was gone.

'Raj,' Jem cried, 'Raj—'

Desperately, Jem swivelled this way and that. Nowhere, nowhere could he see his friend. Waves deluged the terrible colonnades. Clinging to a wooden ladder, Jem called Rajal's name again, but the storm was too loud.

Then water filled his nose and mouth.

And then something grabbed him. It was Scurvy. Through the

wildness of the storm Jem saw the hideous creature flailing, gouging at his calves, then his thighs. Jem kicked and kicked. He swivelled down, grabbing the knife, stabbing and stabbing at the hands, at the face.

He swung up the ladder, choking, gasping.

Then it was there, radiant in the lightning, filling the skies above the stricken galley, howling and heaving immensely on the storm. What could it be but the phantom ship of legend, glimmering and unearthly, crashing through the skies with its sails unfurled?

'The *Flying Zenzan*!' Jem sank down.

Terror, tangible as the storm itself, soared and swooped and plummeted all around him. He screamed. He writhed. He clawed his eyes, longing only for the vision to be gone. Then came a wave mightier than before and Jem was swept into the dark, cascading sea.

Stroke! Stroke! He swam for his life.

Chapter 52

FOOTPRINT IN THE SAND

'Young Lacani . . . Young Lacani, are you all right?'

Jem's words were the merest murmur, the faintest rippling from parched lips. No matter: they made no sense. The old man from the galley was dead; besides, the face that Jem thought he saw hardly resembled Young Lacani's, for all that it may have been old, and a man's. But was the face really there at all?

Jem stirred. No face: no, he had been dreaming.

He coughed painfully. How he ached! Face down, he lay on a dazzling stretch of sand, his nostrils filled with the salt tang of the shore. For now, Jem could barely recall what had happened, neither the storm, nor the wreck, nor the Flying Zenzan. His clothes, the rags he had worn, were gone. His legs were wet, washed by the tide; his torso was dry, blistering already in the rising heat of the day. He felt as if he had just been born, coming to consciousness in this unknown, silent place.

He coughed again, moaning. Through flickering eyelids he saw a clammy, greenish rock, garlanded in seaweed; a grey-gold, curly shell; a large pink crab. Splintered timbers lay all along the beach, painted in a red, enamel-like substance. He remembered something now. He saw a set of manacles; then he saw the footprint in the sand.

A shadow loomed over him.

Jem looked up. It was the man, the man he thought he had seen before. With a gasp, Jem struggled to stand, but why he would flee, where he would flee, he did not know.

He crumpled at once and the stranger caught him.

❋   ❋   ❋

'Wh-where am I?'

'Shh. Don't talk. Drink this.'

'Drink . . . what?'

'Shh. Just drink.'

Jem felt a calloused hand resting lightly on his forehead, and an earthenware beaker pressed against his lips. The beaker tilted upwards. Jem swallowed, for his mouth was parched, then wondered just what the liquid might contain. He did not really care. The taste was pleasant: sweet and warm. Close by, above his head and all around him too, he heard a relentless drip-drip of rain. But Jem was dry and warm, lying on a soft bed in a shadowy hut. Hazily, through a hole in the wall, he made out a greenish, greyish daylight.

He screwed up his eyes. His new companion was a powerful figure of a man, bear-like, with long matted hair and a copious beard. The man's skin was deeply tanned and he seemed to be dressed in animal skins, stitched roughly together. But if his appearance was fearsome, his eyes were kind.

So was his voice. 'A little more – just a little more.' Jem felt the hand on his forehead again, and the beaker at his lips. 'The potation I have given you will remove your pain, but you must sleep longer, my young friend, if the balms which I have applied to your wounds are to do their work. You feel yourself drowsing again, don't you? Just a little?'

The voice was strangely awkward, slow and formal as if, perhaps, it had been long unused. But something about it was familiar.

That accent. Harion? Varby?

Jem's brow furrowed. 'You're an . . . Ejlander?'

The stranger only smiled, his face crumpling into a thousand wrinkles. Jem's eyes blurred, and he felt the stroking at his forehead again. He felt so weak. He felt so . . . *clean*.

'Hush now,' came the kind voice, 'there will time enough for questions. Sleep again, sleep.'

Jem nodded. He lay back, listening to the drip-dripping rain, and wondered incoherently, murmurously, why it was raining.

'Because sometimes it rains,' said his new friend. 'Sometimes it rains.'

And still it rained.

The hole in the wall, the crude window, opened on to a deep, velvety darkness. Jem was aware of flickering candlelight, passing over his inert form; of smoke from a hissing fire; most of all, he was aware of the rain, insisting its way through cracks in the ceiling, slithering down the rough inner walls.

A droplet splashed his cheek. The calloused hand wiped away the water; then came the beaker with its sweet, warm ichor.

Jem drank. 'How . . . how long have I been here?'

A smile creased the stranger's eyes. 'Tell me, my young friend, what do you remember?'

Had Jem's mind been less hazy, he might have been puzzled by this answer, which was no answer at all. Instead he drifted for some moments, listening to the rain, then found himself murmuring, 'Sun . . . light. Light in bright shafts, stabbing though green. Pollen. Insects. Call of birds. And rocking . . . and juddering . . . in someone's arms.'

The hand smoothed Jem's brow. 'And that is all you remember, young friend? – Me carrying you here, after I found you washed up on the shore?'

Jem screwed up his eyes. He blinked, and his voice became strained. 'It's dark . . . and it's light. Blinding . . . lightning . . . and the sea, surging . . . and thunder . . . and waves . . . swimming . . . struggling . . . and there's a ship . . . a ship in the sky.' He broke off. 'But . . . that's mad, isn't it? A ship . . . in the sky?'

The smile again. 'You remember the wreck. And the *Flying Zenzan*. Good, my young friend, good. But is there no more? There *is* more, isn't there?'

Jem lifted a hand to his head, pressing at a point in the centre of his forehead.

With a lurch, he raised himself up on his elbow. The hairy blanket fell down, rasping over his bare chest. By now his heart pounded slowly, and he gazed, gulping, into the stranger's eyes. 'The others . . . were there any others?'

'Only you . . . only you I saved.'

For a moment Jem was silent. But there was another loss too, wasn't there? He touched his chest and said, more to himself than to the stranger, 'And the crystal . . .'

The candle flickered. 'Only you, Prince Jemany.'

Jem gulped. 'You . . . know my name?'

'You spoke in your sleep. You spoke quite a lot.'

Suddenly Jem was frightened. But the potion he had swallowed was taking effect.

'Who are you?' he murmured, as he slumped down again.

And before he passed out, there was just time to hear the wry, almost laughing reply: 'What's this, my young friend? You mean you don't *know*?'

The stranger smoked a clay pipe, filling the air with its aromatic incense.

Sometimes it rains.

And sometimes it shines.

Jem rubbed his eyes. Blades of sunlight, tinged with green, pushed through the window and through the many cracks in the rough, mud-plastered walls. There were rustlings of leaves, cries of birds, animal sounds too – a goat bleating, a cluck-clucking chicken. Heady scents of exotic flowers entwined with the dry, sharp-smelling smoke that still coiled up from the ashy firepit.

Jem looked round him slowly. Was he alone?

Not quite. Catching the sunlight just below the window was a pair of golden eyes, watching him impassively. The eyes belonged to a large marmalade cat, no doubt feral, but also very plump and probably very old.

Hardly, in any case, a fearsome sight.

'Hello,' said Jem. 'What's your name?'

The cat gave a lazy purr.

Jem pulled his blanket round his shoulders and stepped gingerly on to the dirt floor. Standing was strange after all this time – but how much time was that? He half-expected his brain to swirl, or his legs to buckle beneath him. Perhaps the stranger was close by. Should he call to him?

No, Jem was glad to be alone.

His main feelings were two. First, far behind his eyes, was the deep ache of sadness, of a terrible, abiding loss. Second, like a contradiction of the first, was hunger. The pangs were sharp enough to make Jem guilty. How could he be hungry, with the quest in ruins? How could he eat, with his companions dead?

The hut, he saw, was furnished sparsely. His narrow bed was the only one; there was one small table and one hardbacked chair, all of the same rough-hewn appearance. But if the place seemed hardly comfortable, nonetheless it was filled with provisions of one sort or another – firewood, sacks, a net, an axe. There were barrels of pumpkins, bags of potatoes, baskets of plump, rounded fruits. There were carcasses of rabbits and birds and a side of meat – the flank, perhaps of a pig – hanging, smoked and salted, from hooks in the ceiling.

Jem let his blanket fall to the floor. Naked, he lunged at a plucked, crisp turkey, ripping off a huge drumstick. The meat was tough, but he did not care. The cat danced around him, suddenly excited. Jem grabbed the other drumstick, flinging it down.

On the knotty little table was a loaf of bread. Jem dived for it. The bread was surprisingly springy and light. He gorged himself, hacking off chunk after chunk with a big crude knife like a file or a saw. How long since he had eaten? He looked round restlessly. He seized a potato, biting into it. It was sweet and juicy. Then he found a carrot, and was happier still – then a banana, then a mango. But the juice was not enough. He was thirsty, so thirsty!

'Where's the drink, puss? What's to drink?'

On shelves lining one wall were innumerable crudely thrown earthenware vessels, gallipots and pipkins, jugs and urns and canisters. Standing on tiptoe, peering and sniffing, Jem found innumerable preserves, potations, ointments, unguents. There was salt; there was flour; there were seeds and beans. Under a wet cloth was a jug of milk. Joyously Jem drank from it. The lip of the jug was thick and uneven, and much of the milk slid down his chin. In moments, it was all gone.

'Oh dear.' Jem looked down, guilty at his debauch: Puss looked up at him in considerable umbrage. Quickly Jem rubbed spilt milk into the floor, put the jug back on the shelf and, gathering up the turkey-bones, the banana-skin, and the crumbs and crusts of bread, he bundled them into the wet cloth and shoved the cloth, absurdly, behind his bed. He wrapped himself in the blanket again, belching loudly.

'Where's he gone, Puss? Where's your master?'

Jem crossed to the window. Outside the hut was a compound of sorts, its boundaries marked by a gnarled wooden fence. There were vegetable patches and a plot of corn, a chicken run and, penned in little yards, a couple of languid goats and hairy, dark pigs. There was an upended canoe, a wheelbarrow, a cart. From a tall tree hung a twisty rope-ladder, leading to another hut, high in the branches. Perhaps that was where the stranger slept.

Jem bit his lip. Something stirred in his mind, but what it was he could not quite say. The green of the jungle impended all around. The tops of the fenceposts were sharpened into spikes. This place, he thought, had the air of a fortress as much as of a hermitage.

He turned back to the room behind. On a shelf beside the window was a small, dark-bound book, the only one, it seemed, that the stranger possessed. An El-Orokon, sacred book of the Agonists. Jem flipped through it. At some time, the pages had been waterlogged; they were crinkled, crisp, and stained. On the flyleaf was a name, but the ink had run. There were many marks in the margins, barely more legible. The stranger, at any rate, was a man of faith. But did Jem trust him? He only knew that he could not stay here. Somehow, even if it were hopeless, even if all his companions were dead, he must carry on the quest. Somehow he must try to find the crystals again. Or die trying.

But how could he leave here when he had no clothes?

He gripped the blanket, thinking he might tear it, making a loincloth.

But wait. At the end of the bed was a big, shabby, copperbound chest. Jem knelt before it, opening it. Ah yes. Shirts, tunics, breeches such as the stranger wore, made of skins and sacking and thick-spun wool. Leather belts and moccasins. A sunhat, woven from dried reeds. Jem dug deep, pulling out the things he needed.

The stranger had certainly kept himself busy. How long had he been on this island?

It was then, as if in answer to this question, that Jem found the second book, pressed between blankets in the bottom of the chest. A big, heavy, leatherbound book. A ship's log? A journal? A diary?

'What have we got here, Puss, hm?'

Puss's reply was to leap up into the chest, settling himself on the soft, dry clothes. Jem looked round uncertainly. All was quiet. All was still. And no, he could not resist.

At first the book was a disappointment. A ship's log, indeed: page after page of multi-columned reckonings of compass points and star patterns, with elaborately pedantic tallies of cargo – bales of cotton, coffee-beans, tobarillo, &c – and calculations of the crew's pay.

He turned the stiff pages, breathing in their thick, mouldering musk. Only one thing was interesting, and that was just how old this log must be. In places he tried to make out dates, but the characters were spidery and the ink had faded almost to invisibility.

Jem was about to put the book away when something stayed him. He turned another page, then several at once. Now the logbook entries were gone and instead, in ink just slightly darker, were paragraphs of prose – a narrative, a history. He flipped backwards, looking for where it began. He found the place. Then he read the title, lettered in elaborate, archaic script.

'Now, my young friend, do you understand?'

Jem gasped. The stranger – not, perhaps, a stranger now – stood in the doorway, his eyes wry, his clay pipe firm between his teeth. Slung across his shoulder was a big old-fashioned blunderbuss; hanging from one hand, dripping redly, was a brace of dead birds. He thumped them down on the table and looked intently at Jem.

Jem stood awkwardly, the book held before him, covering his naked-ness. He stammered, 'B-But – you can't be . . .'

'Can't be? But I *am*.'

'But . . . you're a character. In a story.'

'And you think you're not?'

Now Jem was confused. He grinned nervously and the stranger crossed to him, laying a comforting hand on his shoulder. Jem flinched, but the stranger only smiled. 'Didn't you know my story was a true one?'

Jem said, 'But . . . it was long ago. So long ago.'

'You're saying . . . you think I'm an *old* man?'

'I'm saying . . . I think you should be dead.'

The smile became a laugh, but a kindly one. Turning away, inviting Jem to take what garments he required, the stranger set about attending to his birds.

But Jem, for a time, could only stand naked, gazing on the elaborately lettered title of his host's autobiography:

THE
L I F E
AND
STRANGE SURPRIZING
A D V E N T U R E S
OF
ROBANDER SELSOE
Of *Varby*, MARINER:

Written by Himself.

Chapter 53

THE LANCING OF A BOIL

'Master Selsoe?'

  'More questions, my young friend?'

  'Well, just one – Blackmoon.'

  'Blackmoon? Is that a question?'

  'Yes. I mean . . . where is he?'

  'Ah, perhaps *you* are Blackmoon now.'

  Jem sighed. These cryptic answers!

  They crashed though the jungle on the trail of a wild boar. Selsoe was certain he could find their quarry, down by a brook he called the River Riel. To Jem, the sunny chasms they wended through were all the same, a bewildering green maze. The castaway, for his part, was certain of their direction, bounding ahead with goat-like agility.

  Already Jem was out of breath.

  Days had passed. Dressed like the castaway in skins and furs, Jem had fallen into the role of companion, assistant – or, perhaps, apprentice. He had whittled wood, built fires, dug turnips, shot hares and once, with much unwillingness, hacked off a chicken's head, hung up the bird by the feet and plucked and carefully collected the feathers. He had listened interminably to the castaway's advice on the husbanding of goats, the construction of tree-huts, and the proper firing of gallipots and pipkins. Did Selsoe – if that was really his name – think Jem would spend his life here too?

  Just yesterday, fishing from the cliff, he thought he had seen a sail, shimmering on the horizon. Excitedly he had rushed back to Selsoe. Should they not light a signal fire? Selsoe had only shrugged and sighed, and said that no ships came here, none; that the sea was a deceiver; that every day there were phantom sails. Since then, the castaway had repeated these assertions many times – too many times. How Jem cursed himself for ever believing them! There *might* have been a sail, might there not?

  His host exasperated him more and more.

  He said now, 'Master Selsoe, you can't just *be* someone else, can you – just turn into them?'

  'Men turn into many things, my young friend. You'd be in, what, your

Fourth cycle, approaching your Fifth? But how many things have *you* been, even in so short a life?'

'But Blackmoon . . . he was real. I mean, if you're real.'

The castaway adjusted the blunderbuss on his shoulder. 'What's this, my young friend? Doubt in your eyes? But you know my story, don't you?'

'Of course. I mean . . .'

'Tell me, what *do* you know?'

They pushed on, the sun dappling their faces in languid, myriad patterns. For three days there had been no rain. Jem wiped his brow. Dark circles of sweat gathered uncomfortably under his arms.

'Your father was a merchant in Varby,' he began, a little flatly. 'A draper.'

'A linen-draper, that's right,' said the castaway.

'Well, he wanted you to follow him into the business, but your one desire was to be a sailor. Your father was furious, so you defied him and ran away to sea. There . . . well, there you had many adventures.'

'Many, many?' Selsoe said archly.

Jem wondered if he was supposed to plod through those inferior adventures, those confusing sallies with slavers and pirates, not to mention the long stretch on the plantation in Somer Maric – all, as everyone knew, dull preliminaries to the one adventure for which the name 'Robander Selsoe' would live for ever in the annals of Ejland. Didn't everyone skip those bits?

Jem would not be drawn. 'But then you were wrecked,' he hurried on, 'far away in the hot tropic seas.'

'Far away? *Here*, actually.'

'Yes,' said Jem, 'but far from Ejland. Far from anywhere.'

'Nowhere, my young friend, is far from *anywhere*. Not if you think about it.'

Jem supposed not.

'But go on, go on.'

Jem had to sigh. 'So for cycle after cycle you were trapped on your island, living alone. At first, you cried out and cursed your fate; you thought you would destroy yourself. But slowly you learnt submission to the ways of the gods. Every day you praised the Lord Agonis, and read from the El-Orokon. You wrote down your adventures, and the "serious reflections" your adventures inspired. But still you were alone; you burned your signal fires, but no ship came to find you, not even a heathen one. Then one day you saw the footprint in the sand. That was Blackmoon. That's what you called him, because that was the day.[1]

---

[1] Once literally the name for the 'new moon' in Ejland, Blackmoon now refers to the

'That's right – Blackmoon,' Selsoe said reflectively.

They had reached the banks of the Riel now, or what Selsoe called the Riel. The castaway had named almost everywhere on the island after some part of Ejland. His compound was Agondon; a mound behind his hut was Holluch-on-the-Hill; a beaten track was the Pale Highway; a finger of rock that jutted up from the sea, just off the shore, was Xorgos Island. There were Groves of Orandy, Ollon Pleasure Gardens (two orange trees and a flower patch, respectively), a Royal Assembly (a tree where many fruitbats hung from the branches), and even a Great Temple of Agonis (the rocky spire where the castaway would worship). There was a Square of the Lady, a Varby Abbey, a Vosper's Loop and an Eldric's Park.

Selsoe trudged confidently along the reedy, slimy bank; Jem slipped and slithered.

'And then . . . and then the cannibals came, Blackmoon's tribe. But you fought them . . . I mean, both of you.' This, though Jem's telling hardly revealed it, was amongst the most exciting parts of Selsoe's adventures. 'And then . . . then the ship came. A ship came at last.'

'Ships don't come,' Selsoe said again. 'Didn't I tell you, ships don't come?'

Jem gritted his teeth. 'But they *do*. A ship came before, and you were rescued. That's how your book ends.' *Did it? Did the journal back at the compound end like that?* 'I . . . I know you were rescued.' *So how come he's here? Ask him.* 'So . . . so how come you're here?'

Selsoe whistled and puffed at his pipe.

Jem was growing strident. 'And where's Blackmoon? If you're Robander Selsoe, what have you done with Blackmoon?'

Selsoe – or whatever his name was – turned, smiling, and rattled his blunderbuss.

'He'll be here, mark my words.'

A moment passed before Jem realised that the castaway referred not to Blackmoon, but to the wild boar. The story had it that Blackmoon, schooled in civilised ways by his master, had been taken back to Ejland when Selsoe was rescued. His career, it appeared, had been a distinguished one. In the highest and noblest drawing-rooms of Agondon, the former cannibal had been a sensation.

But that had been long ago. Very long ago.

Jem pursued, 'Is he dead? Is Blackmoon dead?'

The castaway's voice was hollow. 'There are diseases,' he said, 'diseases we Ejlanders carry in us for cycles, yet still survive. Let's just say that Blackmoon wasn't . . . wasn't so lucky.'

first day of a calendar moonlife: *vide* the Appendix, 'Time in The Orokon', in the first book in the sequence, *The Harlequin's Dance.*

Jem was struggling not to slip. 'Blackmoon . . . caught a disease? What disease?'

Selsoe's eyes blazed. 'Civilisation. Isn't that the disease, the real disease, that lies behind all others? What is our great city of Agondon, that stands so fair in the eyes of all the world? What is it, in truth, but a vile and festering sore, a boil that must be lanced if this world is to be redeemed?'

Jem thought it best not to argue.

Selsoe said, 'That's why I came back, can't you see? They all thought my adventures were over. During my long years as a castaway, my plantation in Somer Maric had swollen greatly in value. I was rich, I was famous – and oh, how I struggled to live my new part! I married; begat children; tended to business. But I knew I could never be happy in Ejland. When Blackmoon died, I saw it all clearly. I knew I must come back here – here, where I belonged.'

Jem looked wonderingly into the castaway's eyes. The brook burbled. Birds cawed.

'But . . . it was all so long ago.'

The castaway smiled. 'What is time, here on my island? What is time, in the world at large? Might you not think of this world as an allegory? And might you not think of me as the spirit of this island? But then, perhaps, you think of me . . . simply as a madman?'

Selsoe laughed. His knives and traps and blunderbuss jingling and clanking, he flung back his head, booming out his merriment to the jungle trees, and Jem's longing to escape from the island welled up uncontrollably inside him.

He lunged forward. 'Stop it, stop it!'

He would have pushed Selsoe, even punched him, but just then there was a commotion in the undergrowth.

The castaway spun round. 'I knew it! Look! The boar!'

Jem fell into the squelching reeds.

'Quick, my young friend! After him!'

Selsoe bounded off. He splashed through the brook. The blunderbuss rang out.

The boar squealed – then crashed on.

'Quick, quick!' Selsoe called.

But Jem was too slow. Then Selsoe was gone.

Jem breathed hard. 'Master Selsoe? Master Selsoe?'

Time had passed. Jem felt the first of the droplets, slipping down through the green, fleshy canyons. At first he thought it was only the leaves, drip-dripping in the humid day; then the drops became thicker, more insistent, and he looked up through the web of branches and glimpsed a patch of sky, clouding, darkening.

'Now that's all I need.'

His voice was muffled in the enveloping green. His head turned, this way and that. He was dirty, sweaty, scratched and breathless. Rapidly the afternoon declined. And now the rain! Where was Agondon? Where was the Riel? Cursing himself, he called again for Selsoe. A bird crashed and fluttered, somewhere close by, with a pealing cry that might have been laughter.

Jem slumped on a mossy log, rain pattering around him. 'He must be looking for me,' he said. 'He knows every jot of this island, doesn't he?'

Yes, Selsoe would find him, of course he would. But the thought only made Jem more miserable still.

He felt something brush against his thigh. 'Puss!'

The big cat peered up at him with golden eyes and Jem saw a chance to salvage his dignity. 'You know the way, don't you? To Agondon? Puss?'

Puss flicked his tail. Jem started after him. The land was running uphill, the vegetation thicker, and soon, in the gathering darkness, Jem could barely make out the flickering stripy coat, weaving its way through the leaves and curtaining vines and thick, long grasses.

'Puss, wait! Puss, where are you?'

He blundered ahead.

Then suddenly the ground gave way beneath him and Jem was tumbling, down, down.

He yelled. He screamed.

He crashed to a halt.

After some moments he moaned, experimentally checking his legs and arms.

Still in one piece. Just.

Just worse off than before.

'Puss, where are you? Puss, did you do that on purpose?'

Puss, as it happened, was nowhere to be seen.

Jem lay at the bottom of a steep rise. Here it was darker, the jungle thicker, but the rain that insisted its way through the leaves was heavier, louder in its unrelenting *drip, drip*.

He struggled back to his feet, more lost than ever.

'You *did* do it on purpose, didn't you, Puss?' (Puss was still absent.) 'Never forgave me over that milk I drank, did you? Huh! Well, you're an ugly thing, as well as mean.' He raised his voice. 'Ugly, did I tell you that? And you've got mange. And worms, I'll bet. And more fleas and lice and ticks than . . .'

Jem saw something up ahead, something glimmering. A lamp? No, a shard of sunset, tumbling down between chinks in the leaves and

381

striking something shiny, concealed deep in the jungle. Jem pushed towards it; at once Puss was by his side again.

'Oh, there you are! You know I didn't mean it about the mange, Puss. Or the fleas. Well, perhaps about the fleas. But ... what *is* this place?'

The light, Jem saw now, was the sun's reflection on a large, fallen statue, or rather a part of it. Close by was an empty, mossy plinth.

Jem tugged at vines. Javander?

Yes, there was a trident, almost buried in the earth.

Puss leapt up on the plinth.

'Now a statue like this,' Jem mused, 'isn't just going to be in the middle of nowhere, is it? What's that, Puss? What can you see?'

Drapings of vines hung just beyond the plinth. Jem parted them. Now he gasped, for in what remained of a jungle clearing he saw the overgrown remnants of a temple, surrounded by tombs.

'Puss, I don't understand. Your master must know about this place, mustn't he? But ... he never said. Even in his book, he never said.'

Jem moved forward, taking in the complex, shattered bas-reliefs, the cracking steps, the nobly fluted columns that lay in ruins all around them. Cautiously, he picked his way over rubble; Puss, a little more fearlessly, padded ahead. The rain kept thudding down. There was a flash of lightning, then all at once the rain was harder, colder.

'Damn it, I'm drenched!' Jem peered ahead. The storm – for it was a storm now – fell in harsh sheets, splattering on the fleshy vegetation all around. Lightning cracked again and he saw a doorway in the temple, yawning open. 'Puss, over there – shall we shelter in there?'

But when Jem reached the doorway, Puss had gone again.

'Puss? This isn't another of your tricks, is it?' Uneasily, Jem looked up at the portico, sagging heavily above the doorway. 'Oh well, it hasn't fallen down in all this time.'

A dark corridor stretched ahead. There would be cobwebs, no doubt. Spiders. Bats.

Gulping, Jem stepped inside.

Something touched him. He cried out, hands flailing.

No, there was nothing. Just cobwebs.

He breathed deeply, relieved.

Then it happened. First came a clang of metal, slamming over the violence of the storm. In the lightning, Jem saw that an iron gate like an intricate web had fallen across the doorway. He blundered back towards it, clutched at it, clawed at it, as if it were really only another cobweb.

Locked. Locked solid.

There was a sound like a roar. Jem reeled, then cried out as, through the murk, there came a looming shape, trundling towards him. What it

382

was, this shape, he could not say, only that it was massive, hostile and rapidly getting closer.

He flattened himself against the bars. Rattled them. Kicked them. Flattened himself again.

Then again came the lightning and Jem saw his assailant, a hideous monster with massive curved fangs, insane goggling eyes and out-stretched claws.

'No! Keep away!'

A shot rang out – then another, pounding into the lock just behind him. A hand darted forward, wrenching back the gate, flinging Jem aside just as the monster – or rather, the stone gargoyle – reached the end of its track and juddered to a screeching halt.

Lying amongst the rubble, Jem looked up. A swaying lantern blurred across his vision, shimmering and refracting in the sheeting rain.

Then came the hand again, extended towards him. 'You do get yourself into trouble, don't you? Come, my young friend, we can shelter in the altar-chamber – just not in these side-tunnels, hm? I thought those old gargoyles were all out of action. Seems I was wrong.'

Jem staggered up, shamefaced and shivering. For a second time, Robander Selsoe had saved him.

He burst out, 'Who are you? Who are you, really?'

Chapter 54

THE FIRE SERMON

'Sometimes,' said Jem, 'it certainly does rain.'

Rain drummed and plashed in the jungle darkness, swirling into rivulets and little eddying pools, turning the undergrowth into an oozing marsh. Rain ran, like a sleek glaze, over the cracking, mossy terrace and the steps outside. Rain beat out its tom-tom on the roof above their heads, insisting its way through a thousand cracks, pinging and plunking inside the temple in a hundred higher, sharper rhythms.

They huddled on the crumbling altar. Lurid in the fire of Selsoe's lamp, the ruins shimmered around them like a sinister dream: the fallen buttresses, the broken urns, the remnants of carvings and candelabra, effigies and icons that once had been the objects of fervent worship.

Jem's teeth were chattering. It was difficult to speak. 'M-Master Selsoe ... why d-didn't you ... s-say?'

'Say, my young friend? Say what?'

Jem hugged himself. He rubbed his arms. 'In your book, you never ... n-never said the island ... never said about this p-place, did you?'

The castaway's look was grave. 'There are things, my young friend, of which it is best not to speak.'

Jem looked round wonderingly. At their feet, trails of water ran across the flagstones. Rats scurried hither and yon, just out of range of the weak, flickering lamp.

'Why?' said Jem. 'Why wouldn't you ... s-speak?'

'Of these ruins? You think I mean only these ruins? Ah, but I refer to *why* they are ruins.'

Lightning flickered distantly.

'Once,' mused the castaway, 'long ago, a thriving people made this isle their home. Now, as you see, almost all traces of them are gone, buried beneath the ground or entangled so deeply in jungle leaves and vines that only the most determined of explorers would find them. What can these rare survivals give us but the merest hint of the glories that once were, and now have gone?'

'But M-Master Selsoe ... what happened?'

'What, but the advent of a certain evil force, a force that has only grown more implacably evil with all the aeons that since have passed? You have heard, my young friend, of ... the *Sisterhood of the Blue Storm*?'

Lightning cracked again, closer this time.

'Sisterhood?' said Jem. Slowly he brought up a hand to his head. Fleetingly, above the wildness of the night, he seemed to hear an ethereal, taunting music. Suddenly, strangely, he felt himself on the brink of revelation.

'You have heard, have you not, of the Daughters of Javander – so-called, though they were never her daughters at all? Those priestly women who ministered on these many Isles of Wenaya, long ago? Then, my young friend, you have heard of the Sisterhood. For the Sisters are what the Daughters became.'

Jem's brow furrowed.

'Long ago, when Javander was free, the Daughters were united in the homage they paid her. In the great empire that was Old Wenaya there were, perhaps, five hundred isles, and on each isle lived a Daughter. Just one; but all the Daughters, thus all the isles, were connected by bands of psychic energy, criss-crossing these Waters of Wenaya like a web. Indeed, they called it the Web of the Divine, and at its centre was the goddess. What an empire she ruled, such as the world has seen but once – an empire truly divine as well as human! Of course, each isle had its secular master or mistress, its particular local despot – but all knew that the real power lay with the Daughters, and ultimately with the goddess they served.'

'But then,' said Jem, 'there was ... Kalador?'

Rats squealed, splashing over the watery floor. Selsoe leaned back, lighting his clay pipe, drawing back deeply on the acrid smoke. In the fiery lamplight, his words flowed forth like a soft, mysterious sermon.

'Three things severed Javander from her Daughters. First there were those Consuls of the Seas, her sons: what could their creation cause but envy amongst those, in the human world above, who had thought themselves her true and valued children? Now the Daughters began to see their folly. The bonds that bound them to the goddess frayed.'

Jem felt raindrops and little slithering slides of masonry landing on the back of his neck. He shifted, intent upon the sermon. Around them, the thudding of the rain was like a mantra; the smoke from the pipe was a lulling incense. Jem breathed deeply, stilling his shivering.

'Those bonds,' said the castaway, 'could only fray more when the goddess devoted herself – with all the cravenness of depraved lust – to her favoured son, Isol of the Shells. But yes, it was with Kalador that the sundering came. As a violent tug snaps the rope that has, until now, borne a heavy burden – yet all the while has been growing weaker, giving way fibre by fibre – so, when the Daughters knew their goddess

385

had taken him for her lover, in a trice all fealty they still held for her, all duty and respect were gone.'

'So what happened,' said Jem, 'when the Web was broken?'

The castaway paused. 'Ah, but was it broken?'

'You just said it was. Didn't you?'

'I spoke of the bonds that linked the goddess with the mortal women who had, in her name, plied their priestly crafts. Did I speak of the bonds that linked those women – linked them, not to the goddess, but to *each other*? In that moment of severance, it was rather as if the Web were lifted free from a burden that till then had weighed it down. Without the goddess, the Daughters did not lapse into helplessness, but came, instead, into their glory. Think of the power they had built up between them over the epicycles of their service to Javander! Now that power was liberated, a psychic network sufficient to generate an astonishing force.

'Rapidly, as the new force crackled round the Web, the Sisters – for they would be Daughters no longer – realised the destiny that lay before them. Embittered by their treatment at the hands of Javander, sensing that Kalador would never let them be, they resolved to come together, and resolved to be invincible.

'Departing in secret from their particular realms, the Sisters converged on Javan Wenaos, an isle famed far and wide (alas, but it is famed no longer!) for its strange fruits and flowers, its sacred groves, its bowers of bliss. Through all Old Wenaya, this isle was known as a paradise. Its peoples were gentle, beautiful, and lived in peace. Ah, but what terrors lay before them! First came Kalador, seeking out the Sisters, bearing down to destroy their isle – then the Sisters, invoking all the force of the Web, raised a storm so fierce, so wild as to uproot the isle from its moorings in the sea. Blue winds whizzed with astonishing force. Blue lightning cracked.

'The storm swept all before it, churning sea and sky into a terrifying eddy. Kalador had no chance. For long days he struggled, focusing all his power, but still he could not breach the swirling cataclysm. He retired, spent and injured. The Sisters exulted. The Web thrummed with joy. Yet still they knew that all was not over. Never could the monster accept defeat. Never could he tolerate so great a rival. And if they had repelled him now, would they repel him next time? And the next? With a conviction that crashed like thunder on every fibre of the Web, the Sisters knew their new defence could never be relaxed. Now, for all the power it would cost them, for all the vast reserves of magic they must expend, for evermore they must be the Sisterhood of the Blue Storm. Their power would come at a terrible price.'

Jem looked down. Reflectively he gazed at a broken urn, a bas-relief, an icon, shifting and shimmering in the eerie lamplight. Then at a rat. 'What about the islanders? Weren't there ordinary islanders?'

'Ah,' said the castaway, 'I spoke of a price. To ask that question is to begin (at least to begin) to understand that price.'

Again he drew on his clay pipe. 'On and on flew the Isle of Javan Wenaos, never resting, never relenting, never returning to its rightful place in the seas. Yet indeed all this time there were ordinary islanders, common citizens swept up inexplicably into this supernatural war. What became of them? I said, did I not, that only vast reserves of magic could keep the Blue Storm whirling? So it was that the Sisters had to draw, as on a supplementary power, first on the psychic reserves of their peoples, then on the thousand natural energies that inhered in the very fabric of the isle.

'The peoples were reduced to mental slavery. Blank-eyed, desiccated, devoid of all will, in time they became mere animated corpses, their spirits sucked dry by the hungry Web.'

Sorrow filled the old man's eyes, and Jem found himself wondering how an Ejlander sailor should know so much of the ancient history of Wenaya – and quite why it should move him as much as it did.

Emotion cracked in the castaway's voice. 'Still the isle flew on; still the Storm swirled; but slowly, the isle itself was consumed. Its fruits and flowers withered and fell. Likewise its trees, likewise its grasses: its sacred groves, its bowers of bliss were devastated. Streams became trickles, lakes shallow pools; then all were dry and dead. No fish swam, no birds flew, no insects chirped and tickered, no animals clambered in the branches, or swished or scurried through the undergrowth. In time the peoples, corpse-like already, began to die, collapsing into dry sacks of flesh or empty, clacking skeletons. Yet still the Web would have their bones, thrumming skeleton after skeleton into dust.

'All was dead or dying, but still the Web needed more energy, more and more, to keep the Storm in place. In the end the very stones and rocks, the very grains of the dark earth beneath were leeched dry of those secret energies that let life flourish here on earth. Where once there were green, blue, red, purple, gold, the many colours of life, now there was only white, blanched white. Javan Wenaos, once a wonder of the world, was a wasteland.'

❋ ❋ ❋

The lamp's fire shivered and plopped. Still the rain fell.

Jem said, 'The island . . . what happened to it then?'

'To Javan Wenaos?' The castaway knocked the ash from his pipe. Then he gestured around them, at the ruins, at the rats. What he said next made Jem shudder. 'Why, this is it. This *is* Javan Wenaos.'

'But it can't be!' Jem protested. 'The trees . . . the vines . . . the flowers!'

The castaway smiled sadly. 'Ah, my young friend, I speak of what happened – oh, aeons ago. Nature in time may recover itself; not so the women and men of this world, when once their spirits have been brutally destroyed. In a sense, perhaps, this isle has flourished again; in another, has it not remained a place of death?'

Thunder crashed. In the ruined portico, masonry fell.

Jem said, 'And the Sisters?'

'But that, perhaps, is the most terrible part of this history. For when they realised their isle would soon be spent, the Sisters, with the last of the force that remained to them, swirled the Blue Storm to new and wilder heights. They let the isle go, released it from their thrall. Javan Wenaos crashed back into the sea; the Sisters, meanwhile, billowed inside the mighty vortex. Like the scythe of a reaper they swept across Wenaya.

'Yet must not all their power now burn out, once and for all? Expectantly, excitedly, Kalador massed his forces. Yet the evil thing was not prepared for what happened next. For now the Sisters converged upon Rica Zeno in the southern seas, once a port as populous, as prosperous as Hora is today – and with the last of their energies from Javan Wenaos, they swept Rica Zeno into the vortex. So it was that a second isle fell. In time, it would suffer the same fate as the first – and later there would be a third isle, then a fourth, a fifth!

'For epicycles, here in these Waters of Wenaya, the Sisters conducted a reign of terror. If at first their intentions had been honourable, to defend themselves against the evil of Kalador, by now they were simply a rival evil, a single mind devoid of humanity, ruled by the Web that thrummed and pounded only with thoughts of power, power and more power.

'At all costs, the Storm must be maintained. Many a war the Sisters fought with their rival; terrible was the devastation they brought to these realms. At last, after the greatest and most cataclysmic of these wars, when Kalador had almost brought the Sisters low, they journeyed far from Wenaya, conducting their depredations in remote waters where the monster, tied as he was to the goddess Javander, could not dare to venture.

'Orbits, epicycles, aeons flew by and the story of the Sisterhood faded into legend. In late generations, few have believed there was ever a time when a flying isle, swirling on its vortex of lightning, wind and rain, terrorised these Waters of Wenaya. But now – now, those who have been doubters must soon believe. Do *you* believe, my young friend?'

Jem nodded gravely. 'I don't believe, I *know*.' He thought of Inorchis. He thought of Xaro. 'They've come back. But why?'

Lightning flashed again. 'It's something,' said Selsoe, 'to do with their power—'

'Well, of course—'

'To do with maintaining it. With keeping it going.'

'I hardly thought they had trouble with that!'

'Jumping from one isle to another, then another? Ah, but it's not quite so simple.' Selsoe paused. The broken curve of an urn rocked and shuddered in a rivulet of water. 'Time and again, my young friend – so the old stories say – back in the days when they haunted these waters, the Sisters would direct the Blue Storm to a certain point in the ocean, a place that sailors much fear and revile – a place they call the *Eye of the Sea.*'

'The Eye?' said Jem.

'It lies to the west, far to the west. There, the waters are of a very different character from those that surround Hora and its empire. First one first must travel to the remote Isthmus of Maric, then through the fearsome Straits of Javander. Further still, braving the Salt Seas of Sardoc, one finds the mysterious Eye, protected by the whirling Maelstrom of the Mandru.

'What is the Eye? Over the epicycles there have been many stories. Some say it leads to the underside of the world. Some say it is the way to the Realm of Unbeing; some that it is a portal to The Vast. For my part, I believe an older, simpler story. What is the Eye, what can it be, but a tunnel in the sea that leads to Javander – to her Briny Citadel?'

'But the Sisters – why would they go *there*?'

'Ah, but why did they go *before*?'

'To do battle? You said they'd given up on that. What, have they changed their minds, is that it? All these epicycles gone by, they've built up their powers again – now they come back to give Kalador the knockout blow?'

'If anything, my young friend, the opposite is the case. In truth, their powers are depleting rapidly.'

'Then why go back? It doesn't make sense.'

'It does if you know why they went there at all. No, not simply to engage in battle did the Sisters venture to the Eye of the Sea – though battle, when they were there, invariably ensued. They went there, I am certain, in the hope that they could kidnap the goddess, snatching her from Kalador's grip. Why, you ask? Of course, they aimed not to give her freedom; rather, they would enslave her for their own ends, to shore up their own power.'

'But you said they didn't *need* Javander any more.'

'They just *thought* they didn't need her. Or rather—'

'What about these islands they've been sucking dry?'

Selsoe's mouth twisted. 'At one time, yes, the Sisters thought they could survive without the goddess. But ask yourself, what is it that channels the psychic energies between the Sisters? What is it that powers the flying island? There is many a tale; but I have heard talk of a lodestone, a mysterious stone that the Sisters have held in their possession since the days when they were the Daughters of Javander. That stone contains great power, but its power in time must fade and die when it is severed from the goddess who gives it life. So it is that the Sisters must return, for a final battle with Kalador at the Eye of the Sea.'

As the castaway delivered these words, Jem's heart pounded harder and harder. The knowledge first glimmered in him, like the fire in the lamp, then burst over him like the crashings of the storm.

The castaway gazed at him intently, expectantly. 'Now do you understand, my young friend? Now do you see that you, too, must venture to the Eye of the Sea? Do you see that you must penetrate the Blue Storm, battle your way up to the flying island, and seize this lodestone? But why do I call it a *lodestone*? You know of what I speak, do you not?'

'The crystal,' Jem whispered, 'the Crystal of Javander!'

'Ah my young friend, you are ready at last!'

Jem's eyes blazed. He leapt up excitedly – then slumped down, almost at once. His hand went to his chest and the emptiness he felt there was like an emptiness in his heart. His next words were for himself, himself alone. 'But how can I find the Crystal of Javander – how can I carry on with my quest, when I've lost the Crystal of Theron? And Raj's crystal, that's lost too! The quest is over – it's already over, and I've failed!'

For some time the lamp had been guttering; now the fire fizzled out and there was darkness. The rain was unrelenting. Vines and leaves slapped against the portico outside. Jem clutched his face in his hands, hating himself; then Selsoe spoke again, and his voice was strangely altered. 'On the contrary, Prince Jemany, you are the world's only hope.'

Jem looked up. If the voice had been different, the castaway looked the same.

But no, not quite. How could he be the same when he reached out his hand and, in his hand, glowing red and pulsing, was the crystal Jem had lost? Jem grabbed for it, in sudden wild jealousy; grabbed, but his companion's fist snapped shut.

Jem cried out. Light streamed through the gaps in the fingers; then Jem saw only the light, searing his eyes as the fist came forward and the knuckles grazed his chest. Thunder crashed and suddenly all the world

390

was crashing, falling, and Jem was falling too, crying as he fell, *'Who are you? Who are you?'*

But the voice – like a mantra, like swirling incense – said only, 'You are ready now. You are ready now, Jemany.'

Chapter 55

AFTER THE RAIN

Jem woke slowly, climbing from dream after shifting dream of storms and great spidery webs, of islands uprooted and spinning out of the sea; of a sea made all of salt, a maelstrom, and a vast, single eye, opening its watery lid and staring up out of the waves. In the dreams, none of it seemed fearsome, only mysterious, almost wonderful, and winding through it all, as if from afar, came slow, ethereal music and echoing voices, whispering curious names: *Eye of the Sea. Mandru. Sardoc. Sisterhood of the Blue Storm.*

And again: *Sisterhood of the Blue Storm.*

Jem felt the warmth of sunlight playing on his face. Greenish brightness flickered around him. He breathed deeply. He sighed. For all his dreams, for all his sorrows, he was aware of a wellbeing such as he had not known for an age. For a moment he wondered why. Then he understood, realising that his hand lay curled upon his chest, that in his hand was a leather bag, and that inside the bag – he squeezed it, feeling the shape – was the crystal he had lost. He sat up sharply, in sudden wild delight.

The quest had resumed!

Quite how it was to proceed was another matter.

Jem, still half in dreams, had forgotten where he was. Only now did he realise that he had spent the night in the temple. He was on the altar, and the bright light came through the cracked, precarious ceiling. He gazed around him, taking in again the smashed, dusty remnants of a lost religion. In the morning they were strangely altered, these carvings, these effigies, not so much sinister as forlorn. On the altar beside him lay a broken curve of urn. Jem reached for it, making out a figure in the scratched and faded glaze. Trident, crown, circling fish: who could it be but the goddess Javander?

He stood, his limbs stiff and aching.

'Master Selsoe? Master Selsoe?'

No reply.

Jem moved cautiously over the rubble-strewn floor, the fragment of urn still in his hand. Avoiding a rat, he walked into a cobweb. He let the fragment fall; but when he had pulled the sticky strands from his face he reached down, picking up the piece of urn again. It had not been on the altar, beside him, last night. Somehow he thought of it as a sign – or a charm.

The jungle pressed, green and dripping, round the temple's mossy portico. Jem peered through the trees. Already the sun was high. Birdsong lilted on the air and the leaves and branches were alive with innumerable invisible rustlings, swishings, tickerings.

'Master Selsoe? Master Selsoe?'

No reply. Jem picked his way past the gate with the gargoyle and the crumbling, overgrown tombs. Strange, to think this isle had once been wholly dead, blanched whiter than these tombs had ever been! Its fecundity was eerie, when one knew its history. How many ghosts must haunt these green bowers?

Jem reached out, parting vines.

'Master Selsoe? Master Selsoe?'

Still no reply; but now Jem thought that there would be none. Selsoe – though that could not have been his name – had gone, his mission accomplished, and Jem was alone.

He should have been frightened, but he only felt the same wellbeing that had filled him upon waking, a calm, clear feeling inside. The stiffness in his limbs was gone; he was warm and happy.

He looked up through the greenery all around him. The temple lay in a deep trough in the jungle floor, as if the ground had subsided long ago. Jem scrambled up the slope, grabbing at vines and branches. Once a bird fluttered past; once he was aware of some larger creature, flitting away from him through the undergrowth. It might have been Puss, and Jem would have called to him; but he did not think he could rely on Puss any more.

Mangy old thing!

Breathless, Jem found himself at the top of a bluff. Here he could see a stretch of sky, blue and dazzling, not merely the green shafts and glimmerings that had pushed through the trees below. He saw the silvery, shifting fields of the sea. Great swards of greenery stretched below him, verdant with fruits and flowers and sloping down precipitously to a curving, bowl-like bay.

And there, in the bay, he saw the masts. The ship, moored against a shelf of rock.

Jem gasped; he whooped; he punched the air. He flung away the fragment of the urn. Suddenly he was running, leaping, tumbling down through the greenery to the sea.

'The *Catayane*,' he cried, 'the *Catayane*!'

393

Jem collapsed in the sand. He rolled over, gazing at the sun. He panted like a dog.

And then there was a real dog, rushing towards him, barking excitedly, leaping on his chest, licking his face.

Delighted, Jem gasped, 'Rainbow . . . Rainbow!'

They rolled and tumbled.

A shadow fell across them.

'Jem – I don't believe it! This is a dream, it has to be!'

Jem scrambled up. 'It's no dream, Raj! I'm real, and so are you!'

For joyous moments the friends hugged and slapped each other, while back on the *Catayane* a familiar nautical figure – not quite up to running on sand – urgently jabbed a far-glass to his eye, bellowed, leapt as best he could, then crashed to the deck.

Arm in arm, with Rainbow loping beside them, Jem and Rajal made their way towards the ship.

'Jem,' said Rajal with a crooked grin, 'is that something I see hanging round your neck?

'That's right, Raj.' Jem patted his crystal, then gasped. His face fell. 'But Raj, what about—'

Rajal reached inside his tunic. 'I found it,' he explained, 'just before they pulled me out of the sea. There it was, lying on a piece of driftwood, as if someone had put it there, ready and waiting for me!'

'Hm,' Jem murmured. 'I wonder.'

'But I don't understand,' Rajal rushed on. 'You were dead, Jem, you had to be!'

'*Me?* It was you who was dead, Raj!'

'Hardly. Porlo picked me up, along with – oh, so many survivors from the wreck. They're all crewmen on the *Cata* now – but you, Jem . . . why, we searched and searched. Where have you been? And where did you get those funny clothes? Jem, you look like a savage!'

'It's quite a story, Raj. But Porlo – what's he up to now?'

'Getting the *Cata* ready, that's what – for what he calls his last and greatest voyage.' Suddenly Jem's friend was grave. 'All this time we thought Porlo was in league with Empster, didn't we? Well, Porlo had his own plans all along. Would you believe he's got a treasure map – and now he's going to follow it?'

They had clambered up on to the rock where the ship was moored. Standing against the salty bows, Rajal dropped his voice.

'Jem, we've got to stop him. Porlo's been a good friend to us, but he's old, he's sick, he doesn't know what he's doing – *and* he's got the Lady Selinda on board! You should see this mouldering old map of this – why, you may as well call it a recipe for suicide. There's a swamp full of crocodiles, by the looks of it; there's a sea that's all salt; there's a – what do they call it? – a maelstrom . . . all on the way to some ridiculous thing – I'm not even sure *what* it is – called the Ear of the Sea, of all things! And *that's* where the **X** is marked!'

Jem laughed, 'Raj, I think you mean the Eye of the Sea!'

'What, you've heard of it? Well, you'll help me, won't you, Jem? We've got to stop the old fool! Eye of the Sea, indeed!'

'*Stop him?* Raj, that's just where we're going!'

And Jem, grabbing a rope-ladder, swung himself up the side of the ship.

Rajal gazed after him, open-mouthed.

END OF PART THREE

PART FOUR

Into the Storm

Chapter 56

DEATH BY WATER

Something about a sea voyage is like a dream. When the anchor rises, when the tethering ropes unravel from the docks, it is rather as if we have entered an alternative dimension. With the wind whipping in the sails above, with the heady smell of salt and the lash of spray, we cannot be as we were before. We pitch our voices over the surge; walking is a trial on rolling decks; our stomachs churn and the rhythms of our sleep are not the same. Slowly but decisively, or so it seems, a strange heartbeat has taken us over. Is it any wonder, as we gaze into the sea, that we imagine ourselves close to mysterious truths? The sea is a place of revelation. When land fades away, we journey not merely in body, but in spirit.

Unless, of course, we just get bored.

'Shaba Lalia. That's next.'

'Shabby what?'

'Not shabby – Shaba. It's a port.'

'Not another one!'

'You haven't been paying attention, have you?'

'And you're sounding like Lord Empster – I mean, when he *was* Lord Empster.'

Rajal rustled the map. 'I hope not! I only meant, we've been through this—'

Jem reached out, gripping the crystal under Rajal's tunic. 'I just want to hurry up, Raj – just get there. That's all I care about.'

Rajal pursed his mouth. 'Jem, no one wants to *hurry* to the Maelstrom of the Mandru. Let alone the Eye of the Sea.'

'They do if they're looking for the Crystal of Javander.'

'Well, all right . . .' Rajal broke off. 'Oh, that boy has no talent at all!'

Their voices low, poring over the map, Jem and Rajal huddled in a corner of Captain Porlo's crowded cabin. Dinner was over for another evening. Filling the air were the squawkings of the squeezebox as Patches attempted somewhat ineptly, and not for the first time, to reproduce the highlights of his master's repertoire. Buby the monkey, like a grotesque icon, squatted in the middle of the laden table, her fingers stuck ostentatiously in her ears.

Time had passed – almost a moonlife – since Jem had rejoined the

Catayane. In this time the ship had zigzagged across ever more distant reaches of Wenaya, putting in at ports which had, indeed, grown increasingly shabby.

And every day, Jem was more restless.

He said, 'This Shabby Island: it *is* the last one, isn't it?'

'Before the Straits? Last chance to take on supplies, make repairs, ready ourselves for the voyage ahead? I told you before, Jem: after this, we're on our own. The end of civilisation—'

'As we know it?'

'Well, probably just the end of civilisation.' Rajal shuddered. 'Actually, I thought the *last* port was that. Oh, the stench of that rotten shark!'

'It was the turtles that got to me.'

'Quite. I'm not looking forward to Shaba Lalia.'

Jem smiled, resigned. 'It *could* be better, Raj.'

'It's more provincial – Jem, it's worse.'

So were the musical efforts of Patches.

'Well, perhaps we won't have any more tars jumping ship.' Jem winced. 'Though they *did* seem to go for that last place, didn't they? Was it the shark, do you think, or the turtles?'

'Hah! At this rate we'll be hauling up the sails ourselves before we get through the Straits of Javander. Not to mention scrubbing the decks, polishing the cannons, and making sure the powder's dry.' Rajal broke off again, exasperated. As a professional entertainer – a Silver Mask, no less – was he not entitled to have his standards? He clapped his hands across his ears. 'That boy, that boy!'

At any time, it seems safe to say, Patches would hardly have turned in a polished performance; but over the last moonlife his voice had begun to break. So it was that his *Pieces of Eight* had degenerated into tuneless caterwauling. The squeezebox shrieked protestingly; under the table, Rainbow howled.

'Stupid boy, give it here!' said the captain, not unkindly, seizing the instrument and boxing the boy, just lightly, on the ears. 'What did you expect, once you went chasing after Goody Palmer and her five daughters? Come on, let me show you how it's done!'

'Oh Faris, not again – you'll exhaust yourself,' said Ra Fanana. 'Here, have a little of your *tea* first. Naughty man, you haven't touched it, have you?'

Scowling, the captain pulled the squeezebox back, pumping in air.

Ra Fanana had to smile. Pencil in hand, the nurse sat bent over a scrap of parchment torn from one of the captain's old charts. She screwed up her mouth. 'Hm, what else? Quinces? Pomegranates? Pears and plums?'

The shopping list was, perhaps, an optimistic one, in view of what was likely to be on offer in Shaba Lalia. While consisting mostly of foodstuffs, it also included entries such as EMBROIDERY FRAME & SILKS, GENTLEMAN'S MUFFLER (preceded by an asterisk), and REPLACEMENT STRAP FOR WOODEN LEG (followed by a row of question marks). 'Oh, and *lots* of bananas for Buby. Salt-pig and mustard can hardly be good for her – no wonder the poor creature's bowels ... well, no wonder.'

'What's that about salt-pig?' said the captain. He seemed a little anxious. 'You won't forget me salt-pig, will you, love? Or me mustard?'

'No, Faris, I won't.' Ra Fanana reached out, patting his hand. 'Of course you can still have your pig *occasionally* – though perhaps you'd try it with mint sauce? Or chutney? Even,' she ventured, 'with some *nice fresh vegetables*, while we've got the chance? I can't see us finding courgettes and spinach in the Salt Seas of Sardoc.'

'A good thing too,' the captain glowered.

But he was not really angry. At her own insistence, Ra Fanana had taken over the cooking for the captain's table, leaving the long-snouted Horan chef to tend only to the common tars. Dear Ra Fa! For a foreign lady she was a good sort, but she *was* determined to make the captain eat healthy food. While the captain had permitted certain reforms, he had drawn the line at any cutting back on his rum ration. Each night, as now, the nurse would serve him a dish of tea; each night, he would let it go cold while continuing to quaff his fiery liquor.

There are things a man holds sacred, after all.

The nurse turned to Selinda. 'You're sure you won't let me buy that slither-silk, my lady? I could whip you up some Hora-gowns *quite* easily, you know—'

The girl seemed preoccupied, even morose; her hand, flopping down from her chair, trailed languidly through Rainbow's fur. She shook her head. 'Ra Ra, really! I'll hardly need gowns where *we're* going, will I?'

'A lady should always look her best,' the nurse said uneasily.

'She should? Why?'

'Well, she must think of ... her prospects, and her—'

'Future?' The girl's voice was sharp; Ra Fanana's heart sank. The nurse's growing intimacy with the captain had made Selinda only more aware of all that she had lost. Try as she might to think of the quest, still the girl languished for Maius Eneo.

She juddered back her chair. 'Excuse me, I ... I—'

'Eh, Miss Selinda, are you all right?' said Patches.

The boy might have followed her, but Ra Fanana laid a hand on his arm.

'Leave her, boy. My lady needs to be ... alone.'

'Really? A *lady*?' Patches coloured, misunderstanding.

But it was time for a song. Lustily, the captain squashed in the squeezebox. If his first chords promised a reprise of *Pieces of Eight*, he then seemed to think it best – after its recent mauling – to leave that particular piece alone. Instead, he launched into the following:

> *Oh say what tar, if tar he be, would languish on dry land*
> *When on the sea adventure be forever close at hand?*
> *What tar would turn away his chance of glory and renown,*
> *When buccaneer meets buccaneer and shoots the other down?*
> *O-oh, for glory and renown, they be waiting there for me*
> *On the day old Faris Porlo met the Ouabin of the Sea!*

Ra Fanana exclaimed, 'Oh, Faris! That can't be a *real* song, can it?'

'Real?' the captain bellowed, over the screechings of his instrument. 'Why, there was a time when tars would roar out this shanty from one end of the five seas to the other! Come on, me lovelies, this time you can all join me on the chorus! Come on Ra Fa . . . Patches . . . Master Raj . . . Master Jem!'

There could be no resistance.

> *That Ouabin came from starboard with his galley's guns ablaze –*
> *Old Porlo's tars were startled when it tore out from the haze –*
> *But Porlo held the line and said, 'We'll blast them, boys, or die –*
> *No Ouabin with a dishcloth on his head gives me the lie!'*
> *O-oh, &c.*

'Of course,' cried the captain, continuing to squeeze, 'this be the *first* time I defeats that there Sea Ouabin. Let's not forget we've done him in twice, eh Patches? That there Ouabin be just food for the fishes now – smashed up his galley we did, good and proper.'

'I think that were the storm,' Patches murmured.

Ra Fanana shot him a warning look. If Faris had decided that he was still a hero, the nurse was determined that none should gainsay him. The old fellow must steel himself for the voyage ahead. It had to be a success: then, she liked to think, when he had found his treasure at last, the dear man might retire to – oh, some pleasant cottage on some pleasant island . . . Why, her lady could live nearby, perhaps with some nice new husband, and . . .

> *That Ouabin fired a broadside aimed to bring old Faris low –*
> *But Porlo was an Ejlander, that's all ye need to know!*
> *That mighty sea-dog fought with all the strength at his command –*
> *No Ejlander would e'er give way to foreigner's demand!*
> *O-oh, &c.*

There was more. The ballad, indeed, continued for many verses; for a time it seemed interminable, and by the end of it no one would have been any the wiser about *quite* how 'old Faris Porlo' had defeated his dishcloth-headed foe. What did it matter? All were swept into the euphoria, whooping out the choruses, while Rainbow beat the carpet with his tail and Buby capered excitedly over the ceiling and the walls.

At last it ended, with much cheering and stamping. It was then, to the captain's delight, that a flushed Ra Fanana seized the pitcher of rum from the table, splashed its contents into various goblets and demanded a toast to Faris Porlo, greatest hero of the five seas.

The toast was the first of many.

'To the *Catayane*, greatest ship of the five seas!'

'To Buby, greatest monkey of the five seas!'

'To Rainbow, greatest dog of the five seas!'

When there had been toasts to all and sundry, including greatest Vaga-boy, greatest Prince of Ejland, greatest nurse, &c., the captain wiped his eyes and turned, his manner suddenly altered, to the future before them, and his wish that all should be well.

The last toast was a solemn one. 'To the treasure hunt!'

'Cap'n,' began Patches, when they were calm again, 'there's one thing I don't understand. Where exactly *is* this treasure?'

'What, boy? You've seen the **X**, haven't you?'

'But Cap'n, it's just an **X** in the sea. The treasure can't be *in* the sea, can it? I mean, under it? I mean, then how—'

'Stupid boy! There be an island there, you mark my words. A small one, under that **X**. What pirate's treasure weren't buried on an island now, answer me that?'

Jem and Rajal exchanged glances; Patches was not sure how to reply. 'But what about this Maelstrom? What about this Eye?'

'Superstition, boy! No, we be headed for a nice sandy island, mark my words.' The captain turned to Ra Fanana. 'Make sure there be a shovel on that list of yours, me lovely. Me old one's rusted through and through.'

SHOVEL × 1, noted Ra Fanana.

'A big one, mind – sturdy. If it's got MADE IN EJLAND stamped on the back, all the better. You don't want none of your foreign rubbish, not when you be on a treasure hunt.'

The captain's eyes glittered, and they all laughed again.

Selinda's tears flowed freely.

She knew she was a fool. What good was it, dwelling all the time on what could never be? Her beloved Maius Eneo was gone, and no mortal power could ever restore him. If only she could at least have said goodbye to him, as the treacherous Glond had promised she would, before she was borne away on this ship!

In the depths of her grief, tracing in her mind the sweet lost face, the taut muscular chest, the rough but tender hands, the girl would fancy that her lover, of whom she had dreamed so many times, had been *nothing* but a dream – and yet, the most splendid, most beautiful dream of her life, promising joys so deep, so profound, that the waking world was only a drab, pallid waste. If only those dreams, those ecstatic visions, would come to her again!

To Selinda, the dangers of the voyage ahead were barely of any moment. What did it matter if she died far from home, in the fearsome realms beyond the Straits of Javander? What did it matter if the Triurge were to rear up from the seas right now, gathering her into the Swallowing Marriage? Already her earlier fears of death seemed distant and unreal. In her heart she had died already, with Maius Eneo on the day that Glond betrayed him.

The wind billowed in the sails above her head. The old timbers of the *Catayane* groaned. Standing in the stern, Selinda stared blankly through her tears, into the ship's dark, rippling wake. It might have been her own life – her prospects, her future – slipping irrecoverably away.

'Lady, why do you sorrow?'

Selinda turned. The voice was a man's, but not one she knew. Tender in tone, it was inflected with an accent she had never heard before. Its owner, silvery-pale in the moonlight – though his skin, Selinda could see, was olive-hued – stepped forward from behind the mast. Of indeterminate age, he was tall, dark-eyed – and extraordinarily handsome.

The girl brushed away her tears. 'Who ... who are you?'

It was a foolish question. The man wore the garb of a common tar. He was a crewman, no more. As a fine lady, she should not deign to speak to him – or rather, *he* should not speak to her.

Yet he hardly had the bearing of a common tar.

Selinda breathed, 'You're one of the slaves. I mean—'

'You mean, I was saved from the Sea Ouabin's galley? Indeed I have been lucky to escape death by water; luckier still to count myself now amongst this noble crew.' The man arched an eyebrow. 'As to whether I would call myself a *slave*—'

'Sir, I meant no insult,' Selinda said quickly. 'I meant only that it had been your fate to be caught, as many were, in the thrall of that wicked Sea Ouabin, who is now deservedly food for fishes. I see at once that you are not a slave in your heart—'

'Lady, is any man a slave in his *heart*?'

The girl flushed. 'I meant, sir, that you were ... of gentle birth.'

The man moved beside her, joining her at the wooden rail. 'Your goodness moves me, Lady, but you are too kind. Indeed there was a time, long ago, when I knew a different life. But think of me as a sailor, the merest of sailors. Does it avail a man to recall what is lost to him?'

'Has he a choice?' Selinda murmured.

'Such doubt in your voice! You are very young, yet I sense that already you have known great sorrow. Ah, but I am right, am I not? No foolish cares of girlhood made your tears flow so freely.'

Again Selinda stared down at the waves. Suddenly, she was not sure why, she was aware that her heart was pounding hard. From below, echoing over the vastness of the night, came the raucous merriment from the captain's cabin. The squeezebox wailed as another verse began, recalling – yet again – the day old Faris Porlo met the Ouabin of the Sea.

Softly, Selinda's new companion hummed the tune.

'You ... you know this song?' she said.

'It used to be famous. Our captain's quite a hero.'

'Or used to be.'

'Now that's unkind.' The man drew closer. 'Don't you think that's a bit unkind?'

Selinda bit her lip. She blurted, 'You understand, don't you? Was there, perhaps, a lady that you loved—'

'And lost? Indeed. Oh, indeed.'

The song carried on. The man hummed again.

Selinda hesitated. 'Sir ... what is your name?'

Was it her imagination, or did the man hesitate, too? He said, 'It's Alam ... my name is Alam. But remember I'm no one. Just a sailor.'

'I'm not sure I believe that.'

'Then perhaps you're right.'

With that, the man drew closer still. Selinda was aware of his hand, brushing hers, and the hardness of his chest, and the warm, sweet flutter of his breath ...

'No! You don't understand at all! No—'

She broke from him. She rushed below.

Alam smiled sadly. Ah, but there was time! If he had nothing now, at least he had time. He thought again of the storm at sea, and how he had been certain he was about to drown. He thought of his struggle to shed his clothes as he clung to the wreckage and the longboats drew near. He thought of all he had been, and all he now might be. Had he not seen the Flying Zenzan? Had he not changed?

Gazing into the ship's rippling wake, again he hummed the song about the Ouabin of the Sea.

Chapter 57

SHABBY ISLAND

'Cap'n, look! They's never going to *eat* 'em, is they?'

'Eh, boy? What else are they going to do?'

'Ugh! Dirty swabs—'

'Foreigners, the lot of 'em! What do you expect?'

Alive but gagged, strapped to what appeared to be a roasting-spit, a brace of orange-furred apes passed by, borne on the shoulders of loinclothed bearers.

Patches clapped a hand over Buby's eyes.

'Take her below, boy. Lock her in me cabin, eh?' the captain said grimly.

Ra Fanana's face furrowed. 'Dear me, this wasn't *quite* what I was hoping for. Do you think they'll have everything on my list, my lady?'

'Ra Ra, do you think they'll have *anything*?'

'Well, I think I might be – hm – some *time*.'

'No! You're not really going down there, are you?'

Rajal said to Jem, 'Provincial! Didn't I tell you?'

'Provincial? Barbaric, more like.'

'Well, this *is* where it ends.'

'Civilisation?'

Rajal nodded; Jem grimaced. From a distance, Shaba Lalia had appeared a place of beauty, a rising mound of rich green, banded thickly by golden sands. Now, as the *Catayane* came into dock, they saw a tumbledown collection of hovels, festering in the equatorial sun. Flies buzzed thickly. The streets were choked with filth. Yet this was a place of thriving commerce. All around them were vessels of all nations, great and small, rich and poor, and all along the seafront were the stalls of busy traders.

The stench was overwhelming.

Ra Fanana scanned the stalls. 'Faris, can you see any embroidery frames? Oh, I shall be so disappointed if I can't get what I need! That cabin wall of yours really *needs* a nice sampler to cheer things up. Something with a nice uplifting message.'

The captain grunted, saying it was shovels he was worried about, not to mention salt-pig – but then, seeing that his companion looked crestfallen, he promised that the tars would knock her up whatever sort of frame she might want.

Ra Fanana brightened, but an altercation followed at once, when the captain said that some of the lads, and not the nurse, should sally forth with the shopping list.

The nurse was shocked. 'Faris, you know how I've looked forward to this! This is my *last chance*—'

'Ra Fa, this be no place for a lady—'

She rolled her eyes. 'You always forget, Faris, that I'm *not* a lady! And no, don't go saying you'll be coming with me – you know your leg's been bad. You save your strength now, do you hear? Patches and my lady can look after . . . can stay with you, and I'll take Master Jem and Master Raj – I'll be safe with *them*, won't I?'

Reluctantly, the captain agreed.

Ra Fanana patted his hand. 'The trouble is, you just don't understand about shopping, do you, Faris? It's not just the list, it's . . . it's the little *unexpected* things, as poor dear Tagan used to say. I'll admit, this isn't the finest of ports, but who knows what little knick-knacks I may find? Who knows what I may come back with?'

'Let's just hope you come back at all!'

A rank smell of burning wafted over the decks. The orange apes were roasting on a spit.

'Did . . . did they kill them first?' said Rajal.

'I'm not sure they did,' said Jem, 'but I suppose they'd scream. If they were alive, I mean.' He fluffed Rainbow's bright head. The dog, panting in the hot sun, rested his shaggy paws on the prow. 'I'm glad Patches has taken Buby. I'm not sure Rainbow should see this either.'

Selinda looked queasy. 'I don't understand. Why do people come to this place?'

'Where else can they go,' said Rajal, 'in these remote seas?'

'Where else,' said Jem, 'for embroidery frames?'

'It's more than that,' came a voice from behind them.

Selinda turned. It was the sailor called Alam. Really, had the man no respect?

He pointed. A large, low edifice of stone – a remnant, perhaps, of colonial domination – lay almost concealed amongst the clustering hovels. 'The Great Market of Shaba. There'll be a sale of ex-certs today, mark my words. That's what keeps this place running. The rest is just a sideshow.'

Jem said, 'Ex-what?'

'Ex-certificates slaves,' explained Alam. 'Slaves without provenance – stolen, mostly, and going cheap. Oh, the Sea Ouabin put in here many times.'

'And how long, good sir, were you in his thrall?' Jem asked.

Alam only shook his head ruefully, as if to indicate a space of many orbits.

Selinda turned away. The girl was fuming. If she was angry with Alam, she was angrier with Jem. The Vaga-boy was a different matter, but was not Master Jem of royal birth, like her? Did he not recognise this sailor's disrespect in speaking to them at all? Whatever this Alam may once have been, he was now a common tar, no more. Clearly he was trying to ingratiate himself – well, he would not succeed!

Helplessly the girl looked to Ra Ra, but the nurse was preoccupied, as ever, with the captain.

Meanwhile Patches was returning from below, where he had locked Buby into the captain's cabin. Bounding up the steps, he cannoned into Whale, the fat first mate.

'Eh, steady on, bum-boy! What's the hurry? Not planning on jumping ship, are we?'

'What? Don't be silly, Whale!'

'Silly? I think we be losing a few more lads, even here.'

'Better not. Why, the Cap'n, he'll—'

'Oh, and what'll he do about it?'

Gulping, Patches stared into the piggy eyes. Only now did he realise that the fat fellow was holding him by the shoulders, rather too tightly, with no apparent intention of letting him go. Not for the first time, the cabin boy's mind flashed back to a certain night, and a certain conversation he had overheard. He had wanted to say something to the captain, but something held him back. He was not sure what. He glimpsed Walrus, Porpoise, Sea-Snake – the looks that passed between them, the grins on their faces – and shuddered, for all the heat of the day.

'Let me go, lard-lump!' he burst out, breaking free.

Whale cried, 'What? Who you calling lard-lump?'

Patches skittered away. 'You, you big lump of lard!'

Porpoise guffawed; so did Walrus. Sea-Snake looked confused, but grinned again when Whale shouldered past him, muttering that he would get that little bum-boy, get him and get him good. Cap'n's favourite he might be, but did he think that set him above the first mate?

'Just you wait and see, Master Patchy-pants,' Whale mumbled, 'just you wait and see.'

Distantly Selinda heard these words, but they meant nothing to her; nor, indeed, did the roasting orange apes, the lowing, skeletal cattle or the stalls laid out with dead dogs and cats and glittering, reeking organs. Oblivious was she, too, to the black, toothless mouths of the old men and

408

women, the festering, mutilated beggars, or the clanking chains of miserable slaves as their masters whipped them into the Great Market. Tears blurred in the girl's eyes as again she thought of Maius Eneo.

How she loved him! How she missed him!

Then she saw the blue raven.

Startled, Selinda wiped her eyes. On a tiny stall, crushed against the water's edge, was a vast selection of birds – birds of all colours, birds of all nations, some living and caged, some dead and stuffed. The blue raven was very much alive. Covering the stall was a faded, striped awning, and it was on the gable of the awning that the raven had come to rest. Intently it stared towards the *Catayane*. Selinda stared back.

Then she cried out. The air around the bird churned like a kaleidoscope, and suddenly the girl was doubling over, moaning, racked by convulsions.

— *With moistened hands I pull away this hood.*
— *Such teasing hands! My heart shall swell to burst.*
— *But other swellings occupy you first.*
— *That flicking tongue! How can this feel so good?*
— *That's good? But now this hardness fills my throat.*

— *Already rise the waters in the moat.*
— *Ah, let them rise, as if to quench my thirst!*
— *I trust this rush of spurting sweetness should.*
— *My love, my love, but if it really could!*
— *My love, how deep in sadness are we versed!*

Ra Fanana cried, 'My lady! Whatever are—'

The captain cried, 'The lass! What—'

Patches cried, 'Miss Selinda!'

But before they could go to her, the girl, leaping up, wild-eyed, made for the gangplank, rushing desperately down to the docks.

At once, all was commotion. Calling for the bird, Selinda flailed forward. Her hands reached out. Other hands, claw-like, reached towards her; the bird-trader, alerted to the blue raven, whipped a net over the valuable find.

Selinda screamed, 'Maius! Maius Eneo—'

The crowd surrounded her. She was going under.

Jem, then Rajal, leapt down after her. Viciously they fought through the seething bodies.

It was no good. Someone punched Jem, hard, in the ribs. Someone drove a fist into Rajal's eye.

The captain cursed. Ra Fanana screamed.

Patches leapt down into the fray.

The girl had surfaced. She fought her way ahead. Now she was struggling with the bird-trader, desperate to wrest the net from his hand.

The man slapped her, punched her.

Wildly the raven fluttered in the mesh.

Then, as if from nowhere, Alam was there. In an instant, as if by magic, the handsome stranger had cleared the vicious crowd, dragged Selinda to safety and knocked the cruel trader to the ground, seizing the net.

He ripped at the mesh. The raven soared upwards, disappearing into the brilliant sky.

Selinda's emotions were a swirl of confusion.

'Oh, Alam – Alam!'

A stone whizzed through the air, striking the mysterious stranger on the side of the head.

He crumpled.

'Do you think he'll be all right?'

'Who, Alam? What about us? My eye's not going to take this sort of treatment, you know. I could be disfigured! At this rate they'll never have me back in the Masks.'

'The Masks? At least you'll be wearing one. But Raj, you're not really going back to *them*, are you?'

'What else am I going to do when this quest is over? I'm a Vaga, Jem.'

'You haven't got much faith, have you?'

'What do you mean?'

'I'm King of Ejland, aren't I? Or will be, one day. You won't be a Vaga then.'

'I'll always be a Vaga – I've got the mark.'

'I mean, you won't be treated like one.'

Rajal sighed. The conversation was a distraction from the considerable burdens they both carried: in Rajal's case, an enormous jar of rum, a basket of bananas, a side of salt-pig and a roll of slither-silk; in Jem's, a second enormous jar of rum, a sack of figs, a shovel and a very fat marmalade cat, which one of the traders had been on the verge of killing. Why anyone would want the thing alive, when there was the chance of having it dead – ready-skinned, too – the fellow had been unable to imagine, adding darkly that the price would be the same. Jem had muttered something about the rats on the *Catayane*; Ra Fanana, with a shudder, had agreed, and hastily opened her purse.

The sun was sinking low at last.

'I can't believe there are no *embroidery frames*,' the nurse said now, shouldering her way between a pair of lingering, ill-clad young women – harlots, most likely, eager for tar-trade. 'And what about straps for wooden legs? Really, it's absurd. Just another go-round, hm, Master Jemany? Master Rajal? After all, it *is* my last chance.'

'Couldn't we take this lot back to the ship?' Rajal gasped, stumbling.

'What, and leave me here?' said Ra Fanana.

'No, I meant—'

'I'll only be a moment.'

The nurse swept ahead again, list in hand; her bearers leaned, breathless, against a wall.

'Perhaps we could rest for a while,' said Rajal.

'I wouldn't bet on it. What'll Porlo say if we let her out of our sight? She'll get herself in trouble at the drop of a *hat*—'

'I'll be dropping more than that soon—'

'Think you've got trouble? Want to take Mouser here?'

'Mouser?'

'Well, *Ratter* doesn't have the same ring.'

'I suppose not.' Dubiously, Rajal eyed their new companion. 'You think Rainbow's going to like him?'

'He'll have to.' Jem shifted the enormous, lazy cat, who seemed neither particularly grateful for being saved, nor likely to be up to much in the way of ratting. Soon enough, no doubt, the furry creature would be taking his meals from a bowl underneath the captain's table. Or perhaps on top of it. But Jem could hardly have let the cat be killed. If nothing else, Mouser – if Mouser he was to be called – bore a striking resemblance to a certain other big, annoying marmalade fellow that Jem remembered now with a strange fondness. 'Say, where's Nurse Fanana?'

'Moves fast, doesn't she?'

'You would too, if you were only carrying a shopping list.' Jem squinted. Between a ferment-seller's stall and a reeking fishmonger's, between staggering cut-throats and dubious-looking harlots, the nurse sallied forth imperiously, obliviously. 'Come on, after her.'

This was harder than it sounded. The harlots, then the cut-throats, who had shown no interest in one plump nurse, showed much interest in two young men. Not only were Jem and Rajal personable young men; the burdens they bore appeared to be evidence of wealth. First the harlots turned to them, leering and pawing; then the cut-throats, envious of rivals; at the same time, the cat spied the fishmonger's and struggled excitedly in Jem's arms. Harlots and cut-throats loomed, threatening violence.

Jem backed away. 'Good sirs, we mean no disrespect—'

Rajal backed away. 'Good ladies, alas we must—'

'What do you mean, *alas?*' burst out one brown-toothed cut-throat. 'You *want* our girls, is that it?'

Rajal blundered, 'Of course we don't *want*—'

'What, not good enough for you, are we?' A painted strumpet sashayed forward.

Rajal gulped. So did Jem. Already a crowd had gathered, pointing and laughing.

Then came the violence. The strumpet pushed Rajal in the chest. He teetered back, cannoning into Jem. There was a cascade of bananas, salt-pig and slither-silk; there was the crash of a jar. Then Jem's burdens dropped too – rum, figs, clanging shovel. The cat leapt for the fishmonger's stall.

A cut-throat cried, 'Get 'em, boys!'

Jem grabbed the shovel. He swung it threateningly.

The crowd was in an uproar. Eager hands scrambled for figs, salt-pig, bananas, slither-silk; then the roll of silk was unwinding; then there was someone wrapped inside it; then it was furling across the ground . . .

Someone slipped. Then someone else.

'Quick, let's get out of here!' said Jem.

But first there was the cat, engaged with the fishmonger in his own battle.

'I'll kill you!' The fishmonger was bleeding.

Mouser hissed, claws blazing.

Jem swung the shovel again; the fishmonger ducked. Jem grabbed Mouser by the scruff of his neck.

'You don't deserve this, Mouser, you really don't!'

They wound their way through the crowd.

Rajal clutched his side. 'But . . . where is she?'

'Nurse Fanana! Nurse Fanana!'

Then they saw her. They gasped.

They were close to the entrance of the long, low edifice that Alam had called the Great Market. With vicious whipcracks, a swarthy slave-master drove forth a party of slaves; the crowd clustered thickly, jeering, pawing; but what astonished Jem and Rajal was the sight of Ra Fanana collapsing to the ground, keening piteously.

'Raj, quick – hold Mouser!' Jem fought his way to her. 'Nurse Fanana . . . what is it?'

Helplessly, the nurse could only gesture. Was she having some attack? Was it the memory of her own enslavement, welling up, overwhelming her?

Jem followed the direction of her hand. 'Nurse Fanana, I don't—'

'Jem, look!' It was Rajal, struggling with the indignant Mouser. 'Look who it is!'

The whip cracked. The slaves, in their clanking irons, disappeared into the Great Hall. But one face – a face they knew, if strange without its paint – twisted back just long enough for Jem to understand.

412

He grabbed a passer-by. 'When's the sale?'
'What, don't you know? It's now!'
The crowd surged forward.

Chapter 58

THE AUCTION

Jem groaned, 'How much longer? I'm passing out.'

'Got a funny idea of *now*, haven't they?'

'I suppose they're getting the slaves in order. Or something.'

'A few last-minute whippings for good measure?'

'Shh!' Jem, with a warning look, jerked his head towards Ra Fanana. But the nurse was intent only on the stage, where soon the stolen slaves would be paraded forth. Not once had she even upbraided her young bearers for losing almost everything they had bought that day.

She clutched her purse tight against her breasts. Now there was only one thing she wanted to buy.

Jem wiped his brow. He could barely move. How he longed to burst from this foetid place, dashing madly towards the sea! But then, he thought gloomily, the sea round Shaba Lalia would be choked with all manner of filth and debris. He leaned on the shovel. Harsh sunlight flooded through long, slatted ceiling-vents, painting the crowd luridly in stripes of light and shade. Everywhere the air was thick with the coarse, greedy talk of customers seeking bargains. A greasy-faced farmer wanted boys to pull his plough; a toothless fishwife wanted girls for her kitchen – especially, as she put it, for the *rough work*; a small-time whoremonger was desperate for *fresh stock*. Just by Jem's ear, a carbuncular fellow, far gone on ferment, muttered ominously about a *nice plump eunuch*.

He grinned at Jem. 'Ever had a eunuch, lad? Once a man's had a eunuch, no woman's ever enough. Sure you don't want to try? You can hire mine, when I'm not *using* him.'

Jem pretended he did not understand.

Awkwardly, Rajal shifted the cat. 'You couldn't take him back, could you, Jem?'

'What? No, you have him, Raj – he likes you.'

'What do you mean, he *likes* me?'

'He's purring – and he's not struggling.'

'He's so hot! I'm boiling, you know.'

'We're all boiling, Raj.'

Rajal looked resentfully at his furry burden. Several times he had endeavoured to set the cat on the floor, but each time the cat had hissed, and Jem had looked at him sternly. Didn't they have enough trouble without this creature? 'I don't think he's really a *Mouser*, somehow,' Rajal said glumly.

'I suppose not. But he *is* magnificent, isn't he? Like a cat king – a king of cats.'

'If you say so. So what shall we call him?'

'I don't know! What was that old cat on the *Cata* called?'

'Bollocks.'

'What's that, Raj?'

'Bollocks, Jem. We're not calling him *that*.' Rajal brightened. 'I know. A king, right? How about *Ejard Marmalade*? Or *Ejard Ginger*?'

Jem said, 'No, I know: *Ejard Orange*. Yes, that's it.'

They both laughed. Ra Fanana glanced at them reprovingly and at once Jem was sombre again. A little shyly, he rested a hand on the nurse's shoulder. 'Don't worry, Nurse Fanana. We'll get him back, I promise you.'

Ra Fanana gulped.

Eager murmurs rippled through the crowd.

'What's happening?' Rajal stood on tiptoe.

'There's someone taking the stage. Well-fed fellow, flashing earrings, golden robes, black gloves – and a silver hammer. Shabby this place may be, but one thing's for sure – this fellow's doing well for himself . . . the dirty pig! He's going to a lectern.'

Twisting in place, Rajal struggled to watch as the auctioneer bade the crowd a curt welcome. There was no delay in bringing forth the first lot, a spindleshanked old man in a loincloth, who appeared to be shivering for all the oppressive heat. Jem writhed in anger. To think that this poor fellow was allowed no mercy, even at the end of his days!

'Fresh,' began the auctioneer, 'from the canefields of Tiralos—'

Cries came, 'Fresh! If that's fresh, what's stale?'

'Look at him shiver! What's wrong with him?'

'He's got the jubba-fever!'

'He's got the pox!'

'Bah, where's the eunuchs? Hurry up with the eunuchs!' said the carbuncular fellow next to Jem.

But the bids came nonetheless, even for the old man. It was simple economics: the reserve price was cheap. The slave would pay for himself by the time he had been worked to death, even if that time were not far away.

Undoubtedly it would not be.

'Going – going – gone! Sold, to the greasy-faced farmer!'

The next lot was an extremely ugly girl in a torn sari who stood twisting her hands and knocking her knees as if she were about to wet

415

herself. One of her legs appeared to be deformed. Jem burned with fury. If only they could buy all these slaves, buy them and set them free!

'From the kitchens of the Emperor of Malaga, famed throughout these many Isles of Wenaya, comes this strong, willing worker—'

Ribald laughter. 'Willing to *what*?'

'To have a bag over her head, I hope!'

'Bah! The eunuchs! Where's my eunuch?'

'. . . And in the far corner . . . yes, toothless fishwife . . . yes, small-time whoremonger . . . toothless fishwife, it's with you . . . going, going . . .'

As the auctioneer's henchmen led the sobbing girl away, Ra Fanana's heart pounded hard. Memories filled her of her own enslavement, of the terrible, annihilating pain and shame and loss. But no, she must be strong. She must think only of Tagan.

Tightly, like a talisman, she clutched her purse.

In place of the girl came a party of children, an ill-sorted band of snivelling urchins dressed in the remnants of fine clothes. These, it was clear, were no common slaves, but the offspring of quality-folk, abducted at sea. All around the hall the ribaldries ceased; bidding grew intense; the price climbed high above the reserve.

Jem was worried. Ra Fanana's purse seemed heavy enough, swollen with the contents of the Blisha doll – but what if Tagan was beyond their means? So young and handsome a fellow would be considered a fine prize, would he not? From the carbuncular fellow, the mutterings about *nice plump eunuchs* did not relent. It was something, at least, that Tagan was tall and thin.

Besides, he had looked *very* bedraggled.

The children fetched a high price, a very high price, and excitement could only grow with the next lot. The auctioneer leaned forward, leering, as he announced three tall, ebony-hued girls, naked but for the muzzles clamped across their mouths and the many rings that circled their stalky necks.

'Often men talk of beauty in women, but what is the beauty of common women, considered against these gorgeous specimens? From the Baba Coast, the stunning Princess Nya and her two luscious handmaidens. Fit equally for marriage or for whoredom, ideally suited for any quality-establishment, these lovely Baba-girls. . .'

The commotion was deafening.

Rajal shouted, 'Jem, I can't stand this! Can't we do something?'

'I wish we could! But what? How—'

Soon the Baba-girls had been led away, to become the wives of a rich local trader; close by, the small-time whoremonger swore and stamped the ground.

Then Jem felt Ra Fanana's hand, clutching at his arm.

416

'And now' – the auctioneer licked his lips – 'to that most prestigious item on our programme today, a prize eunuch, imported direct from Hora's Court of the Triarchs! This, let me stress, is not just the *only* eunuch on offer today, but one of the finest seen for many a long orbit here in Shaba Lalia. There can be no doubt that bidding will be intense.'

Murmurs broke out as Tagan appeared, strutting forth as if of his own free will. Proudly, the willowy figure stood before the crowd. Jem's heart sank; so did Rajal's; Ra Fanana struggled against tears. Tagan, no longer bedraggled, was immaculate as ever – why, he was gorgeous! Somehow he had managed to procure kohl for his eyes, a clean spangly tunic and a tinselly sash. When the auctioneer moved to lift the tunic, to prove the eunuch's status to the crowd, Tagan did not even flinch, but beamed and held up his skirts himself!

Rajal groaned, 'Does he *want* to be sold?'

Ra Fanana moaned, 'He wants to fetch a high price!'

And his plan looked set to succeed.

Cries came, 'I've *got* to have him!'

'Who needs Babas? Give me that eunuch!'

'I could sell him in Vashi – I could sell him in Qatani!'

'He's skinny,' muttered the carbuncular fellow, 'but he'll do – why, he'll more than do!'

'Oh Tagan,' Ra Fanana sobbed, 'couldn't you be shabby, just for today?'

'My friends,' cried the auctioneer, 'be not deceived about the rarity of this lot, the only one hundred per cent genuine *quality*-eunuch to grace this podium in twelve moonlives or more – authentic Horan, from the Triarch's household, no less!'

There were gasps. Tagan struck a pose.

'Oh, many a backstreet trader will offer you *bargain* eunuchs, greasy-arsed street-boys clumsily gelded – often before their time, or too late – and quite untrained in all the arts and refinements of their kind. By contrast, look at this royal Horan eunuch, proud in the height of its youthful beauty, and possessed of an elegance that cannot be feigned. Who says you can't get quality at Shaba Lalia? You want quality? *Here*'s quality!'

Tagan did a little twirl.

Rajal grimaced. 'Oh, the fool! Jem, couldn't we attract his attention?'

'In this crowd? Besides, I think the damage is done.'

The auctioneer smirked, 'I'll start the bidding at three thousand Hora-ducats.' There were exclamations. Bidding for the Baba-girls had *ended* there. 'Do I hear *three*?'

Gulping, Ra Fanana glanced at Jem.

Jem raised his hand, just an instant before Carbuncles.

'Three, to the yellow-haired gentlemen in the far corner. Do I hear *four*?'

Carbuncles shot up his hand.

'And *four* to the carbuncular fellow. *Five*?'

There was a fresh bid from midway down the hall. Then another.

It was back to Jem.

'*Eight*, to the yellow-haired gentleman—'

Rajal gasped, 'Have we got that much?'

Meanwhile, Tagan searched the crowd. Suddenly his hand went to his mouth, and all his foolish posings were forgotten. His kohl-eyes widened. He had seen Jem. He had seen Rajal. Desperately, Ra Fanana waved to her friend.

'*Nine*,' said the auctioneer, 'to the fat lady over there!'

'Oh dear,' said Ra Fanana, 'I hope I've got that much!' Worriedly, she peered into her purse. 'No, it's all right. Twelve thousand, so . . . Surely no one will bid more than that?'

'For Tagan?' said Rajal. 'Don't be so sure.'

He was right. '*Ten*, to the carbuncular fellow. *Ten*, going . . . I declare, this is a record for Shaba Lalia . . . going . . .'

Carbuncles rubbed his hands, leering in anticipation.

Desperately, Ra Fanana shrieked, '*Eleven!*'

Carbuncles swivelled round, murder in his eyes.

Jem could not resist. Quickly he pushed away the clustering crowd, raised the shovel and bashed the fellow over the head, hard as he could. Eyes popped in the ugly face and their rival sank to the floor, tongue lolling. There were cheers, and some were quick to go further, spitting on the fellow, kicking him, stamping on his face and hands. At once Jem wondered what he had started, and was ashamed.

'Jem, get that shovel down!' Rajal hissed.

'*Twelve*, to the yellow-haired gentleman! Why, this is breaking all records!' cried the auctioneer. 'Twelve thousand Hora-ducats for this exceptional eunuch! Do I hear *thirteen*? Only joking . . . *twelve* . . . going – going . . .'

Jem grinned sheepishly. Rajal rolled his eyes, but Ra Fanana was oblivious. Joy overspread the nurse's face, and she beamed ecstatically at the distant Tagan. Eleven thousand, twelve thousand, what did it matter, if her dear sweet friend would be back with them again? Tears burst from her eyes; the silver hammer was about to fall – when a tall, cowled figure rose in the centre of the crowd, extending a staying hand.

'*Thirteen*,' came a booming voice.

The crowd fell silent, astonished.

'*Thirteen*?' said the auctioneer.

'*Thirteen*,' came the voice again, and its owner, holding aloft a clinking bag, made his way rapidly towards the podium, parting the crowd around him like a curtain. A moment more and he had seized the protesting Tagan, slung a rope around the eunuch's neck and dragged him brutally from the hall.

'Tagan, Tagan!' sobbed Ra Fanana.

Jem grabbed a stranger in the crowd. 'Who is that man? Who is he?'

'S-Sir, I don't know, I've never—'

'After them! Raj, quick! Nurse Fanana, come on!'

'Oh Tagan, Tagan—'

'Too late—'

'Damn—'

They hovered uncertainly. After the shadowy confinement of the Great Market, the sun outside was blinding. There were dazzling washes of pallor and dark, hard-edged shadows, simmering and festering in an empty silence. Traders and milling crowds alike had all gone in to watch the auction.

And Tagan and his buyer were nowhere to be seen.

'They can't just have vanished,' said Rajal.

Jem leaned on his shovel. 'I think they could, Raj. It took us a while to get out of there, didn't it?'

He screwed up his eyes. Alleyways lined with tumbledown hovels stretched away in several directions.

No one. Nowhere.

Ra Fanana's face was waxen.

Rajal patted her arm. 'Don't worry, Nurse Fanana. There has to be a way.'

'What way?' said Jem, almost harshly. 'Cowl-face bought him, fair and square.'

The nurse was shocked. 'Master Jem! You can't mean that!'

'Well, no. But what can we do?'

'You've got that shovel in your hand,' said Rajal. 'You did rather well with it back in there.'

Jem grimaced. Didn't they think Cowl-face looked just a *little* more formidable than Carbuncles?

They supposed he did.

Rajal jerked his head towards the docks. 'We could get some tars. A search party—'

'And if we find them?' said Jem. 'What then?'

'Well, that's when we could really use the tars, I suppose.'

Jem shuffled in a circle, moving round his shovel.

Nothing, no one. No one, nothing.

'By the way, Raj, where's Ejard Orange?'

There was guilt in Rajal's voice. 'Well, I had to put him down – on the floor, I mean.'

Jem's mouth set hard. 'You never liked him, did you, Raj?'

'Jem, it was impossible. He's so *heavy* . . . oh come on, don't raise that shovel again—'

'Look!' It was Ra Fanana who cried out.

Jem spun round, Rajal too. Far down an alley off to the left, they glimpsed the cowled form, dragging the struggling Tagan behind him.

They started forward. But an instant later, the figures were gone again.

'No!' puffed Ra Fanana. 'Tagan, Tagan!'

Filth choked the narrow alley. There were vegetable-scraps and scraps of offal, piles of excrement and pools of vomit and the maggoty remnants of a dead dog. Flies swarmed thickly in the heat; sacking hung, shifting lightly, in the doorways of the hovels. A small boy peered at them, blank-eyed.

Ra Fanana tightened her grip on her purse. Jem looked one way, Rajal another.

'This way!' they cried in unison.

They were pointing in opposite directions.

Rajal felt for the crystal at his neck. Had he imagined it, or had he felt a surge, a throb? 'Jem, do you get the feeling that something . . . *odd* might be happening?'

'Odd? What do you mean, odd?' said Ra Fanana, a little too loudly. Her voice cracked into a screech. 'Tagan . . . Tagan!'

Like an echo, the cry came back: 'Fa Fa . . . Fa Fa!'

But where had it come from?

Jem adjusted the shovel in his hand. Yes, something *very* odd was happening. He, too, felt the throb of the crystal at his chest. 'Raj, you're right. It can only mean one thing. Someone's on our trail – someone I don't think we want to see.'

Ra Fanana whimpered, 'Tagan . . . Tagan?'

There came the whisper: 'Fa Fa . . . Fa Fa?'

They turned slowly. The whisper again: then the whisper was a shriek and Tagan came bursting through a sackcloth doorway, rolling into the alley like a ball, tossed contemptuously away.

'Oh Tagan, Tagan!' Ra Fanana collapsed upon him.

Jem brandished the shovel. Steely-eyed, he stared at the flapping doorway.

'Jem?' came a voice. 'Jem, is it really you?'

Jem spun round. Joy overspread his face. 'Littler!'

The little boy ran forward.

Jem held out his arms. 'Littler, Littler, but how did you—'

'Jem, no!' Rajal rushed between them. He flung Jem aside. 'It's a trick! Littler's dead, it's ... it's—'

'Jem, Jem!' Littler broke into piteous sobs.

Rajal grabbed the shovel. 'Back, I say!'

'No!' shrieked Ra Fanana, and tried to intervene.

Scrambling up, Tagan restrained her. 'Fa Fa, look at it! Fa Fa, no—'

The nurse clapped a hand to her mouth. Horrorstruck, she staggered back through the debris. The creature that had seemed to be the little boy was shifting, changing, slipping into other faces, other forms ...

Rajal swung the shovel, hacking at the Triurge.

'You don't think you can win, do you?' said Lemyu, grinning, springing back. 'A Vaga-boy? With a shovel? You don't think you can win, do you, Prince Jemany? And when you lose, I'll have the crystals! Ah, what power shall soon be mine!'

'Power? Yours?' Jem cried. 'Triurge, you've got no power! What are you but just another Creature of Evil, dancing on the wires of Toth-Vexrah? You're not even stable, are you? You're falling apart!'

Glond, or the apparition that had looked like Glond, reared up immensely. 'Take not my master's name in vain! Fool, now I destroy you!'

Jem darted back. Again, Rajal swung.

Glond vanished. Suddenly, behind them, there was Saxis. Tagan cried out his father's name. For a moment he would have flailed towards the apparition, but Ra Fanana shrieked and held him back.

Rajal swung again. But Saxis was gone.

'Raj,' said Jem, 'we've got to run—'

'Which way? He's everywhere—'

'That's right, run!' taunted Leki. 'Key to the Orokon, indeed! Some hero you are, Prince Jemany! Not much better than a *cripple*, if you ask me—'

Rajal struck him. Too late.

Ra Fanana cowered. Tagan screamed.

At Jem's chest and Rajal's, the crystals burned.

'Come on, Vaga-boy! Come on, cripple!' They spun round. It was Glond. 'Take me on, why don't you? You can't win, you know!'

Littler stretched out his arms. 'Jem ... Jem!'

Rajal raised the shovel. He called on his crystal.

But another call came: 'Rajal ... Rajal!'

The shovel fell. Littler staggered forward. In the next moment, he would have clutched Rajal, absorbing him, Crystal of Koros and all, into the sickening morass of the Triurge. There was no time to lose. Jem grabbed the shovel and brought it down, hard, on what looked exactly like Littler's head.

The head, like an overripe fruit, burst in a hot, bloody shower.

❊　❊　❊　❊

It ended quickly.

Jem staggered back, a hand across his mouth. The crystal seared his chest, its heat dying slowly. For moments it seemed that the Triurge was gone. The little party clung together, shaken with horror.

But all was not over. A moment more, and the bloody mess that might have been Littler came slithering back together, cohering, growing—

Rajal turned first. 'Jem!'

Massively the Triurge loomed above them. They tried to run, but there was no escape. Orb-light swept across the filthy alley, filling every foetid, shadowy corner. But all the time the monster, like a guttering candle, flashed in and out of its precarious existence.

Flash, flash!

Tentacles snaked out, reeking, rotting.

One grabbed Rajal. One grabbed Jem.

Flash! Then Tagan.

Flash! Ra Fanana.

Agony surged through them. Jem felt his heart being squeezed and squeezed. Rajal thought his eyes would pop from his head. Tagan fainted; Ra Fanana swooned. Again Jem and Rajal felt the searing of their crystals, but call as they would on the crystal-power, there was nothing they could do. Death was upon them. Jem felt his life ebbing, ebbing . . .

Then there was a screech, and something – to Jem's dazzled eyes, a sack-like object – darted through the air, crashing into the oozing, flashing heart of the Triurge.

It was enough: it flickered out of being.

Heavily, the little party crashed amongst the garbage.

'Wh-what happened?' gasped Rajal, moments later.

'Someone saved us,' said Jem. 'Or something—'

Tagan simpered. Ra Fanana pointed. Where the Triurge had been sat Ejard Orange, purring and licking his big paws, as if at the end of a satisfying meal.

422

Chapter 59

A SEA CHANGE

'*Thirteen* . . .' Tagan sighed again.

'Oh, it was terrible, terrible!' said Ra Fanana.

'Terrible? Fa Fa, it was *marvellous*—'

'What, that I couldn't afford you?'

'Fa Fa,' said Tagan, 'it was a *record*!'

Jem said, 'Tagan, you are a fool. If it hadn't been for your preening—'

'That's not fair,' said Rajal. 'Tagan thought he was going to be sold again, didn't he? Well, of course he wanted to be sold to the richest, finest household.'

The eunuch flashed him a winning smile. 'Precisely.' He held out his long hands. 'You don't think *these* are going to work in the canefields, do you?'

'I don't think anyone had *that* in mind,' said Jem. He shook his head, laughing. 'Tagan, you don't deserve to be saved!'

'I'm glad he was,' Rajal said shyly. A flush appeared in his dark cheeks and he nuzzled, with pretended casualness, at Ejard Orange's fur. The cat had caused Captain Porlo a moment's perturbation; at first he thought it was Bollocks, come back to life. Well, he'd be a good ratter, if so!

Jem said, 'Come on, Raj, let's see Lady Selinda.'

'Oh yes, the mistress!' Eager for the reunion, Tagan would have followed them, but his arm was linked firmly in Ra Fanana's. On her other arm was Captain Porlo. They stood in the centre of the milling deck as the busy tars made ready to leave Shaba Lalia. Red rays of sunset fell around them, catching and flashing in the unfurling sails.

Captain Porlo – perturbed too, it seemed, to have a eunuch on board – said, 'Master Tagan, you didn't have nothing to do with any Caliph fellow, did you? Didn't ply your trade in a place called Qatani?'

Ra Fanana's laughter was awkward. 'Faris, don't be silly – Tagan had nothing to do with those *cobber-as*.' She would have added that the eunuch had not even been born when the captain had his accident, but thought better of it. Instead she said, 'Why don't you come down to the galley, hm? You can talk to me while I make us our dinner . . . I think we're all *very* hungry, aren't we?'

The captain's eyes brightened. 'Well, if there's a drop of rotgut, too!'

There was one task remaining. Patches came scurrying up, a cloth cap jammed firmly over his coppery curls. With coins knotted into a spotted handkerchief, the boy had been charged with going ashore and purchasing, once again, the items that had been bought, then lost, in the course of that afternoon. Ra Fanana had offered to go back, but the captain would not hear of it. He bellowed to Whale and Walrus, instructing them to go along with Patches, and make sure the boy kept out of trouble.

Patches did not seem entirely pleased.

'And lad, when you're ashore,' the captain added, 'no sniffing round any foreign doxies, eh?' Gesturing towards Tagan, he whispered loudly in the boy's ear, 'Let this wretch be a warning to you. It can happen to any lad, if he gets himself a dose of the pox – seen many a bold fellow, I has, cowering under the surgeon's knife! Think of it – not one instant of furtive pleasure, all the rest of your born days!'

Tagan, overhearing, was about to demur; instead, Ra Fanana trod on his foot and he broke off with a squeal. 'Hmph! Well, I'll just go below and see the mistress, shall I? Bedraggled, is she? Dressed as a boy? I'll soon put a stop to that! Come on, Fa Fa, show me the way.'

It was then that something seemed to strike Captain Porlo. He said quickly, 'Not yet, me lovelies. How about dinner first?'

'Yes, after we've looked in on the mistress.'

'No, I think we should have dinner. Let's have dinner.'

'Faris,' laughed Ra Fanana, 'you'll have your dinner *soon*!'

'Oh, it not be healthy for a man to delay. Not when he's changing his diet.'

Ra Fanana eyed him suspiciously. 'Faris, is something wrong?'

The captain looked down, muttering. 'Well, you'll find out soon enough ... I tried to stop the lass, but what could I do?'

Tagan and Ra Fanana exchanged worried glances.

'Lady Selinda?'

No reply.

Jem knocked again. 'Lady Selinda?'

Rajal said, 'She might be sleeping.'

'At this time?'

'Well, a nap.'

'I suppose so.' Jem was eager to see the girl. She knew a lot about the legend of the Triurge; besides, she worried him. For a time, earlier in the voyage, she appeared to have rallied, assuming new strength; then her strength seemed to drain away. Sometimes he thought of her as a spoilt, tiresome girl; then he thought of all that she had lost, and compassion filled his heart.

Besides, she was beautiful, even when dishevelled.

'We'd better look in on her. I hardly trust the captain to take care of her, do you?'

'And how should he do that? Hold her in his arms?'

'What? Oh all right Raj, you can put him down now.'

Relieved, Rajal lowered Ejard Orange; Jem tried the door.

He rattled the handle. 'It's stuck.'

'Lady Selinda? Lady Selinda?'

Hovering around them was the sweet, sharp smell of perfume from within. They thought they heard a sigh; then the door opened, revealing a Selinda altered startlingly from what she had been earlier that afternoon. The girl had resumed her glory. She wore a flowing gown and her hair was dressed in jewels. Her eyes flashed.

Gulping, Jem took a step back. 'I . . . we came to see if you were all right,' he said. 'I mean . . . well, we suppose you must be.'

The girl murmured something.

'We found Tagan,' said Rajal. 'He's on deck.'

'Tagan? Oh . . . Tagan.'

Rajal looked at Jem; Jem looked at Rajal.

'Just the sun, wasn't it, Lady Selinda?' said Jem. 'I mean, before. Gave you . . . must have given you a turn.'

Ejard Orange slipped into the cabin.

'The Triurge came back,' said Rajal. 'Gave *us* a turn, I'm telling you—'

'We wanted to ask you about him . . . I mean, *it*,' said Jem. 'We thought it was seeking only you . . . you in particular, for this Swallowing Marriage. But this time it attacked Raj and me, and Tagan and . . . well, we wondered if the legends said anything about . . . but then, perhaps Toth thought he'd try for the crystals while he had the chance, and . . . Lady Selinda, are you *sure* you're all right?'

A loud *miaow!* sounded from within.

The girl turned sharply. 'No! Keep away!'

'What's she on about?' said Rajal.

They pushed their way into the cluttered cabin. The curtains were drawn, but a chink of sunset danced in a looking-glass and played across the folds of a shimmery, soft fabric. In a heap on the carpet lay Selinda's male costume. Her bedclothes were rumpled; plates and tumblers covered the low table and on the couch on the other side, glistening with sweat, covered only in a twisted sheet, lay the sailor called Alam.

Rainbow hunkered down in the casement-seat, his ears drooping miserably. Ejard Orange miaowed again, and his long tail twitched. Angrily, Selinda pushed the cat away. She knelt by the couch, stroking Alam's hair. She leant close to him, whispering his name.

'Isn't that Nurse Fanana's couch?' Jem said uncertainly.

425

'I didn't think she was *that* sort of girl,' murmured Rajal. 'Fast work, at any rate.'

'Raj, he's sick! She's nursing him.'

Rajal stepped forward. A ghastly greenness played round the sailor's face. 'But what's wrong with him? It was a blow on the head, I know, but . . .'

Selinda looked up, eyes shining. 'Alam's saved me – don't you see, he's saved me?'

'Lady Selinda, are you sure you—'

'What's she talking about?'

Ejard Orange miaowed again.

'Jem – look!'

Jem turned. On a beam above the door, blinking, shifting its skittering claws, was a bird.

The blue raven.

Selinda hummed a little tune, then broke off, smiling. In the shimmering light she was more beautiful than ever; but then too there was a wildness in her face, and dark shadows under her eyes. When Ra Fanana and Tagan appeared in the doorway, their faces registered shock. But the girl only laughed at them and gestured to the bird.

'He came back. Don't you see, Alam brought him back?'

Jem felt a coldness crawling up his spine.

❋　　❋　　❋　　❋

That was just the beginning. Day after day the *Catayane* ventured ever further towards the Isthmus of Maric. And day after day, Selinda sailed on a different voyage of her own, ever further into a rich and strange communion.

Keeping to her cabin, the girl tended to Alam as his illness worsened. His body shook. Sweat matted his hair. His tongue grew swollen and he could not speak. The girl bathed him, fed him, smoothed his brow; sometimes, very softly, she would sing to him. Nothing helped. The handsome face withered; the muscular frame soon wasted away. And all the time, looming above the sickbed, was the blue raven.

The ship was rife with rumour. Tars muttered darkly of the jubba-fever. The conspirators held an urgent conference. Whale said they should burst into the girl's cabin, seize Alam and fling him over the side. Walrus said Porlo must be deprived of his command. But it was not so simple. As Porpoise pointed out, if Alam had the fever, would not the girl have succumbed by now? Besides, the conspirators were still afraid of the captain – and more than a little afraid of the ladies, too. Grumblingly, they agreed to bide their time. Yes, Porlo was senile and a fool, but would any other man lead them to the treasure? They would stick with him – for now. But the time would come when the old fool would walk the plank, and the gorgeous Lady Selinda would first be raped, then kept as a harlot for the crew.

Or rather, for the conspirators.

Had Selinda known of these deliberations, it is doubtful that she would even have registered alarm. Nothing could distract the girl from her duties. Rajal, Ra Fanana, Tagan and Jem took turns to bring her food and drink; only then would she acknowledge them. In the beginning, they would beg her to rest; soon they learnt that it was useless. Instead Rajal would gaze, with an intentness that disturbed him, at the man upon the couch, and find himself possessed by a welling fear; Ra Fanana would shake her head, looking despairingly into her lady's eyes. As for Tagan, he would long for the days when he had dressed the girl, painted her face and arranged her hair. The eunuch's bright manner was soon subdued; his face became drawn and often the kohl round his eyes was smudged with tears.

Jem, for his part, was filled with grave wonderment. Could the bird really be Maius Eneo? And what magic would turn him into human form again? Watching the girl as she bathed the sailor, Jem might have wondered just which man *was* her lover. Sometimes, after leaving her sickly-smelling cabin, Jem would rush on deck to take long, deep breaths; then, leaning over the side, he would find himself staring for long moments at the horizon, trembling with a foreboding he did not quite understand.

It was something about the sailor. Something about the bird.

And then at last came the Isthmus of Maric, like a green band cutting across the sea. How peaceful it seemed! How beautiful! But soon, they all knew, the *Catayane* must weave her way through noxious passages overhung with choking, rampant vegetation. Snapping crocodiles would glide beneath the waters; sharp-stinged insects would hover on the air; dark savages would crouch amongst the trees, spears and blowpipes ever at the ready. What madness was it, to make this journey?

Day after day, the ship sailed on.

Chapter 60

HEART OF DARKNESS

'What about Tagan?

'Perturbed?'

'Probably. And Buby?'

'Piqued. Where is she, anyway?'

'Down below. Locked in.'

'What's she done now?'

'You mean what'll she *do*, Raj. If she swings through these trees, we'll never see her again.'

'Oh? Let's get her, shall we?'

'Not funny, Raj.'

Sinister moonlight glimmered through the darkness. Noxious steam rose from the shore. Jem looked grimly into the jungle. That day the Straits had narrowed alarmingly. Leaves and branches scraped at the bows, caught in the rigging and lashed the sails. They were barely moving. The wind had fallen and the water was a viscous, muddy sludge. At this rate they would be pulling with the longboats soon, bending their backs like the Sea Ouabin's slaves.

Jem sighed, shifting his musket. Heat pressed around them like a tangible thing.

'What about you, Raj?' he asked after a moment.

'Hm? I wasn't planning on swinging through the trees.'

'No, Raj. Buby's piqued – what are you?'

They were discussing certain developments pertaining to the captain – and Ra Fanana. Exiled from her rightful couch, the nurse had been forced to make alternative arrangements. For some nights, accepting a gallant offer from the captain, she had taken his cabin in his stead. But the nurse had not been entirely pleased. Faris was sleeping below with the boys. It was unseemly, she said; it was absurd. So it was that, at her insistence, the captain returned to his cabin – and shared it with her.

Only Selinda was not intrigued. Of the tars, some said that the captain was long past the prospect of carnal delights; others indulged in ribald imaginings, attributing extraordinary powers to an old, sick man with one leg and a festering stump.

Some were merely confused.

'It's so unlike him,' said Rajal.

'What is? Love?'

Rajal was silent. Unseen birds cackled in the darkness. Frogs croaked. There were plunkings, drippings, hissings.

'And you, Jem?'

'Pleased – I'm pleased for him, of course.' Jem sighed. 'Pleased that my watch is nearly over, too.'

'All right for some,' said Rajal.

'Come on, Raj, you only came on halfway through mine. Who's your next partner?'

'Tagan.' Rajal looked down, a little pensive.

'Well, he can't be worse than Patches,' Jem said obliviously. The cabin boy had taken the watch before Rajal's. 'Now there's a boy with a lot on his mind. Pleased, puzzled and piqued all at once, I'd say.'

'Piqued and puzzled I get, but pleased? What, that he's getting thumped in the head less often?

'Haven't you seen?' Jem had to smile. 'When Nurse Fanana's wrapped up in the captain, she lets Patches take her turn with Selinda. I saw him carrying a tray down there before. You should have seen him – beetroot red, he was.'

'Why?'

'Raj, are you blind? He's in love with her.'

'With Nurse Fanana?'

'With Selinda! I'll bet he's dreaming of her right now.'

'Huh! Well, one thing's for sure.'

'What's that, Raj?'

'That she's not dreaming of him.'

Must not sleep. Must not dream.

Moonlight glimmered on the beam above the door. The blue raven shifted. Selinda had lain on her couch just for a moment. But how long ago had that moment been? Her head was so heavy. She must rise up, mustn't she? Prop herself on her elbow? Swing her legs to the floor? Dimly she saw herself doing these things, pacing the carpet, splashing her face. If only she could fling open the casement, gulping clean air. If only she could dive into cool, clear water. But there was no clean air. No clear water. Only mud, marshes, stench and heat. Selinda's brain reeled and her gown was wringing wet.

Must not sleep. Must not dream.

But dear Alam was sleeping, wasn't he? She watched his chest slowly rising and falling. And was he dreaming? Selinda's eyelids flickered. What reveries had come to her, through all the long days and nights of this vigil! Shuddering in her loneliness she knew them again, but this

429

time her lover was sometimes Alam, sometimes Maius Eneo, sometimes both, fusing and parting. Oh, but the girl was burning, feverish! How she longed for a lover's touch! In reverie, she saw herself bursting from her cabin, flinging herself on the dirtiest, commonest tars. They would take her brutally, one after the other, and all the time she would only cry for more, more. It was madness. The thought repulsed her. She loved Maius Eneo, him and no other.

Must not sleep. Must not dream.

Sometimes she would take the raven in her hand, feed it, pet it, ruffle its feathers. Softly she would whisper words of love, but the bird only gazed at her, blinking, impassive, as if it were incapable of understanding. But had it not once spoken in her mind, back on the docks of Shaba Lalia? How Selinda longed to taunt the cold creature, maddening it until it attacked her! Then, perhaps, maddened in her turn, she would clasp the creature to her bloodied breast, crushing it to pulp, or tearing its wings like a helpless insect's . . . Ah indeed, what reveries had come to her, in all these wakeful nights and days! This wakefulness was a horror. But better than sleep, oh far better – this Selinda knew, because after all she had slept several times, while Alam lay on the couch across the way.

Must not sleep. Must not . . .

Selinda slept. Selinda dreamed.

'Ouch!' Rajal slapped his neck.

'Thought you weren't supposed to do that,' said Jem.

'Do what? Scream in agony?'

'Kill things. Didn't the Great Mother say you shouldn't?'

'Well, she wouldn't have been pleased about a lot of things I've done. I dare say I've broken all the Vaga-rules by now.'

'Koros-children,' said Jem, 'Children of Koros.'

'You're telling me the name of my own tribe?'

'*Vagas* is an insult – isn't it?'

'Not when I use it.' Rajal slapped his neck again.

'Haven't you tried that lotion of Nurse Fanana's?'

'Yes, but I've sweated it off by now.' Rajal slumped miserably. 'You know, I've heard of a Sea Ouabin, but I've never heard of a Sea Vaga, have you? No, I think we Koros-children weren't really meant for life on the ocean wave.'

'Or river mud,' said Jem. 'Now where's Tagan? Hope I don't have to wake him up.'

There was the click-click of claws and a sound of panting. Jem turned, fluffing Rainbow's fur. Since Selinda had begun her strange vigil, she no longer wanted her guard dog. Now Rainbow would restlessly roam the decks, sad-eyed and shambling.

'Poor Rainbow, that tongue of yours will fall out soon. Where's his bowl, Raj?'

'I don't know – Ejard Orange has stolen it.'

'What, carried it off in his paws? You just don't like him, Raj, admit it. Remember, if it weren't for him we'd be inside the Triurge now.'

'Rainbow,' said Rajal, 'could have beaten it too.'

'Huh! You didn't like *him* when we first got him, either.'

'No, I loved him. Actually, his bowl's here. Come on, boy.'

The dog lapped eagerly at the brackish water; Rajal hunched sullenly over his musket, feeling the sweat run down his skin. His legs were cramped, his arms too. He would break out in a rash soon; already he was covered in bites.

Around them the jungle was quiet, almost too quiet. Only the croakings, rustlings, scrapings. Swampy bubblings, hissing fumes. Yesterday they had heard the thump of tom-toms. Today they had heard a distant chanting. Captain Porlo had said it must be cannibals, dancing round a cookingpot. And more than once, hadn't they glimpsed skulls, stuck menacingly on rows of stakes?

Rajal tightened his grip upon his musket.

'Hurry up, Tagan,' Jem yawned. 'You can't be putting kohl on, not in heat like this.'

'I wouldn't put it past him,' said Rajal. His voice was almost sour. 'Loves himself, that one.'

'At least he loves someone. Funny, isn't it,' Jem said thoughtfully. 'A voyage like this, and everyone's in love.'

'Perhaps because it's their last chance,' said Rajal.

'Let's hope not.' Jem looked down, thinking of Cata. How he ached to see her again! Night after night he dreamed of the ecstasies they had known together in Unang Lia. How cruel, the magic that had snatched her away! How cruel, the dreams that seemed so real!

But at least he loved someone. Jem reached consolingly for Rajal's shoulder. 'Don't worry, Raj – you're a slow starter, that's all.'

'I'm a *what*?'

At once, Jem wished he had not spoken. 'I mean,' he mumbled, 'that one day you'll meet the right girl too.'

Rajal breathed deeply. He had never told Jem certain of the things that had happened to *him* in Unang Lia. But Jem knew about other things, didn't he? Things that had happened in the Silver Masks?

Perhaps he thought it had all been a phase.

Branches scraped close. There was a sharp hissing.

431

'Jem,' said Rajal, 'there's something you should know. Remember Princess Bela Dona?'

'Raj, you weren't in love with *her*?'

'No ... but remember the sort of girl she was?'

'I'll say. Now if ever there was a *waste*—'

All at once, the hissing was loud. There was a thump. Rainbow reeled, barking. Not for the first time, a tree-snake had fallen to the deck. It writhed. It lashed. Rajal struck out with his bayonet.

His accuracy was surprising.

'Well done, Raj!' Jem flung the coily corpse over the side. 'There you go, disappointing the Great Mother again. And just as well.'

'At least it wasn't a *cobber-a*. Or a cannibal.'

'I say, my dears, what *was* that frightful noise?'

'Tagan! At last!' Jem thrust his musket into the eunuch's hands. But when he had climbed down from the bridge, he looked back up. 'What was that you were saying, Raj?'

Rajal waved a hand. 'Oh, nothing. Never mind.'

❊　　❊　　❊　　❊

In the dream that came to Selinda, during the long nights of her vigil, she would see herself rising from her couch, gliding to the casement, flinging it wide; and there before her, instead of the maddening, hissing jungle, would be a peaceful cove like the cove at her father's house, with waves washing brightly over carved pebbles.

Or, perhaps, there would be a green garden, fragrant with a thousand flowers; or a gorgeous chamber, rich in velvet and jewels. And Selinda, in her fluttering gown, would push her way through the casement, leaving the foetid sickroom her cabin had become. In the cove she would wander the smooth beach, paddling in the warm shallows; in the garden, dappled in the sunshine, she would pass along draping arbour walks; in the chamber, and the chambers beyond, she would trail a hand along soft fabrics or cool, thrilling surfaces of gold and glass. But then the smooth beach would become a place of jagged rocks; the arbour walks became high, forbidding hedges; the beautiful chambers were ruinous, and somehow, she did not know why, the girl could not turn back.

Then, in a rocky cave, in a twisted bower, in a filthy corner she would see them, the naked man and the hunchbacked dwarf. Glowing with an eerie phosphorescence, the dwarf clawed at the naked man, shook him, clutched his chest, slipped across his back, bucked and spurred him like a crazed rider. The creature drew blood, tore out hair in handfuls, but never could the naked man shake him free.

Selinda would try to intervene. She would burst forward, pummelling the hunchback, but the strangely glowing creature would fling her aside.

She would rush in again, beating inexplicably at the naked man, too; then the man would be laughing at her, laughing even as the hunchback flayed him.

And then she saw his face. She staggered back: *Alam*. Of course, she had known. But somehow, every time the dream came, it was here that the horror would burst like a boil; here that she would wake, shaking and sickened.

That night the dream was different. Oh, it began in the familiar way, this time with the beautiful chambers; but then Selinda found herself drifting on and on till the chambers, ruinous now, gave on to the gardens; then came the sun-dappled walks, then the hedges, then the path that led down to the warm cove. Marvelling, Selinda splashed through the shallows; then, as the day darkened, she was slithering over rocks, gasping, sobbing though she was not sure why.

She clambered through the casement of the waiting ship. And there they were, Alam and the incubus, thumping and crashing, grunting, ripping, gouging. *No, not here. No, please.* It was too real. Selinda gasped, starting awake; but that was when the true horror began.

The dream was real. The thing was there.

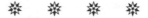

'It's no good, you know. No good at all.'

Rajal said, 'What isn't?'

'Painting. In this heat. Slides off at once.'

'I wouldn't know. I don't.'

Tagan studied his nails. 'Never? Not been tempted?'

Rajal felt a mounting irritation. 'Of course not.'

The eunuch slumped over the prow, unpainted face resting on his fist. He pouted. He flicked sweat from his hair.

'Careful!' said Rajal.

'Sorry, dearie. Are you really a singer?'

'Something of the sort. Well, used to be. In Ejland.'

'Ejland! Isn't that exotic? You wouldn't sing us a little song now? Liven things up a bit?'

'The cannibals might sing one back.'

'Cannibals? Oh, I don't believe in *them*. That's just a story to frighten silly boys.'

Rajal slapped his neck again. Damn, a big one. Still, better a thousand mosquitoes than a cannibal's blowpipe. 'I suppose I'm a silly boy. But I've seen things, shifting round in the darkness. And haven't you seen those skulls?'

'Dearie, now you're *really* frightening me.' The eunuch's tone was wry. 'And I thought we were having an adventure! When are we going to get through this river, or whatever it is? I tell you, I've never been so bored in all my life! Or so uncomfortable. I don't think I can stand it much longer.'

'Captain Porlo says we're getting there.'

'So? He said that yesterday.'

'So? It's a long way.' There was a snapping round the bows. 'Now if that wasn't a crocodile, I don't know what was.'

'I say, you *are* frightening me,' said Tagan, seriously this time. 'Still, I dare say they wouldn't eat *eunuchs*. I mean, not first of all.' He laughed nervously. 'The smell, dearie,' he explained. 'You're a little more *pungent*.'

'What? Well, thanks – I think.'

'You don't much like me, do you, Master Raj?'

Rajal twisted his mouth. 'What gave you that idea?'

'Common observation, dearie. I make you uncomfortable. Didn't you say you'd almost been made into one of my kind?'

'How can you stand it?' said Rajal. 'I mean, how can you stand being what you are?'

'Dearie, perhaps I want to be ... *what I am*.'

The moonlight on the muddy water was sharper. The snapping of the crocodile sounded again. 'What,' said Rajal, 'are you talking about?'

'Father thought I was captured by the slavers. Well, of course, but ... there were others who escaped.'

Rajal shivered, as if his rolling sweat had turned suddenly cold. 'You wanted ... to be what you are? You *wanted* it?'

'You don't believe me? Is it really so hard?'

Rajal screwed up his forehead. He thought of the ladyboys in Unang Lia. Of plump Blubina, of Storkela, Fishia, Cheesia ... He thought of the barber looming over him, razor in hand. 'Yes! Yes, it is!'

Awkwardly, Tagan adjusted his musket. 'No need to shout.' He spoke softly, rapidly. 'Very well, I *wouldn't* choose to be a preening, painted eunuch – that's what you see when you look at me, isn't it? But don't you see, it's the next best thing?'

'To being dead? Some wouldn't agree.'

Tagan breathed deeply. A faraway look came into his eyes and he said softly, 'When I was in the slave market at Hora, before I was bought for the Triarch's household, I met one of the ladyboys from Lania Chor. He was the one – yes, I think he was the one – who told me about the Isle of Vanic. Have you ever heard the legend of Vanic?'

'Why ... why should I have heard it?'

'All our kind hear it in the end. Just where Vanic might be, no one seems sure, but I've heard tell it might be in the southlands, somewhere on the other side of the world. One day, they say, we'll all know how to get there. For now, we're just waiting till one of us finds the way. Then that one will come back, you see – come back and show the others.'

'Show them ... what?'

Tagan smiled. 'There's an enchantress there, they say, who works a great spell, though the price of it is high and the way is hard. It doesn't come in a magic word, it doesn't come in a flash of light. There'll be much to suffer, and all the life you've lived before will still be there in your memory and dreams, never to vanish. There'll always be that – oh, that *wrongness*, that was with you from the first. After all, it's a part of you, part of what you are ... But when a wrong is righted, what happiness comes then? What tears of joy might we shed in the end, could we but find our way to Vanic? Oh, it's a great spell – for our kind, the spell of spells.'

Rajal was aware that he was breathing hard. His companion, he knew in a rush, was more, so much more, than a preening, painted eunuch. What depths of sadness lay inside him? What did it mean, the rolling eyes, the fluttering hands? It all meant nothing, nothing real.

He breathed, knowing already, 'What ... sort of spell?'

Gentle tears flowed down Tagan's face. His words were whispers, vanishing into the night. 'They say she can work only *one* miracle, the Enchantress of Vanic, only this one. In other ways, I'd still be what I am, gangly, ungainly – oh, I wouldn't be like my lady, I know that. But that wouldn't matter, would it? How could it matter? The *one* miracle – that would be enough.'

Rajal reached for the long hand. He said slowly, 'Tagan ... I hope you find that Isle of Vanic. You could be the one to find it, you really could.'

Tagan brushed his eyes. 'How? A silly thing like me? You'd need to be magic, even to ...'

Rajal took the long hand, guiding it to the crystal at his chest. 'You're close to magic now.'

They drew together. Suddenly, marvellingly, Rajal was aware of Tagan's long body pressed against his own, of their hot breath and their heartbeats and the slickness of their sweat. Shuddering, he felt the long hands running down his chest, then down his back, then lingering with practised ease between his thighs. Murmurs welled to his lips, *No* and *You don't understand* and *You've got it wrong* and even, at the end, *There's someone else* – but then his lips were melting into Tagan's and he felt as if he were sinking into a rich, velvety darkness. In merest moments, the spasms might have come, the convulsive release he had suppressed for so long, ever since his last night with Vizier Hasem.

'Oh Tagan, Tagan—'

But the scene ended before its time. Rajal yelped and sprang back, slapping at his neck again. This time, it was not a mosquito. He

435

staggered; he swooned. Then something dropped to the decks, something heavy – then something else again, and something else. Tagan gasped. Then he screamed. War cries filled the night and dark figures swarmed across the decks.

Chapter 61

STRANGE MEETING

'Alam! Alam!'

Blood splattered Selinda's gown. The girl lurched, her thoughts wild. Her hands clawed at the casement. There was a rattling at the door, then a pounding. Terrified, she swivelled back. The lock burst open and Jem crashed through. He had known that something was wrong, known it even before he heard the girl scream. Light from the crystal exploded from his chest. Rainbow bounded behind him, barking. From the decks above came poundings, cries.

The dwarf reeled, cackling gleefully. The raven shrieked and shrieked. Horror filled Jem's face. 'Scurvy! But you're—'

'Dead?' came a crazed voice. The creature glowed with wild, unearthly light. Its eye-sockets had burst, running with jelly; fish had eaten its lips and nose and cheeks; a cavernous mouth opened and shut, but the voice that issued forth seemed to break from the air, to bounce from the walls. 'Foolish boy, could my master let me drown?'

Rainbow cowered, held at bay by Scurvy's powers.

Bleeding, naked, Alam slipped to the deck with a thump. But his name, Jem suddenly knew, was not really Alam.

'The Sea Ouabin—'

'Of course. My conduit into being, my prop and stay—'

'But you're . . . *killing* him—'

Jem could barely speak. Reality was fracturing. The tiny cabin was an immense echoing chamber, all its dimensions at wild, oblique angles. The floor shifted and he struggled to stand. The grinning Scurvy leapt and cavorted.

'Killing him, killing him? I am letting him live! Don't you understand, I gave him a life of bitterness, a life of vengeance, when all other life was lost to him. I made him what he is! Since his vision of the Zenzan he has languished, certain only of death as he struggles to reject me! But shall I let him die? Shall he die for love of a foolish girl? For how many orbits have I sucked at his life-force, leeching at his energies? Long ago, he was all virtue and love. Then he was betrayed by his greatest friend, that monster in human form called Sultan Kaled. Do you not recall the old tales of Unang? Mala – Lord Malagon – was condemned to die. But I made him live! My master Toth sent me to him, and I made him live! He

437

is my *food*, don't you understand? Shall I let my *food* die?'

Now a wilder cackling broke on the air; the deathly phosphorescence glowed and changed; lines of light snaked between Scurvy and Jem, twisting and churning into the rays of the crystal. Jem slumped to his knees. Agony consumed him. Now he knew it all. What had Scurvy been, what had he ever been, but the agent of a greater and darker power? And who was it that spoke through him now, but the puppeteer of all such Creatures of Evil?

'Come, Prince Jemany, the crystal, the crystal—'

'Never! You'll never defeat me, Toth—'

'Fool, I've *already* defeated you—'

Now they were connected by lines of light. But Scurvy, or Toth, was stronger, much stronger. Jem felt the crystal pulling away from him. His flesh seared. His bones juddered. As if in some crazed, violent dream, he was pushed, pummelled round the cabin, smashing against the wide floor, the distant walls, the cavernous ceiling. Far through the air he flew. Distantly, desperately, came Rainbow's barking, and the shriekings of the raven.

And Alam, or Mala, the being that had once been a Sultan's boon companion, the nobleman who had lived with the Ouabin in the desert and loved the lady that his monarch would possess, had surged up, glowing, all recollection of his old life lost. Animated by unearthly powers, the naked creature caught Selinda, flinging her against the wall. She tried to run; he grabbed her; she shook him free; she kicked him, but he kept coming back, and back and back, laughter echoing insanely all around him. The girl, lost in horror, could only shake her head, mouthing *No, no*. She backed against the vast casement; the moonlight behind her pressed through the panes with a wild, unnatural whiteness.

Rainbow, collar glowing, spiralled through the air. Urgently the raven blundered round and round, swooping and plunging through the cabin. Crazed thumpings echoed through the decks. Phantom cannibals marauded all around, clashing with the captain's crew. Then the captain was in the cabin too, cutlass in hand, nightgown flapping, while Ra Fanana screamed and clutched him. She could not hold him back. The captain lunged at the naked man. The Sea Ouabin turned, deathlight streaming from his mouth and eyes. He cried out, but his voice was the same as Scurvy's: '*Porlo! You defeated me once! You shall not defeat me a second time!*'

The cutlass clattered from the captain's hand. He blundered back, his crutch slipping from beneath his arm. Heavily he crashed to the floor.

The Sea Ouabin was upon him.

'No!' Ra Fanana fought her way forward, but the floor lurched. The huge ceiling swooped down, then up; furniture spun through the air;

curtains twisted and snaked across the vastness and the walls zigzagged and bulged. Then the whiteness that was streaming through the casement exploded suddenly into a thousand shards of glass, flying in all directions.

Flash. Jem's eyes burst into blindness; for a moment he thought that all was over; then the blindness faded and he found himself in a green, fragrant garden.

Bright sunshine fell all around him.

❇ ❇ ❇ ❇

Jem turned. 'Captain . . . Lady Selinda?'

There was a stirring of leaves and the blue raven fluttered from one branch to another. Jem looked at it sharply, uncertain if the bird were good or evil. It fluttered again and vanished. Jem put a hand to his temples, aware of a faint pounding, but whether it were inside or outside his head, he did not know. He breathed slowly, deliberately. Leaves rustled. Flowers nodded.Then Rainbow shambled forward, nuzzling and snuffling at something in the grass. In this strange, sunny garden his five-coloured fur was unusually bright, almost dazzling in its beauty. He saw Jem and bounded forth. Jem knelt down, gratefully rubbing the furry head.

'Hello, boy. So you're here, at least.'

A voice said gently, 'And so am I.'

Rainbow snarled; Jem shuddered. But Scurvy had changed; no longer a drowned, decomposing corpse, instead the dwarf appeared much as he had in life. Or almost. His shabby garb had gone, replaced by a costume unusually fine, a brilliant affair of silk and gold braid; then, too, the expression on the little wrinkled face was suspiciously warm and welcoming.

And was there not more? Jem pressed his fingers to his temples again. Could it be the dwarf's face was shifting? Could the little twisted body be changing, too?

Rainbow writhed, as if straining on a leash.

The voice came again. 'Master Jemmy, it's been a long time.'

Jem felt the crystal pulsing at his chest. He moaned, 'No. Toth, this is a trick beneath even *you*—'

'Toth? Master Jemmy, won't you call me by my proper name?'

'It's not your name, anti-god. Do you think I'm a fool?

The little man was crestfallen. He held out his arms. 'Master Jemmy, won't you embrace me? Won't you embrace your old friend?'

Rainbow snarled. His collar glowed, just as the crystal glowed at Jem's chest.

Jem backed away. 'You couldn't speak,' he said suddenly. '*Barnabas*

439

couldn't speak.'

The dwarf smiled. 'Yes, Master Jemmy, and you couldn't walk! Remember your poor, floppy little legs? We've both learnt a lot since the old days, haven't we? But I say, what's that hanging in the bag round your neck? One of the spoils of your exciting adventures? Won't you show me? Won't you show your old friend Barnabas?' The dwarf scuttled forward. He stood up on tiptoes, reaching up a pudgy hand.

Jem pushed the hand away. *'You're not Barnabas.'*

Rainbow circled them, whimpering, growling.

'Master Jemmy, can you be so sure? Oh, but are those tears I see glistening in your eyes? Yes, I knew you'd remember the old days! Remember how I taught you to race in your chair? Remember how I gave you the magnificent sticks? Just think, without *them* you'd never have gone down to the Wildwood, or been friendly with that lovely girl Catayane! Then how would destiny ever have claimed you? Ah, Jemmy, I know you love me, really. After all, you owe me everything. Please, Jemmy . . . Jemmy?'

Appalled, revolted, Jem tried to turn from the pleading face, but somehow he could not twist his head away. The dwarf's eyes – rapidly, thickly, his tears began to roll – seemed to fix Jem in place as he forced the words through clenched teeth, 'Barnabas . . . Barnabas was good and kind. You . . . *you* are a deceiving Creature of Evil. *You* . . . are an agent of Toth . . . you *are* Toth!'

Barnabas – for the little man looked *so* much like him – only laughed merrily. 'Barnabas, Toth, what's in a name? Why, I've been known by many names.'

'What?' Jem said sharply.

The little man rested a hand on Jem's arm. Round and round them Rainbow still circled, his collar throbbing with light. Again and again the dog would have leapt, savaging his master's foe; again and again the dwarf's powers kept him at bay.

The dwarf grinned again, exposing pink gums. 'It's simple, isn't it, Jemmy? In the old days, you knew me as Barnabas. Good a name as any, isn't it? Besides, you *were* Key to the Orokon, weren't you? Someone had to set you on the path of the crystals, and that's just what I did.'

Waves of horror swept through Jem. He broke from the dwarf's grip. 'No! I don't believe it!'

'Jemmy, you must . . . Jemmy, you do!'

Jem reeled away, but the little man skipped after him like a tormenting imp.

'You loved me before, didn't you, Jemmy?' Jem had blocked his ears, but heard the words anyway. 'Whatever else I am, I'm still your old Barnabas! I'm yours, you're mine! Why, Jemmy, you've *always* been mine!'

Jem swivelled round. His fist swung.

There was a piteous cry. 'Jemmy, cruel Jemmy!'

Jem's fist uncurled. Vomit rose to his throat. Suddenly he was collapsing on the grass beside the dwarf, stroking him, clutching him. 'Barnabas, I'm sorry—'

'Jemmy, dear Jemmy—'

A pudgy hand reached out, fingering the crystal. Light glowed like fire in the little man's eyes. Rainbow barked, frantic. It was then, from the corner of his eye, that Jem saw another figure in the garden, looking on, smiling.

The Sea Ouabin!

Just in time, Jem rallied. Suddenly, sickeningly, he was beating and kicking at Barnabas ... at Toth ... at Scurvy, as the scene fractured around them into fragment after fragment. Then Scurvy ... Toth ... Barnabas had vanished, blending into another, more formidable foe. The Sea Ouabin, feverish and stricken no longer, charged at Jem, fists flailing.

Flash. A beach. They were struggling in the sand.

Flash. They writhed in a luxurious chamber.

Flash, flash. Other images crashed and tumbled: of Captain Porlo struggling with the Sea Ouabin too; of Selinda flailing against his assaults, shrieking and sobbing in beach, in garden, in chambers of luxury, between the rocks and the high hedges and in the filthy corners. Yes, they each had their own struggles, and in each reality there was Rainbow as well, collar searing his neck like fire, barking, leaping, scratching, desperate, trapped outside the circle of conflict.

Captain Porlo beat back the Sea Ouabin; then the Sea Ouabin beat him back, or gripped him by the throat. Sometimes the captain was possessed of both his legs; sometimes he was young, sometimes old; sometimes his opponent was naked and gleaming, sometimes in his billowing desert garb. They fought with swords, or hand to hand; ships, like the vision of the Flying Zenzan, lurched in the air in ghostly form, guns blazing on a stormy sea. Could it be, between the wild, rushing sounds, that there came snatches of an old song? What was this, after all, but the day old Faris Porlo met the Ouabin of the Sea, played out again in a wild fantasia?

He was winning, he was losing. Losing, winning.

Different songs accompanied the struggles of Selinda. Naked or clothed, hale and vital or shuddering with fever, in vision after vision the being called the Sea Ouabin or Alam or Mala clutched the girl to him, embracing her tenderly or slapping her, beating her, taking her brutally or reeling back, cursing; in vision after vision the girl gave way or fought back savagely, awash with revulsion, awash with desire. Time and space

441

juddered backwards, forwards, sideways, slipping and skewing in all directions.

Flash, flash. Between the glimpses of chambers, garden, beach, Jem saw slivers of the *Catayane* too, a *Catayane* mysteriously, wildly misshapen, with Rajal, Ra Fa, Tagan, Patches, Buby, Ejard Orange and tar after tar rocking and plunging on the muddy tide. There were blowpipes, muskets, cannons, swords; there were screamings and shots and clashings of steel; there were cannibals and tars, tars and cannibals falling, tumbling, spurting blood.

Flash, flash. And the flashings came faster. Jem kicked and kicked, he beat, he smashed. Flesh tore. Bones crunched. Brains splattered. But flesh and bones and brains were gathered back at once and Jem was staggering, convulsing in agony as Toth's powers seared him. Again and again a hand grasped, tearing away the Crystal of Theron; again Jem snatched it back; again the flesh, the bones, the brains tore and crunched and splattered. And Jem saw himself as if from afar, then close, then far, lost in horror as he killed and killed and killed again.

Flash, flash. It was night, it was day, it was filth, it was splendour; it was garden, beach, chamber. Then, all at once: Toth, Sea Ouabin, Mala, Alam, Scurvy, Barnabas slashing swords in a dazzling arc and Jem, Captain Porlo and Selinda falling, crying out, and in a sickening rush the separate scenes swooping together – then, as if there could be nothing else in the world, the monstrous rising figure of the Triurge! Realities collapsed like houses of cards and everything surged into the reeking, rotting immensity . . . *No, it could not be!*

Selinda spun through the air, limbs waving. In an instant the Triurge would absorb her, completing the Swallowing Marriage at last . . . But then Jem, spinning in his turn, saw Rainbow keening beside him, pawing, clawing – then the radiant light seared from his collar, mingling with the light from the Crystal of Theron, enveloping them, transforming them, as the figures of Barnabas, Scurvy and Toth, of the Sea Ouabin and Mala and Alam careered towards them through the devastation . . . *No, it could not be!*

The cry, the negation burst from Jem's lips and all at once he had seized the Sea Ouabin, flinging the incredulous creature, shrieking, into the all-consuming vastness of the Triurge.

Silence.

Jem tumbled through space, through time. Why had there been no mighty explosion? The Sea Ouabin should have made the Triurge too unstable, destroying it at last. How could it still exist? Somewhere, far away, like a fragment of a dream, Jem saw the blue raven, swooping and darting. Should not the bird have been transformed, blasted back by magic into Maius Eneo?

Silence, silence.

Faces, then bodies in all manner of guises flickered and drifted around him in the air. There was Lemyu, there was Leki, there was Saxis ... Glond, Littler ... Now Jem saw Selinda, Captain Porlo and the raven too, billowing like leaves in an uprushing flame. He called to them, but they could not hear; reached for them, but they could not feel. Then the distance between them grew. Aeons passed, or instants. Up, up they floated like spirits of the dead towards the god-like, terrible majesty of the Triurge.

But where was Rainbow? Jem looked down – or up, perhaps, or to the side, but somehow it seemed that the dog was still below. And before Jem could wonder how that could be, Rainbow's collar shone brighter than ever before, with an agonising, annihilating incandescence – and then, as the last of garden, sand or chamber vanished into the sucking maw of the Triurge, the brightly coloured dog leapt impossibly high, diving into the monster's very heart.

Later, Jem would remember that leap as one of the most beautiful things he had ever seen – and one of the saddest too, as Rainbow, blazing with all the colours of the Orokon, sacrificed himself to save his friends.

And one friend in particular.

Flash. The whiteness came again, and Jem was falling.

To the cove, to the rocks.

To the garden, to the hedges.

To the chamber, to the dusty floor.

And in each place, spinning down beside him, jangling softly or clattering hard, came the dull-coloured, empty circle of Rainbow's magic collar.

Then he fell for a last time, to the deck of the *Catayane*.

It was morning, and the decks were a gruesome scene. Blood was everywhere. The sails were torn and the mizzenmast was down; the ship had run into a muddy bank. Many lay dead. Others were dazed, barely conscious.

But there was something else. This time, a small hand clutched Rainbow's collar.

Jem gasped.

The huddled figure turned gravely, meeting his gaze.

❋　❋　❋　❋

There was one other strange meeting that morning.

Through blurred eyes, as he held the shaking Littler, Jem became aware of others moving sluggishly on the bloodied decks. Of Ejard

443

Orange, piteously miaowing. Of Rajal and Tagan, moaning, sighing. Then there was the slumped figure of Selinda, her arm flung round the body of a stranger. Jem's brow furrowed; but of course, the stranger, a youth, was no stranger at all – and the blue raven was nowhere to be seen.

The girl stirred; the youth stirred; Jem, breathing deeply, watched them as if they were figures in a dream. Languorously, oblivious of the chaos all around her, Selinda rose up, eager to look upon the face of her lover.

She scrambled up. Stumbled back. Slumped down again, a hand to her mouth.

'No,' she whispered. 'No, it cannot be.'

Slowly Jem detached himself from Littler's embrace.

Oh yes, the youth was no stranger.

It was Ucheus.

Chapter 62

ALBATROSS

Oh say what tar, if tar he be, would languish on . . .
When on the sea adventure be . . .
What tar would turn away his . . . glory and . . .
When buccaneer meets . . .
　　O-oh, for glory and renown, they be waiting there for . . .
　　On the day old Faris . . .

'Old Faris Porlo' trailed off, coughing; the squeezebox wheezed into silence. The ballad, once so merry, had taken on an air both sad and sinister. In the captain's voice there was an edge of madness and the squeezebox had lost its tunefulness. Choked with salt, warped in the heat, it produced, like its player, only a broken howling.

Ra Fanana smiled distractedly. Patting the captain on the back, she urged him to drink a little more . . . more *rum*.

She had no choice. There was no fresh water.

'Hah,' the captain spluttered, rallying, 'that Ouabin didn't know what'd hit him, did he? Thought he'd get the better of old Faris Porlo? Hah! Didn't he remember he was taking on an Ejlander? Eh, Bollocks? Eh, Buby?'

Slumped against the mainmast, Buby snickered weakly; under a cannon carriage, Ejard Orange made no response at all. Besides, the big cat – who had, of late, grown somewhat smaller – was toying with a mess of blood and fur. No ratter he may have been, but in these last days he had learnt that it was rats or nothing. And what runts of rats! Had he been saved from skinning just for this?

Patches said quickly, 'The Ouabin didn't remember – why, he couldn't never have remembered you was an Ejlander, Cap'n!'

The captain's fist swung. 'Stupid boy, how could anyone forget I was an Ejlander?'

Patches rubbed his coppery curls. 'Cap'n, I only meant . . .'

'Hah,' blundered the old man, 'the dirty foreigner had old Faris Porlo wrong, didn't he? Thought he'd be helpless without old Lefty, didn't he? Hah! Thought me old rusty cutlass weren't up to much? Beat him back I did, till I had him at me mercy! Didn't I, Master Jem? Didn't I, Master Raj?'

Again it was Patches who rushed to fill the silence. 'You . . . you beat him back, Cap'n!'

Jem and Rajal glanced at each other, wearily, worriedly. Merry mealtimes on the *Catayane* had become a thing of the past. Some days earlier, unable any longer to endure the decks below, they had moved the captain's table up to the quarterdeck. For a time, with the wide white sea stretching all around them, with scraps of breeze rippling in the sails, they had been happier. For moments, they had even forgotten the sufferings they had endured, and were enduring, on the Salt Seas of Sardoc.

But now, if provisions were low, their spirits were lower. The sea was a sludge of wreckage and weeds and slithering, slimy things, glimmering evilly under a burnished, hazy sun. There was not even the hint of a breeze. Distantly an albatross flopped through the sky.

'Hah!' spat Captain Porlo. 'And what did I do then, eh, Ra Fa? Eh, Miss Selinda? Ran him through, didn't I, ran the dirty Ouabin through, and flung him in the sea! Ah, that Ouabin won't be back in a hurry, not when old Faris Porlo . . . not when old . . .'

'Really, my dears, this is unendurable!' cried Tagan, not for the first time. He might have been referring to the captain, to the heat, to the meagre rations, or to the unfortunate sanitary arrangements on the *Catayane*. Perhaps he meant the fact that a certain fellow traveller had barely acknowledged him since the Straits of Javander; perhaps he meant all these things, and more. The bedraggled eunuch sat cross-legged on the deck, a little away from the others. 'Well, won't someone *say* something?' he spat. 'Won't someone *else* speak?'

The captain's head crashed to the table. Ra Fanana winced. 'Tagan, don't be so impatient. Faris is getting us to the treasure, quick as he can – you'll see.'

The eunuch rolled his eyes. 'Fa Fa, you can't believe that.'

'The Cap'n's a hero,' said Patches, affronted.

Tagan, rising on cramped calves, sashayed stumblingly over the deck, a wrist flapping, not quite deliberately, almost as if it were broken. 'Oh, and shall we ascertain the views of the *crew*?' He bowed to the helmsman. 'Master Porpoise, do you think your captain a hero? What about you, Master Walrus . . . Master Sea-Snake? I say, where's Master Whale?'

This dubious foursome were, along with Patches, the only common tars remaining on the *Catayane*. Of the thirty or so who had begun the treasure hunt, all others had jumped ship, died of fever or been killed by the cannibals. Why the others didn't simply refuse to go on was a mystery to Tagan. Why did the helmsman stand at his post, as Captain Porlo had ordered him to do, when for days they had been almost wholly

446

becalmed? That the captain was a senile old fool was not so much a statement of opinion as a fact. How could he inspire such loyalty?

Porpoise studiedly ignored the eunuch. Whale was below, counting the stores. Walrus and Sea-Snake sat with the passengers, nibbling miserably at their meagre portions. By now, with numbers so depleted, old barriers between passengers and crew had fallen away. After the battle Jem and Ucheus had led the repair efforts; Rajal had heaved the anchor-chain; Ra Fanana had hauled the sails. Even the most delicate of hands had become calloused. Had not Littler scurried up the rigging? Had not Tagan plied his needle, protesting frequently at the coarseness of canvas? Selinda, dressed again in her boy's garb, had rolled barrels and swabbed decks, eager for any task, it seemed, to fill the void left by her loss. They were all in this together, as Jem would announce piously from time to time.

But were they?

Tagan said as much. 'There's no treasure, is there? Or if there is, it's not the sort we can just divide up so we'll all be rich. Or rather, we *won't* just divide it up. Come on, Master Jem. Come on, Master Raj. You know more than all of us, don't you? There's something going on, isn't there? I may have lost my manhood, but I haven't lost my brains.'

'Tagan, please!' cried Ra Fanana.

Rajal clutched his face in his hands; Jem was on his feet, wondering how to calm the eunuch. But it was Patches who intervened first. 'Why, you dirty arse-greaser—'

Tagan's mouth twisted. 'What's this? Been dreaming of me, have you, dearie? Or perhaps just *thinking*, while doing other things? In any case, it's sweet.' There was hysteria in the eunuch's voice. 'Isn't it sweet, everyone?' he demanded.

Patches lurched forward, as if to strike him; instead, the boy sprawled to the slimy deck. Tagan laughed; hot, shaming tears filled the boy's eyes. 'The Cap'n said we should never have let you on board,' he muttered, rubbing his knee. 'Not a dirty, arse-greasing, foreign eunuch. Should have made you walk the plank, we should.'

'Well, charming!' Tagan pouted. 'And is that your view these days, Fa Fa? Wish you'd never saved me in Shaba Lalia? You've changed so much, I wonder why you bothered!'

Ra Fanana said nothing. She looked down, shuddering.

Tagan's voice cracked. 'And *you*, my lady? What do you think?'

But Selinda, with Ucheus, was off to the side. What were they murmuring? Oh, it was maddening! Any sane girl would have hated the scrawny youth who had stolen her lover's rightful place. Instead Selinda, perverse as ever, had developed some brotherly fondness for the fellow,

447

and would speak with him interminably of Maius Eneo, eager for tales of her lover's youth.

Tagan reeled round. Littler, dangling his legs, sat on a barrel, clutching Rainbow's collar in his hands. Did he never let the thing go? Was everyone mad? Rainbow was only a dog, a stupid dog!

Starting forward, Tagan would have grabbed the collar, flinging it over the side.

Jem grabbed the eunuch's arm.

'Let me go, let me go—'

'I'll let you go when you behave yourself—'

'You prig! You little *prig*.'

'Tagan, you're drunk.'

'Of course I'm drunk! Aren't you? Though the way we're getting through that rotgut, I dare say it's a temporary problem. What's better, do you think? Drunkenness, or dying of thirst?' He broke from Jem's grip. Reeling to starboard, the eunuch hung over the ship's side, as if about to vomit. 'Look everyone, look at those slithery eels! Look how they glide over the sea's very surface!'

Jem's voice was dull. 'It's the salt. It's so thick.'

'Oh? Then why are we *sailing* though it?'

'You know why.'

'But then, we're *not* sailing, are we? Are we, boys? Hi ho, I'll be below if anyone wants me.'

Jem tried to restrain him. 'Tagan, it's boiling down there.'

'So? It's boiling up here. At least I'll be alone – well, unless any of you boys is up for it. In which case, you know where to find the dirty, arse-greasing eunuch. Usual rates apply, of course.'

Jem winced. 'Tagan, don't be disgusting.'

Tagan waved contemptuously at Captain Porlo. 'What, and it's *not* disgusting to indulge the illusions of that sick, crazy old man? Like you and Fa Fa and all the rest of ... oh, I can't stand this any more!'

The eunuch lurched over the side again, vomit spilling suddenly from his lips.

✻　　✻　　✻　　✻

The squeezebox sounded softly. The captain stirred.

'Tagan,' Jem said slowly, 'you don't understand. Yes, this is no ordinary treasure hunt, but ... I mean, any day now, we'll ...'

'Any day, any day ...' Tagan fell to the deck, sobbing. 'Don't you understand, don't you understand *anything*? Don't you *know* what I mean?'

But the eunuch himself barely knew what he meant.

448

'Tagan, please.' This time it was Rajal. Shame faced, he would have taken Tagan in his arms, there and then in front of them all.

Instead, at that moment, a shriek rent the air. Ejard Orange choked on his rat. Buby leapt up, scrambling into the rigging.

But it was only Captain Porlo, pulling back the squeezebox with a frantic jerk. Alive again, the old sea-dog called for more rum, thumped with his wooden leg, and split the air with another refrain of *The day old Faris Porlo met the Ouabin of the Sea.*

Tagan blocked his ears and rushed below.

Chapter 63

MIDNIGHT VOYAGE

WALRUS: I don't understand. Why are we waiting? Why have
  we waited so long?

WHALE: Too long. Lost our chance, haven't we?

WALRUS (*irritably*): What do you mean, lost our chance?

WHALE: Just what I say – here we are in the middle of nowhere,
  waiting for Porpy to make his move. And he hasn't, has he?
  Shaba Lalia, *that* was our last chance if you ask me. Too late
  now. We're doomed, doomed—

SEA-SNAKE: Eh? What is this, this *doom*?

WALRUS *ignores him*. That's not what I means, Whale. I means,
  why are we waiting for Porpy *now*? I means, where is he?
  On the bridge at midnight, he says, and here we are. It's
  past midnight, and where's he?

WHALE (*glumly*): Oh, he'll be here – got a tummy upset, that's
  all. Not that it matters. I tells you, we're doomed—

WALRUS: That's all we need, a leader with the shits! And you're
  no help, you big lump of lard—

SEA-SNAKE: Alas, the lard! From my kitchen, it is all gone—

WALRUS (*snapping*): Then cut open Whale, you stupid foreigner!
  By Agonis, it's as well you've got something between your
  legs, because what's between your ears is the size of a
  walnut!

SEA-SNAKE: Eh? Now he talks of walnuts?

Pause.

WHALE *sighs*: Some mutineers we've been. It's too late, I tells
  you, mates—

WALRUS: Lard-lump, and I tells you it's not! But one thing's for
  sure – we've got to make our move soon, or I'll burst worse
  than Porpy's stinking arsehole. I tells you, mates, I can't
  take much more of it. All equal now, are we? Have to be:
  and still they looks down on us! Still they treats us like dirt!
  How I hate them all – that senile old fool, that bum-
  greasing eunuch, that Vaga-scum—

WHALE: Forget the Vaga-scum, it's Master Jemmy that gets to

me. Jumped-up little bastard – who does he think he is, Prince of Ejland? I tells you, if we're all going to die, I'd like to smash his smug face in before we do – really have a bash at him!

WALRUS *grins.* Hah! I know which one *I'd* like a bash at.

WHALE *grins too.* You dirty beggar . . . no, she's mine!

WALRUS: Come off it, Whale, you couldn't even find it under all that fat. Right tiddler too, from what I've seen—

WHALE: Hold it, I'm warning you—

WALRUS: Hold it? No thanks! Look, you can have the nurse—

WHALE: Oh? And what about Sea-Snake, then?

WALRUS: The bum-greaser! Won't matter if he splits *that* open, will it?

SEA-SNAKE: Eh? What you say?

WHALE *laughs.* And Porpy?

WALRUS *laughs too.* Patches!

Enter PORPOISE, *unexpectedly.*

PORPOISE: What's that about me? And Patches?

WALRUS *and* WHALE: N-nothing, Porpy!

PORPOISE, *looks between them, scowling suspiciously.* Right, down to business, eh?

WHALE: Thought that's where you'd been.

PORPOISE: Enough of your lip. (Ooh, but me poor guts are fair churning! Another load on its way, you mark me words.) So, you want to know why we don't attack yet? Eh, Whale? Eh, Walrus? Very well, let me tell you—

WALRUS: Enough jawing, I'm sick of it! I say we gets them now.

WHALE: Me too – tonight. You're with us, Sea-Snake?

PORPOISE: What's this? What's this?

SEA-SNAKE *(slowly):* Me . . . too.

There is a silence; then all at once, the conspirators break into furious argument, and what they should do, and how they should do it, is no more decided than it was before. Urgently, guts churning, PORPOISE *manages to hush them, but the arguments continue in muted voices. Sinister moonlight glimmers around them; the slimy sea is still.*

   But wait. Is there a distant stirring in the air?

'Littler? Littler, are you all right?'

   The question, Jem knew, was a foolish one. Shuffling restlessly round the dark deck, he had passed the little boy several times, curled like a question mark on his crumpled bedding. Each time Jem had wondered if Littler were asleep; now he saw the thin shoulders shake and heard a muffled sob.

Jem knelt down. He reached out a hand and Littler turned suddenly, burying his face in Jem's shoulder. For long moments Jem held him, feeling the strength of his young friend's sobs. How Jem wanted to say that it would be all right, that everything would be all right!

But somehow he could not force out the words. Instead he murmured, reaching into his pocket for a rag, 'Blow your nose, hm? Don't want to get snot all over the Crystal of Theron, do we?'

Littler could not quite bring himself to smile. In his hand he still clutched Rainbow's collar; his bedding was Rainbow's old blanket, suffused deeply with a damp doggy smell, and stuck thickly with five-coloured fur. How could Littler ever forget his grief? How could he ever forget his guilt?

He snuffled noisily. The question he asked now was one he had wanted to ask for many days. 'Jem, you know when you find the crystal . . . I mean, the next one? Well, something magic will happen, won't it?'

'I . . . suppose so, Littler.'

'Something magic *always* happens when you find the crystals . . . doesn't it?'

Jem nodded, but uncertainly, fearing where these questions might be leading. In the Unang capital of Kal-Theron, in the moment before he had seized the red crystal, Toth's evil magic had wreaked devastation. When the Sanctum of the Flame had collapsed, the rain of rubble killed everyone within, including Cata, Rajal, Littler and Rainbow. But the unleashed power of the crystal made time run back; Kal-Theron had been restored, and so Jem's friends had returned to life.

Jem breathed deeply. 'It's true, the crystals release a power for good. But it's something different each time, Littler, and . . . well, it's not up to me. I can't *make* the crystals do anything. You . . . you know what I mean, don't you?'

'But . . . what about when we have *all* the crystals, what then? You'll have . . . you'll have the powers of a god, won't you, Jem?'

'I don't think so, Littler. We're trying to save the world from someone else who wants to be a god, aren't we? No, I don't think *I'll* be a god.'

Littler's lip trembled. 'You're saying I'll never see Rainbow again, aren't you?'

'Littler, I . . .'

Tears gathered again in Littler's eyes. 'He was my friend. Remember him when he was just a skinny old, shabby old brown mongrel? He was still my friend even then, my best friend, the only friend I had. And then when he turned magic, it was as if . . . as if I was magic too, and

452

everything changed, and everything was exciting, and . . . oh Jem, he has to come alive again, he has to! Jem, say he'll come alive again!'

Jem's heart thudded painfully, and he held Littler tight. 'Poor Littler, I can't say that, you know I can't.'

'I dream about him, Jem. Every time I go to sleep I dream about him. I see him barking and running and playing and . . . oh, I can't believe he's really dead. Not for good. Not for ever.' Littler's voice grew shrill. 'I keep his collar. See, I've still got his collar—'

'I see, Littler, I see—'

'And I'll *never* let it go—'

'No, Littler, I know you won't—'

'Because he'll need it when he comes back, won't he? After all, it's a magic collar, and . . . oh Jem, where is he now? Where can he be? What if the Triurge is still alive? What if he's in the Triurge, taking my place? I'm worried, Jem! He's lost his magic collar and . . .'

'Littler, shh – shh.'

The child calmed a little, but still his anguish could not be allayed. 'It's my fault,' he snuffled. 'You think it's my fault, don't you, Jem? You never wanted me on the quest, did you? You wanted me to stay behind in Kal-Theron. You wanted Rainbow to stay behind, too. Well, you were right. Rainbow would still be alive if I'd listened to you. I've been nothing but trouble all the way, getting lost and losing things and . . . oh, it's all my fault, everything's my fault!'

This time the sobs were harder, heavier. Tenderly, Jem smoothed the little boy's hair. Lost in his compassion, he did not yet feel the curious trembling that stirred the air, the strange intimation of something about to happen. 'Littler,' he murmured, 'I was wrong when I said you shouldn't have come. You're a brave boy and I'm very proud of you.'

'You . . . you are?'

'Of course I am. And you know something else, Littler? If there's one thing I've learnt on this quest, it's that everything happens for a reason – always. You came on this quest for a reason, Littler. And Rainbow saved you for a reason, too.'

'But . . . why did he have to *die*?'

'He died for us. He died for you. If it hadn't been for Rainbow, you wouldn't be here now, and the Triurge would have killed us all. The quest would have been over and Toth would have triumphed. But Rainbow saved us. He was a hero.' Jem swallowed hard. 'It's terrible, Littler, I know it's terrible. But you're right about one thing. We may never see him again, but Rainbow can't be dead, not really – I know he can't, because there's a place where he's alive right now.'

'Where . . . where's that, Jem?'

Jem touched his hand to Littler's forehead. 'In there, Littler. Oh, perhaps when you're older, you won't think about him every day, not like now. But do you think he'll ever go away? I don't think so, do you? Not Rainbow! Not a magic dog like Rainbow! He'll always be there, Littler, whenever you need him. Safe and sound. For good. For ever.'

'You promise, Jem?'

'I promise, Littler.'

'Selinda . . . Selinda . . .'

It is daring, no doubt, even disrespectful, to say the lady's name like this; it is familiar, far too familiar. But here in the forecastle, here in the moonlit stillness of the night, everything seems strangely disconnected. What has this to do with real life? Nothing. Only with a life of memory and desire, of memory of things that are real no more, of desire for things that can never be.

For too long, far too long, the girl and boy have gazed into each other's eyes. Days have passed, and together they have dreamed, then dreamed again, of the one that they have lost. Yes, had Ucheus been any ordinary boy, appearing suddenly in the place of her lover, Selinda would certainly have despised him, spurned him. But after all, he is a boy her lover loved; he loved her lover; locked behind his eyes is memory after memory of the one that she shall never see or hold again.

'Maius Eneo . . . Maius Eneo . . .'

Ucheus moans, lost in longing. Yes, he is ugly, awkward; yes, he is not desired for himself. But does he want to be? Does he care? How many times has he wished it had been he – *he*, and not Maius Eneo – who had died on that brittle, bright day in Hora! Could he change into his cousin now, he would. He would give up his life for Maius Eneo – but for now, and for Selinda, he knows he must pretend. He tells the girl he loves her; hotly he whispers the words in her ear; trembling, she draws him close, pretending, pretending . . .

Shuddering, they sink to the slimy deck. They sigh first with bliss, then their sighs turn to tears. They cling together, convulsing – and Patches, in the crows' nest, gazes down, devastated. Can this be a vision? A terrible dream? His own tears fill his eyes; he rocks, he shakes; and neither cabin boy nor lovers, if lovers they are, are aware of a different trembling, a different shuddering, a strange convulsing force that is coming ever closer, approaching them stealthily but rapidly through the darkness.

'Faris? Faris, are you all right?'

The old man had turned suddenly, not for the first time, moaning and gnashing his stumps of teeth. Ra Fanana leaned forward, dabbing his forehead with a damp cloth. How she longed for morning! Her chair was hard, the heat was intolerable and the air was foul. If only Faris would sleep on deck! He had moved out of his cabin before, hadn't he, when he had given it up for her? But now the old sea-dog just wouldn't budge.

'Can you hear me, Faris?'

His breathing had become stertorous again. Did he need a drink? If only there were water, fresh water! The nurse sighed, dabbing her own dripping forehead; then she dabbed at her eyes too. Her chair creaked. The casement rattled. Could the wind be rising at last? Pray that it were so!

Despair filled Ra Fanana's heart. That the captain would die soon, she had no doubt. Her dreams of his retirement had crumbled to dust. There was only this voyage, his last voyage, and she must love him now while she had the chance. She had steeled herself easily to his stench, his fleas, his lice. Must she not love them, because they were a part of Faris? Reverently, night after night, she would bathe the senile old man; she would clean the maggots from his stump; she would dress his sores. And when he slept, she would keep this vigil.

But he wasn't sleeping now, was he? 'Faris? Faris?'

There was no reply. Ra Fanana reached for his hand. Did she wonder why she loved him so? He was a coarse fellow, no doubt about it. But then, he was not the first man she had loved. There had been another, the first, who was anything but coarse – at least, in outward manner. But had not the coarseness resided in his heart? Ah, how she had loved him – loved him even long after he had given her up, compelling her to marry another man. In his position, he had told her, he could never take a mere slave-girl as his bride; but if she married this man he had found for her, she would have her freedom, and her future would be safe.

It was a cruel joke. Her husband had been coarse both within and without, and had sold her back into slavery once he had grown tired of her. Sometimes Ra Fanana would wonder which of these two men had brought her the greater sufferings – Vizier Hasem, or Eli Oli Ali?

The nurse would have plunged deeper into these memories, but just then the captain began to speak. His words chilled her, even in the suffocating heat.

'Ra Fa . . . Ra Fa, the time is drawing near.'

'The time? Faris, what can you mean?'

'Me dear, I think you knows what I means.'

The nurse trembled violently, but urged her beloved to go on. For a moment he was silent, and she feared he had drifted away. Then at last he began again, rising up on his elbows, moonlight gleaming in the whites of his eyes: 'See that chest in the corner, me dear? See me old sea-chest?'

455

'I . . . I see it, Faris.'

'Used to be old Cap'n Beezer's, that did . . . been with me all these long years . . . round and round the world, that there chest's been . . . for you know, me dear, the world really *is* round, like a ball, and don't let no ignorant landlubbers tell you otherwise . . .'

'I . . . I won't, Faris.'

The captain reached under his blanket. There was a sound of jingling. 'The key to me chest . . . it's on me belt, on me belt . . . Ah, me dear, I'm getting near me treasure now, I know it. Old Faris Porlo won't last much longer, and . . .'

'Don't say that, don't say that!' Ra Fanana burst out. The casement rattled again, violently this time, as if in counterpoint to her surging emotion. Ah, but the wind must indeed be rising! 'Dear Faris,' she moaned, 'you'll find your treasure, we'll sail back in glory, we'll . . .'

He shook his head. 'Ah me love, if only! I knows you has dreams of settling down . . . what woman don't, answer me that? But you must know by now, old Faris Porlo's never been a one for dry land. Just think, wouldn't his stump be aching something shocking without the swell of the decks underneath, rising and falling like he's used to? Oh, I may not have much in the way of legs, not as much as some, but what I got is *sea-legs* . . . No, you can't be planting *sea-legs* on dry land, me love . . .'

'I know, but . . . Faris, what do I care about dry land? I can sail with you, can't I? Think what adventures must still lie ahead, and . . . and . . .'

The old man only shook his head again. He slumped back, and the moon no longer gleamed in his eyes. 'Me dear, let me say just this. If anything should happen, soon-like, well . . . I just wants you to know there be a letter, a special letter, underneath old Beezer's jacket, down there in the bottom of me chest. Had this letter drawn up proper, I did, back in Ejland before I sets out on this voyage . . . Made a few changes since then, but . . . never mind. When I'm gone, you just get that letter out and . . . you won't forget, me dear?'

Tears streamed down Ra Fanana's face. She nodded blankly.

'You promise, Ra Fa?'

'I promise, Faris.'

❊   ❊   ❊   ❊

Rajal's candle wavered, fluttering and plopping in the humid darkness. Sweat rolled like a glaze down his skin. He had descended to the lower deck. Could the eunuch have come down so far? There was no sign of him above.

'Tagan, it's Raj. You're here, aren't you?'

Ballast shifted faintly underfoot. Hissings sounded through the windowless walls. Rajal cupped a hand round the flame, edging forward, cursing as he stumbled on a coil of rope. He peered at the sinister shapes of barrels, at crates and heaps of canvas, hunched like antagonists poised to strike. A rat flashed across his path and he leapt back, almost extinguishing the flame.

'Dearie me. Where's Ejard Orange when you need him?'

Rajal turned. The eunuch lolled against a small upended boat of the type known as a kayak – a remnant, no doubt, of one of the captain's long-ago voyages. *Twirl, twirl* went a paddle in his hand.

'Tagan, I . . . was worried about you.'

'Oh? Why should you be worried about *me*?'

Carefully Rajal set down his candle. He knelt stiffly, crossing his hands across his thighs. 'Tagan, you know why. You were so upset before, and . . .'

Twirl, twirl. 'Of course I'm upset. This voyage is doomed, isn't it? We're all going to die. It's all right for that old man, but we're young, aren't we? Things to do, places to go?'

'Like Vanic Island?'

Tagan smiled. 'Vanic's a dream.' He turned the paddle slowly now, this way and that. 'Everything's a dream, really. What does it matter? It all means nothing.'

'Don't say that. Here, look.' Rajal touched the bag he wore at his chest. 'It's the Crystal of Koros, see? It's magic. Jem found it, and I wear it, as avatar of my race and my god. Tagan, don't you realise this is the greatest sea-voyage there ever was? Jem's found three crystals so far, and he'll find the fourth, I know he will. We're bound for glory – we all are.'

Tagan looked down at the paddle, motionless now. 'Glory? What do I want with glory? I don't even want Vanic, not really. I just wish things were how they used to be. And what happens? Father turns into a monster, I'm dragged away to sea, my lady doesn't want me, Fa Fa doesn't want me, *you* don't want me, I'm dirty, I'm bedraggled, and I've got no paint.'

The twirling resumed, faster this time. For an instant, Rajal almost laughed. But only for an instant. He grabbed the paddle, flinging it aside.

Tagan turned his face to the wall. 'Go away. Just go away.'

Rajal bit his lip. He shifted closer, reaching for the eunuch's arm. 'Tagan, please. I'm sorry I've ignored you, it's just . . . oh, it was all too much for me, and . . .'

'Call that too much? The other night? Well, *she's* the little innocent, isn't she?'

'Not . . . completely.'

'Oh?' Tagan turned back, eyes flashing in the candlelight.

Rajal became aware of the pressure of his hand, resting too damply on the eunuch's forearm. Distantly he was aware of a trembling, a shuddering, a strange intimation of convulsions to come. A dark, mysterious whirling began in his brain; his hand ran marvellingly down Tagan's chest even as he said softly, 'But there's someone else – Tagan, there's someone else.'

'Someone like me?'

'Not like you, Tagan. Like . . . me.'

'I see. And that's what you prefer, is it?'

'*He*'s what I prefer. His name's Aron – Aron Throsh. Oh, I know I may never see him again, but . . .'

'But what?' There was weariness in the eunuch's voice. The ballast shifted again, no longer so faintly. 'Even if you *do* see him, it won't last. These things never do, you know, not with our kind. What is it, after all, that makes a man a man?'

'Tagan, you don't know him, you can't say—'

'He *is* a man, isn't he? A man – like you?'

By now, Rajal was uncertain what to say; but by now, the power of speech had left him. Dreamily he was aware of Tagan's long hand, guiding his own hand, and his fingers slipping lower, lower, beneath the moist toga. And now the other faint tremblings, the shudderings, the gathering convulsions he heard around him seemed merely the beat of his own blood in his ears, and the new rocking of the ship on the tide was just his body, rocking in the eunuch's arms. Horror and fascination, sorrow and astonishment mingled inside him. His fingers played across the girlish belly, then over the strange, scarred smoothness between the long thighs.

Then came the velvety, swallowing darkness. Rajal's heart thudded massively. The candle guttered; the rat scurried; then the darkness gathered him entire. All through what followed, Rajal was aware of the kayak's juddering canvas, and the hard prow of the little boat knocking, knocking against the tarred timbers of the old ship.

'No, it won't last,' Tagan whispered, hot against his ear, 'I know it won't last, not with one of *his* kind, unless you learn the ways to keep him . . . There are things that make a man a man and you must learn them, play upon them . . . Let me teach you, Raj, please let me teach you . . . Oh yes, I can tell that Aron's going to be a lucky boy . . . But what's this? Well, that *was* quick, wasn't it? Oh my darling, you've so much to learn . . . No, don't pull away, not yet . . . Let's start again, right from the beginning, hm? There's more where that came from, I know it . . .' Tears were running down Tagan's face. '*Much* more . . . Say there's more, Raj.'

Rajal gulped for air. He nodded.

'You promise, Raj?'

'I promise, Tagan.'

The arguments on the bridge – assisted by several jugs of rotgut – have raged for too long, often concerning themselves as much with the rape of the passengers as with the killing of the captain. But as the night is nearly over, so is the time for talking. In moments, startling new events will overtake the ship and all who are on board.
But first, the following:

PORPOISE: . . . Mates, mates! Come on, you sees me point, don't you? (Ooh, this load's getting lower all the time! I can't hold it much longer, I tells you.) Now come on, show a bit of sense. Who knows what risks there'll be, getting this here treasure? Let Master Jemmy and his little friends take them risks, eh? We makes our move when the treasure's safe on board!

WALRUS: Forget it! We'll have the map, won't we, **X** and all? How do we know they won't double-cross us? I says we kills the lot of them now, and be done with it!

WHALE: What about the girl? Not the lovely girl—

WALRUS: *I* bags the girl! Didn't I bags the girl?

WHALE: That's not fair, I want a bash at her, too—

PORPOISE: Mates, mates, we'll all have a bash at her, I promise! Right stuck-up bitch she is, eh? We all want to bring her down a peg or two, eh? (Ooh, this load!) But all in good time, eh?

WALRUS: All? You're not letting Sea-Snake loose on her, are you? What good will she be to the rest of us after that?

PORPOISE: What? She's no tight little first-timer, you can tell!

WHALE (*threateningly*): What do you mean, *tell*? She's a lovely girl! Pure, she is! Innocent-like—

PORPOISE: Come off it, you fat bastard! Can't you see it in her face, that knowing look? Not just a bitch, but a slut, too—

WHALE: Why, you dirty bugger, I'll get you for—

WALRUS: And I'll get you, too! I've had just about enough of you, Porpy! What sort of leader are you, anyway?

PORPOISE (*buttocks clenching tightly*): Mates . . . please! Look, we'll all have our share – I tells you, that little slut's got room enough for all – but when we've got the treasure, eh? (Ooh, this load's fair pushing, fit to burst!) Now, are we agreed?

Pause. PORPOISE, *red-faced, twists and contorts.*

459

WHALE *bursts out*: No, we're bloody well not! I says we gets
them, and gets them now!

WALRUS: I says too!

SEA-SNAKE (*nodding excitedly*): Me . . . too! Eh? Eh?

PORPOISE: You . . . bloody fools! (Oo-ooh, me load!) You bloody,
bloody—

WHALE: Who you calling fools? Walrus, Sea-Snake, you take out
them lads. Leave Porlo to me. I tells you, I's been his first
mate too long not to want to run the old bugger through
the guts! Cutlasses out, mates? Right: *cha-a-a-rge!*

PORPOISE *slumps, struggling with the fastenings of his breeches,
while* WHALE, WALRUS *and* SEA-SNAKE, *all caution forgotten,
clatter down the steps, pistols brandished, cutlasses flashing in the
rising sun. They whoop out their war-cries. But their triumph – for
already, they feel triumphant – is to last but for an instant.*

A screaming comes across the sky. SEA-SNAKE *reels round,
screaming in his turn.* WHALE *stumbles.* WALRUS *drops his cutlass.*
PORPOISE *fills his breeches in a stinking rush. In moments, the Blue
Storm has enveloped the horizon, bearing down upon the* Catayane.
*Suddenly the sky is a churning morass; the sea heaves and swirls.
Blue lightning flashes and the ship lurches, rocks.*

Now all is chaos; there are cries, more cries; now JEM *is there,
crystal glowing at his chest, now* LITTLER, *now* UCHEUS; *now*
CAPTAIN PORLO *struggles from below, but all are helpless, flung
hither and yon. Mighty waves crash across the rippling, bucking decks.
On and on goes the screaming, the roaring; the sea spins, the air
spins, and now the ship is spinning too, gathered up like a scrap of
driftwood into the violence of the Blue Storm. How swiftly it whirls
across the sea!*

In moments it has gone, gone as if it has never been.

And so has the ship.

Chapter 64

TO THE WILD SKY

The *Catayane* lurched and scudded round and round in the Blue Storm. Lightning fizzed and cracked up the rigging. Burning sails crashed to the decks. A cannon broke free from the ropes that lashed it down, skewing wildly this way and that. With one arm Jem clung to a mast; with the other, he clutched tightly to Littler. The crystal burned and burned at his chest. The air was a chaos of water, smoke and fire, fractured in the blinding auroral light. Everywhere, everything, was the Blue Storm, roaring with a violence that might tear the world apart.

And then, quite as suddenly as it had begun, the violence ceased. The *Catayane* bobbed into an area of calm, a billowing cloud of warm, sustaining air, suspended high inside the swirl of the storm. Jem's crystal faded and he staggered to his feet. He helped Littler. Gasping, coughing, they peered through the smouldering debris all around them, shuddering with relief as Selinda, then Ucheus, stumbled down from the upper decks. From below, green and shaken, emerged Rajal and Tagan. Crystal-light played around Rajal's chest, subsiding slowly.

'Now that's what I call a near miss,' said Ucheus.

'A *miss*?' said Rajal. 'That was a *miss*?'

'You're still alive, aren't you?'

'Them cobber-as!' slurred Captain Porlo, dazed, as a harried Ra Fanana pulled and pushed at him, retrieving his crutch, putting his wooden leg to rights. Buby peered fearfully from under a fallen sail. Porpoise looked down, gibbering, from the bridge.

Only Ejard Orange seemed unperturbed. Sitting amongst the devastation, the big cat coolly washed behind his ears.

Jem said grimly, 'We've lost Patches. Did you see him whizzing up into the storm, Littler?'

Captain Porlo hobbled forward. 'What's that about me little cabin boy?'

Jem bit his lip. 'He was in . . . in the crow's nest.'

'The . . . crow's nest?' The captain gazed up at the broken mainmast, then down again to the decks. He turned slowly, broken with horror. Ra Fanana stole an arm around him, but the old man waved her away. On and on whirled the Blue Storm, just beyond the oasis of calm. Far above them, looming immensely, was the rocky underside of the flying island.

461

'So who's next?' Rajal burst out. He clutched his hands to his head. 'Damn it! What can we do, just wait for this storm to kill us, one by one?'

'Not even one by one,' said Jem. 'There were four of us who went then. What about Sea-Snake . . . Walrus . . . Whale?'

'They're gone?' said Ucheus. '*All* of them?'

'There's only one thing for it.' Jem screwed up his eyes. Grimly he gazed into the Blue Storm, then up towards the flying island. 'Somehow we've got to get up there.'

'Jem,' said Rajal, 'what are you talking about?'

Jem might have been talking to himself. 'There're the longboats,' he mused, 'but they're too heavy.'

Rajal's heart pounded with fear. Could this mean what it *sounded* like it meant? He breathed, almost in spite of himself, 'There's . . . there's a kayak.'

'What's that, Raj?'

Rajal gulped, 'There's a kayak – down in the hold. But Jem, you can't be serious – it's . . . it's suicide.'

'Raj, what's he talking about?' Tagan looked worriedly between Jem and Rajal. He would have clutched Rajal's arm, but already Rajal had stumbled closer to Jem, and Jem was speaking swift and low, almost muttering, into Rajal's ear.

'Suicide? And what's this, Raj? You said it yourself. Are we just going to wait here to die? We've been lucky. We've had a reprieve. But how long will it be until we judder into the winds again, or plunge down through the eye of the storm? This pocket of air can't sustain us. And what happens when the island lands? No Raj, it's my plan or nothing.'

Ucheus came forward. 'Plan? What plan?'

'There's a kayak,' Rajal said flatly. 'And Jem wants to get up to the flying island.'

Selinda cried out, 'You can't be serious!'

Tagan slumped down, stricken; Ucheus was aghast. Jem ignored them. Drawing Rajal aside, he pointed upwards. Through the auroral blue, the rocky underside of the island spun and spun like a great wheel. 'Raj, I saw Patches – Patches, and the others – vanishing into the storm. The currents took them upwards – up there.'

'What, so they were smashed against those rocks?'

'Perhaps they made it to the island. Hm? What's that? A big perhaps? Oh yes. But we know the Crystal of Javander's up there, don't we?'

'I . . . I suppose so.'

'And we've got crystals *too*, haven't we?'

'I . . . I suppose so.'

Jem grabbed Rajal by the shoulders, shaking him. 'Raj, pull yourself together! Didn't your crystal glow like fire when the storm took us? It did, didn't it? What is this magic, what can it be, but the power of the crystals, crying for their partner?'

'Don't they glow when Toth's around, too?'

For a moment Jem was silent. Littler looked up at him, wide-eyed.

'Raj,' said Jem, 'listen to me. With the crystals – if we focus their power – I'm sure we can make it up to the island. The storm will whirl us up, then the blue crystal, it'll . . . it'll draw us in, you and me. Oh, don't look like that! Don't you see, we've got to try it? If we don't get the blue crystal and get control of that flying rock, what chance have we got of saving the others? Without us, they're doomed.'

Rajal nodded. Slowly he looked at the faces around him, at Selinda, at Ra Fanana, at the stricken Captain Porlo. Tagan's eyes brimmed with tears; the eunuch hid his face. Littler bent down, gathering Ejard Orange into his arms. Just beyond their bows, the storm seemed stronger, wilder. At any moment they might sheer again into the violent, whirling winds.

Rajal gulped and turned back to Jem.

'You're right. We've got to try it.'

'You can't do this. It's madness.'

Preparations were almost complete. They had taken the kayak up to the bridge, loading it on to an empty gun carriage. For now, the *Catayane* bobbed in the calm zone at a steady rate, dipping dangerously every so often towards the wild whirlings of the storm. Launching the kayak would be simple. A matter of timing, that was all – then paddling hard. Jem and Rajal eyed each other gravely, tunics tightly buttoned at the neck and wrists.

'I said,' came the voice again, 'you can't do this.'

Jem turned, paddle in hand. 'Uchy, what are you talking about?'

'I mean, you can't do this without *me*. There's room in there, isn't there – *and* a third paddle?'

Selinda, hearing his words, exhaled slowly. But the girl made no protest. There in the sweltering tropic heat, her heart was cold inside her. The night before, Ucheus had become her lost lover, as if somehow, strangely, the dead youth and the living one had exchanged places. Now, already, Ucheus seemed far away. It was as if she had never known him, and could only wonder at the strange intimacy that had grown between them, then flourished, then cracked away like a shell. So, he would go: so, he would leave. While Jem protested, while Rajal argued, Selinda knew at once that she had lost him. She turned away, gazing into the dazzling blue light.

'We've got the crystals,' Jem was saying. 'They'll protect me. They'll protect Raj. But Uchy, what about you?'

463

'And what about *you*,' he said, 'when you get where you're going? Have you forgotten, that's Inorchis?' He looked up at the flying island. 'It's my home. I know it. You're going to need me.'

'Jem,' said Rajal, 'he could be right.'

Anguish flashed in Jem's eyes. 'Uchy, you've been a good friend to us. I don't want to risk your life.'

Ucheus smiled. 'I'm risking it now. I'll risk it some more.'

The reply was a paddle, thrust into his hands.

There was no time to lose. They said their goodbyes, but no one had much heart for it, neither the three adventurers, nor those who would stay behind. Hurriedly Jem clambered into the front of the kayak, Rajal into the middle, Ucheus into the back. Tagan, Selinda and Ra Fanana clustered round, sombre-faced, ready to push when the time came. The captain could only look on, bewildered. The old man's mind was wandering; from time to time, he would mutter about the cobber-as.

And somewhere in the background – sinister, stinking in his beshitted breeches – was Porpoise. Buby clung to the remnants of the rigging; Littler still held Ejard Orange in his arms. When Ucheus climbed into the kayak, the little boy swallowed hard. Hadn't he wanted to go too? Hadn't Jem dismissed him, almost impatiently? And only last night, Jem had called him a brave boy! Littler sniffed loudly, angrily.

'The *Cata*'s going to dip again soon,' Jem called. 'Almost time . . . almost. When I say *push* . . . you'll all push, right?'

The blue violence of the storm edged closer. The debris on the decks began to rustle and shake.

Almost . . . but not yet.

'This isn't the end, I swear it,' Jem called, louder now. 'Just hang on, we'll be back.'

Rajal caught Tagan's eye. Quickly the eunuch turned his head. The captain drooled, swaying precariously on his crutch.

'Back with the treasure, I swear it!' Jem cried.

'Treasure, treasure?' Porpoise loomed forward, reeking.

Jem again: 'You're ready, aren't you? All ready?'

Almost. Almost. Blue lightning cracked and fizzed. Buby leapt, shrieking, on to the captain's shoulder; Ejard Orange struggled in Littler's arms. By now, every timber of the old ship shuddered.

Then the hull lurched.

Jem: '*Now! Push, push!*'

Devoid of thought, Tagan, Selinda and Ra Fanana strained, heaved, hauled. The gun carriage trundled, then skewed across the deck and the kayak shot forward wildly, rocketing into the whirling blue.

Suddenly, Captain Porlo came alive. 'Be careful, me lovelies!' he bellowed. 'There'll be cobber-as on that there island, mark me words!'

But the old man's voice was borne away on the storm.

The first buffetings were so violent that Rajal was sure they were about to die. They paddled desperately. There were screams from below. The kayak bucked and skewed, then lurched, veered, almost crashing back, flightless, to the deck. They hovered, spinning, half in and out of the surging vortex.

Selinda covered her face; Tagan dropped to his knees, praying; Ra Fanana cried out, clutching her throat.

In an instant, there was a flurry of action. Porpoise lurched forward, shrieking insanely about treasure, treasure, they wouldn't take his treasure. He leapt up, clutching at the spinning kayak's bow. The kayak knocked him back. He crashed into Littler, then into the captain. He cursed; he would have gone for the captain's throat, but all at once – as if, magically, he were a much younger man – the cutlass flashed in the captain's hand. The mutineer tumbled over the side of the bridge, falling lifeless to the deck below.

In the same instant, Ejard Orange burst like a demon from Littler's arms. He landed in the kayak. Littler screamed. But this was his chance.

The kayak dipped. Littler leapt.

It was the push they needed. With Littler hanging on by his fingertips, the tiny vessel surged into the fullness of the storm, spun like a top, then vanished up, up into the blue fluorescence of the sky.

'Fool, Littler! Fool, fool!'

Like a whiplash, Jem flung back the words.

Rajal moaned, 'We should have tied him down! Thrown him in the brig! Chopped off his legs!'

'He'll get us killed!' Ucheus burst out.

'He's nearly killed us already!' cried Rajal.

Littler twisted back his head. 'I didn't! I set us going! You know I did!'

'We nearly overturned, bundling you in!'

'Fool! Stupid little fool!' Jem flung again.

Littler didn't care. He clung to Jem's back, whooping and laughing, bouncing in excitement as the kayak surged and bucked. Let them say what they liked! He'd had to come, hadn't he, jumping into the kayak as he had jumped on the magic carpet, back in Unang Lia? Yes, it looked touch and go for a while. For a while, both times, it had looked impossible, and Littler had thought he would be left behind. Good old Rainbow had saved the day before; Ejard Orange had saved it now.

The big cat curled in the bottom of the kayak, strong claws lodged firmly in the canvas. All around, the storm roared and howled. They crashed. They cascaded. They pitched and tossed. Wind and rain lashed their faces.

Jem paddled desperately. 'We're climbing! We're climbing!'

Lightning flashed and sizzled. Debris rushed past them, whizzing in the wind. Wilder and wilder raged the storm; all the world was a cataclysm of blue.

Jem shouted, 'Keep paddling, everyone!'

'We're paddling, we're paddling!' Rajal cried.

Under his tunic, the crystal pulsed, ached, throbbed. Jem's crystal burned. They gasped with pain.

Up, up went the tiny kayak. Closer, closer loomed the flying island, rocky, immense, implacable in the violence of the stormlight.

Lightning smashed across their bows.

Littler ducked. Rajal shrieked. Ucheus shut his eyes.

It was a close call. The kayak veered. Zigzagged. Shuddered. For a terrifying moment they were plunging, crashing on a downward current – then the updraught caught them again and they swooped up, up through the dizzying vortex.

'Whew!' said Ucheus.

'A close call!' said Rajal.

Littler wailed, 'I'm going to be sick!'

'Not down my neck, you're not!' said Jem.

Littler swallowed the vomit. Suddenly he was wondering if he had really wanted to come. He crouched, shuddering, behind Jem's back, squashing the protesting Ejard Orange as the kayak rushed ever closer to the spinning underside of the island. In his pocket, jabbing into his ribs, was Rainbow's collar.

Poor Rainbow. Poor Ejard Orange. Poor me.

'We're crashing,' Littler gibbered, 'we're crashing!'

'He's right!' said Ucheus. 'We're going to—'

But no: for all the time the crystals were burning, searing through Jem's tunic and Rajal's, too; now their light came bursting on the air around them, the pulsing rays of purple and red clashing and colliding with the eddying blue.

'Paddle,' cried Jem, 'just paddle harder!'

The crystals burned; the storm lashed; the kayak whirled. Above them, filling the sky, was an immensity of rock, jagged, whizzing and razor-sharp.

'Veer,' Jem muttered, 'please, let us veer!'

'Koros of the Rock, look upon your child!'

'Thunderer, Thunderer, lend us your spirit!'

Burning, lashing, whirling. *Burn. Lash. Whirl.*

Littler shrieked, 'It's no good!'

466

He clutched at Rainbow's collar, clutched it hard. Then all at once, in what might have been the moment of death, came a surge more powerful than any before; all at once the kayak veered to the side, skidded, ripped on rocks, then rushed up and up round the side of the island, gushing and spurting through a kaleidoscope of air – then spinning, spinning through a sudden calm.

❊   ❊   ❊   ❊

Slowly the kayak righted itself; the crystals faded, cooled. Bright purple became dark. Bright red became dull.

Littler was green. 'Sorry, Jem. Couldn't hold it this time.'

'So I see,' Jem muttered. 'Or rather, *feel*.' Disgusted, he brushed his neck. He flicked his hand over the side.

Rajal said, 'So that's Inorchis.'

Ucheus said, 'It looks just the same.'

'You've seen it from the air before?' said Jem.

'No,' said Ucheus, 'but I mean it looks so *calm*.'

'Anything's calm,' said Jem, 'from this high.'

'Oh?' said Rajal. 'I don't like the look of that volcano.'

They billowed softly on the warm air, orbiting the island that lay below. Indeed, but for the dazzling blue of the sky, lapping round the shore where the sea should have been, this might have been any ordinary inhabited Isle of Wenaya, with its neat hill-farms and winding roads and white box-like houses, staggering down towards the bowl of the bay.

But Rajal was right. The volcano was ominous. Dark wisps of smoke drifted towards them.

'Do you see Sarom?' Ucheus was saying.

'The big place on the hill?' said Jem. 'It's more impressive than the one on Xaro.'

'That's the *real* Sarom.'

'Seat of your government?'

'Palace of the Dynasts – well, it was.'

'Jem,' said Littler, 'do you feel something?'

'Yes,' said Jem, 'trickling down my spine.' He turned to the little boy, narrowing his eyes. 'You couldn't reach under my tunic, could you? Sort of pull it out at the back? And I don't suppose you have a handkerchief?'

Littler sniffed. 'That's not what I meant.' Ejard Orange was looking down intently, paws gripping the kayak's side. Round and round the island turned, the town giving way to fields, then forests. The big cat began to miaow. Littler said, 'Jem, I think we're sinking.'

'He's right,' said Ucheus. 'We're going down.'

The kayak dipped, then plunged, scudding over the moving island.

'Damn,' said Rajal, 'why aren't our crystals helping now?'

'Now there's gratitude,' said Jem. 'Haven't they done enough?'

'If we're going to die *now*, then no. Hang on, everyone!'

The volcano loomed near. Smoke, black and choking, filled the air around them.

'Say, haven't we done this *before*?' said Littler.

'It does seem strangely familiar,' said Jem.

'This is it!' said Ucheus. 'Goodbye, my friends!'

They plunged through the choking, sulphurous smoke; then, as if their strange adventure were indeed repeating itself, starting again from the very beginning, the kayak emerged on the other side, hovered and bumped over jungle trees – then tore apart as a cannon-ball came whizzing through the air.

They plummeted to the ground.

END OF PART FOUR

PART FIVE

The Briny Citadel

Chapter 65

RETURN OF THE NATIVE

SCENE: *a brilliant, golden beach. The sunny sky is azure-blue. Surf froths gently, steadily against the sand. Behind the beach is the jungle of emerald green; tall, curving palms hang heavy with coconuts. Enter* WHALE *and* SEA-SNAKE, *looking round with delighted curiosity. Some distance behind comes* WALRUS, *pistol in hand, dragging a querulous* PATCHES.

WHALE: I say, this is the life!

SEA-SNAKE: Eh, what? What life?

WHALE: Use your eyes, you foreign fool! Sun, sand, coconuts, mangoes. Didn't I see a few goats back there, straying through the trees? Didn't I see a fat, juicy pig? (*Placatingly:*) Don't worry, Sea-Snake, in a few days you'll have a new kitchen – think what delights you can cook up then! Why, we'll live like four Robander Selsoes, lords and masters of our own domain!

WALRUS (*grinning*): Four? Don't you mean *three*?

PATCHES: Fools, don't you know where we are? Don't you remember whizzing up on the storm? This island's magic! This is a trick, it has to be!

SEA-SNAKE: Eh, what does Patchy-pants say?

WALRUS: Nonsense, that's what! Shut your noise, brat – there's no Porlo here to protect you. I tell you, we'll need a servant if we're going to live like kings, and guess who we've chosen, eh?

PATCHES: Dirty traitor! Mutineer! I'll never be your slave, I'll—

WALRUS *strikes him with the butt of his pistol.* Shut your noise!

WHALE *yawns, oblivious.* You know, mates, I think there's only one thing missing—

WALRUS: You mean Porpy? Old shit-pants? Who cares?

WHALE: Bugger Porpy, I meant something else. Just as well we got them goats, is all I can say ... But wait – what's this?

Stealing forward like phantoms from the jungle come five dark-skinned maidens dressed in grass skirts – and nothing else. Their eyes flash;

*between their teeth they hold hibiscus flowers; their breasts bob
enticingly as they dance. Enthralled, the mutineers leer and lunge. The
girls pirouette teasingly out of range; then, as suddenly as they have
come, they are gone.*

WALRUS: I knew this was paradise!

WHALE: It is, it really is!

PATCHES: Fools! Can't you see this is some sort of dream? We're
all in terrible danger, I know it!

WALRUS (*lost in reverie*): Think of the concubines we'll have!
Why, we'll breed up our own race – a race of slaves!
They'll build palaces, one for each of us—

WHALE (*worried*): What about Sea-Snake? He's not having them
girls first, is he? He's not *splitting* them, is he? I say we gets
first bash, eh Walrus? Sea-Snake goes last!

SEA-SNAKE (*angering*): Eh? What you say?

*From his belt, the foreigner produces a large and menacing kitchen-
knife.* WHALE *grabs his cutlass. The two men circle each other,
cursing and muttering.* PATCHES *clutches his head in his hands;
disaster seems imminent. But* WALRUS *shoots his pistol in the air,
stopping the fight before it has begun.*

WALRUS: Mates, mates, there's enough to go round!

WHALE (*wagging a finger, muttering*): He'll *split* 'em all, I tell you,
before we've had a go! Met his type before, I have . . .

WALRUS (*suddenly*): Look, mates, look!

*At once, the altercation is forgotten. Before them on the sand,
gleaming in the sunlight, lie pick-axe and shovel, crossed in the shape
of the letter* **X**.
    Can it be?
    At once, the mutineers think only of the treasure.

Ucheus stirred at last.

After he had dragged himself from the stream, the slender youth had
lain, unmoving, on the reedy, muddy bank. The fall had left him dazed.
Barely did he recall tumbling and twirling through the bright smoky air,
or the exhilarating, terrifying blur of fields and tangled trees rushing up
towards him. To crash between the branches of draping willows, into the
glittering, familiar stream – *crash, splash*, like a human missile – seemed
something that had happened long ago, to someone else.

He staggered upright. He looked around him, tugging at his muddy
toga. Bright sunlight shafted through the willows and the stream rippled

and burbled, dancing with light. From the beginning he felt no mystery, no madness, but a deep, abiding calm, as if all the urgency of his mission had been lost. Where were his companions? Oh, he wondered; but more, much more, came the sense that he was home. Between his fingers, he crumbled wet earth. *Home. Inorchis.* Under his feet the ground trembled faintly, pulsing with the Thunderer's comforting deep warmth.

He plunged back into the rippling water, rinsing away the mud; then, slick and sparkling, he set off through the trees, his heart brimming with a strange confidence. Perhaps it was foreknowledge. But of what?

Marvelling, he wandered through a rustling orchard. Didn't he recognise these twisted, hardy trees? Didn't he know every branch, and love them too? His mind filled with memories of the boys who had swung, whooping and laughing, through these green, enchanted caverns. Might they not almost be here still, ghostly presences, peeping from behind the next trunk, or the next? He reached up, plucking a rich, red apple. Juice ran down his chin and he let it run, exulting in its sticky pungency.

He moved faster, taking long strides. The orchard and its cool caverns gave way to stony fields, yellow with tough mountain grass. Dazzlingly the sun scudded through the sky; sweat was streaming down his face, but still his step was steady and he began to smile. He would be running soon, he knew.

He shielded his eyes, gazing with gathering excitement as the familiar prickly hedges, the hayricks, the crumbling walls came into sight, stark against the pale rocks that rose steeply behind. Oh yes, Ucheus would be running soon. He paused, breathing deeply, staring up at a particular, jutting outcrop – Dead Man's Lookout.

Now he did run. He saw the slave-huts and the curing sheds and the big tumbledown barn; he saw the farmhouse with its wide verandah, sprawled and sleepy in the tropical heat.

Over cracking roughcast walls, under gnarled mountain branches, Ucheus hurtled, clutching at his side. At last he sagged, breathless, in a dusty yard. Cabbage-scraps lay around, and straw and bits of timber. Flies buzzed. A donkey blinked, swishing its tail. Ebony slaves slept, propped against walls, wide straw hats covering their faces.

Ucheus lurched forward. One slave, a little girl, stood in his path, dark-eyed and intent. Curiously he gazed at her straggly hair, her ragged shift, her bare feet. Castor-uncle's slaves were usually neater. Something about the child unnerved him; he swallowed hard. For a moment he imagined the child would speak, and he waited, as if her words might be important.

The little girl sniffed and skipped away.

The verandah was deep in shadow. Next to the door was a wheel from a cart. There was a coil of rope; there was a barrel, a box. A golden spray of bananas flared out, catching in a shimmer of sun. Ucheus felt tears pressing behind his eyes. Wildly, just for a moment, it seemed to him that all was as before, and a loved familiar figure would step out to greet him, white teeth flashing in a brown, angular face.

Had this been a dream, that might indeed have happened. But this was no dream; there was no Maius Eneo – but another figure, loved just a little less, was there. Drawing in a long, slow breath, Ucheus moved reverently towards the hunched old man, deep in the shadows in a wicker chair. The old man was sleeping; like a postulant, the youth knelt. Trembling, he touched the withered hand.

No dream, but no nightmare either. In a nightmare, the hand would have been cold; instead, the hand twitched, and breath quickened under the old man's robes. His eyelids slowly opened; his heavy head rose.

'Ucheus, you've come back to us,' said Castor-uncle kindly.

'Jem?' said Rajal.

'Rajal?' said Jem.

Rajal was tangled in a web of vines. Jem peered out from a thick clump of ferns. Green shadows pressed all around them, dancing here and there with the dapplings of the sun.

'How,' said Rajal, 'can the jungle be so thick?'

'Where,' said Jem, 'can this jungle be?'

'It's Inorchis. You've forgotten already?'

'We went all round Inorchis from the air,' said Jem. 'Remember? Houses. Roads. Farms. It's cultivated, Raj. This isn't.'

'Well, that's all right then.'

'What?'

'I thought you might have hit your head. In the fall.'

'I hit my elbow, actually.'

The jungle hissed and steamed. Nearby, a scrap of canvas smouldered, caught on a branch. Jem, rubbing his elbow, staggered up from the rasping ferns. He turned slowly, peering through the undergrowth. Puzzled, frowning, he gazed at Rajal.

All at once, their cries rang out.

'Littler! Uchy! Ejard Orange!'

'Ejard Orange! Uchy! Littler!'

The cries vanished into the thick jungle.

'We've got to find them,' Jem said grimly.

Rajal said, 'This can't be happening.'

Jem pushed ahead, parting leaves and vines. 'Haven't you learnt by now,' he said, 'that *anything* can happen?'

Rajal thought back to the events of last night. 'I have, actually. But this is different.'

'*Actually*, it's the same. Isn't it? Everything, just like before?'

'Not quite,' said Rajal. 'Last time, you were in the vines and I was in the ferns – if I remember correctly.'

'Near enough.' Jem turned back, a little annoyed. 'Raj, are you just going to *hang* there all day?'

Rajal jerked at the vines. 'Well, I was hoping you could help me. I'm . . . sort of tangled.'

'Just pull, that's all I did.'

'I've pulled. I'm tangled, I really am.'

Jem rolled his eyes, trudging back to release his friend. But the vines indeed were tenacious, particularly one which had somehow become entwined round one of Rajal's legs.

'Really, Raj, only you could get yourself in this mess.'

'At least I'm here. Look at Littler. Look at Uchy.'

'I wish we could. Where can they be?'

Jem tugged and tore, cursing. The green shadows were deep, but he began to feel that the web of vines was shifting, changing under his hands. Alarm prickled, but at last, with a hearty wrench, Rajal was free. He staggered into Jem's arms. Jem staggered back and Rajal fell, crashing into the cushioning ferns. For just a little too long he lay there, steam rising around him, gossamer flies buzzing.

'Raj? Raj, come on!'

Rajal lurched up. Fearfully, he caught Jem's arm.

'What . . . what now?'

'See that flower? That red one?'

'Raj, we haven't time to look at flowers.'

'I don't want to *look* at them. But Jem, that one wasn't there before.'

'Last time we crashed in the jungle?'

'Not last time, this time – I mean, just now.'

'What, it's suddenly appeared?'

'Yes.' Rajal was earnest.

So was Jem. He grabbed his friend's arm, compelling him to follow. 'Raj, I don't know what's going on here, but I know one thing. We've got to find the others. I'm worried. They don't have crystals like us. What if they're hurt? They must be here somewhere.'

Jem cupped his hands round his mouth, calling out the names of their companions again.

He turned back. 'Raj, you're not shouting.'

'Jem, we've been shot down again, haven't we? Just like before? Well, whoever shot us down is probably looking for us, right now.' Rajal paused. He looked thoughtful. 'In fact, they might even have found us.'

'What's that?'

Rajal pointed. Standing before them, just as they had been on the Isle of Xaro – spears in hand, muddied, with matted hair – were Leki and Ojo.

'You're . . . dead,' Jem breathed.

Rajal wrenched at Jem's arm. 'Just *run*, hm?'

But Jem reached for the crystal under his tunic, hoping to feel it throb with heat. Defiance blazed in his eyes. 'Who are you? You're Creatures of Evil, aren't you? Puppets of Toth, aren't you? I tell you, Toth, you can't win!'

Leki lunged forward, Ojo too.

Jem blundered back.

'Quick, run, *run*!'

Jem needed no more convincing. They took flight, crashing through the undergrowth. At once, innumerable dazzling flowers appeared and disappeared in the greenery around them, whizzing past their eyes like shooting stars. Branches leapt up, slapping their faces; vines snaked out, urgently, to ensnare them.

Leki and Ojo were hot in pursuit.

Jem gasped, 'But this is *mad*!'

Rajal gasped, 'Just *run*!'

Stripy snakes dropped from the branches, hissing and coiling around their feet. A heavy human form, rotting, reeking, abuzz with flies, swung down before them like a pendulum.

Lemyu's corpse. They battered it aside.

'This can't be real,' cried Jem, 'it *can't*!'

'Who cares? That corpse felt real enough!'

On and on they ran. But their pursuers were gaining, whooping out war cries. Then the cries became anguished shrieks.

Jem reeled round.

He laughed abruptly. 'Everything's just like before,' he said, 'but all mixed up – Raj, look!'

Rajal had doubled over, clutching at his ribs. Then he laughed, too. Through a curtain of vines they saw the Leki-creature and the Ojo-creature too, swaying high above the jungle floor, captured in the mesh of a pendulous net.

'They've dropped their spears,' said Jem. 'Shall we get a little closer? I wonder if they'll talk.'

Still the jungle seethed around them with strange, evanescent life. Jem reached up, clutching the curtain of vines; but as he did so, the jungle darkened around them and the curtain became suddenly thicker, heavier, obscuring what lay beyond. Jem's arm grew heavy and he felt a throb of pain.

He gulped, 'I don't like the look of this.'

A sinister hissing filled the air. Rajal glanced around. 'Well, I don't like that family of snakes that's just appeared under those ferns. Part the curtain, Jem.'

Jem hesitated, then did so.

The jungle was gone. He stepped into a bright silvery light, then drew in his breath. Standing before him this time were neither Leki nor Ojo but a figure still more familiar, still more alarming.

That blond hair. That sunburned skin.

It was *himself*.

Chapter 66

LOOKING-GLASS LABYRINTH

SCENE: *an idyllic one – well, for some. Sun, sand, surf, and* WALRUS, WHALE *and* SEA-SNAKE, *reclining luxuriously, supping on peaches, mangoes, and the milk of coconuts – while a sweaty* PATCHES, *deep in a trench, face redder than his curly hair, labours with the shovel, heaping sand ever higher.*

WHALE: Hurry up, boy, hurry up! Haven't you hit the treasure yet? It'll be a chest, about – ah – *so* big . . .

PATCHES (*muttering*): Fools, fools! What would you do with treasure in a place like this?

WALRUS (*overhearing*): That there Robander Selsoe got rescued in the end, didn't he? Just think, mates – all the pleasures of this island to enjoy, then we'll go home and be rich, rich! Dig, boy, dig!

WHALE: Hm, I wouldn't mind a few of them pleasures right now! Where'd those dusky maidens get to, eh?

SEA-SNAKE: Eh, a maiden, that I should like!

WHALE *bridles.* What you say, foreigner? I knew it, Walrus, he'll *split* 'em all if we're not careful!

WALRUS: Mates, mates, no more of that! There's enough to go round, didn't I say?

Pause. Dig, Dig.

WHALE: But what about something else? Is there enough of *that*, that's what I want to know. Think of it, Walrus: you and me, we be Ejlanders, don't we? Ejlanders, and not dirty foreigners? Gives us certain rights, don't it – certain claims?

PATCHES (*breathless*): I be an Ejlander too, you know!

WALRUS: Shut up and dig, boy! No, you're right, Whale: we Ejlanders, we be the superior race, eh?

They pat their noses. They wink at each other. They glance towards the deepening trench.

PATCHES: Traitors, where does your treachery end?

SEA-SNAKE: Eh? Eh, what? Dirty Ejlanders, you think I'm a fool?

WALRUS: Steady on, matey, what you be talking about?

WHALE: Calm down, Sea-Snake, we didn't mean nothing!

SEA-SNAKE *leaps up, brandishing his kitchen-knife*. No! You think I not understand? You think you cheat me out of my share? I be as good as you, Ejlanders, I be—

A shot rings out. PATCHES *yelps as* SEA-SNAKE, *spurting blood, collapses into the trench he has dug.* WHALE *laughs;* WALRUS *grins, blowing smoke from the end of his pistol.*

WALRUS: You're right, Whale. He'd just have *split* 'em all, he would! Dirty foreigner!

❋　❋　❋　❋　❋

'No, young Ucheus, imagine not that regret fills my heart. Am I to pine for all that might have been, had I succeeded to the throne of Sarom? Am I to regret that it was Pareus Eneo, not I, who assumed the terrible mantle of Dynast-Elect? Why, had I been Pareus-cousin, consecrated to a Dynast's lot, what then would have been my life?'

The old man's eyes twinkled and he gave his own answer. 'Speak to me not of splendour, nor of luxury; were such things mine, so too would be the troubles, the treacheries that every day have beset Pareus Eneo. Was not tragedy enough for one man visited upon him, if we consider but the fate of his son Radenine? Yet what was that but *one*, just one of a hundred, nay, a thousand terrible trials? Better, much better, this Farside retreat, sequestered from care beneath the looking-place of the dead ... young Ucheus, would you not agree?'

Ucheus faltered, 'I ... my uncle, of course.'

The youth was puzzled, but already he was aware of the strangeness of the scene. Had he asked if his uncle regretted his lot? His question had been about Sarom, it was true, but its implication had been very different.

'Hah,' smiled Castor-uncle, 'I think our young friend is far away, for all that he may be with us in body. Hm, my wives? Hm, my seven daughters?'

Ucheus blushed. It was early afternoon. Sunlight spilt goldenly over the long, shabby hall where the family, slaves and all, had gathered round the rough table with its splintery benches. All looked as it had done long ago, but for the absence of Maius Eneo. Myriad faces turned to Ucheus, smiling. Happily, without ceremony, they sat before their rustic luncheon, a goat-and-turnip ragoût with boiled yams and rice. The slaves partook of the same meal, even sipping from the same wine.

'Hm, young Ucheus?' The twinkling came again in Castor-uncle's eyes.

'But perhaps our wine goes rapidly to your head? I dare say, through the course of your Manhood Trial, no such potation has passed your lips?'

By the wall, sitting apart from the others, Ucheus glimpsed the little girl from the yard, the child who had stared at him so intently. He clutched at his forehead, as if indeed the wine was too much for him. 'My uncle, I . . . indeed I have been far away, in body as in spirit. To return here, to this place beneath Dead Man's Lookout, is a benison I thought might never be visited upon me—'

'Indeed, young Ucheus, the Manhood Trial is hard—'

'But my uncle, have you, too, not gone from where you once were? Have things not happened to this isle of ours, things unimaginable in the days before I left? I asked you if you sorrowed for Sarom, for is it not caught in an alien grip? My uncle, my aunts, oh my sweet cousins, know you not that we are flying through the air?'

With a smile, Castor-uncle's eldest daughter rose from the table, clearing plates. His wives blinked amiably; a slave hummed; only Castor-uncle looked thoughtful, even troubled. He stroked his beard. 'Dear young Ucheus, I know what ails you. Convention says we are not to speak of it, but convention sometimes can be a fool, and I would defy it.'

For a moment Ucheus thought the old man understood. Hope quickened in the youth's face, but the hope was rapidly to fade again. He caught the gaze of the little slave-girl. Who was she? Why did she look at him like that?

These were Castor-uncle's forbidden musings:

'Think not that sorrow is absent from my heart, for all that this feast would seem to deny it; think not that knowledge is absent from my mind. Long ago, in the lost time of my youth, did I not submit, in my turn, to the harsh lessons of the Manhood Trial? Young Ucheus, you speak of Sarom in an alien grip, and alien might it seem, now that our beloved Maius Eneo can never take the place that all thought would be his, following the death of Radenine.

'Ah, for all I speak of the burdens of that office, would not my old heart have swollen with pride had my son succeeded to it? It is not to be; my son has not returned to us; but such are the things we must accept. Through all the seasons of your boyhood, young Ucheus, did you not think yourself the inferior of my son? Yet you have returned from the Trial, and he has not: of the boys in your orbit, it is you, and you alone, who is Dynast-candidate. But dear child – rather, dear young man – do you fear that we resent you? It is impossible; you are honourable and true, and I think of you as a second son, a son I never had.'

At any other time, hearing these words, Ucheus would certainly have collapsed in tears; now he barely listened, even juddering back his chair from the table. He crossed to the window, gazing out upon the familiar farmyard as Castor-uncle talked and talked obliviously. The old man's wives and daughters, slaves too, only smiled and blinked, unaware even of the sadness that lay behind their master's words. Only the little girl from the yard was as she should have been. She gazed levelly at Ucheus. His eyes were averted from hers; fear, nonetheless, crawled down his spine. Did he know why? Did he guess?

A goat moved, spindly-legged, across the yard. Ucheus heard it bleat, then the bleating died away. The creature fell to its knees; then to its side; then it was still. Only then did Ucheus consider how thin were the goat's flanks, how sharply the bones were sticking through. His gaze flickered here and there. On the big old ajana-tree by the well, the leaves were almost white – they were wilting, falling. The soil was strangely pale. In the prickly hedges and the fields beyond, in the crumbling stone walls and the hayricks and the barn, everywhere was the same creeping, insidious pallor.

Ucheus gazed up into the rapidly moving sky, into the swirling patterns of blue that neither Castor-uncle, nor any of his family, were able to see. So little time had passed since the youth had come back. Had the farm been like this when he first arrived? Did he see things more truly now? Or was life slipping so rapidly from all he knew and loved, leeched away by the Sisterhood of the Blue Storm?

He turned back to the family. For a moment, just for a moment, he saw them as corpses.

※　※　※　※　※

Jem said, 'I think I understand. I mean, I think I know what's making this happen ... But what to do, that's the trouble. These walls don't even *move* when you push them ...' He turned. 'Raj? You're still here – I mean, really?'

'Of course I'm here – where else would I be?'

'Lost in this maze, perhaps? Or just lost.'

'You really don't trust me, do you?'

'That's got nothing to do with it.'

For too long they had wandered through a labyrinth of looking-glasses. Overhead, the sun beat down; beneath their feet was sandy soil; but all around them, with no exit in sight, was corridor after corridor of silvery reflections.

Rajal's temper had frayed some time ago. He reached out, plucking at Jem's arm. After several attempts, he found the real arm. 'So you *don't*?' he pursued. 'Trust me, I mean? And who was it who saved you from Leki and Ojo? You would have got those spears through your guts, and then where would we be?'

'I told you, I was testing out the crystal,' Jem sighed, whether to Rajal or to one of his reflections, he was not quite sure. 'It should have glowed – I dare say it should be glowing *now.*'

'Then why didn't it? Or why doesn't it?'

'I can think of one reason.'

'What's that?'

'Toth!'

Rajal jumped. Jem's exclamation was not, as it happened, the answer to his friend's question, but referred to the fearsome image that now confronted them as they turned another corner of the maze. If they knew it was not real, still they were alarmed.

Whatever enchantment possessed this place, it was a devious one. At first they had seen only themselves, multiplied in endless array; now, flickering between the Jems, between the Rajals, came images that were not reflections, but pictures. Jem had seen Barnabas, Cata and Uncle Tor; Rajal had seen the Great Mother, Myla and the Harlequin of the Silver Masks.

They both saw Toth.

'Ugly customer, isn't he?'

'Just keep going . . . Look, he's gone again.'

'Jem, my nerves can't take much more of this.'

'They'd better – we've got a long way to go yet.'

'Oh? There might be a way out, just round the corner.'

'I mean till we've found the blue crystal. We're not leaving this isle till we've got it, you know.'

'Leaving? I don't think we've got much choice.'

'I suppose not. And you know what?'

'What?'

'It wasn't Toth.'

'Back there? It was! I've seen him too, you know.'

Jem turned again, patting the air for the real Rajal. He clutched his friend's shoulder. 'Raj, that's what I wanted to tell you. You know about the crystals not glowing? Why? Because it wasn't Toth. That Leki-being and that Ojo-being? *They* weren't Toth. Whatever evil was behind those two, whatever evil's behind these illusions now, *it's not Toth.*'

Rajal's exasperation could only grow. He wiped his brow. How hot it was in this maze, with the sun beating down so brightly overhead! 'Jem, you *didn't* hit your head in that fall, did you? Only . . . of *course* it's not Toth. It's the Sisterhood of the Blue Storm, isn't it?'

'Yes, and all the evil we've met so far has turned out to be Toth in disguise, hasn't it? Or urged on by him?'

'And now it's not. So?'

'So, quite a lot. It means we don't know what we're up against. Worse, it means we've got no defence. Our crystals protect us against Toth, or haven't you noticed? Right here, right now, they're just stones – lifeless stones.'

'I hadn't thought of it that way.'

'Raj, I think you should.'

'All right. Jem?' Images of Polty, then of Sultan Kaled, flared out from the walls. A moment earlier, Rajal had glimpsed the King and Queen of Swords. 'Do . . . do you think something awful's going to happen?'

'Sooner or later. Ugh!' Jem saw Goodman Waxwell.

'I mean *sooner*. Someone's trying to frighten us with these looking-glasses, right? I'll tell you what I think. I think these pictures are going to get more and more real, then more and more frightening – I mean, *really* frightening. Soon we won't be able to *tell* they're just pictures – we'll forget. And what then?'

'I suppose you're going to tell me,' said Jem.

'We'll scream. We'll go mad. We might even go for each other's throats. Oh, I know I'm warning you *now* – but it's no good because you won't be able to help yourself, not then. You'll be crazy. I'd guess your eyes will be popping out of your head, the cords will be straining in your neck, and you'll probably be foaming at the mouth. I suppose we might even kill each other in our insane frenzy – but I don't think we'll go *that* far.'

Jem was surprised. 'You don't say?'

'My guess is that we'll hear a woman's evil laughter echoing in the air, then one of the Sisters of the Blue Storm – several, actually – will step out from behind a panel of glass, gaze gloatingly upon our twisted, gibbering forms, then take us into captivity. We'll be flung into a dungeon. As for what happens *then*, well—'

'Raj, have you quite finished?'

'I'd just started.'

'Well, shut up anyway.'

'I'm just trying to help!'

Rajal might have said more, but he turned sharply, nervously. Could that be Littler he had just seen, flashing in the corner of his eye? Littler, and Ejard Orange too? But then, if that was Littler, might it not be the *real* Littler? And should he tell Jem?

Silvery sparkles danced in the glass, like stars flung off from the inferno of the sun. Jem groped at the walls. A sheer panel of glass blocked the way ahead. Glumly he gazed into his own face, Rajal's, and Lord Empster's too.

'Damn it. Dead end.'

Rajal pushed back his dripping hair. How parched were his lips! How light was his head!

'This is where it starts,' he moaned. 'We'll work our way back, round and round the corners, then just find another dead end, and then another, and then—'

'Raj, enough!' Jem leaned back against the obstructing panel. He sighed again; then his sigh became a startled cry.

The panel swung back. They stumbled from the maze.

Chapter 67

THE BLUE SKYSHIP

SCENE: *sun, sand, surf, but far from idyllic. A bloodied corpse lies under a palm tree, dragged roughly away from the trench where a breathless* PATCHES *still digs and digs. With a desperation they do not quite understand,* WHALE *and* WALRUS *urge on the boy, menacing him with cutlass and pistol.*

WHALE: Put your back into it, boy! Hurry, hurry!

WALRUS: We got to have that treasure, we got to!

PATCHES (*gasping*): You fools, I tell you, this is all a . . . a dream!

WHALE: Dream? Don't look like no dream to me, eh Walrus? There be treasure in that there trench, Porlo's treasure, and it's all ours! To think, we've beaten the old bastard to the punch! Dig, boy, dig!

PATCHES: There'll be nothing here . . . nothing, I tell you!

But just then, there is a loud clanging: the cabin boy's shovel, striking metal. Leaping into the trench, WALRUS *pushes the boy brutally aside.* WHALE, *too fat to follow, can only peer in excitedly as his cohort clears away the last of the sand, exposing the lineaments of an ancient chest.*

WHALE: Can you open it, matey? Can you open it?

WALRUS: No room, no room . . . Patches, help me lift it out, quick, quick!

WHALE *leaps up, with an energy that belies his blubbery mass.* I don't believe it, we're rich, rich!

PATCHES: Fools . . . fools!

WALRUS: Shut up and lift!

With much sweating and straining, WALRUS *and the reluctant* PATCHES *bring the chest to the surface.* WHALE *blunders forward. Seizing the pick-axe, he strikes the rusted lock. Impatiently,* WALRUS *goes for his pistol, shoulders* WHALE *aside and fires. The chest springs open.* WALRUS *and* WHALE *gather round, exclaiming, digging their hands into the gleaming contents.*

485

WHALE: Pieces of eight! Pieces of eight!

WALRUS: Gold and diamonds!

WHALE: Rubies – and silver plate!

WALRUS: We're rich, rich!

PATCHES: You fools, it's sand! It's just sand, can't you see?

It is no good. The conspirators are helpless, lost in illusion. Left to themselves, they would certainly soon argue, disputing how they might share out their useless bounty; perhaps they would kill each other. But the scene is cut short. A high-pitched humming fills the sky, gathering into a mighty roar. PATCHES *gazes up, then staggers back, astonished, as a mysterious flying vessel appears, gleaming and metallic, descending on the sand in a blaze of blue.*

Never in his life has PATCHES *seen anything like it. The vessel is not large – not much larger, perhaps, than one of the longboats on the* Catayane – *but ovoid in shape, entirely enclosed, and with riveted glassed portholes. Strange hieroglyphs cover its surface. How can such a thing exist? How can it even rise in the air?*

Now a panel opens in the side and the illusions of the bright day fade. Harsh, hot rocks replace the golden sands and the cool jungle green; where there was sea and surf, there is now only an eddying, dangerous swirl of air. Instinctively, PATCHES *raises his hands as two* SISTERS OF THE BLUE STORM *approach. They carry no weapons – but at once the boy senses the threat they pose.*

The tall women are dressed in long blue robes. Their heads are shaven and shining, their hands tipped with blue, curling, claw-like nails. But most alarming are their faces. Their eyes are of a dazzling blue, and glitter cruelly. And worst of all, far worse, is the smooth, unbroken flesh where their mouths should be.

And yet the SISTERS *can speak. Their ugly, hissing voices sound in unison, echoing out of the air around them.*

SISTERS: *Intruders, you will come with us!*

PATCHES: We're coming . . . never mind, we're coming!

WHALE: What, more sluts, ready for a tumble? I liked the other
    ones better than these—

WALRUS: Aye, the ones with their tits out! *Proper* women—

WHALE: Where's their hair? Ugly bitches, if you ask me—

WALRUS: Bugger, they got no mouths, too! How can they—

SISTERS: *There can be no resistance. You will come.*

WHALE (*suddenly frightened*): They're not just sluts . . . Walrus,
    they want our treasure! Where . . . where's me cutlass?

WALRUS *whips out his pistol.* Foreign bitches! Back, or I fire!

His threats mean nothing. The SISTERS *advance.* WALRUS *fires, but to no avail. Shaking, he fires again, then again — then, together, the* SISTERS *raise their hands. Blue lightning zaps from their claw-like nails, striking the hapless conspirator. Shrieking, he is borne up into the air, whizzes round, then crashes down, lifeless, to the jagged rocks that he had imagined, in his greedy delirium, to be lush, golden sand.* WHALE *collapses, gibbering.* PATCHES *gulps.*

SISTERS: *You will come. You will come to Sarom.*
PATCHES: Don't worry, I think we will.

✻   ✻   ✻   ✻   ✻

Castor-uncle smiled and held out his arms, reaching for the little slave-girl with the strange, intent eyes. If the girl did not return his smile, nonetheless she went to him, allowing herself to be enfolded in his embrace. Murmurously, the old man asked the child if she would sing. Didn't she know they loved it when she sang?

Trembling, Ucheus turned back from the window. By now the meal had been cleared away, but still the wine flowed. The smiles around the table were broader, merrier. Castor-uncle spun the little girl in his arms. The old man's cares, it seemed, were forgotten.

'This pretty child, young Ucheus, is the greatest songstress I have ever known. It was a happy day when we found her in the slave-market, for she has brought us all much joy.' He nuzzled at the girl's nose. 'Isn't that so, my child? Ah, but how grave your little face appears! Will you always be so grave? Will you never reflect, as in a glass, the joy we all feel as we look upon you?'

But for a moment, Castor-uncle grew grave again too. 'What sufferings this child must have known I cannot guess. To be a motherless infant, caught in the grip of slavers, must be amongst the hardest of this world's fates. How glad I am that we freed her! But who is she? From where does she come? If she knows, she will not say; yet I think, though she is dark of hue, that she is not a Wenayan.'

'No indeed,' smiled one of Castor-uncle's wives, 'but she is a fine child, is she not? How I wish she had sprung from my own loins!'

Another wife extended a hand, petting the girl's black, unruly hair. 'Such a wish might be mine, too. No wonder our benefactors love her so!'

'Benefactors?' Ucheus said sharply. 'My aunt, who are these *benefactors*?'

His aunt only smiled; Ucheus asked his uncle.

The old man appeared not to hear the question, but the little girl turned to look at Ucheus. Again he saw the intentness in her dark, sad eyes. If, from the first, he had sensed something strange in her, only now

487

did he understand that strangeness. He had thought her almost threatening; now he was sure that what lay behind those eyes was, in truth, a mute appeal.

Fascinated, and not a little fearful, he looked on as the child, with no shyness but only the same sombre demeanour, readied herself to perform. In a slant of sunlight she stood by the hearth, eyes cast up to the ceiling, a hand twining in her long black hair. Demurely, one of Castor-uncle's wives brought forth a box harp; a daughter produced an ocarina; a slave appeared with a tabor, another with a gong. Slowly, softly, the music filled the low-beamed, rustic hall; slowly, softly, the girl began to sing. Ah, indeed her voice was celestial, falling in the golden air like a gentle, lulling balm!

But Ucheus could think only of the words she sang.

> *They ride with lightning on a swirling sky,*
> *The strangest strangers sweeping down from high:*
> *What's left for us? What but to say goodbye?*
> > *They come, they come! I see them taking form—*
> > *The Sisterhood of the Blue Storm!*

Ucheus felt fear, gripping him like a hand. How, just a moment earlier, had he seen no threat in the sombre little slave-girl? Now she seemed to him very threatening indeed.

But quite how, he could not be sure.

> *They once united in a sacred chain,*
> *Now what unites them is a Web profane:*
> *What do they bring? What but a spider's bane?*
> > *They come, they come, their evil to perform—*
> > *The Sisterhood of the Blue Storm!*

Shuddering, Ucheus gazed at the faces all around him, some in sunlight, some in shadow. How could they merely smile and nod, registering no shock at the sinister words?

Now he thought even the melody was sinister too.

> *When islands vanish from the oceans blue,*
> *With sands and orchids, jungles and bamboo:*
> *All gone, all gone? What can it be but true?*
> > *They come, they come down like a deadly swarm—*
> > *The Sisterhood of the Blue Storm!*

A crazed urge to violence gripped Ucheus. He might have burst forward, striking the little girl; then turned angrily, despairingly on the mesmerised family. *His* family.

But somehow he was rooted in place.

In lust of power they search and search the seas,
And when they come they will not hear your pleas:
What, plead with them? What man does more than flees?
  They come, they come, and still your trail is warm—
  The Sisterhood of the Blue Storm!

Then it happened. At first he thought it was just the sun. But no, it was a different radiance, shimmering like a halo round the little girl's head; then the halo turned into long, streaming strands of colour.

Purple. Green. Red. Blue. Gold.

But now the lightning fills the swirling sky,
Now come the Sisters sweeping down from high:
There's nothing left! My friends, goodbye, goodbye!
  They're here, they're here! Look, now they've taken form—
  The Sisterhood of the Blue Storm—
  The Sisterhood of the Blue Storm!

Ucheus burst forward, grabbing the child, shaking her.

It was too late. In the same moment a mighty, unearthly roaring split the air. He reeled. It was coming from the yard! He rushed to the window. He gasped. Descending over the farm in a blaze of blue was a metallic, ovoid object, its bright sides gleaming with hieroglyphs.

But only Ucheus registered astonishment. The others seemed entirely unperturbed – all, that is, but for the little slave-girl. She slumped down, rainbow colours collapsing around her like falling ribbons of light. She cowered. She cried out. Ucheus would have gone to her, compassionate now, but fascination gripped him and he could only follow the others. Like sleepwalkers, they filed out on to the verandah, ready to greet those who were, he knew at once, no unexpected visitors.

Dazzled, he looked on as a panel opened in the bows of the skyship, and two extraordinary female figures emerged. Castor-uncle bent low, bowing in reverence, as the strange voices emanated in unison from the tall, blue-garbed, mouthless women:

We have come, Maius Castor. We have come for the girl.

'Jem, can you hear that song again?' said Rajal.

It was a song from Unang Lia, *Marry and Burn*.

'No, but I thought I heard a woman's laughter.'

'I'm getting lightheaded, I really am.'

'That's the whole idea, I suppose.'

This was worse than the maze. After leaving the labyrinth of looking-glasses, Jem and Rajal had found themselves in a market square, surrounded by white, box-like houses. In the square, as in any market, were innumerable stalls, stallholders, haggling buyers; there were slaves for sale, and fish, and skeins of cloth; there were jewels and lamps and incense-sticks and vials of spice, all as expected.

Only one thing was strange. They were all made of stone.

In wonderment, Jem and Rajal wove their way between the statue-like figures that blazed whitely in the sun's heat. More than once, there had been a glimpse of something that was not a statue, a glimpse of something living. Rajal saw a brown, bare foot vanishing behind a thicket of lifeless figures; Jem saw the sudden swish of a robe, a scarlet flash amongst the whiteness. And wasn't that Ejard Orange – just his tail, disappearing round a corner?

Then, more and more, came the teasing music.

Jem turned. 'What's this song? I know it, I'm sure.'

'Of course you do.' It was a song Rajal had sung many times, the song about the King and Queen of Swords. He hummed the lilting, lullaby melody. *Everything is lemon but nothing is lime* . . . He trailed off. That song had proved a sinister one, for all its seeming innocence. In this place, it was more sinister still.

But so was the silence.

'Jem? I was right, wasn't I? About what would happen? Well, in a way.'

'What's that, Raj?' Jem was distracted. There had to be a way out of this trap, he was sure of it. He screwed up his brow. There was an answer, wasn't there? An answer he knew? But why couldn't he think of it? Was he losing his mind?

He peered round a trader's broad, stony back. There came a snatch of the harlequin's song: *Hey ho, the circle is round* . . . Jem felt a terrible sadness, creeping over him like a black, impending shadow. Then the thought came to him that there *was* a shadow, looming over this bright scene. Above the marketplace, or so it seemed to him, was only a white glare. But somewhere in that glare, hidden from him now, the volcano smouldered. He put a hand to his head. He staggered back, clutching Rajal. Something, some knowledge, was struggling to be born in him.

It was the answer. But what answer?

Then, quite without warning, the statues all around them snapped into life. Rajal jumped; Jem started, then leapt back, jostled by haggling buyers, sweaty, shouting, insistent. Helplessly, weakened in the heat, he felt himself swept away through the crush.

He called out, 'Raj! Raj, where are you?'

The woman's laughter came again, distant, faint.

Chapter 68

SAFE IN MY GARDEN

Mandarin. Honeysuckle. Dog-rose. Lemon.

Somewhere within the Palace of the Dynasts lies a garden. Surrounded by high, forbidding walls, it is a small garden, but precious, its borders and shady walks planted with only the finest and most exotic fruits and flowers. Rivulets burble. Fountains plash. Stripy Wenaya-doves coo from the arbour-walks; peacocks strut and preen on the lawns. But the colours of even these gaudy creatures pall beside the wreathing, writhing flowers. In turn, all these rich hues are as nothing to the riotous perfumes that swirl so headily in the tropical heat.

This garden, so the Islanders of Aroc say, was made for a Dynast who had lost his sight, hearing, taste and touch. Here, amidst these thousand tendrils of incense, he would imagine that once again he was possessed of those senses, so vividly did this place strike the one that remained. How then must it affect those without his afflictions? To be sure, it must transport them, as if by magic. Shall you not be transported, child?

The words issued in unison from two Sisters, the two who had borne the little girl from Castor-uncle's farm. The child stood between them now, her hands held fast, by the ornate gateway that led into the garden. No longer dressed in the garb of a slave, now she wore a blue robe like those of her captors, with the addition of a blue trailing headpiece, as if to indicate her status as a novice. Grave-faced as before, she made no response as the tall women propelled her gently forward, then turned back, locking the gate behind her.

Through the mesh of wrought iron came the words: *You will stay here, child, until we are ready. Soon now, another magic shall claim you; first, let these fruits and flowers work their sweet way with you. Compose yourself, and think upon the glory that soon shall be yours, and yours alone.*

For some moments the little girl stood impassively, as if, without the Sisters, she had lost all volition. Since arriving in Sarom she had been their puppet, caught in their strange hypnotic web. As they had shaved her head, as they had bathed her, as they had perfumed her and dressed her, she had made no response. Only now, as the footsteps of her captors faded away, did the child look about her with a stirring of wonderment, taking in this garden that, for a time, was to be her prison. Bright fruits and flowers blurred in her eyes; incense coiled intoxicatingly on hot

491

currents of air.

She breathed deeply; she almost smiled. She staggered forward, falling into the deep, cushioning grass. Scents swirled around her.

Mandarin. Honeysuckle. Dog-rose. Lemon.

Where could they be?

Tail flicking behind him, ears and whiskers twitching, Ejard Orange moved cautiously through the undergrowth, searching for traces of his lost companions. The big cat was in a shabby state. Disproving an old myth, he had not quite managed to land on his feet. Burrs and dry grass stuck to his fur and there was a scratch above his left ear, glittering with blood. His side ached and he limped a little on one of his front paws.

A bird moved on a branch and he stiffened, trying to summon the strength to pounce; but the bird, sensing him, flitted away. Poor Ejard Orange! Already he was beginning to forget his companions. After all, they might have fallen far, far away. Perhaps they were dead. Perhaps he was on his own again. How he wished for some cool, calm place where he might curl up and lick his wounds!

The dry, salty vegetation grew thinner. The earth trembled hotly beneath his paws. Little stones slipped and slithered down, down. Ejard Orange saw a rocky slab below and leapt, this time landing smoothly.

The slab was narrow, jutting out precariously into blue, swirling air. There was a path leading down towards neat fields and farms. And food? Yes, there would have to be food. But in this place, barren though it was, there were pungent smells, smells that aroused the big cat. Blood? Traces of meat? Intrigued, he inspected the pallid rocky shelf with its blackened slab in the centre, and the blackened pit beside it.

A hissing sounded and he swished round, tail jerking, eyes catching in the sun like golden coins. Behind him was only a sheer, rising wall, pocked with innumerable jagged holes, the largest perhaps the size of his own girth.

A longing came over Ejard Orange. Now he forgot the meat and blood and thought only of his wish for calm, for cool. The sun beat savagely on his marmalade fur. The hissing sounded again, so cool, so calm.

He picked a particular hole, tested its width with his whiskers, and vanished inside.

Through the long afternoon the little girl lay, dazed and dreamy, in the soft, sweet grass. The sun caressed her, pouring around her like liquid honey, until at last the sun began to set. Pink, then purple, glimmered in the air, but still the warmth lingered, reluctant to part; the girl, in her turn, was reluctant to stir. Riding on incense, eyes shut fast, her mind descended through strange caverns, purple and flickering with languid, mysterious shapes. Did she understand her destiny? Did she grasp her fate?

In any case she knew nothing of the stranger's eyes that watched her, fascinated, from behind a screen of flowers; nothing of the small arm that reached up at last, pushing aside the leaves and stems, or the small feet that padded across the grass. Only when the stranger knelt beside her, looking down at her, did the girl stir; even then, it was only when a hand touched her, lightly against the face, that her eyes flickered open.

'Who . . . who are you?' she breathed.

'Shh! They call me Littler. But what's your name?'

The girl barely heard the question. 'You're . . . a boy. But how did you get here?'

'I . . . I came out of the sky, I suppose.'

The girl's eyes grew wide. 'But so did I.'

Littler looked down sadly. 'I came with my friends, but I've lost them. I'm bruised all over, and trapped in this garden, and . . . I don't know, it's hard to explain. But what have they done to *you*? I could tell you weren't one of them, just by looking at you. You're their prisoner, aren't you?'

A lost look came into the girl's eyes. 'Their . . . them? But who do you mean?'

'Why, the Sisterhood of the Blue Storm, of course.'

Littler's words had a strange effect. The girl scrambled up, astonishment spreading over her face. She looked about her, this way and that, like a hunted, trapped animal. 'Oh, but you're right! What have they done to me, what will they do? I thought my magic could resist them, I thought I was strong enough—'

'Magic?' Littler began. 'What sort of—'

The girl only rushed on, 'They're strong, ever so strong! And any moment now, they're coming back! They need my magic for some terrible purpose. Oh, I've suffered so much since I was kidnapped, but I never dreamed it would all end like this! They'll grind me up to feed their evil, and there's nothing I can do!'

She slumped down. Despairingly, she looked up into the waning evening light. For a moment it looked as if she was about to cry, but she blinked savagely and gritted her teeth. Suddenly, sharply, she looked up at Littler.

'Kill me,' she said. 'Kill me, now.'

'*What?*' Littler burst out, aghast.

'It's the only way! Don't you see, it's the only way to defeat them? They're too strong. But without me, they'll—'

'I don't understand,' Littler wailed.

The girl would not explain. 'You haven't got a knife, have you?' Her manner, all at once, was quite matter-of-fact. 'Never mind, you'll have to strangle me. Come on, I'll lie down, I'll go limp, it'll be easy—'

'I can't strangle you!' Littler almost shouted.

'Shh! Littler, *please*. Hands around my neck . . . No, not there, *there* . . . Got it? Now squeeze.'

Reluctantly, Littler complied. In the warm evening, the perfumes of the garden seemed ever more fantastical, swirling around them with a wild intensity. Littler swooned as his thumbs sank deeper and deeper into the tender flesh. 'I don't think this is a good idea,' he blurted, 'really I don't—'

'Shh! Oh, you're not trying . . . Harder—'

'But this is awful,' he moaned, as reluctantly he began to tighten his grip. 'How can this be the *only way*? I don't even know what's become of my friends! They could be dead, but they've survived a lot before. And if Jem's here, and Rajal—'

The girl jerked upright. '*What?* What did you say?'

There was no time to answer. Footsteps sounded, ringing over stone.

'They're coming back!' said Littler.

'Quick . . . hide!' gasped the girl.

'I . . . I can't just let them take you!'

'You've got no choice! Hide, just hide!'

The footsteps were closer. Littler scrambled back towards the flowers. Wild thoughts filled him. He would rush at the Sisters, push past them, slam the gate on them, run through the palace, clutching tightly to the girl's hand . . .

Stupid thoughts, stupid.

But there was one thing he could do. In the last moment he lurched forward again, shoving Rainbow's collar into the girl's hand.

'It's all I have! It's magic – take it, please!'

An instant later, as the key clunked in the gate, the girl sat innocently on the perfumed grass, adjusting her headdress with apparent casualness. The Sisters would never guess what she wore beneath, circling her forehead.

Not, that is, until it was too late.

Come, child, come. Your destiny awaits.

From behind his screen of flowers, Littler could only look on, anguished, as the tall forbidding women led his new friend away.

Tell me the measure of an Ejlander,
How long is a tangle of twine?

> *Tell me the measure of an Ejlander,*
> *How deep is a goblet of wine?*

The voice was melodious, sweetly mocking. Jem ignored it. Sweat rolled down his reddened face like tears. He gritted his teeth, clenched his fists, cursed this island and its sinister magic. The ground trembled beneath his feet.

'No, I don't believe this – I won't.'

The figures in the marketplace had turned back into statues. It had happened quite as suddenly as they had come alive. Mysteriously they gleamed in the declining daylight. Stone, all of them, just as before.

And one other, who had *not* been stone.

Gulping, Jem reached out. Didn't he know this was all an illusion? Didn't he know this would change, perhaps in a trice? It didn't matter. At once, the loss that filled him was deep, inconsolable. His fingers splayed over Rajal's chest. Had even his friend's crystal turned to stone? It could not be. He lurched forward, embracing this lifeless thing that had once been Rajal. Tears sprang suddenly from Jem's eyes. But the words that sprang from his lips had been welling for longer.

'Raj, I tell you I won't believe this. They can't kill you, I won't let them. You think I don't care about you, don't you? You think I just take you for a fool. But I don't, Raj. You looked out for me, didn't you, when I was just a silly boy, out of Irion for the first time? Oh, I know a lot about you, more than you think. Don't you think I guessed about you and Bean? I didn't mean that about finding a girl, not really – I don't know why I said it. I love you, Raj, I do. Don't you know that if I'm King one day, you're going to be my wisest councillor?'

He stood back, gazing into the stony face. 'Well, perhaps not the wisest, but the best all the same.'

A song came:

> *Carry me to Sarom, mother,*
> *Let me make my vows.*
> *When I am a man, mother,*
> *I shall live on—*

Jem ignored it. He wiped his eyes.

'The future's all before us, Raj. You're not dead, you're not stone, and I know why. I've worked it out, you see. All these visions, all these illusions, they come from *us*, don't they? Leki and Ojo, back in the jungle. Those faces in the maze, these old songs. It's the Sisters, working on us, reaching into our heads. And this stone? I know what that means, too. Didn't I say the crystals were just stones here, lifeless stones? All that we see now, it's just our fears. But it won't work. And you know why, Raj? Because the magic's not just in the crystals, is it? It's in us. It *is* us.'

He looked up. Defiantly he gazed into the sky.

'Do you hear me, Sisterhood of the Blue Storm? Do you think we're going to be defeated now, after all we've been through? By *you*, when we've taken on Toth? I tell you, we've come for the blue crystal. We know you've got it – and we're not leaving until it's ours!'

Volcanic smoke, dark and wispy, swirled through the hot twilight air. Now Jem might have expected the woman's laughter again, echoing around him. Instead, there was only the murmurous song, Leki's song from a time that already seemed long ago:

> *I shall live on Sarom, mother,*
> *When I am a man.*
> *I must make my vows, mother,*
> *Carry me to—*

Jem slapped the side of his head. 'That's it! Raj, I've got it!'

Before, when Jem had gazed at the smoking mountain above them, a sunny haze had obscured its dazzling slopes. Now, in the shadows of evening, he saw again the long, low palace he had seen from the air. Yes. He knew what to do. He knew the answer. He would turn back to Rajal, slap him, shake him, shout that he was not stone, could never be stone. He would deny this reality, deny it with every fibre of his being. Rajal would come to back to life, and magic would fill them – magic, because they willed it.

They would sweep, like spirits of vengeance, up the mountain road to Sarom, ready to seize the Crystal of Javander.

But before Jem could act, before his hand could even swing back, ready to strike his friend, a sudden high shrieking, then a roaring, split the air. It might have been the cry of a savage beast, descending on its prey. The stony figures in the marketplace burst back into life. All at once the skyship was hovering above them, and the command, the summons, possessed their minds.

Sarom! came the cries. *Sarom, Sarom!*

Only Jem uttered a different cry: 'Raj!'

And now the human throng surged forward, upwards, out of the marketplace. Coins scattered. Beads, bolts of cloth, glittering fish slithered to the ground. Stalls, trading, all were forgotten as the citizens of Inorchis, and the slaves too, thronged up the side of the darkening mountain, helpless in the power of the evil Sisterhood.

'Raj!' Jem struggled to reach his friend.

It was no good. They were pushed apart. Then both were swept away, along, and up with the tide. Dazed, they could only join in the wild, insistent cries:

Sarom! Sarom!

Chapter 69

THE SPIDER'S WEB

Ucheus stumbled through the darkness. He knew that he was delirious. Tears ran down his face and he dashed at them angrily. His toga was torn and so was his skin.

How long had passed since he had left Castor-uncle's farm, he could not say. When the Sisters took the little girl into the skyship, they had turned back, commanding Castor-uncle and his family to follow, hastening to Sarom on their mules and in their carts; even the slaves, they said, must come.

How Ucheus wished he had defied the Sisters! But his terror was too great, and what could he have done? He had cowered back in the shadows behind the barn and only when the skyship rose again, disappearing into the dazzling daylight, did he break his cover, racing out as if somehow, absurdly, he could make it stop.

Instead, the force of the ship flung him back and the next thing he knew he was waking, long afterwards, to find the sun sinking and the farm deserted. At once, he had cursed himself for a coward and a fool. What was he to do? Everyone was gone; there were no mules or carts.

He set out, running, down the road towards Sarom.

That was long ago, and Ucheus could run no more. He looked around him in the tremulous night. Somewhere, in his despair, he had taken a wrong turning. This was not the way to Sarom, was it? This meagre track, winding uphill?

In the old days, before his Manhood Trial, he had known every contour of his beloved island home. He looked up at the sky, but even the patterns of the stars had gone. They shifted as he watched, and so did the moon.

He slumped down. What could the Sisters mean to do? What terrible part was the little girl to play? Blank with despair, he tracked the pale disc of the moon across the sky – and it was then, as he followed the beam of its light, that he saw something familiar up ahead.

Ah yes, he knew where he was now.

❊   ❊   ❊   ❊   ❊

Stretching before the white, low Palace of the Dynasts at Sarom is a great forecourt, where generation after generation of islanders has gathered, obeying the summons of its rulers. In the centre of the forecourt is an immense round dais, patterned in mosaics of mystic design. Here, in the epicycles since they journeyed to Inorchis, abandoning Xaro to the Thunderer's wrath, the islanders have witnessed all the great affairs of state, from the crowning of a Dynast to the obsequies at his death. This is a place where laws are proclaimed; a place where traitors are executed, too. Such has always been the way: on Xaro, long ago, there was another such place, and should the islanders ever return there, this Sarom would be built again, exactly following the old designs.

But for all that has taken place at one Sarom or another, never has there been a night such as tonight. Yes, the crowd is packed tightly, as before. Yes, they gaze up at the dais, as before. But never have the islanders mingled so promiscuously, with adults and infants, women, men and eunuchs, slaves and nobles crushed shoulder to shoulder. Never have they shown this mesmerised blankness. Tapers flicker, drums pound. Rapidly the moon scuds through sky as the hapless inhabitants of the flying island chant, in a monotone, *Sarom, Sarom.*

And somewhere in the crowd is Jem. The words force themselves from his lips too, but he struggles to resist.

Sarom, Sarom. Where is Rajal?

Sarom, Sarom. What can be happening?

In the weirdly leaping taper-light, in the shifting beams of the moon, the faces around Jem are coloured strangely, flickering with patterns of bronze and red and silver; but though he cannot see their true colours, he guesses that already they must be growing paler, draining of life as the evil magic grips them.

Sarom, Sarom. Jem's eyes search the crowd.

Sarom, Sarom. No, it is useless.

But now something is happening; now come the tall, shaven-headed women, emerging from tunnels beneath the dais. This is Jem's first glimpse of the Sisters. He gasps, shocked at their mouthless faces and long, talon-like nails.

And there are so many! More and more of the grotesque figures appear, forming a circle, then circles within circles, all around the rim of the vast circular platform. They face outwards, gazing towards the crowd, their cruel eyes blazing with incandescent blue.

They kneel; they bow their heads; they raise their arms. The actions might almost be those of supplication, but the Sisters hardly worship the Islanders of Aroc.

What *do* they worship?

The answer comes with startling swiftness. Rising through the circle the Sisters have formed comes a tall column of light, glimmering blue, and from somewhere, perhaps from the light itself, comes a booming, crashing voice.

Jem stops his ears, so terrible is the voice. But he cannot shut it from his mind – and with the voice comes a terrible vision. He shudders, almost cries out. Is this a collective manifestation of the Sisters? Is this what their minds, pooled together, have formed? The vision glows and throbs with insane, depraved evil.

It is the vision of a monstrous spider.

And these are its words:

WEBSISTERS, HEAR YOUR SPIDERMOTHER!

RAPIDLY ON THE BLUE STORM WE FLY THROUGH THE NIGHT: RAPIDLY THE TIME OF OUR DESTINY DRAWS NEAR. SOON, THE TREASURE THAT FOR SO LONG HAS BEEN DENIED US SHALL BE OURS: SOON, OUR POWERS SHALL BE LIMITLESS!

FASTER THAN THIS WORLD TURNS, WE CHASE THE GLIMMERING DAWN: WHEN DAWN COMES, WE DESCEND UPON THE EYE OF THE SEA. BUT WEBSISTERS, ONLY WITH A NEW SPIDERMOTHER IN PLACE MAY YOU PLUCK OUT THAT EYE. I AM OLD, AND MY TIME HAS PASSED. PINE NOT FOR ME AS DEATH STEALS UPON ME, SORROW NOT AS I LEAVE YOU NOW: MY ESSENCE SHALL REMAIN, DISPERSED IN THE WEB.

NOW, WEBSISTERS, FOCUS YOUR POWERS. DRAW UPON THESE ISLANDERS, DRAW FORTH THE ENERGIES THEY STILL HOLD IN RESERVE, THAT WE MIGHT MAKE READY THE POSTULANT OF THE WEB: NOW SHE IS A CHILD, BUT BEFORE DAWN COMES, SHE MUST BE A WOMAN, AND A WOMAN SUCH AS WE ARE. ONLY THEN CAN SHE TAKE MY PLACE IN THE WEB, BEFORE WE DESCEND UPON THE EYE OF THE SEA!

NOW, WEBSISTERS, NOW!

WEBSISTERS, GOODBYE!

The vision fizzes out, and the light grows brighter.

Jem's mind reels. Why does this creature speak of dying? Is this Spidermother more than a mere mental picture? Who is this child – and where is she, this Postulant of the Web?

Soon enough, Jem shall know the answers. But now a humming sounds from the Sisters; blue lightning crackles all around them, then around the forecourt too, passing over the heads of the crowd. Weird illusions fill the air – faces, animals, swirling patterns – drawn up like ghosts from the chained, possessed minds.

Sarom, Sarom. Music fills the air. And slowly, strangely, the song begins.

> *They ride with lightning on a swirling sky,*
> *The strangest strangers sweeping down from high . . .*

Jem feels something tearing at his mind. It is as if he is being drawn down into a dark and terrible miasma. He gasps. He chokes.

Sarom, Sarom. Ah, where does it come from, this mysterious song?

> *They once united in a sacred chain,*
> *Now what unites them is a Web profane ...*

Jem feels a thousand contrary emotions. He shivers. He sweats. His consciousness ebbs. He grits his teeth, holds himself back. He must not give way, he must not! But already he feels as if his mind will explode.

Sarom, Sarom. Now, rising up between the prostrated Sisters, Jem sees the singer. She hovers in the air.

> *When islands vanish from the oceans blue,*
> *With sands and orchids, jungles and bamboo ...*

So this is the Postulant of the Web, the child who must assume the Spidermother's place. The girl is dressed in blue robes. A trailing headpiece covers her face. Everywhere the islanders are swooning, swaying, buffeting like corn in a skirling wind. Some cry out; some collapse, flesh withering suddenly on their blank-eyed faces.

Sarom, Sarom. Jem claws at his collar. It is as if someone is strangling him. Nearer, nearer looms the dark miasma.

> *In lust of power they search and search the seas,*
> *And when they come they will not hear your pleas ...*

On and on swirls the blue light, filling the air between the circle of Sisters; on and on comes the zapping lightning, crackling round the crowd. Now the wind grows stronger; now the reaper has come for the corn.

Sarom, Sarom. The child rises higher, revolving in the air.

> *But now the lightning fills the swirling sky,*
> *Now come the Sisters sweeping down from high ...*

All around him, Jem sees islander after islander collapsing; his head jerking savagely, almost snapping, he sees Rajal holding out too, clutching and clawing at the side of the dais. Jem flounders towards him. They grab each other. Agony fills them. They scream.

Sarom, Sarom. The song is over. But it is merely a preliminary. Higher, higher surges the power; higher, higher rises the revolving child.

Of the islanders, some are dazed, some are dead; some have crumbled already to dust. Now only Jem and Rajal still stand. Through dazzled eyes, they gaze up at the child, horrified and marvelling, when the revelation comes. Suddenly, the child reaches up, wrenching at her headpiece. It tears. It flutters away.

On her forehead is a silver band. The band shimmers, surrounding her in its phosphorescence.

Anguish booms in the Websisters. In the same moment, something booms in Rajal's brain, a memory of another ceremony, long ago in a cellar beneath the Great Temple of Agonis. In an instant, he feels again all the pain that has consumed him ever since that night – the guilt, the sorrow, the terrible loss. Can this vision be real? Time and again, Rajal has thought he will never see his sister again.

Her name bursts from him: '*Myla!*'

He rushes the dais. Shocked, Jem follows. Again, again they shriek Myla's name. Oblivious, the child spins faster in the air, faster and faster. Waves of light come pulsing, streaming from the band around her forehead, then surging into a blinding flash.

Then it is over.

Where Myla was, there is nothing.

Only sparks fall down and down, descending like dust through the column of blue. On the dais, the Websisters are dazed, staggering.

But so is Rajal. So is Jem.

And now the Sisters converge upon them, surrounding them as a hideous voice splits the air:

Seize the male-creatures! They are intruders! They have destroyed the Postulant of the Web!

Ucheus scrambled up to the Plateau of Voices. Trembling, he gazed upon the Wall of a Hundred Holes. He turned away, wondering if his plan could succeed. It was mad, wasn't it? For long moments, he held his face in his hands; then, slowly, he stripped off his toga. Reverently, he knelt by the slab, his naked flesh gleaming in the moonlight like bronze. He reached under the belt of his tunic, bringing forth his kos-knife. Cutting into his wrists, he struggled for words.

'Hundred-voiced Sibyl,' he murmured, 'all-wise one, sister of the Sibyl of Xaro, who is daughter of the Thunderer Aroc Xaro, who is brother of the Thunderer Aroc Inorchis ... before you I come with this offering of flesh. Hear me, Sibyl of Inorchis, and tell me what I ask, for you are the last chance that remains for me now. Sibyl, speak to me! How can my homeland be restored? How can the Sisterhood be defeated?'

Ucheus would have gone on, but his strength was ebbing fast. Richly the dark liquid flowed from his wrists, spilling across the sacrificial slab. Yes, this was mad: he knew it was mad. No Sibyl, no Thunderer could help him now. Ah, but his death, that was what he longed for!

He slumped forward, collapsing into his own blood.

The silence pressed around him. The moon shone indifferently. On and on flew the island through the night.

Then two things happened. First, his eyes flashing in the moonlight, Ejard Orange emerged from the Wall of a Hundred Holes. Cautiously, the big cat padded round the bleeding, inert Ucheus. He reached out a paw, cuffing at the youth's face. He miaowed piteously.

The moonlight shifted away and there was darkness.

Then there was light. Ejard Orange leapt back, startled, as dazzling beams shot from the hundred mouths of the Sibyl. And with the light came words, booming and fluting and whistling and whining, words in the human tongue he could barely understand. It was something about the Thunderer Aroc Inorchis, something about a place called Dead Man's Lookout, something about the Sisterhood of the Blue Storm.

It did not matter, none of it mattered. Ejard Orange was aware only of the sudden wild magic gathering him up, possessing him. He shrieked. He howled.

He was changing his form.

And so was Ucheus.

❋   ❋   ❋   ❋   ❋

MALE-CREATURES, HOW DARE YOU INTERFERE? VILE, LOATHSOME ABOMINATIONS OF NATURE, MY VENGEANCE SHALL KNOW NO BOUNDS! YOUR PAIN IS BUT BEGINNING!

Jem blocks his ears, desperate to shut out the hideous, shrieking voice that booms, intolerably loudly, all around him. He lies, almost senseless, on a marble floor; already, pain throbs in every fibre of his body. For an age Jem and Rajal have known only agony as searing goads of mental power have forced them down the steps in the middle of the dais, along dark passages, through bright halls. Chamber by chamber, all the splendours of the Palace of the Dynasts have flashed past their eyes in a scorching blur. Now there is the throne room, and the floor where they have been flung.

Jem rallies first, then gasps, then slumps again, lost in horror as he gazes upon the Spidermother, no longer a vision, but a monstrous reality. What he sees is the head of an old, old woman, withered, mouthless and hairless, staring out from the bloated body of a vast blue spider. The creature crouches in the centre of an immense web, its fibres like huge, juddering cables, each one thick as a man's wrist. Extending from the creature's forehead is a pulsing blue tube, like an umbilical cord, linking her to the vibrating heart of the Web.

The Websisters abase themselves before their Queen.

The blue tube pulses as the Spidermother speaks:

WEBSISTERS, OUR SPELL SHOULD HAVE CLIMAXED IN MY DEATH.

502

NOW, WITH THE POSTULANT GONE, MY LIFE MUST BE PROLONGED: BUT FEAR NOT, WE SHALL YET COMPLETE OUR PLAN. WE STILL HAVE THE ENERGIES OF THE ISLANDERS: THE EYE OF THE SEA IS NEARER: SOON, SOON WE SHALL PREPARE OUR ASSAULT!

AH, BUT THE PAIN THAT WRACKS ME, TO LOSE MY POSTULANT: FOR WHO BUT THAT MAGIC CHILD COULD TAKE MY PLACE? FROM THE MOMENT WE POSSESSED THIS ISLE OF INORCHIS, I KNEW THAT ONLY SHE COULD BE MY SUCCESSOR: WITHOUT HER, OUR GLORY SHALL EVER BE TARNISHED! MALE-CREATURES, PRAY TO WHAT GODS YOU MIGHT WORSHIP: READY YOURSELVES FOR THE TORMENTS OF UNBEING!

The hideous spider moves forward in her Web, malevolence radiating from her withered face:

BUT FIRST, I SHALL DISCOVER WHO YOU ARE: FIRST, I SHALL KNOW WHY YOU KILLED MY PRETTY CHILD.

Only now does Jem have strength to speak. 'Killed her?' he gasps. 'You're ... insane! We wanted to ... *save* her—'

Bitter laughter echoes around the walls; the blue tube throbs as if it would burst:

SAVE HER, MALE-CREATURE? SAVE HER FROM GLORY?

'Glory?' Jem shouts. 'Glory, to be a *monster* like you?'

At once, the Websisters are united in outrage. Blue rays zap from their long, curling fingernails. Jem reels, agonised, clutching his shoulder, but forces himself to resist, resist.

Now Rajal rallies too.

'I'd rather Myla were dead!' he cries. 'I'd rather she were dead than caught in your clutches! But she can't be dead – not Myla! She's escaped you somehow, I'm sure she has—'

The rays zap Rajal too. He sinks to his knees.

The Web judders wildly:

MY PRETTY CHILD IS DEAD, IT IS UNDOUBTED: IS NOT MY MIND ATTUNED TO HERS? IF SHE WERE ALIVE, I SHOULD SENSE HER: ALL I SENSE NOW IS THE ACHE OF HER ABSENCE!

Rajal grits his teeth. 'Your mind – attuned to hers? What do you know about Myla? Nothing, nothing! She's my sister, and I *know* she can resist you—'

Blue rays zap again; desperately, Jem tries to hush his friend, but Rajal sobs, shrieks, 'She's stronger than you! She's resisted you already, when she ripped away her veil! Myla's defeated you, and we will too! You can't win, you monster! We've come for the Crystal of Javander, and we won't leave without it!'

'*No*, Raj!' Jem cries, then slumps down: 'Oh, *Raj*!'

The words *Crystal of Javander* act upon Spidermother and Websisters alike with a force like a blow. At once, the throne room crackles with lightning; the Websisters rise up, hissing and writhing, while the Spidermother scuttles back and forth, shrieking, in her Web:

SISTER? CRYSTAL? WHAT DOES THIS MEAN? WEBSISTERS, FORCE THESE MALE-CREATURES CLOSER: BEFORE I DESTROY THEM, I WOULD PROBE THE SECRETS OF THEIR MINDS AND HEARTS!

The agonies of before are as nothing to what Jem and Rajal must endure now. On waves of mental force they whizz across the floor; now, they writhe beneath the immense Web. In moments, it seems, the Spidermother will rend them apart. Screaming, helpless, they feel as if the creature has entered their very minds, scuttling poisonously through every chamber of their beings. Blue light zigzags up and down the Web. All round the throne room, Websisters writhe in a sinister dance.

At last, the vast spider breaks off, shrieking with wild, triumphant laughter:

WEBSISTERS, WE ARE SAVED! THESE MALE-CREATURES HAVE BEEN SEEKERS OF THE COMPANION CRYSTALS: NOW, AT THIS VERY MOMENT, THEY POSSESS THE CRYSTALS OF KOROS AND THERON! DO YOU KNOW WHAT THIS MEANS? IT MEANS THAT SOON OUR POWER SHALL BE LIMITLESS!

Excitement possesses the Websisters and their writhings become more frenzied. At first Jem does not understand, thinking that the Spidermother seeks to augment the power of the crystal she must already hold. Only as the monster speaks again does he begin to see the truth. Horror grips his heart. Can it be that the blue crystal is not here at all, concealed somewhere on the flying island? Can the quest that has brought them so far across the seas all have been a terrible, terrible mistake? Can Robander Selsoe have deceived him after all?

Relentlessly the words crash around him:

OUR WAY IS CLEAR. HOLDING THE MALE-CREATURES IN OUR MENTAL POWER, WE MUST PLUNGE THEM DEEP WITHIN THE EYE OF THE SEA! THERE, ANIMATED BY THE PURPLE AND RED CRYSTALS, IT IS CERTAIN THEY WILL GRASP THE PRIZE WE SEEK! FOR THIS, I SHALL USE UP ALL MY REMAINING SUBSTANCE! FOR THIS, I SHALL SECURE OUR ETERNAL GLORY! SOON, MY WEBSISTERS, ALL THE WORLD SHALL BOW TO THE SISTERHOOD OF THE BLUE STORM!

At this, blue lightning bursts from the Spidermother, crashing in mighty currents down every fibre of the Web, cascading in terrifying waves around the walls. The Websisters abase themselves; in astonished gratitude, they would pray to their Queen, but impatiently she sets them to new tasks.

SECURE THE PRISONERS IN READINESS FOR THE DAWN.

Spidermother, shall we hold them in mental chains?

WASTE NOT OUR MAGIC. ALL OUR POWERS MUST BE FOCUSED ON

OUR FLIGHT: THIS NIGHT MUST END FASTER THAN ANY NIGHT BEFORE. LOCK THEM WITH THE OTHERS, UNTIL WE REACH THE DAWN.

Spidermother, say the Websisters, *what of the Postulant?*

SEARCH THE ISLAND. IF SHE LIVES, SHE SHALL NOT ESCAPE US: IF SHE LIVES, SHE SHALL YET FULFIL HER DESTINY.

'Oh no,' says Rajal. A chill runs down his spine.

'Now don't you wish you'd kept your mouth shut?' Jem mutters, as two Websisters usher them out of the throne room, just a little less brutally than they had been ushered in.

Chapter 70

TENDER IS THE NIGHT

'What did that thing mean, *others*? Where are they?'

Jem paced the soft, luxurious carpet. The Websisters had locked them not in the expected dungeon, but in a large, sparsely furnished chamber just off the throne room. The chamber was in darkness, but moonlight seeped through a tall, grilled window. There were two sets of doors: large double doors and a smaller, inner door. From under the double doors, which led back to the throne room, came blue pulsings from the Web; reddish flickerings shone beneath the inner door. From time to time the floor trembled as the flying island hurtled through the night.

Jem stopped by the window. He rattled the grille: shut fast. What lay beyond was a densely grown garden, rich in a thousand exotic perfumes. There was a chirruping of insects; nightbirds cooed and cawed. He mused, 'Have they got Uchy or Littler? Are those the *others*? Then what have they done to them?'

Rajal was not listening. He hunched on a couch, shivering. He hugged himself tight. 'She can't be dead,' he muttered, 'she can't.'

Jem went to him. 'Raj,' he said softly, 'if anyone could survive, it's Myla—'

'But Jem, how did she get here? She must have been kidnapped by slavers, and ... oh, think what she's been through! She may be magic, but she's just a little girl! And I couldn't help her ... I was never there for her!'

Jem gripped his friend's hand. 'There was nothing you could do. Remember back in Agondon? Myla was nearly sacrificed to Toth, wasn't she? Whatever's happened, anything's better than that.'

Rajal wiped his eyes. 'Anything? Even being turned into a thing like—'

'But she *wasn't*. You said it yourself, Raj, she has to be alive. I'm sure of it – and I'm sure we'll find her.' Jem scrambled up, pacing again. 'But first, we've got to get out of this place.'

'Some chance.' Rajal looked round glumly. 'I still don't understand all this.' He jerked his head towards the throne room. 'What does she mean about the Eye of the Sea?'

'I'm not sure I follow it all. But we know we've made one mistake, haven't we? We thought *they* had the Crystal of Javander.'

'Perhaps they want it,' said Rajal, 'just like us. What was that stuff

506

about plucking out the Eye – and getting *us* to do it? Do they just mean Kalador – giving him the knockout blow, aided by *our* crystals? Or is Javander's crystal . . . is *that* the Eye? Or is it *in* the Eye?'

'Perhaps not *in* it – but underneath?' said Jem. 'In Javander's palace? In the Briny Citadel?' He thought for a moment, then shook his head. 'But the crystals were scattered so the gods couldn't have them – it says so in the El-Orokon. Javander can't just *have* her own crystal, it makes no sense.'

'Then who's got it? And where is it?'

They would have said more, but just then the air was split by a hideous scream. Jem looked round wildly. The blue from the throne room throbbed impassively; the carpet, greenish-purple in the moonlight, trembled with the tremblings of the island.

Rajal was on his feet. He clutched Jem's arm. 'It's from there,' he whispered, pointing to the inner door. The red light, firelight or lamplight, flickered beneath it with an evil insistence.

Jem started forward. He pressed his ear to the door. Then came another scream. 'Raj, it's torture! They're torturing someone!' He beat against the door with his fists. 'Murdering monsters! Stop it, stop it!'

What happened instead was a cruel mockery. First, as if from within their own chamber, came hollow, echoing laughter; then the door burst open, flung Jem across the carpet, and slammed shut again almost at once.

But the horror was just beginning.

'J-Jem,' said Rajal, gesturing uncertainly.

'Raj?' Jem picked himself up. He looked at Rajal. Then he looked where Rajal was pointing.

They moved forward, appalled.

Two figures, human forms, had been flung into their chamber. One was a huddled, cowering Patches. The other was Whale. He had fallen on his side. But in the shape he made in the sinister light, in the foul stench that filled the air, the fat sailor's fate was evident at once. Whale had been not only stripped and flayed; his torturers had ripped open his belly, too.

The guts trailed, steaming, over the tremulous floor.

'That stench!' Rajal gasped. 'I'm going to gag!'

'He's a dead man, Raj! Show some compassion!'

'What, have you lost your sense of *smell*?'

Rajal could not help himself. He darted to the window. Hooking his fingers through the glimmering grille, he breathed deeply on the perfumes of the garden. How he wished he could push through the grille, escaping into that rich, intoxicating domain!

Patches sobbed, convulsing, on the floor.

'I didn't tell,' the boy kept saying, 'I didn't, I didn't—'

Jem tried to comfort him. 'Patches, shh! It's all right—'

But his words, Jem knew, were hollow. He held the boy's shoulders and said no more.

'They tried and tried,' muttered Patches, when the convulsions ceased. 'Felt them in my head, I did, but I wouldn't let it go, I'd never let it go—'

'Patches, what do you mean? Let *what* go?'

'About the Cap'n – about the *Catty*. They wanted to know where we came from, Master Jem, they wanted to know everything, but I wouldn't betray the Cap'n, I—'

'Patches, of course you wouldn't, I know you—'

'But Whale did! He told them *everything*—'

'Shh, shh. Told them what, Patches?'

'About the Cap'n, about the treasure ... the treasure he's after, in the Eye of the Sea!'

Jem exhaled slowly. 'And what happened then?'

'That's when they killed him.'

'With ... with their minds?'

'With a knife, Master Jem!'

His finger shaking, as if in time with the shaking of the island, the boy pointed towards the reeking corpse. For a moment Jem was puzzled; then he saw the metallic glint. The Websisters, in their murderous frenzy, had left the deadly knife jutting from the guts.

'He deserved it,' Patches spat, suddenly bitter. 'But I deserved it, too – deserved it more than him.'

'Patches, don't be silly. No one deserves *that*.'

The boy sprang up, wringing his hands. 'But Master Jem, it was my fault, don't you see? Plotting against the Cap'n, they were – Whale and Walrus, Porpoise and Sea-Snake. Going to take over the *Catty*, they were – going to take the treasure for themselves, they were ...'

'Not much chance of that now,' Jem said grimly. 'Porpoise is dead, Whale's dead. And the others, too?'

The boy waved a distracted hand. 'Dead, dead. But I knew it, don't you see? I'd heard them, I knew, and ... oh, I kept meaning to tell the Cap'n, I did, but ...' He turned away sharply. 'I hated him, you know. Always hitting me, always calling me names, always going on with that stupid joke about Goody Palmer and her five daughters ... I wanted him to get his come-uppance, I wanted – but I mean ... oh, but I love him too, I love him! And now them Websisters are going to get him, and they'll kill him, and ... I tell you, it's all my fault!'

Jem caught the boy in his arms and let him sob.

Rajal looked on awkwardly. He was almost envious. He turned back to the window.

'I deserve it, don't I, Master Jem? What they done to Whale, why didn't they do that to me, too?'

'Patches, shh, *shh*.'

Rajal breathed the perfumes deeply and said, not turning around, 'The boy's got a point, Jem.'

'What's that, Raj?'

'They've let him live. Why?'

Jem said slowly, 'I have a horrible suspicion.'

Patches stepped back, lower lip trembling. 'M-Master Jem?'

But just then, Rajal gasped.

'Raj, what is it?' said Jem.

His friend stepped back from the window-grille. On the other side, almost obscured against the foliage, stood a small human form.

'Is it . . . Myla?' Jem breathed, astonished.

'It's Littler,' said Rajal.

'Titch, are you all right?'

'Do the Sisters know you're here?'

'Have you seen the others?'

Patches, Rajal and Jem had gathered round the grille. They spoke in whispers; flowers and vines draped caressingly over their small friend, almost overwhelming him in their pungent fragrance. Littler's clothes were crumpled and he was rubbing sleep from his eyes.

'I heard the screams,' he said, 'and I thought—'

'But what are you doing,' said Jem, 'in this garden?'

'I landed here,' said Littler, 'but can't get out. The wall's too high for me, and—'

'Littler, you haven't seen Myla?' Rajal said suddenly.

'A little girl,' said Jem, 'you haven't seen a girl?'

Littler's eyes widened. 'There *was* a girl. I gave her—'

'Rainbow's collar?' Jem said excitedly.

'Jem, what are you talking about?' said Rajal.

'Raj, it explains something, don't you see? That light from Myla's forehead, just before she vanished! She was wearing something, I'm sure of it, a silver band . . .'

'Littler,' Rajal burst out, 'you're a hero!'

Jem explained, 'That little girl is Raj's sister. She's a very special, magical little girl . . . but Littler, she was in the gravest danger. If anyone's saved her life, it was you.'

'You haven't seen her since?' said Rajal.

Littler shook his head.

Patches was pacing. He bit his lip. Moments earlier, the cabin boy had been ready to die; now a new purpose allayed his grief. 'Titch, what was that you said about a wall?'

'It's too high, higher than the treetops—'

'No wall's too high for me,' Patches boasted. 'I'll get us out of here if anyone can.'

'Only one problem,' said Rajal. 'Littler may be a prisoner in the garden, but we're prisoners behind this grille.' He shook the thick, metal bars. 'I don't think *this* is going to move, do you?'

'There are screws,' said Littler, 'on this side.'

'Screws?' said Jem. 'How many?'

Littler peered beneath the window ledge, then stood on tiptoe, craning his neck. 'Three, I think, top and bottom.'

'Three at the top, three at the bottom?'

Littler nodded. 'If I could unscrew them—'

'What?' said Rajal. 'You'd never reach the top!'

'He doesn't have to,' Patches said excitedly. 'Get the bottom free, Titch, that's all we need – then the three of us can push the grille out, at least enough to edge around.'

Rajal was sceptical. 'Has all this perfume gone to your heads? You're forgetting one thing, aren't you? How's he going to get out even *one* screw? With what? With his bare hands? Or do you think the flying island's going to *shake* them out?'

Patches gulped, 'There *is* something.'

Jem knew. Turning, he watched as Patches scuttled back to Whale's corpse. Holding his nose, the cabin boy hesitated, but not for long. He dived down, ripped out the bleeding knife and brought it back to the grille. Jem laughed wryly. Just as well the Websisters were conserving their magic; evidently they were not accustomed to killing people in the usual ways. They had just made a blunder. A big blunder.

Littler's eyes shone as he clutched the knife.

'Oh, just brilliant,' said Rajal. 'And I say again: how's Littler going to get out even one screw?'

Littler shot him an angry look. 'I saved your sister, didn't I?'

'He's got you there,' said Jem. 'Or so I hope.'

Lord Agonis, tomorrow I shall serve you more truly:
I shall look for you with eye-globes so eager that my eye-globes shall crack,
bursting bloody;
I shall work for you with hand-flesh so ardent that my hand-flesh shall
swell, bursting bloody . . .

'What's that you say, Patches?' Jem said kindly.

Resisting revulsion, the cabin boy was kneeling beside Whale's corpse. He turned, glad for the dim light that concealed his flushing face. 'N-nothing, Master Jem,' he said; then, sheepishly, 'just some litany-lines. They're the only prayers I remember, and . . . well, Whale may have been a dirty mutineer, but everyone deserves a prayer when he dies, doesn't he?'

Littler, back at the window, was busy with the knife. Rajal watched, still sceptical.

Jem kept his voice low. 'Who taught you these prayers, Patches?'

'M-my father.' The boy swallowed hard and pride crept into his voice. 'A staunch Agonist, he was, Master Jem, honest he was. Always taught me me prayers, he did, whenever he visited Mother's.'

'He didn't live with her, then?'

'Oh no, he lived with his other family, in the next valley. But he used to visit Mother all the time, he did, and he was ever so kind. It was only when Mother got married – to another father, I mean – that things went wrong. The new father didn't like me. I wanted him to, but he just beat me. So I ran off to sea – what else could I do? But sometimes – you know, I wish I'd gone to my *first* father.'

Jem looked down reflectively. 'Have you a name, Patches?'

The boy was confused. 'My father – my real father, I mean – was called Waxwell.'

'Goodman Waxwell?' Jem thought it best to say no more. From time to time, the thought had come to him that Patches had traces of a Tarn accent. To be sure, the boy's father was the same Goodman Waxwell, surgeon and apothecary, from whose depraved evil Jem had suffered so much.[1] How often had he shuddered with loathing, thinking of that grotesque creature, Aunt Umbecca's sometime paramour, with his twisty smile and unravelling wig and sinuous, soft hands? Strange, that Patches should remember the fellow so differently! Strange – but then, not so strange at all – that Waxwell, that embodiment of Agonist piety, should have had not only a mistress, but a bastard son!

Jem realised that Patches was looking at him quizzically. 'Master Jem? You're from the same part of the world as me. You didn't . . . *know* my father, did you? Didn't meet him?'

Quickly, Jem shook his head. How should he reply? There was only one thing for it. 'I . . . I didn't get out much in those days, Patches. But your father . . . he sounds as if he was a good man. You'll treasure his memory, won't you? Now let's both say those litany-lines.'

'You know them, too?'

Jem thought of his Aunt Umbecca, and swallowed hard.

[1] See *The Harlequin's Dance.*

Lord Agonis, tomorrow I shall seek you more truly:
I shall call for you with voice-cords so tautened that my voice-cords shall
  snap, bursting bloody;
I shall crawl for you across fields of briars until my knees and hands tear
  open, bursting bloody ...

'How's it coming, Littler?' said Jem.

'Two. One more, and that's the bottom done.'

Patches grinned, 'Good old Titch! Any moment now, we'll be over that wall!'

'It'll never work, I tell you,' said Rajal.

Littler bristled. 'Two! Look, two!'

'Titch has got two, he'll get three,' said Patches.

'Oh, and what about pushing that grille *out*?'

Frowning, Jem drew Rajal aside. 'Raj, what's wrong with you? Poor Littler's wrenching out his shoulders for our sake and all you can do is moan! Don't you *want* to escape?'

'Of course I do!' Rajal grew flustered. 'It's just ... well, those monsters are out right now, looking for Myla. What if they *find* her? If anyone's going to be sacrificed, I'd ... well, I'd rather it were—'

'Us?' Jem had to smile.

'Oh, you know what I mean!'

Jem was sombre again. 'It's a noble thought, Raj, but we can't do much for Myla if we're stuck in here. If we escape, perhaps we can find her *first*.'

'I suppose so,' said Rajal.

Littler cried in triumph: 'Three!'

'Good old Titch!'

'Come on, Raj,' said Jem. 'Are you ready to put your shoulder into this?'

'Stand well back, Titch!'

The three captives stood poised, ready to ram the loosened grille. But as they lurched forward, a fearsome, renewed cacophony sounded from the throne room. Blue light fizzed beneath the door. The palace rocked. They crashed to the carpet. Terrified, Littler pressed against the grille; at first, Jem thought their plan had been discovered.

But the commotion in the Spidermother's lair had a different object. Through the harsh crashings of sound Jem made out angry, familiar words, something about intruders, something about treachery, something about punishment and impending death. The words were almost the same as those he had heard with Rajal, earlier that night. The double doors flew open and Websisters goaded new captives brutally inside. Suddenly Jem felt a surge of wild joy.

The survivors from the *Catayane*!

Tagan fanned his face with a long hand. Buby shrieked and leapt through the darkness. Captain Porlo slithered to the floor. At once, Patches rushed to him, plunging back into desperate contrition, begging his master to forgive him, forgive him.

Ra Fanana cradled the old head in her arms. 'Dear Patches,' she sobbed, 'it's no good now. His mind's gone, really gone this time. Poor Faris! He just wanted to go down with his ship!'

Patches gasped, 'The *Catty*'s lost?'

He sank, horrorstruck, beside his master.

Ra Fanana saw Whale's corpse and screamed.

Jem went to Selinda. The girl's face was bruised and her clothes were torn, as if she had been savagely beaten.

'Oh Jem, it was horrible! We were caught up in the Blue Storm, we whizzed round and round . . . we were going to break up at any moment . . . then this thing came down, this thing like a ship, but without sails . . . it swept round and round after us, flashing blue lightning . . . they boarded us and they caught us and they herded us into their ship . . . and we saw the dear *Catayane* falling down and down, spinning down through the calm in the centre of the Blue Storm . . . then the skyship rose higher, and then . . . and then . . .'

The girl hid her face. 'Oh, those creatures! Can they be women? And that spider . . . oh, Jem, it was horrible, horrible!'

Jem held her tightly; Rajal clutched Tagan.

'Tagan,' he urged, 'you're sure you're all right?'

The eunuch was trembling violently, but struggled hard to preserve his old, flip manner. 'Fine, fine. Done us a favour really, those ladies have. That old hulk of ours was about to become driftwood – and really, those blue ships of theirs *are* rather swish. Have your seen the upholstery? And those robes they wear – and those fingernails! Now, *they*'ll be all the rage next season in Hora, if I've got anything to do with it – no, those ladies have done us a favour, dearie, a definite favour.'

'Since *you're* here,' smiled Rajal, 'I have to agree.'

A favour, yes: but for how long?

The red door opened. Backlit weirdly in the light were two Websisters, standing a little apart; gruesomely, the light that spilt between them fell on Whale's corpse. The guts and naked flesh shone richly in the redness.

Tagan, eyeing the corpse, murmured a little less confidently, 'I say, dearie, I suppose that wasn't an . . . *accident*?'

Rajal gulped. 'I'm afraid not.'

He gulped again when the Websisters spoke.

Captain Faris Porlo, you are an enemy of our race. You would seek to purloin the treasure that is ours, and ours alone. Your evil campaign can be punished only by death: but first, before you meet your agonising end, the Spidermother would have us learn your secrets.

'Secrets?' Ra Fanana burst out. 'What secrets can he tell you? Can't you see he's an old man, and sick?'

She would have rushed on the Websisters, but Selinda held her back.

'She's right!' said Patches. 'What can the Cap'n tell you?'

You would question us, flame-haired child?

'Damn right I'd . . . I'd—'

Oh, indeed? But you, we have not forgotten, were hardly willing to answer those questions we put to you. Never mind: perhaps your captain will show greater eagerness when he hears his loyal young servant scream for mercy.

'What? What are you—'

But before Patches could say more, the Websisters had seized him, whizzing him across the chamber on fizzing rays of force. Laughter burst on the air and the red door slammed.

It was only an instant before the first scream came.

Buby leapt, cowering, behind a couch.

Selinda turned, wringing her hands. 'But this is terrible! The captain's lost his mind, he can't—'

Raging, Jem beat at the door. It was shut fast. Again came the evil laughter; again came a scream.

'There's nothing we can do,' moaned Ra Fanana.

'We *can* escape,' said Rajal, then cursed himself at once.

Jem took charge. 'We can't leave Patches! Raj, Tagan, everyone – we were going to break through the window, but now we'll break through the door. Raj, you and me first—'

A third scream came from behind the door; then a different scream from the garden.

Tagan reeled. 'What's happening?'

It was Littler. All night, Websisters had scoured the island, searching for the missing Myla; only now had they searched the secret garden.

And found Littler.

His cries rang out piteously.

Tagan ran to the window, rattling at the grille. Rays zapped him and he staggered back.

Behind the red door, Patches screamed again.

'The door!' Jem gasped. 'Raj, again! It's all we can do!'

They charged against the hard, unyielding wood; they doubled back, charging again, but this time the door burst open of its own accord as a mighty earthquake shook the palace. All night there had been tremors, rocking the surface of the flying island; the Spidermother had shaken the palace with her anger; but never until now had there been paroxysms like this, exploding in wave after violent wave. The floor buckled and twisted; masonry fell; trees crashed in the garden outside.

In the red room, Patches leapt free from his tormentors. Buby rushed in; viciously, the little monkey scratched and bit them. Meanwhile, Captain Porlo bellowed and bellowed, crying out that it was a stormy sea, a stormy sea tonight . . .

Selinda gasped, 'But we're in the *air*—'

'Yes,' said Tagan, 'and not flying smoothly!'

'The flight,' said Jem, 'have they lost control?'

'Jem,' cried Rajal, 'it's dawn! I see the sunlight! We must have reached the Eye of the Sea!'

In the garden, Littler was free too. His thwarted captors were after him at once. Wildly he pounded between the flowers and trees, through the swirling perfumes, through the whirling petals and leaves. Then, before him, was a breach in the wall, shaken open by the violence of the earthquake.

He plummeted through, racing out on to the Thunderer's slopes. Dust and rocks slithered all around him in the fractured dawn.

He staggered. He looked this way and that.

The rocking ceased at last. The palace was in ruins. Jem and Rajal staggered to their feet, coughing and slapping their dusty clothes. For a moment they wondered if they were free.

But only for a moment.

Suddenly the Spidermother's voice echoed around them, booming with wild, insane exultation:

WEBSISTERS, WE HAVE CAUGHT THE DAWN! SHARPLY, EVEN NOW, OUR FLYING ISLAND DESCENDS THROUGH THE AIR, CONVERGING UPON THE EYE OF THE SEA! OUR DESTINY IS UPON US! FORGET ALL ELSE: MAKE READY MY PAWNS TO MEET THEIR FATE! PREPARE THE MALE-CREATURES TO BE FLUNG INTO THE THUNDERER!

WEBSISTERS, REJOICE! OUR TIME HAS COME!

Chapter 71

THE TIGER IN THE SMOKE

'Jem, the pain—'
  'Grit your teeth, Raj—'
  'I can't – I can't *stand* it—'
  'Stand it! This is just the start—'
  'Wait, my crystal! It's glowing again—'
  'Mine too! The light, it's so bright—'
  'Jem, I'm going to throw up—'
  'Raj, the pain, the pain—'
  'Grit your teeth, Jem—'
  'I can't ... *stand* it—'
Booming with energy, buffeted by explosions, the skyship surged up
through the churning air, flashing blue lightning through billowing dust
and smoke. One Websister worked the controls; another, fingernails
fizzing blue, held the captives fast in auroral chains, shrieking with glee
as the red crystal, then the purple crystal leapt into life. Through dazzled
eyes Jem and Rajal took in the shuddering ship, with its plush blue
padding, its gleaming brass levers and dials; outside, through riveted
portholes, they made out the Thunderer's juddering slopes, then the
entire Isle of Inorchis, descending over the sea towards the Maelstrom of
the Mandru and the terrifying, yawning darkness that lay at its core.
  'The Eye of the Sea! It must be—'
  'I don't get it! How are they going to—'
  'Down the Thunderer! It's open underneath—'
  'You mean it's like a funnel, and they throw us down—'
  'That's it! And down we go, sucked into that whirlpool—'
  'And all the time the Spidermother's controlling us—'
  'Like bait on a hook! Bait for the blue crystal—'
  'Jem, I think I'm really going to be sick—'
  'Me too! The carpet was never like—'
  'Carpet? I mean the *whirlpool*—'
Clouds churned wildly, chaotic with light in the surging dawn. Jem
and Rajal struggled to no avail. Nothing could resist the crackling bands
of energy that held them fast. In their minds and all around them, in the
skyship, in the air, filling the world, they felt the presence of the
Spidermother, seething in the knowledge that her destiny was at hand.

Her voice came again, crashing and shrieking:

WEBSISTERS, THE MOMENT IS UPON US! FOR AEONS WE HAVE SOUGHT REVENGE ON THE MOTHER WHO ABANDONED US, VOWING TO POSSESS JAVANDER'S POWER. NOW COMES THE CLIMAX OF OUR QUEST. ALL MY ENERGIES I NOW EXPEND. ALL THE ENERGIES OF THIS ISLE I USE.

WEBSISTERS, IN THIS ACTION I DIE: BUT REPINE NOT THAT I LEAVE YOU. WITH THE BLUE CRYSTAL, I SHALL BE LIBERATED INTO IMMORTALITY. WITH THE BLUE CRYSTAL, I SHALL BE YOUR QUEEN NO LONGER.

WEBSISTERS, I SHALL BE YOUR GODDESS!

Laughter rang upon the air, rang out so wildly it might split the world apart. Below, between the violent clouds, Jem and Rajal glimpsed hundreds upon hundreds of Websisters, blue robes streaming behind them as they scrambled up the slopes. Some slipped back; boulders crushed some, but no Websister helped another. They were blind, swarming insects; all that mattered was this desperate scramble to be present on the caldera at the moment of destiny.

They slumped down, abasing themselves on the rim, as all around them, above the rumblings, the Spidermother's laughter echoed insanely.

'The cobber-as, the cobber-as—'

'Oh Faris, please—'

Ra Fanana wrung her hands. She turned, this way and that, in the ruined chamber, wishing only that there were something she could do. Already the captain had lost his mind; now, as Master Jem and Master Rajal faced death, as the Spidermother's wild words echoed from the throne room, the old man could only writhe on the floor, lost in the terrifying grip of his delusions. Did he even know Ra Fanana was there? He flailed for his cutlass, slashing the air with the rusty blade. Buby shrieked and capered round her stricken master.

'The cobber-as, the cobber-as—'

Sobbing, Ra Fanana staggered out of range.

Tagan embraced her. 'Poor Fa Fa—'

'Poor Faris! Oh Tagan, what's to become—'

'Fa Fa, what's to become of us?'

Dust whirled. Beams and columns, powdery remnants of cornice and ceiling hovered precariously above them. By the double doors were Selinda and Patches. The door frame was twisted, but still the door was shut fast. With chunks of brick, Selinda, then Patches smashed at the lock.

Tagan breathed, 'But the Spidermother's through there—'

He saw sunlight, through a fallen wall.

'There's another way!' he cried. 'Quick, there's another—'

Selinda's eyes flashed. 'Tagan, don't you understand? She's alone in there – she's controlling all this . . . If we can just get to her—'

'Then she'll kill you!' Tagan shrieked. 'Oh, my lady—'

'Don't you want to save Master Jem?' cried Patches. 'Don't you want to save Master *Raj*?'

Tagan clapped a hand across his mouth. He looked round, then round again, in horrified bewilderment. Shouldn't he stay with Fa Fa? Shouldn't he get her out of here? At any moment the ceiling could fall. But already the nurse, sobbing and moaning, had stumbled back through the rubble, longing only to be with the crazed captain. Tagan turned back. Wild, evil laughter pulsed again through the doors.

He lurched forward. 'Give me that brick!'

'Jem, we've got out of scrapes before—'

'Scrapes? We've cheated death—'

'Yes, we've got out of scrapes *before*—'

'So we can get out of this one? Is that what—'

'Actually, I meant this time I think we've gone—'

'A bit too far? Hm – Raj, that's what I was—'

'Oh, Jem! I thought at least *you* wouldn't—'

'Give up? Never, Raj, but just in case—'

'We should say goodbye? Oh, Jem—'

'Raj, let's just say the *moment*—'

The moment is upon them. A panel slides open in the hull of the skyship. Only a fizzing lasso of energy prevents the captives from lurching out at once. A blue column of light – summoned, perhaps, by the worshipping Websisters – sears up through the caldera, streaming through the clouds, striking the hovering, lurching vessel. Beneath the island, the maelstrom swirls faster. How can the island not be consumed?

The skyship descends, closer, closer to the juddering caldera.

Jem gazes below, his heart thudding immensely.

Then his heart stops.

'Raj, look!'

Rajal's eyes zigzag wildly, here, there. His mind reels. He stumbles, zapping painfully against the blue lasso. Can it be? Scrambling up the shuddering mountainside, pushing through the worshipping, entranced Websisters, comes an intruder to the ceremony. Desperately the intruder leaps up and down, waving his arms through the choking smoke, calling out to Jem, calling out to Rajal . . .

Jem curses. 'Oh, Littler, Littler! What are you—'

'The fool! He'll get himself killed—'
'So that makes three of us—'
'The little *fool*!'

'That sound—'
'That light—'
'That pulsing web—'

The throne room was alive with the Spidermother's evil. Crashing through the doors, the chunk of brick falling from his hand, Tagan was almost knocked back by the searing, seething force. All around the walls, projected through the creature's mental power, flickered wild, violent images of the caldera and all that was happening there.

Were they too late? The eunuch flailed forward, gasping, screaming Rajal's name. Selinda jammed her hands across her ears. The Web would drive her mad, drive them all mad. Waves of evil, waves of madness radiated towards them, forcing them back. They sank to their knees. They clenched their teeth. They clawed at the floor.

Patches was the first to rally. With a cry, he leapt up on the Web as if it were rigging. Blue power zapped along the great tensile fibres, burning his hands. The boy was in agony, but would not let go. He swung up his legs. He edged forward. Earnestly he looked towards the thick blue tube that throbbed and surged from the Spidermother's forehead, connecting her to the mighty Web. He whipped the knife from his belt, clutching it in his teeth.

He cried to Selinda, 'Distract her! Distract her—'

The girl swivelled round. The chunk of brick! She grabbed it, flinging it at the hideous wizened head. Shrieks came from the Spidermother and the brick whizzed back, striking the wall, smashing into powder.

The power surged. Selinda crumpled. Tagan could only jerk and twitch. Visions of the caldera churned all around them. Down they stared into the vertiginous depths, then up into the wild violence of the clouds. The skyship shuddered, lurched, swooped. They saw the Websisters, massing evilly, surging forward at the Spidermother's command. They saw Jem and Rajal, about to fall.

Any moment now, any moment now. Still Patches edged towards the pulsing tube; still the knife glittered between his teeth. But still the power exploded all around him. He screamed out, falling. The knife clattered from his mouth. It spun on the floor. He grabbed it, slicing his hands. Again, ignoring his agony, he leapt up into the Web.

On and on came the power, more and more. Tagan and Selinda clutched hands, prayed.

Laughter crashed again, then the crazed command:

WEBSISTERS, THE TIME HAS COME!
WEBSISTERS, NOW, NOW!

But not now: not yet. In an instant, Jem and Rajal would tumble down, down. But through the visions of the caldera, first Tagan, then Selinda, then Patches see something astonishing: a startling apparition, swooping out of the clouds.

They cry out. Can the vision be real?

✳ ✳ ✳ ✳ ✳

'This is it, it's got to be—'
'Goodbye, Jem—'
'Goodbye, Raj—'
The blue lasso fizzes out of being.

But wait! In the skyship, the Websisters scream; a louder scream, the Spidermother's, crashes on the air.

The ship shudders, rocks. Jem and Rajal fall to the floor. Their captors lurch towards the open doorway; one Websister, then another, is sucked out into the whistling, whirling vortex.

The ship reels, spinning round and round.

Rajal shouts, 'Jem, remember how I felt sick?'

'What's that, Raj? Raj, just hang on—'

'Well, Jem, that was nothing to this—'

They clutch at pylons, levers, upholstery; below, round the caldera, the Websisters are in turmoil, pointing up, anguished, at the intruder in the sky.

Littler cheers. Excitedly, he leaps up and down.

✳ ✳ ✳ ✳ ✳

Patches leaps up too.

The Spidermother is reeling, moaning, the Web and all the images round the walls flickering uncertainly. Quickly the cabin boy swings forward, before the creature can send its repelling rays again. Choking with horror, he is clambering over the diseased, bloated body, agony searing through his wounded hands.

Selinda and Tagan look on helplessly, then suddenly they are grabbing up rubble from the floor – bricks, glass, shards of metal. They bash and hack at the fibres of the Web. With one hand, Patches seizes the sickening, pulsing tube; in the other, he clutches the knife. Already, it seems, the Spidermother is dying, her blue light fading.

Then all at once the light and power surge up again, brighter than ever before. The Spidermother scuttles wildly. Patches skews and bucks on her back. Blue violence rocks the throne room. Selinda and Tagan stagger and fall.

Patches screams, the knife whizzing from his hand.

At first, neither Jem nor Rajal sees what has happened, so intent are they on the spinning skyship. In an instant they must crash into the mountainside, or plunge down the caldera.

Only at the last do they see their saviours flashing out of the billowing smoke and the blue, swirling magical lights.

A flying tiger, with a rider on its back!

A shout comes, 'Jem, Raj! We'll swoop again – get ready to jump!'

'Raj, it's Uchy—'

'Jem, it's impossible—'

'Believe it, Raj! And get ready to jump!'

Jem grabs Rajal. They edge towards the door. Now Ucheus and the tiger swoop up, up, ready to dive back, ready to catch them. Ucheus is naked and his skin glows like gold. Power flashes from the tiger's stripes. Its claws are immense and it roars mightily.

Explosions rock the skyship. The Spidermother's rage is palpable, shaking the smoke and the churning air.

'Raj, are you ready? This is our one chance—'

'I'm ready, Jem! Here they come—'

The tiger dives. But now, suddenly, the Websisters rally. Scattered round the caldera, the evil beings rear up. They have no volition, they barely have life – no, they have *no* life; all are mere puppets of the Spidermother's rage.

In unison, they raise their long-nailed hands.

Littler reels, crying out in horror.

Jem cries, 'Raj, now – jump!'

Too late! Blue bolts shoot from the Websisters, blasting Ucheus and the flying tiger, just as Jem and Rajal make their desperate leap.

The tiger howls, hurtling back through the smoke.

Littler loses his balance. Shrieking, he slips into the caldera.

The skyship crashes into the Websisters, exploding in a ball of flame.

Ucheus tumbles down the mountainside.

Jem, Rajal and Littler fall down and down.

In the throne room, despairing, Tagan and Selinda see everything, projected all around them in lurid distortion, image on image, multiplied insanely.

Patches is oblivious to all this. Clinging to the great mound of the Spidermother, as the hideous creature scuttles round its Web, the cabin boy can only scream and scream, his pain greater than any he has known before. He feels his heart is bursting; in the next moment, he is certain, he will die.

Then, as if his heart has burst indeed, a terrible rage explodes inside Patches, for all the humiliations his life has brought him, for all that he has never known and all that he shall never know, if the Spidermother kills him now. He will not die, he will not! Will he not live to be a great man, a hero of the five seas like Cap'n Porlo? Will he not live to love a beautiful girl, a girl like Miss Selinda?

For an instant – but an instant is all it takes – the power in Patches is greater than the Spidermother's power. With one brutal, wrenching tug, he rips out the pulsing tube. Vile blue fluid spurts; the boy drops, spent, almost unconscious.

Now the Spidermother's death throes fill the world in a last cataclysm of sound and searing light. The Web is tearing, collapsing. Gasping, Tagan and Selinda just have time to drag Patches free before the great sagging edifice gives way and the Spidermother crashes to the floor. Revolted, they grab at rocky chunks, pelting and beating at the monstrous body until at last they are certain it is dead.

They rise to their feet; they turn, dazed and staggering. Patches and Selinda clutch each other, hard. The boy's hands are bleeding, but he holds the girl with his wrists, absurdly careful of her ruined clothes.

Shall he kiss her now? Perhaps; but then Tagan utters a guttural sound and points.

Through the clearing dust, they peer through the double doors. In the chamber beyond, the ceiling has fallen, leaving only a mountain of devastation. But what's this? Crestfallen, loping slowly over the wreckage, comes Buby. The little monkey flings back her head. A terrible keening erupts from her lips.

'Fa Fa?' Again, Tagan makes the guttural sound.

'Ra Ra?' Horrified, Selinda gazes into the wreckage.

'Cap'n?' Patches sinks down, covering his face, pressing it deeply into his bleeding hands.

Chapter 72

UNDER THE VOLCANO

'Jem?' Rajal's voice was dreamy.

So was Jem's. 'What's that, Raj?'

'How come we're . . . how come we're alive?'

Jem grinned, 'How can we talk? How can we hear?'

Rajal laughed, 'That's your answer?'

'My crystal's glowing, Raj. So's yours.'

'What about Littler? He's got no crystal.'

'I suppose ours protect him.'

'This is . . . *weird*, Jem.'

'It's fantastic.'

For what seemed like aeons, gorgeous visions had streamed past their eyes, swirling and exploding like slow fireworks; with immeasurable slowness they turned and tumbled, tumbled and turned through the foaming, bubbling maelstrom that held them its grip.

At first Littler had turned faster, but Jem and Rajal, reaching through the currents, had each caught one of his small hands. Down, down the three friends sank together, grinning and laughing at the riotous, crazy beauty all around them.

At last, in a laggardly puff of sand, they found themselves on the bottom of the sea. Mysterious lights played through the currents; exotic fish – striped like tigers, spotted like leopards, patterned bizarrely like the faces of baboons – flickered between blue-green undulating plants and lush, precarious, pink-red coral.

Jem and his friends gazed around them in wonder. They saw the wreckage of an ancient ship; they saw the twisted skeleton of a man, furred thickly with undersea algae. In the trance-like state that possessed them, they knew not even the beginnings of fear. Nor did they feel the desires of the world: they saw a chest, burst open, filled with glittering gold. Could it be Captain Porlo's treasure, lost immemorially on the bottom of the sea?

No matter: there it would lie.

Swishing their arms, kicking back their legs, they moved on like dreamers through the watery silence, their skins weirdly pale, their hair waving upwards, bubbles streaming from their noses and mouths.

The naked youth was bruised and scratched.

Ucheus stirred at last. Where could he be? Already the blue blast that had struck him above the caldera seemed long ago. Had it happened to someone else? Had he witnessed it from afar? In his memory he saw a beautiful, silent efflorescence, enveloping the strange rider; after that he was aware of falling, spinning down and down, not through any undersea domain, but rather, through buffeting chambers of clouds.

Down, down. And what had happened to the creature he had ridden, the creature that had come to him like the answer to a prayer? *Down, down.* It was as if illusion had given way to truth, leaving no answers, no answers at all. *Down, down.* Was he back where he had started?

No. But yes. This was not the Plateau of Voices: Ucheus was back on Castor-uncle's farm.

His heart leapt; for a moment he thought that all was as before, that none of these last events had really happened. But which ones? And how many? Wonderingly his mind reeled in reverse, undoing all the horrors he had known; soon he would be back before his Manhood Trial.

With blurring eyes he gazed upon the homestead, on the barn, on the familiar orchard and the fields beyond, empty and shimmering in the day's rising heat. Ah, but if only he could make time run back! With longing he imagined himself on the cool verandah, curled up in Castor-uncle's big curving chair, waiting for the family – *his* family – to come home.

But Ucheus supposed they never would.

Slowly, inevitably, his gaze rose upwards, towards the jutting outcrop of Dead Man's Lookout. What weariness suffused his limbs! What strange lightness, too! Like a sleepwalker, the naked youth moved forward, his gaze never veering away again from the great precipitous wall of boulders.

He reached up his hands, and began to climb.

At Jem's chest, and Rajal's too, the crystals shine like lanterns. But to where are these lanterns lighting the way?

With the strange, dissolving speed of dreams, the answer comes at once. Now Jem, as if with foreknowledge, gestures ahead; now Rajal, now Littler looks up in awe. Undersea clouds furl back like curtains, revealing the immensity, looming and vast, of the edifice known as the Briny Citadel.

'I don't, I can't believe it—'

'It's so ... beautiful—'

'It so ... ugly—'

'This can't be real—'

'It *has* to be a dream—'

All is as promised in the legends of old: all as promised, but more fantastical still. With its outlandish, luminescent turrets, with its domes, with its minarets and spires sometimes swollen, sometimes tapering, sometimes spiralling or looping, this citadel is unlike any on land has been or ever could be. Castellations zigzag like the jaws of sharks; huge swirling-patterned shells are inset in every strangely curving, strangely angled wall. There are luscious writhing corals, monstrous sparkling pearls, all the most gorgeous treasures of the sea. On and on the palace stretches, glimmering and vast, a place of fabulous darkness, a place of fabulous light.

Marvelling, Jem, Rajal and Littler take in the grotesque, unearthly vision; then, filled only with a calm certainty, they make their way towards mighty gates, garlanded with seaweed and patterned with the shapes of anchors, mermaids and fish. There is no need to announce themselves. The gates swing open; the three friends swim forward, following a route marked by a path of shells.

Undersea gardens shimmer all around them. What treasures loom there! *Look, Jem, there's the crystal*, Rajal almost bursts out, startled at the sight of a rich blue stone; then he sees that it is but one of many precious stones, strewn like strange fruit amongst the bizarre trees and flowers. Do jewels not glimmer, too, in the scales of flickering fish? Can that crab, scuttling on the path below, have a shell encrusted with rubies? Can that lobster, over there, have golden claws?

All this flows dreamily past their eyes. Only as they draw near the mighty, verdigris-coloured portals of the citadel do Jem, Rajal and Littler feel some disquiet. Now, as the twisted edifice glowers above them, they see the sinister tentacled creatures, peering from the windows with glaucous eyes; they see the mighty-snouted sharks, louring like sentinels above the battlements. As if in the afterglow of a drug's hazy illusions, the three friends feel their minds return to them. But this place, they know, is no mere illusion; from this visionary realm, there is no easy waking.

The portals are carved with outlandish bas-reliefs. A huge brass knocker is encrusted with barnacles. Jem reaches for it, as if by instinct, but the portals groan open before he can knock. There is a rapid stream of bubbles, then the water clears. Inside is a dark and mysterious hall.

'Jem, I'm frightened,' Littler blurts.

At once the little boy is ashamed; but relieved, too, when Jem, then Rajal, takes his hand again.

They swim across the threshold.

Nearsider, come. Nearsider, quick.

It was only well into the climb, with his heart pounding hard and his muscles straining, that Ucheus made out the figures above him, gazing down at him through the dazzling sunlight. Could that be Adri – scrawny, nervous Adri? Could that really be Infin Ijas? Of course they were illusions, he knew that; but if they were, he did not care. He wanted them to be real: he wanted to be with them.

Hand after hand, foot after foot, Ucheus climbed, fitting into the familiar holds that Maius Eneo had shown him long ago. If he was naked, if he was crazed, all seemed to him as it had been before, with the sun striking down at him like a hammer at an anvil. His breath came in gasps and the rocks were steeper. But now he saw Nicander, little Nicander. Then there was Juros Iko, or was that Jenas Iko? He saw Zap, boneheaded Zap, and laughed aloud. The dear old follyface!

Nearsider, come. Nearsider, quick.

And now the rocks are sheerer, sharper; now Ucheus grits his teeth; now, all at once, he finds himself frightened, despite the joy he knows he should feel. He flattens himself against the treacherous cliff-face. Blood runs from cuts in his naked skin. How much higher? He turns and looks around. The air is wide and empty, but Ucheus does not scream; he waits; his desperation sinks; he climbs again.

Sheerer, sharper. And there above him is Leki, Leki as he was before he became a madmaster; then dear Ojo, his first friend and perhaps, Ucheus senses, always his best; yes, all the lost boys are waiting to receive him, and all are as they had been long ago, back in the days before their Manhood Trial.

And Maius Eneo? But of course he is there too, and of course – Ucheus imagines it before it happens – his marvellous cousin shall be the one to step forward, reaching down with his strong, firm hand.

Nearsider, come. Nearsider, quick.

Handholds. Footholds. Hammer on the anvil. Must not look, must not turn – and then the hand is there. And at the end, as Ucheus reaches back, he knows for certain that this is no illusion – knows, too, that this has always been his destiny, from the moment he first met his marvellous cousin.

Is he a follyface? Is he a madmaster? No, this is good. No, this is right. He thinks of the summoning that has brought him to this place, and dimly, even now, he is aware that there are those who would think him the victim of a dark, deceiving magic. What does he care? How often has he dreamed of this changing of places? For the last time – he chokes back his sobs so his eyes will be clear – Ucheus looks into the angular, youthful face, shadowy against the bright sun that beats behind. It is a face that he shall never see again.

He whispers, 'I love you, Maius Eneo.'

And grips, hard, to the triumphant hand.

Rajal says uncertainly, 'Jem, I'm wondering—'

'What's that, Raj?'

'Well, don't you wonder who's controlling all this? I mean, this strange descent of ours – these dreamy feelings – these opening doors. Is the Spidermother still in charge, dangling us like bait? Or could it be—'

'The goddess Javander? I don't know, Raj. But I can't feel the Spidermother in my head any more, can you?'

'You think she's lost control?'

'Perhaps. But if she has, then—'

'Then what, Jem?' Littler shrills.

'Then she's left us to face this alone.'

But quite what they are facing is not yet clear. They keep tightly together; all around them, the darkness is deep, illumined only by fleeting glimmerings. Littler thinks of the tentacled things in the windows; Rajal thinks of the sharks; Jem tries to remember all he has heard of the fugitive goddess who built this place.

Littler gulps, 'You don't think we should turn back?'

'Funny, I was just thinking that,' says Rajal.

'Well, it's not a *bad* idea,' says Jem.

But then, perhaps to comfort them – or perhaps to mock – there comes a respite from the fearful darkness. First it is just more of the glimmerings – purple, red, blue – in a cluster this time; then, very slowly, there is a gathering of brightness and soft, strange music drifts towards them on the currents.

Brighter grow the gleamings; louder grows the music; brilliant chandeliers shine down and Jem, Rajal and Littler see that they have entered a massive ballroom, a gorgeous place of shimmering looking-glasses, golden cherubs, soaring fluted columns and there, on an ornate podium, the strangest band of musicians ever assembled.

It is the ORCHESTRA AQUATIC, of which legends tell. Seals, poised plumply, sit at twin virginals; octopuses strum at many-necked guitars; rays, their tentacles dishevelled, saw at fiddles; crabs stop the holes in recorders with their claws. There are swordfish, blowing trumpets; porpoises, puffing tubas; sea-snakes, fizzing with current, scrape across bass-viols; sea-urchins roll back and forth on xylophones fashioned from oysters and cockle-shells. A walrus presides pompously over the timpani; a baby whale holds cymbals in his fins; a big blunt-headed shark butts, a little too insistently, at a gleaming gong. Clams click-clack back and forth in rhythm; a vocal trio of bobbing sea-horses bubble out their *oohs* and *aahs*.

Swishing to the fore – a conch-shell clutched, like a megaphone, in his fins – a slender swordfish sings, his long proboscis glittering, sweeping mournfully back and forth.

The Swordfish's Song

In the circle of light from my lamp
I would study ancient scrolls,
But ah, before my eye there rolls
A hieroglyph of startling stamp:
My gaze I sweep towards it,
But ah, what then should fall?
My long proboscis overturns my ink—
My spirits sink
In choler!
   I would be a scholar
   But how can I be a scholar
   With my sword,
   With my sword,
   With my sword?

In a grotto of coral I wait
With a pounding, aching breast,
For how I long to ask the quest-
ion crucial to secure my fate:
My pretty cod swims forward,
But ah, what then should fall?
Upon my pointy nose I pierce her heart –
In shame I start
For cover!
   I would be a lover
   But how can I be a lover
   With my sword,
   With my sword,
   With my sword?

This moving ballad proceeds through many verses, in which the swordfish successively comes to grief in his attempts to be a physician, a lawyer, a preacher, a farmer, a tavern-keeper, a whoremonger and even a soldier, in each case betrayed by his troublesome sword.

But if the singer is sad, then never mind: the music that surrounds him is a merry cacophony, and the scene that fills the ballroom is one of joy. Appearing as if from nowhere, sea creatures of all kinds swish and jig above the watery dance floor, creating all manner of swirling currents. Sea-lions waltz with squid, jellyfish with sturgeon; there are carp, brill, cod, hake, haddock and herring-fish, coming together and parting in stately quadrilles; eels twist and gyrate, fizzing in rhythm; cuttlefish jig up and down, squirting ink excitedly; starfish come together, cluster, then burst out like joyous, undersea fireworks.

Watching, Jem and his friends are lost in wonderment. Littler's eyes shine and he claps his hands. But then the swordfish relinquishes his conch-shell, and the music subsides to a discreet murmur. The dancers disperse – but in their place come creatures still more astonishing.

'They're . . . boys!' says Littler.

'Boys,' says Rajal, 'with tails like fish!'

'And blue scaly skin – and seaweed hair!'

Jem remembers a myth he has heard. 'So it's true what they say – when Wenayans die, they come down here to serve Javander.'

Rajal is appalled; Littler cowers, frightened. But what is there to fear, Jem wonders, when the scaly servants, like servants in any great house, merely bring forth goblets, plates and cutlery? With tails flicking here and there, deftly they lay out a long banqueting-table that has risen from the centre of the floor.

The table is strangely shaped, with many irregular curves; the top is a huge, swirling-patterned slab of rock, supported by a plethora of waxy-looking legs, like ancient stalactites in a sunken cave. Spaced around the table there are only four chairs. Each one is grotesquely ornate, encrusted thickly with shells and pearls; the one at the head of the table is the most ornate of all, a vast, golden, rococo throne laden with many cushions that are fashioned, it would appear, from seaweed and lichen.

In moments, the scene is readied: the lights are low, the orchestra plays softly; flame in gnarled, many-branched candelabra flickers impossibly through the undulating currents. On the podium, the blunt-headed shark butts the gong again, this time just once; uncertainly, exchanging glances, Jem and his friends make their way towards the table – and it is then, as they pass the servants, now stiff at attention, ranged in a formal line, that Jem begins to share the unease of his friends. One by one the fish-boys bid them welcome, as if in a promise of fine service to come; one by one, they bow and say their names.

There are nine of them.

'Greetings, sirs, I am Adri.'

529

'Greetings, sirs, I am Infin Ijas.'

'Greetings, sirs, my name is Nicander.'

Jem can guess the names that come next. The twins, Juros Iko and Jenas Iko. And this burly fellow with the merry, dancing eyes? The joker, of course: boneheaded Zap. Even under their blue scaly skin, the human origins of the lost boys can hardly be forgotten; unnervingly, their faces remain unchanged. But what do they recall of their old lives?

'We meet again, Leki,' Jem says now; Leki, like the others, only bows respectfully.

Ojo is next; Jem and Rajal glance sadly at each other.

And next? Through the dim blue current, the face looms forward. Jem's eyes widen. Littler cries out. Rajal reels back. Should this not be Maius Eneo?

But no. It is Ucheus.

Jem gulps. He thinks of their last sight of their friend, swooping down to save them from the maw of the volcano. Stricken, he whispers, 'You've . . . sacrificed yourself.' *For nothing*, he thinks. The pain throbs hard in him. 'Ucheus, you've sacrificed yourself . . . for *us*.'

Does Ucheus understand? Would he laugh, if he did? Now, perhaps, Jem would grip him by the hand; perhaps he would embrace him, breaking down in tears. But there is no time. A fanfare sounds. Great doors open and advancing towards the throne, trident in hand, comes the awesome being that is the goddess Javander.

Jem turns, astonished. Flanked by guarding sharks, the goddess is clad in a costume of netting, shells, sea-plants and the iridescent skins of fish. Behind her billows a long blue cape – from the flesh, perhaps, of a blue whale; on her head she wears a crown of coral, gold and precious stones.

The servants abase themselves; awkwardly, Jem and his friends would do the same, but the goddess, reclining on her gold and seaweed throne, merely smiles and, with a wave of her hand, commands her guests likewise to sit, sit.

Jem takes his place at the foot of the table; Rajal and Littler sit at the sides. The servants flurry round, furling out napkins, filling heavy goblets with fragrant wines. Can that be Ucheus, waiting on Jem? But Jem cannot think of their lost friend now; entranced, he can only gaze down the long, shimmery vista of the table, the crystal throbbing painfully at his chest.

Javander is a vision of strange beauty. Though a weird, green-blue luminescence surrounds her, she is quite without traces of scales or fins or gills. Her skin is of a creamy pallor, like those of the finest Ejland ladies; her flowing tresses are of extraordinary luxuriance, and their colour is a flaming auburn, not blue.

But is there not something more entrancing still? Is there not something particularly, profoundly blue? Indeed, for what is this that burns at Javander's breast – burns, and throbs too, in time to the throbbing Jem has felt, ever since he arrived in this undersea domain? When, at last, Jem turns to Rajal, he will see that Rajal knows, too. The mystery is over.

At last, they have reached the object of their quest.

Chapter 73

THE FIFTH ELEMENT

Purple, red, blue.

Purple, red, blue.

Richly the three crystals throb in time. Softly, in the background, the ORCHESTRA AQUATIC plays. By now, with immaculate refinement, the fish-boys have presented the guests with exotic dishes of seafood, garnished extravagantly with strange flowers. But Jem can have none of it, and neither can his friends. Javander, for her part, favours different food. Languidly she reaches with her trident, skewering a jellyfish that passes by; when she beckons to a lingering lobster, the creature scuttles down the table towards her, waving its feelers excitedly, offering up its bulbous, juicy claws.

The goddess reaches out a hand and tears.

Gulping, Jem avoids the eyes of his friends. Now the throbbing possesses him entire; he trembles, as in a fever; he would sink, floundering, from his ornate chair. Can the goddess be mocking them? Will she not speak? Ah, but Jem sees that it is *he* who must speak – *he*, as the Seeker after the sacred stone. Briefly, nervously, he clutches his throat. He struggles for words, but when the words come, he feels them taking on a strange configuration.

Littler and Rajal gaze at him, astonished, as, at last, there begins the fifth and final act of *The Javandiom*.

JEM:

Most welcome have you made us, Mighty One,
In this your sacred undersea domain:
Such miracles and wonders fill this place!
And yet, must not all these storied turrets,
Domes, castellations, minarets and spires,
With all the many splendours they contain,
Yet fade against the splendours, greater far,
Of she who has created all we see?
  Old tales speak profusely of the beauty
Of this place; of the beauty of the one

Who calls it home, the tales, alas, are dumb.
Goddess, to you we bow.

JAVANDER:

                    Young Ejland Prince
(For such I sense you are), am I to think
That ready is your tongue to gallantries
Of such a kind that mortals of my sex
Might fear, with reason, your seductive wiles?
That loyalty and honour rule your heart
I can be sure: and yet, such wiles you seek
To practise on *Javander* all the same.
  No, speak not to me in words beguiling,
For as you know my story, so you know
That many are the ruined kitchenmaids,
That many are the milkmaids big with child
That might, when viewed in parallel with me,
Yet seem to be the less deceived in love.
  Speak boldly to me, Prince, of why you came
To this my citadel beneath the waves:
For think you not that at your chest I see
The truth behind your mission, glowing bright?

JEM:

O Mighty One, I swear I would have none
Of arts – so mean, so shabby – such as base
Deceivers would employ: and as you see,
My purpose here can hardly be denied.
For goddess, though fantastic is this place
In which you dwell, fantastic more by far
I find the crystal that you wear; and yes,
Though beauteous your face and form appear,
To me that crystal glowing with its blue
Unearthly light must ever be possessed
Of beauty greater. – Yet, is not it strange
To find this sacred stone against the breast
Of she for whom it was created first?
Deceived how sorely have I been to think
That from the Sisters I must snatch my prize!

Deceived yet more to think (as scriptures say)
That when the earth's first age had reached its end,
Then all the Crystals Five were lost, flung far
Upon the winds! – And yet, there is one thing
Of which I can be certain: that I come
To take away that glowing stone you wear.
   Deny me not: for am I not the one
Foretold in ancient prophecy, the one
Whose destiny it is to reunite
The Crystals Five, defeating *Toth* at last,
And bringing to an end this present age?
Javander, sacred one, you know my name:
Jemany am I, Ejland's rightful heir,
And to the Orokon I am the Key –
Deny me not!

JAVANDER:

            Hah! But Prince of Ejland,
Why do you think denial is my way?
Let not surprise o'ercloud your fair visage.
'Tis true, 'tis true, that at my breast you see
This prize which long ago my father-god
Invested with the powers of my domain.
Until this day, concealed this stone has been
Beneath the garments covering this breast,
A secret known not even to my sons:
Only now in open pride I wear it,
Yet you mistake me if you think I seek
To clutch it to my breast for evermore.
   There was a time when differently I felt:
In aeons past, when in The Vast on high
I languished in the bondage of my first
Unhappiness, did not I look below,
Defying all my father-god's commands,
In desperate hope to find again this stone?
Could I but hold it in my hand again
And focus all its powers, I foolishly
Believed that I could win back *Theron*'s love.
   Yes, this is what your legends do not tell
(For legends are but fragments of the truth),
That back to earth I came for this alone –

534

Vain hope! This crystal I could not remove
From deep within the ocean where it lay.
    The truth, in time, was evident to me:
None but the rightful Seeker could that task
Achieve; the crystal, though it bore my name,
No longer could be mine – that is, not mine
Entire. Yet could I not its keeper be?
Ah, yes – I saw that this must come to pass.
Beneath the waves my crystal would I wield,
And build, with its great powers, this citadel
Where I might live divided from the one
Who loved me not. – And here I might have been
Contented (contented as a woman
Without love can ever be), had not I
Fallen, like a fool, into the clutches
Of my brother's instrument, that monster
By the name of *Kalador*. – *Kalador!*
The name is like a bell, to toll me back
To sufferings still worse than in The Vast.
Kalador! – What devious arts he practised,
Cruelly to betray a heart that loved him!
Kalador! – And yet for all his wicked
Wiles and ways, still his hands could never clutch
This crystal, nor all his violence rend it
From my breast, though much he tried. (For although
I kept this stone a secret from my sons,
How could I keep it from a lover's gaze?
Impossible!) – Ah, *Kalador!* But all
Is over now: I would end this vigil,
End it. My exile in this world is done:
Of all that I have made I have grown
Tired; no longer does my self-creation
Move me. To The Vast then I return,
To face whatever fate I must endure.
    Enough, then: for this sacred stone of mine
No longer, Prince Jemany, need you quest.
Seeker, take your prize!

Jem gasps. All the time as she has spoken, the goddess has clutched a
hand around the blue crystal. Now, with no sharp, sudden gesture but
with all the grace of a diver, she tears it free, and with the same slow
grace – turning, tumbling, refracting its long lines of light through the
currents – the crystal drifts down the table towards Jem.

His eyes blur as he watches it; the lines of light become a swirling, patterned haze; the music of the ORCHESTRA AQUATIC becomes stranger, distorted, the rhythms booming cavernously, the melodies writhing and bulging. Harder, brighter throbs the red crystal he wears, in time to the blue crystal's turnings, tumblings; the moment seems protracted endlessly. Light from Rajal's crystal streams out too, cutting purple through the blue, the red. Can it all be so easy?

Then it happens. All at once comes a mighty rumbling, shaking the floor. The long, rocky table cracks apart and in a bubbling upward rush comes a monstrous, misshapen, serpentine form!

Javander cries out, clutching her face in her hands. The orchestra scatters. Jem darts back. Littler and Rajal look on, horrorstruck – but in an instant, the hideous serpent has metamorphosed into the beguiling, red-hued Kalador.

With casual ease the evil creature reaches out, plucking the spinning blue crystal from the current. His eyes glow; mockingly, he looks at Jem.

KALADOR:

                    Well may your visage
Register astonishment, *Jemany*!
Well may your weak companions quake in fear!
Foolish whelp (like unto a bantam-cock,
Puffing out your chest in vain delusion
And thinking to prevail with casual ease),
I scorn your insolence! For all your pride,
See you now the recompense? *Javander*
Is my puppet, that is all! – This crystal,
It is true, I cannot own: this crystal,
In my hands, would fade into inertness,
If boldly I should take it from this place.
But what of it? *Javander* I can force
To feed me with its might, to channel all
Its glowing, sacred power into my being!
   And my power shall grow! *Javander*, never
Shall you leave this place! *Jemany*, never,
Though ages of the world might rise and fall,
Shall you possess this stone! I shall have yours –
Yours, and your companion's, and feed on all
Their force, until I rival with my power
Not just this paltry goddess that I scorn
But even mighty *Theron*, god of fire!

Yes, greater than my father will I be,
I must – and all the world will bow to me!
Fools, prepare to die!

Jem would shout out his defiance, but cannot. As the evil words churn towards him, he feels his strength draining suddenly, terribly away, and can only hover, helpless in the current, as Kalador assails him. With one hand, the creature grips the blue crystal, clutching it tight against his chest; with the other, he reaches out, zapping Jem with zigzagging lines of power.

Jem cries out as the rays strike him. Agonised, his body jerks and snaps as the red crystal tears free from his chest. Slowly over the ruined table it spins towards Kalador's waiting hand.

Jem doubles over, stricken, moaning.

But all is not over. There is a mighty crash. The portals burst open and a new figure swirls into the scene, blue, majestic and blazing with anger.

Littler claps his hands in glee.

OCLAR:

Spawn of evil, hold!
You cannot kill this sacred one who comes
Before us now. You cannot keep the stone
That he demands. It's over, *Kalador*,
And nothing, no, not any of your schemes
Can now prevail. – My mother? Think you still
To keep her in your thrall? No more: at last
She shall be free, to return to The Vast!
    Vile creature, see you not that now your reign
Is out? For long, too long, I could but flee
From you, for after all, alone and deep
In sorrow have I lodged, since in your cruel
Campaign against the fair *Javander*'s sons,
You took the one I loved far more than life:
The golden one called *Uvan of the Sands*,
For whom my heart shall ever more repine.
    There was a time when I could only curse
My brother's murderer, imagining
The torments he deserved, yet knowing, too,
That all these gruesome phantoms of my thoughts
Could serve me not. That time has passed, for now
This Prince of Ejland stands before your sight:

The destined one has come, and destiny
Can never be supplanted or denied.
    Prepare, then, for the battle of your life:
A battle I am certain you will lose.
As you may draw upon my mother's power,
So I draw on the Prince, and beat you back.
For *Uvan of the Sands* I fight today.
No longer but in dreams shall justice lie:
Your reign is out, I say, and you must die.
    For all who seek on evil's wings to soar,
Death comes – as now it comes for *Kalador*!

Astonishment, then rage fills Kalador's face. The scene has been held
in a strange suspension as Oclar speaks. Still the red crystal spins
towards Kalador; still the evil hand reaches out, but now Oclar hurtles
forward, striking the searing stone from its path. The two beings
struggle, grappling madly. Turbulent currents rock the great chamber.

Javander cowers. Jem reels.

For moments, Rajal is the only one with a crystal. Terrifyingly,
exhilaratingly, its power surges through him; he rushes forward on its
pulsing rays. At any moment, it seems, he will be drawn into the battle.
Desperately he struggles to focus his powers, to turn his crystal, and its
streaming purple light, against Kalador's deadly force.

Savagely, Kalador flings Oclar down.

Oclar rallies. He twists back, striking the monster.

But Oclar is weakening.

Meanwhile, the red crystal hurtles towards the walls. Littler thrashes
after it. There are cracks in the walls. Soon, they will crumble; the red
crystal will spin out into the open sea, to be lost again, perhaps this time
for ever. Littler screams for it. He flails. He flounders.

He is too small. The crystal is too far away.

But Jem cannot help him, nor can Rajal. Littler forces himself forward,
straining with all his childish might.

The crystal whirls redly away.

Lost. For ever.

But no. In the last moment, the crystal seems to hover, as if some occult
force holds it back; perhaps this force is Littler's own desire. Exultantly,
he surges forward – and clutches the mystic red stone that he shall bear
now until Jem's quest reaches its end.

Littler turns, the fiery orb blazing in his hands, to see Oclar reeling
under Kalador's blows.

Kalador raises the blue crystal. Javander screams. Energies surge from her, feeding the monster. In the next instant, the blue crystal will destroy her son.

Jem struggles to intervene, but is powerless.

Crazed laughter bursts from Kalador.

But then come Rajal's rays and Littler's too, clashing together, there under the waves, into a hurtling ball of fire. Kalador screams. The fireball flings him back. The blue crystal shoots from his hands.

Jem grabs it.

At once, the chamber is alive with swirling light. Earthquakes shake the floor. Walls crumble. Fresh terrors burst in Jem, in Rajal, in Littler. The power is building, building and cannot be controlled. Round and round they reel through the violent currents. What can be happening? Where is their victory?

Through churning waves, Jem sees the truth. Kalador has seized Javander. The evil thing is shaking her, slapping her, wrenching her limbs. Will he tear her apart? Wildly he cries that she will not leave him, that she will never be free; insanely he screams that she will feed him and feed him, that his power will grow and grow, that he will destroy the world before he dies.

He, Kalador!

He ... the *Mandru*!

For already the creature has left behind its deceiving form, resuming the shape of the hideous serpent; now the serpent – the monster called the Mandru – is growing, growing, while on and on the power keeps surging, all of it surging, surging into the Mandru ...

By now, the walls, all of them, have crumbled.

By now, the battle fills the open sea.

Where is Oclar? Where is Littler, where is Rajal? All around him, Jem sees only the sea itself pulsing, flashing back and forth with blinding, annihilating light. A monstrous rumbling, a roaring fills his mind.

Now, the explosion.

Now, screaming in every fibre of his being, Jem feels himself hurtle upwards through the churning sea, spinning in the wild, magic light that sears and burns from the crystal in his hands. What can this be but the downward journey in reverse, in all its swirling, hallucinogenic madness, but this time in a terrifying, ecstatic rush?

Jem bursts up from the waves, into the dazzling brightness of the sky.

Chapter 74

WHAT THE THUNDER SAID

'The cobber-as? The cobber-as?'

'Oh Faris, please—'

Ra Fanana was sobbing, but almost laughing, too. Bruised, scratched, she sprawled across Captain Porlo in a low dusty space, a fortuitous cavern beneath fallen beams and columns that had protected them from the avalanche of rubble.

How lucky could they be? When the ceiling had crashed down, the nurse had been certain that death was here at last. But if she were astonished to find herself alive, still greater was her astonishment – her joy, too – that the captain was alive. It was as if he had been saved for something, as if it were a sign! Tenderly she embraced the old man. What did she care if he were mad or sane?

Whatever he was, she would be by his side.

They sat up awkwardly. If Faris was muttering about cobber-as, at least he was docile. He looked about him, blinking, like a big, stupid baby. Smiling, Ra Fanana wiped away her tears. How funny Faris looked, covered in dust! Why, he was white all over, like a ghost!

She supposed she was the same; supposed, too, that they were trapped. Should they call out? Would anyone hear them? Distantly she wondered about the others but they seemed unreal. There was only this place, this cavern in the rubble.

Again the nurse embraced her beloved captain. Would their lives end, not in a sudden moment but in a long, slow expiry in this secret place? The thought was almost comforting; but then Ra Fanana realised that – of course – she was a fool. Daylight shone clearly between the beams. Could they not see the world beyond? There was space enough to get through, she was sure of it.

She reached for Faris. His crutch was broken; she would have to support him. If they stooped, there was just room enough to stand.

With much straining and stumbling, Ra Fanana helped the old man upright. Tightly he clutched his rusty cutlass as they made their way outside. What would they find there? Who was to say? Poor Captain Porlo! Poor Ra Fanana! Now, more than ever, she loved him desperately.

'Are you all right, Faris?' she asked, several times.

'The cobber-as,' was all the old man said, 'the cobber-as!'

❋ ❋ ❋ ❋ ❋

Could this be the end?

When his mind came back, Jem found himself revolving high in the air, cross-legged in a bubble of blue, transparent light, gazing, transfixed, at the Crystal of Javander, cupped in his hands.

Then he looked about him. Far away through the fractured brightness – billowing, like him, in the air – Jem saw Rajal, in a bubble of purple.

Then Littler, in a bubble of red.

Jem exulted, thinking their adventure was over at last – over, and a triumph!

Slowly they were descending to the Isle of Inorchis. Then Jem's heart hammered hard. The flying island had crashed back into the sea and now revolved, in a great wheeling arc, around the still-turning maelstrom. For now, the island moved slowly; but soon, Jem was certain, it would turn faster and faster, smashing up in the whirling waves.

But their friends were still down there!

And the islanders! Were any of them still alive?

Jem gasped. What a fool he was, to think their trials were over!

Instead, things could hardly be worse.

Except that, in the next moment, they were.

For now there came a new, wild foaming in the maelstrom, a bucking, a thrashing, a writhing – and now, glittering in the sunlight, there erupted the mighty form of the Mandru!

The sea serpent had swollen immensely. Already the scaly, seething behemoth was almost as large as the Isle of Inorchis, and still increasing in size. Helplessly Jem gazed at the crystal in his hands – but all the magic that should have been unleashed when he had clutched it had only been channelled into the Mandru's crazed evil.

Down, down towards Inorchis went Jem in his bubble of light – down went Rajal and Littler, too – as the monster reared up hideously above the waters.

Huge coils convulsed. A roar, crashing through the air like thunder, burst from the monster's dripping jaws; what the thunder said was that the sea serpent wanted power, power, and would not be denied.

Now Jem knew what was about to happen. The Mandru would devour them, swallowing the crystals. Then, indeed, its power would be infinite.

But first, Inorchis.

Slithering forward, leaving a foaming wake, the Mandru wrapped its coils around the island, ready for the descent of Jem, Rajal and Littler.

But the drama had one last scene to play.

'The cobber-as! The cobber-as!'

'Faris, no, no—'

Ra Fanana screams, clutching at the captain's arm, but the old man hobbles forward alone, supporting himself on the rubble that lies all around them on the mountainside.

Where it has come from, this sudden terrible rumbling, Ra Fanana does not know; what it is now, this monstrous thing that writhes past them, gathering up rocks and leaves in its slime, she cannot begin to understand. The nurse knows only that she would drag Faris away, but new cascades of rubble crash down in the ruined palace behind them. There is no way back; all they can do is look on helplessly while the monster surges around them.

Captain Porlo slumps down, gasping. Dazzled, he gazes up into the immensity of the Mandru. Does he really see it? All he knows is that the cobber-as have returned, come back to torment him one last time.

Yes, on the rocky slopes before him; yes, in the air all around he sees them, cobber-as seething – *sss, sss* – and arcing back their hoody heads. How many times have they defeated him before? How many times have they made him a coward, mocking all his pretences to manly bravery? The cobber-as have ruined him, ruined everything.

Rallying, struggling to stand again on his wooden leg, the old man slashes his cutlass through the air. Terror consumes him. *The cobber-as, the cobber-as!* If Ra Fanana screams, he does not hear her; if the Mandru's deadly coils come closer, ever closer, still he does not see them.

'Faris, no, *no*—'

The Mandru sweeps past, its huge jaws slavering, its huge yellow eyes glowing like fire, intent only on wrapping itself round and round the island. Against its monstrous form, they are the merest insects. Ra Fanana sinks down, paralysed, unable even to scream any more as the monster, unknowingly, gathers up the captain into the slimy scales of its head, as if he were just a rock or shattered branch. The old man's wooden leg tears away; it clatters back to the mountainside. Ra Fanana weeps and prays. Round and round coils the Mandru.

But all is not over: not just yet.

It is Jem who sees it first, looking down from the blazing sky; then Ra Fanana is leaping up, exclaiming, for all the world as if Captain Porlo is not, after all, about to die.

Ah, for he is not dead yet! Echoing in the air she hears his cry – *The cobber-as! The cobber-as!* – this time not a cry of terror but a brave rallying-call. Now she sees his tiny figure, cutlass in hand, slithering and scrambling on the Mandru's mighty head. But can it be true? Can the Mandru be rearing back, enraged at the torments of so small a figure?

The monster uncoils from the island, thrashing the air. Captain Porlo sticks to the slime of the scales. His rusty cutlass waves back and forth.

But now Jem's blue bubble descends, descends. Through the brightness of the air he sees Littler, then Rajal too, ever closer to the Mandru's steaming fangs. The creature roars and roars.

But now Captain Porlo is hacking at its head, stabbing with his cutlass at the fleshy interstices that lie between the scales, opened by the creature's reckless expansion. The monster rears wildly through the air. The captain slithers downwards on a cascade of slime.

The creature pauses, its massy coils arrested in midair. Now the crazed old man rears up on his knees, gazing into the huge, golden eyes. The golden eyes blink. The captain is exhausted, ready to slip, ready to die. But with the last of his strength, he hurls himself forward and the cutlass slashes open a golden eye.

A roar breaks from the creature; the captain falls.

But what he has done is enough. In the pause, the Mandru has already shrunk, its stolen magic seeping away; now Jem, Rajal and Littler billow around it, striking it with the dazzling radiance of their crystals.

Slowly they descend to the surface of the island.

Slowly, as they descend, the Mandru shrinks.

Chapter 75

THE SHADOW LINE

It is over.

Jem wonders just where it is that he is lying. All around him are bodies, the bodies of strangers; at first he thinks they are dead. But no, not all of them. There are stirrings, here and there; then Jem sees the great ruined dais, where the Websisters tried to sacrifice Myla. Ah yes, now he remembers. He has come back to Sarom. These people are the islanders; the survivors look round, dazed.

One side of the forecourt is sharp in shadow; in the other, the sun beats hotly. Rising, Jem staggers out of the shadows into the light. In his hands he holds the blue crystal; to his surprise it still glows, pulsing like a tiny rival to the sun. He gazes upon it. Mysterious, mystic light bathes his face.

He wanders beyond the forecourt, out into the road that leads away from the palace. Boulders and rubble lie all about. Aching with sadness, he looks out across the wide, empty sea; then his gaze draws in closer, and his heart thuds hard. Can that be the *Catayane*, sloshing and knocking in the ruinous docks? Oh, but she is unmistakable! If the old ship has been battered by her fall through the storm, nonetheless she has survived again.

Jem feels a wild joy; but it is then, as his gaze sweeps up the slopes of the island, towards where he stands, that he spies the broken figure, lying bloodied on the rocks below the palace. It is Captain Porlo, cutlass still in hand, sprawled across the shrivelled, serpentine thing that is all that is left of the Mandru.

Ra Fanana is on her knees, sobbing; Jem sees Buby, clambering urgently down towards them.

He turns away, thinking only, in the blankness of his grief, that the Mandru now bears some resemblance to a cobber-a. A *cobber-a*: for a moment the word echoes in Jem's mind as if in the captain's rough voice. But now it is only in his mind, Jem realises, that he shall ever hear that voice again. Tears prick his eyes and he wishes the crystal in his hands would stop glowing, pulsing. To what end? Its magic, or promise of magic, seems like a cruel mockery.

A hand touches his arm. It is Rajal, and clutched in his friend's arms, to Jem's surprise, is Ejard Orange.

Jem gulps, 'I didn't think you two got on so well.'

Grimacing, Rajal sets the big cat down on the ground. 'Let's just say I was glad to see a familiar face. Sitting on a rock in the sun he was, washing behind his ears as if nothing had happened. Fat, lazy thing! I dare say he's just been lying low somewhere, all this time.'

A thought comes to Jem, and he flashes Ejard Orange a curious glance. 'Lying low? I think that would have been difficult, just lately.' Jem tries to smile. 'But Raj, it's not fair: how come your crystal's stopped glowing?'

Rajal shrugs. 'I suppose it's not a new one, like yours.'

'Ho ho. You haven't seen Littler, have you?'

'Actually, I was wondering about Myla.'

'I know, Raj, I know.' Jem looks away.

'Well, here's someone,' Rajal says uncertainly, looking back towards the forecourt. It is Tagan, dishevelled and limping, emerging from around a heavy chunk of stone that gleams palely on the sunshine side.

Rajal takes a step towards him, but the eunuch's manner is distant; secretly, Rajal is relieved. Already, the events of some nights ago seem far in the past; Rajal can barely believe that they happened. Does he wish that they had not? Oh, he likes Tagan well enough – but not the way he likes Aron Throsh!

He says only, 'You're alive, Tagan.'

'Dearie, it was terrible,' the eunuch says flatly. 'After that ceiling fell, there we were, trapped in the throne room with the big squishy spider. Ugh! Stinking something dreadful it was, let me tell you! Oh, and now I'm scratched all over! Still, I suppose I should be grateful to our patchy-panted friend – finding the way out, and all that. Quite the little hero.'

The eunuch jerks his head behind; coming towards them now are Patches and Selinda. They are holding hands. Tagan raises an eyebrow; Rajal glances at Jem, but Jem is looking the other way.

He whistles slowly. From the shadowed side of the forecourt, weaving their way between stirring islanders, come an old man in regal robes and a tall, handsome youth. The old man leans heavily on the youth's arm.

Who are they? Jem has seen only one of them before, and then only briefly, from a distant window; but this old man and this youth, he knows – this father and this son – have been amongst the most important figures in this story all along.

The old man is Castor-uncle; the youth, Maius Eneo.

Soon enough, inevitably, the cries ring out, echoing between the sunshine and the shadow; and it is on the line between sunshine and shadow that Selinda falls into her lover's arms, exclaiming disbelievingly, sobbing and gasping.

The youth only embraces her, long and hard, while Castor-uncle looks on, a little bewildered, a little bemused, at this girl who will soon be his son's bride; as for Jem, as for Rajal, they think again of Ucheus, and exchange worried glances.

Patches lingers in the sunlight, eyes cast down. He turns away; he scuffs the dusty ground.

* * * * *

Jem said, 'So where *is* Littler, then?'

He raised an enquiring eyebrow at Ejard Orange, but the big cat merely purred and buffed his head against Jem's calves, then Rajal's, almost as if demanding to be fed – which, they supposed, he probably was.

They would have called Littler's name again, but just then, and for the last time, they heard a mighty rumbling and the ground shuddered beneath their feet. Startled, they gazed towards the Thunderer's summit, which was almost clear now of its dark, obscuring clouds. Rising from the caldera came a radiant blue form, spinning and spinning in a spiral of light. The strange being rocketed up through the sky like a meteor in reverse, disappearing at last against the brightness of the sun.

'Goodbye, Mother,' came a voice close at hand.

'Oclar!' Jem turned excitedly to the Prince of Tides, who had appeared as if from nowhere. 'I thought – well, I didn't know what to . . .'

Oclar's look was wry. 'You will have noticed, my young friends, that Mother's instinct for the theatrical appears to have survived unscathed? Since this isle no longer hovers over the Briny Citadel, she must have gone to some effort to make her departure through the Thunderer's vent.'

A confusing memory stirred in Jem's mind. Had he forgotten something? He would have asked what Oclar meant about the island hovering no longer, but the Prince of Tides went on, 'No, Kalador's evil did not manage to claim me. I live, as they say, to fight another day. Unlike my brothers,' he added sadly.

Rajal gestured skywards. 'So she's really going back? But what will happen to her?'

'I wish I knew,' said Oclar, 'but alas, such powers of divination as I possess cannot reach to The Vast. Still, I suspect she won't be in Theron's thrall. Not any more.'

'Not if she has any sense,' said Rajal.

'Well, yes,' Oclar murmured doubtfully.

'And what about her servants?' There was harshness in Jem's tone. 'She's just gone and abandoned them, hasn't she?'

'I see you have a low opinion of gods, Prince Jemany. But Mother's servants were never there for *good*, you know – even she didn't need that many. After a time, they would be liberated to The Vast – or, I suppose, to the Realm of Unbeing, if that's where they were destined to go. I dare say your friend Ucheus has found his proper place, even as we speak.'

Jem and Rajal looked down, sighing. But Oclar's blue hands touched both their chins, and he smiled, '*Up*, I think – *up*, for Ucheus. I'm sure of that, at least.'

They smiled, too; then it was Oclar's turn to sigh. 'Poor Mother – in a strange way, I shall miss her. Still, I dare say I haven't seen the last of her. I've a feeling she'll be descending into this world again before too much time has passed.'

Jem's brow furrowed. 'How so?'

'Aren't you nearing the end of your quest, my young friend?' Oclar indicated the crystal that, even now, after its goddess had left the world, still flickered and pulsed in Jem's hands. 'Only one more to go, hm?'

'But why,' said Jem, 'is the crystal still glowing?'

'You haven't guessed that?' said Oclar. 'The crystal always unleashes a good magic, doesn't it, just after you've found it? This time it's been thwarted by the Mandru, but the power's still there – still there, waiting.'

'A good magic?' Jem glanced at Rajal; then both glanced down to the rocks below the road where Ra Fanana still sobbed over the corpse of Captain Porlo. By now, not only Buby but Patches had joined her, too. The cabin boy had turned away, hugging himself as if he were cold and staring down towards the *Catayane*; the little monkey keened in despair, her teeth bared, her head flung back.

The sadness in Oclar's voice was deep. 'A magic,' he added, 'for the particular race to whom this crystal belongs. But this, I suspect, will be magic of which, at present, we are all in need. You'll recall, Prince Jemany, that this isle no longer hovers over the Briny Citadel?'

Jem looked puzzled; then he gasped as the memory crashed inside him. Wildly he looked out to the sea again, aware that the dazzling horizon was turning, turning in a great arc. 'The maelstrom! We're headed straight towards it!'

Suddenly Oclar was closer. 'Shut your eyes, Prince. And open your hands.'

Jem did as Oclar asked. He felt the large, strange hands twined around his own; he felt the crystal's heat growing and growing, and registered, through the red caverns of his eyelids, the great slow flash that all at once enveloped the Isle of Inorchis. After all the violence of before, this last great feat of magic happened calmly, silently.

When he opened his eyes, Jem saw the crystal fading, becoming only a hard, dark stone. He turned slowly, perhaps expecting to see Inorchis as it was before the horrors of the last night, with the ruined palace and the city restored. They still lay in ruins; but indeed, Jem realised, Inorchis had been restored. He gazed down over the city; his eyes roved over the docks where the *Catayane* still sloshed and knocked. Then he looked further. No longer was the sea wide and empty, not on this near side of the island, at least. Across the bay rose familiar, jungle-covered slopes.

'Back where we started,' said Jem. 'Well, almost.'

On the forecourt, the islanders pointed and stared; they turned towards the Thunderer; they dropped to their knees and prayed.

Of the Arocans, Jem noted, only Maius Eneo neglected this observance; the handsome youth remained with Selinda in what appeared to be an endless embrace. A little sourly, Jem wondered if they had even noticed what had just happened. It was rather as if some strange communion were taking place between them, beyond any ordinary meeting of lovers. What words might be passing between their minds, words they had no need to speak aloud?

Perhaps they might have been words like these:

> — *Beloved, can it be we dream no more?*
> — *What need of dreams, when dreams at last are real?*
> — *And yet what ecstasies such dreams reveal!*
> — *Come, leave our dreams like wreckage on the shore.*
> — *Come? Yes, I come to know your love forsooth.*
>
> — *But yet you feel an admixture of ruth?*
> — *But yet across my flesh sensations steal.*
> — *And soon that flesh with bliss shall ache full sore.*
> — *Beloved, soon I open wide a door.*
> — *But think, but think, of all you soon shall feel!*
>   *Ah, come my lady, come my stranger-youth:*
>   *An end to lies: now you shall know the truth.*

Oclar said, 'Ah, but here is one I was about to seek.'

'He's in rather a hurry,' said Rajal, 'for this heat.'

It was Littler, scrambling up the road from below. As he came closer, they saw that he was sobbing.

Jem raced forward, stuffing the Crystal of Javander into his tunic. 'Littler, what's wrong?'

'It's my friend – she won't move, she's . . .'

'Friend?' A shudder, a wild hope, ran down Rajal's back.

Breathlessly, Littler pointed down the road. He turned, flailing back, and Rajal followed. Jem raced after them.

Oclar watched them go, his eyes blazing strangely.

❄ ❄ ❄ ❄ ❄

The figure, the black-garbed form of a woman, lay in the shadows of a shattered tree, face-down and inert.

At first Rajal thought the tree had crushed her, but this was not so.

Leaves obscured her head, but no part of her lay beneath the trunk; this place beneath the tree was merely where she had fallen, some time during the violence that had shaken the island. But was she dead? Rajal clutched her shoulder, fighting down his disappointment, struggling to think only of this stricken person.

For of course, this was not Myla; this was a grown woman.

But what had Littler meant, speaking of his *friend*? The little boy only sobbed and gulped.

Jem, floundering behind them, crashed through the branches. There was a new shaft of sunlight and Rajal saw that the woman's gown was not black, but blue. Then, through the chinks in the obstructing leaves, he saw that her head was shaven.

A Websister!

'I thought they were all destroyed,' said Jem.

But Littler only shook his head, sobbing more loudly.

'She's breathing,' said Rajal. He pushed away the foliage from the woman's head; gently, he turned her over.

Then he cried out.

Was it the Lichano band, gleaming on her forehead, that he registered first? Or the face that was still so familiar, though so much older?

At her brother's cry, Myla's eyelids flickered open.

'Hello, Raj,' she murmured, 'it's been a long time.'

'But Myla, you're ... But Myla, how ...'

The eyelids came down and again she was unconscious.

Rajal would have shaken her, desperate to wake her, but all at once Oclar was with them. Gently, the Prince of Tides reached a staying hand to Rajal's shoulder.

'Oclar,' urged Jem, 'what's happened to her?'

'The Sisterhood of the Blue Storm may be gone,' was the reply, 'but their evil lives on after them. In the ceremony at Sarom, would they not have brought this child to a forced maturity, so that she could take the Spidermother's place? Alas, I fear the process continues.'

Horror filled Rajal. 'You mean ... it hasn't *stopped*?'

'She's already our age,' said Jem, 'or older. In one night!'

With tender fingers, Oclar touched Myla's forehead. 'How fast it will happen, or how slowly, I cannot say. The child's powers will hold it back for a time, aided by the Lichano band. Do you see, she has lapsed into a coma again, the better to preserve herself? But ah, for how long? My friends, in the time to come you must wake her as little as you can; be especially careful not to let her perform any magical feats, unless you would have her soon be an old, old woman, lingering on the brink of her natural death.'

'And ... and dying?' said Jem.

Oclar looked down sadly.

'But what can we *do*?' cried Rajal.

Littler was sobbing. He clutched at Oclar's hand. 'You'll make it all right again, won't you, Oclar? You'll make her the way she was before?'

Oclar sighed. 'If only I could! But if I could counteract the evil of the Sisterhood, I should have done so long ago – no,' he said, 'there is only one way. When the five crystals of the Orokon are assembled at last, the magic that is then unleashed shall be greater than all you have witnessed thus far. Only such magic can combat this evil, and restore this child to her natural state.'

Jem punched a fist into his hand. 'Then we just *have* to get back to Ejland,' he declared, 'as fast as we can – and find that last crystal!'

Rajal looked up. 'Back to Ejland?'

'But of course,' said Jem. 'It's the Crystal of Agonis next, isn't it? Where else will it be, but in the land that worships Agonis?' He covered his face in his hands. 'Oh, but it's so far!'

Unexpectedly, the Prince of Tides smiled. He pointed through the trees. 'I suppose it all depends on how fast you travel.'

Wonderingly, Jem looked through the shattered, dappled branches. Catching in the sunlight was a blur of blue. He wondered what it could be; then he realised, and was startled. Hieroglyphs blazed out, and a riveted porthole. Could Oclar be serious?

'This one looks a bit battered,' said the Prince of Tides, 'but at least it's still in one piece. I think I can get it working again. Oh, don't worry – it won't be hard to fly.'

'It won't?' Gulping, Jem gazed at the skyship.

Chapter 76

SEA BURIAL

'You're *sure* you won't stay, Prince – you, and your dear friends?'

'But Jemany – Jem – we've so much to *talk* about!'

'Oh Jem, please – just a little longer. For *me*.'

Jem could only smile sadly, shaking his head. The speakers were Castor-uncle, Maius Eneo and Selinda. Evening was drawing in. After a banquet at Castor-uncle's farm, an affair at once strangely solemn and merry, they had gathered on the decks of the *Catayane*. With a scratch crew of islanders, and piloted by Oclar, the creaking ship had sailed out on to the Bay of Inorchis; she would venture just a little further, into the open sea. If she was barely seaworthy, her sails in tatters and a mast snapped, for now it did not matter: the sea was calm and the voyage would be short.

'In these Isles of Aroc, Prince, you shall always be welcome.'

'Jemany – Jem – we *must* see you again.'

'Jem, oh yes – say you'll come back one day.'

Jem said he would, though whether the promise was an empty one, he could not yet know. At a different time it would have intrigued him to see what would happen on these Isles of Aroc, with the old regime in ruins and the people reeling from so devastating an experience of enslavement. Would they build a new and just society, freeing their own slaves? Would they abandon such cruel rituals as the Manhood Trial? Would they open themselves to the world, forgetting their old insularity? Perhaps, but who could say?

Jem embraced the three nobles, one by one.

'Maius Castor,' he said warmly, 'Maius Eneo, Selinda – you've all been so kind. Believe me, my friends and I should like nothing more than to linger. But alas, crisis upon crisis presses upon us, and we must away.'

Neither the Inorchans, nor Selinda, said more. There had been too much talk of crisis, too many bewildering facts to take in.

Castor-uncle gestured about the shabby decks. 'Won't you at least wait for this noble vessel to be repaired? Why, in such a little time this *Catayane* can be ready, with the best crew we can muster. That skyship – I just don't trust it.'

'Me neither,' said Maius Eneo. 'Rather my coracle, any day!'

At this, Selinda had to smile, thinking of how she had first met her

551

lover, washed up on the cove in Hora. Often, since he had come back to her, she would smile and smile, unable to help herself; this time she was quickly sober again. 'Jem, you're sure you know what you're doing? It's madness, taking that thing!'

Jem shrugged. 'It's not the maddest way we've travelled, believe me! But we can't delay with Myla – really, we can't.'

The girl, still in deep sleep, already lay on one of the plush couches of the skyship; Rajal, no doubt, was still beside her, clutching her hand.

Jem gazed towards the upper deck, where the mysterious vessel stood ready for their departure. Close by was Oclar, turning the great spoked wheel of the *Catayane*, directing her rudder to the place where, soon enough, the sea would receive a certain sad offering; perched beside the blue man was Littler, with Ejard Orange in his arms. For the moment, the little boy looked almost happy.

Poor Littler: he would miss Oclar.

The sky was turning red. Already tapers blazed on the shores of Inorchis, where the docks were being hastily repaired. They sailed between the flickering lights of one isle and the dark, hunched silence of the other.

Jem said, 'Maius Castor, though Inorchis has been restored to its rightful place, so much of the isle lies in ruins. Will your people start afresh on Xaro?'

'Perhaps,' said Castor-uncle, 'but I've a feeling that many of the old ways are changing. We may live on both these isles of ours, who knows?' He turned to his son. 'Should we ask our noble young Dynast-to-be?'

Maius Eneo flushed. 'I can barely believe it – the Dynast dead, and . . . all this.'

All this, and Ucheus, was he about to say? More than once, since he had realised what had happened, Jem had wondered how Maius Eneo could bear the sacrifice his friend had made. In times to come, would the noble Dynast lie awake in the night, with all his new happiness, all his worldly power, useless against wave after wave of sorrow?

Perhaps; but something about Maius Eneo, for all his looks and charm, nonetheless left Jem feeling uneasy. How Selinda had dreamed of the handsome youth! But how would she find the reality as opposed to the dream?

'Patches?' Jem turned to the cabin boy who had come to stand, alone, by the railing nearby. The boy's eyes were hollow and thick bandages covered his wounded hands. For all the voyage until now, he had been hunched over the funeral barge where Captain Porlo lay in state. 'Patches, are you all right?'

'Oh yes, Master Jem.' The boy, though his manner was subdued, appeared to be bearing up well enough. Only during the banquet had he seemed to show emotion, and then only fleetingly, gazing for just a little too long at Selinda's beautiful face. Then he would turn away, ashamed, almost baffled.

'You're sure you won't come back to Ejland?' Jem said kindly.

Patches shook his coppery curls. 'No, my place is here – with the *Catty*.' Dropping his voice, he gestured to the nobles of Aroc. 'I suppose someone will buy her when she's fixed up – some stranger, some foreigner.' He shuddered a little, pronouncing the last word in tones which could almost have been Captain Porlo's. 'Never mind, Master Patches will be signing on, just as soon as these hands are good again. Cabin boy again, or the lowliest tar, I don't care – not so long as I'm sailing on the *Catty*.'

Jem reached consolingly for the boy's arm, then thought of a certain hint, a certain speculation that he had heard from Ra Fanana. Some time earlier the nurse, breaking her vigil over the funeral barge, had gone below decks, wiping her eyes in a practical way and saying that she must look through the captain's things.

'You're right, Patches,' said Jem, 'I think you'll be sailing on the *Catty* again. But I think it might be . . . well, here's Nurse Fanana now.'

'Master Jem, I think you can read Ejland writing?' She reached out, offering a crumpled parchment. 'No, stay, Master Patches – this concerns you too. Indeed, I think it concerns *you* most of all.'

Patches looked puzzled, almost alarmed, but crowded round with the others as Jem unfolded the document. Screwing up his eyes in the glimmering twilight, he could just make out the tight, formal script of a notary, scored through with corrections in Captain Porlo's hand. What legal status such a much-corrected document might have seemed doubtful, but the captain's intentions were clear enough. Jem skimmed over long paragraphs of verbiage, looking for the substance.

'*To my wife* – no, that's crossed out – *to my . . . more-than-wife Ra Fanana, who, foreigner though . . . though she may be, and therefore in defiance of all I might have expected'* – Ra Fanana smiled uncertainly; Selinda smiled encouragingly – '*has been the comfort of these my . . . my last days, I leave all the treasure and worldly wealth accumulated in this my . . . my last voyage'* – Selinda exclaimed, hugging her nurse – '*with the exception of one fifth's part of said treasure, which I . . . which I leave to my . . . my faithful* – there's a few things crossed out here – *my faithful cabin boy Scabs* – no, that's crossed out, too – *my faithful cabin boy Patches, whom I'* – Jem drew in breath; the others held theirs, desperate with impatience – '*whom I* – unsomething, ah – *unequivocally . . . declare my successor as sole owner, master and captain of the* Catayane!'

There were gasps, there were cheers – from all but Patches. The cabin boy – the former cabin boy – could only sway, as if he might collapse.

'Steady on, Patches!' Selinda hugged the boy, and he burst into tears.

'He'll have a big task ahead of him,' said Jem, grave for a moment, turning back to Castor-uncle and Maius Eneo. 'And he's still so young—'

'Don't worry about him,' said Maius Eneo. 'Selinda's told me how brave he's been, and we'll take care of him. Never fear, this noble Ejlander captain will have a place to stay, while he's getting ready for the life that lies before him.' The young Dynast-to-be clapped Patches on the shoulder. 'In the meantime, I've a feeling we'll be building up a fleet of our own. We haven't put to sea much in the past – but that's going to change, I think. And I think we may have invaluable help from so experienced a seafarer as Captain . . . Patches?'

'Captain Waxwell,' Patches said, sniffing, struggling to regain his dignity.

'Noble Ejlander captain,' Selinda echoed fondly.

'Or Ejlander pirate,' Jem murmured. He turned to Ra Fanana. 'I'm afraid your treasure doesn't come to much, Nurse. Nor your worldly wealth.'

The nurse smiled sadly. 'There's only one treasure I hoped to have, and it's . . . and *he*'s gone now. But then, I have my memories, don't I? Besides, my young lady's going to be married. I think I'll have enough to fill my days, soon enough!'

'And Tagan?' said Jem. 'What's to become of him?'

The eunuch stood a little apart from the others. He was speaking with Rajal, who had emerged, at last, from the skyship. Deep sadness filled both their faces, and Jem noticed that their hands were linked. His brow furrowed. A thought came to him, but he dismissed it at once.

With Tagan? No, he didn't believe it.

'This afternoon,' Ra Fanana confided, 'Tagan seemed sadder than I've ever seen him. *Things never last*, he kept saying, *things never last – not for my kind*.' The nurse shook her head. 'Then he started talking about the Isle of Vanic again.'

'Vanic?' said Jem, not understanding. 'Where's that?'

Ra Fanana did not quite reply. 'Oh, it's just silly talk – how many times have I heard his silly talk? Wait till he has to do my lady's hair for the wedding, that's all I can say – there won't be time to think about the Isle of Vanic then. Or about other things,' she added sadly.

Jem would have comforted her, but all at once he was aware of Oclar beside him, then Littler too, with Ejard Orange in his arms. Ra Fanana turned away; but the nurse's gaze lingered, just for a moment, on the little boy. A strange fluttering came to her breast, as if some hope, or longing, had possessed her. But only for a moment, a foolish moment. She shook her head. Now where was Tagan? Really, they must think about their lady's wedding!

Jem fluffed Littler's head.

'Oclar's been telling me the strangest things about the sea,' said the little boy. 'And about Ejard Orange, too.'

'Oh, what about him?' Jem said curiously.

But another question was only left hanging.

'We're almost in place,' Oclar interrupted. 'After the ritual, you must leave at once. But Prince of Ejland, there are a few things I'd like you to have – you, and the Koros-child, and . . . and your small companion. I think now is the time.'

He drew Jem aside, Littler too; Rajal joined them.

'My young friends,' said Oclar, 'the way before you is hard, and I only wish I could help you more. But perhaps,' he smiled, 'I shall help you enough if I give you back certain items you seem to have . . . *mislaid* in the course of this adventure.'

Kneeling down, the Prince of Tides held his closed hand before Littler's face. Then, like a conjuror, he opened his big fingers, revealing the Orb of Seeing.

Littler's eyes grew wide.

'Magical things can cause a great deal of trouble, Maro, when they fall into the wrong hands,' Oclar murmured. 'Or into the wrong monsters.' He raised his voice sternly. 'Perhaps you'll remember this in future, hm?'

Gulping, Littler promised that he would; so intent was he on the promise, and his prize, that he did not even think to ask about the name by which Oclar had called him, once again. An endearment, no doubt, in some strange language of Wenaya.

Oclar rose. With the other hand, he repeated his trick, this time with Rajal.

'You'll recall this object, Koros-child?'

'The Amulet of Tukhat!'

'Yes, I don't think you much appreciated it before. Let's just say you're going to need it now – *really* need it,' Oclar added ominously, 'after what's happened to your sister. You won't forget, my young friend?'

Rajal shook his head, and it occurred to Jem that there was something curiously familiar about the way in which Oclar used the phrase *my young friend*. He might have asked if the Prince of Tides was acquainted with a certain castaway, but now Oclar turned to him; at once, Jem could think only of the closed fingers, and what they might contain.

'For you, I am afraid, I have nothing so magical. But then perhaps you may regard *this* as magical enough?'

Gold flashed in the sea-god's hand.

'The harlequin's coin!' Jem cried. 'Oh, Oclar!'

Gazing lovingly upon the precious prize, Jem thought it an object every bit as valuable as the crystal that now lay dormant at his chest. To him, more valuable: after all, the coin was a symbol of Cata. Once more Jem gazed up at the skyship, and wondered impatiently how soon it would be before he could see her. How desperately he loved her! How he longed to sweep her into his arms again!

Then fear gripped Jem, as he thought of all that might have happened to Cata while he had been away. She could take care of herself, he knew that well enough – but she was a headstrong girl, even foolhardy. She would hardly have been lying low, merely waiting for Jem to come back. Who knew what scrapes she might have got herself into – scrapes, and worse than scrapes? What if Cata had got herself hurt? What – what if she had got herself . . . *Oh Cata, Cata!*

Jem closed his hand around the coin, gripping hard. But if he struggled to push such fears away, other fears came crowding in swiftly enough.

What had happened to the Kingdom of Ejland, strife-torn and languishing in the grip of Toth-Vexrah? Already, Toth's evil powers had massively increased. For now, Jem could be certain of only one thing: that he had not seen the last of the anti-god. Toth would be back, and this time would stop at nothing to prevent Jem from finding the fifth crystal and reassembling the Orokon. The final confrontation was soon to come, and without doubt it would be more terrifying than anything Jem and his friends had yet endured. In Ejland, at the epicentre of his power, the anti-god would have no need to project himself through distant Creatures of Evil. This time, Toth would be immeasurably more powerful. This time, he might be invincible.

Jem shuddered, and his heart thudded hard.

Perhaps fortunately, Rajal broke the moment. A little sheepishly, he gestured towards the wooded slopes of Xaro. 'I don't suppose you found any *more* coins over there, did you, Oclar? Not a whole bag, by any chance? It's just that, if we come across a nice comfortable tavern somewhere . . .'

Jem stood heavily on his friend's foot.

It was a little later. Jem still clutched the harlequin's coin, but his impatience to start for home was in abeyance, temporarily at least. First must come the ceremony that he could not miss – no, not for all the world.

It was an event he would remember for ever afterwards, and always with the same welling sadness. For now, he would banish all other thoughts, even of Cata, even of the trials that lay ahead, and think only of the cowardly, drunken, crazy, exasperating, pig-headed, good-hearted, brave old sea-dog with whom he had shared so many of his adventures. One day, Jem vowed, if ever he were really King of Ejland, he would have a statue built in Agondon Harbour – a statue of Captain Faris Porlo, looking out to sea. Yes, one day the captain would be acknowledged by all as one of Ejland's greatest heroes. Perhaps, to generations yet unborn, the thought of him would always bring joy, instead of this sorrow that filled Jem and his companions now.

Open sea stretched before them and the sun was setting rapidly, glimmering redly on the horizon's edge. When the moment came, it was Oclar who took charge, directing the crew of islanders as they lowered the barge in which the captain lay, dressed in his finest coat and breeches and three-cornered hat. There were words, too, a solemn oration by Castor-uncle, and the sad wheeze of the squeezebox, which was played with surprising ability by Patches, even though he struggled with his bandaged hands; still, the words were mere formalities and the music was a vapour, fading to nothing as it drifted away on the air.

For Jem, and for his friends too, there was only the funeral barge, drifting slowly away from them on the tide. How noble the captain looked, lying there so still, so cold, with his rusty cutlass laid across his breast!

Ra Fanana tried to be strong, but soon gave up, weeping helplessly in Tagan's arms. Patches relinquished the squeezebox, struggling instead with the stricken Buby. To get the little monkey out of the barge before it was lowered had been hard enough; now she longed only to leap back down to it, still refusing to leave her master's side. Patches, wincing at the pain in his hands, could only grip Buby by the tail until at last she subsided on his chest, trembling and making guttural sounds much like human sobbing.

Jem moved to assist Patches, then steadied him, clutching an arm firmly around the boy's shaking shoulder; meanwhile, Rajal comforted Littler, who was squeezing Ejard Orange very hard indeed. Castor-uncle, for his part, looked solemnly into the glimmering sunset, honouring this man he had never known, this foreigner who had saved his life, and saved the Isles of Aroc. Selinda and Maius Eneo exchanged glances, their arms around each other, sad for all that had passed, but happy, too, for the lives that stretched before them.

At last, unseen by the others, Oclar slipped away, climbing back to the bridge where the skyship, no longer blue but purple in the sunset, stood ready for its long flight. He bent down, looking through a porthole, checking on the girl who lay inside. The poor child! Would she survive, even if her companions found the last crystal in time? Oclar could not be sure, and looked away. His task here was done. His young friends knew how to fly the skyship; the crew would take the others back to Inorchis.

There was just one thing more. Out at sea, the funeral barge was vanishing into darkness; the great disc of the sun had almost sunk entirely. Oclar stretched forth a hand; he pointed, and the barge burst into flames.

Now, with only the faintest splash, unheard by the others, the Prince of Tides slipped away, returning to his natural element. Loneliness and deep sorrow filled his heart; far and wide through the seas he would travel, seeking to assuage them.

On the *Catayane*, Jem and his companions remained watching, silent and unmoving, as the burning barge sank slowly into the darkness of the deep.

Here ends the Fourth Book of THE OROKON.
In the Fifth Book, *Empress of the Endless Dream*,
Jem's adventure at last reaches its shattering conclusion
as Jem, his friends, and his enemies too, confront
their fates – and the fate of the world.